Eve of Redemption

Salvation's Dawn

by

Joe Jackson

Follow the author:
http://Citaria.wordpress.com
www.Twitter.com/shoelessauthor
www.Facebook.com/shoelessauthor

This book is dedicated to Mrs. Raftery, who told a strange kid with a stranger imagination to let it take him anywhere he wanted it to, and to the men and women of the U.S. Armed Forces, the true defenders of freedom.

The Eve of Redemption Series

Salvation's Dawn
White Serpent, Black Dragon
Serpents Rising
Legacy of the Devil Queen
The Huntresses' Game (due in 2017)
Preludes to War [Working Title] (due in 2017)

Legend of the Blackscale Series

Ashanti (due in 2017)

Want to keep up with updates and new volumes? Join my mailing list here: http://eepurl.com/cbviiD

Contents

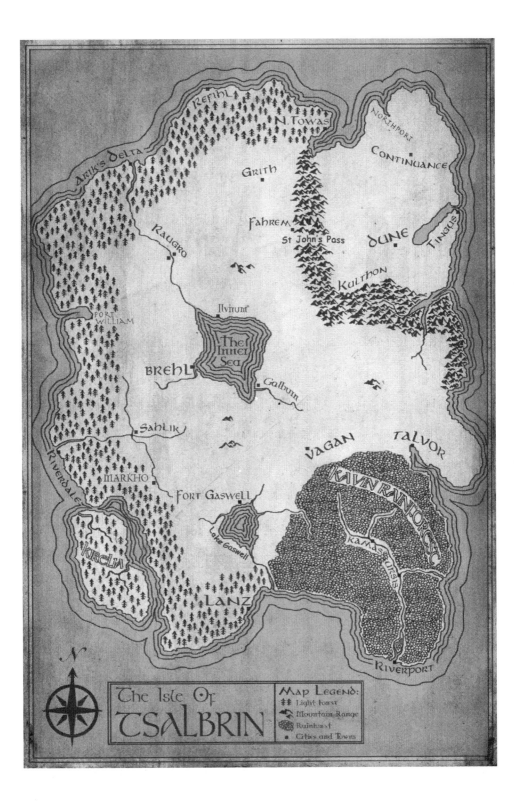

Chapter I – Opening Move

The fortress rose before her, a strong silhouette against the rising sun of a new morning. Finally, after a few days of walking, her destination was within sight. She was unaccustomed to dealing with outsiders, but still she was confident she could get the answers to her peoples' many questions, and she reminded herself that in this situation, she was the outsider. Her people and those she had traveled to speak with were related distantly, but she reminded herself that her people were feared by outsiders.

She was kirelas-rir, a mystical race whose inherent grasp of arcane magic, attunement with nature, and innate powers of the mind led others – even of the other rir species – to fear them. While they were, at their core, still just rir – a semi-draconic but mammalian folk – they were different, and that led the other rir species to treat them with either deference or contempt. She held hope in her heart that those she traveled to speak with were of the former variety, but history kept her cautious.

The man she went to speak to – one Braxus Gaswell, a General among his kind – was the descendant of a man who'd tried to conquer her people several generations before. She and her people found it unlikely that he sought to repeat his ancestor's actions, as they had resulted in the death of Gaswell's forefather, but she had traveled here to make certain of it. Her people were not a warlike people, and though they had tremendous strength as practitioners of the arcane, they preferred not to use that strength to bring harm to others, even in self-defense. She found it far more likely that Gaswell was simply organizing a standing army in the face of what was going on in the world.

Only days before, the Apocalypse had come to an end: the Devil Queen's forces were decisively defeated and the Devil Queen herself met her end. While most of the fighting had been contained to other continents far from her home, its effects rippled through the ether and could be felt by those attuned to power, whether divine, arcane, or natural in origin. People were uncertain what the future held, and uncertain people frequently made errors out of fear. And that was what she had come here to investigate and, if necessary, prevent.

It was also possible that Gaswell sought to lend aid to one of the factions on the mainland, where a civil war had waxed and waned for nearly two centuries. She knew little enough of the war, its purpose, or its results, and thankfully, the fighting had yet to touch this island of Tsalbrin or her own peoples' small island home. She thought perhaps that there had been some major turning of tides in the mainland war, and that perhaps Gaswell sought to either join the winning side or bolster the losing side. There were many possibilities.

As she approached, she could see that there were several uniformed officers out before the fortress' front gates, and by the regal dress of one of them, she assumed she had already found General Braxus Gaswell. There were only slight bristles of anticipation amongst the men as she made her approach: they apparently couldn't see that she was kirelas-rir from the distance between them. If they could, she thought it likely they would be much more on their guard, but she was conscious to not make any sudden or threatening moves, and she kept her hands in plain sight outside the wide sleeves of her robe.

There was a vague sense of danger, a tickle of warning in her mind and below her skin as she drew closer to Gaswell and his men. Something was out of place: she could feel an immense arcane power close by, one that easily rivaled her own. Gaswell's recruitment letters and fliers had not mentioned seeking those of arcane or divine power, so she was somewhat surprised to find he had an archmage amongst his followers. Her gaze swept side to side as she sought the source of the power, but she had a hard time pinpointing it; it seemed to come from all around her. She slowed and then stopped altogether when she sensed a trap about to be sprung.

Her senses did not deceive her: she detected the unnatural tang of demonic power below the surface of that massive arcane power. Gaswell and his men backed away, alarmed, as her hands began to glow and lightning crackled up her sleeved forearms in preparation to defend herself. Her mind worked to pierce the veil before her, to peel it away and reveal the presence of the demon that she had thankfully detected before it was too late. Even as she began to unravel the arcane veil, a wave of concussive psychic force struck her, battering her senses to the point where she lost all sense of equilibrium and the grasp she'd had on her arcane power. She collapsed and had to work to keep the contents of her stomach down while the world spun violently around her.

At last she got most of her wits back about her, but her eyes widened as they fixed on the demon before her. It grinned at her, a chilling flash of fangs, and she quickly realized that this was not one of the minor demons native to her world: this was a minion of the underworld, a demon in pure form. It instilled only the slightest of fear in her, though; she was a master of the arcane, and prepared to demonstrate such to her foe. Even as she thought so, a second wave of that concussive psionic force slammed into

2

her mind, and she fell to her back, prone, and conscious only by a tremendous amount of will. Her eyes fixed on Gaswell and his men as they approached.

She was vaguely aware of the demon standing over her, and even in her shattered mental state, she still found herself surprised when the voice she heard was that of a female. "This one may yet be of use to us; keep her subdued and alive in the dungeon," the demon commanded.

A set of manacles was locked about her ankles, wrists, and neck, connected by sturdy chains, and her mind immediately went blank. She was stripped of all will and nearly all conscious thought. Though her body wouldn't respond to her desire to cry, she did so inside: she had failed her people, and now there would be no one to warn them of what was to come.

There was a demon on Tsalbrin.

Chapter II – The Calling

Kari turned and looked westward.

Her companions slowed in their walk as they saw she'd stopped. "Colonel?" Captain Machall prompted.

Kari ignored him for a few moments, in part to listen for the sound to come a second time, and in part because she still wasn't used to being called colonel even after eight years. She was a demonhunter, not a soldier, but she, like countless others, had been conscripted to fight in the Apocalypse against the Devil Queen and her forces. Owing to her being one of the highest-ranking demonhunters, she was afforded a position as an officer, and had been named lieutenant colonel by the brigadier general under whom she'd served. Still, in her mind she was always just Kari, and she'd preferred even those under her command to call her such. Military decorum, however, had dictated otherwise.

After a brief pause, she heard it again: the faint but unmistakable sound of a summons. It had to have come from the city of Barcon, a few hours to the west, and Kari grimaced. She and her companions had avoided the city on their way down from the mountains, and her intent was to go with her subordinate and friend, Captain Lawrence Machall, to his farm on the outskirts of Gavean to help with the late harvest. That plan was dashed as she realized her deity's priesthood was summoning her, likely for a hunt, and she would have to separate from her companions.

The War was over, the Devil Queen Seril cast down, and her defeat and destruction had brought eight long years of grueling fighting to a close. As she'd walked with her companions toward the town of Gavean, though, Kari wondered what that really meant. For so long her people had battled the Devil Queen's demonic creations; what would no longer having such an enemy really mean? Would Seril's death mean the extinction of her creations, or would they continue to be a problem, led by some other evil? Worse yet, would the absence of such an enemy mean that some other evil would arise to fill the void – perhaps even another war among the mortals themselves? Was it too much to hope that they had not just found victory, but peace?

Kari sighed. She had hoped to push aside such questions for a while, to take up a simple life helping on Captain Machall's farm, but the summons of her deity's priests meant she would enjoy no such respite. The War might have been over, but a part of her understood that as a

5

demonhunter, it would never end for her. She glanced at her companions, who waited patiently for their former lieutenant colonel to give voice to her thoughts, and her draconic lips tightened into a line. It came as little surprise to her that, even after the death of the Devil Queen and the technical 'end' of the war, there would still be work to do and demons to be hunted. It further came as little surprise that she, Karian Vanador, one of the highest ranking demonhunters in the world, was being summoned to look into whatever the priesthood had set their focus upon.

"Is everything all right, ma'am?" the captain asked, still maintaining the discipline and respect for chain of command he'd honored all throughout the war.

"I'm being summoned by my church," Kari said at last. "I guess I'm not going to be helping you and your family after all."

Captain Machall and the others were disappointed: that showed plainly enough in their expressions. In those expressions, though, Kari could see that they understood what she'd been thinking just moments before. "You've got more important things to do than harvesting," the captain said. He straightened up and saluted her respectfully, and the others followed suit. "It's been an honor to serve under you, ma'am."

Kari returned their salute by bumping her fist on her breastplate over her heart and bowing her head: the typical salute of the Demonhunter Order. "It was an honor to serve with you," she returned. "I guess it was silly of me to think we'd get any rest after the war. Would you do me a favor, captain? Take this sword back to your farm and keep it hidden somewhere. With any luck, I'll never ask for it back. But let it collect dust somewhere."

She handed the captain a sheathed katana with a brilliantly carved handle of a black dragon with red crystal eyes. His brows rose immediately; there was little mistaking whose it was, but he asked anyway. "Is this the sword you took from–?"

"Yes," she interrupted, in no mood to hear his name. "If someone comes after me looking for it, I want to make sure it's someplace safe. So keep it out of sight."

"Understood," he said, and he saluted her again. "Stay safe, colonel."

"You all do the same," she returned. She bid farewell to her companions, former members of the Thirty-fifth Light Division, and turned to head back west to the city of Barcon.

Kari began to jog at a brisk pace. She gathered her hair into a tail to keep it out of her face as it swung about, and she threw it over her shoulder to settle between her black, leathery wings. She turned her ebon eyes

6

skyward briefly and saw that rain was imminent, so she picked up her pace even more. She could smell the rain on the wind and the temperature was dropping; she did not want to be alone on the road when the full storm descended. Reaching the city before nightfall would mean she could find out why she was being summoned by the priests and then indulge herself in a warm bath and a good, solid meal.

Winter came early this far south, a fact attested to by the chill wind that danced cruelly across her shoulders, sending her hair whipping to the side. The chill bit deeper than that of the wind, and Kari realized why accompanying Captain Machall back to his family's farm and helping with the harvest had appealed to her: it would have served to cover up the fact that she had no family of her own, nor even a permanent dwelling. As a demonhunter, Kari's had always been a life lived on the road, but here and now, so far removed from the life she had known, she felt out of place and out of touch with the world she had just helped save. She had no idea where her road would lead her once she was put on assignment by the priests, but she knew whatever it was would do nothing to dispel eight years' worth of battle fatigue.

Barcon would've never been her first choice of refuge, but it was the closest city to where her battalion was stationed at the war's end. The call of the priesthood would have echoed from every church and temple of her deity until it found her, and thus the church in Barcon had been the first one she'd heard when summoned. Barcon was a haven for organized crime and had been for as long as Kari could remember, but even still it had a well-established temple district, and her deity, Zalkar, the patron of law and the Demonhunter Order, maintained a church even in the corrupt city. Kari figured that for all its problems, Barcon also had warm inns and taverns, which meant baths and strong drinks – both of which she planned to indulge in for as long as she could before heading out on whatever new assignment she received. It had been years since she'd had a bath that wasn't taken in a river or lake and in the company of several hundred others, and alcohol had been all but banned in the battalion throughout the War.

The very thought of a potent double-godhammer in her hand as she relaxed in a steaming tub warmed her blood, and Kari tucked her wings close to her back with the thumb claws lightly gripping her shoulders, her head down into the wind. She was able to keep up her brisk pace for some time, testament to a life of physical activity and conditioning, and Barcon came into sight after a while. The first few drops of rain began to pelt Kari on her draconic snout, and her clawed feet kicked up dust from the dirt road

7

as she approached the city. Within minutes she closed the remaining distance, just as the skies opened up and the steady beat of rain upon the earth began. She hoped the guards at the gate would let her through quickly and she'd be in a bathtub by the time the rain became a steady downpour.

She slowed her approach as she reached the edge of the firelight from the gates. The rir people had strong eyes and could see well in the dark, but Barcon was a primarily human city and the two guards posted at the southeast gate were both human. Kari was a terra-dracon, a subspecies of the rir people that mutated to grow leathery bat-like wings. They were very rare and, because of the wings, they were quite often mistaken for half-demons, a product of the rir people being crossbred with the Devil Queen's demons. Even as a high-ranking demonhunter, Kari made certain not to provoke the guards by appearing to be a charging half-demon warrior, especially not so soon after the War's end.

As she approached the gates, the two human guards posted at ground level prepared to stop her. They both had the look of green recruits, and they wore the expressions of men who were not at all happy to be stationed out in the cold rain while their comrades sat inside the warm tower or up in the covered archers' post. Hands went to hilts as the one on the left held his hand up, and Kari came to a stop before them once she stepped into the firelight. The guards seemed to study her for a few moments before exchanging a glance, and then the one on the left spoke.

"Half-demons are not welcome in the city," he said with the accent common in the southern plains. He was dressed in dull gray chainmail, with a tabard depicting the standard of the city of Barcon – a black heart upon a red field – upon his breast. His pale-skinned, unscarred face was covered with stubble, and his bright green eyes fixed Kari with an unwelcoming stare.

Kari reached behind her neck and drew up the chain of her dog tags so that they fell across her breastplate. They were the tags of a demonhunter, enchanted with a latent aura that marked them as authentic to anyone sensitive to the arcane or the divine. "Karian Vanador, Shield of the Heavens, by Zalkar's grace," she responded as she stood straight before the men. The guards were no taller than she, though when she expanded her wings she cut a much more imposing figure than either of them. Kari grinned so that her black lips peeled back to show off her pearly-white teeth. "I'm not a half-breed."

"She got white teeth," the other guard said, approaching. "She ain't half-demon, she's terra-dracon."

"I can see that, McKinley," the first said with a roll of his eyes, but then he saluted Kari respectfully. "Begging your pardon, ma'am, we were just nervous what with…"

The demonhunter waved off the explanation. "No need to explain," she said. "When a winged soldier approaches in the dark, I usually have the same reaction." She smiled and the guards chuckled as they waved her through the gate.

"Enjoy your stay, ma'am," they said, and Kari stepped into the city.

As the gate closed behind her, Kari paused a moment in the shadow of the portal, where she was partially shielded from the increasing beat of the rain. Barcon was a walled city several miles east of the southern end of the great forest, and was surrounded by farmland. The interior of the city was broken up into four districts, and Kari had entered through the southeast gate into the temple district. She wondered if the city had changed at all since her last stay so long before, but she knew of one thing that had not changed: Kaelin Black -- the Earl of Southwick County, the city's mysterious ruler, and alleged head of the Black Dragon Society -- was still in power. His criminal syndicate was one of the worst in the world, and had a horrid reputation that stretched back over two hundred years. They made Barcon a dangerous city, particularly for those who served in the temple of Kari's deity. That her deity's people had maintained a temple to Law in a city of lawlessness so long was a testament to their dedication and courage.

Kari looked down the long main avenue of the district and the well-kept facades of the temples stood proudly on both sides of the road. Eternal flames stood in crackling vigil on each of the front terraces, illuminating the white-washed walls and the carved symbols of each deity: the golden axe of Garra Ktarra; the gold cross of Bek the Pious; the shield with the lion's head that represented Ambergaust and Carsius Coramin; the winged focus of Kaelariel; and at last the light blue balanced forces symbol of Zalkar the Unyielding. There were many more deities amongst the pantheon, but these were some of the most prominent and widely-served amongst humans, who made up the overwhelming majority of Barcon's population.

Kari considered going to the temple first, but she wanted to be clean and smell pleasant when she finally went. She looked left and right down the streets that ran along the outer walls of the city, but saw no obvious signs of an inn, so she walked up the main road. She passed the temples, the places of worship were dark and quiet within as evening settled and meditations began. At the end of the road was an intersection, and a neat and clean inn stood directly across from Kari. There was a sign hanging over the front porch, where several older humans sat smoking pipes as they watched the growing intensity of the rain. As Kari moved closer to read the sign, she saw it was emblazoned with a golden axe coated in black blood, and read *The Bloodied Blade*.

Glad to find an inn dedicated to the god of explorers, Kari nodded briefly to the humans on the porch as they regarded her curiously. She knew it was because of the wings, but soon enough they went back to smoking their pipes and Kari entered the warm interior. A clean, smooth wood floor creaked slightly as she stepped inside and tucked her wings tight to her back, and the eyes of not quite a dozen patrons looked up to mark her briefly before they returned to their mugs or conversations. The clientele was completely human, and Kari took a moment to remind herself that Barcon was a primarily human town; the number of her kind, the rir, was small here. She wiped her wet feet on the rug by the door and proceeded toward the bar.

An older, slightly portly human pulled up a tankard and began polishing it as Kari approached, and he marked her with a mostly neutral expression. Once she sat down on one of the high stools before him, he hung the towel over his shoulder and placed the mug down in front of her. He was of fair complexion: the humans of the southern region didn't have much in the way of skin color, though when compared to her own ebon skin, she guessed the same held true for almost anyone who wasn't rir. His hair was thinning and beginning to match his grey eyes, and he rubbed his moustache thoughtfully as he flashed a smile at the terra-dracon woman. "What'll it be?" he asked.

Kari ran a hand back through her damp black hair and sighed lightly. "I'll need a room for at least the night, and a warm bath and a double-godhammer for right now," she said. She produced a gold coin from her belt purse, set it down, and pushed it toward the innkeeper, but she was surprised when he pushed it back her way. "I'm not a half-demon," she clarified. The declaration drew interested gazes from the other patrons again momentarily.

The barkeep laughed. "Figured that much," he said with a nod, and he pointed briefly at the dog tags that still hung over Kari's breastplate. "Don't see many half-demon demonhunters. But your coin is no good here." He reached under the counter and produced a long, slender iron key. "The inn's empty right now; most folks that have been holed up here in recent months have finally begun making their way home, what with the war being over finally. So you can have the master suite, up the stairs at the end of the hallway. I'll have Millie fix you a hot bath."

"Thank you," Kari said. The barkeep pulled up a glass from under the counter to replace the tankard, and he began pouring shots of dragon's breath, furean vodka, "elven moonshine," gutsplitter, fire-ice, and good old-fashioned tequila. It wasn't unusual for the common folk to provide basic goods and services to demonhunters free of charge, but Kari found it surprising that the barkeep could afford to so soon after the War, which had no doubt severely hurt the man's business. "You got a name?" she prompted him.

The man fixed her with a curious gaze before the smile returned to his face. "David Marrack," he said. "Folks around here just call me Dave. Welcome to the Bloodied Blade. Forgive my manners; it's been an interesting week in the city. I was just trying to figure out your accent – it's new to my ears, and these ears are pretty old. Had 'em all my life."

Kari chuckled. "Solaris, over on Terrassia," she said, and the barkeep acknowledged his surprise with an appreciative nod. "I was born and raised on Terrassia," she continued, "Only came over here to Askies to attend the Academy at DarkWind and more recently for the War."

Dave fixed her with another curious stare, and as he put the finishing touches on Kari's potent drink, he slid it toward her. "If you'll forgive my saying so, ma'am, you look a tad young to have attended the Academy *and* fought in the war."

Kari couldn't argue that, but didn't feel like explaining. "It's a long story," she said. "And if you don't mind, I'd like to take my drink up to my room and bathe now."

"Not at all; I'll send Millie up with the hot water right away," David said, and he turned toward the door to the back room.

The demonhunter rose from her stool and made her way to the stairs in the corner of the inn, and she marked well the eyes of the other patrons as they followed her. Always it was the same: initially they saw the wings and the solid black coloration and assumed she was a half-demon. When it came to light that she was not only terra-dracon but also a demonhunter, the suspicions and hostility melted away immediately, giving way to both trust and admiration. Kari figured she should be used to it, as it was something she had dealt with for so long, but then she wondered if anyone ever got used to such treatment.

The first sip of her potent drink sent a burning heat down the center of her chest as it slid into her belly like liquid fire, and she let out a contented sigh as she reached the top of the stairs. The upper level was comprised of a single, long hallway that ran lengthwise across the inn, with four doors on each side and a single door at the end. Based on the size of the inn from the outside, it was apparent the smaller rooms were single-person domiciles, and she wondered exactly how large the "master" suite at the end was going to be. At the very least it would be large enough to house a bathtub, as the innkeeper didn't tell her to take a bath in the commons, if indeed there even was one.

Her quiet footsteps brought her quickly to the end of the hallway, and the door swung open easily as she unlocked it, revealing a large bedroom of impressive décor. The bed, large enough for two, was centered along the right hand wall, flanked by small nightstands with lanterns, and it was covered in clean, crimson sheets. Four pillows sat up against the headboard, and just looking at them tempted Kari to lie down to sleep as she took another intoxicating sip of her drink. Instead she crossed the room to the large double window that looked out over the edge of the bazaar, the neighboring shops, and the eastern part of the city, and after a moment Kari closed the crimson drapes.

An armoire stood against the left wall from the doorway, along with a reading chair upholstered in the same color scheme as the rest of the room. Kari moved to the wardrobe and placed her traveling pack and cloak within, then secured it. She took another sip of her drink, its numbing effect beginning to loosen up her sore muscles, and she inspected the pictures that hung at precise intervals on the bare white walls, but she had no idea who any of the people pictured were. She walked around the bed and placed her drink on the nightstand before she began to remove her armor and lay the pieces neatly on the floor beside the bed. She decided she would wash the entire suit later, and then perhaps stop in one of the local smithies to buy something to polish it with the next day.

Kari's padded shirt and pants came off soon after, and she tossed them along with her undergarments into a pile by the window. They were filthy, and she failed to suppress a grimace at how dirty she was, excusing herself only because she'd spent the previous couple of weeks coming down out of the mountains and through the riverless portion of the southern forest. Indeed, the only washing she received in those weeks was that of the autumn rainfall, which was neither sufficient nor pleasant. She stood naked and impatient as she waited for Millie – who she assumed was the innkeeper's wife – to deliver the hot water for her bath. She rubbed her grimy arms once each as she approached the bathtub, only to find there was already water in it.

It was nearly halfway full, so she tested the water briefly with her fingers: it was clean and lukewarm at best, but she climbed in anyway and lay back on the angled end to put her feet up on the other edge. A knock came at the door and she called for whomever it was to simply come in. An elder human woman approached and smiled at her. She handed the demonhunter a bar of soap and then poured a bucket of hot water into the tub, and Kari swirled her hands around to mix in the warmth. After staring at Kari for a moment, Millie walked over and retrieved the drink off of the nightstand, and placed it on the floor beside the bathtub.

"Would you like more hot water?" Millie asked, the southern accent much more homey and charming when combined with the sweet voice of the older woman.

Kari looked the human woman over briefly and didn't miss the stare she was receiving in return. Among the rir, nudity was neither taboo nor shameful, but it was something that the humans still found curious and awkward, even after three thousand years of assimilation. Millie was not an unattractive woman, though it was sometimes hard for Kari, as a rir, to judge what humans considered attractive. Millie was aging well, and based on her figure she lived both well and comfortably. Her sharp green eyes were studying Kari carefully, and the terra-dracon woman accepted it as the curiosity of a human who probably rarely saw rir in the inn, let alone in the bathtub.

"Just to rinse, and a couple of towels and a scrub brush if you have one," Kari replied at last. "Wings are a pain to wash, you know?"

"Of course, m'lady," the human woman said, though Kari reminded herself that the woman certainly wouldn't know. Millie bowed her head and made her way from the room.

Once Millie left, Kari began washing herself in earnest. The soap was smooth and smelled fruity, and she practically purred as the grit and the smell of sweat and weeks on the road began to be replaced by something lady-like. She almost laughed at herself as she thought the last; she always considered herself closer to being one of the boys than a lady, and her muscular build usually made others feel the same way. Kari stood up so she could properly wash her tail and backside, and then bent over to soak her hair. She stood up straight again and began washing her mane, using her small claws to untangle what knots she could before taking a brush to it. While she let the soap settle on her scalp, she reached over the side and picked up her drink, and she finished it in a single, long swallow before placing the glass back down on the floor.

A knock came at the door a minute later as Millie returned with the towels, scrub brush, and a bucket of water for rinsing. Kari wasn't sure whether to make any effort to cover herself as she stood there, but

13

ultimately she decided against it. There was a brief moment where the human woman simply stared at her, but it was a stare Kari was fairly used to: the one that clearly said the person was impressed by her muscular build and chiseled stomach. Kari reached to take the brush from the human woman, but Millie instead walked around behind the demonhunter, took up the soap, and began to gently lather and scrub the backsides of Kari's wings. Kari thanked her and took up the bucket of water from beside the tub to rinse the soap from her hair. She stood still for a couple of minutes while the human washed her wings, and then Millie left once again to get more rinse water.

Kari sank back down into the tub but made sure to keep her hair outside, and she scrubbed the insides of her wings. Being clean made her feel like a woman, but as the thought entered into her mind, it brought with it the disturbing reminder that she was a lonely woman, without a home or a family, and she wondered exactly where her assignment would take her. Her thoughts turned to her commander, Brigadier Kris Jir'tana, who'd made no secret of his attraction to her throughout the eight years they worked together in the war. Why had he disappeared so suddenly after the war, when she was finally ready to consider courtship? Why did her refusal to start a sexual relationship in the middle of a war surprise him?

Kari sighed, closed her eyes, and rested her head against the warming metal of the tub, and she wondered why she was in such a position again. Hadn't she already served her time, giving the world and the gods a lifetime of selfless service once before? Hadn't she earned that rest, in that place of warmth and sunshine, apart from the struggles and pains of mortality? What right did Trigonh have to rip her from there, to thrust the mantle of war upon her shoulders once again, to drag her back down into a lonely life lived on the road for who knows how long? What right did he have – indeed, what right did even the gods possess to allow him to bring her back against her will, citing some misguided belief that he was in love or that she could ever love him in return?

The alcohol settled in deeper, warming her even further, and Kari wiggled her numbing toes in the water. But the amusement didn't soothe the ache in her heart or the uncertainty of her future. She'd been lucky enough to survive the eight year war, and only days removed from it, she was already about to be assigned to another dangerous hunt that could cost her her life. While she wouldn't be averse to returning to that place of warmth and comfort, she recalled the amount of pain that had preceded going there the first time. She had *died*, a slow, horrible, rotting death that took twenty-seven years to come to fruition, and though she was with

14

friends when it finally came, it was something she had faced alone.

Alone.

The demonhunter sighed again, and she held her dog tags up to read their inscription: *Karian Vanador, Shield of the Heavens, T03172849.* Was that the entirety of what she was to her own deity? Why did the thought of serving a higher power not bring her comfort? Why did she feel apart even from him, from his church and his power, when as a demonhunter she was supposed to be an extension of his right hand, his justice, and his mercy? She closed her eyes and shook away the thoughts; if the Unyielding got the impression her faith and conviction were falling apart, she wouldn't even have a job – and her job was all she had. She was simply tired, and assumed Zalkar would understand.

Millie knocked on the door again as she returned with two more buckets of warm water in her left hand, and another drink in her right. "Something about you seemed off, so I thought maybe another drink would help you relax. It's just not right for a pretty thing like you to look so out of sorts," she said as she placed the buckets beside the tub and handed the terra-dracon woman the drink.

"Pretty?" Kari repeated hesitantly. She'd never considered herself very pretty, but to be called so by a human was even more unusual. Though the two species assimilated easily and got on well, they were still vastly different in terms of physical attractiveness.

"Och, don't kid yourself, girl. You're gorgeous as rir go," Millie answered with a sincere smile. She looked about the room. "Did you finish your wings, or can I help you rinse off? And would you like me to clean your clothes and your armor?"

"Wings are done," the demonhunter replied, and she stood up once more. "Would love help with everything else. I have to warn you though, my clothes are pretty gross."

Millie hardly seemed put off. "I wash the linens here," she said. "Dirt and sweat are nothing new to me." She helped Kari rinse and dry herself, and then she gathered up the dirty clothes and armor as she prepared to leave. "My word, this armor is light. Is this paluric?"

"Aye," Kari said, and she moved to sit on the corner of the bed to let the air dry her more thoroughly. "It was a gift from a friend, a long, long time ago."

The human woman's eyes widened slightly, and she let out a short laugh. "Must've been some friend," she said with a wink. She closed the door behind her as she left. The reaction was not completely unexpected: paluric armor was exceedingly rare and worth a king's ransom, and few people could ever believe that someone had *given* it to her. It was extremely lightweight, almost completely unrestrictive, and near-impenetrable; that particular suit had protected Kari throughout much of her previous and current lives.

Kari took a sip of her new drink, and chuckled quietly as another knock sounded on the door. "What did you forget?" she called.

She was surprised when a male terra-rir came through the door instead of the human woman. The terra-rir were the most common of the rir species, and the one from which terra-dracon were an offshoot. The man was about a hand taller than Kari, well toned and handsome, with the white hair and green eyes most common to their people. His hair was trimmed short, which was typically a way of saying one was not a fighter but perhaps a professional soldier; rir fighters wore their hair long as a testament to how long they'd been fighting without being beaten or killed, while soldiers tended to wear their hair short in a military cut. Kari wondered if this man had been a soldier at some point. He wore a tunic and a pair of off-white trousers, and he stepped into the room and closed the door quietly behind him.

"Hello," he said softly. "My name is Aaron, and I was wondering if you might like some company for the night."

Kari's brows rose; she had used the services of prostitutes before in her prior life, but never had she had one come up to her room and proposition *her*. She took a sip of her drink to stall. To find a male rir prostitute in a human city was unusual for several reasons. "You're a mule?" she asked rhetorically, and he nodded silently in response. A *mule* was what a male rir prostitute who'd had himself *fixed* in some way was called; they were uncommon anywhere. As a species the rir were not very sexually active, but there were always exceptions and mules made their living providing services to females who wanted a partner for a night rather than a mate. On occasion they even provided their services to human women, though the differences between the two species made such an event rather rare. "I'm not interested, but thank you."

Aaron smiled and made no effort to mask the fact that he was admiring her naked form. "If it's the price that concerns you, my lady, I would offer myself to you freely," he said.

Kari blushed, and then she laughed and nodded at the compliment. "No, it's the sex I'm not interested in, sorry."

"Does my lady prefer to be alone then, or would she be content with some company for the evening?" he pressed.

It was clear he was attracted to her, which struck Kari as odd since as a

16

mule, he was unlikely to ever attract a mate. Why he was interested in spending an evening with a woman who wanted nothing sexual from him was a mystery, and the fact that he would do so for free only compounded the point. Ultimately, Kari figured he was probably just as lonely working in a human town as she was stopping in it. She took some pity on him, though she wasn't really interested in anything he could provide her with. "I'll only be in town for the night, most likely," she said, trying to be tactful.

"A night with a beautiful woman of my own kind would still be more than welcome, my lady," he said, confirming her suspicions about him simply being lonely. Part of her wondered if he really found her beautiful or if that was simply flattery. She guessed he might try to persuade her to indulge in his other services later in the evening, but decided not to dwell on it. There was something else that caught her attention more at that moment.

"Stop calling me *lady*," she said. "My name is Kari."

He approached and knelt down before her, and she had to make a conscious effort not to brush his hands aside when he took up her dog tags to inspect them. "You are a demonhunter?" he asked. "That makes you more a lady, not less."

Kari shook her head, put her drink on the floor and rose to her feet, intending to politely show him to the door before he could say anything else. Aaron straightened up before her but kept his hands to himself, and there was something in his smile and his eyes that put her at ease. Kari put her hands on his chest, and she could feel the sculpted muscle beneath the fabric of the shirt. She pulled him close to her just by touching him, and he put his hands gently on her hips as though preparing to dance. For a moment she felt a release from some of her tensions as she remembered the simple joy of a man's warmth under her hands. She expected him to make his case for her more forcefully, but he was a perfect gentleman, his hands maintaining their soft perch on her hips as he breathed lightly against the side of her neck. After a couple of minutes, he slid his hands up her back, and his fingers traced curiously along the muscles of her wings before his hands met between them and pulled her close into him. He smelled good, he felt warm, and for a moment, Kari thought perhaps she should indulge herself.

Her thoughts were interrupted by yet another knock, and Millie came in without waiting for Kari's invitation. She stopped in surprise as she saw the two embracing. "Oh, dear me! Forgive my interruption," she said. Kari waved off the apology as she separated from Aaron and motioned

17

toward the buckets and brush. "I see you've met Aaron. He's a sweetheart."

Aaron motioned Millie out of the room with his eyes, and after nodding politely to the two, Millie left and closed the door behind her. Aaron turned back to Kari, who sat on the corner of the bed again. He stared into Kari's eyes and leaned down to kiss her on the base of the neck. She practically melted at his touch, and he knelt before her. He kept his gaze steady with hers, smiled, and took her hands in his. "If you are not interested in sex, how about a bedmate to at least keep you warm?"

"I'm not sure that's a good idea," Kari returned honestly. She knew how to enjoy a night with a man, but to her thinking, now was too soon after...

Aaron shook his head. "I am not trying to force myself upon you, lady, I am simply lonely. Few had money to spend during the war, and this city's inns have been largely empty since the war's end. If you find reason not to trust me, I will leave, only say the word."

Kari took his face in her hands. "It's not you I don't trust," she said. She started to elaborate, but bit her lower lip, sighing lightly.

Something changed in his expression, though Kari wasn't sure he quite understood, even as he answered, "I understand. Have you eaten? Would you care to share a meal downstairs?"

"Maybe after I get back from the church," she answered, which drew a curious look from him. "I've been summoned by the priests; I shouldn't keep them waiting. I only came here to have a bath before I go see them."

Aaron nodded. He sat on the edge of the bed and watched Kari open her pack and pull out some leisure clothes. She got dressed quickly and belted on her swords despite the fact that she had no armor. Soon she was ready to travel across to the church, and Aaron followed her to the common room but no farther. Kari exited the inn hastily and crossed the intersection to Zalkar's church, the first one on the left as she came out from the inn. She climbed the steps to the front porch slowly and placed her hand over the blue eternal flame burning brightly on the top step. After a few seconds, she withdrew her hand, unharmed, and she breathed a sigh of relief: Zalkar was not displeased with her for her nagging doubts.

The front door of the church swung open quietly, and as Kari closed it behind her, her eyes adjusted to the lower light inside. Most of the people within were seated with their heads bowed in prayer, while a couple of acolytes whispered over the altar. Everyone in the church was human, which came as no surprise in the human town, and doubly so because Zalkar himself was a human deity. As the god of law and justice, he attracted many who worked in the judicial systems, city watch, and other law enforcement to his service, and nearly all those who worked in the justice system at least paid homage to the human deity. He was likewise the patron of the Demonhunter Order, which worked alongside his clergy.

Kari wiped her feet on the mat inside the door and looked around for whoever might be the head of the church. The inside was simple and to the point, just as its patron preferred: the walls were bare and white with long, unstained windows high up to let the sun in. Benches were arranged around the room in a horseshoe-like pattern, with the altar at the open end of the arrangement and the center of the floor kept clear for the head priest when he wished to give a sermon. High upon the wall behind the altar, in light blue, was the image of a sword with balanced forces striking it from opposite sides. This symbol of the balanced forces, Zalkar's personal insignia, depicted the Sword of Truth and the two balanced tenets of his most holy doctrine: *Love justice, but do mercy.*

After a few moments, Kari approached the altar and bowed down. She rose and fished her dog tags out from beneath her shirt, and upon seeing them, one of the acolytes gestured toward a door on the back wall. Kari nodded and made her way to the door, where she knocked politely and was welcomed to enter.

Beyond was a simple study lined around with bookshelves, with a hearth on the north wall that had a warm fire going. The walls showed a near-purple reddish color where there were no shelves. The floor was covered with a masterfully-crafted rug of beautiful design, and it almost shamed Kari to put her dirty feet upon it. A mahogany desk stood centered near the far wall, covered with papers and more books, with a lantern on each corner. An elder human sat reading in a padded chair that matched the coloration of the walls. After a few moments he looked up and studied Kari briefly before a smile creased his face and he gestured toward one of the padded chairs before the desk.

Kari moved forward but stopped before she seated herself. She saluted the human by touching her fist over her heart and then bowing her head. "Karian Vanador, by Zalkar's grace, Shield of the Heavens," she said formally, and the man rose to his feet.

"I am Devin Sanstrom, head of this small church," he said. "I am no high priest, so you needn't salute me, young lady. Please, have a seat." He gestured toward the chairs once more, and Kari sat down. She guessed Devin must have seen at least sixty years, his hair gray but well tended, while his eyes and the corners of his mouth were creased with what could have been worry or laugh lines. Given the work that Zalkar's church

19

performed, she guessed it was more likely the former. Light blue robes completed his look, its style and color popular among priests of the pantheon.

Devin unlocked a drawer to his right and pulled out a small bag, the coins within jingling, and he placed it on the desk before the terra-dracon female. "Firstly, I understand you haven't been paid since the start of the war," he said. "Unfortunately, the work of the Unyielding and the plight of the common people in the wake of the war have left little in our coffers. I can offer you but a single month's pay."

"I wouldn't expect more than that," Kari said. She tied the small purse to her belt just behind her right scabbard. "Honestly I'm surprised the church can afford to give me this much."

"It was good of you to answer our summons so quickly," Devin said, sorting through the papers on his desk before he picked up one in particular and read it again thoroughly. "Master Attir Surallis in Sarchelete has requested you travel there to meet him at the earliest time. It seems that even with the end of the war, individual problems not necessarily related to the Devil Queen or her schemes are already arising. Master Surallis has something he would like you to look into, as you are now among the highest ranking hunters in the Order."

Karian swallowed uneasily. She was only one of the highest ranking demonhunters because most of those higher in rank had been killed in the war, not the least of whom was Jason Bosimar, the former head of the Order, called the Avatar of Vengeance. She was also being sent to see Attir Surallis, the high priest of Zalkar's entire church worldwide, based in Sarchelete, the most holy city of the rir people. If Kari was being called to speak directly with him, then the mission she was being assigned was not only being kept a secret, but it was also exceedingly dangerous. She considered that it spoke volumes about how much her deity trusted in her, which gave her a bit of comfort after the doubts she'd felt earlier in the night: she realized the potential to bring glory to her lord and thus further meaning to her life and future.

"I'll do as our lord commands, of course, Master," she said formally.

"I can tell you this much, also," the human said as he rose to his feet. "The Unyielding offers you a promotion should you be successful in this endeavor."

That took Kari by surprise as well; promotions within the Order were not handed out arbitrarily, but only after consistent service or overwhelmingly important missions. While it was possible her work during the War was considered service enough, it was the only thing she'd done since her resurrection, and then not directly for the Order or the church. "As he wills, so shall I do," she replied formally as she shook the offered hand of the priest, and he came around the desk to walk her to the door.

"Our lord preserve you and guide you to victory. Love justice, but do mercy, lady."

Kari bid Master Sanstrom farewell and, after bowing once more at her lord's altar, she made her way outside to the streets. The foot traffic coming down Temple Street was heavier, as those who could afford their dwellings in the nicer part of the city made their way home, either from the bazaar or their jobs in other parts. Kari considered her orders and realized the safest way to cross the mountains to Sarchelete would be to sign on as a guard for either a merchant or pilgrim caravan. Pilgrims heading to the holy city were quite common, especially when winter was approaching. Most made their treks during the deep winter, to coincide with the traditional New Year which occurred on the day of the winter solstice, but the holy city was very crowded at that time, leading many to make their journeys when things were calmer. Kari had only ever been to the holy city once before, in her previous life, but she'd seen it as a glowing speck on the horizon as she looked out from the rocky highlands where her unit was stationed near the end of the War.

The issue with signing on with a caravan was that they usually left from the northwest district: the seat of Kaelin Black's power and where his ebon tower stood in silent vigil over the city. As a demonhunter, Kari was also a law enforcement agent, expected to uphold and enforce the law wherever she went even if the local authorities couldn't – or wouldn't. She thought it likely that a trip into the northwest district of what was, since the fall of Oge, probably the most corrupt city in the world could very easily turn out to be more dangerous than hunting demons.

Kari chuckled at herself and returned to the inn. Aaron sat alone at one of the tables in the commons, and Kari joined him. The two shared a meal together. The common room had emptied out since Kari had gone to the church, so they had the service of Dave and Millie to themselves. The innkeeper served them roasted pork with buttered greens and fresh bread, things Kari had not enjoyed at all during the eight years of the war. Among the camps her unit had set up during their almost continuous movement through the mountains, she had eaten little but tough bread, old cheese, and whatever meats the hunters and scouts could fell without depopulating the wildlife. While she, as an officer, never wanted for food during the entire war, neither did she ever eat to excess, and rarely did she allow herself to

21

enjoy even such a simple thing as food in the middle of what she'd considered a massive tragedy.

Kari and Aaron made small talk, though he was shy about himself, and Kari guessed he didn't want her to feel as though he was bragging about his sexual adventures. He was more interested in her descriptions of the war, or at least what little she was willing to share. Kari stayed fairly quiet on the fighting, as the vast majority of things she had seen were things she would rather forget. Her unit, traveling through the Barrier Mountains, avoided most of the attrition-based war that had so dominated the open plains and lighter forests of the heartlands. In the more mountainous terrain, their objectives were to free those cities already captured and occupied by the Devil Queen's forces, or to waylay serilian demons as they tried to cross the mountains toward the holy city of Sarchelete on the west coast.

Aaron listened enraptured as Kari described Brigadier Kristofer Jir'tana, more commonly called simply The Warlord and whose brilliance on the battlefield was already widely known. Son of the archangel Kaelariel, he was a student under the brilliant Celigus Chinchala – a demon king considered by many to be the greatest tactical mind across the cosmos – and Kris led his brigade on a spectacular campaign, suffering less than a thousand casualties over the course of the eight year war. Kris' instincts and ability to remain calm and collected even in the face of a blitzing assault saved the brigade from certain destruction on more than one occasion, and Kari was very proud to have served under him, something she made sure to accentuate.

Aaron seemed especially interested in how she spoke of Celigus Chinchala, and Kari knew that it was because Chinchala was a demon king and she was a demonhunter. While most people knew that Chinchala had long ago turned on his own kind and allied himself with the pantheon, most people were still surprised to hear how demonhunters reacted to such a creature being their tentative "ally." Aaron said it reminded him of an old saying about war making strange bedfellows, or something of the sort. It was a close enough comparison; Kari had met Chinchala once in her prior life, but even still she was at a loss as to what to make of him. A part of her believed that no demon – or demon king, for that matter – could ever truly be turned, and that he would one day betray the pantheon. That being said, he'd been instrumental in the Light forces winning the Apocalypse, and thus Kari granted him the same respect she would anyone else, demon king or not.

Three more drinks and a comical tale about her friend Captain Machall

22

later, Kari felt quite relaxed and retired to her bedroom. Aaron followed after her but stopped in her doorway, and only after staring at him for a couple of minutes did Kari realize just what her hesitation was. *Kris isn't here anymore,* she thought. *He left without a word.* With that, she invited Aaron in. Millie had emptied the bathtub some time during dinner, and fresh towels sat on the reading chair for the next day's bath. The pillows were fluffed and the blankets turned down already, so Kari undressed herself, and Aaron did likewise and slid smoothly under the sheets. Kari moved around the bed and slid in, and she lay on her side to face him.

"What are you thinking?" he asked her, leaning on his elbow and a pillow to prop himself up. He touched her hair lightly, fiddling with the shorter strands in the front that curved over her forehead while the rest of the long, smooth silky black lay straight across her pillow.

"Can I trust you?" she asked simply.

Aaron ran his fingers along her jaw and nodded silently. He put out the lantern on his side of the bed and Kari did the same. He gave Kari a single chaste kiss on the side of the snout. She turned away from him on her side and he pulled her in tight, laying one hand protectively over her belly with his other arm folded under his pillow. He bid her sweet dreams, and within minutes the two fell asleep, thanks in part to the amount of alcohol they had consumed. Aaron had no problem cuddling with her, as she kept her wings tucked tight to her back as she slept.

The night was quiet except for the occasional toll of a bell to mark the hour and the gentle tapping of the rain on the roof and window. Around the fifth hour, Kari awoke with a start, and she sat up slowly and wondered why there was a naked man with her. She looked around for a few minutes to get her bearings, and then lay back down beside him as she recalled where she was. She had grown so accustomed to being awakened halfway through the night for watch duty that not being disturbed caused her to wake up nervous. The room was quiet and the bed was warm, and Kari took advantage of both and went back to sleep.

Chapter III – Under Orders

The morning came with muted sunshine, even once Kari rose and opened the drapes. The rain had stopped but the sky still remained cloudy and threatening. The sounds of the city as people made their way to the churches for morning prayers filtered up to her as she opened the windows to the breeze. It was still chilly and bound to get colder, but because of the shared heat of sleeping rir the room was a bit stuffy, so she welcomed the cool breeze. Aaron awakened not long after she did, and when she turned back to the bed she saw he was watching her. She was thankful that he had remained a perfect gentleman throughout the night, lending her comfort rather than suspicion, and she smiled at him. He returned it, and then he rose to a sitting position on the edge of the bed as he reached for his trousers. Kari looked around but didn't see her armor or clothes, so she put her leisure clothes back on and motioned toward the door.

Aaron joined her for breakfast in the common room, and a few tables were already full with local temple workers stopping in for their own meal before attending to their duties. Like the night before, the entire clientele was human, and the two took a table near the bar as the other patrons scrutinized them. Aaron seemed to pay them little heed, but Kari didn't appreciate the attention, specifically because she was with a prostitute and imagined that was why most of those present were staring at them. The others returned to their meals soon enough, though, and Kari loosened up a little. It was just as likely they were looking at her because she had wings, tucked tight to her back as they were, and she stifled a sigh, realizing it would do more harm than good. Instead she turned her attention to a young human girl as she approached.

"G'morning," the girl, also of the pale complexion common to the other humans, said amiably. "Would you like breakfast or just some coffee?"

"I'll take some breakfast and a DarkWind Sunrise," Kari said, and she received a curious look from both the barmaid and Aaron.

"Breakfast and coffee sound just fine, thank you," Aaron said after a moment. He stared across at Kari. "Do you always drink so early in the morning?"

Kari fought for something to tell him and wondered what she could say. She had started drinking heavily when she was just a teen, and it only got worse after she'd been diagnosed with a terminal disease. Nothing had changed: while she'd been forbidden to drink during the war campaign, she felt no inclination to put it aside as she tried to pick up whatever pieces of her shattered life she could. On the contrary, the way she'd felt the night before, and the way she felt at that moment…no, a drink was exactly what she needed by her reckoning.

"I don't know how to explain it," she said after a few moments. "I've always enjoyed a strong drink. It's the only release I really have."

Aaron waved his hand, cutting her off. "You don't have to justify yourself to me," he said. "I suppose if I worked as dangerous a profession as you do, I might feel the same way."

Kari nodded shortly, but her work had little enough to do with it. She hunted and killed demons because it was something that needed to be done, and something she was quite good at. When it came to her work, drinking was simply a way to wind down, to relax and shake off the tension of the hunt. During the hunt itself she never touched alcohol, not being able to afford coming face to face with her quarry while intoxicated. Drunken demonhunters in the field soon became dead demonhunters. The fact that she'd spent the previous eight years engaged in skirmish after skirmish was no better than her usual lifestyle of hunting: she was battle fatigued, and she wanted a drink to keep herself wound down as much as possible.

To Kari, drink was a silent partner: a celibate mate who made her feel good without consequences or an awkward goodbye the following morning. Her brow furrowed as the thought crossed her mind, and she rubbed her arm across her eyes in exasperation. She found that she was thoroughly confused, hardly able to put one thought in front of the other where her long-term goals were concerned without wondering if she had felt that way before her untimely death. Had life always been so bleak, even when facing a terminal disease? Or was it just that back then, she had no future to consider?

"You seem pensive," her companion said, piercing her thoughts, and he leaned back in his chair as the barmaid returned with their meals and drinks. He studied Kari, but her attention was on her own thoughts and she paid his words and stare little heed. She had woken before dawn and sat staring at Aaron, and she wondered if he had perhaps merely kept his eyes nearly closed and pretended to still sleep. She was just as glad for that; she didn't want to answer any of the awkward questions the incident may have prompted.

After bidding them have a good meal, the barmaid left the two alone to their silence once more, and Kari's finally met Aaron's eyes. She wondered if he ever thought about his own long-term future, and whether he thought he could continue in his line of work indefinitely. She wasn't sure why she even cared, but the curiosity of whether others faced the same uncertainty she did nagged at her. Was he saving money to retire, or did he plan to get more "honest" work when his youth and attractiveness abandoned him?

"It was easy enough to not think about the future during the War," she said quietly after another minute, and she took a sip of her drink as Aaron nodded. "When you're in a war, all you really think about is doing your duty, making sure there'll be a tomorrow without worrying about what it will bring. Now that I don't have a war to consider, I have a lot to think about."

He smiled as he began to eat, and Kari did likewise. She didn't want to elaborate too much on the subject and sound like she was whining. Breakfast consisted of eggs and some of the roasted pork from the prior night, and though it wasn't her favorite, Kari ate it gladly. After eight years of eating trail rations or whatever the hunters managed to fell, a good solid meal was a blessing no matter how much she didn't like it. Her drink was good but weak, but that was just as well: she had a busy day ahead of her and didn't want to give any potential caravaneers the wrong impression when she asked them for a ride to Sarchelete.

"I don't think about the future much," Aaron commented between sips of his coffee. "I suppose when my days of selling myself are over, I might have to find work in a temple paying for it."

Kari laughed, nearly spitting out her drink. "You might want to avoid Ambergaust and Carsius' church," she joked.

He laughed in turn, picking at his food. "You think prostitution goes against the tenets of marriage, childbirth and womanhood?"

"Just a little," she answered, but then she shrugged. "Then again, they're among the more forgiving of the pantheon." He nodded to that comment, and they continued their meal in silence until Millie came out of the back room and approached. She had Kari's armor in her arms, with the clothing folded neatly on top of it. She placed the garments in an empty chair beside the terra-dracon female and smiled, lightly patting Kari's shoulder before she returned to the back room. Aaron took one look at the armor before his eyes swung up to meet Kari's.

"Is that paluric?" he asked simply, his question drawing the attention of others in the common room even at its low volume.

"Yes it is," Kari said, watching as he ran his fingers across its smooth but segmented surface. "It was a gift from an old friend."

His eyes widened in shock, and he whistled softly. "You realize you

27

could sell that armor and live comfortably for the rest of your life? Probably allow your children to do so as well? That is, if you ever got tired of hunting demons for a living."

"I don't hunt demons for the money," Kari said quietly. She finished her drink and her eyes slipped down to the table as she gripped the empty glass between both hands. She looked away from him, out one of the front windows of the inn, lost in thought again.

"Did they hurt someone in your family?" he asked, but she didn't respond. "Did they hurt *you*?"

Kari turned back to him and shook her head lightly. "Nothing so personal," she said. "It's not something I think I could put into words." She rose from her seat, took up her armor and clothes, and met her companion's eyes once more. "I'm going to get dressed and then I've got things to do. I may be in town a few days, but I don't think it's a good idea for us to see each other again."

Aaron sat back in his chair and fought to hold her stare. "Did I do something wrong?" he asked.

"No, it's not that at all," she said, waving a hand. "I'm just...not looking for a mate, Aaron, and neither are you. I appreciate your company, but the more time we spend together, the harder it'll be when I leave and don't come back."

He sighed, rose to his feet, and forced a smile. "You're right, of course, my lady," he said, and he gave her a chaste peck on the side of her snout. "Thank you for the pleasure of your company, and the gods preserve you as you head back out into danger."

"Thank you," Kari returned, and she made way up to her room to get changed. The upper hallway was quiet behind her, and she could clearly hear the front door of the inn close as Aaron left the building. Kari closed the door to her room behind her, put her back against it and slid down to the floor. She sat there a few minutes, stifling the urge to cry, and instead she reminded herself that it was better that way. Walking the path of the demonhunter was lonely and dangerous, but it was the life she had chosen and would not walk away from. She knew that one day, perhaps the timing would be right and she wouldn't have to push men away, but for now, she had a job to do, and she had to keep that her priority.

She rubbed her hands slowly across the black skin of her forearms, and could still feel Aaron's gentle touches from the night before. She rose to her feet and stripped off her leisure clothes. She dressed quickly in her undergarments, padded clothes and paluric plate armor, and after strapping on her sword belt, she made her way downstairs and out of the inn.

The rain brought slightly warmer air with it, but Kari imagined it would be the last breath of warmth the southlands felt until the spring. The temple district was fairly busy, and a lucky few vendors set up carts with the last of the harvests along the streets in the nicer part of the city. The main merchants' square was at the center of the four districts, but there were so many carts, stalls, and people pressed into the area that oftentimes unwary merchants lost more to shoplifters and pickpockets than they made from honest folk. In the temple district, such was not usually a concern, and Kari understood being allowed to open shop there must have been quite a privilege.

Kari set out to the central bazaar, where she figured someone would know whether any caravans had stopped in the city to resupply recently. She briefly considered returning to the inn to get her pack, but she realized it would be both a ripe target for pickpockets and more weight to be carried when she wasn't even sure a caravan would be leaving that week, let alone the same day. She turned left from the inn's front door and followed the road to the northeast until another turned back toward the northwest and into the market square proper.

The bazaar was the largest instance of organized chaos she had seen in her life, even more so than the initial war camp where the various Light divisions were assigned to their respective commanders at the start of the war. Everywhere there were merchants in stalls, standing protectively before carts, hawking wares, haggling, yelling at children who swiped small goods, yelling at guards for not doing anything about it, and in some brave cases, openly counting gold and silver coins. Instinctively, Kari flattened out her coin purse and tucked it inside her girdle; it wasn't comfortable, but it was a relatively heavy purse and a tempting mark for pickpockets. She remembered well that even demonhunters were not immune to the wiles of pickpockets and street urchins.

Kari walked into the bazaar and most of the people cleared a path for the winged, dog tag-wearing woman as she made her way through the crowd, except for one merchant who tried to sell her some alchemical concoction that would let her fly farther. She'd heard that claim enough times and, despite her lack of understanding of such things, she knew that unless whatever he was selling made her weigh significantly less, it wouldn't help her fly at all. Her lack of staying power while flying was a product of her weight coupled with the low strength of her wings: she could glide well enough, but actual flight was very difficult and rarely lasted more than a couple of minutes. She ignored him as he vied for her attention.

As she dodged shady-looking characters and merchants desperate to make a sale, Kari spotted a fruit vendor stationed in the northwest corner of the bazaar. She guessed he probably lived in the northwest district if he was able to secure such a prime spot for his cart, and she headed towards him, hoping he might know something of the caravan schedules, or at least someone else who would. His clothing gave the impression that his business was prosperous, as did the fact that he was somewhat overweight. A smile creased his face as she approached, and he readjusted an utterly ridiculous-looking hat that sat high on a bald spot.

"Greetings," he said to her as she came to a stop before him. "Can I interest you in some of my apples or oranges?" He gestured toward his rather generous fruit selection, which seemed out of place given the cold weather that was gaining a tighter grip on the region daily. Kari assumed he was benefitting from the late harvests of the more northern orchards, which would have been overstocked with produce while the majority of laborers were still away at war.

"How are the apples?" Kari responded, and she took a closer look at the odd combination of fruits and autumn pumpkins and gourds on his cart.

"They were harvested late, but I have only the best of what the orchards had to offer among my selection," he said.

"Excuse me mister, can you spare a coin?" came the high-pitched voice of a child from behind Kari as someone tugged lightly on her tail. Kari turned to behold a young rir child. The girl put her hand to the end of her little snout as she realized Kari was a woman, and her green eyes widened as she blurted, "Whoops!"

"Chelsea!" a terra-rir woman called as she came up behind the little girl. The woman's green eyes took in Kari quickly and then she blushed, the black skin of her face paling around the eyes and cheeks. "Oh, I'm so sorry officer, my daughter didn't know..."

"That's all right," Kari said. She knew that most demonhunters had a rather intimidating reputation, and that beggars and the poor might be afraid of them in such a place as Barcon. Kari smiled down at the little girl, who looked like her mother minus the obvious years of toil, and Chelsea's cute little green eyes stared up in wonder at the muscular woman before her. Chelsea began tugging on her hair and grabbed her mother's leg for comfort under Kari's scrutiny.

"I just wanted a apple," the little girl said.

"Yes, but you ask me, don't go begging other people, Chelsea," her mother berated her. The woman looked toward Kari again, but had a hard time making eye contact. "Apologies again, m'lady, I don't mean to impose, it's been difficult since the War…my husband never returned…"

"I understand," Kari said. She fished inside her armor and into the purse, a deft finger bringing up a single platinum coin. A platinum coin spent wisely could feed a family for weeks, and Zalkar's church paid her up to five of them a month for her service. Demonhunters were rarely in one place for long and frequently needed to pay for food, lodgings, travel supplies, and oftentimes healing. Kari made further money from actually performing the hunts she was given, as even the serilian demons she killed sometimes had coins to transact business. Though Kari never accumulated any real wealth, neither did she ever seem to want for anything. She held the coin out toward the woman, who stared at it tentatively before shaking her head.

"I can't," the woman said meekly.

"Don't give anything to the beggars, it just encourages them," the merchant grumbled.

Kari turned and flashed him a scowl, her pointed ears angling back sharply, and the man backed up a step. "You just shut your mouth," she said shortly, and then she turned back to the woman. "Take it. Just don't tell anyone you have it, or where you got it."

"My lady is too kind," the woman said and she took the coin, but still she avoided eye contact. "Did you fight in the War?"

"I did," Kari answered. "All eight years."

The terra-rir female perked up at Kari's answer, some glimmer of hope entering her eyes, and the once-dull orbs glittered. "What unit?" she asked hopefully.

"Thirty-fifth Light Division, up in the Barrier Mountains," Kari said with a nod toward the west, and the woman's shoulders slumped.

"Ah, my husband fought through the heartlands in the Eleventh Light Division," the other woman said. "Maybe he is still alive. It's only been a few days…maybe he's still on his way home to us."

Kari sighed silently, shook her head slowly, and put a hand to the woman's shoulder. "The Eleventh Light Division was lost," she said softly. "I'm sorry, if your husband was assigned to that brigade, he's not coming home."

The woman sank down to her knees and wrapped her daughter in a tight embrace as both began to cry, but she looked up to meet Kari's eyes as the demonhunter squatted down. "Do you know how it happened?" the woman asked breathlessly. "Did he die bravely?"

"Yes, he did," Kari said. "I don't know the details, but the Eleventh Light Division broke the siege of DarkWind. The brigade was lost, but the entire city of DarkWind was saved, and they owe their lives to men like your husband. We all do, really: had DarkWind fallen, the War might still be raging, or we may have already lost."

Kari hugged the woman tightly, holding her until her crying subsided into short sobs, and then Kari fished out the rest of the purse she'd been given by the church. "Take this," she said as she pushed the pouch into the woman's hand and closed her fingers around it. "This is the Unyielding's gift for your husband's sacrifice."

The terra-rir female hid the coin purse quickly, but her eyes came right up to finally meet the stare of the demonhunter. "Who are you?" she asked quietly.

"Karian Vanador, Shield of the Heavens, by Zalkar's grace."

"Karian Vanador...?" the woman muttered, and Kari wondered if a slew of questions was forthcoming. None did, however, the woman merely adding, "I...I will never forget this." She bowed to the demonhunter, and then she picked up her daughter and made her way out of the bazaar. The little girl's eyes never left Kari even as her mother carried her away, and the woman looked back over her shoulder once before she disappeared into the traffic heading into the northwest district.

"You're very trusting for a demonhunter," the merchant said when Kari turned back to him, a look of doubt clearly splayed across his weathered face. "The beggars around here, they all have a similar story. The War just gives them something else to use as a weapon."

Kari fixed him with her aggravated stare once more, silencing him. She considered his pot belly, his fancy clothes – even the ridiculous hat – and guessed he knew nothing of being poor, ragged, or hungry. "Did you lose anyone in the war?" she asked, but he shook his head in response. "Then don't tell me how to recognize someone who has. That was no act, I could see it plainly in her eyes. I lost enough friends in the war to know."

The human shrugged, and then placed a few of his better-looking apples on the cart's shelf before her. "You have other coin, I assume?" he asked.

Kari stared down at the apples for a few moments before shaking her head. "I've lost my appetite," she said simply. She turned and headed up the northwest road out of the bazaar. She would have liked to ask the merchant if he knew anything about caravans coming through the city, but his demeaning tone of voice when speaking of the other woman made Kari want to punch him. She guessed that if his tone didn't change while she was asking directions she might do just that – better she go elsewhere, and find someone a bit more accommodating.

The northwest district was clean and well kept, and Kari assumed it was because the majority of its inhabitants were cronies of the infamous crime lord who called the district home. The houses demonstrated the wealth and affluence of their owners much more prominently than even those in the temple district: here the homes and buildings were constructed of brick and whitewashed stone. Most even had windows free of the iron bars she expected in such a city, which told her even more of the iron-fisted rule of the Earl.

The main avenue ran from the bazaar straight out to the city gates, passing through a square which housed the Earl's black tower. Across from the black tower was what appeared to be a church, which Kari found curious; all the other churches and temples were located in one district. When she reached the square she realized it was not such a curious thing as she thought, for over the church's door, displayed for all to see, was a swaying wooden sign marked with the symbol of a burning parchment. Kari balked, shocked that any city, even one so corrupt, would have a church to Achirun, the silver-tongued devil, out in the open for all to see.

She stared at the structure in contempt for several minutes and spared a glance over her shoulder at the black tower and its two well-armed guards before she continued in her trek. She wondered how her deity could stand to have a temple in a city that housed one to a *demon lord* from the underworld, and how the den of evil had not been burned out. The only conclusion she could reach was that Kaelin Black himself had ordained the church's construction, and that while Zalkar might have no tolerance for such things, her deity would not abandon those who tried to lead honest lives even in the heart of such a city. Zalkar's duty to his people, like theirs to him, transcended his own likes and dislikes – and so his small church stayed. It was hard for her to fathom, but gave her further pride in her job and the master she served.

Kari ignored the wolf-whistles of the black tower's guards and continued up the main avenue toward the gates. Demonhunters were generally not welcome in the city of Barcon, and it was no mystery that they were trying to bait her into doing something that would allow them to arrest her. Kari wondered why Black surrounded himself with humans when he was half-demon. It further gave her pause as she considered the previous night, when the guards had nearly denied her entry because they thought *she* was half-demon. Why would Black refuse entry to his own kind? His heritage was no secret; when one considered his already centuries-long life, it was pretty much a given: he was certainly no elf, and the rir people, like humans, rarely lived more than a century. It was possible to use magical means to extend one's life – it was quite common among the wizards and other arcanists of the world – but his species had been confirmed on many occasions, reclusive though he was.

The only reason Kari could come up with was that he found humans easier to control, and that his own "kind," as it were, had the potential to be far more corrupt than even him. That thought gave her a laugh as she considered just how despicable one would have to be to give even Kaelin Black pause. While there were many different types of half-demon and they were all unique from the others in some way, she had a hard time imagining many full-blooded serilian demons that could compare to Black. Granted, he was only "suspected" of doing many of the things he had a reputation for, but he did nothing to dispel such rumors, which lent credibility to them and suggested his reputation was likely well-earned.

The northwest gate was a double portcullis, forming a square that extended beyond the normal wall, and the area was comprised of numerous stables and parking areas for wagons and carts. An outer gate with a complement of half a dozen guards allowed caravans and other travelers into the stable square, while the inner gate was guarded by four more who would require identification before travelers could enter the city proper. An inn was nestled on one side of the large square, allowing travelers simply passing through to stay within the outer wall without identifying themselves to the guards.

Inside the inner portcullis were two more guards, whose main job was likely to dispatch rioters attempting to storm the gate and to alert further squads of militia should any serious trouble arise within the stable square. Atop the portcullis on either side was a pair of towers, where several more guards with crossbows were stationed up high to provide cover fire in case of trouble or to open the portcullis to let people through. They paid the demonhunter little heed, their attention focused almost completely on the other side of the gate.

After speaking briefly with the guards, Kari passed through the gateway and crossed the plaza toward the inn. The square was dominated by stables and the smells associated with them, and Kari chose her path carefully, padding across the unpaved dirt grounds, and she headed into the dim interior of the inn's common room. The guards mentioned that traffic was heavy lately, and their description was apparently no exaggeration: every table and chair in the common room was full, leaving barely enough room for the woman to make her way to the bar. Kari scanned the crowd and saw that the clientele was quite varied: more of her own kind was present than humans, so she figured it was almost certainly a pilgrim

34

caravan. Even a few terra-bengals sat around one of the smaller tables, their white tiger-like stripes standing out among the plain black skin of the other rir present. Engrossed in their conversation as they were, they looked up when the winged female crossed the room, as did most of the crowd.

A young human with tan skin and a high brow greeted Kari when she reached the bar, and his chestnut eyes studied her briefly. Once he noticed her dog tags, he smiled. "What can I get for you, officer?" he asked.

Karian waved off the question. "Just looking for information," she said and he nodded, wiped his hands on the white towel at his belt and leaned forward on the bar so she could keep her voice down. "I'm looking for a caravan or group of travelers headed to the holy city. I'm guessing the bengals over there are headed that way, are they part of a caravan?"

"All of these people are," he answered. He pointed toward a table where a mixed group of rir and humans sat. "See that rir fella over there with the golden hair? Name's Nurrik Orndrom; he's the caravan master for the pilgrimage to the holy city. I'm sure they'd be happy to have a demonhunter with them."

"Thank you," Kari said. She moved toward the table and received a few curious stares from Nurrik and those seated around him, but they seemed to loosen up when they saw her dog tags. "Are you Nurrik?" she asked as she came up next to the man.

"I am. What can I do for you, officer?" he replied, sitting back in his seat so he could look up at her face more easily. His emerald eyes were full of a mixture of curiosity and awe, and perhaps appreciation for her feminine form. Kari tried not to dwell on the last.

"I'm looking to travel with someone headed to the holy city," Kari said. "The barkeep said you were the caravan master; would you let me sign on as a guard in exchange for a ride?"

"Will we have supplies to support another?" Nurrik asked the man seated to his left, an older human dressed in a hooded blue robe, who nodded. He looked back up to Kari's face with a crooked smile. "We have a couple of half-demons with us, so they won't let us into the city to re-supply," he said. "It's not going to be an issue if you have to travel with them, is it Miss...?"

"Karian Vanador, Shield of the Heavens, by Zalkar's grace," Kari said formally, and then she shook her head in answer to his question. "And I've no problem with them if they behave themselves." She realized that much of the common room had gone silent, and she found herself the target of several dozen stares. She wondered if it was the comment about the half-demons behaving themselves, which she had intended as a joke, and she

35

scratched absently at a pointed ear as the silence grew thick.

"Karian Vanador?" Nurrik repeated after exchanging looks with the others at the table. Kari expected a slew of questions, but only one came forth. "You served under Brigadier Kris Jir'tana during the War?"

"Yes," she replied. "We came down from Atrice in the north, through the Barrier Mountains, and weren't far from here when the War ended."

The older rir nodded his head appreciatively, a muted but not insincere smile on his features. "Yes, the accomplishments of the Warlord and his company are well known around the southlands. Very well, you are welcome to travel with us so long as you are willing to lend your blades should any trouble arise. We were planning to take our leave this afternoon, as they will not allow us into the city to resupply, as I mentioned. If you wish to travel with us, I'll make room for you in my personal wagon."

"That's perfect," Kari said. "How long do you expect the trip to take?"

"Assuming all goes smoothly, no more than two weeks. Possibly three if we have any problems with the wagons or the mountain passes prove difficult. We should be supplied for four, just in case," he said, his unspoken question answered by another nod from the human.

"Great, I'll just get my things from the inn and be back shortly," Kari said, and she bid the man and his companions farewell and started toward the door. She had thought they knew who she was based on their reaction - and everyone else's - to her name, but thankfully, no one asked about her death and apparent resurrection. She expected most people wouldn't know what to make of such an unprecedented event, and in any case, it wasn't something she really knew how to explain, anyway.

As she left from a different angle, Kari saw the half-demons Nurrik had spoken of for the first time. They were watching her with wary eyes, and she knew that even though her job was to hunt and kill their progenitors, prejudice and hatred were things they lived with constantly. Kari tried to stay as open minded as possible: she knew they had certainly not chosen to be born half-demon and that they were as free-willed as any other peoples. While half-demons could be as big a problem as full-blooded serilian demons and many half-demons had fought on the Devil Queen's side in the war, she had to be careful not to alienate possible allies and friends.

When she passed closer to them, she could see that both were half-elite, their fathers of the elite variety of serilian demon. The serilian demons were the Devil Queen Seril's creations, the soldiers she had made for her endless war against the rir and the other mortal races of Citaria. The elites, however, had been the first of the serilian demons to break completely free of her influence and choose to go their own way. For the most part the elite demons had assimilated themselves into mortal society in the frontier towns, and even in the major cities in some cases. During the Fifth Demon War, they turned on their creator completely, throwing in their lot with the mortals, and they were one of the reasons the mortals' victory had been so complete.

Kari smiled at the two as she passed, and they bowed their heads shortly in greeting. No words were exchanged, but it was clear her smile spoke volumes to them. Half-elites were usually the product of truly loving relationships, as elite demons quite often took rir females as mates and settled into an almost mortal lifestyle, at least until war came. When war came, they were fearsome fighters, strong and durable and without a shred of surrender in them. Banded together, they were incredible shock troops, and among the best allies one could hope for. Kari knew from experience: Jir'tana's brigade during the war had half a dozen elite demons and numerous half-elites among their number.

Based on Nurrik's hesitation, Kari had assumed they were half-brys or half-corlypsi: half-demons of the lesser types that were normally the product of force. The lesser types of the serilian demons were thoroughly evil, created solely for destruction or to spawn half-breeds that would live among mortals until they were powerful enough to undertake destruction themselves. While many of the brys had betrayed their creator and served Kaelariel, their children were enigmatic and didn't often fit in well in mortal society. And the half-corlypsi – the spawn of the thoroughly evil corlypsi demons – grew up to be as stupid and violent as their fathers more often than not. Had Nurrik's half-demon passengers been of those varieties, Kari would've had a more guarded outlook toward them.

Kari headed back out into the square, squinted skyward at the sun breaking through the cloud cover, and was thankful for the clarity of her immediate future. She was content knowing that she would travel with the pilgrims, do her duty as a guard, and once safely in Sarchelete, she would receive orders likely to keep her busy and focused for at least a few months. After a moment of quiet contemplation, she moved out of the way of a couple of people heading into the inn, and set her feet back on the road to the Bloodied Blade in the temple district.

~~*~*

Kari stopped in the church to let Master Devin know the approximate

37

timetable for her arrival in Sarchelete so that he could pass the information on through prayer to Zalkar. She thanked David and Millie for their hospitality and left them several gold coins despite their insistence that a demonhunter not pay. She returned to the stable square as quickly as possible and met with the caravan. As promised, Nurrik provided her with a bedroll in the back of the lead wagon. He also welcomed Kari to sit on the driver's bench with him whenever she wished. His mate, a pretty middle-aged rir woman with the typical white hair and green eyes of their kind, welcomed the demonhunter to their traveling home and let her know to simply ask when she wanted something to eat. Thus her journey to Sarchelete began.

The morning hours passed quietly. Nurrik was busy passing orders to get the caravan moving steadily and all together. After lunch, Kari's traveling companions became more talkative. Kari did her best to dodge personal questions, and the Orndroms seemed content to listen to stories about her career as a demonhunter, apparently unaware of the fact that the things Kari told them of had happened two centuries before. It was just as well, since the tale of her return from death was one most would be hard-pressed to believe or even understand – as it was, she could hardly believe or understand it herself. Based on Nurrik's and the rest of the tavern's reaction to her stating her full name, she had expected many to recognize her the previous day, and in a minor way was thankful that such had not been the case.

"So you're a Shield of the Heavens?" Nurrik asked. "That's rather high up in the ranks, isn't it?"

"Twelfth order," Kari confirmed with a nod, unsure if the caravan master was aware that there were sixteen total ranks in the Order. "I advanced pretty quickly since my work was all I really ever did. No family or anything to divide my time with."

"Did you train with Jason Bosimar, before his unfortunate death in the war?" he asked.

"I only ever met him at the war camp up in Latalex," she said. "And I only got to speak to him for a few minutes, which was too bad. Seemed like a really good man. A lot of times reaching the rank of Avatar of Vengeance has a tendency to change people: to harden them and make them a lot less open. I could tell that wasn't the case with Jason. He was a friend to nearly every man and woman he spoke to up in the war camp. A leader like that is a rare thing."

"Indeed," Nurrik said. He spared a glance around the side of the wagon to inspect the train behind them. When he returned his attention to the road ahead and his conversation with the demonhunter, he asked, "Does your Order have a new Avatar?"

Kari shook her head and picked up her canteen to take a careful sip of water. By all accounts the caravan had plenty of supplies despite being turned away at Barcon, but Kari's time in Jir'tana's brigade taught her to conserve even when it didn't seem necessary. "No, no one is even close to attaining the rank," she said after a moment. "Right now Lord Allerius is the head of the Order, at least admina..." She paused again, her brow furrowed.

"Administratively," Nurrik prompted as she stuttered, and she nodded.

"Yea, he's the administrative head of the Order," she finished. "But he's only a rank above me, still several ranks below becoming an Avatar and true head of the Order."

"So you're in line to become an Avatar sometime in the near future?" he asked with a raised brow and an impressed smile.

Kari shrugged but couldn't suppress a smile of her own. "It's always been a dream of mine, but I have a lot of work ahead of me to reach that point," she said. "And sometimes, I still have doubts...the Avatar has to be above such feelings."

"Hogwash," Nurrik said, his declaration echoed by a giggle from his mate in the back. "Everyone has doubts. Don't ever let anyone tell you any different. Nobody's faith is perfect."

"You have doubts, even though you're making a pilgrimage to the holy city?" the demonhunter asked curiously.

Nurrik took his eyes from the road to fix Kari with a steady stare for a few moments before he swung his gaze back ahead. "Our creator died at the end of the War," he said, and Kari's stomach dropped at his words. "I go to the holy city to see what direction our people go from here, what his will was for us prior to his destruction. We all have doubts, young lady."

Kari swallowed uneasily; how could she have forgotten such an overwhelming truth? Gori Sensullu, the creator of their world and all of its indigenous peoples except the serilian demons, was destroyed along with his evil counterpart at the War's conclusion. How did such a thing slip her mind, that her *creator* was *dead*? It was almost unfathomable, and she realized that she was far from being alone in her doubts and confusion: likely the entire world was suffering the same uncertainty she was. Though their creator's son, Kaelariel, had assumed leadership of the pantheon, the faith of the people was still shaken at best, or completely torn asunder at worst.

"I hadn't really thought about it," she said. "I've always served

Zalkar, but I've never really worshipped him. I've always served him and I love serving him, but I feel…apart from the pantheon for some reason, as if something else drives me, but lets Zalkar steer my course."

Nurrik put a hand reassuringly to Kari's shoulder. "Perhaps you'll find more than just orders in the holy city," he said. "Even with Zalkar guiding your career, it's not unusual for you to still have questions or even doubts. Maybe in the holy city, you'll find your answers."

Kari nodded but remained silent, and the caravan rolled on into the afternoon. The journey was quiet and uneventful; the serilian demons knew to stay far from the Barrier Mountains, where they'd suffered defeat after defeat at the hands of Jir'tana and his brigade. The warm front that had come in while Kari was in Barcon did little once they headed up through the mountain passes, but the weather remained mostly favorable nonetheless. There weren't many things in the wild that would attack something the size of a caravan, so they passed harmlessly through the mountains and onto the coastal plains on the far west side. Just as Nurrik had promised, they came within sight of the holy city after two weeks, and as they crested a hill, Kari stepped down from the wagon.

From the hilltop, Kari looked out over the massive city. Its north end was dominated by the towering white marble temples of the pantheon and capped by what was the most holy temple to Gori Sensullu, the rir peoples' lord and creator. She looked over the temple, and even from such a distance she drew one of her blades, placed it tip-down to the ground and knelt, and she bowed her head in silent prayer. She prayed for the unity of the pantheon, and that Kaelariel would be as strong and benevolent a leader as his father. Others climbed down from their wagons and followed in Kari's example, and began their memorial before ever setting foot in the city itself.

Kari rose, caught up to her wagon, and climbed back up into the driver's seat. Nurrik fixed her with a curious stare but said nothing. By the end of the day, the procession reached the gates and began the long and tedious process of checking in with the city watch. While pilgrim caravans were common, the holy city was particularly careful not to let large bands of potential assassins or terrorists within its walls. It had been ages since anyone dared attack the city in any way, but Kari assumed the guards knew that complacency was the seed of disaster.

"You won't be mad if I enter the city on my own, will you?" Kari asked her benefactors.

Nurrik shook his head lightly. "Not at all," he said. "You obviously have more pressing concerns than filling out paperwork or answering questions for hours. By all means, go."

Kari shook the hand offered to her and thanked the rir couple for their hospitality. She made her way to the gates where she was stopped only briefly. The rir guards there saw her dog tags and waved her through without question. The massive city gates, made of reinforced wood, had a door in the base for pedestrian traffic, and Kari slipped through quickly when the guards opened it for her. The other gates to the city were far less stringent in their entry requirements from what she had been told, as all carts, wagons, and caravans were diverted to the east gate to lighten the load of the checkpoints at the other entryways.

Kari stepped into the city and found herself in the eastern quarter, which she remembered housed mostly military personnel and city watch. Just inside was an open, circular plaza with half a dozen guard towers stationed around it at even intervals, each with an archer platform atop it should any trouble arise at the checkpoint. The towers and the plaza were empty. The process of entering through the busy east gate took most far longer than it took Kari, and for a moment she was thankful that being a demonhunter tended to let one avoid thorough questioning. With a deep breath she took in the scent of the city: dusty and heavy with the smell of wood fires as the weather began to turn colder, with the slight smell of salt water from its western side.

Avenues ran along the inner wall to the north and south with another main road leading toward the center of the city. Kari headed down the middle road. The eastern quarter was quiet and near-deserted, and she guessed that those guards and soldiers not on duty were likely sleeping, awaiting their own shifts. She took advantage of the clear streets and quickened her pace toward the center of the city. She remembered that there was a main boulevard into the heart of the north quarter, where the grand temples were located.

Sarchelete was the seat of rir civilization: the very first city their people had built with bare hands when they were created over three thousand years before. The city was much smaller then, when the species was young and still getting its feet beneath it. Once the attacks of Seril's demonic servants were turned back more steadily and the rir began to thrive, the city began to slowly expand, and the walls gradually moved outward as more and more homes and workshops sprung up throughout. After several centuries, when the pantheon likewise began to grow with those handpicked mortals Gori Sensullu promoted to deity status, the lone temple to their creator was joined by more and more marble temples to his helpers.

Kari's own deity, Zalkar, ascended in the late fifteenth century, and was anointed the patron of demonhunters, the law, and justice, areas to which he had dedicated his mortal life. Each of his fellow subordinate deities had likewise been brought up from mortality, each being given control over the domains their lives most closely followed. The only exception was Karmi G'Dorrinn, the goddess of the seas, who Gori Sensullu had created whole as a deity. In the years leading up to the Fifth Demon War, the gods of another world called Koryon had joined with the Citarian pantheon to aid in the Apocalypse, but that had happened after Kari's death. She knew there was less attachment between the Koryonites and the people of Kari's world, and though that was changing over time, Kari had seen enough during the War to know that her people didn't relate as well to the Koryonite deities who had never been through the trials of mortality.

The central square was a massive, sprawling plaza with a titanic fountain in its center. In the heart of the fountain was a flawless marble statue of Kris Fletcher, a human paladin more commonly referred to as the Ghost. The statue commemorated his victory over a squad of brys during the third century, when the assassin demons were newly created and sent to infiltrate the holy city in an attempt to destroy it from within. History spoke of Fletcher fearlessly facing the demons, calling upon his lord to protect him and turning aside their every attack. He was well known as a master with a two-handed sword, and made short work of the faster, deadly demons. In the end, he had won not only the battle but also the adoration of the rir people as a whole, and had been named Lord Protector of the holy city. He served that post with honor and courage throughout the remainder of his life, and upon his passing he was anointed the patron deity of paladins and the god of honor and purity. Despite the fact that he was human, many rir who took up the sword to follow the path of the knight or paladin took easily to the Ghost's service, and he quickly became a very popular deity.

Kari stared at the fountain in silence and let the sounds of the city flow through her, the groan and hum of the passing masses giving life to the marble scene before her and further meaning to its existence. This city stood because of the efforts of great men and women like the one depicted before her. It was part of the reason she became a demonhunter: to help preserve civilization against those who refused to become a part of it and would therefore see it destroyed. For a moment, Kari wondered if her own life measured in any way against the accomplishments of men like Kris Fletcher: whether the history books spoke favorably of her short life, or if they mentioned her at all.

Kari coughed quietly into her hand and spared an embarrassed glance skyward as her thoughts turned toward hubris. Her fame and fortune, even her name had almost nothing to do with why she had undertaken a life of service, why she continued to do what she did despite her doubts and loneliness. Kris Fletcher didn't become a hero because he'd set out to be a hero: he became one by doing what needed to be done despite his own doubts, fears, and desires. At her core, Kari knew the same must be true of her: those who set out to become heroes failed far more often than not, succumbing to ego and jealousy, and quite often became the embodiment of what they'd set out to fight.

Kari met the frozen stare of the marble statue. It held its sword in a defensive posture, and for a moment she saw the smile beneath the scowl of determination. The artist had captured what the Ghost stood for so well in this rendition, somehow hiding the smile of a mind and spirit at peace beneath the look of determination that marked the heart of a warrior. Kari glanced around the rest of the plaza. Its outer edge was lined with quaint eateries and well-kept taverns, and no smithies or hard goods shops made their home amongst such beauty. People of nearly every race she knew sat at small tables or on benches around the circular central plaza, enjoying the sun and what remained of the fairly warm weather, knowing that winter was on its way and would be brutal as always. Life in the holy city and the surrounding region had never been easy: the creator had placed his people in such a place to make them strong and adaptable, and when they fell short in those areas, the humans had bolstered them.

The demonhunter dipped her fingers in the water of the fountain, uttered a silent prayer to her deity's ally, and touched her wet fingers to her forehead. She made her way up the wide northern boulevard that headed toward the raised plazas of the temples higher up on the hill against which the city was built. She glanced briefly at the humans she passed and marveled at how well they integrated themselves into rir society, and the feat was no less impressive for being three thousand years in the making. Kari wondered where it was they came from and who created them. History said they had crashed near Sarchelete in the latter half of the first century of her people's existence, in some type of craft that traveled among the stars. At the very least it was a good story, and certainly no less believable than the counter-reports that they arrived via magic – it all sounded like magic to her.

The cobblestones of the northern road soon gave way to marble steps, and Kari moved to the side of the street where a man sat on a simple folding wooden chair beside a pan of water. Without a word, she washed her feet and dropped a silver coin from her purse into the box at the man's feet. The human smiled and nodded his head, though he said nothing, and Kari began to ascend the marble staircase into the first temple plaza.

The northern quarter was shaped like a clover, with each "leaf" comprised of two temples, and the grand marble stairway up the hillside representing the stem. Between the two central temples at the very north of the quarter was a narrow staircase leading farther up to the hilltop, where Gori Sensullu's temple sat. It was crowned by a massive sandstone statue of the deity's upper body with its hand outstretched to the northeast. Legend said that if one knelt on the topmost step to the temple at the marking of the New Year, the eclipsed sun appeared to sit in the palm of the statue's hand. It was something Kari had always wanted to see for herself, but she'd never found the opportunity.

When she reached the top of the grand staircase, Kari looked around the broad plaza at the columned, marble fronts of the six major temples. Though there were far more than six deities in the pantheon, the newly joined deities of the Koryon pantheon had no temples in this most holy place. Only the eldest and most revered among the Citarian deities had a grand temple, and Kari looked to the symbols carved into the face of each from left to right.

The leftmost temple on the west side of the plaza was to Kerry Kijana, known as Garra Ktarra, the terra-rir god of the night, explorers, and skill; it was marked with the sign of the golden axe. He was among the first generation of rir born to parents rather than created whole, and had served as both a priest of Gori Sensullu and a battle commander in defense of the fledgling race and city. He was widely accepted as one of the greatest fighters among the pantheon: his skill with the dual twin-bladed golden axes he wielded was terrifying to behold and earned him the adoration of warriors and soldiers alike.

Beside it stood the temple to Kaelariel, marked by the sign of the winged focus – a black cross within a circle wrapped in the bat-like wings of a serilian demon. Kaelariel was Gori Sensullu's son, the deliverer who destroyed the Devil Queen at the end of the Apocalypse. He was regarded as an archangel, but his body was that of a guardian demon, the strongest type created by the archdevil. It gave many pause upon seeing him, but Kaelariel's purity was without question, and his life was one of unending dedication to his primary sphere of control: freedom. He also shouldered the mantle of death and, after his father's demise, the coordination of the pantheon.

44

The left of the two middle temples was that of the Ghost, marked with a golden cross. The symbol was a remnant of Fletcher's own faith, an ancient religion the humans brought with them when they arrived on Citaria so many years before. The Ghost also shared the symbol with one of his Koryonite counterparts called Bek Coramin, who adopted the symbol for a different reason. It was often confusing that the two shared the same holy symbol, but those who knew the deities and their doctrines well understood just how similar they were. Fletcher controlled the spheres of honor and purity, and his counterpart controlled the sphere of piety. It was also well known that the two deities shared much in common personally and were good friends.

To the right of the center stood the temple of Sechre Tori, which was marked with a simple red-bladed and black-hilted longsword. Sechre Tori was the god of righteous battle and the greatest of the warrior gods among the pantheon. Tori had lived during the first century and served alongside Kerry Kijana, his mentor, when both were mortal. Though slain in combat with Seril early in his life, Sechre Tori was nicknamed "First In Battle" and quickly became the patron deity of the military and professional fighters. His was a tradition of honorable combat that many aspired to, and his followers through the years worked with the paladins of the Ghost.

Two more temples stood on the right side of the plaza, on the eastern edge of the hill. The east-most temple was different than the others, constructed of black marble streaked with white, which made it easily recognizable as that of Tisa Ch'Brakkh. Named Deanna Jir'tana when she was mortal, Tisa was a descendant of Garra Ktarra and served as queen of the terra-bengals for two decades before ascending directly, rather than after dying. Her gift to Gori Sensullu was to bear Kaelariel, and the common consensus was that her beauty had a large part to do with being chosen. Others argued it was the blood of Garra Ktarra in her veins, but whatever the case, she fulfilled her duty and was anointed the goddess of beauty. She worked closely with her son and her mate upon ascension, and was well loved by all of the deities of the light pantheon. High over the doorway of her temple, carved into the marble, was her symbol: a black cross with the white stripes of a terra-bengal.

Nestled between Tisa and Tori's temples was that of Kari's deity, Zalkar the Unyielding. His balanced forces symbol was carved into the marble over the doorway and painted in the light blue common to his church. Kari paused before heading to meet with the high priest; something else nagged at her, and instead she walked up the final staircase to Gori Sensullu's now defunct temple. Her steps were hurried, as she understood

45

the dinner hour was fast approaching. She wanted to meet with the high priest before he took his evening meal and began his nightly prayers and meditations.

She dodged traffic and reached the top of the final stairs, and Kari approached the white marble structure slowly. Standing at its base she felt very small, staring up at the titanic statue atop the temple that stretched its hand away toward some undefined point. The creator was dead, she reminded herself, and yet still the traffic into and out of his temple was relatively heavy. Groundskeepers tended to the gardens on either side of the wide path leading inside, and it was clear the temple itself wasn't suffering from any neglect in the weeks following the loss. It brought a pained smile to her face.

Kari walked inside and immediately drew the attention of nearly every other pilgrim and mourner within. It was unclear if it was the wings or the dog tags, but she paid their stares little heed. Almost without thought, she approached the slain deity's altar and knelt before it, and she hardly noticed that all the others within knelt with her. She felt a strange urge to cry, but she stifled it. She steeled herself and realized the eyes of all those gathered were upon her. There were no clergy in attendance: the priests of the temple must have converted quickly to the service of other deities to consolidate the strength of the pantheon in the wake of the loss. Only then did Kari realize that as a demonhunter, the others might be looking at her as the only one present with a direct connection to any of the gods.

After a few silent moments, Kari took a deep, silent breath, and spoke quietly. She was neither well educated nor particularly well-spoken, and the words that came forth seemed out of place even to her as she intoned, "Gori Sensullu, our father and creator, we dedicate this time to you. We, your children, don't understand where it is you've gone to, but we'll always remember you. We have you to thank for our lives, for the beautiful world in which we live, and for the strength and perseverance of our people. Wherever it is you've gone to, lord, our love and our thanks go with you. May peace be with you, wherever you are."

She sighed lightly as several *Amens* sounded from around the crowded room, the response to the close of prayer having become popular since the arrival of the humans. Kari turned as someone touched her shoulder, but no one stood there, and a shiver coursed through her momentarily. As odd as it was, it was not a shiver of cold, but instead it left a warmth below her skin that she couldn't explain. She glanced briefly at the others in the temple, but if they had touched her or seen anyone do so, it wasn't apparent in any of their expressions. After another reflective moment, she rose and exited the temple, and made her way back to Zalkar's temple.

The inside of the temple was no different than the church in Barcon, though it was much more spacious given its larger congregation and status as the main temple of the faith. The benches toward the center were full with worshippers listening to the teaching of a middle-aged human in a white robe trimmed in light blue. The priest looked up at Kari while he taught and gestured toward one of the benches, so she sat down to wait and listen. Most of the congregation seemed to be city watch and lawmen, and the priest continued to teach for a few more minutes. As always, the lesson revolved around upholding the law while observing the church's central doctrine regarding justice and mercy.

Once the lesson was complete, the worshippers rose and made their way out of the temple, and many nodded their head to the demonhunter. The priest leaned against the altar and pulled back the hood of his robe to reveal the same military crew cut their deity wore, and which was consequently quite popular among his followers. He studied Kari quietly and paid little heed to the acolytes who came out to clean the temple after the service. After a couple of minutes only the terra-dracon female and the human remained.

"Karian Vanador," the man said when at last they were alone. "It's good that you've come, I've been waiting for you."

"I just wanted to pay my respects to our creator, or I would've been here sooner, Master," she said. She rose and approached the man, and she touched her fist to her breast in salute.

He waved off the explanation. "You only missed more of the same I'm sure you heard countless times in the Academy," he said and extended a hand, which she shook. "I'm Attir Surallis, as I'm sure you've guessed. It's a pleasure to meet you."

"It is?" Kari asked before she realized what she was saying, and the human chuckled as he gestured to the padded chairs at the rear of the chapel. He turned one to face the other and sat down across from her as she took her own seat.

"When the Unyielding told me you were coming, I was quite excited," he said. "I studied your career in detail when I was a younger acolyte in this church. I've been in Zalkar's service for over twenty-five years now, but I have continued to study your career through the years – yours and Turik Jalar's specifically; amazing contemporaries."

"I always regretted never getting to know him," Kari said quietly "We were classmates at the Academy, but he was a couple of years ahead of me in our studies."

47

Attir nodded. "I'm sure being brought back from death has been quite a shock to you," he said. "Understand: it's been a shock to all of us – but a welcome one. We have something quite alarming and urgent to look into, and the Unyielding has asked me to pass along this task to you specifically. Though our lord had no hand in your return, he is *thrilled*, to say the least, with having you back in his service, and hopes that your career will pick back up where it was tragically cut short so long ago. As do I."

"I am my lord's to command," Kari said formally, and she bowed her head toward the high priest. "If he's brought me to you for orders, Master, I'm sure it's something important."

The human nodded once again and held his hand out, and he took Kari's offered hand in both of his. "I'm sure this isn't going to be something you want to hear, given that the War just ended for you a couple of weeks ago," he said. "Just understand how important this is to our lord. There are rumors of the threat of war to the west, on the island of Tsalbrin – a civil war, not another war with the serilian demons or anything of that sort."

"So you're sending soldiers over there to help fight?" she guessed, assuming her service as a lieutenant colonel under Kris Jir'tana meant more to others than it did now to her.

Attir shook his head, releasing his hold with one of his hands to make a dismissive gesture. "Not at all," he said. "No war has actually broken out yet, and the gods want it kept that way. I'm sure you understand that after an event like the Apocalypse, another war would only serve to weaken the pantheon, strain relations, and perhaps even open the door to unrest from the underworld. No, you will head to Tsalbrin with a small group of elite war veterans and do whatever – and I stress *whatever* – is necessary to stop this war from actually happening."

"Tsalbrin? Isn't that halfway across the world?"

"Indeed it is, but as unlikely as it may sound, you're the closest of our champions strong enough to take care of this for the gods," he answered.

"What's the root?"

The priest smiled, and Kari was unsure what amused him. "A terra-rir general named Braxus Gaswell is said to be bolstering his garrisons and recruiting for his army for an as-yet unknown reason. Some speculate that he intends to invade Kirelia, much like his great-great-grandfather did, but that theory ignores a couple of very important facts: firstly, he is only recruiting terra-rir."

Kari considered the priest's words and her brow furrowed. "You think it's a racial war, Master?" she asked.

48

Attir nodded. "That's what it looks like at the moment," he said. "We haven't anywhere near the full picture, so there's only so much I can tell you, but rest assured that a racial civil war will tear the island apart and quickly spread to the mainland. This has the potential to explode into another world-wide war, perhaps bad enough to rival the Apocalypse. The involvement of the kirelas-rir also has many concerned; those people are best left alone and to their own devices. If Gaswell upsets their society and the bakatur of Dannumore become involved, things will get out of hand very quickly. And, of course, there is one other thing..."

"You suspect there's demons involved," Kari stated. There was no other reasonable explanation for why she would be chosen to try to stop a civil war on a remote island.

"Zalkar's faith in you is well placed," the human commented, and he released her hand to sit back in his chair. "We're not certain of their type, but it's not a serilian demon. We've only received bits of information at this point, and most of it is second- or even third-hand knowledge. There's definitely a demon involved, but they're keeping themselves out of sight for the most part, so while we suspect they're involved with Gaswell's sudden interest in an uprising, we don't know exactly where they are or what they're up to. What we're afraid of is that it may be the start of another invasion like the one Arku attempted on Terrassia during the War. If that's the case, then they need to be stopped before they gain even the slightest foothold on Tsalbrin."

"I understand," she replied.

"You obviously won't be working alone on this mission," he said, rising to his feet, and he paced back over to the altar to lean against it. "Have you heard of Erijinkor Tesconis?"

Kari thought to herself for only a moment, trying to recall things she'd heard during the War. "One of those half-guardian kids out of Latalex?"

Attir nodded. "Yes, Erik's a half-guardian and only two generations removed from both Cylestor and Cerberus," he answered, and Kari's eyes widened. Cylestor was the lord of the guardian demons, and Cerberus was an extremely powerful guardian demon so named because of his station guarding the hellgate. A half-guardian who had them both for grandfathers would have to be quite the man of renown. "He'll be your partner in this. I'm not sure how well you know of him, but he's rising through the ranks of the Order very quickly. The Council has faith in him, but at the same time, they want to be sure this young man's quick ascension is deserved. So we would like you to work together to investigate this demon activity on Tsalbrin, and then you may brief us on just how good a demonhunter you think he is."

"Half-demon demonhunter, isn't that a little weird?" Kari asked, her mind flashing back to what David Marrack had said in Barcon.

The priest smiled again but didn't answer. "He won't know you're mentoring him," Attir said. "In fact, it's quite possible he'll think he's mentoring you. If that's the case, do nothing to suggest otherwise; if anything, it'll tell us how good a commander he is on top of his skills as a demonhunter. He may not make the connection that you're the real Karian Vanador, either; a lot of people may find it hard to believe you've been resurrected, since this has never happened before. So if he comes across as somewhat arrogant or demeaning, just give it time. The way he conducts himself is primarily what we're interested in here."

"Of course," she said with a nod. "Is there anything else I need to do while over there?"

"Just aid any victims of demons you come across," he said. "You know your job well enough, I'm sure I don't need to tell you what to do. You're one of our best, Karian, and that's why you've been chosen for this. We know you won't let us down."

"I appreciate your confidence, Master," she said. She stood and shook the human's hand once more. "When does transportation leave?"

"There's a ship at the port in the west quarter," he said. "We've had it waiting for your arrival. Erik and his siblings have been in town for a few days; you should be able to find them at Land's End. Gather what personal things you'll need and look for the ship called *Karmi's Sword* at the north pier in the morning. Don't worry about supplies, the ship is fully supplied and will be making a stop on the east coast of Terrassia on the way to Tsalbrin."

"How long a trip is it?" she asked.

"About two months if the weather stays favorable," he said. "The crew of *Karmi's Sword* is among the best on the high seas, so I don't expect any trouble will slow down your journey. I just hope you handle sea travel well."

The demonhunter shrugged. "I'm sure I'll get used to it," Kari said. "Thank you, Master; should I return here to give my report when the mission is complete?"

Attir shook his head. "No, your return trip should take you around the north coast to DarkWind, so you can give your report to Lord Allerius and Master Bennet at the Academy when your work is complete. They will have the authority to promote you when all goes well."

When *all goes well, not* if, she thought. Kari smiled and touched her fist lightly to her breast in salute. "When all goes well," she repeated. She bid the high priest farewell and made her way to the western quarter and the inn known as Land's End.

Chapter IV – The Silver Blades

Evening had fallen when Kari left the temple plaza and made her way to the docks in the western quarter. The smell of the open ocean overpowered even the smoky warm scents of wood stoves, and the terra-dracon female was pleasantly surprised at how clean and secure the docks seemed. Port towns were normally rough, even more so by the docks, but there was a full complement of guards keeping watch over the area. It was quiet, and the calm about the port was such that the lapping of the water against the pier was nearly the only sound in the air.

Kari turned up the road to her right, toward the north-most pier where she would find the inn Master Attir had mentioned. Guards of several different races watched her as she passed, marking the intentions of the winged, well-armed woman, unable to see her dog tags in the sparse light of the streetlamps. She ignored their stares for the most part and quickened her pace, and she dodged the few people milling about enjoying the breeze off the water. It was a little too chilly for Kari's liking, but fortunately she soon found herself at the north end of the docks. A massive sailing ship was secured to the pier, and directly across the street from it was a homey-looking inn called *Land's End*. It was well tended and all of its doors and windows looked intact, which she assumed meant it didn't see many barroom brawls: a rare thing for port-city inns and taverns. All of the curtained windows showed firelight from within, and without further hesitation, she shouldered her way quickly through the front door and shut it behind her.

The inside was far more crowded than the quiet outside suggested, and Kari noted the many faces that looked up as she entered. The air was clear of the smoke that clouded many inns' common rooms, and most of the tables were full, with a good mixture of races making up the crowd. Kari guessed that many were waiting for a transport to someplace warmer, either farther north along the west coast or else one of the northern continents, where spring would be settling in. A lone half-demon stood chatting with the innkeeper while waiting for his drink, and Kari approached the men.

The innkeeper was human, and the worry lines and weathered features of his face suggested retired military or adventurer. His grey brows rose only briefly before a smile appeared, his stark blue eyes taking the woman in as she approached the bar. "What can I do for you, ma'am?" he asked amiably.

"I'd love a double-godhammer, please," Kari said, which drew a grunting laugh from the man as he pulled up a glass from underneath and began placing bottles on the bar. Kari regarded the half-demon beside her; he'd only glanced briefly at her from the corner of his eye. He looked like he could be half-guardian, but he wasn't what she was expecting if he was Erijinkor. "You wouldn't be Erijinkor Tesconis by chance, would you?"

"By the grace of the gods, no," the half-demon answered. He stood up straight to face Kari. He was probably the most handsome half-demon – and probably rir of any type, for that matter – that she'd ever met, barely taller than she and not quite as muscular except in the legs. He was dressed in black trousers and a shirt that she could barely distinguish from his flesh, and his eyes and hair were ebon like her own. His mane was long in the back but cut in a fashionable style on the top, and he flashed a boyish smile as Kari looked him over. "Erik's my older brother; you're looking for him?"

"My name's Karian Vanador," she said, deciding against her typical introduction. "I was told I could find him here, seems we'll be working together."

"Ah, well, I'm Aeligos," he said, extending his hand. "I take it you're joining our little pleasure cruise over to Terrassia?"

There was a distinct change to the light in his eyes as he spoke, and Kari figured that their mission was supposed to be kept secret as much as possible. "I guess so," she said as she shook his offered hand. She took the drink from the barkeep and reached down to her purse, but was waved off by the half-demon.

"I've got it," Aeligos said. "If you want to meet the rest of my siblings, they're seated in the corner over there." He gestured toward a large table that occupied an entire corner of the room, where almost half a dozen half-demons sat playing cards. "Erik's the blue-eyed one."

"Thanks," Kari said, raising her drink in salute, and she patted Aeligos on the shoulder as she turned toward the table. He went back to speaking with the barkeep, apparently about the fact that he was stuck in a single room with all of his brothers. Kari chuckled and guessed the inn was likely full due to the imminent voyage of *Karmi's Sword,* and that the rooms were being rationed out rather than offered to the highest bidder as might normally be the case.

She looked over the group at the table. There was a single empty chair where Aeligos had apparently been sitting. There were three men and two women at the table, all half-demon, though one of the females was a half-brys, while the others were all half-guardian like Aeligos. The half-brys

54

was tiny by comparison sitting amongst the half-guardians at the table, but if she was intimidated at all, she didn't show it – hardly surprising for a half-brys: they were calculating and near-fearless. Kari doubted the woman stood even five feet tall, and she had the long, silky black hair and crimson eyes prominent among her kind.

All three of the males at the table were impressively large. The blue-eyed one on the far side of the table was very tall and broad through the shoulders, but well proportioned and with a long, thick mane of black hair tied back in a tail. With his attention on his cards and a stone-faced expression on his features, Kari saw he had a strong chin and an imposing countenance. To the right of Erik sat an even taller, stronger male with thick, curving black horns on the sides of his head, long, straight black hair, and dull red eyes. On Erijinkor's other side was a slightly shorter but barrel-chested male that looked as though he could crush the life out of someone with his bare hands. While it was not unusual for half-guardians to be tall and strong, all three of them seemed well beyond the norm. Even more intriguing than the massive muscles of the shorter brother was his shock of blonde hair, unkempt and wild, and which was complemented by emerald eyes. He was handsome, though his coloration was unusual for a half-demon, even of the half-guardian variety.

The second female, also a half-guardian, was the only one to look up at Kari when the demonhunter approached. The half-guardian woman was also tall, falling somewhere between the shortest of the three brothers at the table and the blue-eyed one as far as Kari could tell while they were all seated. She had the red eyes common to half-demons of all types, and a full head of scarlet hair tied down in lovely twin braids. She smiled at Kari and motioned her forward, and the others at the table finally took notice of the terra-dracon woman.

"Hello," Kari said, suddenly feeling out of place and somewhat overwhelmed for some reason she couldn't put her finger on. "Is this the table for the pleasure cruise?"

The others laughed, and the blue-eyed male rose from his seat and approached. He saluted Kari by bumping his fist on his chest. She returned the gesture, and he extended a hand, which she shook. His grip was powerful yet careful, as he was obviously mindful of his strength. "Erijinkor Tesconis, Demonhunter," he introduced himself formally. "Most folks just call me Erik so they don't confuse me with the guardian demon of the same name."

"Karian Vanador," she said, introducing herself more casually again. She motioned over her shoulder with her thumb. "I already met your little brother Aeligos." It felt odd to refer to Aeligos as "little," but with the way Erik towered over her, it was somewhat fitting. Erik was easily two hands taller, perhaps more, which put her face in line with his muscular chest. He was wearing a light grey tunic with cuts in the back to allow his wings through, and she could make out his dog tags hanging below.

"Nice to meet you, Karian," he said, a question in his eyes though none came forth from his lips. Kari guessed it was because she didn't introduce herself formally; she assumed he'd know who she was anyway, and if not, that she should honor Attir Suralis' request.

"Kari, if you please," she corrected. "I don't like being called Karian."

He bowed his head deferentially and gestured toward the seat his younger brother had vacated. "Kari it is," he said and moved back around to his own chair. "Do you gamble?"

"I'm a demonhunter," she said. "Every time I leave town it's a gamble." The group got a laugh out of that comment, but Kari didn't like the way the blonde looked at her. When she tried to meet his gaze, he looked down at his cards and returned a neutral expression to his face.

"What's the game?" Kari asked.

"Poker," the blue-eyed male answered. "We can deal you in on the next hand. We can play for money if you prefer, but at the moment we're playing for the right to choose which watches we keep during the nights on the ocean."

Kari sat down. "Whatever's fine," she said. "I heard a little about you and your siblings during the war, but I don't remember names very well unless I connect them to a face."

"Oh, of course," Erik said. He gestured first to the scarlet-haired beauty beside Kari. "This is my sister Sonja; she's the brains of this group. Next to her is Eryn. She's not actually one of the group but she's got Aeligos enthralled so she's traveling with us for the time being."

The half-brys woman half-smiled at the comment, and Kari beheld her curiously for a moment before she looked back over her shoulder at Aeligos. It seemed an odd couple to her, but she remembered that half-demons were always more like each other than any other race, so in a way it made sense, even if it was a bit of a mismatch. Kari looked to the horned male to Eryn's right as Erik introduced him as Serenjols, or just Jol as he was more commonly called. The horned male nodded politely but said nothing, and Erik explained that Jol was usually shy, so Kari shouldn't take it personally if he didn't speak to her.

"And my blonde brother here is Typhonix," he finished. "We usually call him Ty, though *loudmouth* and *jackass* get used as often as not." Erik

56

took a backhanded punch to the chest for the last comment. It nearly knocked the wind out of him, and he rubbed the pain away with a crooked smile. Sonja laughed at the exchange, and Kari gave a muted smile, though in the back of her mind she marveled at how quickly and powerfully the blonde had struck.

"You traveled with Kris Jir'tana and his brigade, did you not?" Sonja asked, fixing Kari with a sparkling ruby gaze. Her voice was a little on the deep side but still musical and definitely feminine.

"Yea, the Thirty-fifth Light Division, we traveled down through the Barrier mountains, starting with the liberation of Atrice," Kari answered.

"You were the ones that found what was left of the city of Seren?"

Kari didn't answer. She closed her eyes and blew a long, quiet sigh through her nose. Of all the things she'd gone through either in her previous life or during the War, that was the single worst thing she'd ever seen. The entire city, still and lifeless, its streets littered with the shredded and rotting corpses of every man, woman, and child that had lived there. Not one survivor had been found, and Kari remembered all too well spending days helping to bury the dead. "Yes," she answered at last. "I'd really rather not talk about it."

"It never made any sense; all of the cities and towns we came across had been occupied and enslaved," Sonja said. "We could never figure out why Seril had the people of Seren slaughtered to a man."

"Nothing she ever did really made any sense," Erik said with a shake of his head. He rolled his eyes and dropped his cards face down on the table. "Fold. Anyone else notice I lose every hand that Eryn deals?"

Kari was glad for the abrupt departure from the subject and turned toward Eryn. "Aw, is the big demonhunter getting his feelings hurt?" the half-brys female taunted with a wicked little smile. Her voice was cold and confident, which was common for her kind, though Kari had rarely ever encountered female half-demons, let alone two at the same table. That cold, expressionless look returned to Eryn's face after a moment. "It's just luck. If I was cheating, I'd at least make it look good so I'd stand to win more."

"And she'd probably cheat someone that was more likely to beat her," Ty added without lifting his eyes from his own hand. "Not the one who bets on a pair of fours."

"You're not doing much better," Erik told his shorter brother, and he leaned to the side to try to get a glimpse of the blonde's cards.

Typhonix put his cards against his barrel of a chest and glared at his elder brother, and Kari wondered if another punch was forthcoming. "I

57

don't usually gamble unless someone's going to get their head broken," the blonde grumbled.

Kari was amused at the exchange, as rude as it sounded. She'd never had any brothers, so it was always amusing to her to see the way brothers behaved toward each other. She looked down at her own cards. It had been ages – literally – since she'd played cards, and the mention of pairs brought the game back to her only slightly. She remembered having all of one suit or all numbers in a row was good, as was having a lot of picture cards. She shook her head at herself, knowing she was likely to get crushed. As it was, her hand wasn't particularly promising.

She was surprised as someone lightly touched her shoulders, and Aeligos whispered in her ear. "They think you're clueless. Make sure you use bluffs to your advantage. Ask for two cards, drop the five and the seven, and try to get a flush. Odds should be pretty good."

"Fold," Serenjols grumbled, and he dropped his cards on the table. After smirking at Aeligos, Sonja did likewise.

"To hell with this," Typhonix said, tossing his cards down on the table, and he rose to his feet. "I'm going to get a drink. If anyone wants anything, they're welcome to get it themselves."

"Such a gentleman," Eryn muttered without looking up, and the gruff blonde's siblings chuckled. "How many cards?"

"Um, two," Kari said, and she dropped the cards Aeligos had indicated face down and slid them to the center of the table. She picked up the cards the half-brys woman dealt her and grimaced, realizing she hadn't gotten the ones she was looking for. She glanced over at Eryn and the half-brys woman was watching her intently. Kari realized she had just given away her bad hand, and she rolled her eyes, which drew chuckles from the others. She folded. "I think I'm a little out of practice."

"You're too easy to read," Eryn said. "Stick to friendly games, and don't play with *Pretty Boy* behind you. He cheats."

"I do not," Aeligos said with a wounded expression.

"We've got a long trip ahead of us, and an early morning tomorrow," Erik said as he rose to his feet. "I want everyone in bed within the next half-hour. No exceptions."

Sonja nudged Kari's arm lightly. "You can stay with Eryn and me. There are no more rooms available anyway. You'll have to sleep on the floor, but it beats sleeping down here."

"That's fine," the terra-dracon woman said, sitting back to enjoy her drink.

"Will you be down here for a little while?" Eryn asked Sonja and Kari, and the two women gave non-commital shrugs. Eryn looked up toward Aeligos and nodded her head toward the stairs, and the two made their way up to the rooms.

As they moved toward the stairs, Kari saw the stark contrast between the two. Aeligos stood at least two hands taller than his mate. Kari could only imagine what it was like for Eryn to look up at either Erik or Jol. Kari turned toward Sonja, but the woman appeared lost in thought, sipping her own drink from a tankard. From the smell on her breath Kari guessed it was just ale, and Sonja didn't seem anywhere near intoxicated. Erik and Jol said goodnight and made their way upstairs.

"If you think sleeping on the floor is bad, imagine what it's like in their room," Sonja said, breaking the short-lived silence once the men left.

"All four of them are in the same room?" Kari asked.

"Four?" Sonja repeated. "Five. Our other brother, Grakin, is already upstairs sleeping. He hasn't been feeling well these last few days."

"Why doesn't Aeligos just sleep with Eryn if they're mates? Or did you just not want your brother in the same room with you?"

Sonja shrugged. "They're not mates," she said. "Far from it. They just have sex a lot. Give it a few days, and you'll see what I mean. Eryn's a bit open about her sexuality, but she's a fiery girl and very private where just about anything else is concerned. Try not to take it personally if she's short with you, it's a half-brys thing."

"I know it," Kari said, and Sonja chuckled for some reason. "Why's Jol so quiet?"

"We're not sure," Sonja said with a shrug. "He's never been talkative, but he's been even quieter these last few years. I figure it's to balance the fact that Typhonix never shuts up."

Kari chuckled at the sibling rivalry. "You have a lot of brothers," she said, but then she looked sheepishly at the larger woman. "Sorry, I didn't mean any offense."

"None taken," Sonja said with a half-smile. "Our father wanted a big family: he wanted to name his many sons after the twenty-one guardian demons."

"Tell me you don't have sixteen other brothers...?" Kari returned, shocked.

The scarlet-haired beauty laughed and crossed her muscular arms lightly over her ample breasts. "Thank the gods, no," she said. "It's hard enough being the only girl in the family, if I had any more brothers I think I'd lose my mind."

Kari nearly asked about the woman's mother, and why she had said

59

she was the only girl in the family, but she went quiet instead. It was probably a rude question, whether Sonja minded or not, and the intended questions brought up too many memories of Kari's own past. She pushed down the thoughts and took a long sip of her drink, and Sonja patted her shoulder as she rose. Kari beheld Sonja curiously, knowing that her brother and his girlfriend were upstairs in the girls' room.

"Finish your drink, I'm going to use the commode, then we can go kick Aeligos out," Sonja said.

Kari chuckled in response. She sat back in her chair, finishing her drink and savoring the warmth and relaxation of the alcohol as it coursed through her. The inn was fairly quiet for how crowded it was, and no one bothered Kari while she sat alone at the table. She pictured each of the men and women she'd been introduced to in her mind and sorted them by name, and found they were distinct enough that it wasn't difficult. She assumed that unless Grakin was a twin of one of his brothers, she could keep the six siblings straight, and Eryn was so different that she was simple to remember.

Before she knew it, Kari had dozed off in her chair, and she woke with a start when Sonja touched her shoulder. She had only slept a few minutes, but the larger woman told her it was best that they all head to bed, and with a nod the terra-dracon woman rose and followed her new friend. As they entered the small and inadequate room, Kari quickly imagined five large men sharing a similar one, and laughed into her hand. Sonja and Eryn chuckled with her, apparently knowing exactly what she was thinking.

Kari dropped her pack to the floor, unrolled her bedroll, and began digging through her pack for a few moments. She pulled out the dark blue blanket she kept rolled up, set her pack down on its side near the head of the bed as a makeshift pillow, and lay down under the blanket. Sonja had the bed closest to Kari, as Eryn was already in the second one against the far wall, and soon the scarlet-haired woman was looking at the demonhunter over the edge of her bed.

"I'd offer to let you sleep with me, but this bed is a little small even just for me," she said with a sheepish smile.

"I've been sleeping in the wild or in the back of a wagon for the last eight years, it's no problem," Kari said, waving off the larger woman's concerns. She assumed that Eryn wanted her bed to herself despite her tiny frame, which was just as well in Kari's mind. She chuckled at the thought of Aeligos visiting again during the night. Sonja soon joined her, as if the larger woman had read her mind. The three women made small talk but soon fell asleep, and though she woke up in the pre-dawn hours as she usually did, Kari slept fairly well.

~~*~*

The air was cool and heavy with fog in the pre-dawn gloom, so Kari pulled the cloak from her pack, tucked her wings tight to her back, and then wrapped herself in the warm, thick garment. Her half-demon companions had all done likewise, and their glowing eyes surrounded her in the darkness as they made their way from the warm interior of the inn and down the pier toward *Karmi's Sword*. Kari's eyes glowed, but their luminescence was muted because her eyes were black, as was the case with Aeligos and Grakin.

Kari saw Grakin only briefly in the inn's common room, as he'd spent quite a bit of time sick in the latrine. When she finally saw him he looked a lot like Aeligos, though his hair was shorter and of a uniform length rather than stylized like his brother's. He wasn't unattractive but there was a gaunt and tired look about him, and Kari figured it was due to the fact that he'd been sick for several days, as Sonja said. Whatever the case, he was unresponsive to the suggestion that he introduce himself to the group's newest member, and he simply paid the innkeeper a couple of gold pieces for a pot of hot coffee that he could take with him.

Erijinkor led the group down the pier to *Karmi's Sword's* gangplank, though most of the features of the massive ship were obscured in the blanket of fog that hung over the port. Kari wasn't sure how comfortable she was getting on a ship that would be setting out under such a pillowy covering, but she resigned herself to the will of the ship's captain. She knew nearly nothing about sailing or ships and tried her best to curb the doubts and fears that crept up on her from all sides. She reassured herself that though the rir weren't fond of traveling across the oceans, the humans had been sailing the ocean routes between the continents for over two thousand years and were well accustomed to doing so.

Erik spoke briefly to the guards at the base of the gangplank, a pair of burly human marines who were well armed and armored. One made his way up the wooden walkway after a moment, while the other continued to make small talk with Erik. Kari took the opportunity to look around. She had expected the pier to be crowded: the large number of people in the inn the night before suggested that the ship would have an ample number of passengers. Only she and her half-demon companions stood waiting to board, though, and when she thought about it, she realized there also hadn't been any cargo waiting to be loaded on the ship the night before. She wondered just what sort of vessel *Karmi's Sword* was.

"Where's everyone else?" Kari asked Sonja quietly, but Sonja waved off the inquiry and beckoned for Kari to follow as she headed up the gangway after Erik.

The group assembled on the quarterdeck of the ship and Kari looked around at all the white uniform-clad humans standing at attention along both rails. Many of the humans had the pale skin she was most accustomed to, but some were of the darker varieties, their tan or smooth chocolate-toned flesh standing in stark contrast to their bright uniforms. There was only a single rir among the crew, sitting on a small platform a few feet up from the base of the main mast, and she looked down over the gathered group with the darkest blue eyes Kari had ever seen. She was dressed in some sort of uniform, though in the dark and with her in a seated position, it was hard to make out any details. The rir woman had red hair not unlike Sonja's and a somewhat unwelcoming expression on her face, though it could have just been the darkness combined with her ebon flesh that made it seem so.

Near the stern, by the door to the aft cabin stood a fairly tall and well toned human who still looked somewhat short standing before the massive Tesconis brothers. His face, easier to see by the light coming from the lamps beside the cabin door, was tanned and weathered, a testament to a life sailing the seas in the sun and wind, and was augmented by a well-kept, short black beard and moustache. His outfit was slightly different from the others: his white uniform was augmented by the decorated blue overcoat of a naval officer, and over his short-trimmed dark hair he wore a black hat that marked him as the captain. He stood straight with his hands folded behind his back, and as Kari looked him over, he did the same to the group before him with an obviously discerning eye.

Beside him stood a thinner and less muscular man, clean-shaven with dark eyes that studied the new passengers warily. He wore a different uniform than either the sailors or the captain, which designated that he was an officer, though of what rank was not immediately apparent. He wore no hat, and his short black hair was receding, but he had a dignified and officious look to him. Every so often his eyes clearly went to the rir woman sitting up on her little platform, and it seemed to Kari that the two were having a silent conversation regarding their new passengers. His stare, too, seemed rather unwelcoming, but in his case Kari was able to attribute it more to the morning chill.

"Welcome aboard *Karmi's Sword*," the captain said as the group dropped their packs to the quarterdeck and stood waiting. He kept his voice somewhat low, mindful of it carrying across the water even given the early hour. "I am Captain Galdur, and I will be in charge of getting you lot safely to Tsalbrin. I'm sure you're wondering why none of the other guests of Land's End are with you; they're not going. This ship is under direct orders and contract from the temple of Zalkar to get you folks to Tsalbrin as quickly and quietly as possible. We know a little bit of your mission, and that's all we need to know. You can speak freely of it around the crew, as we've all been sworn to secrecy and I trust every one of the men under my command."

"Now," he continued, "as I'm in charge of your safety, that means you're under my command, and must follow my rules. There are no exceptions to my rules: break them and you'll be put to work maintaining the ship. Continue to break my rules, and you'll find yourself swimming to Tsalbrin. I'm sure this seems like a harsh welcome, but since I understand you each have a military background, I'm sure you can understand the need to keep order on a ship. Though we sometimes run freight and passengers, this is a military vessel and is run as such."

"The man next to me is Master Bryan Calhoun, and he is in charge of logistics and the navigation of the ship. He'll see to the ship's operation while we're underway. Most of my time will be spent with him, plotting our course and making sure we avoid known pirate waters and other trouble. While *Karmi's Sword* is a military vessel and pirate-hunter, our orders are to get you safely to Tsalbrin, which means avoiding trouble along the way. Getting the Unyielding's people killed before they reach their destination would rather defeat the purpose of this trip."

"The final officer you should become acquainted with is Jori-an Stormrider, the rir woman you see seated up on the boatswain's nest. She is the ship's First Mate, but she also serves as my bosun and morale officer. She's in charge of the deck and everyone on it. You cause trouble, you answer to her. And if she hasn't walked you off a plank or hanged you from a yardarm, then you answer to me. We expect all of you to be on your best behavior while aboard my ship. You let us do our job, and we'll get you to Tsalbrin safely. Any questions?"

"No questions, captain," Erik said. He tapped his fist over his heart in salute and Kari did likewise, and Captain Galdur returned it with a military salute that was repeated and held by all the members of the crew save Jori-an. Erik stepped forward and extended his hand. "I'm Erijinkor Tesconis, and I'm in charge of this group. Most of these are my siblings, except for the dark and short girls." The two shook hands and Erik gestured over his shoulder with his other thumb. "Any of them give your crew any trouble, you just let me know. They'll answer to *me* first, and your crew can take care of whatever's left."

Galdur let out a chuckle and patted the much larger man on the shoulder. "I knew that aiding Zalkar's people would be easier than usual," he said. "The only other thing I will go over with you is quarters. Most of you men will be in general quarters with the crew; the guest cabins will be reserved for the ladies. However, if any of you have a problem sleeping in a hammock, now would be the time to say so."

"Grakin," Erik said and his younger brother approached, taking a sip of his coffee and shaking visibly. Erik turned back to Galdur and said, "This is my brother Grakin. He's been sick for a few days, so a steady bed in one of the guest cabins might be helpful."

"What's he sick with?" the captain asked. He regarded Master Calhoun and Jori-an, and his expression left no doubt that the prospect of a sick passenger alarmed him.

"Nothing contagious, captain," Grakin answered, the first words Kari had heard him speak. He sounded bad, his voice gravelly and quiet, and Kari couldn't tell if he was shaking from the cold or because he was sick. It generally took prolonged exposure to the cold before a half-demon would even feel it, so she guessed it was the latter. "It is simply fatigue from my work during the War. I am a healer of Kaelariel; were it something that would endanger your crew, I would channel my lord's power to cure it."

"Ah, I see. And you're certain that you wouldn't rather sleep in a hammock so the ship's motion doesn't make your troubles worse?" Galdur prompted.

"A bed would be more suitable for my evening meditations," the priest replied. "That concerns me more than the issues with my stomach."

"Fair enough," the captain said with a respectful nod. "Crewman Mallory! Escort our sick guest to one of the cabins so he can lie down while we get the ship ready to leave port."

"Aye, captain!" said one of the dark-skinned humans as he approached and saluted Galdur. He led Grakin by the elbow down below decks.

"Is there anything else my officers should know about?" Galdur asked. Erik glanced to Kari, Eryn, and each of his other siblings before he shook his head in response. "Good. My crew and I are wary of magic, so if any of you use it and plan to practice it during the journey, be sure to check with either my first mate or myself before doing so. If there's nothing else, Crewman Mallory will show you down to your quarters while my officers get us underway. It's going to be a long trip, and once we set sail, there will be no turning back."

64

"We're ready, captain" Erik confirmed. The captain made his way up to the stern deck along with Master Calhoun, and soon Crewman Mallory returned to lead the others down into the cabin.

The cabin was fairly dark, its gloom pierced every so often by hanging lanterns, revealing narrow doors on each side of the long central hallway. After passing the first few sets of doors, which were spread farther apart, Mallory gestured to the next four which were closer together, and told the women to go ahead and choose their rooms however they liked. He left Kari, Eryn, and Sonja to divvy up the three remaining rooms and led the men farther into the forward section of the ship, the general quarters.

The ladies came to a consensus, and each opened the doors to their cabins to look in. As Mallory had said, they were all virtually identical, each equipped with a narrow bed, a secured night table with a securable drawer, a hanging lamp, and a footlocker at the base of the bed. Each also had a small porthole to allow some air and light into the somewhat cramped quarters, and a polished metal plate attached to the wall served as a makeshift mirror. Kari smiled at her two companions and then headed into her room and closed the door behind her.

Kari opened the footlocker and deposited her pack within, and she lay down on the bed to test how comfortable it was. It was soft and she sank into it, though not far enough to touch the hard wooden frame beneath, and while it was slightly damp, it wasn't as bad as she expected aboard a ship. She found it amusing that there was a board attached to the side to assure that she didn't fall out while sleeping, something she hadn't seen since she was a child. She fluffed the pillow, then shook her hair to the side and lay back, closing her eyes. She smiled, realizing that unless sea conditions were exceptionally rough, she would have no trouble falling asleep on her bed. She sat up quickly, not wanting to doze off, and inspected the rest of her quarters. The table, bed, and footlocker were affixed to the floor, and she gazed briefly at the black-eyed woman staring back at her from the surface of the metal mirror for a moment.

Kari started to rise but fell back to her rump as the ship pitched, and when she looked out the small window she realized they had already left the dock and the vessel was making its turn northward. Her cabin was on the port side of the ship, so she couldn't see the lightening of the horizon as the sun began to rise; instead all she could see was the foggy gloom hanging over the dark water to the west. After thinking about it a moment, she decided it would probably be best to stay in her quarters at least until the ship was fully underway. While Kari knew virtually nothing about sailing, it wasn't hard to figure out that clueless warriors underfoot

65

wouldn't be very helpful to the crew when getting the ship onto its course.

Kari lay back down on the soft bedding and started to doze off until a knock sounded at her door. She called for whomever it was to come in, and Sonja opened the door and peeked around it before she slipped inside and closed the door behind her. The scarlet-haired woman was already chuckling before a word had been spoken, and Kari curled her legs so the larger woman could sit on the end of the bed. "What's so funny?" Kari asked.

"These beds are smaller than the ones in the inn," her friend said. "I have to sleep with my knees bent just to fit in mine."

"But they're nice and comfortable," the demonhunter said, folding her arms behind her head. "Certainly has to be better than sleeping in a hammock in a room full of men."

"True enough," Sonja said with a shrug, looking out the porthole briefly. Kari guessed Sonja had had as little privacy during the War traveling with five brothers as Kari'd had in the company of her brigade. "It's going to be a long trip, and I imagine I'll be spending a lot of time going through my spell book and guides, so having a bed to curl up on while reading is nice."

Karian beheld the muscular half-demon woman curiously. "You're a wizard?" she asked, and Sonja gave a knowing smile and nod. "I'd guessed you were a warrior."

"I am," Sonja said. "You don't have brothers like mine and not know a trick or two with the sword. I try to stay on par with my siblings as much as possible where martial combat is concerned, but I spend most of my time studying. Most of my spells are defensive enchantments and utility cantrips, but I know a few destructive spells as well."

"What about transportation?" Kari asked. "Can't you just teleport us or whatever over to Tsalbrin?"

The scarlet-haired female shook her head. "Tsalbrin is sealed off from magical transport, probably because of its proximity to Kirelia. The only way to get there is by boat, and my spells wouldn't be strong enough to move a group of this size anyway."

Kari remained quiet for a minute, listening to the sound of the water as it glided along the hull, and then she turned to put her legs high up on the wall to stretch. With her head hanging over the side of the bed, she got a good look at just how muscular Sonja's legs were; the woman wasn't as built as her brothers, but even Kari's own muscular form seemed scrawny compared to Sonja. Kari wondered if all half-guardians were so muscular: whether it was natural for their kind or if the Tesconis siblings had a rough childhood, leading to such strength. She thought the latter unlikely, since Aeligos and Grakin were far smaller than the others, though Aeligos looked like a dancer and Grakin had mentioned he was a healer.

"How's Grakin doing?" Kari asked as she thought of the priest, and she looked up to the distant eyes of the half-guardian woman.

Sonja didn't answer immediately. She glanced out the window one last time before she seemed to register that Kari had spoken at all, and gave a noncommittal shrug. "He gets sick a lot," she said. "He'll be fine in a few days. He just burns himself at both ends sometimes, channeling so much of Kaelariel's power to heal people. There was a stretch of days a few months ago, when we were in Oceana, where he would get up in the morning and spend a few hours healing people before he nearly passed out from the exertion, and had to go back to sleep."

"That can't be good for him," Kari said. "Channeling divine power takes a lot out of me, and I can't even do much with it."

Sonja nodded. "The power of the gods is an incredible thing to wield, but it's not something for mortals to trifle with. It's intoxicating and addicting, and if you take it for granted it can quickly be your undoing."

"Is wizardry so bad?" Kari asked.

The larger woman nodded with a half-shrug. "It's taxing, but different. The more I use it, the harder it is to focus on the rituals I *see* written in my mind. As I lose focus, I lose the ability to draw forth that power, so it limits itself before it does me any harm. I'm still careful to use it sparingly unless the need is great."

"How did you learn to use it in the first place?" Kari prodded, and she returned to an upright position and sat cross-legged to face her friend.

"I was taught by Archmage Gareth Maelstrom of DarkWind, if you know of him."

"He's still around?" Kari asked, a brow raised in surprise. "I used to hear about him when I was training at the Academy, and he was pretty old then."

Sonja beheld Kari curiously, but then her scarlet eyes suddenly widened and lit up with wonder. "Wait a moment, you're Karian Vanador? Like, *the* Karian Vanador?" Kari nodded, and Sonja practically cackled with glee. "My word, but how?"

"As I understand it, Trigonh used some sort of divine favor he was owed, and I was brought back to fight in the Apocalypse," Kari answered. She drew her knees up to her chest and wrapped her arms around them.

Sonja considered Kari's words for a minute, obviously all at once surprised and awed by the revelation. Trigonh was an erestram – or a wolf demon, as they were sometimes called – who had come to Citaria as an advance scout preceding an invasion by Celigus Chinchala. Before the demon king turned and allied himself with the gods, he sent the erestram known as Trigonh Cabra to evaluate and begin smashing the world's defenses, but the wolf demon shocked his master by defecting to the service of Kaelariel. Trigonh had been Kaelariel's most trusted servant ever since, and the erestram even reconciled with his former master once Celigus was also turned. It was simply amazing – even given the erestram's remarkable history and personality – that a demonhunter would share such a friendship with him as to drive him to use a divine favor on her behalf. Given the fact that he was still a demon, it was hard to fathom that he had bestowed such a boon on a mortal woman when there were doubtless many, many things he could have asked for himself.

Sonja was apparently considering exactly that, and her face began to crease into a smile. Kari figured Sonja was coming to the same conclusion as she had with regard to Trigonh's actual motivation. Sonja's smile disappeared when she saw Kari's reaction to her own words, though, and she touched a hand gently to Kari's shoulder. "You didn't want to come back?" she stated as much as asked.

Kari sighed. "I wasn't asked," she said with a shrug. "What can I do but make the best of it? At the very least I still have my duty to Zalkar. And thankfully I don't have the disease that killed me."

"Disease?" Sonja echoed. "You must mean Dracon's Bane?"

Kari nodded and the larger woman grimaced, giving her shoulder a squeeze of comfort, which brought a slight smile to Kari's face. Dracon's Bane wasn't so much a disease as a genetic defect, one that was quite often attached to the genetic mutation that occasionally caused a terra-rir to grow wings. Terra-dracon was not a species but a mutation of the terra-rir, though the science behind the facts did not often change peoples' perception. The terra-dracon was considered a separate species, and Dracon's Bane was considered an incurable disease. It was a wasting condition that drained the vitality of the afflicted like a cancer until there was nothing left for it to consume.

"How old were you?" Sonja asked. She immediately regretted pushing the issue, and she waved her hand to dismiss any reply.

"Twenty-seven, and please don't tell the others," Kari answered, blinking back a few tears. She let out a long sigh when Sonja silently agreed. "It's fine if they figure things out for themselves, but I prefer to keep it quiet. The amount of questions I get otherwise is just too much." She stayed silent for a few moments, but then she finally raised her head off

68

of her arms and fixed her friend with a mischievous look. "So you don't have a boyfriend either, huh?"

Sonja laughed. "No, not as such," she said. "Then again, I was only seventeen when the War started, and after its end not two days passed before Erik was assigned this mission to Tsalbrin, and the rest of us with him. I've never even been with a man; again, I've had no real opportunity...or desire to dally with someone I didn't care about."

Kari nodded. "You're not missing much," she said. "Better off waiting. Are any of your siblings mated or even involved, other than Aeligos?"

Sonja shook her head. "Serenjols is the eldest, and he's still only thirty-eight," she said. "I know it might sound old to still be unwed or even looking, but you have to remember our lifetimes are stretched out much longer than normal rir. Mostly my brothers simply haven't had the opportunity to look, and in some cases – like Ty's – the desire."

"What's his story?"

Sonja waved off the question. "Mostly he's just still young and stupid, but it's a longer story than that," she said. "Try not to take it personally if he's rude to you, because if he is, it's likely it has nothing to do with you at all. So Trigonh pulled some divine strings to have you returned?"

"Ugh, don't remind me," Kari said, and she lay her head back down in the pillow, but she kept her legs bent so she didn't put her feet in Sonja's lap. "He and I knew each other back before...I died. I think he always had this crazy idea that we could have a life together. How weird is that? An erestram falling for a rir, and a demonhunter at that."

"These days, I've heard stranger things," Sonja said, looking out the porthole once more. The ship had broken free of the fog, and the sky was finally beginning to show signs of life as the sun spread its warmth in vibrant colors. "I'd ask if you want to take a walk up on deck, but I'm not sure the crew will want us underfoot so early in the journey. We'd probably best give them a few days to get used to our presence before we start wandering the deck."

"I was thinking the same thing," Kari said, "though there's not much to do in these cabins other than sleep."

"I have some books you're welcome to borrow," Sonja said, and she smiled in response to Kari's dubious look. "Not all of them are about magic. I have a couple of history books and a great biographical about Kaelariel during the Fifth Demon War. Typhonix has some books too, though he reads about strange things."

"I can imagine."

Sonja chuckled. "Not like that," she said. "He reads about politics and economics, and he's a bit of a student of history too, even given his age."

"Economics?" Kari echoed.

"Weird, isn't it?" Sonja replied before she seemed to realize that Kari simply wasn't familiar with the word. "How marketplaces work."

"Really? Typhonix? You're right, that is strange," Kari said.

Sonja excused herself and rose with a smile, and she left Kari's cabin for a couple of minutes. When she returned, she had a couple of heavy books with her, and she left them on the end of Kari's bed. "I'm going to do some studying, I'll see you in a while or tonight at dinner," Sonja said, and Kari thanked her before she left.

Chapter V – The Company of Strangers

Just after sundown, Kari was summoned to the captain's quarters for the evening meal. She was surprised at how large the room was, as it apparently took up the entire first level below the sterncastle. Were it not for the motion of the ship, the room's impressive décor and spaciousness might have led her to believe she was in the home of a minor noble. She gave herself a few moments to take in her surroundings, and found that most of the lavish décor was outdone by the desk in the near starboard corner. Its polished oak surface was littered with maps, papers, and leather-bound books, and carved into the front was the crossed sword and flail of the sea goddess, Karmi G'Dorrinn, with the sword more prominent.

In the rear starboard corner was a long, oval-shaped dining table apparently made of the same polished oak as the desk, with nearly a dozen chairs of the same make around its perimeter. Apparently the captain's quarters were not just his sleeping chamber. Kari looked more closely and could see that all of the furniture was affixed to the floor, just as in her own cabin, and the arms of the chairs appeared to lift up and down to allow their occupants to get in and out easily. Captain Galdur, Eryn, and the Tesconis siblings were already seated, and were being attended to by an apron- and hat-clad sailor placing large plates of steaming food on the table, while a second placed pitchers of drink. The captain waved Kari over, and she moved toward the table slowly as she scanned the rest of the room. Soon, she took a seat next to Sonja.

"Have you started reading the books I gave you?" Sonja asked as Kari sat down beside her. There was such a warmth to her smile that Kari couldn't help but smile herself.

"Not yet," Kari answered, looking over the large selection of hot food curiously. She had expected that the majority of the food served during the voyage would be salted meats, bread, and cheeses. To see so much hot, freshly-cooked meat and vegetables spread out before her was almost like a dream. "I took a nap, actually. I didn't sleep well last night."

"I noticed," the scarlet-haired female said, picking up one of the larger plates of meat effortlessly and holding it near Kari's. "You woke up a few times like you didn't know where you were. Bad dreams?"

Kari helped herself to several pieces of roasted pork, and then waved away the dish while she took up another full of some sort of leafy, roasted greens. "I think it's mostly from living on the road my whole life," she said

71

quietly, not meeting Sonja's eyes. "When you don't sleep in the same place more than a couple days, you really don't know where you are when you wake up a lot of the time."

Sonja looked across to Erik, who half-smiled, and she poured herself a glass of cold wine. She seemed about to say something else, but remained quiet and took a sip from her glass before beginning to eat. Her siblings were all silent as well, taking their meal with no conversation, and though he looked from face to face, Captain Galdur didn't seem intent on making any of them talk. His expression was a mixture of curiosity and suspicion, and he looked somewhat out of place even in his own quarters surrounded by these large, dangerous people.

"Thank you for the meal, captain," Kari said before she began to eat.

Captain Galdur nodded curtly with a slight smile but said nothing. The servants came in and cleared away the empty plates once the captain and his guests finished eating, and the empty wine pitchers were replaced with full ones. Contentedly well-fed, the group sat back in their chairs and looked up at the captain as he produced a deck of cards. Aeligos and Eryn grinned even as the cards hit the table's surface.

"I thought perhaps you would all enjoy a game of cards," Galdur said. "Normally my officers would join us, but they will have time enough to become acquainted with you during our voyage. I likely won't, so I thought to share a game of cards with you and get to know you a little better, so in addition to coins, we'll all be betting a little bit of ourselves, too." He gave that small, muted smile again as he was fixed with furrowed brows from every side of the table. "The winner will receive their coin, sure enough, but when you win, you have to tell the table something about yourself – and no lies or tall tales."

Chuckles sounded around the table, and Captain Galdur produced a sack of silver coins. He handed out a like amount to each of his guests and himself, and set rules as to how little and how much could be bet on each hand. He seemed to be more interested in the game continuing for a while than for anyone to actually make any serious money, and Kari saw Eryn and Aeligos shrug to each other. It seemed they realized it was more of a social game than a serious gamble.

"Are you going to let the ladies buy more coins with their clothing if they start losing?" Typhonix asked nonchalantly, which drew laughs from his brothers.

"You just concentrate on winning a single hand," Eryn shot back, and she scratched the underside of her jaw toward Typhonix when he grinned.

Captain Galdur chuckled lightly, apparently trying to maintain

72

decorum even in the face of such a bawdy comment. He dealt cards to each of the players and then set the deck before him. It was far larger than any deck Kari had seen before, and as she considered the number of people around the table, she guessed he must be using multiple decks. She scratched the side of her snout absently as she picked up her cards, assuming such meant her odds of getting difficult hands was better, as was everyone else's. She was careful to guard her emotions as she looked over what she had been dealt, and organized the cards slowly as she sat back in her chair.

"Left of the dealer bets first, two silver ante," Captain Galdur said, looking to Grakin. The priest looked much better than he had the first time Kari saw him: he was awake and alert, if a bit worn-looking. He twisted his draconic lips to the side slightly as he looked at his cards, and tossed two silver coins to the center of the table. They bounced off of the polished surface, but were slapped down almost reflexively by Erik, whose eyes never left his own cards.

Eryn followed suit, pushing two of her own coins to the center, Sonja did likewise, and Kari looked over her cards with a finger to her chin. After a few moments, liking all the picture cards she was holding, she pushed two of her own to the center. It continued all the way around, and Captain Galdur put in his own two. Grakin called and the others followed suit; it seemed to Kari that no one had an overwhelming hand, or if they did they were simply biding their time to increase the pot. The captain dealt cards to each player in turn, and Kari asked for only a single card. She worked very hard to suppress a smile, not wanting to give away what she had.

Bets went around the table twice, and along the way all four of the Tesconis brothers on the far side of the table folded, along with Sonja. Captain Galdur, Grakin, and Eryn continued to raise the stakes, and Kari met their bets each time, not sure exactly what she had but pretty sure it was a winner. Eryn watched Kari intently each time it came around to the demonhunter, but Kari made sure to always give a little smile whenever she fell under the half-brys' scrutiny. At the very least, she thought she was doing better than she did the prior night. Captain Galdur called a halt to bets due to the limits he had set on the game, and the players revealed their hands. Grakin had a full house of eights over fours; the captain revealed two pairs, eights and tens; and Eryn laid down a three of a kind - nines.

"Lots of pictures," Kari said as she laid down her cards: a king, a queen, and three jacks. The eyes of nearly all the other players widened when she showed her hand.

"King's court," Erik said, amazed. "That's a lucky hand."

"I see it's a good thing I put a limit on the bets; she'd have cleaned us half out," Captain Galdur said with a chuckle.

Kari collected all of the coins in the center of the table, and looked to the captain to deal again, but she found the entire table staring at her. She realized she was supposed to share some intimate detail about herself for having won, and silently cursed her so-called good luck. Kari wasn't interested in revealing or proving who she was and then spending the entire voyage telling everyone all about her past life. She smiled to stall for a minute while she thought of something she could tell the gathering that would satisfy the captain's requirement without exposing herself to too much interest.

"My name is Karian Vanador," she began, stalling a little more. "I was born and raised in the city of Flora on Terrassia, and lived in Solaris for about five years before attending the Academy at DarkWind. During the war I fought in the Thirty-fifth Light Division, where I served directly under Kris Jir'tana."

"And I'll bet he had a smile on his face every morning on account of it," Typhonix muttered, stunning the table into silence. Erik put his hand over his face, trying his best not to laugh, and Aeligos turned away with a chuckle. Jol and Grakin didn't seem to know what reaction to have; they were clearly amused by the comment but refrained from demonstrating it considering how rude it had been. Captain Galdur pursed his lips, obviously sensing a shift in the mood, and though he'd found Ty's previous comment funny, he wasn't amused now.

Eryn and Sonja were obviously disturbed by the rude comment, and they scowled at Ty, but they didn't seem to realize that Kari wasn't even sure what he'd meant. She stared at him for a minute, unsure how to react. She puzzled out what he'd meant after a few moments and felt her blood boil as she saw the laughter around her from the corner of her eye. He'd just insulted her quite personally, and after another few silent moments, Kari stood up, tossed her cards to the table, and made her way for the door.

"Kari," Sonja called after her, but Kari kept walking. Before she left the captain's quarters she overheard Sonja tell Typhonix, "I ought to break your snout!"

Karian left the captain's quarters and ignored the curious stare of Jorian, and she suddenly felt quite trapped on the ship. She made her way back down to her cabin and slipped inside. She closed and latched the door behind her and sat down on the edge of the bed. Tears rolled from her eyes and down the length of her snout as she looked at her hands, and she clenched and unclenched them to calm herself. The insult was so much worse for how long it had taken Kari to understand it; on top of Ty making her look like a fool, the fact that she looked too stupid to understand his insult only made it worse. She wasn't sure why the comment itself even bothered her; Ty was an ass and his siblings had even told her so ahead of time.

It was because she still felt as though she'd missed the opportunity to court Kris Jir'tana, she realized. There was no denying she had feelings for him: the way her emotions had gotten the better of her over what was honestly just an obnoxious comment made that quite clear. Kari was still dealing with whether or not she regretted not sleeping with Kris during the War. She huddled into the corner of her bed as a knock sounded at her door, and she closed her eyes. On top of everything else, now she felt embarrassed by how easily Ty had made her cry.

Memories of her past life crept up on her and the trapped feeling intensified. The knock came again more insistently and Sonja asked to be allowed in, but Kari ignored her, lost in a fog of pain. She ignored a third and fourth knock and plea from her friend, and in the ensuing silence Kari could clearly hear her heartbeat. For all the haziness of her distant past, there was one facet that started to become clear: men would hurt her, and then she would walk away, alone. Her separation from Kris Jir'tana at the end of the war had continued the cycle, and her brief encounter with Aaron in Barcon had done so as well in the opposite sense.

After several long moments of silence, Kari heard the sound of Sonja's footsteps receding down the hallway, and tears flowed freely from her eyes. It pained her to push Sonja away, as Sonja had been the closest thing to a real friend Kari had made since her return. While she had plenty of friends among the Thirty-fifth Light Division during the War, they had been temporary: passing acquaintances in a time of common trouble. Sonja was more what she would consider a *true* friend: someone who, given more time, would more than likely become as a sister to her. Shrouded as she was in pain, Kari knew that she would have to apologize to her friend, but not until after she sorted through her emotions.

She worked to steady her breathing as she lay down and closed her eyes again. What bothered her so much about Typhonix' obnoxious comment was that it reminded her she was still alone. In her prior life, she had pushed people away because she knew her days were numbered: that the disease that was slowly draining the life from her was too much to bear and that she didn't want anyone else to suffer with her. Once again she found herself in a similar situation, though not of her choosing: she was alone because the life she had chosen didn't allow her any personal consideration. And what she had lost was not just a handsome man, but a great general and, not the least of all, the son of a deity.

Kari's thoughts wandered briefly to her sisters, and she wondered if either of them had ever found the peace in life that had evaded her. The last time she had seen either of them was on a trip through Flora, the city where she'd been born and raised, sometime after her twenty-second birthday by her reckoning. Fresh tears rolled down her cheeks as she recalled the incident: her sister Beth-Ann recognized her in the market square and was so excited to see her again, and had called to their mother to come see the daughter who'd run away some eight years before. But Kari had told them they were mistaken, that their sister and daughter had died eight years earlier, and that she wanted nothing to do with them.

That had been the end of it: her travels never took her back through the city of her birth, and she had never seen or heard from her family again. She wondered briefly why that was so important to her, but her past life was still shrouded in that mental fog. Large portions of her past were shrouded so that she couldn't properly recall them; it had been that way since she'd been returned. On the other hand, she was able to recall how she'd found a new family twice: once with a handsome king, another time with her best friend. Her breast heaved with the memories, and a deep breath got stuck for a moment before it came out in a rush, and Kari moaned softly as her entire body relaxed. The memories faded quietly but left her with a feeling of peace, and after a few minutes she dozed off.

Kari dreamed lightly of her training under King Suler Tumureldi, the only male to ever sit on the throne in Aurun Ch'Gurra, capital of the shakna-rir empire on Terrassia. Kari had gone to the shakna-rir capital to inquire about attacks upon the city and whether any sort of demons were behind it, and the king took an instant liking to her for some reason she didn't understand at the time. He took her under his wing and taught her an intricate, intense fighting style that he'd created and mastered. The people called him the *Emerald Scorpion*, a nickname based upon his green shakna-rir skin and because his blades struck at seemingly impossible angles and as blindingly quick as a scorpion's sting. It had been one of the best times in her life and, as she dreamed of him, she remembered the first night he had come to her bedchamber – and the feel of his breath against her neck as he kissed her for the first time.

Kari awoke with a start as a knock came at the door, and she stopped herself from telling Sonja to go away, afraid of being as rude as Typhonix. Kari rose, wiped her face clear of the tear tracks streaking her snout, and

76

moved to the door. She took a deep breath to make sure her emotions were still in check, but she was surprised when she opened the door and found Eryn standing there. The shorter woman was leaning against the frame and looked up when the door opened. She held up a large bottle of tequila and said, "You look like you could use a friend, so I brought you one. But you have to let me chaperone you." She nodded up toward the deck, and Kari laughed despite herself and fell into step behind the half-brys woman.

The two sat on a bench beside the door to the captain's quarters, and Kari looked at the portal warily. "They already left," Eryn assured her. "I think the boys all went down below to sleep." She patted Kari's shoulder but seemed unaccustomed to comforting others. "Don't worry about what that meathead said. It's just nature's way of making sure he never breeds."

Kari laughed and put a hand over the end of her snout. She took a long swig from the liquor bottle and grimaced after she swallowed the burning liquid. She gazed briefly at the bottle before giving the shorter woman an apologetic look. "This stuff is terrible," she said.

"That's because I finished it already and then pissed in the bottle to refill it," the half-brys woman said dryly. Kari stared at her for a few moments before she broke into laughter once more, and as Eryn joined her, they were both joined in their mirth by Jori-an in the boatswain's nest. Kari and Eryn turned their gazes toward the normally silent, vigilant rir female, and Eryn asked, "Don't you ever sleep?"

"Tenth hour until first light," the first mate said but added nothing more, and a neutral expression returned to her face.

"What time is it now?" the half-brys woman asked.

"Nearly half-past nine," the rir female said. "I would appreciate you being off the deck before I retire for the night. The deck and the passengers are my responsibility, and I prefer to sleep without worrying about either."

"Fair enough," Kari said. "Where are you from?"

Jori-an shrugged. "All over," she said cryptically. She remained silent for a few moments before she sprang down from the platform, hurried to the port side, and then practically ran up the rigging to the crow's nest higher up. Kari and Eryn watched her move, amazed at the fluidity and sureness of her steps while running up what amounted to a rope ladder, and when Kari looked at Eryn, the two shared an appreciative nod. Kari wasn't sure if Jori-an actually needed to go up to the crow's nest or was just dodging personal questions, but since Kari didn't like personal questions herself, she didn't give it too much thought.

Kari and Eryn each took another long swig from the bottle. Kari was at a loss as to the look she was getting from the half-brys woman. She guessed that Eryn was trying to figure her out, just as she was doing in return, each gauging how much they could trust the other. Kari wondered how long Eryn had been with Aeligos, how long she had been traveling with the Tesconis siblings, and exactly why she had chosen to go along on their dangerous mission. She wasn't naïve enough to think that the half-brys woman couldn't be a war veteran – after all, the half-brys were undoubtedly the best archers among the mortal races – but rather she wondered why Eryn was there if the mission was a secret.

Kari soon came to the obvious conclusion: for her to have the surname Olgaryn, Eryn's father must have been Olgaryn, the lord of the Five Clans and second-in-command among the brys. There was little doubt that the half-brys woman was likewise an assassin, and Kari considered it was likely her mission was to assassinate Braxus Gaswell. While in the end it had little bearing on Kari's own mission to Tsalbrin, it meant the civil portion of the entire affair might be ended without a blade being raised in combat. If anything, it would at least be efficient.

"How long have you and Aeligos been together?" Kari asked at last, wanting to change both her line of thinking and the silent subject between her and the shorter woman.

"We're not together," Eryn muttered, and she took another draw from the bottle. She started to elaborate but stopped, sighed, and took another sip before handing the bottle back to Kari. "If you'll excuse me being blunt, I'm good in bed, so he stays around. But it doesn't stop him from letting me know how he feels about my father, my allegiances, or what exactly I do for a living. In short, I'm good enough to fool around with, but not to marry."

Kari sipped the liquor and chuckled silently as she saw the bottle was already nearly half gone. "Why don't you just stop sleeping with him, then?"

Eryn sighed. "Because I love him," she said. "Against my better judgment. I'd have been better off falling in love with a paladin."

That drew a laugh from Kari, but her companion joined her. "Doesn't anyone just have normal relationships?" Kari asked.

The half-brys woman fixed her with a curious look. "Do you think you could find five people who agree on what's normal?" She looked up briefly as she saw Jori-an gliding down the rigging with her unnatural grace, and the assassin nudged her friend. "We'd better get below decks before we get yelled at."

Kari nodded and the two women headed down to their cabins, where they shared one last sip of the potent liquor before they bid each other goodnight and entered their quarters. Kari closed and latched her door behind her, and she brought up the flame of her lamp before she undressed. She stretched out on the bed and picked up the books Sonja had given her. Stifling a yawn, she glanced at their titles: *The Lord of Demons*; *Sole King of the Matriarchy*; *Incineration: A Mage's Mistake*; and *The Ascension of Saint Bakhor*.

She placed the extra books in her footlocker, and she settled back into the soft bedding with *Sole King of the Matriarchy* in hand. She found it odd that she'd dreamed about Suler Tumureldi only to find a book about him among those Sonja had given her, and she scratched her head absently as she thought about it. Shrugging, she opened the well-kept tome to the first page to find it was written in the rir language, and she began to read.

~~*~*

The first week of the voyage passed sleepily and predictably. Kari spent her days either reading or being lulled to sleep by the ship's gentle rocking, took her evening meals with the captain – and consequently Typhonix, though he behaved himself at dinner after the first night – and the later evenings were spent drinking with Eryn on a bench up on deck. Kari made sure to apologize to Sonja for the way she'd reacted to the larger woman's attempts to comfort her, but Sonja had simply waved the incident away with a smile and hugged her. It served to ease Kari's spirit during what was a boring week, though the tedium was no worse than the trip to Sarchelete with the merchant caravan, and much better than any of her time served during the War. Eryn wasn't overly chatty about her past, just as Sonja had said, but she was pleasant enough to make small talk with, and Kari was pleasantly surprised to find that Eryn had a good sense of humor, however wicked and blunt it could be.

As the second week of the journey unfolded, Kari ascended to the deck one morning to behold a sparring exercise between the Tesconis brothers. It was unusual to see anyone but the officers on the quarterdeck during the day, but the siblings had apparently obtained permission to use the open area for training during the voyage. Grakin and Sonja sat on the bench that Kari and Eryn normally shared during the evenings, and their three larger brothers formed a loose triangle with Aeligos at its center. Aeligos was telling them something about keeping their guard up, but was getting frustrated by Typhonix' constant interruptions.

"Listen, you stupid ox, if you're not going to pay attention, go read your history books and find out what happens to idiots who never listen,"

Aeligos said at last.

Typhonix took a swing at his shorter brother, but Aeligos bent smoothly at the hip to dodge the blow. He lightly hooked Ty's arm as it sailed by, and he dropped to his rear, wrapping his legs around Ty's. Aeligos caught Ty's foot in his armpit and soon brought the larger warrior down to the ground, and Kari could see the contortion Aeligos was putting on his brother's leg. Ty tried to reach up and punch his brother while locked in the hold, but there was an audible pop, and Ty fell to his back.

"Damnit!" Typhonix yelled, gritting his teeth. "Let me go, you slippery little bastard."

Aeligos released Ty's leg but quickly rolled over backwards to come up on his feet in a defensive stance. Typhonix rose but didn't lunge for him; the blonde was limping gingerly on his injured leg. "Speed will beat strength every time, Ty," Aeligos said.

"And try not to get baited so easily," Erik commented dryly. Serenjols snickered.

Kari marveled at how quickly and precisely the young man moved. She realized her error in judgment: he had the legs of a dancer because he was a wrestler or other unarmed combatant. She looked Aeligos over and realized that he and Eryn had more in common than she had thought. If he was the group's spy and infiltrator, then he likely applied similar skills as the assassin – though by the looks of his submission-based fighting style, he didn't have to kill everyone in his way.

"Where did you learn that?" Kari asked Aeligos as he approached and took a drink of the water his sister was holding.

He took a few sips before facing Kari squarely and putting his hands on his hips. He gave one of his boyish smiles, and Kari had to wonder if that was what made Eryn fall for him, or how the two had met. "It's a human martial art," he said. "Actually, more of a combination of several. It's all about leverage, joint locks, chokes on the ground, and kickboxing on the feet."

"You seem very good at it," Kari complimented honestly.

He nodded in thanks to her praise. "Well, I've been studying and practicing it since I was six," he said. "I'm sure your skill with the sword is just as impressive."

"I'd like to think so," Kari said.

Aeligos' gaze dropped down, and Kari looked toward her feet, wondering what he was looking at. "Would you like to learn? With those legs, you look like you'd be pretty good at it. Not to mention those arms," he said. He gripped her upper arm, but Kari shook him off, the feeling more than a little uncomfortable. He seemed shocked by her reaction, but a sheepish look crossed his features as he muttered, "Erm, sorry."

Kari guessed he was used to the casual way he could speak with or touch his siblings and even Eryn, so she waved away the apology. "It's ok," she said. "Just don't grab me like that until you're actually teaching me. Instincts, you know."

Aeligos smiled again and chuckled, apparently at himself. "I can start teaching you whenever you like," he said. "We've got quite a trip ahead of us."

"We can start tomorrow," Kari said, and she excused herself and headed over to the rail where Eryn sat by herself. She tapped her shorter companion on the shoulder, and the half-brys woman flashed a brief smile when Kari sat down. "How'd you sleep?"

"Comfortably atop Aeligos, and without the lecture on my lack of morals this time," Eryn said with her typical dry humor. "How about you? Still having bad dreams?"

Kari shrugged. "Still not used to being on this boat," she said. "I wake up every night wondering where I am, and why no one's come to wake me up for my watch. Still used to the war schedule, I guess."

"That'll take a while to grow out of," the half-brys woman said. She leaned her elbow on the railing and rested her head in her palm as she fixed Kari with an appraising look. "You realize there're four other good looking men on this boat, right? Well, I guess you can forget about Typhonix, but Aeligos is still technically available, to be honest. And there's plenty more if humans tickle your fancy. I'm surprised you haven't tried taking any of them to your bed."

Kari tapped her fingers on the rail and shrugged. "It's not quite that simple," she said. "Most of the relationships I've had, if you can call them that, were the type where I could simply walk away from them. There's nowhere to go on this ship, and it's not something I think about all that often, really." She paused and met Eryn's intense gaze, and wondered just how easily the woman could read her. Eryn always seemed to know what Kari was up to when they played cards, and the terra-dracon woman could tell the assassin was a tough one to keep secrets from. "Was Aeligos your first love?"

Eryn shook her head with a sour look, and turned her gaze out over the waves. "Nah, I had a boyfriend years ago, well before the War," she said. She seemed as though she were about to elaborate, but her eyes became distant and fixed upon the horizon and she stopped speaking. She seemed to think to herself for a few minutes so Kari kept quiet, not wanting to interrupt whatever introspection the shorter woman was going through. "What about you?" Eryn asked as she finally turned back to Kari.

"I've been with a few different men; mostly mules," Kari admitted quietly. "Since I'm on the road all the time, I can't really afford to get attached, or let anyone get attached to me."

Eryn nodded. "I know the feeling," she said. "Aeligos is as close as I've ever let anyone after that other bastard."

She paused again with a sigh, and Kari touched her shoulder lightly. "Don't talk about it if it bothers you," Kari said.

"Yea, it does, sorry," the half-brys woman said.

"Any brothers or sisters?" Kari asked, trying to keep the conversation going while only changing the topic slightly. She wasn't sure why, but she found Eryn's candor refreshing. Most people either took a long time to get to know, or otherwise were so open that they quickly became obnoxious. In keeping with the efficiency of their forefathers, the half-brys just seemed to know how to hold a conversation without being too open or too closed. Like everything else in their lives, their answers were direct and to the point, leaving unsaid what they did not desire to share and being brutally honest on the things they did.

"Just one, by adoption," Eryn answered. She produced a flask, took a sip and then held it toward Kari. She waved it around for emphasis and told Kari it was simply brandy-milk. Eryn sighed lightly as Kari took and tried a sip from the flask, and Kari nodded appreciatively before returning it. "My brother was human, believe it or not."

"Your father adopted a human?" Kari asked, surprised. It was not all that rare for rir to adopt human children and vice versa, but it was fairly uncommon. It was unheard of for a serilian demon to adopt anything, though.

"Maybe you've heard of him: Buk Denning?"

Kari thought about the name briefly, and came up with only a single reference she could recall from the War, something about an enforcer who worked for the Five Clans out of Oge. Oge was the heart of the Devil Queen's empire during the Apocalypse: the city was her base of operations for centuries, and the assassin's guild had thrived there for many years. Something changed during the war, and the Five Clans' endless fighting with a rival guild called the Blood Order came to a head during the War itself. The Five Clans collapsed: Olgaryn, their leader, was assassinated, and the remaining members of the clans had either folded into the Blood Order or else been conscripted into the Devil Queen's army.

Buk Denning, as far as Kari had heard, was Olgaryn's right hand, a utility man who was skilled at either assassinating his lord's – or rather, his father's – enemies, or else meeting them on the field of battle in mounted combat. He was killed at some point during the Great War, but Kari knew few of the details surrounding his death, other than the fact that age had a lot to do with it. Buk was not a young man when the War began, and with the chaos surrounding the seat of evil and the fierce fighting between the clans, he had apparently lost his life.

"Only briefly," Kari said after a silent minute. "He died during the Apocalypse?"

Eryn nodded. "Just as well," she said, though it was clear from her expression that she was not pleased. "He was getting older, and there was no telling where his loyalties would lie after I killed our father."

"*You* killed your father?" Kari repeated with surprise.

"You didn't know that?" Eryn confirmed. "He was going to use me as some sort of bargaining chip with the Blood Order. It was only a matter of time before he betrayed me, so I beat him to it: I sold him out to the very people he was trying to sell me out to."

"So you're a member of the Blood Order now?"

The half-brys woman nodded. "Unfortunately," she said, and she shrugged in answer to Kari's curious stare. "I've wanted out of this life for a long time. Never wanted into it, really. But after everything that happened..." She paused and let out a long sigh. "What about you, any siblings?"

"I had two sisters," Kari said. "They've both been dead a long time: Beth-Ann and Marian."

"Your parents really liked the sound of *Ann* names, didn't they?" Eryn asked with a chuckle. She looked Kari over, and Kari could tell her half-brys companion was trying to put together all the pieces Kari had shared with her over the previous week. Eryn let out a sigh and gave an appreciative, lopsided smile, something she seemed unaccustomed to doing.

"What're you smiling about?" Kari asked suspiciously. She assumed Eryn was trying to dig up secrets, all the better to help her beat Kari at cards. The half-brys woman was clever and deductive, and Kari imagined no secrets were safe around her for long.

The half-brys woman shrugged. "Everyone on this ship has secrets," she said. "You've got a lot, I can tell."

Kari studied her companion for a minute and gave a soft shrug as she looked out over the water. "In your line of work, I'm sure keeping secrets is an important skill," Kari said at length. "If there's something you want to know, ask. Just don't repeat what I say if I choose to answer."

Eryn looked over her shoulder and noted no one within earshot – certainly not with the wind that was blowing past as the ship plowed through the water. "Who are you, really?" she asked, wiping a few drops of mist from her snout as the seas became rougher and the ship's smashing through waves began throwing water even farther back.

"I'm exactly who I said I am," Kari answered quietly.

The half-brys woman shook her head. "You're either a liar or you're a reincarnation of someone who's been dead for hundreds of years," she said. "I've become an expert at reading people over the course of my career, as it were: you're not a liar. So are you the same Karian Vanador from the twenty-ninth century, or are you an impostor like Erik and Typhonix think?"

Kari looked over her shoulder toward the sparring males and shook her head lightly. She could scarcely believe that either of her demonhunter companions, let alone both of them, would suspect her of such deception. Considering how rare the mutation that created a terra-dracon was, she couldn't believe that so many coincidences could come together to even allow such a deception. If they had doubts, why hadn't either of them asked their superiors? Or even she herself? After all, she wore dog tags that very clearly had both her name and date of birth, not to mention her rank, on them. And what did they think she stood to gain even if she *was* pretending to be someone else?

"Do you know Trigonh?" Kari asked.

"Of course," the half-brys woman answered. Kari wasn't surprised: probably everyone in the world knew of the erestram's name, if not all of his deeds.

"He used some sort of divine favor he was owed to return me to life," Kari said with a sigh. "He said it was because he thought I could help turn the tide of the Apocalypse, but I think that's a bunch of crap. He brought me back because he wanted me to be his lover, and the Apocalypse gave him a good excuse if things didn't work out."

Eryn laughed, and Kari's first instinct was to draw away from her. The half-brys woman looked Kari up and down for a moment. "You're very pretty, but I can't see why he would be attracted to you...giant wolf-demon falling in love with a rir? That's just crazy."

Kari's tensions eased up at Eryn's words. "I'll drink to that," she said, prompting Eryn to share another sip from her flask.

"It's quite a story you tell," the half-brys woman said after they shared the drink. She waved her hand as Kari started to hold up her dog tags and added, "I don't need to see those; I believe you. I had my suspicions, but someone coming back from the dead...that was something even Seril never managed to pull off. If you don't want me to tell the others, I won't."

"I'd appreciate it if you didn't," the demonhunter replied. "It's better for me to see how Erik and Typhonix treat me if they don't believe me. Not to mention, by the look of things, at least two of the brothers have an eye for me."

"Only two?" Eryn said, a brow rising inquisitively, and the two shared a laugh. Eryn rose to her feet as the splashing mist blowing back from the bow became heavier, and she and Kari walked over to stand beside Sonja and Grakin. They watched Erik and Typhonix spar with weapons under the stern but equally impressed gaze of Jori-an. While the rir first mate clearly wasn't happy with the men swinging sharp weapons around on her deck, she was appreciative of both their skill and their caution, as they made sure not to strike the ship or anything else besides each other. Even with the captain's permission to spar on the quarterdeck, it was clear that the men were mindful of damaging the ship or hitting passersby.

Kari was surprised at Typhonix' skill with the massive axe he wielded, despite the fact that such weapon mastery came with membership in their Order. She didn't expect much from the strapping brute, but as she watched the way he twirled and spun his axe to keep even his larger dual-wielding brother off-balance and out of reach, she had to admit to herself that his mouth was not the most dangerous of his weapons. He was a student of the great-axe in the tradition of Turik Jalar, Kari's legendary contemporary. Ty moved gingerly, his leg recovering from whatever damage Aeligos had done, but he still posed quite a threat to Erik. If nothing else, it was a pleasant surprise from a man she had found completely unpleasant during the first week they had spent together.

She found Erik's fighting style intriguing: he dual wielded a combination of longsword and scimitar. The curved blade of the desert-dwelling shakna-rir had many notches and pits on its backside, and he was using it primarily to distract or attempt to pull his brother's weapon out of position. His longsword came up for stinging thrusts and brutal swings whenever he had successfully broken through Ty's defenses, but he stopped his attacks short or turned the flat of his blade whenever it was clear he would strike home. Ultimately, he had to respect the raw strength of his shorter but stockier brother, as the butt end of Ty's axe often came up and nearly caught Erik in the face whenever he thought he'd found an opening.

Their sparring session came to an end, and the two saluted each other in the demonhunter way. Erik sheathed his swords while Typhonix stood his axe up against the wall beside Sonja's seat. Erik took a towel from his sister, wiped his face, and hung it over his shoulders. Ty fixed Kari with a piercing gaze. He seemed to be thinking of something to say, but simply snorted, took up his axe, and headed down below decks. His siblings watched his egress, and then they all turned what looked to be apologetic glances toward Kari. Kari was dumbfounded as to what the brute's issue was, but she tried to keep Sonja's words in mind.

"You and I will spar tomorrow," Erik said to Kari after a moment. "I'm sure I don't need to worry about you, but I'd at least like to see how well you fight before we get to Tsalbrin. I already know what to expect from the rest of my siblings."

Kari nodded. She kept in mind the fact that Attir Surallis was curious as to how well Erik could lead as well as hunt and fight demons. If he wanted a demonstration, she would give him one, though as she thought about it she realized the potential to damage her monitoring should she best or humiliate him. She decided she would push him just enough to ease any doubts, but let him think himself superior – it wasn't improbable that he was better than she anyway. He would push her, and she would push him in return, and both would learn a lot about their partner.

"Just don't wear her out," Aeligos commented, stretching his legs now that their workout was done. "She wants me to show her some of the arts, and I can't do that if she's exhausted."

Erik chuckled lightly through his nose. "I'm going to take a nap. Wake me for dinner, please," he said before heading down into the cabin.

"I didn't think half-guardians even had to sleep," Kari commented as he left, and she received a nod from Sonja.

"We do not have to all that often, but we are certainly healthier and more active if we do," Grakin said quietly. He still hadn't fully recovered from the fatigue that had dogged him since the end of the War, but he was looking a little better each day. "Not to mention that once they are tired from sparring, there is not much else to do on this ship."

"That's because your brothers are too dense to try to bed Kari," Eryn said. Kari put a hand to the end of her snout as she blushed, and the half-brys woman waved away her own comment. "I'm sorry, I was just teasing."

Kari understood that. It wasn't what Eryn had said so much as who she'd said it in front of, Jori-an and Sonja not the least of them. "It's ok," Kari said trying to laugh at herself as the others smiled. "I'm just not used to people being so frank about such things."

"Welcome to the half-demon corps," Sonja said with a giggle.

"You'll get used to us eventually," Aeligos said, and he rose to his feet as he finished stretching. "Well, off to wash up and then a nap for me. Have a good afternoon, ladies."

"Actually, reading in my cabin sounds like a good idea," Kari said. "It's too windy and damp up here to bring a book." She bid the others farewell and headed below decks.

Chapter VI – Salkorum

Another week and a half passed as the ship continued its steady and swift course across the ocean. Kari now spent most of her time reading, training with Erik and Aeligos, and chatting with Eryn, dealing with the tedium as best she could. Typhonix continued to be miserable toward her, taking nearly every opportunity to insult or harass her, though she gradually began to shrug off his cruelty and learned to ignore him altogether. Dinners were taken nightly with the captain and his officers, as Galdur continued to do his best to ease the discomfort of the long trip while getting to know his semi-famous passengers. In all things, Kari and the others did their best to simply stay out of the way of the crewmen.

Kari learned that the Tesconis siblings had begun referring to themselves as the Silver Blades during the Apocalypse, and much of what she had heard about them fell into perspective. She had heard much about the work of the Silver Blades during the War, and likewise the work of the Tesconis siblings, so to find out they were actually the same group was impressive. They hadn't served in an established battalion during the war, but instead performed self-imposed covert missions to take out high-profile but isolated targets wherever and whenever they could. News of their victories had always brought a bit of joy and hope to Jir'tana's brigade, and Kris had spoken of the Silver Blades in high esteem quite often.

The most specific instance Kari could recall involved a minor underworld demon lord named Curlamanx, who by all reports was a vassal of a demon king called Arku. Arku had attempted an invasion on Terrassia during the war, seeking to use the chaos and confusion of the conflict to slip through the dimensional barriers uncontested, but was thwarted. Kari was ignorant to the details of how Arku was stopped, but she knew that at the same time, Arku created a diversion on Askies by sending Curlamanx to fake an invasion there. Apparently the Silver Blades had foiled the demon lord's plans, and sent him fleeing back across the planar boundaries to his master. For a half-dozen people who were mostly under the age of twenty-five at the time, it was an impressive feat.

Kari was not one to enjoy another's suffering, but the thought of the years of punishment Curlamanx would doubtless be subjected to for his failure, particularly when that failure came at the hands of a relatively young group of mortals, brought a smile to her face. She had little patience for the demons: they had chosen their lot in the grand scheme of things, ultimately choosing to become what they were rather than repent the things that had earned them such a fate in the first place. She did not feel sorry for them at all, and it was that absence of sympathy or mercy for them that fueled her as a demonhunter. Her Order's tenet of *love justice, but do mercy* applied to the demons she hunted, but the mercy she gave them was that of the sword.

For ten days Kari trained with Aeligos, and the flexible, acrobatic male taught her the basics of his unarmed combat style. Though Kari was a formidable boxer – boxing was a fundamental training block at the Academy, as one could not always expect to keep their weapons in hand – Aeligos showed her how to avoid and minimize the damage of incoming blows rather than simply blocking or taking them in anticipation of a counterstrike. He further showed her how to take fights to the ground: to throw, tackle, or drag her opponents down where she could use leverage and contortion rather than strength to win.

Ignoring Typhonix's numerous suggestions that they try their exercises without clothes and behind closed doors, Kari learned a lot even in a week and a half. By the end of five days, she was able to mimic the leg-lock she witnessed the first time she saw Aeligos practicing with his brothers, though not as fluidly or quickly. By the end of ten days, she was grappling with the larger and stronger Erijinkor, and forcing him to submit as often as she was submitted by his strength. Even Jori-an, whose expression normally said little to her guests, was clearly impressed by Kari's advancement.

"Speed will always beat strength," Aeligos impressed on her over and over, and the lesson was always driven home by his speed and agility. Though Kari was also very quick and stronger than Aeligos, he always seemed a step ahead of her even before taking his technical prowess into account. Even still, he was clearly impressed by her athleticism, and he watched intently one afternoon as Kari demonstrated considerable dancing skills. She explained how dancing was the basis of her movements both while fighting with swords and while practicing the techniques Aeligos was sharing with her. Aeligos' obvious pride and the way he spoke of her advancement lent Kari a sense of acceptance that had been lacking from the siblings – with the exception of Sonja – and reminded Kari of the way Suler Tumureldi had treated her.

Kari spent further portions of her days sparring with weapons against Erijinkor, who proved to be a deceptively skilled adversary. Though Kari was already impressed by his demonstrations against Typhonix, she soon discovered that he had been holding back, and the more she pushed him

90

during their sparring sessions, the more of his skill surfaced. When combined with his inhuman strength, his prowess left her with little doubt as to why he was advancing so quickly among the Order. She couldn't imagine anything less than an elite or guardian demon standing much of a chance with him in single combat, and figured the weaker of the underworld demons would find themselves overmatched by him as well. Kari didn't recognize his fighting style, but the more she was exposed to it, the easier it became to stifle him in their training. She was careful not to push him too hard, though, as she didn't want to either tip her hand or let him know that she was evaluating him.

On the eighteenth day of their journey, the ship approached a small chain of tropical islands in the middle of endless water. Kari wasn't sure what to make of it, as Master Surallis had only mentioned a stop on the west coast of Terrassia along the way. It was clear the rest of the group was excited by the prospect of feeling solid ground under their feet again once the news that land was ahead spread, but Captain Galdur requested a meeting with his passengers before the ship made its final approach. At his request, the group met in his quarters, and sat around his large table. In the center of the table was a partial map of the world that showed Askies Island on the right southern half and Terrassia on the left northern half. Between the two was the small chain of islands Kari assumed they were approaching, and she looked to Captain Galdur curiously when he entered the room and sat at the head of the table.

Captain Galdur looked over each of the adventurers before him, and then gestured toward the map. "As you can see from the map, we're approaching the islands known as Salkorum," he said. "Now, as we've agreed to keep your mission a secret, I am requesting that you make this stop a secret. These islands are home to a people that many don't know exist. And they prefer to keep it that way. You won't be welcome on the island until I've had time to talk with the elders, but after that you'll likely be allowed to go down and meet the people. Just understand: they're going to be suspicious of you, and the greeting may not be warm."

"How long do you plan to stay here?" Erik asked irritably. "We are scheduled for a stop at Flora and then nothing more until we reach Tsalbrin, so what is this?"

Captain Galdur held Erik under an impatient gaze but gestured for calm. "We will be here for one night only," he said. "We're here on a mission of mercy, for these islands are home to the seterra-rir."

A collective gasp rose from the group, and Sonja's eyes went wide as she tapped her small claws on the table in recognition. "Of course!" she exclaimed. "Jori-an is seterra-rir, isn't she? That's why she keeps her belly covered and she has those odd blue eyes."

Captain Galdur nodded with a suppressed smile, and his passengers began muttering amongst themselves. The seterra-rir were thought to be extinct or extremely close to it, as they'd been the target of a genocidal war that broke out after their creation. They were what was described as a "more human" type of rir: they had red blood and were connected to their mothers via umbilical cords during gestation. Rir were normally born of a magical process that involved a pregnancy but no umbilical cord connecting mother and child, and thus they had no navels. The seterra-rir had navels and thus were easily identifiable apart from their other rir cousins, even before their red blood gave them away.

The results had been horrific: the general rir populace assumed the appearance of the new race was some sort of plot by the Devil Queen to further weaken and infiltrate their bloodlines. War broke out on the fledgling race soon after their creation, and the seterra-rir were chased from the Isle of Morikk, where they had been created. They were thought to have been killed off – at least to the point where their bloodline could not sustain itself – but if what Captain Galdur said was true, they had escaped to the tropical islands and survived. Even still, two centuries later there remained no records of who they were created by or why, and Gori Sensullu had long been silent on the matter, even to his most trusted priests. And though all this had happened after Kari's death, she'd heard all about it from Kris during the Apocalypse: it was something even he and his father were still at a loss to explain.

Kari studied Captain Galdur and wondered if perhaps one of his forefathers had aided the seterra-rir people in their escape. The rir people as a whole were uncomfortable traveling across the oceans, so Kari assumed when the seterra-rir escaped, they likely had the help of the humans. A smile creased the demonhunter's face as she stared in wonder at the captain, and he smiled in return as he noticed her gaze. As he'd said, it was a mission of mercy: Captain Galdur was there to deliver supplies to them, to help them survive.

"What did you bring for them?" Kari asked after a silent minute had passed, and the others regarded her curiously before looking to the human.

"Lumber, bricks, mortar, weapons, foodstuffs – just the things a people hanging on for survival would need," he answered, and he folded his hands on the table before him. "You must understand that these people are afraid of strangers: any word of their existence reaching the mainland could be disastrous if your people decide they still want to finish what they started.

They may not be as scared of you half-demons, since your people have been persecuted in the past and still are, somewhat. Karian, you may not receive the same benefit of the doubt if they recognize you're not half-demon. To them, you're a rir, and your people were the agents of their destruction."

Kari pursed her draconic lips and sighed. "I understand," she said. She was saddened to think her very presence might cause the people discomfort, but she was thrilled to hear that their people had survived, and Sonja seemed just as excited. The others looked mostly indifferent: it was clear they understood the need to exercise caution when dealing with the people, but Kari saw no signs that they had any interest in the seterra-rir themselves whatsoever.

"If you'll excuse me, I will go make ready to head onto the island," Captain Galdur said, rising from his seat. He bowed his head curtly toward his passengers and made his way quickly from the room.

The others rose and began to follow, but Kari stayed where she was and let out another sigh. She wondered briefly if her people had ever truly *won* anything: whether the defeat of the Devil Queen and her demonic creations simply meant that now mortals could concentrate fully on killing each other. While there had been few major wars among the various rir races in their just over three thousand-year history, the ones recorded were brutal, usually resulting in some nation being completely wiped out, as the seterra-rir nearly were. It was hard to dismiss the possibility when she was on her way to prevent racial civil war only weeks after the Apocalypse ended.

Sonja stopped at the door, and she came back to stand across the table from Kari as she sat thinking. "Are you all right?" the scarlet-haired woman asked.

Kari looked up. "Will this ever end?" she asked. "People killing each other; will it ever end, now that Seril is gone?"

"No," Sonja said, shaking her head lightly. "Kari, Seril was evil but she wasn't the source of evil. I know your Order concentrates on fighting demons, but they're not the source of evil, either. It doesn't take a demon to turn a man bad. All it really takes is a selfish heart, and enough people who are either the same or just not strong enough to fight against it. The history of the humans is full of examples dating back to before they even came to this world."

"I guess I'm still a little bit naïve sometimes," Kari said. "I had hoped when the War ended that maybe we'd find peace, for just a little while at least."

Sonja gripped the back of the chair. "I'm not sure what it's like for someone who's been fighting as long as you have, but Kaelariel said something during the Apocalypse that I've always carried with me," she said, and she tapped her fingertips over her heart. "'You carry your peace in here; if you keep looking around you for it, you'll never find it.' We fight against evil, Kari, not against men. You can kill men, and demons, and whatever else, but others will just take their place. That's why the fight never ends, but it's also why we can never give up what we do. We're not expected to win, Kari. Victory belongs to the gods; our place is to fight the good fight."

Kari beheld her friend curiously. She'd heard that same tenet before, but she couldn't put her finger on where at the moment. "You're right," she said, rising to her feet at last. "Let's see if we can undo some past sins."

Sonja half-hugged Kari as the two headed out to the deck. The ship sat at anchor in a horseshoe-shaped harbor on the south side of the largest island. Beautiful, white sandy beaches ringed the islands, with tropical trees on the interior and quaint villages built up in the rocky hills that made up the centers of each island. The villages weren't large, comprised of a mixture of low, flat-roofed wood and brick buildings, and the one at the center of the largest island appeared to be home to a few hundred people. Kari and Sonja watched as a rowboat manned by two sailors carried Captain Galdur and his first mate to the shore.

Already a small band of seterra-rir had gathered on the beach waiting for the rowboat to land, and Kari figured it had to be nice for Jori-an to return home to her people now and again. Judging by her own life lived on the road, Kari wondered if the sailor woman had a family or a home on the island, or if she was simply happier on the high seas. At the very least, it was quite an advantage for the captain to have a seterra-rir among his crew when making stops among the doubtless xenophobic people.

Kari watched from the deck of the ship while Captain Galdur and Jori-an headed ashore and were led through the tropical forest and up to the village. The men got impatient and began sparring lightly as they awaited the captain and first mate's return. Kari received permission from Master Calhoun to take a short swim on the far side of the ship. Salt water or no, it felt good for the woman to take a makeshift bath, and to clean her armor and clothing in the process. The work with Aeligos was intense and sweaty, and while the ship was in motion she had no opportunity to take a swim.

Sonja and Eryn joined her, and the three women splashed around for a

94

little while. They climbed back up a rope ladder to the deck just as Captain Galdur was returning to the ship in the rowboat. Jori-an wasn't with him when he returned. Kari, Sonja, and Eryn stood under the strong, hot sun, and the ocean breeze dried them quickly. The captain stepped before them on the deck and fixed the group with a smile. He gave the three women a curious glance, but then chuckled away whatever he was going to ask.

"I have good news for you all," he said. "I spoke with elder Elleraus and told him about each of you – even that you're terra-dracon, Karian. They have no reservations, and have invited you all to spend the night on the island. As the crew will be busy bringing up the supplies we've brought, I'd like you all to head ashore now, so you're not underfoot as the work begins."

"Should we bring our weapons or armor?" Erik asked.

Captain Galdur shook his head. "There's nothing dangerous living here, just the seterra-rir people, and while you're their guests they'll make every effort to keep you safe. This is probably the last chance you folks will get to relax on dry land until we bring you back home: the gods know you won't want to let down your guard in Flora. So go ashore, try to be pleasant and polite, and let them fawn over you a little bit. They don't have visitors often, so if they're this excited to see you, you may as well enjoy it."

While the distance to shore was short enough to allow all of them to glide across on their wings, such an act might have seemed hostile or at the least intimidating, so it went without saying that they should take the rowboat. "I wonder what kind of booze I can buy from them," Eryn mused as the women lined up at the rail to take the first rowboat to shore.

"Rum," Captain Galdur said with a knowing smile. "And fine rum it is."

The ladies laughed and climbed down into the rowboat, and soon the two broad-shouldered sailors brought them to the shore. The men hopped out as the rowboat approached the sandy beach and dragged the boat full of women carefully through the shallow water to beach it. The women hopped out, looked back toward the ship momentarily, and were greeted by a pair of seterra-rir males. The young men looked to be brothers, as both had bright red hair and pale purple eyes. They were somewhat tall – though not so much as Sonja – and broad through the shoulders, and had the appearance of warriors, though they wore little other than loincloths and a few sheathed knives. They gestured for their female guests to follow and made their way up a dark-soiled path that led through the thick trees and scrub before it wound up to the hilltop village. Kari looked to the trees and noted that many bore coconuts, while others bore fruits or what appeared to be large nuts.

The soil of the path was cool compared to the sun-soaked sand of the beach, and the party padded toward the village while the rowboat shoved off to go retrieve more of their companions. Kari and her two friends walked up the incline to the cozy community behind their two escorts, and looked over the first few structures as they came into the village proper. The buildings were well-made box-like structures that were almost invariably painted white, and as they came up to the top of the hill, the women could see that the village had a main avenue and a central square.

Little shops seemed to dominate the square but the rest of the buildings appeared to be homes, and as Kari got a closer look at the village, she realized that the population was probably around five hundred at best. It depended on the family structures mostly, as larger families living in the domiciles could easily push the population over one thousand, but Kari knew little of the seterra-rir and whether they took single mates. With a population that had once bordered on extinction, the demonhunter understood enough about genetics to know that small populations often required taking several mates to keep the bloodline from becoming too inbred.

Several seterra-rir appeared on front porches and doorsteps as the three walked by, offering friendly waves or simply curious stares, and Kari and Sonja did their best to smile as much as they could. The seterra-rir people all seemed to have shocking hair and eye color combinations, from red hair with sapphire eyes to sapphire hair with purple eyes. They tended toward deep, rich colors, and the combinations – unusual for rir – were stunning to behold. The people were beautiful, and the prospect of them fighting so hard just to survive nearly brought a tear to Kari's eyes. She simply couldn't imagine what it must have felt like, even given the consequences that had awaited everyone if the Light forces had lost the War. To fight for survival against an evil force was one thing; to do so against your own people was quite another.

At last the two males brought them to a house near the central square, no larger or more luxurious than the others from what they could see, but the village elder was standing on the front step waiting. He was an older seterra-rir with weathered features, still handsome in a rugged sense, and had the deep red hair that seemed prominent among his kind. He was dressed in a dark blue robe belted at the waist, a garment that appeared light but durable. He gave a warm smile of welcome, and his intense amethyst eyes studied the three women as they drew near. Wordlessly, he held his

96

front door wide and gestured them inside.

The interior was larger than it seemed from the outside, the single-story home partitioned by half-walls and well furnished. A sleeping area with a double-sized bed told the demonhunter that he had a mate who was not present, and the numerous chairs around the single, oval oak table near the kitchen area told her that he saw many visitors, possibly his own children. She was surprised to see windows in the homes, as their presence further told the terra-dracon woman that at some point Galdur – or those who worked charity with the captain – had brought glass, likely from the shakna-rir of Terrassia. The white walls were decorated with shell mosaics and small woven-grass pictures that lent it a sense of warmth that went beyond its tropical location.

"I welcome you to my home, and to the islands of Salkorum," the elder rir said as he bowed before the women, and then he gestured to the chairs around his table. He offered them cups of water, and he went to get them from his kitchen area while the women took seats. Kari continued to look around, noting a hand-loom and woodcarving tools near the sitting area. There was a rear door with a lantern sitting on a high square table beside it, and in the center of the home was a sprawling hand-woven rug. As she had guessed from looking at the outside, it wasn't particularly luxurious for the leader of this particular village, but that wasn't surprising if the people were fairly destitute.

"So you ladies are on your way somewhere with Captain Galdur?" Elleraus asked as he brought them their cups of water. The cups were made out of carved-out coconut husks with the bottoms flattened so they sat properly on the table.

"Yes," Sonja answered. "We're actually on our way to Terrassia, and the good captain was kind enough to let us buy passage aboard his ship. We were rather pleasantly surprised to find he'd be stopping here to deliver supplies."

Elder Elleraus nodded and took a seat at the head of the table with his own cup of water. "Galdur is a good man," he said. "He has been bringing us supplies whenever his course has allowed him to for a little over fifteen years now."

"Do you know Jori-an, his first mate, well?" the scarlet-haired woman asked.

"Of course; she is my niece," Elleraus said, and then he chuckled. "Then again, so is about two-thirds of our female population. Given the number of our people, most of us are related at least a little bit by blood."

"I assume you mate with men and women from the other islands in

97

turns?" Eryn asked. Kari was surprised that the half-brys woman would ask such a question, even given her blunt nature, and Sonja seemed shocked as well.

"Yes," Elleraus said with an appreciative smile. "Very rarely we introduce some fresh blood into the population when outsiders come and decide to stay, though we lose our youngsters to wanderlust far more often."

"I can't tell you how sorry we are for the way your people have been treated," Kari said.

Elleraus waved away the comment. "Please, do not burden your hearts with such thoughts. You had nothing to do with it, and what is done is done and past. We are simply moving forward now, hoping for a day when we are accepted for what we are. Much like your own people have done for so long," he added, looking to the two half-demon women.

Sonja nodded. "Things have been changing over the past few centuries, particularly since the Fifth Demon War," she said. "I think as the mysteries surrounding Gori Sensullu come to light, things will change even more. It may not be soon, but your people will be welcomed among the rest of us eventually."

"I know, I simply hope I live to see that day," the elder male said. "Until that time, we will work to grow stronger as a people, for what else can we do?"

"Die," Eryn said evenly. "And that's not really much of an alternative."

Elleraus was shocked, but when he realized Eryn was just making a blunt observation, he gave a short nod and let forth an uneasy chuckle. "Indeed," he said. "While I would love to hear all about the outside world and your adventures, I am sure you would all like to walk around and feel solid land beneath your feet again. Take some time to see our little village, visit one of the shops, or spend a couple of hours down on the beach. I will be here, waiting to greet the rest of your friends."

The three women rose, thanked their host for his hospitality, and left his cozy and comfortable abode to explore the village. It was quaint and homey compared to the cities that each of the three women had grown up in. There were a few score houses, a handful of shops, and numerous gardens where food was grown. The life was simple, Kari could tell, and in a way she found it appealing, as alien as it was to the lives she had led. Kari had done most of her growing up in Solaris, a transition city between the rolling plains and the deep forests of Terrassia. It was a waypoint for caravans crossing from the desert kingdom of the shakna-rir to the elven kingdom of the east, the northern kingdoms of the humans around Dira Ch'Tori, and the fures-rir homeland in the frozen north. Solaris wasn't as affluent or beautiful as Sonja's home city of Latalex, but it had a large, static population, and saw that swell with the constant traffic headed in almost every direction across the continent.

The seterra-rir village, whose name was nowhere to be found among its stone streets or the signs that adorned the few shops in the square, was the type of little town that many dreamed of retiring to but never found. The fact that it sat on a tropical island only added to its allure, and Kari sighed wistfully, thinking that perhaps when her adventuring days were over, she might like to live in such a place. She assumed if the people of Salkorum were ever openly accepted in the world she came from again, the island would become quite a tourist attraction as well as a home to those who enjoyed bright sun, open seas, and beautiful beaches.

Kari excused herself when her two friends stopped at a little general store, and she made her way back down the path to the beach. Along the way she passed the rest of her companions, except for Grakin, being led to the village by the same two seterra-rir brothers. Kari thought about knocking down a coconut to bring back to the ship but decided against it on the off chance the people considered it stealing. She figured it best to ask first and let them either give her one or welcome her to take one for herself. She remembered the taste of coconut well from the few times she had stopped in the shakna-rir city of Awlsabre on Terrassia's southern coast.

The white sand of the beach was warm under her feet as she crossed down to the crystal-blue water, and she stepped out to nearly knee-high depth and walked along the strand. Grakin was sitting alone farther down the beach, his black wing-wrapped form a stark contrast to the sands he sat upon, and she moved slowly toward him. The warm ocean breeze caressed her sun-drenched skin and Kari smiled. The beauty of the place reminded her of what she and her friends had fought so hard to preserve. Sonja's words to her shortly before they left the ship came back to her, and she found there was little place for the shadows of her past under the sun.

Kari approached Grakin but he didn't look up at her. She drew up beside him and began shedding her clothes. Even her naked form didn't earn a glance from him so, suppressing a chuckle, Kari made her way back down to the water and dove under its crystalline surface. The harbor was warm and felt comforting compared to bathing in the mountains for years during the War. The water glided across her skin and she beat huge blasts of water behind her with her wings. The stress was a bit much for her to continue, but she propelled herself with unnatural speed below the surface.

99

She came up nearly a third of the way to the ship and treaded the water, and she waved to Grakin to see if his stare registered her at that distance.

He waved back at last, and after he sat still for few more moments, Kari beckoned for him to join her out in the water. He seemed to hesitate for a moment, but he removed his own garments and swam slowly out to meet her. Kari moved in so he wouldn't have to swim out too far: she didn't want him to exhaust or possibly hurt himself trying to match her distance if he was still fatigued. They met halfway between the shore and where she had initially waved, and she was surprised as his black eyes met her own for the first time since their journey together had begun. His eyes were full of fire and life despite his quiet and seemingly detached nature, and as she stared into their depths Kari could see – almost feel, in a sense – the warmth and love of the man. She could see the passion that drove him to become a healer, and to follow a deity whose domain – death – often frightened even those who knew what he was like. She could see the burdens Grakin bore, as he was the one ultimately responsible for the life or death of his siblings in their dangerous line of work.

What surprised her was that she didn't see the love for her that she had supposed his evasive gaze held. Over the years, Kari had found that men who were enamored with her and not just looking for a night of irresponsible carnal pleasure were unable to take their eyes off of her until she tried to meet their stare. And so she had assumed that Grakin's evasive gaze meant he felt something toward her. Staring into his eyes, though, she could see that she was only partially right. He cared about her in the same sense that he cared about his siblings, and more than likely all the people he came into contact with. He cared about her life, her comfort and well-being, and her happiness, but if there was romantic love, she didn't see it now.

"How do you feel?" she asked him quietly.

Grakin looked back toward the shore briefly, but then he met her gaze once more and flashed the first true and genuine smile she had seen from him. "The warmth and the water seem to be good for me," he said. "I feel better than I have in months, or even years."

"All that time healing people, and you keep ignoring the most important of them," she said. She lifted her dripping hand out of the water to stroke his face. He seemed to almost melt at her touch, leaning his face into her palm, and she wondered briefly if what she had thought a moment before was off-target.

"Service is its own reward," he said softly, and his ebon eyes filled her with wonder. There was a light in their depths that told her quite clearly

100

that he was not just repeating a tenet he'd heard in temples, but something he truly believed in. "I may put myself last, but my time will come. Everyone's does, if they but wait; everything comes in its own time. Even death will not stop us from being exalted when it is our time."

Kari tilted her head curiously as a smile appeared on the handsome male's face, and she couldn't help but chuckle. "You know who I am, don't you?" she asked.

Grakin blinked slowly and nodded. "To me it was obvious not long after I heard your name," he said. "My brothers, they are not as trusting: they still require their eyes and ears and hands to believe things. I am a priest: I take things on faith, because in the end the truth will always be revealed. It was difficult to believe it was truly you, but any doubts I may have felt at first have since dissipated."

The terra-dracon woman laughed. "I'm not sure how Erik and Ty could think I'm an impostor," she said. "I'd have to have been born terra-dracon with black hair and eyes, trained to become a high-ranking demonhunter, and stolen a name without anyone taking offense. It seems a little ridiculous."

Grakin dipped under the surface, tilting his head back as he reemerged so that his hair was out of his face. "Jealousy may be a part of it, as sad as I am to say so," he replied. "Anger is also an issue in Ty's case. We have been through much as a family, and Typhonix does not like women very much, hence his disrespect toward you in particular. I cannot apologize enough for the way he treats you..."

"That's not your mistake to apologize for," Kari said, waving off the comment, but then she let him continue.

"Erik...has a very particular way of viewing the world around him. To him, things are what they appear to be, and many times he fails to look below the surface of what he sees to find what is truly at its core. When he looks at Eryn, he sees only a cold-hearted killer. When Captain Galdur brought us to a strange port and asked us to swear secrecy, he suspected piracy. When you say you are someone who died hundreds of years ago, he sees a liar."

"And what do you see?" Kari asked.

Grakin remained silent for a minute, studying her face and her eyes in particular, and Kari waited to see what he would say. "Salvation," he said simply.

Kari was taken aback and waited to see what else he would say, but after a silent moment, Grakin simply leaned forward in the water and kissed her chastely on the side of her snout. The terra-dracon woman almost melted, her ebon eyes wide in shock, and she stared at him in wonder. She wondered what had prompted such a statement, or the kiss that had tickled her to the core. Her emotional compass was spinning heedless of direction, and she was unsure if her initial thoughts were correct. Was he not interested in her, as she had assumed when they'd first met in the water? Was the chaste kiss one of friendship and admiration, or was it his gentlemanly way of telling her he was, in fact, interested?

His eyes were near impossible to read, showing wonder at knowing who she was, but there was something darker behind them, something she couldn't read because he was preventing her from doing so. She reached up to touch his face again, and tears welled in her eyes as he rubbed his cheek against her palm. Kari realized in that moment that he was, in fact, interested in her, but there was something else that kept him from pursuing her. It took her only another moment to recognize what it was he saw in her, what he didn't want her to see in him, and what his siblings apparently never saw. "How long have you known?" she asked quietly.

Grakin looked down, but Kari slid her hand under his chin and lifted it so that he was forced to look into her tear-laden eyes once more. "I am sorry, this is my burden to bear; you have already been through this once before," he said, trying to look away once again.

Kari shook her head, grabbed his chin more forcefully and met his gaze more intently. "No," she said sternly. "Don't turn away, that's the same mistake I made as a young woman. This is your burden to bear but that doesn't mean others can't help or comfort you. I pushed everyone out of my life because I didn't want to hurt them, when pushing them away *is* what hurt them. Don't push me away, Grakin. Let me be here for you."

His own eyes began to well up with tears, but he steeled himself and sighed, and met Kari's gaze evenly. "All right," he said quietly, forcing a smile, and he wrapped his arms around Kari as she hugged him.

Grakin held her for a few minutes, and with the warmth of the sun, the water, and his tender embrace, Kari lost herself in the happiest of her memories. It brought to mind the love that she had shared with Suler Tumureldi, and how safe she had felt with him, the first and only man she had ever truly loved. Nine months of bliss saturated her being as she clung tightly to the priest, and she even recalled Trigonh, who – though she'd always felt his love was misplaced – had guarded and protected her during their time together. She separated from Grakin slowly, and when their eyes met, a part of her understood that she had found something special once again.

Kari leaned her head to the side slightly. After the barest of hesitations

Grakin took the invitation and leaned in to kiss the base of her neck. His arms encircled the small of her back and he pulled her in tight to him again. She lost herself in his embrace and the softness of his tender kisses again, and she laid her head on his shoulder, keeping her eyes closed as she soaked up the moment. He stroked her wet hair and kept one hand between her wings, keeping her close to him, and he kissed her again at the base of her neck. She moaned contentedly against his shoulder, and drew back to run her hand along his jaw after a few more moments.

"Would you like to find someplace more private?" she asked him. He was clearly shocked at the suggestion, and Kari regretted asking. She was relieved when his expression melted back into a warm smile and he stroked her cheek.

"If you wish it, I would like nothing more," he said simply. She led him back to the shore to collect their clothes, and after looking around for any of their companions, they headed into the woods to find a more secluded place.

A while later, after taking a short dip in the water to wash themselves and their clothes, Kari and Grakin sat at the tidemark. They cuddled in the warm afterglow of their passions, and Kari leaned against him while they watched the sun make its way to the western horizon. "Do your siblings know?" Kari asked quietly, taking his hand. She didn't want to ruin the afterglow that surrounded them both, but wanted to be sure she didn't break his trust by accident.

"No," he said with a slight sigh, but the smile remained on his face. "No, our work is important, and I have never wanted to impair or slow down the group because I am ill. I do my best to take care of myself, but other considerations have to come first."

"I know that feeling," she said, and silence fell between them. They watched the waves slide up onto the sands. Though Kari clearly remembered suffering from the illness, there was a numbness that surrounded those memories, and she wasn't sure how to share them with Grakin.

"Was it painful?" he asked suddenly.

Kari met his gaze and knew that it would do no good to lie. "Sometimes, especially when I got close to dying," she said. "Most of the time you just feel weak or tired for no real reason." She sighed and touched his face tenderly, and he rubbed his cheek against her palm again. "When you die, you'll stand before your lord alone, but you don't have to die alone. Let your siblings and your friends be there for you."

She was amazed when he smiled and kissed her lightly on the side of the snout, which he already seemed fond of doing. He took her hand in his and held it tight to his breast, and Kari could feel the strength of his heartbeat. She didn't understand how a half-guardian contracted Dracon's Bane in the first place: she assumed it was something specific only to terra-dracons. Whatever the case, she was pleased to see that knowing his fate didn't dampen his spirits – at least not in her presence – and she figured his service to the god of death had a lot to do with it.

"You pushed everyone away when your time came?" he asked.

"Not entirely," she said. "I was with Trigonh and my friend Carly Bakhor when it happened, but I spent a lot of effort keeping people at a distance for years so they wouldn't be as shocked when I was gone. I knew Carly could handle it. She was probably the strongest woman I've ever known."

"*Saint* Carly Bakhor?" Grakin asked, looking at her sideways. "You knew Saint Bakhor when she was alive?"

"We traveled together for over a year and a half. Our group even killed a red dragon once," Kari said. Grakin's eyes went wide and his jaw dropped in astonishment. "We only stopped working together when she got pregnant and settled down in the elven lands of Laeranore to have her baby."

Grakin shook his head, his smile growing even wider. "You are just full of surprises," he said, squeezing her hand.

"I know, but don't you be," she said, her expression becoming more serious. He looked at her quizzically, and she took up both his hands in hers. "You need to tell your siblings. This isn't something you want to go through alone, and you'll want their strength to keep you going. This is a path you have to walk, but you don't have to walk it alone."

"I walk no paths alone. Kaelariel is with me everywhere, always," Grakin said. He held his hand up to stifle her reply and continued, "I will tell them, I just do not know how or when. I do not think my brothers are ready to face such a thing, but Sonja might be. Just please say nothing until I have. Please?"

"Of course. You have my word," she said, and she pulled his snout down slightly to kiss his forehead. She saw so much of her younger self in the way he was dealing with his illness, and she was determined to keep him from making the same mistakes she had. "I'm always here for you if you have questions. I'm here if you need me."

Grakin stroked her face affectionately, and in his eyes she could see that he felt the same way she did. "You are a good woman, and a good friend," he said, but he stopped speaking when they heard a call from down the beach.

Erik approached, and he slowed to a stop a few feet away when he noticed the two were naked. His brow furrowed momentarily and he folded his arms across his chest, looking out over the water briefly before meeting their gazes. "Elleraus would like us all to gather for a meal, and to assign us to some of the citizens' houses for tonight," he said. "If you two are done swimming, I want you to come to the village now."

"Of course," Grakin said, and he and Kari rose to their feet to get dressed. Erik's scrutinizing gaze stayed over them the entire time, but he said nothing. Once they'd dressed, they walked with the larger male back to the village, silent and apart, though Kari's thoughts remained fully upon Grakin.

~~*~*

The island cooled off nicely as night descended. The air was thick with the sounds of birds and insects, and the western horizon was painted a fascinating array of purples and pinks. Kari sat on a rooftop with the seterra-rir couple that had agreed to house her for the night, and she sipped from a cup of rum as she sat with her gracious hosts. They were young – she guessed not much older than twenty – and the female was obviously carrying a child. She and her mate reclined together on a towel, watching the sunset along with their guest.

"When are you expecting?" Kari asked, making small talk, and the woman put a hand to her belly with a smile.

"Just a couple more months," she said, beaming as her mate wrapped an arm around her shoulders. "It's our first. Do you have any children?"

Kari shook her head but had to smile as she thought about it. "No, not me," she said. "As a demonhunter, I've lived my whole life on the road. Never really had time to think about it before…but I am now."

"There was already talk when the large man came back to the village with you and the darker one in tow," the woman said, and a mischievous smile crossed her face. "Rumors and gossip spread quickly about outsiders."

"Oh?" Kari prompted, curious.

"The initial assumption was that you might be mates," the male said, pushing purple hair back from his face. He had matching amethyst eyes and hair, an intriguing combination, and as his eyes began to glow softly in the twilight, they were wondrous to behold. "Once word spread that he is serilian-rir and you are not, the gossip dried up rather quickly."

"Serilian-rir?" Kari repeated. "You mean half-demon?"

"If that is how your people call them," the male said with a shrug. "Our people cannot breed with serilis-rir or serilian-rir, and were unsure if the same held true for your kind."

"Well, yes, we can," Kari answered, trying not to sound condescending. "Half-demons – or serilian-rir – can come from any of our people. Well, except yours, I guess."

Erik called to Kari from the street, and Kari walked to the edge of the roof. "Come to Elleraus' home, there's something we need to discuss," her companion said as though there was little choice involved.

"I'll be right there," Kari said. She already felt defensive simply based on his tone and the way he'd looked at her and Grakin earlier. She thanked her hosts and excused herself to go speak with the elder and her friends, and then she descended a ladder to jog down the street. The windows of the elder's home were aglow with the warmth of candlelight, and she found the door left slightly ajar so she could enter.

Kari expected to find all of her companions in the elder's home, but when she saw only Erik, Sonja, and Aeligos along with Elleraus and his mate, she wondered if being summoned had something to do with Grakin. Erik had made only a poor attempt to mask his aggravation at finding the two naked on the beach, and Kari was at a loss as to why it would bother him. He hadn't seen anything except for two naked people drying on the beach after swimming, unless he'd been watching them for several minutes before he approached. In any case, he had made no indication that he was interested in Kari, so she wondered what the issue could be.

Erik had an exasperated expression on his face when he looked at her, as did Sonja and Aeligos, and Kari shook her head lightly. She quickly decided that if there was any sort of attempt at *disciplining* her for making love to their brother, she was going to let them know exactly what she thought of their nosiness, and possibly even more than that. She paused in her thoughts, however, as Elleraus smiled and gestured for her to sit on one of the low padded chairs around the central rug of the living space.

"How are you enjoying the company of your hosts?" the elder asked Kari. His mate approached from the kitchen, and the elder seterra-rir woman touched her forehead to Elleraus' shoulder and then took a seat across from Kari.

Kari smiled, stalling while she let her heartbeat slow down a bit. "They've been great," she said, shrugging sheepishly. "I already forgot their names, though."

"Dowain and Saisha," Elleraus said with a smile. "They are expecting their first child."

"Yea, they said as much," Kari returned. "Is the child his or did she have to have a baby with a man from a different island?"

The elder waved his hand and shook his head. "No, the firstborn is always with our mate," he explained. "After that, we will normally have one or two with another couple, then again with our own mates if we desire more."

"How many children do you have?" Kari prodded, ignoring the impatience she could clearly see building up in Erik. She wasn't sure if it was because he knew she had been with Grakin, but she found the topic something she was giving a lot of thought to now. "And how many do your people normally have?"

"I have three by Minaara," Elleraus said, touching his mate's shoulder, "and four more by women on other islands. Minaara has three more by other males, so it gets a little confusing as to how many children *we* have." He chuckled shortly. "Each of our women generally tries to have six, but their health or the availability of unrelated males sometimes makes it less. Rarely do they have more."

Kari's eyes went wide and she chuckled despite herself. "That's a lot of babies," she said, trying to imagine herself with so many children.

"Yes, but we tend to have them all young," Minaara said, her voice vibrant and sweet. Like all of her people, she had a fascinating combination of hair and eye colors: her eyes were a stunning orange, while her long, straight mane was of a deep red. She had age-lines on her snout as was typical for an elder rir, but was still quite lovely. "Usually by the middle of our fourth decade, our babies are all having babies of their own, so life is quiet except when the little-little ones are around."

The group shared a laugh. "Why don't we get to the reason we're all here," Erik said, clearly trying to keep his tone neutral. Kari noted that he wasn't looking at her: his stare was fixed on Elleraus. That eased Kari's tensions.

"As I am sure you have heard, either from our people or from Captain Galdur, these islands receive supplies from ships running the lanes between Askies and Terrassia," he said. "What he might not have told you is that sometimes those ships also bring refugees of one sort or another, escaping a life on one continent to start over on the other. Rarely do they choose to stay here, but sometimes they leave things here that they feel they cannot take with them."

"Why do I have the feeling I'm not going to like this?" Erik asked somewhat irritably.

Sonja glared at him, shutting him up. "Erik, for the love of Kaelariel, these people have been nothing but generous and accommodating to us, stop being so suspicious of everything," she berated him, and he held his hands up in silent apology. Sonja turned to Elleraus and asked, "What would you have of us?"

Elleraus waved off Erik's outburst, took a seat beside his wife, and sipped from the mug of rum he was holding. "Many years ago, twin children were left with us by a human couple trying to escape their past. They were on the run from something that threatened their lives, and hoped to spare their children by leaving them with complete strangers in a place few ever visit." Minaara took his free hand in hers and gave it a squeeze. "Though we love them, there is no future here for these youngsters."

"So you want them to travel to Terrassia with us?" Kari asked. During the dinner they'd shared with their hosts, it had slipped that the group was truly headed to Tsalbrin, much to Erik's annoyance. An embarrassed expression suddenly crossed Minaara's face, and the seterra-rir woman rose and crossed to the kitchen. Elleraus didn't respond. Instead he waited for Minaara to return and hand Kari a mug of rum, and the terra-dracon woman smiled her thanks.

"No," Elleraus said when Minaara returned to his side. "No, what I ask of you is much more specific. We have done our best to shield these youngsters from the past of their parents, and the results have been a mixed blessing."

"You didn't tell them the truth about their parents?" Sonja asked, though her tone was non-accusatory.

"We thought it best not to," Elleraus said. "They were left here nearly seventeen years ago, and their parents have never returned. Our assumption has always been that whatever their parents fled from eventually caught up to them. We thought it best not to expose the children to whatever that might have been, so we told them that their parents were crusaders who left them here for their protection. It was not entirely true, of course, but we felt it would be less hurtful – or dangerous - than the absolute truth."

"Understandable," Aeligos said, and Kari and Sonja echoed his sentiments.

"Of course, when they *learned* that their parents were crusaders, they likewise began to strive to the same ways of knighthood," Elleraus said. "Now, I am no expert on the ways of knightly honor, but I believe with a little refinement, they may champion the people as paladins."

"Both of them?" Kari asked, surprised.

Minaara nodded. "When you meet them, you will know it to be true," she said.

"How old are they?" Erik asked.

"They are twins, roughly seventeen years of age," Elleraus answered.

The blue-eyed half-guardian shook his head. "Forget it," he said, waving a hand dismissively. "This isn't a pleasure cruise and we don't have the time or luxury to babysit a couple of teenagers."

"Erik!" Sonja barked. "Don't disrespect our hosts."

Erik sighed but then apologized again. "This is just not a good idea," he said. "Maybe we could leave them in Flora, but taking them with us to Tsalbrin is a bad idea. A possible civil war is no place to bring a couple of inexperienced seventeen-year-olds."

"How quickly you forget that Typhonix and I were that age and younger when the Apocalypse came upon us," his sister countered. "No one is saying we should take them out to the battlefield, but we're being asked to show them how agents of the gods operate. I don't think that's too much to ask, but your irritability is making me think I may be wrong."

"What do you think?" Erik asked his younger brother.

"I'm not sure there's a lot I can teach them," Aeligos said. "Somehow I don't think the kind of work I do or what I've been teaching Kari will be very helpful to them. But if they really have received the calling, maybe being around you and Kari would be good for them."

Kari was surprised: she'd never assumed she had anything in common with a paladin other than perhaps a *crusader* title. She had met only a few paladins in her lifetime. The chivalric, knightly defenders of the faith simply pursued different goals and went about their quests much differently than the demonhunter did. While they had occasionally enjoyed each other's company, contrasting styles, and fighting prowess, she had never really found much in common with them on a personal level. Paladins were simply a different type of person and represented strength of character that even Kari aspired to.

"Kari?" Erik asked, and she started. "What do you think?"

Kari shrugged, surprised that Erik would even ask. "As far as I'm concerned, more help can't be a bad thing," she said. "Honestly, I had no idea there were going to be as many of us as there are. Worse comes to worst, we leave them somewhere if the fighting gets too intense or they're in danger. They're still kids but they're also old enough to make their own decisions. Maybe we should just tell them where we're going and why, and let them decide."

Sonja nodded with Kari's assessment. "I couldn't have said it better," she said. "If we tell them where we're going and why, their response should pretty much tell us where they stand as far as becoming paladins is concerned. I know you don't like variables, Erik, but you have to keep in mind: we may not succeed at our primary task."

It was clear Erik hadn't really considered that point, and he nodded after thinking about it for a few moments. "Yes, you're right," he said, rubbing a hand thoughtfully across his wide chin, and he looked to Elleraus. "Can we meet them first?"

"Of course," the elder said. "I will have them meet us here for the morning meal, and you can make your final decision then. Better that you rest on it and give it more thought."

Erik nodded, bid everyone goodnight, and made his way quietly from the home back toward his temporary abode. Sonja and Aeligos soon did likewise, and after thanking Elleraus and Minaara for the drink, Kari returned to the roof of her hosts' home. She found them still there, romancing under the young stars, and let them know that she would be turning in for the night. They graciously offered to let her share a side of their bed, but she turned them down politely and headed indoors.

The interior was set up much like Elleraus' house. After failing to get comfortable in any of the padded chairs, Kari spread her clothes out on the central rug and lay down under her cloak. She fell asleep rather easily, as the rum loosened her up a bit and the consistent drone of the tropical island settled down around her like a second blanket. She slept soundly, dreaming of Grakin's soft touch, the smell of his body, and the feeling of his half-guardian warmth pressed against her.

Morning came with a slightly damp but not unpleasant heat, and when she saw her hosts cuddled in their bed, Kari dressed and left quietly. She was the first to arrive at Elleraus' home, and found him and his mate already preparing a morning meal for their guests. The rear door of the house led to a common area with an outhouse, and when Kari returned from her trip there, she found that Sonja and Aeligos had arrived. Soon all of the Tesconis siblings and their half-brys companion sat around Elleraus' dining table, and they took their breakfast.

The group made small talk, joking about the joys of returning to the ship, and after a while a pair of young humans arrived in the elder's home. It was immediately apparent that they were siblings, and it only took a moment to confirm what the elder had said about them being twins. Both were a little taller than Kari and had long, sun-lightened brown hair with chestnut eyes. The young man was starting to grow a beard, his face covered with well-maintained stubble and his long hair tied back in a tail

110

while the young woman's hung in long, wavy curls.

The two bowed respectfully to the elder and his mate, and moved to the sitting area when Elleraus bid them take seats. Soon, the elder and his mate rose and moved to the sitting area, and Erik walked over to stand before all of them. Kari and the others took seats around the rug or on unoccupied chairs. The two humans studied the many half-demons before them with the same amount of interest as they were receiving in turn.

After a few moments, Elleraus finally spoke. "Katarina, Sherman, these are the adventurers we spoke of last evening who may be taking you with them," he said. "They wanted to meet you first to see if they felt you could handle the dangers of the road ahead, or if perhaps you would simply like to accompany them to Flora and remain there."

Erik spoke up. "The first thing you have to understand is that we're headed into a possible war, far to the west on the island of Tsalbrin," he said, his muscular arms folded tight across his chest. "While it was only rumored when we left home, it's still going to be another month and a half or so before we reach the island. By then, who knows how far the situation will have devolved. The entire island could be in the throes of war, destroyed, or maybe untouched – we don't know at this point."

"We're all war veterans: every one of us fought in the Apocalypse, which you were thankfully shielded from, living out here on the islands," he continued. "I understand you've self-trained a bit in the ways of knightly honor and combat and that's a fine start, but if I'm going to be responsible for you, then you have to respect and obey my commands. I can't have people who don't listen to me traveling with my siblings: ultimately, I'm responsible for all of us. So the decision you need to make is whether you want to travel into a possible war, if you think you can handle that and obey my orders, or if you would rather just be left in Flora. If we leave you in Flora, you're on your own. We have no idea how long we'll be on Tsalbrin and will not come looking for you when the war is over. Sorry if I seem a bit like a drill sergeant, but I want to make sure you know what it is you're getting into should you leave the islands with us."

"We understand," Sherman said, and he shared a glance with his sister. They both smiled after a moment. "If anything, you're just what we were hoping for. Elleraus has told us about our parents being crusaders, and we want to follow in their footsteps."

"We want to make a difference," Katarina added, and Kari was already impressed by the look of determination on the young woman's face. It didn't mean the twins were ready to face the dangers of the world or a war, but it at least gave Kari the impression that they weren't walking into the situation blindly. "If you go to divert or fight in a war at the direction of the gods, then I think there's a reason you're here now. And if Elleraus wants us to go with you, he must think you can teach us something of the way of the crusader."

It was clear even to Kari that Erik liked what he was hearing despite his reservations about bringing youngsters with them. "None of us are paladins, but there may be a bit we can teach you since three of us are demonhunters," Erik said. "My elder brother Jol can teach you about some of the more exotic creatures we might run into. Aeligos is our tactician, and though he's mostly an infiltrator, I'm sure there's a lot you can learn from him. I'll leave this decision to you; Kari was quite right on that. Unless anyone else has something to add?"

"How do you fight?" Typhonix asked.

"We've trained quite a bit with the greatsword," Sherman answered. "Obviously, there are no master swordsmen here on the islands, but our friends here have many warriors among them and they have trained us as well as they were able."

The blonde demonhunter nodded and pointed his thumb toward Serenjols. "He and Sonja will probably be able to teach you a thing or two," he said, and the two youngsters nodded.

"I have seen no temple here, what deity do you two serve?" Grakin inquired, and he was surprised as the two shared a glance before shaking their heads. "Well, I see I will have a part in your training as well, then. The lifeblood of a paladin is the strength of their faith. Who you have faith in is not the issue, so much as that you *have* faith. We can discuss it further later."

"Then we are free to join you?" Sherman asked.

Erijinkor nodded. "Gather your things, I believe Captain Galdur wants the ship to set sail at midmorning," he said. "Has anyone seen Jori-an since we landed?"

"She has a home on the next island over," Elleraus said. "She has family there that she was visiting. I am sure she will be back in time to set sail."

"I had no doubts about that," the blue-eyed male said with a grunting laugh. "If anything, she'd be setting sail without us, not the other way around. You all know what I expect. Go thank your hosts and be back on the ship within the next hour."

His siblings all rose and made their way from the home, as did Sherman and Katarina. Eryn nudged Sonja and the two lagged behind with Kari. Kari looked to the other two women curiously as they followed her toward Dowain and Saisha's home. After a few moments, Kari stopped and turned to face them in the street, wondering what they wanted.

"So?" Eryn asked.

"So, what?" Kari returned.

"How was it?" the half-brys woman prompted with a smile.

Kari couldn't believe it; how did Eryn find everything out so easily? She folded her arms across her chest and tried to take up a stern posture, but the smirk on Eryn's face made it nearly impossible. "It was amazing," Kari said at last.

"What was amazing?" Sonja asked, confused.

"She had sex with your brother," Eryn told her.

"Wait, what?" the scarlet-haired woman blurted. She looked back and forth between her two friends. "With who??"

"Grakin," Eryn said.

Sonja fixed Kari with a wide-eyed stare. "You and Grakin had sex?" she asked, putting a hand to the end of her snout. "Oh my, that's...that's amazing." She looked around suddenly to make sure no one else was around. "Oh, you'll have to give me all the details when we're back on the ship! How did this happen?"

Kari waved her two friends away. "I'll tell you about it later," she said. "See you down on the beach." She tried to ignore the giggles of the two women as they turned and headed the other way, but she had to smile, thankful that at least two of her friends didn't share Erik's feelings. She returned to Dowain and Saisha's home, thanked her hosts for their hospitality, and promised to stop by and see their new child if the timing worked out. After gathering her things, she headed down to the beach to join her companions.

Already the Tesconis siblings were being ferried across to the ship by the sailors and their rowboat, and as the women stood waiting, Kari turned and looked over the island again. It was wondrous and beautiful just as its people seemed to be, and she offered a silent prayer to Zalkar, asking him to watch over and protect the shattered folk. She hoped that the return trip would give her time to return for a night or two, and turned away to board the rowboat and get her journey underway once more.

Chapter VII – Dedication

Kari spent most of the morning and afternoon sitting at the rear of the ship, watching the Salkorum islands disappear over the horizon. She couldn't shake the feeling that she'd left something behind on the island, but at the same time she knew it was nothing tangible. She had left all of her belongings on the ship during their visit, so she had no doubts that what she felt was more of an emotional loss. It was Grakin, she realized: everything felt right when she was with him, but since Erik had interrupted them on the beach, everything felt wrong. A part of her was wondering what she had missed out on for not having given herself to Kris Jir'tana the way she had with Grakin, and she felt she was already betraying Grakin's trust by thinking about another man.

As night fell and the first of the three moons rose over the eastern horizon, she stared across endless water to a far point where the islands had dropped out of sight. She wanted to turn the ship around, return to the island, and forget the responsibilities that sat on her shoulders. She wanted to take Grakin by the hand – his impending doom be damned – and make a life for herself. For the first time Kari understood just how emotionally tired she was, and how it was compounding the physical fatigue that had plagued her since the war began.

She let out a sigh and looked up to the crimson gaze of Eryn as the half-brys woman laid a hand on her shoulder and sat beside her at the rail. Eryn handed Kari a flask, and she took a long draw from it without even asking what it contained. Thankfully it wasn't the same acidic tequila the women had shared earlier in the trip: it was some mixture of coconut and rum. It was strong but had a decidedly sweet quality to it, and Kari took a second swig before handing it back to her friend.

Eryn didn't speak, and Kari realized that was what she liked most about the half-brys woman: Eryn simply didn't feel the need to fill an enjoyable silence with worthless banter. She could see that Kari was sorting through something in her mind, and was content to simply lend a physical presence without the prying that normally went with it. Kari had never been one to make friends easily, and so she was amazed at how likable most of her traveling companions turned out to be. The fact that one of the nicest was an assassin struck her as comically ironic.

Kari studied her companion for a few minutes, wondering if the assassin had ever thought about settling down with Aeligos. Eryn had already mentioned that she never wanted into the life she led, so Kari had to wonder why she had continued to pursue it after her father's demise. Kari remembered Sonja saying that Aeligos and Eryn weren't mates, which likely meant neither of them had any intention of having children with the other or getting formally married in the human tradition. But that left Kari with little doubt as to how she really felt about Grakin.

After a few minutes of being stared at, the half-brys woman cocked an eyebrow and offered another drink. "Go ahead," the assassin said when Kari took another sip from the flask. Kari was confused, and the half-brys woman continued, "It doesn't take a genius to figure out why you're sitting back here alone."

Eryn looked back over her shoulder, apparently to see who else was around. When she turned back to Kari, she said, "Go invite Grakin to your bed. No one is going to say anything, and anyone who does is probably best ignored anyway."

Kari looked back to the horizon and took another sip from the flask before handing it back to her companion. She sighed, began to speak, but then she closed her mouth: she wasn't really sure what to say. Her feelings were jumbled, but it went beyond even Grakin or their wonderful lovemaking. Everything had been jumbled since she was returned by Trigonh's favor. There were things in her past that were slowly returning to the surface of her thoughts, and at times she was having difficulty keeping everything chronologically sorted. "Life is cruel," she blurted after a few more introspective moments, and her declaration drew no protest from her companion. "The gods must really hate me for some reason."

Eryn patted her shoulder and gave it a squeeze of comfort. "What happened?" she asked. "Or is this just about having died?"

Kari shook her head and laid it on the railing as it seemed to become very heavy. She nearly laughed at herself: she was a drinker, but she'd had too much of the deceptively sweet alcohol too quickly, which was made worse by the fact that she hadn't eaten since the morning meal. She waved a hand and the motion looked as weird as it felt, so she closed her eyes. "That's the center of it," she said slowly to make sure the right words were coming forth. "But it's more than that."

"Did something bad happen with Grakin?" Eryn asked.

"No, no," Kari said, sitting up at attention. She waved away the half-brys woman's question. "I'm not sure how to even explain it. I've just been so confused since coming back, and I don't even know why or what about. Everything just seems unreal, like being in a dream, and a lot of it is just the world being different...I'm in a different time, a different place, and all of the people I used to know are dead and gone. Well, except for that overgrown, flea-bitten mongrel that brought me back."

"Such gratitude," Eryn said with a brief smile.

Kari shook her head. "I spent my life fighting for Zalkar's ideals, but I have to be honest, I felt and still feel betrayed that he just let me die," she said, looking back out over the water. She laid her head down on her folded hands atop the railing and let out a long sigh. "I don't know how long I can stay dedicated to this way of life. I never thought about it before since I knew I was going to die, and the War was all I thought about after I was brought back, but I want a mate, I think I want to have children, settle down somewhere. I can't live the rest of my life on the road like this."

"So don't," the half-brys woman said with a shrug. "You can rest assured that when I'm done with this way of life, I'll be walking away from it without a second thought."

Kari beheld her curiously. "What do you mean, when you're done with it?" she asked, shaking her head to try to keep it clear. The jarring motion didn't help, and in fact seemed to multiply the effects of the alcohol.

"I can't really say too much," Eryn said, "but this isn't a life you can just walk away from unless you're very sure that it won't follow you. It's something you have to plan and build towards for a long time before the way to freedom becomes clear." She shook her head. "But in your case, why don't you just complete this mission, and then tell your superiors you're taking some time to make a family? Then take Grakin by the hand and go have some babies with him."

Kari shook her head again. "The gods hate me," she said. "I've gotten two chances at life: first I died young, and now I've fallen in love with a dying man."

Eryn's face dropped. "Grakin's dying?" she asked quietly.

Kari tensed up and put a hand to the end of her snout. She cursed in the back of her mind: she was sure Eryn would've figured out Grakin's secret, just as she figured out everyone else's. "I wasn't supposed to say. Gods, please don't tell his siblings! He asked me to let him," Kari said. She tried to keep her emotions contained. Betraying Grakin's trust was something she wouldn't be able to forgive herself for if Eryn let it slip to his siblings. But Eryn nodded her agreement and squeezed Kari's shoulder gently. "He has Dracon's Bane, like I did."

The assassin swore under her breath, her gaze swinging out over the water, and she shook her head. "How long does he have?" she asked.

Kari felt like she sobered up quickly as their conversation turned

117

serious. "I died when I was twenty-seven," she said. "But half-guardians are a lot tougher; maybe he has a lot longer than I did? Maybe he'll even survive it...hard to know, since I thought it was something only terra-dracons could get."

"He must have picked up the recessive gene from one parent or the other," Eryn said, but she didn't bother to explain exactly what that meant. "I'm sorry, Kari."

"For what?"

"That is pretty horrible," Eryn said. "When I saw you two in the water and on the beach, you looked very good together. I thought maybe you'd gotten lucky running into him."

Kari steeled herself. "I did get lucky meeting him," she said. She sighed and shook her head. "I'm sorry you had to listen to me whine, Eryn. You're right, I did get lucky and I shouldn't be crying about what I've been given. All we can do is make the best of what we're dealt, and considering I've been given a second life, I guess I shouldn't complain."

The half-brys woman smiled, leaned over, and kissed Kari on the side of the snout, which surprised her. "That's the girl I met two weeks ago," Eryn said, and something flashed in her eyes that Kari didn't quite recognize. "I know from experience: it's not easy to always be strong. Don't be afraid to cry or be weak; just work to make sure that what makes you cry or what makes you weak also makes you stronger in the end."

"Good advice," Kari said, surprised as she considered the source.

"Good, then maybe you'll listen to my other advice," Eryn said with a grin. "They're planning to give Grakin's cabin to Katarina and put him in a hammock. You should ask for one of the larger cabins, maybe Jori-an's, and share it with Grakin. She's seterra-rir, I think she would understand."

Kari shook her head in disbelief. "You talk about these things like they're simple," she said. "Like I could really just ask to sleep with Grakin in front of his siblings?"

"Things are only complicated if you make them that way," the half-brys woman said, cutting off Kari's train of thought. "You and Grakin enjoyed having sex, and who knows, maybe you two will actually become mates. To hell with what everyone else thinks, you've got to do what makes you two happy, and not worry about what his siblings think." She held her hand up to further stifle any reply. "I know 'normal rir' are supposed to be different, but if you enjoy the sex, there's nothing wrong with that."

"It's not that," Kari said. "I honestly don't care what any of them think of me. As long as they trust me enough to get this mission done, that's all

118

that really matters. I'm more worried about what they think of their brother. I'm not interested in making his life any tougher, given what he's been through – and what he has to look forward to."

Eryn slapped Kari's rump, shocking her. "What he has to look forward to is making love to you on that sandy beach back there," the half-brys said evenly, gesturing toward the horizon. "Maybe having the joy of raising a little boy or girl, or both, before his time here is done. He has to look forward to waking up beside this beautiful woman every morning, fighting by her side in the afternoon, and making love to her at night. Just because he's going to die doesn't mean that dying is all he has to look forward to."

Kari thought about it for a minute and wondered why she'd never had that perspective in her prior life. "What about you and Aeligos?" she asked at length. "What do you two have to look forward to?"

Eryn grimaced, clearly not expecting Kari to turn things around on her so easily when she was tipsy. "I don't know," she answered. "He doesn't seem to understand that I was forced into the life I lead, and that to me, it's just a means to an end. I don't intend to kill people for a living for the rest of my life, but I have obligations I have to satisfy before I can break away. After that, honestly…I want to have his children, move to a nice place in Latalex, maybe open up an archery school or something. But sometimes he's just such an ass…"

Kari was intrigued. Everything she'd seen and heard suggested Eryn and Aeligos would never be much more than lovers. Something else stuck in her mind, though. "Well he certainly *has* a nice ass," Kari joked. "I've gotten to put my hands on it enough times while he's been teaching me that grappling technique of his."

Eryn laughed aloud. "Doesn't he?" she said. "Anyway, you can learn a lot from him about grappling; he's practically a master of it already. And if he tickles your fancy, I won't take offense if you two end up in bed together."

Kari wasn't expecting that, but she waved off the comment. "Not interested," she said. "I like him, but I don't really see him that way – and not just because he's yours. And from the amount of self-control he shows when he's on top of me or between my legs, I'm guessing he's not really interested in me anyway."

"He's just very professional," the assassin said. "I'm sure he has eyes for you, but he's not going to insult you by getting aroused while you trust him to train you. And I can't say I blame him: you'd probably tear his arms off if he did."

"Sounds like an interesting conversation," Sonja said. She approached

119

with a smile. "Dinner is about to be served in the captain's quarters, and he wanted to discuss cabin assignments due to our new guests."

"We can talk more later," Eryn said. She offered Kari one last drink from the flask before they departed, but Kari declined. They rose and shared a short hug, then followed Sonja to the captain's quarters.

~~*~*

Dinner was a wonderful assortment of roasted meats and steamed vegetables, and the air was almost festive as the Silver Blades and their companions welcomed the two newcomers to share their first dinner with the group. Captain Galdur spent most of the mealtime giving his new passengers an in-depth explanation of what to expect while aboard his vessel, as well as a good description of where everything on board could be found. To Kari, it was quite a gesture coming from the captain, as any of his subordinate officers or crewmen could've and probably would've been given the responsibility under normal circumstances.

The meal lasted for well over an hour, and everyone simply took their time, still relaxed and unhurried after their stay on the slow-paced island the night before. As the servants brought fresh cold wine and sweets for the group, Jori-an joined them, and she looked as content as Kari had seen her during the trip. She took a seat at the far end of the table from Captain Galdur, folded her arms before her and waited for the captain to begin the discussion she had been invited to take part in.

After introducing his new passengers to his first mate, Captain Galdur took a sip of his wine, cleared his throat and brought the conversation to the topic at hand. "Now, as I'm sure you're familiar with after your arrival on board, the rules of my ship give guest cabins to women first," he said, eyeing Grakin. "As we now have the lovely Katarina aboard, you'll be required to surrender your cabin so she may have one. Do you feel well enough to sleep in a hammock?"

"Yes, that will not be a problem," Grakin said. "As I had said, the bed was simply better for my evening meditations, but I have found that this ship is more than accommodating when it comes to quiet places for me to pray."

Captain Galdur nodded to Grakin's words. Kari glanced at Jori-an briefly, then sat forward in her chair and leaned her arms on the table. "I actually have a question," she said. "I know it might be a bit forward of me, but I understand the officer cabins are quite a bit larger than the ones we've been assigned to?"

120

"Aye, that's true," Galdur said.

"Would any of your officers be willing to swap rooms with Grakin?" she asked, receiving a curious glance from Galdur and Jori-an. "Then Katarina can have my bed."

"I'm not sure I understand. If you want to sleep in a hammock, then Katarina can just have your bed," the captain said, and he took his hat off and ran his hand back over his hair. "Why would one of my officers need to switch beds with Grakin?"

"Well, if he has a larger room and bed...I can stay with him," Kari said quickly before she could lose her nerve.

Sonja put her hands to the sides of her snout, and the smile Grakin turned on Kari nearly melted her heart. Erik did a double-take, a smile crossed Serenjols' face, and a silence spread over the group for a minute until it was pierced by a loud – and surprisingly jubilant – *HA* from Typhonix. Erik didn't seem to share his mirth at first, but after he stared at Kari for a minute, the blue-eyed male squared his jaw and nodded. "You two did have sex on the island," Erik stated as much as asked, and he nodded again when he received an affirmative response from both. "I thought as much."

Kari's eyes were drawn to the blonde demonhunter sitting next to the blue-eyed male, and she couldn't believe Ty was smiling at her. Ty turned his eyes away when their stares met, but the smile remained undiminished and he gave Grakin a thumbs-up. It was the first time Kari could think of that the obnoxious brute had smiled without first insulting her or making some lewd comment. Given the way he had harassed her throughout the trip, she found it strange that he would find her a suitable mate for one of his siblings. Kari supposed that perhaps she wasn't the only one full of surprises amongst this bunch.

Kari was thankful for it whatever the reason, and she turned her attention back to Grakin. Eryn rose and moved down to her friend, and gestured for Kari to go take her chair. The terra-dracon woman felt a little exposed as she stood with the eyes of everyone gathered upon her, but she walked over and sat down next to the priest. After a moment, they shared a passionate kiss, and Captain Galdur nodded appreciatively while smiles sprouted on the faces of the rest of the gathering. Under the table, where the others could not see, Kari and Grakin's hands interlocked. She gave him a strong squeeze, and received one in return.

"I'll relinquish my room to them and take Karian's cabin, Captain," Jori-an said. She turned her attention to the couple. "I only ask that you not disturb any of my belongings while you are in my room. I will move my clothing and such to the footlocker in Karian's cabin, but my wardrobes and bookshelves should remain untouched."

"That is more than reasonable, thank you," Grakin said.

"Then it seems as though everyone is satisfied," Captain Galdur said. "Sherman, you will be afforded a hammock with your half-demon friends in the general quarters. Grakin, if you'd be so kind as to show Katarina to her cabin when you go to clean out your things? For now, we can welcome our new guests with a game of cards."

"I think I'll pass, but thank you, Captain," Kari said. She kissed Grakin again and made her way out to the deck. She hurried up the stairs to the sterncastle and the back rail, and she looked east toward the horizon. The second moon was just cresting the edge of the world, and she looked to its radiance and that of its sister with a smile. The sense of loss that had dogged her since they left the island was gone, and she closed her eyes as the wind slid over her shoulders and through her hair.

Soon Grakin's hands took the wind's place, and he ran them over her shoulders and down her arms gently, kissing the side of her neck as his fingers interlaced with hers. She tucked her wings tight to her back, and he pressed close to her and held her in a gentle hug for several minutes. Kari turned around and Grakin stared deep into her dark eyes, and she did the same to him. The lantern light from the pilot's station showed in the depths of his ebon eyes, and Kari could also see her love for him reflected there as well. They kissed again briefly, and she wrapped her arms around his neck as his encircled her lower back. "I love you," she said. "And I'm sorry I didn't say so when we were on the island."

"But you did," he said quietly. "In the way you made love to me, I could tell. If there is any blame for things not being said, then it belongs to us both. I love you too, Karian Vanador."

She poked the end of his nose. "*Kari*," she corrected. "I don't like being called Karian. I know I introduce myself that way, but I prefer my friends – and my lover – to call me Kari."

"Lover?" he repeated.

"Mate," she corrected herself, and she kissed his cheek affectionately. "I offer myself to you as your mate. When we are finished with this mission, I will bear you children."

Grakin cupped her face in his hand and touched his forehead to hers for a moment before he met her gaze once again. "It is my honor to have you as a mate," he said. "But let us not make plans beyond tomorrow. We have a very long, very dangerous task before us, and our focus must be on it and it alone."

122

"Of course," she agreed, but then she flashed a mischievous smile. "Can we make plans for tonight?"

Grakin laughed and sat down at the rail, and Kari sat down beside him. "May I ask you a question?" he asked, and she nodded. "Why did you choose me? Why not Erik, or Aeligos?"

Kari's brows knitted, and she shook her head. "I'm not sure how to answer that," she said. "I guess it's because...you remind me of someone I loved a long time ago, in my past life. Someone that kept me safe and made me feel like I was more than just a demonhunter. You're a healer, a gentle man driven by compassion. I...probably sound silly right now. Erik and Aeligos are both handsome, but both of them just...I don't know how to say it. Neither of them *interests* me. Erik's too damned big and hard-nosed, and Aeligos strikes me as a bit of an opportunist, at least when it comes to finding a woman. Not to mention he's already involved with someone."

"So it is not because you feel sorry for me?" Grakin asked, though it was clear he already knew the answer and simply wanted to hear it from her.

"Of course not," she said, laying a hand on his thigh. "I'm not like that; I wouldn't do that to you."

Grakin waved his hand. "I was not suggesting that," he said.

"I know," Kari replied, cutting him off. "I just want to be clear. What we shared was special to me, and *you* are special to me. If you were going to die tomorrow, it wouldn't change the way I feel about you."

Grakin closed his eyes for a few moments, and when he opened them again he smiled and leaned in to kiss her. He rose to his feet and held his hand out to her, helped her to stand, and then he took both of her hands in his. "Would you like to make love tonight?" he asked.

Kari touched his face gently and he rubbed his cheek in her palm. "Just understand: I won't always be interested," she said, to which he nodded knowingly. "In a few days, depending on what I smell like, you may not be, either."

Grakin laughed and turned toward the stairs down to the lower decks with her beside him. "I guess you did not know that the officers' quarters have bathtubs in them? Or Jori-an's does, anyway."

"They do?" she asked. "I didn't think they would waste water on a ship."

The priest shrugged. "They have another stop planned along the way, and this ship holds quite a bit of cargo. I would not worry about water or any other type of supplies. You cannot bathe nightly, but we can share a bath every few days at the very least."

"This trip is getting better and better," Kari said, and Grakin joined in her mirth. The two were met by Jori-an once they descended to the cabins, and the terra-dracon and seterra-rir women swapped the contents of their footlockers while Grakin brought his own pack into the larger cabin. Kari sat on the corner of Jori-an's bed and watched Grakin place his pack with hers. They looked up as Jori-an returned one last time.

The seterra-rir first mate closed the door behind her and put her back against it. "Let me be a little clearer," she said, and Grakin sat beside Kari on the bed. "I didn't want to be crass in front of your siblings and friends, but I have some very specific rules about your usage of my cabin. Remember that this room is my home. Be clean: if you make a mess, I expect you to clean it up. Keep your lovemaking confined to the bed or the bathtub, and do not touch the clothing or other articles in my wardrobe under any circumstances."

"The bathtub?" Kari asked, looking at the secured metal tub – not unlike the one she'd used at the Bloodied Blade but for the fact that it could rock within its frame upon rough seas.

Jori-an rolled her eyes but did not elaborate. "You may read my books, but they are kept in a specific order, so mind where you got them and return them there when you are finished. Do not read them while bathing. I already put the spare sheets on the bed, so do as you will in them…I'll just burn them when the voyage is over."

Kari chuckled, embarrassed. "Thank you, Jori-an," she said. "How did you enjoy the short stay on the island?"

Jori-an smiled, though briefly. "It's always a pleasure to return to see my mate and my children," she said, "but my home is on this ship. Now: do you want to ask me questions, or do you want to use my quarters? Get to your lovemaking."

Once Jori-an closed the door behind her, Grakin began undressing while Kari walked over and secured the latch. When Kari turned around, she glanced at their new abode and gave an appreciative nod for how well-furnished it was, given its size. There was the bed, which was large enough for two, with efficient night stands on both sides, a secured wardrobe on the wall between two portholes, short but well-stocked bookshelves along the inner wall, and, of course, the secured metal tub.

Kari glanced at the bathtub and then fixed her mate with a curious stare. "The bathtub?" she asked.

Grakin cocked his head. "Certainly not something I feel inclined to try. If you had said in the water at the beach, then perhaps, but in a bathtub?" he asked, and he looked at the metal tub with contempt. "I cannot imagine one person can get comfortable in that, let alone two."

They got undressed and slid into the soft bed, and Kari smiled as they snuggled under the blankets and he stroked her hair. She kissed him gently and met his stare. "Your brothers took what I said better than I expected," she said.

"What makes you say that?" he asked.

"I expected some of them to be angry, or at least jealous," she clarified.

Grakin propped himself up on his elbow. "Why would you think that?" he asked, but he touched his finger to the end of her snout to stifle her reply. "The only ones I could understand you thinking about that way are Erik and Typhonix. Ty is a jerk sometimes, Kari, but he is my brother, and in the end he is actually fairly protective of me. All of my brothers are, as they are fighters and I am not. I know Ty is suspicious of you, but despite the way he acts, he is not determined to make us miserable. As for Erik, he is just protective of us all."

"It was more the way Erik looked at us when he found us on the beach," she said. "Almost like he couldn't believe I was with you rather than him."

"I do not think it was that," Grakin said, stroking her cheek softly. "It may have more to do with his suspicions about your past and, again, his overprotective nature, especially where I am concerned."

"Oh," she said, considering his words for a minute. "I would've thought he'd confront you about it, and that you would've told him the truth about me."

"I am having sex with you," the priest said with a slight frown. "He would not believe me any more than he believes you. I do not think it will be an issue, given that we are now mated, but it may still take a while before he accepts the truth of the matter in his heart."

"Good," Kari said, and her words drew a curious glance from her mate. "I'm supposed to report on his abilities as a leader and as a demonhunter when this mission is complete. If he still doesn't believe me, then it means he won't rely on my experience, and I'll learn a lot more about him than I normally would."

"Ah, I see," Grakin said with a slight smile. "I will keep that in mind and make certain not to try to change his mind in the future, then."

"Aeligos and Serenjols seem happy for us," she commented.

"Do not be fooled by Jol's silence," the priest said, stroking her cheek again. "There is much love in that man; he simply does not know how to express it. Erik is more headstrong, but Serenjols is no less protective of us

125

in his own, less direct manner. He wants us all to be happy and safe, and ultimately together. You should have seen him during the Apocalypse; you would hardly know the man you have seen was the same man who fought in the War."

"As for Aeligos," he continued, shaking his head lightly, "whatever you may think of him on account of his relationship with Eryn, he has a good heart."

"Your parents must be very proud of you all," Kari said, and she kissed him. "I hardly know you all very well, but I'm proud to call you my friends. Well, most of you, anyway."

Grakin chuckled and hugged her tightly. "May I make love to you, my wondrous mate?"

Kari answered wordlessly. Their lovemaking was no less passionate than the first time, and afterwards they fell asleep nestled in each other's arms. The gentle rocking of the ship further eased them into blissful slumber, and the only sounds were the muted wind as it passed by the room's two portholes and the rush of water along the hull. For the first time in years, Kari slept the whole night through.

~~*~*

Kari stirred lightly the next morning as Grakin's hand traced up her side softly, and he kissed her on the cheek before rising. She stayed asleep a while longer and found her mate gone when she awakened fully and sat up. Kari assumed he had headed up to the ship's deck to pray with the sunrise, and she stretched out, pulled the blankets close to her snout, and drew in the scent of his body. She marveled at how perfect he was for her, and the way her body and soul had reacted to his presence and his touch. She considered the chain of events that had caused them to meet, and as her mind flashed across the previous weeks, she thought about how Grakin must feel, considering that she'd been returned from the dead.

She was Grakin's first lover, of that she was sure, and yet it made little difference to her. Somehow, he seemed to already know her so intimately, reacting to her every thought and desire without her having to speak a word. He was amazing; there was little other way to say it, and Kari ran her hand down her side, following the spectral path of the remnant of his touch. The feel of his skin set her own on fire, and she understood just what Eryn had meant the prior evening.

Kari sat up and dressed herself, but she didn't bother with her armor, which had proven unnecessary aboard the ship. The leisure clothes she

126

kept in her pack weren't fashionable, but they were comfortable and the only other thing she had to wear. Once dressed, Kari made her way up to the deck, and as she approached the quarterdeck where her companions normally congregated, she could hear the sound of a guitar being played.

Kari stepped up to the quarterdeck, looked up, and politely saluted Jori-an, as seemed to be the custom. Jori-an kept her seat but returned the salute crisply. On the quarterdeck, Kari found Sonja sitting before their favorite bench, and the scarlet-haired woman's hands were pressed to the sides of her snout in awe. Behind her, Erik and Typhonix were practicing their combat routines while Aeligos and Serenjols watched. Grakin sat on the bench with a guitar in hand. Kari had no idea he – or any of his siblings, for that matter – played, and certainly not with the degree of skill he displayed. His eyes were closed and yet his clawed fingers danced across the strings with such grace, his left hand caressing the neck of the stringed instrument with the same precision as it had Kari's body.

Kari didn't recognize the piece he was playing, having had little contact with music outside of the occasional bard she heard perform in taverns across Terrassia. The piece was lovely and moving, and it struck a chord somewhere deep within her. Kari closed her eyes, listening to its structure, feeling its pulse, and she sighed lightly when it came to a close. Sonja hugged her suddenly, and Kari's eyes came open as she was nearly knocked from her feet. "Don't hug me, hug the bard," Kari said as she regained her balance.

Grakin laughed – it was such a beautiful sound, and seemed so commonplace now – and his sister turned so that she could look at both of them. "He hasn't played...gods, since he was fourteen? It's been ages since I heard him play and his skill hasn't diminished at all." Sonja met Kari's gaze and her ruby eyes sparkled. "It can't be coincidence that he's started playing again after everything that happened in the last two days."

"I hear music when I touch Kaelariel's mind," the priest said pensively, and he sat back and stood the guitar up alongside the bench. "He seems to always have music on his mind, and sometimes, when I meditate on his thoughts, rather than hearing instructions, I hear such music."

"His son is very fond of music too," Kari said with a nod. "He entertained our battalion with a song or a guitar piece a number of times during the war."

"With Kaelariel, it is more than just a fondness," Grakin countered. "His thoughts seem to be arranged like music, if that makes any sense. It is as if his every thought, every action, is carefully constructed so that it follows a rhythm and a pattern, like a piece of music. It lends a cadence and a canon to his ways that brings me strength and comfort, even in the midst of something like the Apocalypse."

"What's it like to touch the mind of a god?" Kari asked as she sat beside her mate. Sonja sat cross-legged before them with a warm smile on her features.

"Humbling," he answered. "The gods think much like we do, as they were once mortals, but the things that occupy their minds…it is humbling to touch such power and responsibility, and muster the strength to ask for even the simplest of things. In the morning, when I pray, he is asking and I am listening. When I meditate in the evening, I am asking and he is listening. At times, though, when he is satisfied with my current goals and my work, what I hear is music…as if even he, as a deity, sometimes needs to indulge in simple beauty."

Kari kissed her mate and he kissed her in return, and when Kari looked at Grakin's siblings, they were all smiling at the couple. Kari was surprised at Typhonix' sudden change in demeanor, but she stayed guarded where he was concerned, as it had only been a day. Of all of her mate's siblings, only Erik seemed to harbor even the slightest of unhappy feelings toward them, and she wondered if it was just jealousy, and whether it would pass. She had to work directly with him on Tsalbrin, so if he was covetous of his brother's relationship, she imagined it could cause many problems.

Eryn eventually joined the rest of the group on the quarterdeck. She asked where the twins had disappeared to, and once informed that they were having breakfast with the captain, she muttered something about being left out. The group and even Jori-an got a chuckle out of the half-brys woman's reaction, but once Eryn returned below decks, the men all followed after her. Grakin gave Kari a parting kiss before leaving her alone with Sonja.

Sonja sat down on the bench beside Kari and patted her leg. "This has been such a surprise," she said simply.

"Not just for you," Kari said. Just scant weeks before, she thought she'd missed the best opportunity of her new life when Kris Jir'tana had left.

"How did all of this happen?"

The demonhunter shrugged. "It's hard to put into words," she said. "It may sound weird, but Grakin…reminds me of Suler Tumureldi."

Sonja beheld her curiously. "He *reminds* you of Suler…?"

Kari glanced at Jori-an before she continued, "That 'mistress' mentioned in the book you loaned me…that was me. I was Suler's mistress

128

for about nine months, before my training with him came to an end and I had to get back to my work."

"*You* were mated to *Suler Tumureldi*?!" Sonja blurted.

"I was his mistress," Kari corrected. "He couldn't take me as his mate; that would've made me queen and the people wouldn't allow that. Neither would I, for that matter."

Her friend chuckled. "Gods, girl," Sonja muttered. "I need to find a book about you. Mistress to King Suler Tumureldi...and you say Grakin reminds you of him?"

Kari nodded and met her friend's eyes. "People think of Suler and they think of his fighting style and all the duels he won, but Suler was a gentle man. He looked at fighting as an art, not an act of violence, and he was a very good king to his people. Grakin is the same in many ways...he's gentle, he puts others ahead of himself, and he loves me. And it only took me a couple of minutes to realize it when I looked in his eyes and spoke with him."

Sonja smiled more broadly, the telltale traces of tears of joy in the corners of her eyes. "Is it still as magical?" she asked. It seemed Eryn's bluntness may have rubbed off on her.

"I'm still glowing from the first time," Kari said, rubbing her hands up her arms with a gentle sigh. "I don't know what it is about him, but he's perfect for me."

"Are you two mated, then?" Sonja asked. If Kari and Grakin were 'mated,' it was the rir equivalent of human marriage. Being mated was closer to a common-law marriage, but among rir it was a very strong bond and rarely did two who became mates split up and go their separate ways. Occasionally rir married in the human tradition, but most felt the ceremony unnecessary.

Kari thought about it for a few moments, and though she shook her head, she said, "Yes. I can hardly believe I'm saying it; it still doesn't seem real."

Sonja hugged Kari, and the demonhunter returned the strength of the embrace in full. "I'm so happy for you two," Sonja said. "Even Ty is already beginning to look at you like a sister. I think he's still a little suspicious, but you're his brother's mate now, and that seems to be taking priority over whatever he feels. You're family now."

"Yea, I guess you finally have a sister," Kari said, and the two women hugged again.

"Well it took my idiot brothers long enough for one of them to get it right," Sonja huffed. "Shall we go get some breakfast, too?"

"You go ahead," Kari said and motioned for Sonja to go. "I'll be down in just a couple of minutes." Sonja nodded and descended below decks, and Kari turned to meet the sapphire gaze of Jori-an up on the boatswain's nest. Once Sonja was gone, a smile spread across the first mate's face. "What are you thinking?" Kari asked. She was honestly curious how the entire thing looked to a total outsider.

"Many things," Jori-an answered in her typical cryptic fashion, but after a moment she seemed to reconsider. She bobbed her head to one side for a moment. "I am foremost thinking that you are either very lucky or very foolish. I hope it is the former."

"What makes you say that?" the demonhunter asked.

"I've sailed the oceans for many years," Jori-an said, "and I adventured across the lands for many more before that, in my youth. I've seen people fall in love when they're confined to a ship, out on the road, or else in a position where they spend a lot of time close to someone. A lot of times, once that confinement or journey ends, they suddenly find that their relationship was one of convenience and need, rather than love."

Kari nodded. "If you knew me, you'd know I don't fall in love easily," she said. "It's not a matter of convenience or need from my side; I meant everything I just said to Sonja. I'm pretty sure the same holds true for Grakin."

The first mate bobbed her head again. "Yes, for you I can tell this is the case. Grakin is a little harder for me to read. I've spent little time in the company of serilian-rir – half-demons, if you prefer. I traveled with one when I was younger, but he was so much different than these Tesconis siblings, especially Grakin. Grakin certainly seems to be in love with you, but there is something about him that just seems…off. It is as though he is hiding something."

"I know," the demonhunter replied. "I know what he's hiding, but it's not something I can share, by his request." Jori-an nodded. "It has nothing to do with his love for me, though."

Jori-an gave a sincere smile, but only for a few moments. "Then you are lucky," she said, the strength of her eye contact stating quite clearly that she believed what she had said. She bounded down from her platform suddenly and practically ran up the rigging to the crow's nest, leaving Kari to marvel at the woman's dexterity. Once again Kari wondered if the woman's sudden need to visit the crow's nest had more to do with avoiding showing any emotion, and Kari headed for the general mess to share breakfast with her friends.

The rest of the day passed quickly, which surprised Kari since she spent most of it looking forward to spending the evening alone with Grakin. She took her lessons from Aeligos and spent a little time sparring with both Erik and Typhonix. She found the blonde male's style simple but brutal. The sheer power behind his massive, arcing swings was too much to take lightly or underestimate. Like when she watched him spar with Erik, Ty also used the butt of his axe haft to keep Kari at bay when she came in from odd angles. She was confident she could penetrate his defenses with ease and score a killing blow if she wished, but instead she took the time to acclimate herself to his fighting style and brush up on her two-weapon defense against a larger, crushing weapon. Her seemingly hesitant, tentative nature when fighting Typhonix also served to mask her true abilities from Erik.

Dinner was taken with Captain Galdur, and she passed the early evening playing cards with her friends. Eryn and Aeligos took no small amount of pleasure educating Sherman and Katarina in the ways of gambling, and cleaned the youngsters out easily. It was all in good fun, as they continued to play with the captain's coins once it became obvious how overmatched everyone else was compared to Eryn and Aeligos. The coins were all returned to the captain after the game, and each player was given the same amount to start each night to keep the games friendly and fun.

Kari was getting better at masking her feelings as she became more familiar with both the game and her fellow players, and consequently she began to hold her own even against the more skilled gamblers. She had always considered poker a liar's game, but when she said so, Aeligos explained that it was a game of deception, which was not the same as lying. He illustrated by pointing out that in Kari's profession, she worked hard to never show weakness to her enemies, while at the same time masking her strength to make it more effective. He explained that poker was very much the same, and even admitted that the majority of hands he won had little to do with his cards and more to do with everyone else's behavior. The twins took Aeligos' words in with great interest, and his lesson was punctuated by a sage nod from Eryn.

Kari spent the later evening sitting at the rear rail of the sterncastle, where she shared drinks with Eryn and Sonja and watched the moons come up over the horizon. Much to the delight of the three women, Katarina joined them on the second night. She was full of questions on nearly every subject regarding the outside world, and Kari, Sonja, and Eryn were glad to see that the young woman was not intimidated by their stature or reputations. They tried their best to make Katarina feel like she was one of the group – even Eryn, who normally seemed closed-mouthed around the

131

twins. Not surprisingly, Kari found that even Katarina was curious about the demonhunter's new relationship, and she shared as much as she was comfortable with.

As the night grew older, Kari retired to her cabin to find Grakin reclining on their bed, reading one of the books Sonja had loaned Kari. Kari undressed and joined him on the bed, and she gave him a quick kiss on the side of his snout. She looked over the page he was reading and could tell he had chosen *The Ascension of Saint Bakhor*. Apparently he hadn't been reading very long, as he was only a couple of dozen pages into the volume, and Kari smiled when she recognized the point in her friend's life that he was reading about.

"How do you like the book?" she asked when he paused and looked up at her.

"I have always been fascinated by her story," Grakin said, "though details of her life have always been a little sketchy. It strikes most people as odd that she took up worship of the Beast, and that fact leads to a lot of speculation as to what race she was, since his followers tend to be shapeshifters and lycanthropes."

"It was an unusual choice," Kari agreed. A sylvan beast - sometimes called a sylvan demon - was a massive, minotaur-like variant of a serilian demon, but unlike their destructive cousins, they lived in and defended the woodlands wherever they were found. Their leader and deity – who had been a mortal named Carlos Bouron before being reincarnated as a sylvan beast – was most often simply called *the Beast*. Those who swore to his service were usually other sylvan beasts or shapeshifters who lived in the wilds, or even lycanthropes who had mastered their curse and come back to some semblance of sanity.

"You said you knew her," Grakin said. "What race was she?"

"Shakna-rir," Kari said. "And she took a fures-rir as a mate."

The priest's brows rose in surprise. The fures-rir were one of the least populous of the rir races, were nearly impervious to cold climates, and they made their homes in the frozen lands of the far north and south. The shakna-rir were desert dwellers with a dislike of cold climates, but they thrived in heat that was unbearable to most. For members of the two different races to mate was uncommon, to say the least. "And they had shakna-fury children?" he prompted, naming the hybrid of the two races.

"Just one," Kari said. "A beautiful little girl with red hair like her mother, and the most solidly black eyes I have ever seen; even more so than mine or yours."

"What was it like to travel with someone so famous?" he asked.

132

Kari shrugged. "She wasn't really *famous* when we traveled together," she said. "But she wasn't anything like what you'd probably expect from a *saint*. She was cocky: she had the Beast's favor and she wasn't afraid to let people know it. She had this giant sledgehammer, and woe to anyone she actually swung it at."

Grakin chuckled. "Yes, I have heard she had a bit of a fiery temper, but she would not have been sanctified if her dedication to the gods was not complete."

"Dedication wasn't even the word for it," Kari said. "The group she traveled with always wanted to go dungeon delving, and I usually tagged along with them to get from one place to another because I always had some mission or other from Zalkar to take care of. Carly would always end up deciding to follow me, and would tell the rest of the group to go die in a lost tomb if that was the best they could think to do."

"A little headstrong?"

"Why do you think we got along so well when I was younger?" Kari asked with a shrug. "She didn't really take orders from anyone since the Beast doesn't have established churches, but when she got a cause to follow there wasn't a thing in the world that would stop her. Half the time I think she was more serious about my missions than I was, and with the kind of power she wielded, it made my life a lot easier. She just had a dedication that few ever realize: she knew what was right and just tried to do the best she could in every situation, regardless of the risk. She jumped into everything with near-reckless abandon and never looked back. I think the only regret that woman ever had was that she couldn't cure my illness."

Grakin nodded. "I can sense that Kaelariel feels the same way," he said quietly. "It is no disease that is killing me, but a defect in the way I was made, and there is nothing he can do to fix it. I feel his sorrow when I touch his mind, but you…you remind me just how much I can do with the time I have. Thank you for that, Kari. Thank the gods for you."

The two shared a kiss, and Kari fought off the urge to cry. "I'll never leave you," she said. "Just as Carly never left my side except when I pushed her away."

"Do you suppose any of her descendants are still alive?" he asked, apparently trying to keep the conversation light.

"I know her daughter is," Kari said, the dark feelings fleeing. "I heard her mentioned in the war camp when the Apocalypse was just starting. Karinda Bakhor: it's the same name. They mentioned she was a war wizard or something like that. Carly named her somewhat after me. I'm pretty sure it's the same girl."

133

"It might be nice to meet her some time," Grakin said. "Did you know her?"

Kari nodded. "Yeah. Carly's mate, Hrothgar, died adventuring before my time came, and Carly settled down in the elven lands with her baby. Karinda was only a toddler when my own time came, but I remember her very clearly: such a beautiful girl. Maybe someday when I can take some personal time, we can go see her. If what I heard is true, she still lives in the elven lands of Laeranore, near where her mother's home was."

"I would be honored," he said with a smile. "So what do you think this book will have to say about you?"

"Hard to say," she said with a shrug. "Towards the end of my life, when I was traveling with Carly, I think I was a lot like what you see of me now. Maybe a little more impatient, since I felt the sands dwindling, but otherwise the same. Hmm, I wonder if it will mention Fireblade."

"Fireblade?" the priest echoed as he reclined on his elbow and put his head in his palm.

"The red dragon," she clarified. "Fireblade was her nickname among the people of Terrassia. We killed her mate and one of her children, and scattered the rest of her brood. We never got to plunder her hoard, but that was among the biggest accomplishments of my old life, even considering all the demon kills."

"I can imagine," he said, still shocked. "How did you manage to kill two dragons?"

"Well, having a priestess who wielded her god's power certainly helped. A lot of people think when you fight a dragon, you just kind of surround and beat on it. That's a great plan if you're trying to get eaten. If you're fighting them in the open, you've got to ground them, and then it's a matter of confusion and trickery that gets the job done. They're too well-armored for brute force to work."

"Serenjols would love to hear about this," Grakin said. "He spends a lot of time studying and researching creatures and how to kill them if they attack. Knowing how to survive or even defeat a dragon attack would probably be the bright spot of his year."

"This is the killer strike," she said, touching Grakin just above his groin. "If you can avoid getting kicked by their hind legs, get their attention focused on someone else, and groin them, they'll bleed to death before you ever do any real damage to their armored fronts or flanks. Hamstringing them," she added, running a finger across the back of his leg, "really hurts their ability to defend themselves too, but getting through the armor there can be tricky."

134

"Where ever did you learn to fight dragons?" he asked, fascinated.

"Actually, from Suler Tumureldi," she answered, which drew another wide-eyed stare from him, and Kari shrugged knowingly. "I knew a lot of people back then."

"Did Tumureldi teach you his fighting style?" Grakin asked, surprising Kari but only for a moment, and she nodded with a barely-suppressed grin. "So you have been holding back when you spar with Erik?"

"A bit, yes," she said. "Like I said before, our superiors want to know how good a leader he is, and if I embarrass him or make him doubt himself, he may just follow me and I won't learn anything."

"I understand," he said, putting a finger before his snout. "I will say nothing." He closed the book and put it on the floor, and then he looked Kari's naked form up and down. "Would you like to make love?"

Kari smiled, leaned in with a kiss, and let that answer his question.

Chapter VIII – Storm of Memories

The next two weeks for Kari passed lazily and predictably, following much the same schedule as the first couple of days out of Salkorum. Eryn and Aeligos started fighting less than a week after the ship left Salkorum, and it got to the point where Galdur and his officers had to step in to force the two to tone things down. They stopped sleeping together and could hardly stand to be in the same room. Eryn joined the group at the captain's table for less and less time, barely taking her meal before leaving, and eventually stopped going altogether. Kari had no idea what started the entire mess, but she knew that with Eryn's volatility and Aeligos' habit of prodding her on moral issues, it had only been a matter of time.

The half-brys woman stopped joining her three girlfriends for their evening chats as well, and Kari could honestly say she missed the woman's company. She knew Eryn was a very private person, so Kari was torn as to whether she should try to coax her friend back out of her shell. Kari procrastinated about it for a few days, but once the lookout spotted land on the western horizon she made the decision to go see how Eryn was doing. For how little she actually knew the half-brys woman, Kari was able to talk her down from the place she'd stranded herself mentally, and convinced Eryn to give things another try.

The rest of the group smiled and greeted the assassin when she came up with Kari, and though he said nothing, Aeligos did flash his part-time lover a smile. The men were practicing their respective combat arts except for Grakin, who sat beside his sister on the bench as usual. When Kari and Eryn stepped up onto the quarterdeck, Sonja relinquished her seat so Kari could sit beside her mate. The scarlet-haired woman sat on the deck and watched Sherman and Katarina take turns attacking Serenjols, each being rebuffed easily.

Kari watched Eryn approach Aeligos. The half-brys woman touched his shoulder while he did a split on the deck. She crouched beside him and the two kissed lightly. Neither said anything, but Kari understood that an apology was in the making. It was almost wonderful to behold, though in the back of her mind, the demonhunter thought that no matter how many times the two made up, they would only end up hurting each other again. Her thoughts were punctuated by Typhonix letting out a sarcastic *awwwww*.

Eryn and Aeligos fixed Ty with icy glares, but he simply began making kissing noises until he had chased them from the deck completely. "Speed may beat strength every time, but sarcasm beats a cheap relationship every time," he said, drawing chuckles from Erik and even Serenjols. "One of them is going to kill the other, and I'm not sure which to put my money on."

"Okay, Ty, that's enough," Erik said, prompting the blonde warrior to laugh again.

"How long until we reach port?" Kari called, attracting the first mate's attention while she had a brief moment between yelling orders to the crew.

"About two and a half hours to reach, and probably another half hour before they let us dock at one of the piers," Jori-an answered. "You may want to get your things together. Unlike Salkorum, we'll be spending a couple of nights here while we resupply."

Her final comment put the group into motion, and they made their way below decks to relax, get out of the way of the busying crew, and make sure their armor and packs were ready to head ashore. Flora was a wealthy port city, the primary landing site on Terrassia for ships coming from Askies, but it also had its fair share of the seedier element and could be a dangerous city. It was imperative that the group go ashore ready for trouble on the off chance they found it; Kari knew trouble often found those who did not expect or prepare for it.

"Everyone should be armed and armored when we head ashore," Erik said before the men continued to the general quarters. "We'll all be heading to an inn farther into the city than the docks, and we'll let Aeligos sniff around to see what sort of trouble we can expect. Don't bring too much money or anything that's going to attract attention – we don't want trouble either finding us or warning anyone where we're going and what for. Mouths should remain closed as much as possible. Other than that, have a good time."

Kari chuckled. Erik's warning sounded a lot like those the drill instructors at the Academy gave when the cadets were allowed to spend time in the city proper. She and Grakin spent a few hours cuddling and reading from the books they had chosen. Soon enough the feel of the ship's movement lessened and then stopped altogether, and not long after that the call came down that they would be free to disembark soon. After grabbing her coin purse and getting dressed in her armor, Kari belted on her scimitars, drew on her cloak, and followed Grakin outside.

Twilight was settling in around the port as the group gathered on deck, waiting for Galdur to wave them ashore. Captain Galdur and Master Calhoun were down on the pier, speaking to a customs agent who was flanked by two armored guards. Jori-an stood at the top of the gangway to bar anyone from passing until the port authority had given permission, and she watched with folded arms while Calhoun went over the contents and passengers of the ship. The customs agent – a short, balding, bespectacled human – carefully marked off a checklist he was holding and nodded every so often.

Eventually the questioning stopped and the customs agent left, and Captain Galdur turned and motioned for the crew and passengers to come down off the ship. Twenty armed marines and Jori-an remained on board while the rest of the crew waited behind the passengers to disembark, and the Silver Blades and their companions headed down the ramp. Kari remained at the top, looking out over the city as it sat bathed in the deep purples of twilight, and she hesitated. Old memories crept to the surface, clawing their way free from the deep recesses of her mind as she looked out over the city she hadn't visited for so long. She couldn't shake the feeling her life would be in danger if she entered the city, though she couldn't remember why.

Grakin returned to her side after a minute and touched her shoulder lightly. Kari couldn't help but smile when she met his gaze, bolstered by the presence of her mate. He said nothing but simply took her hand and waited for her to regain her composure, and the two stepped aside to let the crewmen pass by. Kari glanced down to the pier and the curious, glowing-eyed stares of her half-demon companions further encouraged her to swallow her fears and join them. Kari closed her eyes with a sigh, squeezed Grakin's hand, and then headed down the gangplank to join the rest of the group.

"Is everything all right?" Erik asked softly but sternly, obviously at a loss.

Kari frowned, unsure as to what she could even say. She didn't want to answer a lot of questions, particularly when she wasn't sure what the answers were. Something about the city of her birth spooked her, but like with many other facets of her past life, the memories were cloudy and indistinct. She remembered having run away from home, but the reason why was still buried beneath the sands of resurrection. She finally glanced at Grakin before she answered. "I was born and raised here," she said. "I've never liked this city; it was a bad place to grow up."

Erik clapped her encouragingly on the shoulder. "There's nothing this place can throw at a demonhunter that she can't handle," he said, and Typhonix nodded his agreement.

"Come on, sis, I'll buy you a double-godhammer," the blonde warrior

139

said, jabbing Kari lightly in the shoulder as he passed by. Such treatment coming from Typhonix of all people helped to ease Kari's tensions, and she relaxed a little bit, surrounded by her friends. She couldn't remember what it was about the city that frightened her so. Her memories were jumbled and disjointed, and she had a hard time figuring out which were real and which were shadows or dreams. She had no problem remembering the things she had done after she'd left the Academy in her previous life, but her life before that was hazy and ethereal, a conglomerate of ghosts and specters of old fears.

Erik led the group away from the docks, and the companions looked over the city. Flora was lovely, named for its botanical gardens and the trees that lined its street, and it was built into the side of a rolling hill that wound up to a rocky cliff to the north. It was a perfect port: a naturally sheltered deep harbor ringed on its third side by a rocky outcropping that likewise protected it from storm surges and other swellings of the sea. Though it was on the eastern coast of Terrassia, ships seeking shelter in its harbor had to approach from the south, as the east side was blocked by the crumbling cliff wall.

High up along the hill were large homes, likely those of the wealthy and noble, built of white stone – possibly marble – that shone in the combined moon and firelight. Zigzagging roads led up the hillside, as the climb was much too steep for a straight road. Even from down on the docks Kari could make out the wonderfully complex waterways that prevented heavy rains from washing away the terraced homes. At the highest point of the cliffs Kari could make out a large fire signal, flanked by several catapults that must have served to destroy hostile vessels that ventured too close to the bustling port.

Kari remembered that the eastern coast of Terrassia had long been a favored hunting ground for pirates. The trade route north out of Flora to Dira Ch'Tori and even Castle Tenari – the capital of the tundra-based fures-rir kingdom – was too ripe a target for the raiders to pass up. As the first stopping point between Askies and the rest of Terrassia, Flora was the launching point for imports to pass north to Dira Ch'Tori and the fures-rir people, as well as south and west to Awlsabre and eventually the shakna-rir capital of Aurun Ch'Gurra on the west coast. While gold and silver were rarely to be had, Kari had no doubt that there were syndicates like Kaelin Black's that could turn a profit off of nearly anything.

Farther down the hillside were less affluent but still impressive homes built of wood or brick, with flat rooftops that allowed their occupants to look out over the port and ocean. They likely belonged to the more well-to-

140

do among the merchant class, the lesser nobles, and possibly even the priests of less-philanthropic churches. While it was unusual for any of the Citarian pantheon's clergy to use donated wealth for personal gain, the same couldn't be said of some of the Koryonite deities. Kari didn't know much about the Koryonite deities, but she had heard about some of their less-than-honorable brethren, and her Order made it a point to watch the clergies and worshipper bases of those deities.

The rest of the city, set on the flat land at the south end, was where the commoners and peasants lived. Flora had farmland to the southwest and a fair number of livestock ranches in the meadows to the northwest, and many of those who worked there either made their homes or had shops in the lower district. They were mostly built of wood with a few made of brick or stone when they formed an intersection or square. The streets were slightly dirty but not unbearably so, a byproduct of the terracing system that washed some small amount of trash and other debris down the hillside when the rains came.

Eventually, Erik stopped in one of the squares that marked an intersection of larger streets and indicated a brick-faced inn called *The Ranger's Respite*. Its namesake was an obvious nod toward the god Zitenius, a lesser god who had been a mortal ranger and whose work on Askies was legendary. When the group entered the inn, the innkeeper looked overjoyed to see such a large group of customers arrive, but his face turned to unmasked trepidation upon seeing they were almost all half-demon. He looked the group over slowly and thoroughly, and moved back behind the bar as if it might shield him from possible attack. He was visibly relieved when all but Erik moved to push a few tables together and seated themselves. Kari took a seat with the others while Erik approached the innkeeper. He stood patiently at the bar for a minute while the man continued to stare at him but said nothing.

"Generally, this is where you say 'what can I do for you,' and perhaps introduce yourself," Erik said.

"Of course, of course," the human said after another few moments, and he pushed his fingers back through his thinning grey hair, only to have it spring right back into place. He was tall and thin, his face decorated with a sparse beard that matched the color of his hair, and he had brown eyes that had no doubt seen nearly every kind of traveler and group imaginable – except the one before him. "Err, what can I do for you?"

"We need rooms for two nights, preferably one for each of us if you can manage that," Erik said, drawing the light silver chain that held his dog tags forth so that his status became obvious to the nervous man. Kari saw him put three platinum coins on the bar before the innkeeper and the man's eyes widened, though he didn't reach for them. "I expect this should cover our stay, including food and drink. If anyone starts to get drunk, you're to deny them anything but water. I'm not asking you to babysit them, just to make sure *you're* not the reason they do something stupid."

"Certainly. Right now the inn is nearly empty, so you're welcome to each take your own rooms," the human said, and he glanced at the group before producing a like number of keys from behind his counter.

"My name's Erijinkor Tesconis, but you can call me Erik," the demonhunter said, shaking hands with the innkeeper as the man's fear dissipated completely, likely due to Erik's dog tags. "If anyone here gives you trouble, you just let me know and I'll handle it."

"Understood, officer," the innkeeper said. "I'm Clinton Darby, but most folks just call me Clint. My serving girls are Celia and Oksera. If you need anything, you just let them know. I can provide food and drinks for you and your companions now if you like."

"Please," Erik said. "Just ale for everyone. They can get stronger drinks after if they like. Did you say one of the serving girls was named Oksera?"

"Yes, she's fures-rir," the human said. "I'll have her bring you your meals."

Clint walked toward the kitchen door and Erik returned to his companions and took a seat at the head of the combined tables. Kari wondered if ordering ale for everyone was a wise thing to do, and apparently the same thought occurred to Erik when he looked over the human twins. "Food and drinks are coming, and everyone will have their own rooms," Erik said. He glanced at Kari and Grakin and seemed to blush, adding, "Eh, you two may want to tell the innkeeper you'll be staying together."

Grakin smiled at that, but both he and Kari were surprised when Typhonix piped in, "When are you having a baby?"

"Ty," Erik said admonishingly.

"What?" the blonde demonhunter asked. "I'm not trying to be a jerk, I'm just curious when I'm going to have a niece or nephew to play with."

His clarification seemed to ease everyone's nerves, Kari's not the least of them. Ty seemed to be warming to her, forgetting whatever suspicions he had over her identity, and it made her glad to fit so well into her mate's family. Even Erik's jealousy had finally simmered down into what she assumed was a calm acceptance that he simply missed out on an opportunity, and each day he seemed a little happier for her and Grakin.

142

Kari looked over the large group and realized that if Eryn and Aeligos ever actually became mates, then all but the human twins would be related. That thought warmed her blood a little more.

"We have yet to discuss it," Grakin said, piercing through Kari's thoughts. "We certainly will not be trying until after this mission is done."

Kari nodded. It was no mystery that Grakin's declaration was intended to satisfy Erik. "I'll have to ask the Order for some personal time after we finish with this business," she added. Not only had she and Grakin not discussed it other than her declaration that she would bear him children, but she hadn't really thought about it. She lived on the road and the thought of settling down and having a family was alien to her; pleasant, but still alien. Ty could barely conceal a grin, and Kari was surprised that such a burly and foul-tempered man would be looking forward to having nieces and nephews to play with. The thought of that sight made her smile.

"You've been smiling a lot lately," Eryn commented, and she leaned her face in her hand as she put her elbow on the table, an amused smirk on her features.

"I know what I said a few weeks ago," Kari answered. "I was wrong. Life is beautiful."

"And it'll look a lot better once ye've got some of this in ye," came the oddly-accented voice of Oksera the barmaid as she approached the table with all ten steins of ale in her hands. She placed the drinks in the center and then made her way back toward the kitchen. She was tall and slender, her eyes and long, straight hair the pale blue that nearly all of her people had – a characteristic that many found odd. It was difficult for most untrained eyes to tell one fures-rir from another, but those like Kari who had spent time among the race knew that observing other features still made it fairly simple. Oksera's hips were curvy but her breasts were small, which marked her as unmated, and she had a slight overbite, which was common among the lower class. She was attractive, which left Kari to wonder why she had moved so far south to the warmer climate, away from the cold tundra of her homeland.

It didn't escape Kari's notice that the stares of Erik, Typhonix, and Serenjols all followed the scantily-clad woman's swinging hips as she returned to the kitchen. Due to their cold-impervious natures, the fures-rir were the least likely of any of the rir races to wear clothing, even in their frozen homeland. It made for humorous situations many times, Kari could remember, as they walked around nude or nearly nude while guests to their kingdom were so bundled in clothing that their species couldn't be recognized. Oksera herself wore a flimsy but colorful outfit that spoke

143

more of modesty than fashion.

Soon enough, Oksera had served dinner to all of them and stood near Erik, looking over the strange group with interest. Her gaze lingered on Kari for a minute. "Ye're terra-dracon?" she asked simply, and Kari nodded. "First time I've ever seen one of yer kind."

"Would you care to join us?" Erik asked. He was having a hard time moving his stare up the curvy line of Oksera's hip to eventually meet her eyes.

Oksera laughed. "Ha! That's not the kind of service Clint pays me to provide. Come up with twenty gold and *maybe* we'll talk," she said with a devilish grin, and Erik put his hand over his face, chuckling lightly. Oksera clapped his shoulder and turned to head back to the kitchen. "That's what I thought. Enjoy yer meals, I'll be back to check on ye shortly."

Kari had a laugh at Erik's expense. It was the first time she could remember seeing anyone have him at a disadvantage. His siblings laughed at him more openly, and even Eryn and the twins got a good chuckle out of his reaction.

"Twenty gold? She'd have to be coming to Tsalbrin for *that* kind of money," Typhonix commented, which drew further laughter from the others. "Hey Grakin, how do you get a woman without having to pay her?"

The question hardly seemed to catch Grakin off guard. "Well, I believe you start by making her think it is not simply sex that you are after," he answered with a smirk.

"So you lie?" Ty returned in a serious tone. Kari put her hand over her face and shook her head while the rest of the table erupted in further laughter. "Hmph, I thought honesty was supposed to get you somewhere."

Kari half-shrugged and leaned her face in her palm. "You're a big, strong, dangerous-looking man, Ty. You're going to scare most of the girls you ever try to talk to. The way you talk doesn't help, either: you're not afraid to say what's on your mind, and that's going to turn a lot of girls away, too. If you want to find a woman, honestly…you need to make sure she's not going to think you might hurt her."

He seemed surprised by her candor, but Ty nodded after a moment. "I'll keep that in mind," he said quietly.

"And don't be such a jackass around them," Sonja added evenly. Ty gave her an impatient look, but the others laughed again at the exchange.

"There's one thing I want to add before dinner is finished," Erik said. "I don't want anyone walking the streets of this city alone. If you go out to visit another tavern or a shop or what-have-you, make sure you go with someone else. I know all of us are war veterans with the exception of the

144

twins, but we can't afford delays or accidents. Make sure you're safe at all times, and the best way to do that is to travel in pairs or packs."

Everyone nodded their agreement, and once they finished their meals, they all headed upstairs to check their rooms. Kari and Grakin's dormitory was nearly the same size as the suite Kari had stayed in at the Bloodied Blade, with a private tub and a double-sized bed. Grakin turned up one of the bedside lanterns, undressed, and lay down on the bed with his book, and he looked up to Kari as she stood beside him, still armored. "I'm going to look around the city a little," she said. "Probably with Sonja or Eryn. Maybe we can share a bath when I get back."

Grakin smiled and bid her farewell, and when Kari met Eryn in the hallway, the two women descended to the common room and then headed out to the streets. Quiet blanketed the city like a burial shroud, and Kari was immediately put on her guard by the utter lack of activity. The night was still fairly young, and it was hard for her to imagine that the streets emptied out so thoroughly after dusk. Two of the moons were high in the sky, illuminating the city in a bright heavenly glow while their darkened sibling lagged beyond the horizon, and yet the shadows seemed deep and dangerous. Kari found that tinge of fear she'd felt on the boat sinking in again.

"It's all right," Eryn said after a minute, her glowing crimson eyes taking in the entire square. "This is eerie, but the streets really are as empty as they seem."

Kari nodded and fell into step beside her companion. Though Kari could see well in the dark and especially in strong moonlight, her eyes were nowhere near as sharp as those of the half-brys woman. While all rir had the ability to see in low light much like a cat, the half-brys could see body heat when the light was insufficient for hunting; it was nearly impossible to hide from their all-seeing gaze. Still, Kari had lived for years on the streets of Solaris, and even so many years removed from that life and with her memories jumbled, the instincts remained just below the surface, keeping her alert and vigilant.

The two walked the city, crisscrossing the lower district, and noted where all of the shops and taverns were, where to find the stations of the constable and city watch, and where the other inns were. Eryn was insistent on stopping at every other inn they could find, merely having a glass of water at each while she watched what kind of traffic they saw. She explained that how crowded the inns were could tell one much about the city, whether there was excitement, danger, or even civil unrest coming. Kari took the lesson in attentively, appreciating the older woman's willingness to share some of her experience.

Eventually the friends ventured into the middle district farther up the hill, and as Kari had suspected, the streets were cleaner, as were the homes and the gardens. Eryn was not so intent on visiting the inns there, and she further explained that the middle and upper classes generally didn't head to inns and taverns when there was trouble. Instead, she explained, they barred themselves inside their homes and convinced themselves that nothing could touch them within their little fortresses. In the nicer district Eryn was more intent on finding clothing shops, food stores, and other businesses whose quality would meet a much higher standard in the classier neighborhood.

The two walked up the main avenue that led farther north to the zigzagging roads, but Kari stopped suddenly as something caught her eye. She looked up to behold a wooden sign that swung lightly in the ocean breeze. It was perched above the door of a school, intricately carved to read *The Apple and the Tree*, and was further marked with a picture of an apple tree with several loose fruits around its base. Eryn was staring at her, but Kari hardly noticed.

"Did you go here when you were a kid?" the half-brys woman asked at last.

"Yes...I think so, but...they never listened to me," Kari said. She wasn't even sure what she meant with her own words, her memories still cloudy.

Eryn touched Kari's shoulder briefly and Kari flinched and backed away a step before she regained her composure. There was something about the city and the school sign that pierced the foggy veil of Kari's distant past, but she was still having a hard time piecing it together. She shook the thoughts away after a moment and motioned up the road with her head, and Eryn fell into step as Kari continued along.

"Did the other kids make fun of you when you went to that school?" Eryn guessed, but she didn't wait for Kari to answer. "I got picked on all the time as a kid. The other half-demon children were all bigger and stronger than I was, so even they picked on me."

"I tried to tell the teachers...but they never listened," Kari said quietly. She scratched the side of her head and cast one last glance back at the school and its wooden sign. There was a vague sense of anger that simmered below the surface, as though whatever hurtful shadows were concealed in the hazy recesses of her mind involved the teachers and administrators of the school. Eryn's suggestion of bullying didn't seem to fit, but Kari still couldn't remember fully. She sighed and went quiet again, and she and Eryn quickened their pace.

"Teachers never wanted to hear it from me, either," Eryn said. "They always insisted that being picked on and hurt made you stronger, so it was good for you. Even my father's status as head of the Five Clans never seemed to make them think twice about it. I sure didn't feel bad when that whole city was burned to the ground."

Kari stopped and turned to look at the school once more. Eryn's mention of her father disrupted the waters of Kari's hazy mind like a brick being tossed into a puddle. When Kari looked at the school again, she recalled what it was she'd told the teachers, and the fact that they'd never listened struck her so much more poignantly. Kari was acutely aware of Eryn's stare and worked hard to keep from breaking down. She fought with every ounce of her will to keep herself together, afraid to break down in front of her half-brys companion and end up the target of far too many questions from her other friends. "I shouldn't have come back here," Kari said steadily. "Let's go back to the inn."

It was clear Eryn wanted to see the higher-class neighborhoods of the city while it was night and few were out and about, but she seemed to understand that Kari was uncomfortable and needed to see Grakin. Eryn kept silent as they walked back through the city, showing once again that though she was perceptive toward others' thoughts and feelings, she simply lacked the ability to properly express sympathy. Kari remained completely silent as they passed along the slightly dirty streets to the inn. Eryn offered to share a drink with her once they returned, but Kari waved her off and simply asked the innkeeper for a double-godhammer. Once she had the drink in hand, she retired to her room.

Grakin was still reading when Kari entered, but he smiled, closed his book, and put it on the night table. His face took on a look of concern when Kari swallowed the entire glass of liquor in a single long swig. "Is everything all right?" he asked. He sat up on the edge of the bed and reached out to touch her elbow.

Kari shied away from his touch and placed the empty glass on the night table. She still struggled to keep herself together. Despite the love between her and Grakin, she found she didn't want to talk about what she'd felt with him, either. "I'm not feeling well," she said. "I think I'm just going to try to get some sleep."

Kari undressed and crawled past Grakin to lay down on the other side of the bed with her back to him. Grakin simply brushed her hair away from her cheek and kissed her softly. He lay down beside her, but Kari kept her wings slightly fanned, so he kept his distance. As the alcohol settled into her, Kari drifted into a troubled sleep. The night was quiet, but the alcohol only kept its grip on her for so long before the memories of her childhood smashed through the barriers that had kept them at bay since her resurrection.

Kari sat upright in the bed and looked around in a panic. Grakin startled awake at her sudden motion and reached up to lightly touch her elbow. "No!" Kari cried. "No, no, no, no..." Grakin sat up and put a hand to her shoulder, but before he could even say a word, Kari ducked away, jumping awkwardly to the side, and she fell out of bed and landed on her rump. Grakin moved to the edge of the bed and started to sit up, but Kari pushed herself away from him, shuffling to put her back to the wall below the window. For years she had been unable to tap into her memories, but now she was caught in the worst of them.

"Karian?" Grakin asked gently, moving toward her slowly.

Kari put her hands to the side of her bed as the bell tolled the fifth hour. She kept saying *don't* each time the bell tolled, trying to push herself away from Grakin, even with her back to the wall. She curled into an upright fetal position as he got close to her and he stroked her face gently. "It is all right, Kari, you are all right."

She punched him, sending him onto his side, and she screamed, "MAMA! MAMA!" Kari sprang to her feet, ran to the door, and put her back to it. There was nowhere to run; she was trapped, and despite crying out for her mother, she knew the woman wouldn't come. Kari slid down to a crouch and wet herself, completely terrified as years of abuse flooded to the surface of her mind. Grakin rose to his feet unsteadily, rubbing his aching jaw, but as he started to approach, Kari bared her teeth in a snarl.

Someone banged on the door and Kari perked up with a small glimmer of hope. "Mama? Mama, help me!"

Someone hit the door from the outside with their weight, and it nearly came off of its hinges but for Kari leaning against it. The shock of the pain clutched her like a clawed hand, dragging her further into the nightmare and refusing to relinquish its hold. "NO! Mama, help, please...mama...."

Wild panic overtook Kari and she sprang to her feet again. In the span of a heartbeat she opened the door and rushed out, pushing near-blindly through the strange forms gathered in the hall. She paused at the top of the stairs, but when she turned back to the door of her room and saw the people approaching, her eyes widened in terror and she panicked again. "No, no, no!" Kari shouted, and she rushed down the stairs and out the front door of the inn before anyone could even yell for her to stop.

Kari sprinted down the long, near-deserted moonlit streets of Flora, oblivious to the fact that she was still naked or that there were people who stared after her as she ran. Her heart was pounding but she kept her pace, putting as much distance between herself and her attacker as she could. She ran until she came to the edge of the city, her breathing and her pulse heavy as she crested the hill that separated the city from its cemetery. She glanced across the tombstones, but her gaze whipped back over the city, trying to discern movement or any pursuit. In the light of the moons she couldn't see anyone approaching. She had escaped.

Her heartbeat eventually slowed and her breathing did so as well, and Kari's mind cleared when she realized she was cold and naked and standing on a hill outside of town. She put her hand to her temple, trying to figure out if what she'd just experienced was real or if she'd run out here in the haze of a waking nightmare. Far in the distance, Kari could just barely make out the masts of *Karmi's Sword* sitting in the harbor, and she realized it had been a dream – a very real, very wakeful one, but a dream nonetheless. She wondered why she was alone, though, and how she had gotten so far from the inn without at least Grakin following after her.

Kari considered what she had just gone through, and she turned and walked into the graveyard. The short, dew-laden grass was cool under her feet. She followed the tombstones, arranged by year, and she was able to find the area she was looking for. The moonlight filtered in between the trees, illuminating even those headstones that stood under the shelter of the branches, and within minutes, Kari found what she was looking for. The tombstones were all in one place: the entire family's except for Kari's own. Her breath was shaky as she read the inscriptions, and when her eyes passed over the words *beloved husband and father*, Kari put her hand to the end of her snout and sobbed.

She wasn't aware of the two people that approached, too wrapped up in the pain of her past which, though it had subsided a bit, still stabbed deeply when she read the insulting epitaph on her father's grave. When she realized she was no longer alone, Kari turned and saw Eryn and Typhonix through the blur of her tears. The two seemed unsure of how to approach, and only then did it occur to Kari what she'd done: she'd struck her mate forcefully and fled. Her heart skipped a beat as she considered that having hit him would only compound the darkness of her past, and she wondered: would he ever accept her again?

"Help me," Kari whispered. "Please, help me."

She sank to her knees, and the last thing she remembered was Typhonix picking her up.

~~*~*

Kari slept until midmorning. When she sat up in bed, Grakin ran his hand gently down her arm. She tensed up at first, still not completely free of her nightmares, but Grakin took up her hand and interlaced his fingers with hers. He didn't try to hug her or get too close; he gave her some space, and Kari sighed quietly as she considered what to say. She took some comfort in the fact that he'd apparently slept beside her throughout the night, and even now was making an effort to get close to her. Had she woken up alone, she wouldn't have been surprised.

Kari turned to look at him at last, and he stared at her in his loving, gentle way to let her know he was worried about her. She reached toward him tentatively and Grakin happily rubbed his face in her palm. "I hit you last night, didn't I?" she asked, nearly choking on the words.

Grakin sat up beside her and maintained strong eye contact. "Do not concern yourself with that," he said with a shake of his head. "You were scared; I know you did not mean to. Do not concern yourself with it."

Kari began to cry, and Grakin pulled her into his tender embrace. He held to her tight but didn't ask any questions. He made soft sounds to hush her and soothe her, and the soft caress of his hand stroking her cheek helped ease her tensions and her fear. He had not forsaken her, and he was trying to bring her out from her private hell. Kari wasn't sure he understood, and was even less sure about how many of the others would know or suspect what had broken her. She decided after several long, comforting, quiet minutes that Grakin deserved to know. She rose up to a sitting position again, and though she had a hard time maintaining eye contact, she began to tell him what had happened.

"It was a sign," she said quietly, and she closed her eyes and blew out a sigh. "A sign outside the school I went to when I was a little girl; it was still there." Grakin stayed silent but held her hand in his with the fingers interlaced. "I told the teachers there. I told them all the time, but they never listened," she said. "No one believed me. They all knew, but they pretended not to. So I had to run away."

Grakin let out a short sigh, and Kari lay down with her head in his lap. He stroked her hair softly and she put her hand on his thigh. "What did you have to run away from, my love?" he asked. "What happened?"

"I was dia...diagnosed with Dracon's Bane when I was a little girl," she said. "My parents never told me. But my father took out his frustration on me...I remember now, he used to beat me when I was little. But after a while, beating me wasn't enough anymore; he said he wanted to break my

150

heart the way I'd broken his."

Grakin cocked his head and Kari paused, closed her eyes, and let out another sigh. "I was nine the first time he raped me," she said, and it almost sounded like someone else had spoken. She had never told anyone before, not in her past life and not in this one. She had buried that ugly truth for years, but the confusion and disorientation that had come with being resurrected had fractured her will. The broken shards of the memories stabbed ever more painfully, and despite her fear that Grakin would reject her, Kari felt like she needed him to know, needed his strength and his comforting love to quell the pain and the fear. And if he wouldn't give it....

It wasn't often that Kari saw Grakin at a complete loss for words. "Your father...molested you?" he practically hissed. "Gods, Kari...I had no idea."

She shook her head, trying to dislodge the memories' grip on her heart, but still she continued, "When I was fourteen I ran away. I hitched a ride with a wagon train headed up to Solaris and never looked back. I had forgotten it for a while...after I spent the time as Suler's mistress" – there was an unmistakable look of shock on Grakin's face, but he didn't interrupt – "I was happy for a time, and I'd pushed the memories down. After I was brought back, I had the shadows in my dreams, but they were never real. But when I saw the school sign, it all came flooding back. These aren't just nightmares, Grakin: they're memories. Now I remember: this is why I didn't want to come back. I never should have come back here, and I...I shouldn't have deceived you."

"Deceived me?" he echoed with a confused look. "About what?"

"Being dirty," she said. She looked away from him, ashamed.

Grakin grabbed her chin softly but firmly and turned her face back to him, and he kissed her nose to nose. "You are *not* dirty," he insisted. "You are one of the best women – no, one of the best *people* I know. You are my mate, and nothing will ever change that: not my brothers, not your father, nothing short of death itself. And even then you will still be a part of me."

"Then you're not mad at me?" Kari asked.

"Mad?" he repeated, and he put his hand over his mouth as he bit back a sob. "Kari, I love you! The only thing that makes me mad is the thought of losing you."

Kari hugged him tightly, and Eryn's advice shone through the jumble of thoughts and emotions that washed through her like a rainstorm: *Don't be afraid to cry, or to be weak; just work to make sure that what makes you cry or what makes you weak also makes you stronger in the end.* Kari

151

quietly gave thanks to the gods for the circumstances that had led her to meet so many good friends, and most importantly her gentle and loving mate. After a few minutes, Kari pulled lightly away from Grakin's embrace and met his stare evenly.

"Grakin, it...may be a few days before we can make love again," she said before biting her lip. "I have to...make sure this doesn't happen again, and that I don't hit you again."

Grakin waved off the comment and ran his fingers smoothly along her jaw. "Whenever you are ready; when you feel safe," he said with a comforting smile. He rose from the bed and began to get dressed, and he turned to face her when he finished. "We should go down and join the others for breakfast so they know you are all right."

Kari shook her head. "I'm not ready to share this with them, Grakin," she said. "I think I can keep this in check, but it was hard enough to tell you about it. I've never told anyone else. Not even Suler, or Carly."

"I understand," he said. He sat down on the edge of the bed and touched her shoulder tenderly. "You need not give them the why of it, but you should let them know you are all right. You are part of our family now, and they are all worried about you. Take your own advice to me: let your friends be there for you."

Kari didn't bother to try to stop her tears. "You're right," she said, managing a smile. "I'll be down in a little while; I'm going to take a bath. Can you just explain to them that it was something private, and that I'm sorry?"

Grakin glanced at the bathtub, and Kari wondered if he was considering what she'd said about being dirty. He waved off her comment. "I will tell them you are fine, and to leave it at that," he said. "They will not butt into your business where there is no concern of theirs and they are not invited. And there is nothing to apologize for, Kari."

Kari nodded and Grakin went to join his siblings for breakfast. Kari climbed into the tub, which was still full with now room-temperature water from earlier in the morning. She'd taken a hot bath when Typhonix and Eryn got her back to the inn the night before, to warm her back up after her naked jaunt through the cool evening. The shock of the water felt good, awakening her a little more fully after a poor night of sleep, and Kari washed herself off quickly before she lay back in the tub. She relaxed as much as she could and tried to keep her mind clear; Grakin had not rejected her. After a few minutes there was a knock at the door, and she called for whomever it was to enter. She looked up to behold the barmaid from the night before.

"Brought ye some fresh hot water," Oksera said. She approached the tub and, once she received a nod from Kari, she slowly poured a bucket away from Kari's flesh or delicate areas.

"Thank you," Kari said, swirling the water around to mix the temperatures.

"My pleasure," the woman said in her wondrous accent. "Would ye like a drink?"

Deep in her core, Kari thought that drowning her sorrows in a double-godhammer sounded like a wonderful idea. "No, thank you, I'll be coming down to the commons soon enough," she answered, resisting the temptation. She wondered if her abuse was what had driven her to drink or whether it was knowing she had Dracon's Bane; strangely, she couldn't remember. With Kari lost in thought, the fures-rir woman bowed politely and left. Kari closed her eyes and massaged her feelings with Grakin's words: he'd said she wasn't dirty, and that she was one of the best people he'd ever known. Typical sentiments coming from a mate, and Kari honestly had to wonder if he really understood everything she'd told him. In the end, she supposed it mattered little: he loved her, and hadn't rejected her. That was as much as she could've hoped for. It made her wonder briefly how Suler Tumureldi might have reacted had she told him; she imagined in much the same way.

After a short bath, Kari rose from the water and pulled a towel from the nearby wardrobe to dry off. She dressed slowly and did her best to keep her thoughts in order. It was hard not to imagine that little wooden sign outside the school and the memories of her father it evoked, but Kari countered her fear and her pain with the love of her mate and how she'd felt when Grakin held her. It reminded her of Trigonh and the way he'd held her hand tightly until she fell asleep for the last time in her previous life. She remembered how Carly Bakhor had followed her into battle, the way thousands looked up to her as she relayed the orders of Kris Jir'tana, and of Suler Tumureldi, the only other man who'd ever made her feel as beautiful as Grakin did.

Finally Kari rose to her feet and reminded herself that she was one of the highest ranking and, more pointedly, most respected demonhunters *in the history of the Order*, that Zalkar stood with her, and that she had survived and succeeded despite all that had happened to her as a young woman. Such a perspective only countered the memories so much, but Kari smiled at the woman that looked back at her from the full-body mirror that stood in the corner of the room. Her image reminded her pointedly that she was a woman of strength, and that though the scared little girl her father had abused lived within her, that girl was now protected by someone even the demons feared. Satisfied that her emotions were in check, Kari made her way downstairs and joined her friends in the common room.

"Hey, there she is," Typhonix said with a genuine smile. For some reason, of all the looks of concern Kari received from her companions, Ty's was one of the most important to her.

Erik rose from his seat. "Are you all right?" he asked. Though he normally had an imposing countenance, Kari could tell it was more than just the leader in him asking.

"I'm sorry about last night," she said somewhat sheepishly, trying not to fidget. "I guess I owe you all something of an explanation."

Erik grabbed Kari's snout lightly to close her mouth and said, "You don't owe us a thing. We all have things we don't want to talk about. Just tell us you'll be all right."

Kari met the blue-eyed stare of the larger male evenly. "I'll be all right," she said confidently, and from Erik's reaction, she could tell that confidence shone through in her eyes.

"Good," Erik said. He gestured toward her seat. "We'll be out of the city first thing tomorrow morning. If you like, I'll give you a bit of coin and you and the girls can go look for some leisure clothes at one of the nicer shops today."

Kari was a bit confused by that. "I have money," she said as she took a seat.

"I know," Erik said with a shrug. "But you're my sister-in-law now."

A comforting warmth spread through Kari when Erik smiled at her, and Grakin patted her knee beneath the table. She leaned over and gave him a kiss. Celia, the human barmaid, brought over hot buttermilk biscuits, honey, and coffee for breakfast. Kari enjoyed her meal while the group chatted about their plans for the day, and she felt her spirit lighten considerably. The more time she spent among her friends and with her mate, the more the shadowy figments of her childhood dispersed, giving way to the strength and conviction of a veteran demonhunter. Once the morning meal was done with, Eryn guided Kari, Sonja, and Katarina to one of the richer districts up the hill to do some shopping.

Kari was nervous about walking through the city again, but Eryn and Sonja kept the air light with chatter, discussing bra cuts and lace panties that Eryn was looking forward to picking up. Katarina seemed just as amused by the topic as Kari did, and Kari wondered if perhaps she should get something sexy that Grakin might enjoy removing. She had never owned anything she considered sexy, but as she thought about it, she realized it was largely because she'd never had a reason to. She considered what Grakin's reaction might be if she shed her armor back at the inn to reveal some sexy lingerie. When she glanced at Eryn and Sonja, the two women were staring at her, and Kari blushed, sending all of the women into a fit of laughter.

They spent most of the day in a couple of fancy clothing shops, though only Kari and Katarina had any luck finding clothing or lingerie in their sizes. Sonja, who stood six-foot-seven, was simply too large for what the shops had in stock, and they didn't have time to get measured clothes tailor-made. Eryn stood only four-foot-eleven, so she had the same problem, but the two women seemed to have enough fun watching Kari model sexy clothes. Despite the fact that she was a tomboy, Kari had a beautiful figure that was only accentuated by the purple garments her friends helped her pick out. Initially Kari had been looking at something in black, but Eryn changed her mind by suggesting she just go naked if she was going to wear something the same color as her skin.

The late morning and afternoon passed calmly and amusingly, and with the urging of her friends, Kari bought some sexy undergarments. Both of her half-demon friends also helped her pick a couple of sleek dresses and casual outfits. Katarina picked up a couple of additional outfits as well, though she seemed more interested in their utility than their fashion, which didn't surprise Kari given where the human girl had grown up. Kari was content, thinking it would be nice to wear something on the deck of *Karmi's Sword* other than the old leisure clothes she'd had stashed in the bottom of her pack for eight years. She knew Grakin would like all of the pieces she'd purchased: he was content when she wore nothing. The true test, she mused with a chuckle, would be what Jori-an said the first time she wore the new casual clothes up on deck.

Just before dinner the women stopped in a jewelry shop, where Eryn and Sonja bought small golden hoops for their pointed ears. Kari didn't wear jewelry other than her dog tags, but she had always liked the way earrings looked and caved easily to the suggestions of her friends to get some for herself. Katarina's ears weren't pierced either, but Eryn and Sonja suggested she give earrings a try. Eryn pointed out that Katarina was no longer living among rir and might want to start trying to attract a mate, and despite the fact that it was mostly an attempt at humor, the young paladin agreed.

Kari had to admit she looked less *tomboyish* when she was wearing earrings, and she decided to try turning Eryn's sharp sense of humor back on her. "Do either of you have piercings anywhere else?" she tried to ask nonchalantly, but she ended up giggling as she finished the question.

"Not I," Sonja said with a hearty chuckle.

"What, like nipple rings?" Eryn asked, cocking an eyebrow. "Forget it. Honestly, if what I've already got isn't enticing enough, sticking jewelry through it isn't going to help."

Kari cackled and put her hand over the end of her snout. It seemed impossible to outdo Eryn when it came to humor. Eryn and Sonja shared a chuckle over Kari's reaction. Katarina remained silent, but she was trying very hard to suppress an impish grin. "I was just wondering," Kari said. "I look kinda plain, and thought maybe a body piercing would give Grakin more of an eyeful."

Her three friends exchanged looks and shook their heads when their gazes fell back over Kari. "Trust me, you don't need one," Eryn said, her words echoed by nods from the others.

They joined the rest of their companions for dinner, and they passed the remainder of the evening quietly playing cards. Most of them had enjoyed the opportunity to get off of the ship, but to Kari, spending a night and day in the city didn't compare to the calm and beauty of the tropical island they'd visited beforehand - even before taking her waking nightmare into account. She spent the evening getting to know their two human companions further. As it turned out, Sherman mentioned that he was an apprentice smith when he lived on the island, so he found that he and Serenjols had that in common. The largest of the Tesconis siblings didn't speak much, but he listened to Sherman's stories and seemed to understand much of the underlying humor better than his siblings did. Katarina, on the other hand, had a fondness for woodworking, and she chatted a bit about the art of the bowyer with Eryn while they played cards.

Later in the evening Kari and Grakin retired to their room. Kari had trouble suppressing a grin as she removed her armor and padded clothes to reveal the purple lingerie she bought earlier in the day. Grakin's eyes lit up and he smiled broadly, approached, and traced a finger curiously along the fabric of her bra and then her panties. His eyes were drawn to the way the panties hugged her curves, and he spent nearly a minute admiring her before he straightened up and lightly touched her long, silky black hair. She waited for him to take her undergarments off, but instead he moved away and sat on the edge of the bed, looking at her curiously. After a moment, she moved over to him, pushed him onto his back, straddled him, and leaned down for kisses.

Kari told him clearly without saying a word that despite what she had said earlier in the day, she was expecting a night of passion. Grakin recognized it and didn't disappoint. They fell asleep in each other's arms, and Kari prayed that her thoughts and dreams would remain calm and centered on her mate. She woke around the five o'clock hour, but it was that expectation of being awakened for guard duty, and not due to a nightmare. Kari turned to look at Grakin and found him watching her, concerned. She kissed him to ease his worries, and then she returned to sleep.

When Kari woke the following morning, she found Grakin seated cross-legged before the window in prayer, and she had little doubt that he had many things for which to thank his lord.

Chapter IX – Arrival

Kari and her companions boarded the ship and got underway without any attention from the city, and began the final leg of their long journey. *Karmi's Sword* sailed off the south coast of Terrassia for over a week, but passed by the massive port city of Awlsabre without stopping. Soon enough the entire continent disappeared over the horizon and it took the hurtful memories Kari had relived with it. Though they stayed with her and the monotony of the ship threatened to help break them free, she did her best to concentrate on her training and her relationship with Grakin instead. As Eryn had advised, Kari drew confidence from her efforts and strength from her confidence, and she kept the memories walled up.

It took another couple of weeks to reach Tsalbrin once they left the currents around the southern end of Terrassia, and Kari and her friends began to bristle with anticipation as their destination drew closer. Kari spent the final weeks of the voyage training exclusively with Aeligos, no longer sparring with either Erik or Typhonix. She wanted to learn as much of Aeligos' unarmed technique as she could before they landed. Kari continued to demonstrate her incredible adaptability and hunger to learn, and Aeligos told her that she was learning in days what may have taken other students weeks or months. Kari had the legs and grace of a dancer but the strength and grip of a long-time warrior, and the two skill sets combined made her a fierce opponent.

Aeligos hurt her more than once, hyper-extending joints and nearly breaking bones as he fought to stay a step ahead of Kari's speed and reactions. Kari hurt him nearly as many times, and once caught him in an arm lock so tight she nearly tore his shoulder apart when he tried to escape. Grakin was forced to minister his healing arts to them both on several occasions, but as much as he showed impatience toward his brother for hurting his mate, he was still clearly proud of Kari's advancement under Aeligos' tutelage.

As for the priest, he spent most of his time educating the young paladins about the pantheon: he explained the histories, areas of control, tenets and doctrines, and relationships among each of the deities. Grakin's dedication was to Kaelariel, the god of freedom and death, but Kari soon learned that he was well-educated when it came to the pantheon as a whole, and he was able to properly teach the youngsters about all of the gods equally well. He seemed to be very careful not to push his own beliefs too strongly, as he apparently wanted to make sure the youngsters chose a path that reflected their beliefs and motivations rather than simply choosing the one their teacher had. Grakin spent the most time speaking of Kris Fletcher, Carsius Coramin, and Carsius' daughter Bek, all of whom were paladins or very close to it. Kari was pleased when, based on the diligent instruction of the priest, the twins decided to take up service to the Ghost and his primary spheres of control: honor and loyalty.

The others practiced their combative arts during the remainder of the trip: Eryn wowed crew and passengers alike as she shot down bottles hanging from the crow's nest with her bow. Her hand-eye coordination was phenomenal, and the fact that she could adjust her shots to take the constant motion of the ship and the speed of the wind into account was astounding. Sonja received permission to begin spellcasting on the ship's deck, and she frightened the marines more than a few times as she arced lightning bolts through the night sky or across the surface of the water, where they were mirrored on the waves as they flashed toward the horizon. Sonja eased the crew's worries by demonstrating her defensive enchantments: one night, she conjured a water shield that kept dangerous swells from washing over the deck but still allowed the wind to pass through and keep the sails full. Sonja never spoke of her wizardry with great confidence, but it was clear to Kari that Sonja would bring a lot of utility to the group with her arcane power. All together the group practiced and encouraged. Erik worked hard to make sure everyone was ready for the trials that lay ahead, especially the twins, whose swordplay improved dramatically over the weeks training under Serenjols with help from Sonja.

After nearly four weeks out of Flora's port, the island of Tsalbrin appeared on the horizon. The call arose that land had been spotted, and Captain Galdur called his passengers together for one last speech. He looked them over and cracked a smile, and Kari figured he must've been happy that they'd proven such an easy lot to manage. Only Aeligos and Eryn's fighting had proven to be any concern whatsoever, and though it waxed and waned over the last month of the trip, it was quite bearable. Discipline came naturally to Kari as a demonhunter, but she imagined that when confined to a ship for months, even the best-natured of land-dwellers usually became antsy and, consequently, troublesome.

"As you've heard, we have reached our destination. We'll be docking in the city of Riverport, on the southeast coast," the captain said as his passengers stood at attention before him on the quarterdeck. "Riverport sits at the mouth of the Ursis River and is a busy trading port for ships coming from Terrassia, or Dannumore to the north. However, it's unlikely you'll want to start your actual journey in Riverport: there's nothing but rainforest around it, and it would take you considerable time to pass through the jungle. If your presence here is for the reasons I've heard, then most likely you'll want to find a ship to take you up the coast to Tingus."

"Why don't you just take us to Tingus, then?" Erik asked.

"I would if I had the time," Captain Galdur said, and he removed his hat and ran his fingers through his hair. "Unfortunately, what it comes down to is this: our job was to get you to Tsalbrin, and bringing you here is not the only reason we've come this far west. We've other things to attend to and a strict timetable for doing so, so we must continue on our way quickly."

"So you're just abandoning us, then?" Erik pressed, and he folded his muscular arms across his chest. Kari sucked in her lower lip; Erik could be very bull-headed at times, and he was about to throw away what had been a good relationship with the captain and his crew over something that was a minor inconvenience at worst.

"Watch your tone," Jori-an said from up on her platform, "or you'll be swimming the rest of the way to the island. We were contracted to get you here, and we've done that. We've upheld our end of this bargain."

Erik sighed and turned back to Galdur, but Sonja put a hand on his shoulder and spoke before he could. "And we appreciate your help," she told the captain. "I don't imagine it will be difficult to find a ship heading along the coast from Riverport to Tingus, will it?"

"Not at all," Captain Galdur said with a semi-apologetic look. "There is a major shipping lane along the east coast, from Riverport up to Dannumore and back, for bringing supplies and trade goods back and forth to the mainland."

Erik gave a curt nod, though he was clearly not happy with the turn of events. "Then that will have to do. Very well, thank you for your hospitality, captain," he said before he turned and fixed Jori-an with a squinting stare. "And that of your crew."

The first mate fixed Erik with a smile that could have said any one of a hundred different things, but she held her tongue. Kari wasn't sure what the issue was between the two; whatever had transpired that made them dislike each other had happened when Kari wasn't on deck. Kari followed her companions back down below decks to gather their belongings. When she returned to the quarterdeck, she dropped her pack, approached Jori-an, and shook the first mate's hand.

"Thank you for letting us use your quarters," Kari said. "I'm sure it's not something you're used to doing. Or required to, for that matter."

161

"You are paying passengers," Jori-an said with a shrug. "Making sure you're happy and comfortable is a part of my duty."

Kari shook her head. "You have the heart of a romantic," she said, pointing at the first mate, "whether you'd ever admit to it or not."

Jori-an said nothing and smiled only slightly, but a deeper one showed in her eyes. The mysterious look returned to her face after only a moment, and Kari had to wonder how good the seterra-rir first mate would've been at their poker games. On a hunch, Kari reached down as though pulling a coin from her purse, and she held her pinched fingers before her face before turning her empty palm and moving it away in a dismissive gesture. Jori-an's expression changed only slightly, but Kari could tell she was surprised and intrigued. As Kari expected, the first mate answered her gesture by reaching behind her ear as though pulling something forth, and then repeating the same end to the gesture as Kari had.

"Be safe," Jori-an said quietly after a moment. "And good luck in your mission."

"Will you be picking us up when we're done here?" Kari asked her.

"Possibly; it will depend on the timing of your success and our return."

Kari nodded, having received as detailed an answer as she expected, and she sat down on the bench across from the seterra-rir first mate. Soon Grakin and the rest of the group returned to the quarterdeck, and they waited patiently while the ship made its final approach to the island and eventually pulled into the port. Like in Flora, the passengers were required to remain on board while the captain and Master Calhoun went down to speak with the port authority, and Jori-an blocked egress. Nearly a half hour later, with daylight beginning to wane, they were invited down onto the pier and allowed to head into the city to find lodgings.

Their farewell from the captain was short and cordial, and they watched only briefly as he walked back up onto the deck and gave Master Calhoun the signal to get the ship underway. Erik waved for the group to follow him and made his way farther into the city. There were no inns down near the dock, so after looking around, he began to lead his companions higher up into the city. His stare drew Kari's back over the ocean to behold *Karmi's Sword* turn and begin heading farther west, and the blue-eyed male gave a tight-lipped sigh and beckoned for the group to follow. He muttered something about the importance of whatever Captain Galdur was on his way to do, but dismissed his own words with a shake of his head.

Riverport was a tiered city. The wooden docks constituted the lowest of the tiers, where the gapped planking showed slick rock below and there were no shops or services to be found. The only doors Kari saw on the lower tier were those of the port authority and harbor patrol, with a station on the centermost of the five piers for the guards. Farther to the west, she could see that there were other, angled piers for boats coming down the river. The mouth of the river was much larger than Kari expected after Captain Galdur first described the city and its location. There was a delta, suggesting the depth was insufficient for deeper-running ships like *Karmi's Sword* to head farther inland, and her thoughts were further enforced by the flatboats, barges, and skiffs she could see at those other piers. She wondered briefly how far inland the river went and whether she and her companions could find what they were looking for at the next port upriver.

Erik led everyone up a wooden staircase to the next tier of the city, and from there Kari could see much more of Riverport. The second tier was comprised mostly of warehouses and storage facilities, and the outer rim was lined with wooden cranes to ease the transport of cargo from the holds or decks of ships up to the higher level. Laborers lined the edge of the wooden overhang, which was set farther back than the lower level, and human and rir alike watched the group pass before turning their attention back to their work. From the higher vantage point, Kari could see there were two more tiers, and she wondered how much higher up the level ground was from the water. Erik quickened his pace, motioning with his hand for the others to keep up. Kari understood that he wasn't interested in being exposed with the possibility that Gaswell had eyes in the port city.

They reached the next stairway upward and ascended to the third tier of the city, and Kari saw this level was comprised of shops, inns, and taverns. In an uncharacteristic display, Erik headed into the first inn he could find, a ramshackle place with a little painted sign that simply read *The Port*. It seemed to matter little to Erik, and it was obvious he just wanted to get the group off the streets as quickly and quietly as possible. He gave the inn's interior only a cursory glance before he waved his siblings and friends in and then shut the door behind him as he entered last.

The inside was only slightly less dreary than the outside suggested, and it was obvious even from a glance that there weren't enough rooms for everyone. The common room was efficient but a little too cozy, with only half a dozen tables spread throughout, a hearth on the far right wall, and a bar that took up half of the back wall. The inn was unoccupied but for a single terra-rir standing behind the bar. He looked bored and cast a curious but neutral glance at the large party. He appeared to be fairly young: his long, vibrant white hair was tied back in a ponytail, and his ruby eyes were full of youth that was still obvious despite the boredom that filled them. He stood up straight and waited for the group to approach, so Erik gestured for the others to be seated and moved over toward the terra-rir. Kari followed him. When they reached the bar, Erik towered nearly a foot taller than the apparent proprietor.

"Welcome to the Port," the man said with a distinct lack of emotion. His accent was unfamiliar, thick with a drawl that Kari had never heard before, though it was not unpleasant. "Name's Marshall Landrie, proprietor. What can I do for you?"

"Erik Tesconis," he said, extending his hand, though the man simply stared at it a few moments before meeting the larger man's gaze again. Erik pulled his hand back and continued, "We could use lodgings, at least for the night, and would appreciate some food and drink in the meantime."

"And why should I let you stay here?" the man asked evenly. Young or not, his facial expression was quite unwelcoming, and he leaned back and folded his arms across his chest. Kari found the reaction strange, given the size of the man he was speaking to.

Erik was taken aback. "Why wouldn't you?"

"Because you're obviously half-demons," Marshall said. "It's dangerous to associate with your kind these days."

Typhonix started to rise from his seat but Erik motioned for him to sit back down. Kari had little doubt what Typhonix' solution to the innkeeper's attitude would have been. Erik simply reached into his coin purse, pulled forth three platinum coins, and set them down before the man. It was an exhorbitant amount of money to spend on a single night's stay at an inn, but Marshall looked the coins over for only a few seconds before he picked them up and slid them into his pocket. He studied the group briefly once more, pulled a number of pewter mugs from under the bar, and began filling them with ale and placing them before Erik.

"Excuse my manners, but with all this nonsense going on with Gaswell, my inn's been empty for weeks. Having it suddenly fill with half-breeds won't look good," Marshall said after he'd filled the last tankard. "Let me give you some friendly advice: I'll let you stay here the night, but be out of the city by morning. Likely the local goons have already either noticed your presence or been told about you. Rest assured that trouble's going to find you if you stay here more than a day."

Erik ignored the *half-breeds* comment. "Do you have any news?" Erik asked, and Aeligos approached when he overheard the conversation.

"You just land here?" the innkeeper asked, and Erik nodded. "If you've ever heard of Eric Gaswell, one of his descendants has been pushing to 'purify' the island by removing anyone not terra-rir from it. Even our

164

brother races – shakna-rir, fures-rir, even you half-demons – to him, no one else is welcome."

"That much we know," Erik said. "What's been happening more recently?"

"So far, nothing," Marshall said, and he began polishing the bar despite the fact that it was spotless. "Most of what he's done so far is just posturing, but rumors started spreading around the city recently that he's holding some kirelas-rir war wizard or such. Most folks seem to think he's going to use her as a hostage, but since nobody's really sure what he's after, it's hard to know what to expect."

"Anything else you can tell us?" Aeligos asked as he leaned forward against the bar.

"About what?" Marshall returned.

"Have you heard anything regarding demonic activity of any sort?" Erik asked. The question seemed to catch the innkeeper off guard, and Kari took a chance and pulled out her dog tags. When Erik did so as well, Marshall seemed to immediately grasp the reason he had a room full of half-demons. His demeanor changed, though still not to a friendly or welcoming one.

"Thankfully, I haven't," he said with a shake of his head. "I think there's a church to Zalkar up on the topmost tier of the city, if you're here for work. If we're lucky, Gaswell's little crusade will include the serilian demons, too. We don't see many of them around these parts, especially since you foreigners won the war, but if there's a church to Zalkar here and a bunch of demonhunters sitting in my inn, I guess there's enough of them to be a problem."

"Well, thank you for the information," Erik said, though Marshall simply shrugged. "How many rooms do you have available?"

"Six," Marshall answered, casting a glance toward the doors spread at even intervals along the north side of the room, and there were two more on the back wall beside the bar. "You're free to take them all. As I said, I haven't had a customer in weeks. But the rooms will not be available tomorrow night, if you catch my meaning."

"Clearly," Erik said, and he, Kari, and Aeligos took up the drinks and headed over to the rest of their companions. "We've only got six rooms, so a few of us are going to have to pair up. Kari and Grakin can obviously share one room. Sonja and Eryn can take another, and…"

"Eryn can stay with me," Aeligos said.

"Are you sure?" Erik asked. "You two can't have a fight and draw attention to us. From what the innkeeper said, we've already attracted too much attention and are likely to attract a lot more before we can get out of the city."

"There won't be an issue," Eryn said evenly.

"Fine," Erik said. "Ty and I will take the third room, Jol and Sherman can take the fourth, and then Sonja and Katarina can have their own rooms." There were nods all around the table, and Erik paused a moment to take a sip of his drink and look over his shoulder at the innkeeper. Marshall seemed to remember something that needed tending in the kitchen and left the group alone.

"All right, we need to go over some things," the blue-eyed male said, scratching absently at the side of his snout. "First thing being our mission here: you'll have to forgive me but I haven't exactly been forthright with you all regarding the reason we were sent here. In addition to everything else going on here, my superiors have reason to believe there's demonic activity as well. Since we don't have a lot of details, we're going on the assumption that it is somehow connected to Gaswell's sudden interest in purging the island."

"Why didn't you tell us this during the trip?" Sonja asked, flustered.

"To avoid weeks of argument," Erik said. "There's no room for debate on this. Kari and I have been assigned to look into the situation while the rest of you start gathering information and allies to quell the brewing rebellion."

Sonja was clearly not happy with the revelation, but it was Typhonix who spoke up next. "They don't want me to help you?" he asked with a disappointed look. Kari could imagine how he felt, being the only one of the three demonhunters that was not a part of the plan.

Erik took a long sip of his ale and let the silence hang for a minute before he continued. "The Order assumes that Kari and I will be enough to handle whatever the problem is," he said. "With the amount of actual detail they've received, it's obviously nothing so powerful that it requires three of us to look into. Ty, I need you with the group for this: they're going to need your muscle and your brains. Getting information is not going to be easy, especially if Gaswell has as large a following as I'm starting to suspect. Be sensible: let Aeligos and Sonja do the talking when there's talking to be done, and if that doesn't work, then you can try strong-arm tactics. This innkeeper's not exactly chatty, so we still need to learn a lot before we can establish a plan. You know I don't like leaving you all, but I've got orders and my first duty in this situation is to Zalkar and what he needs done. I trust you to get the rest of our mission started, and Ty – I trust you to keep the others safe."

Typhonix nodded and leaned forward on his elbows as Sonja spoke. "Do you know where you're going to start looking?" the scarlet-haired woman asked.

Erik looked briefly to Kari, and she nodded her head upwards. "As I said, we don't have any details, really. But the barkeep said to check farther up in the city for a church of Zalkar, so we'll start there. The rest of you should head farther north to Tingus like Captain Galdur said. If I recall correctly, there's a shakna-rir kingdom to the north, and I'm sure they won't be too happy about some warlord wanting to push them off the island."

The others laughed. The shakna-rir kingdoms were matriarchal but tended to be heavily militaristic, and when threatened, they didn't hesitate to crush their enemies. The only advantage one could realistically gain over them was that of climate, as they couldn't tolerate the cold for very long and their armies generally failed under wintry conditions. In almost every other circumstance, thanks to their highly organized militaries and considerable populations, they had virtually no equal in war. The thought that Gaswell might actually challenge them with an army comprised of only one race was baffling. He surely would have no luck gaining an advantage due to the climate here on Tsalbrin.

"That's probably our best place to start," Aeligos said. "If all else fails, we may be able to prod the shakna-rir to spearhead south and crush this rebellion before it gains any momentum. They won't like what Gaswell's planning."

"Agreed," Sonja said.

"It shouldn't be too difficult, either," Typhonix said. "War is good for the social and economic systems the shakna-rir have. If they get an excuse to leave the desert and look at the lands to the south and west, they will." Kari wasn't the only one to fix him with an amused gaze, and he shrugged. "What? You don't think I read those books because they're exciting, do you?"

That drew further laughter from the group. "Remember, our goal is to *avert* war if we're able," Erik said. "If they wanted the shakna-rir to crush Gaswell and conquer half the island, they'd have sent different emissaries to accomplish that. I think the assumption we're to go on is that the demon is somehow behind this, and that war is probably the demon's ultimate goal. War on the island will attract the attention of the larger nations of Dannumore, and if *they* decide to go to war, it'll look like the Apocalypse all over again."

"I wonder if traveling up the river will take us anywhere near Tingus?"

Kari mused.

"I think Captain Galdur would've mentioned it if it did," Erik answered. "Likely it just leads into the heart of the rainforest, or maybe the island...hard to know without seeing a map. From the way the captain mentioned it, I'm guessing the entire southeast of this island is nothing but rainforest, so taking a ship to Tingus is what you all should do. Kari and I may join you depending on what information we get from the church."

"Is there anything else our illustrious host was willing to share?" Typhonix asked.

"Something about Gaswell taking a kirelas-rir war wizard hostage," Erik said, but he shrugged. "We can't be concerned with that at this point. As callous as it may sound, we're not here to save one life, we're here to save many. Risking everything to try to save one woman would be a fatal mistake. It's unlikely he'll do anything to her if he hasn't already, but we'll worry about that when we have more information."

"So we are planning to leave by the morning?" Grakin asked, and he glanced at Kari.

"Yes," Erik said. "Aeligos, I want you to head down to the pier and see if you can find a ship that will take all of us, if necessary, to Tingus. Captain Galdur sounded confident that it would be easy to find passage, so we shouldn't delay. Kari and I will head farther up into the city and see if there really is a church up there, whether to Zalkar or any of his allies. At the very least we should be able to get more reliable information than we have so far."

"I'll head down now," Aeligos said. He took a last sip of his ale, and then he deposited his pack in one of the rooms before he left the inn.

"Shall we go?" Kari asked.

"Not yet," Erik said, eyeing her briefly. "I don't want too many of us going out all at once in case the inn is already being watched. You should all get your things settled in your rooms, make sure there are no unsecured windows for anyone to slip in through, and then stay out here in a group once Kari and I are gone. Ty, watch the door. If trouble shows up, break someone's back, and if that's not enough to dissuade them, you and Jol do what you need to."

"Understood," the blonde warrior said, and Serenjols nodded his agreement.

The twins looked shocked to hear Erik speak so frankly of possibly killing strangers, but it seemed to fade fast as they realized the gravity of the situation. Katarina and Sherman glanced at each other, and the young woman nodded at her brother. Kari got the impression that though the twins were green, they understood what was at stake and were fully prepared to follow the lead of their more experienced companions. Everyone stowed their packs and secured the windows of the rooms they chose, though the portals weren't large enough for anyone to climb through. The rooms were narrow, as were the beds, and it quickly became apparent that the non-couples sharing rooms would have at least one person sleeping on the floor. It was an easy enough choice in all cases, as the larger Tesconis siblings wouldn't fit in the beds anyway.

Kari and Grakin got acquainted with their bed, and figured they could both sleep in it at the same time, though it would barely be comfortable. Kari smiled and Grakin returned it: they would just have to make the best of it. They had just begun exchanging kisses when Erik knocked on the door and asked if they were busy. Grakin invited his older brother in, and the blue-eyed male pushed the door open, leaned against its frame, and looked the two over.

"Are you ready?" he asked as his gaze swung to Kari, and she was on her feet near-instantly. She put her dog tags back inside her breastplate and Erik did the same after a moment. Kari gave her mate one more kiss before she and Erik left the inn.

Evening was closing in on the port city as they exited the inn, and the sun, sitting just above the horizon, bathed the west-facing tiers with its glory. The demonhunters looked around briefly, trying to be nonchalant about it, and Kari didn't see anyone who was obviously watching the inn. They made their way quickly to the wooden stairs up to the next level and found that it was the final of the main tiers that ringed the port. There was another tier built atop the peak of the hill to the east, and from their new vantage point the two could see that the hillside the port was terraced into dropped off into a lush, misty woodland that appeared to be without end.

Erik pointed to the final tier on the hilltop, and Kari followed him along one of the wooden-planked streets leading in that direction. The tier they were on seemed to be for homes, and though the hillside was mainly stone, the builders had apparently chosen to craft scaffold-like structures rather than carve the rock face. The homes at the top were all fashioned of wood and looked to be cheaply made compared to what Kari had seen in the cities she'd visited. Kari regarded Erik for a moment, and found that he seemed to be thinking the same thing.

"I think it's because of the weather," he said. "They get those powerful tropical storms here...probably have to rebuild parts of the city fairly often."

Kari nodded and the two continued on their way, and at last they came to the final staircase that led up to the peak of the hill. When they reached the top step, they could see that *churches* was a relative term. They were shrines: open-faced structures with an eternal flame in the center of each, marked with the symbols of the major temples in Sarchelete, and there were only a half-dozen in total. A human in a hooded robe was tending to the shrines, watering flowers that had been left by visitors and cleaning up debris that had been blown across the hilltop by the coastal winds. He looked up when the two approached and his expression was cautious, but Kari pulled forth her tags, assuming that a human was unlikely to be serving a warlord that wanted to remove humans from the island. The man's gaze turned respectful when he saw Kari's dog tags, and Erik pulled his forth as well.

Erik and Kari came to a stop before the man. "Good afternoon," Erik said. The human was older but had the look of a retired adventurer for what little the demonhunters could see of him. "Are you an acolyte here, or just the groundskeeper?"

Emerald eyes sparkled as a smile creased the human's thin, weathered face. "Just the groundskeeper for the shrines these days," he said. "What can I do for you, officers?"

The demonhunters shared a brief glance. "Just wondering if you've heard about any demonic activity on the island," Erik said. "We've been sent by the Unyielding to look into some rumored trouble, but details were sketchy at best."

"Demon activity?" the human repeated, rubbing his chin for a moment. "Nothing I've heard about from any of the other ports or towns we trade with. If there's anything out there causing trouble of the sort Zalkar would be interested in, it's keeping to the shadows. Of course, most of the news and talk is about Gaswell these days."

"Is there anyone else we could check with that might know?" Erik asked.

"Closest church to Zalkar would be over in Talvor," the man answered. "As I said, though, no news has come from there or any other ports regarding demons. I suppose you could always check with the czarikk. They control most of the rainforest to the north and east, though not so much near the Ursis River or to the west of it."

The czarikk were reptilian people who kept mostly to the swamps and deeper forests of the various continents around the world. Generally they weren't troublesome, as they preferred to only trade with outsiders when absolutely necessary, and they very rarely made war on their neighbors. They were a people of the bow and the spear: they fished, hunted, and gathered to sustain themselves, and history spoke of very few times when territorial disputes had broken out involving the czarikk. Overall, they seemed most happy when left alone, and the rir, humans, and demihumans of the world were just as happy to leave them be.

"How do you mean 'control?'" the blue-eyed male asked.

"The rainforest, or at least the eastern half of it, is generally respected as theirs," the man clarified, and he sat on a stone bench. "They allow us to maintain this port here, and they keep their distance from the city of Ursis farther up the river. In return, we leave them be. There were some frontiersmen years back that started to clear some of the forest to establish farms...that hasn't been tried again since. The czarikk may not like to make war but they're certainly a force to be reckoned with when their lands are threatened."

"Do you know where their tribe is based?" Erik prodded.

The man shook his head. "Afraid I don't," he said. "You'd be best served either finding a guide or just following the mule trail down the backside of the hill into the forest. If you've got a compass, you can just keep heading north until you find what you're looking for. Chances are if you don't find the czarikk, they'll find you. I hope you can speak their language."

"Speak it? I've never even *heard* their language," Erik said, and he glanced toward Kari. "Have you?"

Kari nodded. It had been years since she'd encountered one of the lizard-folk, but she remembered several of the incidents quite well. "Can't speak it, but I've heard it before," she said. "You've never met a czarikk?"

Erik shook his head. "Never been down near Mandar-Czar," he said. "Or anywhere else they call home. What're they like?"

Kari waved off the question; there would be a better time to fill him in on the lizard-folk. She turned her attention back to the human, who rose to his feet. "Thanks for the information," she said. "May I ask your name?"

The man shook his head and waved a finger. "No, you may not," he said. "And I don't want to know your names. The less we know of each other, the better. I don't need any trouble for having spoken to a couple of half-demons, demonhunters or not."

"I'm not half-demon," Kari said.

"You explain that to Gaswell's men and see if they care to make a distinction," he said. "I have no love for Gaswell or his goons, obviously, but I have to live here and I don't need any trouble from them. You'd best keep away from the heartlands and the southwest of the island, that's where he and his men have the most influence. If you're smart, you'll do as your lord asked and get off this island before war erupts."

"Will do," Kari said. She thanked the human once more, and then she and Erik made their way back to the inn. They still didn't notice anything suspicious along their route, and soon they were back with their companions in the common room of *The Port*. Aeligos had returned from his own task, and Marshall was just beginning to serve his guests dinner with the same bland expression that had dominated his features since they'd arrived. Erik and Kari took seats with their friends and waited for the innkeeper to finish serving the meals before he disappeared into the back room.

"Any luck?" Erik asked his younger brother.

"There's a ship leaving for Tingus tomorrow," Aeligos said. "It's not as big as *Karmi's Sword*, so it won't be cheap to get eight of us on board, and less so if it's all ten of us."

"That won't be an issue," Erik said, holding a hand up. "Kari and I will be heading into the rainforest, as the czarikk out there are the only lead we have to find any real information about the demonic activity we're looking for. I assume you already reserved your spots?"

Aeligos nodded. "Of course, but only for eight since they seemed unlikely to refund our money if you two decided not to come along. Something else I should mention: the city of Ursis upriver seems to either be a Gaswell bastion or just full of sympathizers. I asked about transport up the river, but most of the boatmen found excuses why they couldn't take us. One even suggested that 'someone like me' wouldn't last very long there. So if you've been pointed to the rainforest to find the czarikk, that seems like a much better option than going upriver to Ursis."

"What are the sah-reek?" Sherman asked.

"Lizard-folk," Kari said. "I used to run into them in Solaris and other cities on Terrassia now and then. They take a little getting used to, but I've always found them to be a handsome and friendly folk once you get to know them. The thing you have to keep in mind with them is they have a strong sense of personal honor – in other words, pride – so you've got to be careful with sarcasm and teasing with them. If you insult the fact that they're reptilian, you're going to make a quick enemy."

Erik regarded her curiously but said nothing, and the others were also clearly curious as to how much Kari knew about the reclusive czarikk. She told them about the rare times she'd met one in the city of Solaris, which they passed through from time to time, and filled in as much detail as she could about what the lizard-folk were like. Once everyone finished eating and Marshall cleared away their plates, Erik produced a deck of cards.

They played a friendly game, wagering imaginary coins that Aeligos kept tallied on a piece of paper. Erik wanted everyone to relax, particularly him and Kari, so they could get a good night's sleep before their journey took them into the heart of trouble.

They played cards for a few hours before Erik ordered everyone to their rooms. Grakin closed the door to his and Kari's room, and Kari sat on the edge of their bed. He approached, dropped to his knees before her, and looked up to her eyes, and she could clearly see the worry in his dark gaze. She stroked his cheek lightly and leaned down to kiss his forehead, and then she stood to undress. He began to undress as well after a moment, and soon he lay on the bed with Kari straddling him in the smooth purple lingerie she had purchased in Flora. "This may be our last night together," he said solemnly.

"Just for a couple of weeks," Kari corrected, leaning over him on her arms to meet his gaze evenly. "Nothing's gonna stop me from coming back to you, Grakin. I want to have your babies, and I don't care if it's Celigus Chinchala himself out there causing trouble, I'll find a way to kill him and come back to you. That's a promise."

Grakin chuckled but it was uneasy. Kari undressed the rest of the way and they took comfort in their love. Their lovemaking was passionate and needful, and they clung tightly to each other, knowing that despite what she'd said, it was a very real possibility that they wouldn't see each other again. Kari wondered how long it would take Grakin to get used to her being in such a dangerous line of work, and whether his trust in the gods would let him simply be proud of what she did rather than constantly worried for her safety. They made love for a while before the size of the bed forced them onto their sides to sleep. Kari turned her back to Grakin as he preferred, and he pulled her into his embrace and wrapped his left arm over her protectively. She found it easy to fall asleep with his warm chest against her back and his arm lovingly around her, and she slept soundly through the night, to the relief of both.

They rose the next morning to the sound of voices outside their door and dressed quickly. When Kari opened the door she found Aeligos pacing back and forth while Erik tried to calm him down. The larger male's efforts were for naught, as Aeligos seemed to just get more and more upset, and soon the rest of the group joined them in the common room. With the urging of his sister, Aeligos finally took a seat, as did the others, and Marshall appeared with fresh biscuits, honey, and fruit juice for his guests.

"Where's Eryn?" Kari asked after their charming host had left.

"She's gone," Erik answered, obviously hoping to prevent his younger brother from starting another tirade, but it was no use.

"I *knew* she would do this," Aeligos said. "I knew from the start she wasn't going to work with us and she'd take the first opportunity to slip off and try doing things on her own."

Kari held her hand up, which brought her companion's rant to an end, and she kept her voice down. "She's probably been hired by someone to assassinate Gaswell," she said. "If anything, she could make our mission here easier."

"Not likely," Erik said. "If anything, history has shown that when someone like Gaswell actually attracts followers, they'll just pick up right where he left off if he's killed. I'm confident Eryn knows that, and she won't do anything rash, but if she's just getting paid for his head and the end result doesn't matter to her or her sponsor, then we don't know for sure."

"We cannot concern ourselves with any of that," Jol said, but he didn't elaborate.

Sonja nodded and picked up her eldest brother's train of thought. "No, we must proceed the way we would if she never came: all we've lost is the cost of her spot on the boat."

There was an uneasy, silent agreement among the group, but Kari and the others all knew they had lost far more than a gold deposit. They shared their breakfast quietly. Once finished, they took their packs and headed to the docks, where Aeligos led them to a single-mast ship called *Coastrunner*. He spoke briefly with the guards at the base of the gangplank, and then waved for his siblings and human companions to join him. Erik and Kari remained on the pier, and after their companions had put their belongings in the ship's cabin, Grakin returned. He approached Kari and they hugged, holding each other tightly for several minutes before they separated slightly for a long, passionate kiss. Grakin stroked Kari's face affectionately and she tousled his hair, and both ignored Typhonix as he leaned on the railing, staring at them and trying to be funny about it.

After another minute, Kari nodded toward the ship and Grakin hugged her again before he rejoined his siblings on deck. "I'll be back, I promise you," she said.

"And I will be waiting," the priest said, smiling at her from near the railing.

"We'll see you soon," Erik said, and the others waved goodbye. Kari and Erik watched the ship set out from the port, and once it turned with the wind and made its way around the southern cape, the blue-eyed male turned toward Kari. "You have everything you need?"

Kari hefted her pack and gave a confident nod. "Yes, but I don't carry a compass; do you have one? The human up top said we'd need one to get through the rainforest."

Erik nodded. "Let's be off, then. We've got a demon to kill."

Chapter X – Bond of Trust

They ascended to the topmost tier of the city, and Kari took a moment to smile down at the ship carrying her mate before she and Erik found the mule trail down the backside of the hill. It was steep and the footing was rocky, but after a while they managed to reach the bottom, far below the canopy of the jungle. The base of the rocky cliff was wet and litter-strewn, as rainfall, wastewater, and debris apparently dropped off the backside of the city-capped hill. The two avoided the obvious muck and refuse, and looked at the thick maze of trees before them. Erik regarded Kari and she nodded, and they set off into the jungle.

The coastal breeze was cut off immediately, giving way to an oppressive, sticky heat that soon had Kari sweating. She shed her cloak, rolled it up, and tied it down to the top of her pack, and looked to her companion. Not surprisingly, Erik was completely unfazed by the heat, with not a drop of sweat upon his half-demon form. He didn't seem particularly fond of the humidity though, and he tied his hair back tightly in a tail before motioning for Kari to follow.

The trees here were thick and ancient, and many of their trunks were covered with heavy vines and other hanging plants that could survive with less sunlight. The trees' crowns formed a blanketing canopy overhead that allowed little light through to the ground, lending a thick shade to the misty floor. There was more than enough light to see, but the murky mist made it even more difficult than the density of the trees themselves. The forest floor was damp and covered with a thinner carpet of leaves than Kari had expected: she was used to the deeper drifts of leaves in the southern portions of Terrassia's forests. Here, however, the leaves – at least those that fell – seemed to decay at a faster rate, leaving rich soil but not much that would give away their footsteps or conceal natural and man-made hazards.

Kari regarded Erik, and he looked to his compass briefly before pointing them in the right direction. She fell into step beside him and they walked along in silence for several hours. The air was thick with bird calls and other, unfamiliar animal sounds, and they tried to keep their pace steady. Both were accomplished fighters, and Kari was confident that little the rainforest could put in their way would prove troublesome. Kari also wanted to spend as little time in the rainforest as possible on account of its name: while neither of them had ever visited such a place before, Kari was able to point out the signs that the place received a substantial amount of rain. Erik seemed surprised at her familiarity with such things, but took her points attentively: they didn't want to be exposed to the elements for too long regardless of the island's tropical nature.

Night fell early, as the thickness of the canopy and their location on the island's eastern end meant the light was choked out far sooner than they were accustomed to. They decided against traveling in the dark and instead collected what little dry wood they could and set up a small camp. They started a fire only long enough to cook some food, and once their hunger was sated they doused the flames and nestled between the exposed thick roots of a massive tree. Kari decided it would be easier to simply sleep in her armor, since it was light and supple and she had no idea if anything would decide to investigate their presence while they slept.

Erik didn't have the luxury of sleeping in his armor: the heavy plate and chain suit he wore was far too restrictive to get any sort of restful sleep within it. Kari figured it had to be exceedingly uncomfortable in the sweltering humidity, but fortunately his half-demon heritage meant it wasn't an issue for him. Erik took off his armor and then sat back against a sizeable protruding root, and Kari noted that the garments he wore under the armor were still mostly dry. When she glanced at him, he looked her over curiously in turn, and he finally spoke when she laid out her bedroll and bunched her cloak up as a makeshift pillow. "Is that paluric?" he asked.

Kari looked down at her armor briefly before she folded her hands behind her head and lay back. "Yes, it is," she said. "You had to have noticed it before."

"I did," he agreed, shrugging. "I just wasn't sure; I've never seen paluric armor before. Where did you get it?"

"It was given to me a long time ago, by an old friend," she said.

Erik gave her a doubtful look and then shook his head. "I find that hard to believe," he commented.

Kari was pointedly reminded of the fact that he even doubted who she was: Eryn had told her that Erik apparently thought Kari was an impostor of some kind. "You find a lot of things hard to believe," Kari returned. "Doesn't make them any less true. If you only believe in what you see for yourself, you're not going to make it very far as a demonhunter."

Erik's brows arched before settling closely over suspicious eyes. He scratched behind a pointed ear for a moment and looked as though he were about to speak, but instead he pulled his pack between his legs and started digging through it. He came up with a thick-bristled brush, and after

178

loosing the tail he'd kept his hair in, he began to brush it silently. It was clear from his expression that he knew exactly what she meant, and she wondered why he didn't press her on the issue or admit he had been foolish.

Kari sighed, closed her eyes, and attempted to find the quiet within to fall asleep. Her thoughts turned immediately to Grakin: she missed his touch and his presence that acted so much like a child's security blanket, and his warmth that had so easily eased her to sleep over their many nights together. She nearly laughed and the corners of her snout creased up into a smile as she considered that she didn't miss the heat of his half-demon body at that moment. While the jungle had cooled off slightly, the heat was still oppressive and pushed down on her like an unseen hand.

"So who was this friend?" Erik asked after the long silence between them deepened and she had nearly fallen asleep.

Kari opened one eye and fixed him with an impatient gaze, and she snorted. "Goodnight, Erik," she said simply, and she turned on her side to face away from him. She could tell by his tone that he wouldn't believe anything she said anyway, so she felt no desire to waste her time telling him about it. She could feel the weight of his stare on her back, but he said nothing, and soon she fell into a light but sweaty sleep. She awoke with a start as he touched her shoulder and asked her to take watch so he could get a few hours of sleep. She had no idea how long she'd been asleep, but she had slept well despite the temperature.

Kari sat up against one of the roots while Erik bedded down on his cloak. She recalled how her friend Carly had always told her that one could tell a lot about someone by watching them sleep, and she kept her attention on the dozing half-demon for several hours. He seemed calm: he was certainly at peace with himself and his duties enough to allow him to sleep without interruption. No dreams or nightmares rocked him from his slumber, and there was no trace that he faced anything similar to Kari's hellish memories. It made her wonder what Carly had meant, since by watching her companion, the only thing she could tell was that he was asleep.

She looked over his muscular form, from his powerful arms to his thick legs, and finally to his belly, which was as sculpted as hers. Physically he was a perfect specimen: he looked as though he were carved from a solid block of ebony. She imagined many would disagree, unable to see past the wings that marked him as a half-demon, but Kari had wings as well and found him undeniably attractive. He had a wide snout and a powerful chin, and she knew from experience that both lent him an imposing countenance that served him well as the group's leader. His hair was long in the tradition of rir warriors, and he kept it straight and tended to it well. Erik was perhaps a bit too big for her – in more ways than one – but all told, he was a fine looking male.

He had stripped down to his loincloth, which told her that he at least trusted her to keep him safe while he slept. Considering half-guardians could go for days or even weeks without sleeping, that said a lot. Such trust came naturally to Kari after an eight-year war: if one wanted to sleep at all, it required trusting someone, whether one liked them or would ever trust them outside of war or not. As she thought about it, though, she wondered if his near-nudity had any other purpose: whether he was trying to tell her *look what you missed out on by choosing Grakin*. She nearly laughed at the thought: if that was his intent, it'd had the opposite effect.

Her gaze swung to his carefully piled equipment: the fine set of plate and chain armor that she assumed was steel, along with the masterfully crafted scimitar and longsword. She could tell by the craftsmanship of the hilts that both weapons were made specifically for him, and she remembered being told that Serenjols had crafted all of the siblings' armor and weapons himself. Erik's scimitar was unlike the twin ones Kari wielded: his had notches and grooves on its backside meant to disarm foes or pull weapons out of position. Her own had a sharpened backside up by the tip, a handy part that allowed her to land a chopping strike when necessary – such as cleaving through plate armor. Hers also had two notches for fingers should they ever need to be used two-handed for defense, though such a situation had never arisen.

Kari suddenly realized that one of his eyes was open and he was watching her as intently as she was studying him and his equipment. Neither of them spoke for a few minutes, and then Kari noticed the strange calls and songs of the night had switched over to those of awakening birds. She hadn't even noticed the night passing, but she smiled after a minute when she realized Carly had been right: she had learned a bit more about her partner simply by looking at him and his things while he slept.

Erik arched an eyebrow. He sat up and looked Kari over briefly but said nothing, apparently still annoyed by her words earlier in the night. He began to put on his armor, and then he stood and belted on his swords. Kari still sat looking at him, so he sat on the root he'd leaned against earlier and stared at her in return. "What is it?" he asked.

"Just wondering what your parents fed you as a child," she said, allowing a cheeky grin to see if his attitude would improve or if it was going to be another long, silent day.

180

Erik rolled his eyes, and she wondered at the reaction. "Our grandfathers were both guardian demons," he said.

"I know that much," she said. "It just seems strange that you and Jol are so big, and Grakin and Aeligos are, well, not small, but closer to normal."

"They're more like our mother; Sonja and Typhonix...fall somewhere in between," the half-demon said dryly. Kari nodded, and Erik folded his hands before him and leaned forward. "What exactly attracted you to my brother?"

His tone set her on edge immediately. "Jealousy doesn't fit you well," Kari said, making it quite clear that her words were a warning.

Erik waved a hand dismissively. "This has nothing to do with jealousy," he said. "This has to do with protecting my brother. Grakin's a little on the frail side. He's been shy and quiet ever since he became a priest, and he wears himself out far too often helping other people. He's changed a lot since you laid him and I'm left to wonder what your intentions really are. There's far too much potential for you to hurt him."

Kari was stunned, and her jaw fell open slightly. "I did not *lay* him, you arrogant bastard," she said, and she rose to her feet and began to pack her things. "What's this about? Why bring this up now? Why not when he was with me?"

"I don't trust you," he said evenly, and when she turned to look at him, his features were hardened into a scowl. "I don't believe you are who you say you are, and I don't appreciate you taking advantage of some false fame to try to seduce my brother."

"False fame? What the hell...?" Kari began, and she shook her head. "Just who do you think I am, anyway? Do you think I'm really Annabelle Sol'ridachi, that I'm sleeping with your brother to irritate you, and when we find this demon I'll need you to protect me because I'm just some stupid woman?"

Erik waved his hand dismissively again. "Look, I get it. Bosimar got killed during the Apocalypse and the Order needed a hero to keep morale up. I don't blame you for that, but continuing to pretend you're Karian Vanador now...it's not amusing anymore. If you want my respect, you're going to have to earn it on your own merits, not by charading as someone else."

Kari tilted her head, astounded. "Are you serious?" she asked. She pulled the dog tags from her neck, threw them at him, and growled, "What do you think, I went and dug these up in Laeranore?!"

Erik caught the tags easily and his mouth tightened into a line. He held

181

the dog tags up and read their inscription, but then held them back out to her. "What's that supposed to mean?" he asked.

Kari started to walk away, but stopped herself. They were in a rainforest, and though she was pretty sure she could get back to Riverport without much trouble – or at the very least, find the coast and head back to the city – she realized she really couldn't walk away. "Laeranore, Erik," she said, trying to keep her temper in check. "That's what the elves call their homeland. If you studied my life at the Academy, I'd think they'd have mentioned where I was *buried*."

"Wait, what?"

Kari turned around and pushed his hand with her dog tags back towards him. "Keep those," she said. "When we get back to Askies, you can go tell Master Bennet and Lord Allerius that you don't believe I'm really Karian Vanador." He started to speak, but she waved her hand in a dismissive gesture. She nearly clipped the end of his snout with her fingers, and a part of her wished she had: she wanted to punch him in his arrogant chin. "You know what? Forget it. Take them back to our superiors and tell them I quit. When they ask where I am, tell them I'm on Salkorum 'laying' your brother. Maybe you can even keep the disgust out of your voice."

Erik stared at her in shock. "I don't understand; you mean to say you really *are* Karian Vanador?" Kari rolled her eyes and looked away into the forest. "Honestly, how can this be? I studied your career when I was in the Academy, and now here you are, alive and well, serving as my partner? How was I supposed to know that…that…you were resurrected? Assuming that's what happened…you were resurrected?"

Kari nodded and folded her arms across her chest, biting down her urge to either slap him, scream at him, or simply walk away. Master Surallis had warned her that people might find it hard to believe that she was resurrected, but after spending two months with Erik aboard the ship, Kari could hardly believe he was still this ignorant. "Gods, Erik, didn't you pay attention to anything that was said on the ship?" she asked. "How could you have listened to the stories, the way Sonja and Eryn and I interacted, and even sparred against me and still had no idea?"

"I thought…I thought it was all part of your 'act,'" he said. "I thought it was weird that the Order would've gone to so much trouble to prop up some false hero to boost morale, but it's even stranger to think you're a dead woman come back to life. I'm not sure which should be harder to believe. This is all…more than a little strange."

Kari cocked her head. "Try having it happen to you," she said evenly.

Erik looked back up, let out an uncomfortable chuckle, and acknowledged the point with a nod. He stared at her for several minutes as though seeing her for the first time, and despite how upset she was, Kari could see the wonder and confusion written plainly on those normally hardened features. "I can't believe this...you're the girl that killed an erestram single-handedly?" he ventured.

Kari wondered what it was that made that point in particular hard for him to believe. Was it that she was smaller than him, not as strong, or was it because he'd seen her cry on a few occasions? Whatever the case, she shook her head. "*Defeated*," Kari corrected, "not killed. You wouldn't believe how hard they are to kill."

"But if you're really Karian Vanador, then you're a Shield of the Heavens," Erik said, and Kari nodded. "Why would they put me in charge of you? You're three ranks higher than I am, and if what our history books say about you is all true, you're certainly more qualified."

Kari sighed and closed her eyes. "Several reasons," she said. "They want to know if you're as good as your rank suggests. They also want to know if you're a good leader, probably because they see you becoming Avatar at some point. And frankly, my mind's been foggy since I was brought back, for some reason I don't understand."

"Honestly?" he asked, surprised.

Kari opened her eyes again and nodded. "Honestly," she said. "I know it's hard to believe a dead woman is standing in front of you; I don't really understand it all myself. But the Order wants me to watch you, Erik: they want to know if you're good at leading people. Right now I'd have to say the answer is 'no.' Your siblings may do what you tell them to and the twins may be willing to follow along, but that doesn't make you a leader. You need to learn to trust people, and trust the people under you, and they have to be able to trust you in return. I served under Kris Jir'tana; he was a brilliant leader. You...you're too suspicious for your own good, and you don't give people a chance to prove themselves before you just pass judgment on them."

She half-expected Erik to get defensive, but he said nothing as he held her gaze steadily. Finally, he glanced at her tags once more. "I guess I owe you an apology," he said quietly, but he shook his head. "Why didn't they tell me you're *the* Karian Vanador? Why keep it a secret?"

"It wasn't kept a secret, Erik. They wanted to see what your reaction would be, and I just don't like the attention or the prying that comes with people knowing who I am...or was," Kari explained. She was amazed at how well she was keeping her emotions in check. "Like you said, my career gets studied by recruits at the Academy. Everyone in Jir'tana's brigade knew who I was. And whenever someone knows who I am, they expect me to start telling them all about my life as if we're friends. Like you said, you know? 'Oh wow, you killed an erestram? How did you do it? What's your secret?'"

Erik nodded and Kari sighed, tightening her mouth into a line. "The Order didn't tell you clearly because they didn't want you to just follow me, and they didn't want you to know you were being watched. I really shouldn't even be telling you this. I don't know why they kept promoting you if they don't trust in your abilities, but that's not for me to say. Whatever the case, I'm here to help you, and you can depend on me to do exactly that."

Erik grunted a laugh. "That'd be the one thing I don't doubt at this point. This is all still very hard to believe, but..." he said, but then he cocked his head. "Does Grakin know? Gods, am I the only one who didn't?"

"Grakin, Eryn, and Sonja know; I'm not sure if everyone else knew. I don't like letting people into my life, Erik, but there's something about Grakin," she said. She made an effort to hold his powerful gaze steadily. "I love him, Erik, and he loves me. I'm not using him, and our relationship isn't just 'a matter of convenience,' as Jori-an put it. He also knows a lot more about me than the rest of you do, especially after...after what happened in Flora."

Kari's heart skipped a beat; she still wasn't ready to share that, not with Erik, and not here. She shook her head and began to head off into the forest, and Erik jumped to his feet and fell into step beside her. He remained quiet for a few minutes, studying her, but Kari didn't look at him. "What did happen in Flora?" he asked softly, which was unusual for him. "Nobody wanted to pry into your affairs after that happened, but...I won't lie, Kari. I need to know if you're going to be all right to hunt this demon. That can't happen out here; I need you."

"I'll explain some time, but not now," she said. "It won't happen again, though: it was something about the city, and I've been fine since we left there."

Erik accepted her explanation and touched her shoulder lightly, and Kari finally managed something close to a smile. He smiled in return, squeezed her shoulder comfortingly, and said, "I'm really sorry. I hope you can forgive me for being such an ass. I just..."

Kari sighed and looked ahead once more. "You're a half-demon," she said. "And I'm smart enough to know that has an effect on how easily you

184

trust people."

"That has nothing to do with it," he said, though his tone was not overly defensive.

"Doesn't it?" she asked as she looked higher up into the trees. "People treat your kind with mistrust or even outright hatred, and it makes you just as hesitant to trust them. But you're a half-guardian, so you've got the same protective nature as your, well, grandfathers I guess. I'm no expert in psychology – I couldn't spell the word if you asked – but I figure mistrust and over-protectiveness makes for a very strange combination of emotions for you to sort through."

Erik chuckled. "I guess that's fairly accurate," he admitted.

"You're very protective of your siblings, and I admire that," she continued. "And I guess it must be weird for some woman you think is either crazy or an impostor to take an interest in one of the quietest of your brothers."

"Exactly. I know you think I was jealous," he said, and he shrugged. "I guess I am, to some extent. More than that, I was just afraid of Grakin getting hurt. He's quiet and shy enough as it is, and if someone were to hurt him…"

"I understand," she said. "I tend to be the same way. It was hard for me to let him in. It'd been years since I let someone into my heart."

Erik stopped, so Kari paused as well, and the two faced each other squarely with the air of the rainforest an uninterrupted cacophony of sound about them. "We got off to a bad start," he said and held his hand out to her. "I'm Erik Tesconis, and I understand you and I are going to be working together."

Kari chuckled lightly but shook his hand. "Karian Vanador, Shield of the Heavens, by Zalkar's grace," she said formally. It struck her as odd that he turned his attitude around as quickly as Typhonix had, but she hoped it was genuine and would hold. Kari took her canteen and sipped carefully from it, and then she reached up and wiped the sweat from her brow. "We need to find water. At the rate I'm sweating, this canteen isn't going to get me very far through the jungle. As far as I can tell, it won't be long before the next rainfall, but we should find another source just in case. I figure there should be some creeper vines that store water, but I'm not sure if they'll be the same type as I used to find on Terrassia."

Erik nodded and checked his compass before leading them in the right direction. All around them they could hear the chirping, clicking, and chattering of life, though they saw nothing at ground level. Higher up in the trees they could hear the movement of creatures both large and small, and rarely they were able to catch a glimpse of shadow as it sped through the canopy. The day passed uneventfully. They failed to find a source of water, and like the previous night, they set up a camp nestled in the roots of a massive tree.

They pushed through for another two days with the heat continuing to weigh down upon them. Kari continued to sweat and Erik gave her his own canteen. He could go much longer without food or water thanks to his half-guardian heritage, and he was insistent that she take his drink and not endanger herself. As she expected, Kari was able to get water during a heavy rainfall on the third day, but she wasn't sure how often they could depend on rain, so she suggested they stay alert while they traveled. Kari began to suspect there was a grade to the land that was too slight for them to detect, as they continued to have no luck finding rivers or streams. Erik was amazed that such a lush landscape could be so lacking in running water, but Kari explained that they were likely to find some deep rivers once they reached the lower portions of the rainforest. Instead, Kari described some of the water-storing plants she was familiar with.

Their search continued into the fourth day. When they prepared to stop for a short meal around what they assumed was midday, Kari noted that the forest had become very quiet. She looked around suspiciously and Erik finally noticed as well. They both drew their blades and crouched down defensively near a tree, and Kari watched the jungle around them intently. With the unnerving silence growing thick around them, Kari worked to keep her breathing slow and steady. She centered her mind within herself and prepared for battle. Her nerves ached as every fiber of her being bristled with the sweet release of adrenaline. When she finally spotted the culprit, she burst into action. She dashed toward a large trunk directly ahead of her, and Erik followed close behind. They circled the tree and found a single corlyps, and Kari motioned for Erik to engage it while she looked for its companions. The corlyps was a fearsome fighter but was generally a cowardly creature, and they rarely traveled – let alone attacked – on their own.

The corlyps appeared somewhat like a red-skinned rir, though their crowns were covered with small black horns rather than hair, and they had heavy, black leathery wings. They were muscular, with terrible claws and fangs, and were intelligent enough to wear armor, though they preferred their natural weapons to man-made ones. The demon hissed menacingly and hopped around as it circled Erik and looked for an opening to attack. "Watch your back, Erik," Kari called, and she moved away from her partner around another tree, following a set of tracks that could have belonged to the demon they had already engaged.

"Watch your own," he yelled back.

Kari followed the tracks around the wide trunk before her, and she kept her blades up defensively to prevent being pounced upon. Sure enough she found two more corlypsi on the far side of the tree, apparently hoping to ambush her and Erik while they engaged the first serilian demon. Kari sidestepped to square up with the two demons, who hissed at her and split apart to try to flank her. "Two more," Kari called. She could hear a pained grunt from around the tree, and she hoped Erik didn't get blindsided by even more of them.

Kari stepped between the demons, and they were not expecting such a foolish move. She turned and cut three times at the one on her left before she spun and repeated the combination at the other. Each hopped away from her short flurries, and Kari dashed to her right to confront one and square herself up to the other. The corlyps she engaged hissed menacingly but kept its distance. The corlypsi were cowards, but they were clever and vicious, and Kari knew that they wouldn't engage her solo without weapons of their own. When fighting with tooth and claw, the demons relied on pack tactics like hyenas or wolves. Kari knew that when their counterstrike came, it would come from behind her.

Kari swung high and then low with her scimitars and sidestepped again, and she turned to confront the other corlyps. It backed away a couple of steps as she bore down upon it, but its attention was in the wrong place: Erik came from around the tree and ran the creature through from behind. His longsword came out neatly between the creature's ribs and the wind came out of it in a rush as its lung was pierced. Sensing the coming attack, Kari turned and hit the corlyps approaching from behind her with a crouching swing, slicing open its thigh. The creature stumbled in pain and Kari turned to the side, straightened out fully, and relieved the foul creature of its head.

Erik kicked the dying corlyps impaled upon his sword in the back and turned around as though expecting further trouble. The third demon, the one Erik had initially engaged, came around the tree but stopped short when it beheld its slain companions. It hissed and faked a threatening step forward, but then it jumped and clawed its way slightly up a tree trunk before it took wing and flew off into the rainforest.

Kari watched to make sure the demon hadn't simply circled to attack from another angle. Once satisfied that they were safe for the moment, she decapitated the one Erik had impaled. Kari saw that Erik's armor was torn on the back of his left arm, and the steel armor was coated in his black blood. Erik removed his left vambrace so Kari could inspect the wound. The demon had caught him solidly and the lacerations were fairly deep, so Kari channeled a bit of her deity's power to stanch the bleeding. While the healing magic she had access to as a demonhunter wasn't strong, it was useful for stanching bleeds so that the wounded would have time to seek proper healing. She dug through her pack for a minute before she found some clean bandages. She wrapped Erik's wounds as well as she was able and helped him replace his vambrace, damaged as it was.

"Is that going to be all right?" she asked. She wasn't sure where they'd have to go if he needed the services of a proper healer, but Erik picked up his scimitar and swung it around a couple of times with a grimace.

"I think so," he said, though it was clear he was trying to mask the pain. "It stings and it burns, but I can still move my arm well enough. We heal fast; I'll be fine in a couple of days."

Kari trusted in his assessment and patted his armored shoulder. "Thanks for the help," she said. "Corlypsi can be a pain when you're fighting more than one."

"You seemed to handle yourself just fine before I came," he said, eyeing her. She could see he was more than satisfied with her combat abilities, even moreso than he'd been on the ship. "If you hadn't held its attention, I'd have been stuck between two of them and, well, you can see how that would've ended. You remind me of Aeligos in a fight: he's not a swordsman like you, but he's a hell of a tactician, and always seems to be in the right place at the right time."

Kari smiled at the genuine compliment and studied the forest around them for several minutes, watching for the slightest sign that the last corlyps had returned or that anything else might have been attracted by the sounds of battle. She was fairly certain the demon would not attempt a second strike: corlypsi were easily demoralized and unlikely to try again unless they had an advantage of numbers. Unless the rainforest was crawling with demons – which she doubted – it seemed safe to assume that they would not encounter the creature again. Once the nearby birds and insects started up their cacophonous chatter again, she relaxed.

Kari turned her attention to the corpses of the dead corlypsi and grimaced at the prospect of leaving them exposed to rot under the elements. Demon flesh was foul and their blood was poisonous, so it wouldn't benefit the local wildlife for them to be left as they were. On the other hand, she and Erik didn't have the luxury of time, energy, or water to waste the precious hours it would take to bury the dead. Burning them was out of the question for the same reasons, not even taking the danger of forest fire into account.

"Guess we leave these," Kari said as she slumped the corpses against the base of a tree, and Erik agreed.

Silently, the two put some distance between themselves and the site of the battle and then sat down to have their lunch. Kari ate her trail rations sparingly and took only a few sips of her dwindling water supply. Erik didn't want to eat at all, but Kari pushed him to so that his wounds would heal faster. He couldn't argue with her logic, but he picked lightly at his own rations. He kept looking at Kari while they ate, and she wondered what he was thinking. She figured he was probably still embarrassed by their conversation from a few days before, perhaps especially after being in a battle with her.

"So you really received that armor as a gift from a friend?" he asked, clearly intrigued. Like Aaron in Barcon, Erik could hardly believe that anyone had given away such a valuable set of armor. Paluric armor was made of an odd metallic substance that didn't behave like a metal: it was nearly impervious to heat and therefore rumored to only be workable by a smith who had access to dragon fire or hellfire. It required similarly massive heat just to mine it, since it turned aside metal and magic alike. Not surprisingly, armor, weapons, and other tools made from the metal were exceedingly rare, and therefore worth a fortune.

"Are we back to this again?" Kari asked irritably, but she chuckled when Erik started to stammer an apology.. "You probably wouldn't believe the tale if I told it to you."

He eased up when he realized she was teasing. "I'm talking to a woman returned from the dead," he said with a smirk. "Let's see how much more unbelievable your story can be."

"Ever heard of Ashurinax the Black?" she asked. Erik shook his head negatively. Kari rocked back slightly with a sigh, and she looked off into the past rather than around them. "I guess I have to start from the beginning. You know I was born and raised in Flora, eventually moved to Solaris, and then went to the Demonhunter Academy. After I finished my training, I asked to be assigned to duty on Terrassia and my request was granted. I moved around a lot, accepting and carrying out orders whenever I came across them, and finding my own as I wandered between the four kingdoms."

"Four kingdoms?" Erik prompted.

"Yes, Terrassia used to be divided among four kingdoms, though I think that's changed since Arku's invasion in the later years of the

189

Apocalypse. There were the fures-rir kingdom of Tenari in the north; the humans of Dira Ch'Tori and its territories in the northeast; the elves of Laeranore in the east; and the shakna-rir based in Aurun Ch'Gurra in the south and west."

"I spent most of my time moving between Laeranore and Aurun Ch'Gurra, traveling with…," she started, but she paused as she considered he would probably be overwhelmed if she told him she'd traveled with Saint Bakhor. "Traveling with some friends that knew following me would usually lead to some type of adventure. They weren't welcome in the elven lands, though: the elves don't like outsiders, and I only gained their trust by rooting out a nest of demons that were using the elves' territorial nature to keep hidden. Anyway, outsiders avoid setting foot in Laeranore, but the place is far from empty and elves aren't the only thing that inhabits the forest."

Kari finished her lunch and stowed her things in her pack once more. She beckoned for Erik to follow and they set out to the north again. "Back in the summer of seventy-three – erm, twenty-eight seventy-three, that is – I came across a cave with a nasty stench coming out of it. It smelled like rotting demon corpses."

"So naturally, you decided to investigate what was killing demons," Erik said. "With absolutely no concern for your own well-being, I'm sure."

Kari shrugged. "You'd be surprised how brave being diagnosed with a terminal illness makes you," she said.

Erik did a double-take. "Terminal what?"

Kari glanced at him. "Oh, I thought you'd know. I…died of Dracon's Bane when I was twenty-seven. Never knew I had it until I graduated from the Academy. Up til then, I could never figure out why I was always sick."

Erik considered her, amazement plainly written on his face, and Kari wasn't sure just what about her surprised him the most. "You didn't find out until you were…?" he prompted.

"Twenty-one," Kari answered. She remembered that day well: she was so proud to have graduated from the Academy, but then the headmasters had pulled her aside and told her the truth. They had only allowed her into the Academy as a mercy because they didn't think she would survive the training. They told her of her illness, that her longevity was unusual, and that her success in spite of the illness made them very proud of her. But only then had Kari figured out why she was abused and treated as a throwaway child by her own parents, and it remained a painful subject. She swallowed her feelings, though, and continued, "My parents knew when I was a child, but they never told me. Even the headmasters didn't tell me til

190

I graduated; they were surprised I survived the training. I guess it was a shock to most that I lived as long as I did: most born with Dracon's Bane don't live to see puberty."

"Something tells me you're a little too strong-willed to give up so easily," he said.

Kari nodded solemnly. "So anyway, yes, I decided to look inside the cave, against better judgment. There were a few dead demons: mostly corlypsi, but there was a brys as well. The smell was awful, as they'd been dead for at least several days, but part of the smell was from the infected wounds of what they'd been fighting."

She went silent a few moments, and Erik took the bait. "And what was that?" he asked.

Kari looked at him from the corner of her eye, gauging his reaction. "A black dragon."

"Alive?" he asked, his eyes wide with shock, and she nodded. "So what, did you kill it and find the armor amongst its hoard?"

"No," Kari said. She hesitated to tell him what she had done, but figured it would let her know how much he really trusted her. "That's what he expected, but he was too weak to defend himself. So…I healed him."

Erik's brow furrowed. "You healed a black dragon?" he asked. Black dragons were generally violent and antisocial, and were a popular target for adventurers because they were also among the "weakest" – a relative term – of dragonkind. Kari having healed one would normally go against everything the Demonhunter Order stood for: they were expected to defend the people not only from demons but from anything that threatened society in general. Kari watched Erik sort through the thoughts, though, and he seemed to realize the one loophole that allowed her to heal the beast in good conscience: her duty to aid those attacked and wounded by demons.

Kari shrugged. "It was either that or kill something that was defenseless," she said. "I suppose I could've just left him to die, but I thought we were supposed to be better than that – you know, all that nobility they try to push on us at the Academy. They don't realize that you can't be taught to feel that way; you either do or you don't. I do."

Erik thought about it for a minute but then bobbed his head approvingly. "Frankly, I'm just surprised he didn't burn you to a crisp when he regained his strength," he said.

"It took him a while," Kari returned. "Our healing power isn't very strong, so all I could really do was keep the bleeding in check, wash the wounds, and try to keep them from getting infected again. It took over a week before he could even lift himself off the ground, and since I'd spent that time feeding him and keeping his wounds clean, he'd taken a liking to me. He felt he owed me – something about a 'draconic debt of honor' – and asked me what I would have of him. So I made him swear to not harm the elves or their neighboring kingdoms."

"Are you serious?" Erik asked.

"Quite," she answered. "He felt he had no choice but to honor my request. But he felt something else, too: surprise, I guess you could say, that I didn't ask for gold or any of the trinkets he kept in his den. So he gave me this suit of armor."

Erik shook his head, clearly surprised himself. "That's amazing," he said. "Though I wonder where he got it from."

"It belonged to his daughter," Kari said. "He told me he had a half-dragon daughter named Ashanti S'Laviolor who adventured for a couple of centuries. Ash – the dragon – said I reminded him of his daughter, so he gave me her armor as a gift for sparing his life. She was only slightly taller than me so the suit fits well, but the gauntlets are for someone with much longer fingers, and the helmet has so many holes for horns that it doesn't offer much protection."

"I was wondering why you didn't wear them," he commented. "You'll need to see Serenjols – the demon, not my brother – back in Latalex if you want them refitted. He's worked with paluric armor before. So, were all of your adventures in your…past life so amazing?"

Kari shrugged, at a loss. "You tell me. You're the one that studied them," she said, to which he chuckled. "Knowing I only had a little bit of time made me restless, and I guess pretty reckless, too. I tried to get as much done as I could with the time I had."

Erik nodded silently and simply stared at her for a while, and Kari understood that he must be reconciling everything he'd seen and learned of her over the course of the voyage with what he knew of her from history books. They continued on their way. Later in the afternoon Kari found what she was looking for: a type of vine that curled sinuously around one of the ancient trees. She hacked through it easily with one of her scimitars, and soon it began to drip water to the forest floor. She filled her canteen slowly before repeating the process with Erik's, and then she took a drink from the end of the severed plant. The water had a slightly bitter taste, but it was better than going thirsty. Kari explained a bit about the vine and why it was so rich with water, and Erik took note of what the vine and the tree it was wrapped about looked like in case they needed to find one again in the future.

They traveled for two more days before they finally came to a wide, fast-running river that appeared to head southeast toward the coast. Kari spent several minutes scouting both sides of the river, watching for movement or any signs of life other than from the canopy overhead. The sunshine was strong here, bathing the river in light, but it only served to deepen the shadows where the forest thickened on each side. Once Kari was satisfied that there was nothing else around, she asked Erik to keep watch while she took a quick bath. The scent of her sweat was grating on her after several days. He agreed and sat near a tree.

"That staff on the side of my pack has a folding bow in it," Kari said while she shed her armor and clothes. She waded out into the water and it took a moment to get her legs underneath her. The current was stronger than she had anticipated, and she had to go a fair way out to submerge herself to the waist. Fortunately the bottom was fairly rocky where she stepped out, so she was able to brace her feet against a solid bottom.

"Did you get these for Grakin?" Erik called from behind her, and Kari blushed when she realized he was looking at her purple undergarments. She didn't answer, but she assumed her silence did so well enough.

After washing quickly, Kari emerged from the river and sat down on a thick root near the water's edge. Erik stared at her curiously, and Kari figured that even though nudity didn't faze the rir, he was not only half-demon but her brother-in-law, so he was likely surprised that she walked around naked in front of him. Kari sat for a minute but then decided not to wait for her undergarments to dry. She figured they would take too long with the humidity anyway, so after slipping them on, she motioned for Erik to go ahead and bathe. He was hesitant, but Kari was insistent: while he didn't smell bad, she hadn't seen him bathe at all during their entire trip. At the very least, she figured he'd best wash his wounds and make sure that he smelled presentable for the czarikk, who she remembered had much keener noses than rir or even half-demons.

Erik began removing his armor while Kari sat back down on the root, where she waited for her undergarments to dry a bit on her before she'd put on her padded clothing. She watched him strip, but he paused before he removed his loincloth. He seemed to acknowledge that he had done the same to her, so he slipped off the garment. Kari continued to stare at him, curiously impressed, but he soon became aroused by her stare. He swore quietly and made his way into the cool river. "Sorry about that," he blurted and waded out into the water.

Kari waved off the comment, though he had his back to her. "Nothing I haven't seen before, especially during the Apocalypse," she said near-truthfully. There'd been no such thing as privacy in the camps of Jir'tana's brigade, and she'd shared the command tent with Jir'tana himself. Given his attraction to her, she'd seen him naked more than a few times, and Erik's muscular masculine form wasn't all that different than Kris'.

"Still, if word gets back to my brother that I was standing aroused in front of his mate...," he said with a chuckle. "I'll never hear the end of it. Certainly not from Ty."

"I doubt he'll have much trouble inventing stories about what we did all alone in the jungle, anyway," she said. "Not that it matters. Grakin knows me better than that."

Their eyes met when Erik emerged from the river, and he nodded as he stood nude before her once more. His self-control was better this time, and he took a few steps away from her before his form was suddenly lined with black flames that evaporated the water from his flesh near-instantly. Kari was shocked; she knew guardian demons commanded hellfire, but she wasn't sure if their children and other descendants did. Erik's command of it was considerable, and Kari was shocked that none of her companions had ever mentioned being able to use it during the entire trip. She couldn't help but wonder if her mate could do similar things.

Kari helped her partner don his armor, and then she moved over to begin putting on her own. Soon they were underway again, and they followed the river to the northwest while they looked for a suitable place to cross. While bathing, Kari became aware that there was a sharp drop-off in the depth, and the current in the center was much too swift to attempt swimming. It would have been easy enough to fly the distance, but Kari wanted to conserve her strength, and she explained that flight taxed her much more than it did her half-guardian companion. In the end the decision was a simple one: they were no less likely to find the czarikk by following the river than they were by crossing it. Daylight began to wane when they found a fairly safe crossing point where some rocks and boulders formed a makeshift bridge across the currents. It required hopping from rock to rock, but with the help of their wings they made the crossing quickly. When night descended, they found themselves a good distance from the water. While their trek had been uneventful where wild animals were concerned, Kari explained that the proximity of the river might change that, so they moved farther inland before setting up camp.

They made only a small fire to cook some meat and then doused it, and they settled in at the base of one of the larger trees. As usual, Erik allowed Kari to sleep first, letting her rest through the majority of the night before he would get a few hours of rest himself. Kari lay down on her cloak, watching her companion as he sat vigilantly scanning the forest around them. "Do you think I'm pretty?" she asked.

Erik turned a surprised look on her. "What? Why would you ask me that?" he returned. "Of course I think you're pretty, as does anyone else with a working pair of eyes. Or a single eye, for that matter. Why, did Ty say something to you?"

Kari shook her head. "No," she said. "I was just wondering."

"Both of my parents will be proud of Grakin's *catch*," Erik said, and it was clear from his expression that he was, too. "Though I'm sure I'll catch hell for not finding one of my own."

"Why are you still unmated?" she prodded.

Erik fixed her with an unreadable gaze, but he swung it out into the forest after a minute. "I imagine for the same reason you are...or were," he said. "This job isn't exactly conducive to finding a mate and starting a family."

"Condu-what?"

"We're demonhunters, and that always has to come first," he said as he looked back to her. "I at least – theoretically – have the luxury of a much longer lifetime. I'm not sure how the rest of you make your peace with the demands of this career."

Kari thought about it, and a deep silence grew between them that was still only slightly uncomfortable, and only because it demonstrated that no matter how much alike they were, they were still vastly different simply on account of race. While Kari didn't mind half-demons, they certainly took some adjusting to get used to on account of their differing outlooks, lifestyles, and lifetimes. They thought on a different level, on the one hand seeming unhurried due to their slower aging, yet on the other always seeming like they had to run to keep pace with their less long-lived friends.

"It's about commitment," she said quietly. "I guess in the end, if we can't commit to the life we chose as demonhunters, then we won't likely be able to commit to the bonds of a mate that are supposed to last much, much longer."

Erik didn't disagree, but his expression said he wasn't entirely satisfied with her answer. "Can I ask you something, honestly? And I don't ask this to make you upset, but doesn't it bother you to know that Grakin will outlive you, that he'll likely have other mates and children long after you're gone?"

Kari shook her head. "No, it doesn't," she said. "Maybe I see things differently because I've already died once, but the only thing I really worry about is what's right in front of me. There's no sense worrying about a future I may not live to see."

Erik was surprised, but he seemed to like that response much more. "That's practical," he said. "You'd best get some sleep. If we don't find the czarikk by tomorrow, I'd like to start traveling into the night as well."

Kari agreed, turned on her side, and closed her eyes. She tried to push what Erik had said out of her mind. Grakin had still not shared his burden with his siblings, and she knew from experience it was just going to hurt more the longer he waited. It was bad enough to know a loved one was going to die, but far worse to find out from someone else, or long after the fact. In her case, the opposite had been true: how painfully it had stung to find out in retrospect that the reason for her abuse was something her parents – even her sisters – knew and never told her.

Silently Kari whispered into the night air, wishing her mate a sound sleep and a night's freedom from his pain.

Chapter XI – Strange Bedfellows

Kari and Erik traveled for three more days but still found no trace of the czarikk or any sign that they inhabited the forest. They began to wonder if the old man's words were true, or whether he'd been some sort of spy: a confidence man in the employ of Gaswell set to misdirect possible troublemakers out where they might become lost and die. If the czarikk controlled the rainforest and there had been such dire consequences to the humans of Riverport trying to raze the woodlands to build farms, then it was hard to understand how they were so difficult to find.

The obvious conclusion was that the czarikk didn't want to be found, and having lived in the rainforest for uncounted generations, they were experts at being untraceable when the situation demanded it. Kari began to wonder if the movement overhead in the canopy that she had been largely ignoring since they'd entered the forest could in fact be the very people they were searching for. Her limited knowledge of the czarikk didn't include whether or not they liked to climb trees or travel among the boughs like the elves were so fond of doing.

It seemed unlikely as she thought about it, though she supposed it depended on what type of czarikk they were. The *mulrassa* were more humanoid and unlikely to be walking around in the trees, but the *sulrassa* were more reptilian, so for them it was entirely possible. Initially she had assumed that the forms whose shadows she saw moving overhead were animals – monkeys or such – but she began to suspect something more sinister. If her nagging concern that the old man in Riverport had been a spy was well-founded, it was possible they were being tracked from above by an elf, possibly, or even something worse like a brys.

They kept their wits about them and pressed onward, and Erik made sure to check his compass regularly. In prior days they'd found that following even the simplest curve of a hill or skirting around a thick cluster of trees and growth turned them around easily. By the compass' readings they knew they were still heading north, though neither knew how deep into the massive forest they were. They didn't come across any other rivers, just some narrow, slow-moving streams that at the very least supplied them with plenty of water to drink when combined with the common rainfalls. Kari couldn't smell the ocean, so she was likewise unsure how far inland they were. She wished more than once that there had been a cartographer in Riverport who could've shown them a map – or better yet, sold them one.

Night settled in but they continued their travels, and they marched until Kari's legs began to cramp. They set up their camp at the base of the largest tree they could find, but they didn't bother to build a fire since the fresh meats they'd brought were long since gone. Kari nibbled on trail rations but Erik skipped his meal. His wounds were nearly fully healed, and he said he'd ration out his own food supplies more strictly in case Kari's ran out.

Kari slept soundly through most of the night, and she rose and belted on her swords when Erik woke her so he could get in a few hours of rest before dawn. She sat upon a rock near the base of the tree and scanned the dark around them, and she listened for anything out of the ordinary among the sounds of the night. Her surprise was complete when she turned her attention straight out before their camp once more to behold a brys standing not twenty feet away from her.

Kari was on her feet in a moment's time and slid her blades from their scabbards with a distinctive ring, and she barked for Erik to wake up. Though the demon held his bow in hand, he made no move to threaten either of them; he merely stood across from Kari regarding her and Erik curiously. He backed up a couple of steps when Kari approached warily, but then he took up a confident posture and continued looking the two over with his glowing, dragon-eyed stare. Sensing that he was not immediately hostile, Kari lowered her guard somewhat and halted her advance. She heard Erik pick up his weapons and approach her from behind.

Like all of his kind, the brys was short, standing just under five feet tall: nearly the same size as Eryn. He was well-toned but lean, as though he'd never known an idle moment. He wore a set of blackened leather armor which, if Kari's eyes did not deceive her, was made from the skin of other serilian demons, and a pair of rapiers hung sheathed from his belt. He had three rows of small, rear-curving sharp horns on his head and an overbite that caused his black front fangs to stick out slightly. When Erik stepped beside Kari, the brys tilted his head curiously.

"Are you lost?" he asked. His voice was slightly high-pitched due to his size, and it lacked the malice Kari expected from a brys. There'd been a number of brys loyal to Kaelariel who served in Kris Jir'tana's brigade, and though technically they were all on the same side, Kari had never gotten to know any of them. Brys were vicious, vengeful assassins who had little in the way of personality, by all accounts, and the ones in Jir'tana's brigade had been far from eager to spend time with the demonhunter.

"Why do you ask?" Erik returned. He touched Kari's shoulder lightly

198

and she nodded that she understood he wanted to handle the talking.

The creature waved his unoccupied clawed hand briefly, and said, "Worry not: I will not assault your mate."

The two demonhunters exchanged a glance, and Erik stepped away from Kari, removing his hand from her shoulder. "She's not my mate," he said.

"How unfortunate," the brys responded immediately. "I have been tracking you since you slaughtered my corlypsi cousins on your way down from Riverport. This jungle is not a place I would expect to find half-breed lovers wandering, though I know that she is neither half-breed nor, as you say, your mate. So I ask you again: are you lost?"

Kari squared her jaw as the brys confirmed her suspicions: she had let her guard down too easily during their journey. Though the brys were nearly impossible to track or detect when they didn't want to be, Kari had spent enough time amongst the elves in their woodland home to know the telltale signs when someone was following her. The fact that the canopy here was so much higher and the forest was damp and misty was no excuse: she had failed herself and her partner, and had the demon meant them harm they would certainly have been killed already. The one positive, she thought, was that they knew that the creature didn't mean them harm.

"We're trying to find the czarikk," Kari said quietly, and her words drew a glance but then a nod from Erik. She wasn't exactly comfortable telling their plans to a serilian demon, but since he hadn't harmed them and had taken the time to speak with them, Kari gambled on the chance that he might know where the czarikk were located and be willing to tell them.

The creature cocked his head again. "So you thought to wander around until you found them? Did no one in Riverport tell you where to find them?"

"They gave us general directions, but we were hesitant to ask too many questions; there's war brewing among the mortals of this island, and we can't be too careful," Erik answered. He turned his back – foolishly, Kari thought – and moved over to don his armor. Dawn was coming, so there was little point to him returning to sleep.

The brys nodded shortly. "I have heard there is the threat of war to the west, but with the troubles here in the east, I have had little time to investigate the other side of the island."

"Who are you?" Kari prompted.

"I am called Makauric," he said with a strange gesture of his clawed hand. He leaned back against a tree, stood his bow on end before him, and continued, "I range these woods and north to the mountains claimed by the

199

Tuvurasti. If I am not mistaken, you are Kari and Erik. I am curious why you have come to my forest."

"*Your* forest?" Erik echoed with a chuckle as he worked to don his armor by himself.

"*My* forest," the creature repeated, and his eyes flicked only briefly to the side before his unwavering, nearly unblinking gaze settled once more on Kari. "If you are here to help, then I will guide you to the czarikk. They will not welcome my kind into their village, but they may feel differently about you – time will tell, I suppose. Unless you know how to communicate with them, you should not expect a very warm welcome. I can tell you from experience that they do not speak the words of either of our creators."

"You know where to find them, then?" Kari asked.

"I do," Makauric said. "Your course will take you out of the forest and into the savannah before you ever find them. Someone in Riverport could likely have given you directions; the czarikk are not far from what the mortals call the Ursis River. They draw their territorial lines quite firmly, and the other mortals of the island respect those boundaries."

"We were told to avoid the city of Ursis because of the threat of war," Kari said. "How far from here are the czarikk?"

The brys studied her for a moment and gave a noncommittal shrug. "A week, perhaps more, given how fast you have been moving to date," he said. "Then again, if you know where you are going, then perhaps a little less than a week."

Erik approached again once he finished putting on his armor, and he looked the brys over skeptically as he stood beside Kari. "You *do* know we're demonhunters, don't you?" he asked.

Makauric stared at him a moment, his impassive expression unchanged, and then gave the same shrug again. "I could have killed you many times had I wished," he said. "I think you owe me at least the courtesy of keeping your threats to yourself. I sense the hand of the gods behind your presence, so I offer you my aid. This is my forest, and my island, and what I cannot protect myself I welcome the aid of others – even demonhunters – in so doing."

"Aid in what? What trouble is there here in the east?" Kari prompted.

The brys looked around for a few moments and then gestured for the two to follow him as he headed off between the trees. It was strange for Kari to see a serilian demon turn its back on her willingly, but she fell into step behind the brys, with Erik behind her. Eventually the brys slowed his pace and moved to the side so Kari walked abreast from him. They continued for several minutes and the brys' crimson eyes darted around while the sounds of the forest awakening rose around them, though he said nothing.

Kari noted as they walked that Makauric appeared very young for his type: his flesh was smooth and almost shiny, like a newly created demon, and there were no scars upon his deep red skin where it showed through the black leather he wore. She knew little about the creation of her enemies: she recognized the types by sight, could name their leaders and important figures within each type's hierarchy, and knew where to hit each to have the most effect, but when it came to how, when or where Seril had created them, Kari was oblivious. It was well known that aside from Askies Island and Terrassia, the other continents were relatively free of the presence of serilian demons, so to find several on Tsalbrin so soon after their arrival took her by surprise. Her orders from Zalkar had suggested that the demonic influence they were looking into likely originated in the underworld, and she didn't expect to find serilian demons operating in the same area as an underworld breed. It made Kari wonder how many more there might be, and what effect their presence might have on the overall mission.

After walking for several minutes, the brys finally began to speak. "Several weeks ago, I went to hunt in the mountains to the northeast, as I do every spring when the rams come down from the higher peaks with their mates and young. The hunting is always good, and the flesh of the rams is lean and makes for good salted jerky for my travels. When I arrived I found entire flocks of them already slaughtered, though none of them had been even partially devoured. The marks upon them were from a blade, but it made little sense: even if bandits or frontiersmen had made a home in the foothills or the peaks themselves, they would be fools to not take the meat and skins these animals provide. My suspicions were further aroused when I began trying to track whatever had killed off the animals: there were no footprints, only long drag marks, so at first I believed that perhaps it was a poor attempt by the perpetrators to cover their tracks. It was also possible that it was a group of men traveling in single file to hide their numbers but dragging a wounded comrade or even a dead animal on a litter. Both of those theories were dispelled when I found the first traces of dung."

Kari regarded the brys curiously, and he continued. "The creature is very careful about where it leaves its droppings, but my sense of smell is difficult to fool," Makauric said, tapping the end of his snout. "Based on the droppings, the creature is some sort of reptilian."

"Did you see the creature yourself?" Erik asked.

201

"Patience," the brys said with a glance over his shoulder. "I will tell you all I know, but I will not overwhelm you with details. I must tell you everything in order, and in context, so you may decide what it is that must be done."

"So after you found its droppings, what did you do?" Kari prompted.

"From there I tracked it farther, though it began to travel atop the rocks to try to hide its path. I located a cave in the foothills before the higher mountains, and the refuse pile outside left little doubt that I had found its lair. Much of the remains outside the cave consisted of destroyed armor and weapons along with the bones of humanoids of many different types. The bones were picked clean but had fang marks on them. The markings on the ruined pieces of armor again suggested a bladed weapon, but there were also puncture marks – roughly as wide as the length of my thumb, and a little more than a hand apart."

"Sylinth," Kari said, and her words prompted an *mm-hmm* from Erik behind her. The brys looked to her expectantly, so she explained. "A sylinth is a type of serpentine demon native to the realm of Sorelizar in the underworld. They're about fifteen feet from the tip of their snake-like snouts to the end of their tail, but slither upright, sort of like a man."

"I see," Makauric said.

"Did you engage the sylinth at all?" Erik asked.

"No," the brys answered. "I did not get the chance. Something clouded my mind and I left that place quickly, afraid I was soon to be forced into the service of whatever inhabited the cave. I have not returned since, but I have tried to monitor its behavior from a distance as best I can. To my knowledge it has not troubled the Tuvurasti to the north, but the czarikk seem to be even more hostile in recent weeks, so I suspect it may be bothering them. It is difficult to know, as the czarikk are quite adept at finding me when I attempt to get close to their settlement."

"Perhaps we'll have better luck," Erik said, and then he moved up beside Kari. "We should meet the czarikk and make sure it's the sylinth that's bothering them, if it's something demonic at all. Could turn out it's more of those corlypsi, or something else."

Kari agreed with a nod, and then turned back to the brys. "Do you know what's going on in the west at all?" she asked.

"I am not certain," Makauric answered. He stopped briefly and sniffed the air a few times, and he scanned the canopy above them. Soon he shrugged off whatever he was thinking and continued ahead. "When trouble brews among the mortals, I make myself scarce. Trouble always seems to get blamed on my kind – rightfully so, many times – so normally

202

it does not benefit me to be visible when the mortals are looking to harm someone, or blame someone for harming each other. All I can say with certainty is that there is talk of a war, and I have no plans to be anywhere near the western side of the isle when it comes."

"Where's your partner?" Erik asked. Brys typically lived and worked in pairs, which made them so much more dangerous an adversary. To find one operating alone was unusual.

"I have none. My brothers on the island live in the forests on the western edge and I seldom see them," Makauric answered. He turned his attention back to Kari. "So what exactly is a sylinth doing on my island?"

"That's what we're here to find out," she answered but didn't elaborate further, and the brys didn't press.

"You should take your morning meal and relieve yourself before we go any farther," Makauric said, and he stopped in a small clearing and looked around. He made certain the area was safe and then met Kari's curious stare. He shrugged. "I have been tracking you for nearly a week; I know your schedule quite well now."

Kari blushed slightly. "So you saw us down by the river...?"

"I did," he said with no change in his expression. "That is why I assumed you were mates. I should warn you: you must be careful when drinking or bathing in this forest. The waters are full of many types of parasites and dangerous fish. Have you felt ill at all?"

"No," Kari answered. She sat down and pulled out her rations, but she stared at her canteen suspiciously.

"Taking the water from the vines was clever," Makauric said. "If you need take water from the rivers, you should boil it before putting it in your canteen for drinking."

Kari nodded and ate her stale but filling breakfast quietly, and Erik did the same while the brys stood by stoically, watching the forest around them. Kari met Erik's gaze and the two demonhunters held a conversation with their eyes. The brys certainly seemed helpful, but Kari wasn't entirely sure just how much they could trust him. Kari couldn't easily dismiss the fact that he had followed them for days without attacking, though: brys were not known for subtlety or being overcautious. If he had wanted them dead, he would have watched them, waited until nightfall, and killed Erik while he was on guard before slitting Kari's throat in her sleep. If he was one of the more vicious varieties of brys, he may have killed Erik while Kari slept and merely disarmed her, so he could harry her for days before taking her life.

They finished their meal and traveled on in silence. Makauric made no attempt at small talk, and Kari understood his breed well enough to not bother trying. His claim that he knew their schedule was no boast, and the timing of his stops to take meals and take care of their other needs aligned nearly flawlessly with Kari's body clock, which was finely tuned after eight years in Jir'tana's brigade. The demon himself ate salted meats during their stops and drank carefully from his own canteen, and he began to follow Kari's schedule rather than his own.

He marched them well into the night before he could walk no farther, and as Kari and Erik set up a small camp, the brys clawed his way up a wide trunk and looked around the forest. Once it seemed he was satisfied that there was nothing nearby that might cause them trouble, he descended and took his meal with his traveling companions, though he remained silent. When he finished eating he clawed his way back up the tree and reclined in its lowest branches, and Kari and Erik looked up at him with interest. "Wish I could climb a tree like that," Kari said.

"I don't think I could sleep up in a tree," Erik commented. He spared the brys another glance before he turned to Kari. "So I meant to ask, did you get your scimitars from that black dragon…Ashurinax, did you say his name was?"

"Ashurinax the Black," Kari confirmed, but she shook her head. "No, I didn't get these from him. His daughter used one of those weird double-ended swords. I found these among a demon's things when I was young and freshly returned to Terrassia after graduating."

"Really?" Erik asked, and he took one of the blades Kari offered for inspection. Kari knew her weapons well: their craftsmanship was beyond superb, the curve of the blades and every nuance of their backsides and pommels spoke of a master craftsman who had put every ounce of skill and passion into their making. The blades were inlaid with a weave design that was blackened so that it stood out from the silvery brilliance of the metal itself. Near the hilt was a marking that Erik recognized immediately, and his eyes went wide. "This was made by Terx!"

Kari nodded. Terx was a harmauth, a type of underworld demon also commonly referred to as a ram demon. They typically served as generals and bodyguards to the demon kings and nobles, and were masters over all of the lesser types of demons in the underworld. Terx himself was an oddity among his kind, as he had never served as either a general or bodyguard, but as a master smith who created weapons of unmatched quality for the highest bidder. According to the stories Kari had heard, sometime during the twentieth century on Citaria, Terx was captured during a battle between angels and demons that spilled over into his homeland in the underworld. Taken back to the celestial realm, he was placed under a compulsion by his angelic captors and began making weapons for them: weapons to destroy his own kin. For over a millennium he served that function in the celestial realm, and occasionally his works found their way to Citaria to fall into the hands of exceptionally lucky adventurers. By all accounts, he still worked daily to equip his celestial "allies" with flawless weaponry.

"Who did you kill for these?" Erik prodded.

"A valiras called Alcuron," she said, referring to another type of underworld demon also commonly called a vulture demon. "I'm not sure how he got here or why he'd come, but I found him in an old abandoned bunker where he'd set himself up as a god among some gnolls north of Dira Ch'Tori." Kari chuckled and took a sip of her water. "Let's just say the gnolls didn't think he was a god when I was done with him."

"I wonder where he got them," Erik commented, and he handed the weapon back to her.

Kari shrugged and slid the scimitar back into its sheath. "Not sure; I guess maybe he either killed an angel or whoever had the swords," she said. "Or he was just lucky and found them. I wasn't really familiar with scimitars at the time: I trained almost exclusively with a longsword and either a shortsword or long dagger at the Academy. But when I found out these were made by Terx, I knew I'd found something special. When I trained with Suler Tumureldi, he made a master out of me rather quickly."

"You trained under the Emerald Scorpion himself?" Erik asked with wide eyes, and he shook his head. "I have to say, the history books at the Academy didn't do your life any justice, just based on what you've told me in the last few weeks. They went into a lot of detail about all of your demon kills, but not so much about you, or that you trained under the Emerald Scorpion. I'd think something like that would bear mentioning."

Kari sighed wistfully. "Honestly, Erik, I've never seen anyone fight like that man since," she said. "Tumureldi had a gift, and I was blessed not just to learn from him, but to learn the very fighting style he created."

He fixed her with a stern gaze, but then he put his palm over his face and grunted. "Well thanks for not embarrassing me in front of my siblings," he said.

Kari waved off the comment. "You're a hell of a fighter," she said. "I don't think I *could* embarrass you. In fact, I was wondering whose style you used?"

Erik nodded in thanks to her praise but then he shrugged. "Not any one person's, really," he said. "I learned the traditional shakna-rir scimitar style from Headmaster Akiveldi at the Academy, and was already proficient with the longsword thanks to my father. I just…not to brag, but I hit a lot harder than most people, and the half-demon speed and reflexes don't hurt."

"I'll say," she agreed. "You and your siblings are all very talented for a bunch of kids."

"Kids? I'm older than you are, if what you've told me is true," he said, and he nodded when she looked at him curiously. "I'm thirty-six; if what you say is accurate, you were twenty-seven when you were resurrected, and it's been eight years since then."

"I guess I hadn't thought of it that way," she returned pensively. "I feel so old because I lived so long ago…everyone feels like a kid to me now." Erik conceded to her logic with a chuckle and a lopsided smile, and Kari lay on her cloak to sleep. She was surprised to find that with the brys perched high up in the tree above them she felt safer than she had when she and Erik were alone. It was strange, but she took advantage of the calm feeling and fell quickly into a light but restful sleep.

~~*~*

By the time Erik woke up the following morning, Makauric had a small fire burning with a game bird roasting over it. Makauric was seated across the fire from Kari in silent vigil as they waited for the meat to cook, and Kari nibbled lightly on some of her rations, intent on having something hot herself. She regarded Erik briefly as he awakened, and Makauric climbed quickly up the tree and scanned the forest before he came back down and removed the cooked bird from the spit.

"I didn't think your kind cooked your food," Erik commented as the brys sliced up the bird and handed each of his traveling companions a portion wrapped in a thick leaf.

"Eating birds without cooking them is foolish," the demon said before he began tearing off a strip of the meat. "Meat that has been cooked does not benefit us nearly as much, but is still better than something diseased, or nothing at all."

"Thanks for the meal," Kari said. She took a careful bite, the juices still bubbling.

"You will need the strength of both meat and grains," Makauric said, not acknowledging her thanks. "The road ahead is long and I must push you to your limits to reach the czarikk quickly. We do not want to dally in this forest long enough to draw the attention of its dragon."

206

Erik and Kari both looked at their companion at the same time, and Kari could see the worry in Erik's gaze. "Dragon?" he echoed simply after a few moments.

Makauric nodded. "Its lair is on the other side of the Ursis River, but it considers this entire rainforest to be its own and patrols fairly often. It is young but powerful, and certainly not to be trifled with. Accordingly, we will need to be on our guard for its presence – though it flies overhead much of the time, it also walks through the forest since it knows it is easy to hide under a canopy such as this."

"Do you know its name?" Kari asked.

The brys shook his head briefly. "I have not managed to speak to it, and honestly have little desire or reason to try. I only know that it is green, ill-tempered, and well-armored enough that I would only kill it if I were exceedingly lucky. And I do not believe in luck."

Kari nodded with his assessment. She understood that the brys were not risk-takers and generally didn't engage in any battle they didn't feel they had a very good chance of winning. If they felt the odds were against them, they fell into the shadows, watching and waiting for the most opportune time to strike. They were master assassins and possessed an almost supernatural stealth, but they also knew their limitations quite well and were not prone to foolish or impatient mistakes. If there was a dragon in the forest and the brys had not vacated the area, then he must have studied its patrols and hunting habits thoroughly.

The three finished their meal in silence, and once the demonhunters were ready the brys led them farther into the heart of the jungle. His steps were sure, and he halted the group every so often to climb a tree and gaze around their immediate area or scare off an animal shadowing their movements high in the canopy. His tracking skills were amazing even to Kari, who'd traveled with and among the elves for several years in her previous life; Makauric had no need for Erik's compass or any direction whatsoever. He led them around both terrain and animals that posed a danger to them, and kept them on a steady pace.

They traveled for several days without incident and came upon a river on the fourth day, though it wasn't as wide, deep, or fast-moving as the largest one the demonhunters had found. The brys halted their march and told them to bathe if they wished, though he warned them not to relieve themselves in the river itself. Erik motioned for Kari to go first, but Makauric waved them both in. He took up his bow and squatted on a log at the river's edge, keeping vigilant while his companions stripped and waded out into the water.

The demonhunters washed off quickly and hand washed their undergarments as well before they emerged from the river. Erik donned his armor immediately so Kari could sit and let her clothes dry. Once Erik was armored, the brys removed his own leather armor and waded out into the river, which Kari hadn't expected. Brys didn't sweat and their bodies carried no scent, so it was surprising that he would also take the time to bathe unless something was bothering him. Kari watched the demon strip completely but, as she expected, he didn't seem to care at all, and waded out into the river under her scrutiny. Confirming her observation from the first day they'd met, he seemed underdeveloped, like a young man who was just hitting puberty, though his lean, muscular build told her otherwise. She wondered if it was a common trait among the brys: in her experience serilian demons were normally better endowed than mortal males. It made sense given the brys' slight frames, though nothing in her training had suggested that such would be the case.

Makauric emerged from the river silently, put on his leather armor, and took up his bow while he waited for Kari to get fully dressed. Once she was fairly dry, she put her clothes and armor back on and followed the brys farther into the forest. Makauric skirted the edge of the river for nearly a mile, and then he turned and beckoned for his companions to crouch down and be silent. He crept soundlessly to the river's edge, and after a minute he motioned for the two demonhunters to do likewise. When Kari and Erik reached the embankment that dropped off to the water's surface, Makauric pointed to the west, where Kari could see the dragon drinking from the river. It was the first time Erik saw a dragon, and he slunk back behind the nearest tree to watch the massive beast from around the trunk. Kari had seen several dragons in her lives, and though she had never met or battled a green, she recalled one facet of all strategies that was the same when dealing with dragons: don't engage unless you have to.

Kari watched the emerald reptile drink from the river, and its sharp eyes didn't notice the three where the brys had led them. After a few minutes the creature rose up, took wing, and lifted off over the treetops in a massive rush of wind. The trees bent and swayed with the force of the dragon's passing, and it flew southwest, away from where Makauric was leading them. Makauric watched it fly away and then motioned for the demonhunters to remain still, and he climbed the nearest tree and watched the dragon's egress. He descended a minute later and beckoned for his companions to follow once more.

"It seems to have returned southwest, back across the Ursis," he said. "It likes to patrol the rivers, as that is where it normally finds animals to hunt and bothersome people to remove from its forest. I am not entirely confident that we will not see it again, but my instincts tell me that having seen it on this river now means we will not see it again in the near future."

"How long does its patrol of the forest normally take?" Kari asked.

"Three days," Makauric answered. "It will normally patrol, then hunt, and then it will return to its lair for several days of sleep."

"How far through its patrol is this area?" Erik asked.

"If it has flown back across the Ursis, then its patrol is complete," the brys said. "I believe it will return to its lair to rest, as it did not see us. If it had, it would have attacked."

"Does it attack the city on the river?" Kari asked.

"No. The dragon seems content to let the mortals use the waterways, but does not tolerate anyone living in the forest itself," he answered. "The city of Ursis is the only settlement it has allowed them to build within the heart of the rainforest."

"What about the czarikk? Does it bother them at all?" she prodded.

"No," Makauric answered. "I am not certain it even patrols the forest near their home. I assume it is because they are both reptilian, though I have little evidence that such is the case."

Their journey continued uninterrupted for two more days, and the rainforest took on a certain charm when they weren't lost. Makauric's guidance was quiet but without hesitation, and he led them across streams and gullies, avoiding the wildlife flawlessly, and the brys even hunted and cooked – albeit simply – for his companions. While he normally ate his meat raw, he always cooked birds before eating them, and fowl made up the majority of what he was able to kill that wasn't wasteful for the size of their group. Erik never seemed to fully trust the brys: he treated Makauric respectfully but rarely took his eyes from the demon except when it was time to sleep.

Kari, on the other hand, found herself beginning to trust the brys. While her training and instincts told her it was unwise at best, she found no reason not to trust him: he hadn't attacked them, and unless he was leading them into some elaborate and immensely subtle trap, he was keeping his word and helping them. Subtlety was not a trait of the brys: their methods were direct and deliberate, so Kari doubted he was up to anything. On the contrary, he could have led them into the waiting maw of a dragon. Not only had he not done so, but he'd even taken the trouble to show the beast to them – something few got to see in their lifetimes.

Kari always trusted her instincts, but in Makauric's case she ignored their gentle warning. If he intended to misdirect or harm them in some way, she figured they would be best served to have him at close range rather than be an unseen enemy at distance. It seemed he was trying to befriend them, though such a gesture coming from a brys was awkward and not something Kari, let alone Erik, could properly appreciate if it were so. He made no secret that his eyes took in Kari's every detail, particularly when she was nude, but he also did nothing to suggest he was anything but curious. Kari assumed she just might be the only woman Makauric had ever seen naked or spent an extensive amount of time with, so she took his curiosity in stride.

Kari's contemplations came to an end abruptly as Makauric jumped sideways and clawed his way up a tree in the span of a few heartbeats. She and Erik found themselves surrounded by spears: czarikk had appeared out of the jungle without warning, and had surprised even the brys momentarily. Before they could even train their weapons on Makauric, though, he was already on his way up to perch on a tree branch with an arrow aimed at the closest lizardman. Two other czarikk watched the brys, ready to throw javelins at the slightest provocation, but the bulk of the group hedged in Kari and Erik, thrusting their spear tips threateningly.

"Wait, wait," Erik said, holding his hands up.

The largest of the czarikk, a broad-shouldered obvious veteran of many hunts, stepped forward and began hissing at them in a sibilant language that Kari didn't understand. It wore no clothing, and the others were likewise completely nude. Their reptilian heritage hid their gender but for the relative size and musculature of the warriors, which Kari assumed pointed to their being male. The only articles it wore at all were a necklace of clawed finger-bones that looked humanoid, and a couple of hand-woven grass bracelets on its left wrist. Kari noted the coloration of their scales and was amazed how easily they blended into the jungle.

Kari looked up to Makauric, but she recalled he said he couldn't understand the lizardman's speech, and he shook his head and never took his aim from the apparent czarikk leader. Kari held her hands up and the largest of the czarikk continued its questioning, the language fascinating but also disturbing for Kari's lack of understanding it. Kari looked around at each of the lizardmen and noted that many looked young and quite frightened by the encounter. She dismissed the idea that they might understand the rir tongue based on Makauric's words, and she assumed if they didn't understand rir, then they didn't understand the common human language either. On a hunch, Kari tried something else.

"Peace," she said boldly in the language of the elves, and both Erik and the czarikk leader tilted their heads in surprise. "We would have peace with you, noble czarikk: we are here to help. Please do not harm us."

Their leader's scaly brow rose briefly in recognition, and it seemed to try to translate her words for a minute before it waved for its warriors to lower their spears. The other czarikk came to attention, standing the spears on their ends, and even the two javelin-wielding lizardmen touched their weapons tip-down to the ground while they kept a wary eye on the demon above. The leader stared at Kari for a few moments, chewing on its reptilian lip before it spoke very slowly. "No make elf speak good," it returned in broken elvish. "Come village, elder talk."

The czarikk leader glanced up at the demon, and Kari turned her attention to Makauric on his perch, his bow bent in a deadly arc as he waited for any hostile movement. "Makauric, stand down," she called up to him. He nodded and put the arrow back in his quiver. Kari turned her attention back to the czarikk patrol leader, pointed up toward the brys, and spoke slowly in elvish once more. "Friend; he will not harm you."

The czarikk beheld the demon for a few moments, and then he fixed Kari with a wary eye before nodding shortly. "You fault," it said, and then it gestured for the three to follow its group.

Erik stepped forward and touched Kari's shoulder lightly. "I should have guessed you speak elvish," he said. "What did you tell them?"

"There's still a lot about me you don't know," she said lightly. "But anyway, I told them we're here to help. I'm not sure they understand exactly, but they're at least willing to take us back to their village so we can speak to someone more fluent in elvish. I think they understand that Makauric won't hurt them either, if they're letting him come along."

They followed the czarikk for several hours, and eventually came to a high embankment where more spear-wielding lizardmen stood vigilantly. The breastwork was several feet high with sharpened stakes planted firmly into the side the group approached from. When they drew near, another czarikk with a bone necklace and the woven-grass bracelets moved to stand atop the earthen wall and greet its companion. They spoke briefly in their racial tongue, and the leader of the patrol gestured toward its guests several times before it pointed to the brys and then Kari and Erik in what was obviously its way of saying *he's their responsibility*.

Soon enough they were waved through, and after carefully climbing the embankment, Kari could see the closest edge of the czarikk village. The jungle was thinner here, and between the more widely interspersed trunks were quaint wooden huts, animal-skin teepees, and even a few simple stone structures. The stone and wooded homes were nothing like those of the cities Kari had lived in and passed through: simple yet well-constructed, and a bit primitive for lack of a better term. The teepees were fairly impressive, much like those described in human history as the trademark of aboriginal tribes of a semi-nomadic nature.

The czarikk marched the demonhunters and the brys into the center of the village. Kari could see that the homes were arranged in a wide circle around a clearing that had been made by the removal of a large tree. In the depression where the stump had been chopped below ground level and dug out was a fire pit, one which saw frequent use judging by the amount of ash and charred wood that lay within. It was ringed with stones, and the entire village around it had been cleared of the carpet of fallen sticks and leaves that was more common throughout the northern portions of the jungle. Near to the central fire pit were smaller ones with crudely fashioned but serviceable stone cooking hearths built over them.

Many czarikk scurried around the smaller fire pits, and Kari decided in her head that the patrol they encountered was indeed all males. The czarikk tending the hearths were more slender through the shoulders, and though they had no breasts, they had pinkish colorations across their chests and bellies, and fins down the back corners of their heads as opposed to the spiky ridges of the others. Kari guessed the ones tending to the cooking were female, and that the larger ones lacking the pinkish coloration were males. It was a guess, but she thought perhaps the pinkish coloration might also denote that the females were in season, as it was still spring on the northern half of the world. That thought gave her pause, and she wondered if that had something to do with the czarikks' more agitated state of mind according to what Makauric had told her. It was quite possible that their recent intolerant nature might've simply had to do with not wanting a brys around during their mating cycle, or when they were laying their eggs. Of course, it was quite possible that they simply didn't want the brys around at all – few ever did.

The patrol leader bid them stay by the main fire pit and set his warriors to watch over them. He made his way to a decorative teepee that had many simple but bright, colorful designs painted upon its walls. He scratched at the door and disappeared inside after a moment, and Kari took the opportunity to look the younger males of the patrol over. They fidgeted under her scrutiny, and she had to stop herself from laughing, reminding herself that the honor-driven people might not understand her amusement and take it as an insult.

"Do any of you young men speak elvish?" she asked in that tongue, but she received no response from the males as they looked to each other in confusion. It left her to wonder why the patrol leader was able to understand some of it, and how the tribe as a whole might have come into contact with it. Were there elves here on Tsalbrin, possibly in this same rainforest?

She turned her attention to the females then, and watched as they worked to prepare the gathered foods and hunted meats for the tribe's evening meal. They paid almost no attention to the newcomers, and set about their tasks with grim-faced determination. Like the males they wore no clothing, but many had decorative bone hoops in their pierced fins or, in a few cases, string belts around their waists that were punctuated by a single bone circle that hung down before their lower bellies. Kari wondered at their meaning, but her thoughts came to a quick end when the patrol leader returned with another male at his side.

"You are she who speaks the words of the elves?" the other male asked in elvish as he drew up before the small group. His accent was wondrous, retaining the sibilance of his native language even while speaking the flowing tongue of the elves.

"I am," Kari said, and she touched her hand palm-up to her breast before waving it slowly in the direction of the elder. "I am called Karian Vanador; I am a hunter of demons in service to Zalkar. The male to my right is called Erik, and the demon to my left is called Makauric. The demon has served as our guide so that we could find you easily; he will bring you no harm."

The elder considered her words for a minute, after which he motioned for the patrollers to return to their duties. He waited for the others to depart, and Kari looked over what she assumed was a tribal shaman. The male wore brightly colored woven garments, though they still didn't quite classify as clothes. They appeared more like vestments of priesthood, embroidered simply with depictions of a large lizardman with a sun behind him, holding a hand out over many smaller lizardmen who knelt in supplication. His face had small yellow and red designs painted under his reptilian eyes, and a feather-adorned headdress covered his crown, its plumage comprised of a myriad of tropical bird feathers arranged in a careful pattern that was impressive to behold. He didn't have the woven-grass bracelets that Kari assumed denoted authority, but she guessed that it was because his shamanistic vestments did that well enough.

After a few more moments, with the patrol well out of earshot and the females behind them busily tending to the cooking meal, the shaman spoke once more. "I am called Savarras," he continued in elvish. "I am the high shaman of our family, and speak for our chieftain. For what purpose have you come among the people?"

213

Kari nodded appreciatively for the creature's fluency in the somewhat stilted and overly formal speech of the elves. She wondered again where he had learned to speak it, but decided not to dwell on it: she was simply thankful that he did indeed understand her. She looked to Erik and then Makauric briefly and let her expression tell them to relax and wait for her to explain what was being said afterwards. The brys shouldered his bow, and the czarikk in the area were all visibly relieved.

"Erik and I are hunters of demons," she answered, and then she gestured lightly toward Makauric. "This one has earned our trust for the time being, and indeed led us to you. We have been tasked by our lord to hunt a much larger and more dangerous demon called a sylinth. We have come among your people to ask if you have any knowledge of such a creature."

Something flashed in the shaman's eyes, but after a moment he blinked whatever it was away. "Remain here at peace," he said. "I shall return to you shortly."

Savarras returned to the teepee from which he had come. Erik approached and touched Kari's shoulder and she turned to face him. "What happened?" he asked.

"Just introductions so far, but did you see him flinch when I asked about the sylinth?" she asked, and Erik nodded. "He's probably asking his chief how much to tell us, and letting him know we're here to help. The one I've been speaking to is Savarras; he's the tribe's shaman."

"I am not certain it was your sylinth," Makauric said, "but looking at these people, they have clearly been hurt by something. Look at the faces of the females."

Kari followed Makauric's gaze to the czarikk tending to the cooking, and Erik did the same. The females didn't bother to even acknowledge the guests, so Kari studied them for several minutes. Though she had only met czarikk a few times in her life, as she watched the females closely she could see there was truth to Makauric's words. There was something about the downturn of their reptilian mouths, the slight narrowing of their eyes, and the tightness in their throats that suggested anger, fear, or pain.

After a couple of minutes, Kari turned back to the brys. "How did you know those were females?" she asked. Makauric simply tapped his slitted nostrils. Kari tilted her head, and she glanced at Erik as he snickered quietly into his hand.

Savarras soon returned and held his hands out to the sides with the palms up. "My chieftain has tasked me with showing you what it is you have inquired about," he said to Kari. "First, however, he has welcomed you to stay with the family for the evening, to share in our meal, and even to watch as we perform a fire dance for Sakkrass."

Kari touched her hand to her breast and bowed her head. "We are grateful for your hospitality," she said. "Is Sakkrass your deity, then?"

"Indeed," Savarras said. "We believe our lord is displeased with our family, so tonight we will perform a fire dance to attempt to return to his good graces."

That piqued Kari's interest, and she folded her arms across her chest. "Your women appear to be in pain," she said quietly. "Is this related to Sakkrass being displeased?"

The czarikk shaman nodded with a sigh. "Come, and I will show you," he said, and he led the trio across the village. They came to a dome-shaped skin hut, but the shaman pulled up short before the door. "I cannot enter until the time for the cleansing rites is upon us, but look you well upon what has happened to us."

Kari steeled herself, opened the flap to the tent, and crouched to step inside, and she was immediately assailed by a horrid stench. When her eyes adjusted to the low light within, she saw that the wider tent had a depressed, sand-covered floor that served as a rookery. All of the eggs within were smashed, and it appeared some of them were near to hatching at the time they were destroyed. Kari put her hand to the end of her snout, trying not to be sick or burst into tears as Erik came in behind her. In all her years as a demonhunter, even with all of the atrocities she had come across, never had she seen something so base and horrible – not even the massacre in the city of Seren during the Apocalypse.

"By the gods," Erik muttered as he came in, and he gave Kari's shoulder a comforting squeeze.

She stayed only another moment, fighting hard not to burst into tears, and she scrambled out of the tent to get back to fresh air and away from the gruesome scene before them. "Forgive me, I was not prepared to see such a thing," Kari said to Savarras. She took a deep breath and rose to stand straight before the shaman, whose eyes showed the telltale traces of withheld tears in their depths. "What happened here?"

"I do not know," the czarikk shaman said. "Sakkrass has hidden his face from me and I cannot divine his wishes for the people. He allowed a snake to kill our children, like the old gods did to the people many generations ago when we turned our backs on them."

There was clearly a lot more to the story, but Kari's attention was fixed on the shaman's mention of what could've been the sylinth. "A snake?" Kari repeated. "Tell me: was this snake twice the length of a man, and did

215

it slither upright like a man?"

"We did not see," Savarras answered with a shake of his head. "This was done in the dark of night when we were in our sleep cycle. We assume it was the snake, as it has previously attempted to make us bend knee to it: to make us turn our backs on Sakkrass as he has turned his on us. Its scent lingers, though we have not seen it since our refusal to swear fealty to it."

Kari didn't know how the shaman would react to her trying to touch him, but she slowly laid her hand on his shoulder and met his stare evenly. "Sakkrass did not do this to you," she said confidently. "This was done to you by a creature we call a sylinth, a demon that shares the characteristics of a snake. This is the very creature we have come to hunt."

Savarras shook his head. "But Sakkrass ignores my pleas…"

"No, he does not," Kari said forcefully, but she softened her gaze. "His answers are being blocked by the sylinth. They are crafty adversaries, and they confuse and blur the minds of men to attain their evil ends. It wants you to believe Sakkrass has turned his back on you so that you will serve its own master."

Savarras considered her words for a minute, trying to keep up with translating what she'd said, and recognition filled his eyes. "Like the old one!" he exclaimed. "Then Sakkrass has not turned his back on us, I have simply failed him?"

"No, no," Kari shushed him. "You have failed no one! This is something beyond your control, and this is why my lord has sent us to the aid of your people. Sakkrass has likely asked my lord for our help," she said, for though she hated to lie, she knew the shaman needed to be bolstered. "Sakkrass will want to see your fire dance tonight. Honor him and stay true to his service, and when we remove the sylinth, you will feel his joy again."

Savarras studied her eyes for a few moments, and she could see the joy spread through his own. "I must inform my chieftain at once," he said. "Please, make yourselves comfortable near to the fire pit, and I will join with you as soon as I have spoken with Oshasis."

Kari nodded and the shaman made his way hastily to the chieftain's tent. She led her two companions back to the fire pit and sat on a nearby log. Erik knelt before her and Kari fell into his open arms, and he hugged her tightly and stroked her hair. She felt foolish, or even a little weak, and she figured that he probably expected someone much tougher in a partner, especially now that he knew who she was. If he felt that way, though, nothing in his touch showed it. He pulled away from her lightly after a couple of minutes and met her stare evenly, and Kari could see there was no judgment or disappointment in his eyes, only concern.

"Are you all right?" he asked.

Kari shook her head. "Gods, Erik, it killed their *children*," she said, blinking back a few fresh tears, and Erik nodded solemnly. "It's going to pay, Erik. This thing will beg for death when we're done with it. I swear it."

"Yes, it will," he agreed with a grim smile.

"The czarikk think their god turned his back on them," she continued. "The sylinth tried to force them to serve it, and killed their children when they refused. But it was too cowardly to fight them. It slipped in during the night and smashed their eggs when they weren't awake to defend their young. That kind of cowardice doesn't seem to fit a sylinth; it sounds more like something a corlyps would do."

"Or a brys," Erik said, turning his stern gaze to Makauric, whose own eyes narrowed.

"This was not my doing," the brys said simply.

"So you say," Erik returned, "and I'll take you at your word for now. But I'd better not find that you've lied to us, brys. If this *was* your doing, in whole or in part, you'd best disappear before I find out."

"Save your threats," Makauric said evenly, his voice impassive even in the face of the accusation. "I am not afraid of you, and regardless, you have no cause to suspect me."

"Let it go," Kari said, touching the end of Erik's snout to silence him before the argument could get any more heated. She glanced at Makauric and he nodded, and he climbed a tree, apparently wanting some time alone.

Kari sighed, turned back to Erik, and stroked his face. "I'm going to swear a Blood Oath," she said, and his eyes widened. "If our guide was responsible, it'll become obvious immediately."

Erik was speechless for the better part of a minute. "You're a better person than me, Karian," he said, and she didn't bother to correct him. "While these people have my sympathies, I don't think I could muster the fury to swear the Blood Oath. Does that...make me weak?"

She regarded him curiously in light of her thoughts only minutes before, and she cradled his cheek. "We all became demonhunters for different reasons," she said. "I don't know why you did, and I was confused about what would drive a half-demon to despise his father's kind enough to hunt them for a living. I think I understand that now, but honestly, I don't really care. You're a good partner, and I know I can depend on you." She paused with a sigh. "But what we saw in that tent...that's why *I* became a demonhunter, Erik. That kind of pain is something I can identify with, something that no one should ever feel. And we have to make the ones responsible pay for it; that's why I do what I do. I've walked across a good bit of this world, and everywhere I can see the hurt and pain the demons cause written on the faces of nearly every person I pass. If we didn't stand up and do something about it, *that* would make us weak."

"Did they kill someone in your family?" he asked, and she was shocked. "I only ask because when you ran away in Flora, Eryn and Ty said they'd found you in the graveyard." Kari bit her lip and looked away as tears welled up in her eyes again. Erik touched her face gently and said, "I'm sorry. Forget I asked, I didn't mean to hurt you again after what we just saw."

Kari shook her head; she wasn't ready to tell him the whole of it, but she realized it wasn't fair to keep it from him altogether. "I had an abusive father," she managed quickly. She closed her eyes and fought to keep her emotions in check, and she took a deep breath after she'd said it. "I went to the graveyard to remind myself that he's dead, and that he can never hurt me again. And despite everything he put me through, I'm a good enough woman to impress a man like you...and more importantly, your brother."

Erik smiled and gently pulled her into another embrace, and he held her tightly for a few minutes. "I suppose I am rather hard to impress, but that's a product of my character more than others'," he admitted. "But Grakin...he's a better judge of character...and a very lucky man."

Kari wiped the traces of tears from around her eyes when Erik released her. She fought for something to say, but ultimately just smiled, and Erik returned it in full. "So what's our plan?" he asked, cocking a half-smile. "I know I'm supposed to be in charge, but since I don't speak elvish, I've no idea what you two have been talking about."

"We've been invited to share dinner with them and then watch them perform a fire dance to Sakkrass," Kari said. She elaborated, "Sakkrass is their god, but I can't say I've ever heard his name before. After their fire dance we're welcome to stay the night in the village."

He nodded. "Well, that's helpful. We should have Makauric lead us to the sylinth's lair at first light. Once it's dead we'll come back and let these people know, and then try to find out where the rest of my siblings and the twins are. We've got a lot of work to do, but these people deserve whatever help we can give, even if it's just the strength of our presence, right?"

"Well said," Kari agreed.

The two waited for nearly a half hour before Savarras returned with the chieftain at his side. Kari expected the chieftain to perhaps have a more elaborate headdress or facial markings, but instead he was clothed with short, tanned animal hide breeches and an open leather-like vest of a similar color. He had golden bands around both of his upper arms and a bone necklace that hung down over his breast, and the clothing and simple jewelry distinguished him greatly from his people. The outfit reminded Kari of the wolf people of southeast Terrassia, called luranar: she remembered that golden bands were their way of denoting royalty, and that the tanned leggings and vests were very popular among them. She found it curious that a czarikk would be wearing a similar outfit, and wondered if it meant there were luranar here on Tsalbrin.

Kari rose and bowed before the chief, and Erik did the same in turn. The czarikk male held his hands up before bringing them quietly together before his face and nodding his head. He said something in his sibilant tongue to his shaman, and then he folded his arms across his chest and waited for his shaman to translate his words.

"This is our chieftain, Oshasis," Savarras said, gesturing toward the other male. "He welcomes you to the home of the people."

"We are honored to be welcome among your people and share in the comforts of your village," Kari returned with a bow of her head.

Savarras translated her words to Oshasis, and the lizardman's expression changed enough that Kari understood he liked her formal greeting. The two czarikk males exchanged words a few more times before Oshasis uttered what Kari assumed was the czarikk phrase for *excuse me* and made his way to sit on one of the logs around the fire pit. Savarras approached Kari and Erik and said, "Oshasis is deeply thankful for your promised efforts to rid us of the snake. His thoughts and prayers go with you, and the spirit of Sakkrass will watch over you."

Kari thanked Savarras and his chief for the blessing, and they took their places around the fire pit at Oshasis' direction. Kari explained what Oshasis had said to Erik. They shared in the evening meal when the rest of the tribe came out to join them, though Makauric stayed perched up in his tree. Not including those on patrol, there were well over one hundred czarikk, and all of them came out to share dinner with their chief and shaman. They sat in a cozy but large circle around the central fire pit. Kari spent most of the mealtime telling Savarras a little bit about herself and her partner, their adventures, and their mission to find and strike down the sylinth. Kari swore to them that she and Erik would not let them down.

Dinner gave way to the lighting of a massive bonfire in the central pit, and soon many of the czarikk began painting each other with festive,

219

colorful markings all over their bodies. Males and females painted each other, and as each one's body painting was finished they began a dance around the fire. Not all of the tribe took part in the painting or the dance, but a score danced and the others sang in their beautiful language, a chorus of voices filled with joy but tinged with pain. Kari watched as male and female alike danced past her and Erik, spinning, stomping their clawed feet, throwing their heads back in elation, and joining the others in singing the joyous exultation.

Kari felt her heartbeat quicken as her eyes drank in the bright light of the fire and the intoxicating motion of the dancers. She wondered at the display: her love of her profession and dedication to her own lord never once drove her to any sort of emotional release. She had known nothing of Sakkrass, but watching the czarikk, she learned that he was benevolent. In learning of a new race and its customs, finding that their patron was a loving one was always a positive first step. So many of the primitive humanoid races in the far reaches of the world bent knee to those that reveled in war and destruction; to find a people whose deity reveled in song and dance gave Kari a warm feeling.

Kari felt her heart swell and she closed her eyes for a few moments as the veil of her past split again. She remembered dancing around a fire when she visited with the elves, and though that had been a different type of dance and celebration, her participation had made her feel as though she belonged among the elves. When she opened her eyes, she was near-mesmerized by the dancing flames and reptilian bodies. She stood, removed her armor and her clothing, and waited patiently while two czarikk females approached and began to silently paint her body. The reptilian women seemed to enjoy painting her nude form, and they traced designs up her legs and across her breasts, down her arms and even across her face, back, and wings. Once they were finished, Kari stepped into the steady stream of dancers and began to flow along with them.

Kari danced among them for hours until the fire began to burn low, and little by little the dancers left the circle. Eventually most of the tribe returned to their homes to sleep, leaving only Kari dancing around the dying fire. Oshasis had retired to his own teepee, but Savarras remained with Erik until Kari's performance came to a close. She was covered in sweat when she returned to the log where the two males sat, and she took up her swords before returning to the fire pit.

She knelt before the fire and held her swords inverted with the tips to the ground before her, and Kari lowered her head. "Zalkar!" she called, her voice echoing in the night. It had been some time since she'd sworn the

Oath, but the words flowed from her lips effortlessly. "I ask of you the right to vengeance on behalf of these people. Fill me with your strength and make me an instrument of justice: grant me the power of your avatar that I may strike down the demon that has caused these people harm."

Kari stood up and turned to face Erik and Savarras, and she crossed her swords before her. Zalkar's symbol, the Sword of Truth and the balanced forces of Justice and Mercy, drew itself across her chest in light blue and then pulsed once before it faded into the blackness of her skin. Savarras sat agape, stunned beyond words though his mouth began to move. Erik regarded Kari with a gaze that clearly said he was impressed, and he nodded in recognition that her prayer had been answered.

"What have you done?" Savarras finally managed when Kari moved to pick up her clothing and armor.

"I have enlisted the aid of my deity himself in our cause," she answered, her smile one of confidence and comfort. "Would you prefer we sleep out here near the fire?"

The czarikk shaman was still shocked by what he had witnessed and by her words, but after considering her for several moments he shook his head. "No. No, you may have the use of my home this night," he said. He looked off into the darkness on the far side of the village. "My mate and I...we have not shared a tent since our egg was destroyed. It is forbidden for male and female to mate until the rites of cleansing are performed over the dead. However, if Sakkrass is not displeased with us, then the rites are merely a formality. I will go to my mate, and leave you two to take our home."

Kari sniffled but did her best not to cry when it was the shaman who was in pain. She squatted down and touched Savarras' face lightly, still unsure if it was taboo to do so. He didn't shy away from her touch, but met her eyes. "I am sorry for your loss," she said, to which he nodded in thanks. "Go to your mate; she needs you."

Savarras rose to his feet and touched Kari's face in return as she stood. "My tent is the one beside our chieftain's," he said. "Goodnight to you both, and rest you well."

Savarras moved off into the darker portions of the village, and Kari looked up to see Makauric's glowing eyes watching over her. She waved for Erik to follow and moved toward the tent Savarras had indicated. Kari was surprised that the brys had not come down from his tree during their stay thus far, but attributed it to him wanting to stay out of sight to ease the tension in the czarikk village. Kari entered Savarras' teepee with Erik behind her, and found it spacious and warm, decorated with trinkets and

221

charms that hung from its wooden supports. Its floor was covered with animal skins and furs. It was clearly the home of a holy man, and was accordingly clean and efficient.

Erik undressed down to his loincloth, piled his armor and his weapons neatly near the doorway, and lay down on the surprisingly soft nest of furs and hide blankets. Kari lay down beside him and touched his face lightly, and she kissed him chastely on the side of his snout. Erik smiled and looked at the painted designs that adorned her naked body, and his eyes returned to meet hers, searching. "That was amazing," he said simply.

She searched his eyes in return for a few moments, and she blew out a calm sigh. "It took me back to another life, when I traveled among the elves," she said quietly. "I'm not sure what came over me. Watching the fire dance...it was like it awakened something in me, something that's been asleep since I came back. Maybe it was the shock combined with the moment...I don't know. I just know I feel more alive, I guess you could say. It's like I'm connected to this world again, rather than just walking on it."

"And now our god's strength rests in you," he said. He was impressed, and made no attempt to mask it.

"We will not fail these people, Erik. I swear it."

In the depths of his glowing blue eyes, Kari could see his confidence was the same. He touched her face lightly and kissed her forehead. "I know," he said. "Tonight that sylinth feels a chill, and the shadow of death closing over it."

"I have to ask you one thing, though," Kari said. "I know you're not fond of Makauric; I'm obviously not fond of brys myself. But he's helping us, so try to be polite to him."

Erik chuckled but conceded her point with a nod. "I will," he said. "I was caught up in the moment a little, as you were. It won't happen again."

Kari was satisfied with his answer and the expression on his face that said it was genuine. With that the two fell asleep among the warmth and security of the czarikk village. The jungle was quiet around them, and Kari slept soundly throughout the night.

Chapter XII – Uncertainty

The journey to Tingus was uneventful, and the crew of the *Coastrunner* seemed anxious to get their half-demon passengers off the ship as soon as possible. Unlike Captain Galdur and his crew, the sailors of the smaller vessel lacked the courtesy or accommodating nature Aeligos and his companions had gotten used to over the length of their previous voyage. It led to a very boring and tense trip, and the group passed most of the time reading in their hammocks, as they didn't want to be underfoot on deck. They arrived in the port city of Tingus after a little more than ten days, and when the ship docked around midday, the half-demons and their two human companions were the only ones to disembark. The ship left port again immediately after, on its way to Northport.

Tingus was quiet for a port town, and only a few other ships were in its sizeable harbor when the group disembarked. Unlike the other ports they had visited on their journey, Tingus wasn't built on a hill, but instead extended into grassy plains. The docks themselves were clean and well-maintained, and there were armed, uniformed guards stationed at the end of each pier while others patrolled. It gave Aeligos hope that the city wasn't as rough as Flora was reputed to be, or as unwelcoming as Riverport had been. At the very least, the guards were of varied races, from human to terra-rir to shakna-rir, which said the city wasn't likely a bastion of Gaswell sympathizers.

The Silver Blades received many a strange stare from the locals when Aeligos led his siblings and two human companions to the nearest inn, but he shrugged it off as curiosity. The closest inn to the docks was a three-story hotel called *The Sand and the Strand*, and Aeligos motioned for the others to head inside. Aeligos lagged behind and scanned the docks and piers in both directions to see if anyone was watching them. Other than the dissipating curious glances of the guards, there didn't appear to be any obvious trouble. He nodded to the nearest passing guards, who returned the gesture, and Aeligos stepped inside with his siblings.

The inside was spacious and cheery, with the windows left open to let in the smell of the ocean breeze, and the pleasant aroma was augmented by the scents of baking bread and roasting meat. There were several dozen other patrons within, and each spared the large group a glance, several eyebrows rising in surprise before they returned to their own conversations. Like the guards, the patrons were of many different races, which reinforced

Aeligos' initial assumption. Aeligos spotted a couple of empty tables near one of the front windows and motioned for his siblings to push them together and sit while he approached the innkeeper.

The proprietor was shakna-rir, and the green-skinned rir looked over the approaching half-demon with a measured, red-eyed gaze. His hair was dark brown and a little longer than shoulder-length, tied back in a high conservative tail. He made busy polishing the bar as Aeligos approached, but when the dark male drew close, the innkeeper stood up straight and smiled. "Welcome to *The Sand and the Strand*," he said with the soft, flowing accent common to the desert peoples. "Ieyok Melurasti, at your service. What can I do for you this fine afternoon?"

"How many rooms can you spare?" Aeligos asked, and he slid a couple of gold coins the innkeeper's way.

Ieyok picked the coins up and dropped them in a bucket on the shelf behind him, which to Aeligos was a telling gesture. "We've more than enough if your friends would like one apiece," the innkeeper said.

"We'll take seven, then, if you please," Aeligos said. He looked around the common room for a few moments before returning his attention to the host. "We could also use seven ales and seven meals. How're things in the city, calm?"

"How long do you plan to stay?" the shakna-rir male asked.

"Tonight and tomorrow night," Aeligos answered, and he leaned forward on the bar so that he had to look up slightly to keep the innkeeper's gaze.

"Rooms, meals, and drinks for seven over two days will cost seven gold," Ieyok said. He reached under the bar and pulled up seven simple iron keys. "You may take the third floor to yourselves; all but the back left room."

Aeligos produced seven more gold coins and placed them on the bar while the shakna-rir began filling tankards from a tap behind him. Aeligos picked up the keys, deposited them in a pocket of his cloak, and waited for the barkeep to finish pouring the drinks. He looked around the common room again; none of its occupants were staring at him or his companions, and he breathed a silent sigh of relief. He was more accustomed to doing reconnaissance work on his own, when he could use minor magic to alter his looks to better fit in and didn't have a large, conspicuous group with him.

The shakna-rir turned back around once he finished filling the last tankard, and he scooped up the gold coins and put them into the same bucket as the first two. "Things in town have been very calm," Ieyok said.

"Not much in the way of trouble or even gossip on the wind, except of course for the situation in the west."

"Oh?" Aeligos asked, feigning surprise. "Something going on in your homeland?"

Ieyok shook his head. "No, no, I suppose you folks are newcomers to the island?" he asked, though he didn't wait for an answer. "General Braxus Gaswell is raising an army in the west and threatening to push all but the terra-rir from the island. The consensus seems to be that it's a lot of posturing and wind, and I haven't heard of any serious responses to the 'threat.'"

"Oh, I see," the dark male said with a nod. "How far to the west are your people?"

The shakna-rir's brows rose momentarily. "Thinking of visiting the desert?" he asked with a short, grunt-like laugh. "I didn't think your kind liked it out there, despite your heritage. It's about three days around the bay to Dune, or about a week to the kingdom seat of Kulthon at the base of the mountains. Even if you don't pass through Dune, it's best if you head west once you've passed the bay until you come to Dune Road, which will take you to Kulthon, if that's where you're headed."

Aeligos straightened up. "Great, thank you," he said. "Do you have women here?"

Ieyok fixed him with a curious stare for a moment, but then shook his head. "Not for the purpose you're asking," he said. "I'm sure you can find one at any of the taverns around town. But to be honest, I try to keep mules and such away from my inn."

"Understandable," Aeligos returned. "Is there hot food for us?"

Ieyok nodded and gestured his guest to the table where his companions sat. "Of course; I'll have one of my serving girls bring meals right over," he said.

Aeligos returned to the table, took a seat beside his sister, and looked over his group. Serenjols and Typhonix both looked bored, as though they were half-tempted to go out looking for trouble just to have something to do. Sonja was studying the other patrons in the bar, likely trying to detect any undertones of fear or anxiousness, and Aeligos was thankful to have her vigilant assistance. Grakin looked tired: he was sick a couple of times during the trip up from Riverport, and Aeligos suspected Kari not being around might have had something to do with it.

The two human teenagers looked excited, and Aeligos reminded himself that it was their first time away from home, and that everything – no matter how trivial to their companions – was going to seem new and

225

exciting to them. It also occurred to him that the group was going to have to take the time to have armor made for them and make sure that the weapons they had were of suitable quality in the event of a battle. Since they grew up on a tropical island that only received metals by the graces of Captain Galdur and similar supply runners, it was unlikely their weapons were of good quality.

Sherman noticed Aeligos' stare and smiled. "Something on your mind, sir?" he asked.

He didn't show it, but Aeligos was shocked to be called 'sir' by anyone. "We need to get you two armor and some better weapons," he said, and the twins agreed. "I don't mean to pry, but is there anything I should know about you before we undertake an overland trip?"

"Such as?" Sherman asked, rubbing a hand through his facial hair, which was much more unkempt than it had been when he joined them on Salkorum.

"Anything that would make our trip longer or inconvenience the rest of us, absolutely anything at all," the dark male said without pause, and the two shook their heads. "Good. We move quickly, so when we get you armor, you'll want to take into account speed, comfort, and how well you'll handle it while crossing the desert. We'll be in town at least until the day after tomorrow, or as long as it takes to get you youngsters outfitted. Ah, and here come some meals."

One of the shakna-rir barmaids brought over roasted chicken and pork with greens. After a few trips back to the kitchen, she had served them all and the friends enjoyed a hot lunch. Aeligos gave a subtle gesture to keep the reason behind their presence a secret as much as possible, so they kept the small talk mostly about the quality of the food or sightseeing in the city. Aeligos assigned them to pairs: he partnered each of the humans with one of his own siblings so they could be watched closely, and he left himself as the only one not paired with anyone else so he could get some snooping accomplished. He passed out their keys so they could get situated before they went out to see the city, and Aeligos warned them to stay out of trouble and not leave their partners while they were out and about.

Aeligos entered his room and stowed his travel pack inside the wardrobe, and then he checked the window's security briefly. It was a locking window with latching shutters that would allow a double layer of protection if he deemed it necessary. Satisfied that no one would be breaking into his room through the window without a lot of work, he turned and looked at the rest of his temporary abode. The rooms were set up simply but furnished with quality goods, and as Aeligos looked over the bed he squared his jaw and sighed. It had been an uncomfortable ten days aboard the *Coastrunner*, due in no small part to Eryn's absence. As much as her profession and her unapologetic pursuit of it annoyed him, her absence was what really hurt. He couldn't deny the fact that he loved her; not in quite the same way as his brother and Karian loved each other, but deep down he knew he did. He and Eryn were so good together, both in bed and outside of it, but only until they began to speak of the future.

He sighed again just thinking about it. He wanted her to be his mate and become a part of the Silver Blades so that they would always be together, but she insisted on sticking with her evil and spiteful career until she was "finished." She always went back to the assertion that she couldn't just walk away, and Aeligos wasn't naïve enough to think otherwise, but whenever she talked about *working* to get away from her life of crime, or of how she had no choice in pursuing it, she always left out some detail. His only conclusion was that there was something else, and the way she pursued her goals led him to believe that what it ultimately came down to was that she enjoyed her work. In the end, whether that was the case or not, Erik absolutely despised Eryn, and being caught between them, it laid a lot of stress on Aeligos.

Aeligos grunted, frustrated, and tried to clear his mind of the thoughts as he made his way downstairs and out of the inn. He thought of Grakin and Kari and how perfectly – seamlessly, he might go so far as to say – they went together, and considered that perhaps he should simply give up trying with Eryn and find someone like Kari. Kari and Eryn shared many characteristics, but their biggest difference seemed to be their past: while Eryn succumbed to the evil of her father and his lifestyle, Kari had risen above whatever she hid like a wounded heart. Aeligos smiled as he thought of his sister-in-law, and wondered if she and Grakin would decide to *tie the knot*, as it were, taking part in the human tradition of marriage. While a rir mating was much the same, the rir had taken to the human custom quite easily, appreciating the symbolic and physical tokens that each swore to the other. Aeligos' own parents had taken part in such a ceremony, and though their relationship ended quite bitterly after Typhonix' first birthday, Aeligos still had an enduring respect for the commitment.

He intended, as the innkeeper had detected, to find himself a woman for the night. His siblings – and everyone else, for that matter – never took his 'lifestyle' well, but they never understood his reasoning. Aeligos loved Eryn and his dedication was to her; the other women he slept with were simply a means to an end. He always found that a warm, happy, satisfied woman lying in bed beside him was far more willing to divulge sensitive information and secrets than anyone he could bribe with coin. Sonja and Erik were by far the most judgmental of his siblings about it, but none of them understood the big picture. Eryn knew why he did what he did, and it didn't bother her in the least: he always went back to her.

Aeligos passed into the heart of the city, and he looked around at the cozy structures that marked it as a community rather than a loose conglomerate of people sharing the same living space. It was a warm town: he could sense it simply by looking at the way it was built and laid out, with its main avenues stretching in the eight cardinal directions from a circular central plaza. There didn't appear to be any richer districts, the city uniform in the quality and beauty of its structures, and he wondered if he would even be able to find what he was searching for. His travels took him to the outskirts of town on its western edge, from which he could see sprawling farmlands where the plain extended to the horizon to the southwest and a glittering, breathtaking inland bay to the north and west. The city sat at the end of a short peninsula that jutted to the northeast, and he got a good look at the road leading off of it, presumably toward the cities of Dune and Kulthon. He turned back into the city after a few minutes to continue his search.

He walked the city for a while, looking for any suspicious characters or other signs that the city might have a thieves' guild or at least a gang that acted like one. Shockingly, his efforts turned up nothing, so instead he decided to check with the common citizenry to see if they could offer up similar information. He found a general goods store and headed inside. There were no customers within, so he approached the counter and was greeted by a young female shakna-rir in a simple tunic and breeches. "Good afternoon. I'm wondering if you carry information, and how much you charge for it," he said bluntly to gauge her reaction.

She looked him over for a few moments before responding, and he did the same to her. She was pretty, with bright scarlet hair and matching eyes like Aeligos' sister. She smiled after a minute and leaned forward on the counter, crossing her arms on its surface. "What did you want to know, handsome?" she asked.

He looked around again to make sure no one else was there, and there was concern on her face when he turned back to her. He smiled to ease her tensions, and said, "I'll be honest: I'm interested in what you know, or even just what's being said about Braxus Gaswell."

"Oh!" she exclaimed. She stood up straight, the smile fully returned to her face. "And what would you be willing to trade for such information?"

Aeligos laughed and rolled his shoulders back so that his wings popped free of his cloak, and he folded them behind himself. "What is it you'd like?" he asked evenly. He wanted it quite clear what she would be getting if she decided that a personal favor was in order.

If she was at all deterred by his demonstration that he was half-demon, she didn't show it. "I close shop at sundown, how about dinner and dessert, unless you have other plans?"

"I don't," he said with his boyish grin. "And that sounds fine, but we can't go back to my place unless you want to dine with my siblings."

The girl laughed. "What's your name, dark-eyes?"

He thought to himself for only a moment; in this situation, it would be harmless to use his real name. "Aeligos," he said. "And you?"

"Ellena," she said, her red eyes sparkling. "Ellena Illurasti. So you want to know about Gaswell...well, not much news about him comes up this way since he's so far to the southwest, but I'll tell you what I know. He's trying to push everyone who's not terra-rir off the island either by threats or by force, though he hasn't actually attacked anyone yet. There's a lot of talk that he wants to attack the Isle of Kirelia like his ancestor did, but since he chases off anyone not terra-rir, it's hard to get any real information. So, did that buy me dinner and dessert?"

Aeligos chuckled. "Not just yet," he said. "Tell me about your people; what do they think of all this?"

Ellena shook her head. "I was born and raised here in Tingus, so I don't really know what the queen thinks of Gaswell," she said, and she glanced at his wings. "You know, my people aren't afraid of your kind, so if you went to Kulthon, I'm sure either the queen or one of her people would be willing to talk to you. Why all the interest in Gaswell?"

"I'm interested in helping to stop him, if anyone has already taken the initiative to do the same," he said somewhat honestly. "So, where do you like to take your meals?"

"There's a nice little inn around the corner called *The Lonely Shepherd*."

Aeligos nodded and flashed her one last smile. "I'll see you there a half hour after sundown," he said. Once she agreed, he made his way back out into the city.

Ellena followed him to the door and leaned against its frame, watching him stride across the plaza and down the eastern avenue, and once he was out of sight, Aeligos laughed to himself. He hadn't gotten much in the way of information that he didn't already know, and he found it comical that he *had* found the one thing he didn't really need. He checked the position of the sun, judging when he would need to return to the inn and let his siblings know he'd be out for the night. He wondered if Sonja would be suspicious of his excuse that he was working on getting more information, and that brought a less amused chuckle from his lips.

The afternoon passed quickly, the half-guardian taking in nearly the entire city to find that his earlier observations regarding a thieves' guild had proven mostly correct. It was a nice city, but a bit too quiet for him. Aeligos had always preferred the hustle and bustle of Latalex and its extraordinary nightlife that was always full of intrigue, adventure, and danger. His was the life of the infiltrator, the rogue, moving in the shadows and finding what he sought without leaving a trail back to himself. In Tingus, it seemed that despite a fairly large population, it still had a small-town feel to it, and he got the impression that not much stayed a secret for long. Such might have meant that using his real name or expressing his intentions might be foolish, but he dismissed it; it seemed news came to and left Tingus slowly.

He returned to *The Sand and the Strand* just before the dinner hour and found the others already there waiting for him. The humans were both dressed in fine suits of chainmail with white tabards to help deflect the sunlight. They had well-crafted greatswords leaning against the wall, and the twins looked to their leader expectantly, waiting for his judgment. Aeligos wasn't sure how the locals would view the group being well-armed and armored, but with the rumors of trouble to the southwest, he assumed it wouldn't seem out of place.

"You look good," he said with a nod as he approached the table. "The armor's not too heavy for you, is it? Chainmail isn't the type of thing you can wear all day."

"It will take some adjusting, but it's not too bad," Katarina said with her disarming smile. "At the very least, we're used to the heat from back home."

Aeligos looked around the common room. There weren't many patrons in the dining area, so he turned back to the group. "I'll be out working this evening, so have a meal and don't stay up too late. Pretend Erik is here to yell at you. I'm not sure if I'll be back, so don't wait for me. So far I haven't found out anything that we didn't know, but I'm hoping that will change."

"Do you need any help?" Grakin asked.

The rogue shook his head. "No, in fact, it's better if I'm the only one asking," Aeligos said. "Best that all paths lead back to me, if they lead anywhere at all."

"Be careful," Sonja told him, and Aeligos bid them goodnight before leaving again. His legs were getting sore from having walked the length of the city several times over the course of the day, and he looked forward to having a relaxing dinner. His thoughts turned to the shakna-rir woman he was on his way to meet, and her charming smile and sparkling eyes stood out most prominently in his mind. He wondered if he could ever have a meaningful relationship with such a woman. His was a life lived on the road and in the shadows, and unlike Eryn, the girl probably didn't have the background or experience to know how to handle it. Eryn understood Aeligos, and she could not only live with the stress of his dangerous role among the Silver Blades, but also deal with the other demands of his work; Ellena likely couldn't. Of course, the entire train of thought was irrelevant: he would be gone within another day and likely never see her again.

Aeligos pushed the thoughts aside, determined to at least enjoy the time he would spend with her. His footsteps took him toward the western side of the city as the sun dipped below the horizon, and it didn't take him long to find the inn Ellena had described. He nearly laughed aloud when he saw the sign above its door swinging in the breeze, depicting a shepherd sitting on a rock, head in hand, with a pool of blood on the ground before him. Aeligos imagined the mutton must be especially good, but before he stepped within, he ducked into the shadows of a alleyway nearby.

He watched the inn for nearly twenty minutes before he saw Ellena enter. She was alone when she approached, and she stepped inside without even looking around, which eased Aeligos' tensions. He stepped out from the alleyway and walked silently into the inn's common room, and he joined the young woman at the table she'd chosen by the hearth. He wondered for a moment why the inn would even have one given its geographical location, but shrugged off the thought and took the seat across from her.

Ellena smiled when he sat down, and he touched her hand lightly. The barmaid brought over two ales and then two plates of – as he'd guessed – hot mutton and potatoes. The two ate and chatted lightly, and she told him as much as she could about the island and her people. She related that Tingus was the name of a general from Kulthon who'd captured the city several hundred years before, and that the peninsula was called Kroth's Point after the shakna-rir warlord who'd previously held it. Aeligos listened to her brief history lesson while they finished their dinner and their drinks, and once they were done she stopped talking and looked at him as if waiting for him to talk about himself.

"So what kind of dessert do they serve here?" he asked, in no mood or position to reveal anything that might be potentially damaging.

Ellena grinned, put her elbows on the table and brought her hands together beneath her chin. *"You* are the dessert, silly," she said.

Aeligos laughed, his mirth serving to mask the more appraising glance he gave the girl. She seemed younger than he'd initially thought when he met her at the shop, and the way she nursed her ale ever so slowly confirmed his suspicions further. He ran his hand through his hair after a moment, looked up at her from a strange angle, and flashed his boyish grin again. He didn't want to give her the impression that he was judging what he saw. "So why did you want to come here, are your parents at home?" he ventured.

"Aye," she said as she leaned to the side and crossed one leg over the other, her smile still broad and enchanting. "I'm hesitant to ever bring young men home; you know how fathers are about their little girls."

Aeligos grimaced inside but kept his expression neutral; that was not what he wanted to hear. "Especially when it comes to half-demons," he said.

Ellena chuckled. "No boy is ever good enough for papa's little girl, but you...well, let's just say that should I bring a half-demon home, my father would have a fit, regardless of how my people feel about yours."

That was the typical reaction for a rir woman to a half-demon, and what Aeligos had expected when he first spoke to her in the shop. His boyish smile and good looks could usually get him past that hesitation, but he found Ellena's lack of hesitation alarming. "That's where being a half-demon has its advantages: it's hard to find something less desirable to bring home to one's parents," Aeligos said with a chuckle before he picked up his mug and took a sip.

Ellena laughed, and between the sound and the look in her eyes, Aeligos could tell she was already getting intoxicated. "So, is it true what they say about half-demons?" she asked.

"You'll have to be more specific," he said, "since a lot gets said about my kind."

"I've heard that other races aren't nearly the lovers that half-demons are," she said, barely able to stop herself from giggling.

Aeligos chuckled again through his nose and then finished his drink, and he cast his dark-eyed gaze across the common room. The other patrons appeared to be paying no heed to the couple or their conversation, and he raised a single finger toward the barmaid when she met his wandering stare. He turned back to the young shakna-rir woman before him and waited for the barmaid to bring him another drink. His warm smile settled into a more measured, intent gaze. "A lot of what *they* say is just conjecture," he said, "but some of it's true. I don't think I put any other men to shame, but let's just say I've never left a woman unsatisfied."

Ellena leaned forward on the table and a giggle escaped her as the alcohol settled in a little more. "Oh, so you're experienced? You're not mated, are you?"

"Not as such," he said, and he gave a nod of thanks when the barmaid placed his ale on the table and quickly departed. He took a slow sip from the drink, keeping his eyes locked with those of the young girl. He placed the mug back on the table and licked the foam from his chops. Ellena continued to smile at him, oblivious to the intent behind his stare, and Aeligos turned a sigh inward as he considered his next words. "So, shall I go get us a room?"

The young woman seemed to sober up a bit. "A room?" she stuttered. "I...I'm not sure I'm quite ready for that."

Aeligos leaned forward on the edge of the table and nearly burned a hole through the shakna-rir girl with the strength of his gaze. "Oh, come now, you didn't honestly ask me here for dessert just to tease me, did you?" he asked. Her reaction clearly told him that she had, and that now she was growing nervous. "I'm only going to be in town a few days, and was hoping to sample the local fruit before I move on to your capital city."

"Gods, my father would kill me!" the girl blurted.

"Then what are you doing here?" he asked evenly. Ellena straightened up as he took a tone akin to what he expected her father might sound like when angry. "Let me be quite clear, young lady: if I were a half-demon of another kind, I might not take *no* for an answer. This is a dangerous game you play, and your father would throw a fit for good reason if he knew you were out here doing this. There are a lot of men – and not even half-demons – who would be fully willing to take advantage of you, when you think you're just being cute and teasing them. Your father's job is to keep you away from men like that, and like me. How far away do you live?"

Ellena was nearly on the verge of tears. "Not far from here, sir. Just up the road."

"I'll take care of dinner. Thank you for your company, but I want you to head straight home, right now," he said. The girl rose without hesitation and scrambled from the inn as quickly as she could, given her state. The others in the tavern regarded the girl as she left and then their gazes fell over the rogue briefly before they returned to their own business. One of the barmaids followed Ellena out the door, and Aeligos hoped she would escort the girl home.

Aeligos sat back in his chair and blew out a long sigh, and he'd only closed his eyes for a moment before the hand of the other barmaid fell on his shoulder. The human woman gave him an appreciative nod when their eyes met, and she left a fine cigar on the table before she made her way over to the other patrons. Aeligos tucked the cigar in a concealed pocket on the inside of his leather breastplate and took a long, final sip of his ale. He left two gold coins on the table and made his way silently back to *The Sand and the Strand*.

~~*~*

The Silver Blades spent the following day and night in Tingus, and then took to the road. Aeligos decided it would be best to travel to Dune first and see if they could find a caravan headed into the desert. He knew little of desert travel other than the obvious, and was concerned that his human charges would be less prepared for the moisture-sucking heat. He further had a nagging worry about sandstorms and such, and knew a caravan would be better prepared for such an event.

Just as the innkeeper told him, it took them three days to reach the city of Dune by following the road out of Tingus. The bay was on their right the entire time, and they took the northern fork when the road split from its path into the heart of the desert. The farms extended for miles and miles outside of the port city, and once they passed the edges of the cultivated lands they found wide expanses of grazelands for livestock. The landscape only began to change once they drew within a day's travel of Dune, where the plains began to give way to a dry, rocky and sandy expanse.

Dune itself was barely a city. It was a transition and stopping place for caravans and travelers more than anything else, and was comprised of a good mix of humans, shakna-rir, and terra-rir. It was smaller but busier than Tingus, with structures built of adobe and sandstone, and painted white or left the natural color. There were numerous wells throughout, which suggested a large amount of water far beneath its sands and rock, and there were vegetable gardens and even a few fruit trees. The Silver Blades expected a fairly barren city but found a jewel instead, and were pleased to find that the terra-rir population held no sympathies for Gaswell or his crusade.

The Silver Blades remained in Dune for only a couple of days before they were able to accompany a caravan headed into the heart of the desert empire, on its way with trade goods from Northport and the continent of Dannumore to the north. Using Typhonix' status as a demonhunter, they signed on as guards but asked for no pay, which got them easily approved.

The caravan left the city without delay once dawn broke on the third day, and soon the group was on its way to Kulthon.

Aeligos wasn't sure what to expect from the shakna-rir queen. The desert peoples tended to be militaristic and even a bit warlike at times, but the fact that they had not made any move to counter Gaswell's threat left him to wonder. He'd hoped that the young shakna-rir woman he'd met in Tingus would be able to tell him more, but neither she nor Ieyok was able to tell him anything he didn't already know. Something about the whole situation struck him as quite odd, and he wondered if it was just his experience with Seril's tactics during the Apocalypse that made Gaswell's more patient approach seem out of place.

The rogue took the point for the caravan and advised them when to slow and let him go ahead to scout out dangerous-looking areas. Wherever dunes piled on both sides of the road to form a natural bottleneck, he rode on ahead to make sure that no bandits or marauders awaited them. He wasn't sure how common brigands were in the hot, unforgiving wastelands of the desert, but Aeligos wasn't one to take chances, particularly when he was expected to help keep his hosts safe. He was quietly thankful that they encountered no trouble on the first day of the journey, and that his precautions proved unnecessary.

The temperature dropped considerably at night, and the group bundled up under the wagons, staying close to conserve heat. Aeligos shared a blanket with his sister, and the two lay on their sides face to face so they could speak, voicing their concerns for both the road ahead and their impending work in the shakna-rir capital. Sonja hadn't said anything to him about his *work* in Tingus, but he was able to tell by her expression that she "knew" what he'd been up to when he came back before she retired to sleep.

"What do you think we should do when we reach Kulthon?" Aeligos asked her. "No one seems particularly concerned with what Gaswell is about, or eager to go and start a fight with him, and he hasn't mobilized at all. I'm left to wonder what it is we're even doing here."

"Well, our most prudent course of action will be to let the shakna-rir do the talking," she said. "We should see what their intent is: how they plan to react either to the current situation or to Gaswell's imminent first attack on a neighboring city. They may be slow to move now, but once actual fighting breaks out, I doubt the shakna-rir will remain idle for long."

"That's what worries me," he said. "We've been tasked with preventing a war, but how exactly are we expected to do that? We're too few to take Gaswell down by force even if we use covert means, so what do

Erik's superiors really expect? I think at the very least we're going to need allies to take the fight to Gaswell. If I know history as well as I think I do, he's not going to disperse without first testing the strength of his army."

"We can only do our best," Sonja said. "Erik's superiors don't want a war to break out, but if we can't stop that from happening, then we do the only thing we can: try to make sure the right side wins."

Aeligos nodded. "I hope he and Kari finish their other duties quickly. I'm fine with leading this bunch to carry out diplomacy and explore, but I'd rather Erik were here and in charge when there's going to be fighting."

"You'll do fine, if it comes to that," she said. "Erik trusts you with our safety, and for good reason. How you behave when you're on your own time, that's another matter entirely."

"What's that supposed to mean?"

Sonja didn't bother keeping her voice down; it was a safe bet the others were all listening to their conversation anyway. "Don't lie to me, Aeligos. If you're going out to have sex, then say so. Don't tell me you're going out to gather information and have me worried for your safety when you're out satisfying yourself. That's not fair."

He sighed but didn't deny her words; she didn't understand and he wasn't sure she or the others ever would. "I didn't think you'd like it," he said.

"I don't," Sonja answered, her red eyes sparkling even as they glowed in the darkness. "But I like being lied to even less. I don't have to like what you do or who you choose to do it with, but honestly it's not my business anyway. But as I said, I don't appreciate sitting up at night worried because I think you're out probing the shadows of a city for answers."

"I'm sorry," he said. It was easier to ask forgiveness than permission, as they said.

Sonja nodded, and then a slight smile came to her face. "Was she cute?"

Aeligos chuckled but shook his head. "She was pretty, but also just coming of age, so I walked away," he said. Sonja beheld him curiously. "I know you probably don't understand, but sleeping with experienced women...they know what it is they are and aren't getting into. A young girl like that doesn't, and I wouldn't do something like that to her, or her father." She held his stare evenly but said nothing, and he touched the side of her snout. "It's why if any man slept with you and then was gone with the sunrise, I'd find him and cut his throat."

Sonja was clearly shocked by his declaration. "You're right, I don't understand," she said. "But it helps to know that there is at least a rhyme and reason to the way you behave." Aeligos sighed and fell quiet, and the two went to sleep among the droning of the other members of the caravan and the quiet whisper of the wind.

Sunrise came early and the caravan got back underway, and continued its trek for three more days along the sandy but well-traveled road. The desert heat was oppressive, but most of the group was able to sit inside the wagons while they traveled and didn't have to wear their armor. Out of the sun and without the extra weight upon them, the heat seemed not much worse for the human teenagers than the normal climate of their tropical home on Salkorum. Aeligos continued his vigilant scouting, and guided them all the way to the seat of the shakna-rir empire without incident. He was shocked when the caravan master paid him for his vigilance, and Aeligos took the offering of gold coins graciously. It was an odd day for him to take another man's money without a card game or a good deal of subterfuge taking place.

Kulthon was a massive city, much larger than any of the Silver Blades expected. Its outer edges stretched onto the arid rocky plains of the desert, while the heart of the city rose up into the foothills and the crook of the mountain range. The mountains extended from east to west and then curved around to the north, and the shakna-rir capital was nestled defensively into the elbow. Its back was securely against the base of a titanic peak and the city was surrounded by a wall in the front, while still more dwellings sat outside the wall. Aeligos had heard of the defensive structure of Aurun Ch'Gurra – the capital of the shakna-rir kingdom on Terrassia – and wondered if it was as impressive as the sight before him.

The caravan slowed to a stop outside the city proper, and the Silver Blades bid their gracious hosts farewell and made their way in. The lower section of the city, out on the arid plain, was comprised almost entirely of residences: flat-roofed one-story homes made of adobe and sandstone like their counterparts in Dune. Like in the smaller city, there was an abundance of gardens and wells, and the group even came across a fountain in the first circular plaza, though it was dried out. The roads were dusty and unpaved, though relatively well-kept, and each home seemed to have a rain barrel in addition to their access to the local wells, which the companions found odd.

Just as Ellena had suggested, Aeligos and his siblings received few stares as they entered the city. Aeligos took in their surroundings and studied the people as well. The shakna-rir were dressed simply in bright, light flowing clothes. They were naturally impervious to the heat of their preferred homelands, and wore their clothing as much for modesty as to protect themselves from the elements. The people had a simple look about them, but their expressions spoke of contentment stemming from the security of a strong kingdom.

Aeligos looked to the west, where he could see that the sun would be cut off early. The skies likely remained light well into the afternoon and early evening, but the high peaks would shade the city. It made him evaluate the homes around him a second time, and he took note of the glass windows that the shakna-rir had become famous for crafting, as well as the stone the homes were built from that likely trapped heat during the day and slowly released it at night. He gave a smile for the peoples' ingenuity that allowed them to thrive in a place where others would simply perish trying to carve out a life.

They passed through the lower portion of the city along a main road to one of the broad iron portcullises that led into the walled upper city. The portcullis was raised, and a squad of scimitar and spear-armed guards stood two to a side and watched the traffic passing into and out of the upper city. They glanced briefly at the approaching half-demons, but Typhonix touched Aeligos' shoulder, stepped to the forefront, and laid his dog tags over his chest. The guards gave courteous nods when Ty saluted them, and they allowed the group to pass without question.

The upper portion of the city was far more heavily populated, and the homes and buildings were constructed of the same materials as those of the lower section in most cases, though there were a few made of wood and brick. Many of the buildings were also two or three stories, and the wide streets of the lower city gave way to narrower, shadier roads in the upper district. The streets here were made of carved stone, and as soon as Aeligos' feet touched them he could feel what he suspected: the stones stored and gave off heat in turn to keep the city and its cold-sensitive residents warm at night. The plazas of the upper city were shopping centers with general stores, taverns, and inns cornering the alternating square and circular intersections. Aeligos found a respectable-looking inn called *Desert Wind* and led his companions in. They were able to get several rooms, but they paired up to conserve funds, and Aeligos bid his companions stay and have something to eat and drink while he explored the city. He exchanged a wry smile with Sonja and they both laughed, and the others joined in soon after.

Aeligos made his way farther into the city and was surprised at how homogenous the population was. While he fully expected it to be mostly shakna-rir, instead it was almost entirely shakna-rir: since leaving the caravan he'd seen very few people of other races. He wondered if it was the heat or if it had something to do with the shakna-rir and the way their kingdoms were organized and run. Ultimately he guessed it was a combination of the two: humans normally adapted to even the most inhospitable environments, but the rigid and matriarchal order of the shakna-rir may have made it more trouble than it was worth.

Aeligos continued up a steep road that was clearly for foot traffic only, and he saw other roads cut into ramps up the mountain to allow carts and animals to make their way up more easily. His road led to a second wall with an open portcullis, though there were more guards and they halted his approach. Looking through the portcullis, he could see that it safeguarded the royal palace and a few other buildings that appeared to be temples or homes to the nobility.

"State your business," one of the guards said. He rested his hand on the hilt of his scimitar, though Aeligos could tell that it was a formality and not a threat.

"Is this the way to the palace?" Aeligos asked, and the guard nodded curtly. "How would one go about requesting an audience with Her Majesty?"

"What is the nature of your request?" the guard prodded.

Aeligos looked the guards over briefly, and they clearly did not appreciate his appraising glance. It told him a lot in only a few seconds, though: he noted that the guard speaking to him was an officer and not just a nosey grunt. "I am here at Zalkar's request," he said after a few moments, and the officer's brows knitted suspiciously. "Two of my brothers are demonhunters and were sent here to the island on official business. As my elder brother is busy taking care of something else for his superiors, he entrusted me to come speak to your queen."

The guard studied the half-demon before him for several minutes, holding him under a blazing red-eyed gaze. Aeligos didn't so much as twitch, but met the officer's stare evenly. Satisfied that Aeligos was telling the truth, the officer nodded. "Continue up the road to the front door of the palace and inside, and then ask the guards within to direct you to the chamberlain's office. He will listen to what you have to say and decide if you are deserving of an audience with Her Majesty."

Aeligos thanked the guard and was saluted crisply as he headed through the portcullis and into the palace district. The area had much larger buildings than the upper city and was cloaked in shadow even early in the afternoon. The main road circled around to the north and then northeast to a second gate, with the palace on the outer edge and the temples and dwellings on the inside. He paid little attention to the temples and homes, and made his way to the massive castle with its sky-tickling towers and beautiful stained glass windows. A pair of guards opened the wooden double doors at his approached, and Aeligos continued inside.

The entry chamber was not what he expected. It was a spacious but sparsely furnished foyer with many doors leading off in every direction and staircases leading up to a second level on both sides. The floor was covered in an intricate, eye-catching carpet of crimson and gold, and suits of elven plate mail stood at attention around the perimeter, which he found curious. There were two guards inside the doorway dressed in finery with ceremonial rapiers at their belts. They gave the newcomer a couple of minutes to survey the beauty of the entry chamber, and once his eyes turned to them, they greeted him. After a short conversation, Aeligos was led upstairs and to the chamberlain's office.

The chamberlain's office was efficient, with only a couple of well-stocked bookshelves, a beautiful polished-wood desk, a crimson plush chair in which the chamberlain was sitting, and a pair of similar chairs in front of the desk. The chamberlain was middle-aged, his hair cut short and layered in such a way that suggested he was too busy with palace details to worry about grooming. His red eyes regarded Aeligos only briefly before he gestured shortly to the chairs across from him, and once the half-demon had taken his seat, the chamberlain put down his quill and sat back in his chair. He studied his guest for a minute before speaking, and his voice was clear and strong when he did. "Half-demon?" he stated as much as asked. "We don't see many of your kind out this way. What brings you to Her Majesty's palace this day?"

Aeligos didn't respond immediately, but instead leaned forward and extended his hand across the desk. After hesitating for only a moment, the chamberlain shook it. "My name is Aeligos Tesconis," the rogue said. "My older brother is a demonhunter under orders from Zalkar, and part of those orders is to weigh the intentions of the kingdoms here with respect to Braxus Gaswell. He asked me to come and speak with your queen while he sorts out another matter for his lord."

The chamberlain weighed Aeligos' words for a moment before he bobbed his head appreciatively. "That's probably the best reason I've heard for anyone to see the Queen in quite some time," he said with a muted smile. "I am Haicer Dorsereldi, chamberlain and advisor to the Queen. I'm sure I can arrange an audience with Her Majesty based on what you've said. I know the situation in the southwest is becoming of concern to the warlord, so the Queen will be interested to hear what you have to say. However, Her Majesty is a very busy woman, so it may take some time before she can give you her attention."

"I understand," Aeligos said, his brow furrowing slightly. "I hate to waste your time, but I'm curious…every other shakna-rir I've met here on the island has a surname ending in –asti, but yours ends in –eldi. Did you come from Terrassia?"

Haicer's smile broadened. "Very perceptive," he said. "My great-grandparents moved here from Aurun Ch'Gurra after they were married. You are correct: the bloodlines here carry the –asti ending, whereas those from Terrassia carry the –eldi ending. It relates to the matriarchal lines that are the beginning and source of our empires."

"Interesting," the dark male said. "How long to gain an audience with the queen?"

"Give me just a moment," the shakna-rir male said. He turned to one of his bookshelves and pulled forth a large tome bound in red leather. He flipped to the place marked by its leather thong and began studying the pages, and then he flipped two more before his mouth tightened into a line. "I can put your petition before Her Majesty this afternoon, but she wouldn't be able to see you until three days from now."

"Only three days?" Aeligos echoed, masking his impatience to make it sound as though he were pleasantly surprised. It still struck him as odd that a potential war wasn't getting more attention from the shakna-rir – or anyone else. It was the sort of complacence that had let the Devil Queen conquer a good deal of Askies at the start of the Apocalypse before the mortal armies could react. "That would be great, though if you could arrange it so that my sister, Sonja, can see the queen with me, I would appreciate it."

Haicer scribbled notes into the red leather tome and nodded his head. "That would be acceptable," he replied. "I will set your audience for high noon three days from now. Be aware that you may not enter Her Majesty's presence armed, and the use of magic in her presence is punishable by death. I don't mean to sound threatening, I just don't want you to walk into the situation unprepared. It would be best for you to come formally attired, as coming dressed as you are may put Her Majesty and her guards ill at ease."

"Of course," Aeligos said, rising to his feet, "I will see you again in three days. Thank you for your time." Haicer stood up and shook his offered hand, and escorted Aeligos out of the office and to the front door of the palace.

Aeligos headed back to *Desert Wind* and found Sonja sitting at a table in the common room, reading one of her books. "Where's everyone else?" he asked quickly as he took a seat across from his sister.

Her sparkling eyes came up to meet his after a moment. "Typhonix and Serenjols went to see the arena in the northwest of the city. They wanted to see if there are fights to watch…or compete in," she said with an amused shrug. "Grakin's at the local church, and I believe he took the twins with him. It's their first opportunity to see actual temples."

"You and I have an appointment to see the queen at noon three days from now," he said, and he held a hand up as her brows rose. "I know, I don't want to sit around three days waiting to find out if we're wasting our time here, but until Erik and Kari rejoin us I think we have the luxury of time."

Sonja nodded and turned her attention back to the book she was reading. "Will you be going out again tonight?" she asked, making an effort not to chuckle. "I hear these shakna-rir girls like half-demons to keep them warm at night."

He shrugged. It was unnecessary – not to mention potentially damaging – here if he was going to be speaking directly to the queen and her advisors. "Are you going to get mad at me if I do?" he asked anyway.

Sonja glanced up at him briefly and returned to reading her book for a minute before she responded. "No, not really," she said. "As long as I know you're just out enjoying yourself and not in any danger. Though honestly, you might want to think about Eryn a little before you do. Specifically, whether or not you're serious about having a relationship with her."

Aeligos sighed but didn't argue. "Join me for a drink?"

Sonja looked up. "Aeligos, we're at an inn."

"Exactly. Come on, let's go find a trashy tavern and see if there's any excitement to be found in this city," he said, turning the tables on her for a change. "Maybe you'll find the shakna-rir boys like half-demons to keep them warm, too."

Her mouth fell open. "You jackass!" she said, but she chuckled and slapped his forearm before she gathered up her books. She took them upstairs to her room, and once she'd come back down, the two set out into the city to take in its sights.

Chapter XIII – Snake Trail

Kari and Erik departed with their brys guide the next morning, and the czarikk gathered to bid them farewell as they headed farther to the northeast. The tribe's trackers gave Kari general directions to the city of Talvor, the first bastion of civilization beyond the edge of the rainforest, and Makauric confirmed what the czarikk told her. He assured her that he knew the way not only to Talvor, but also to the foothills of the eastern mountain range where their enemy made its lair. Satisfied that they would not be wandering blindly during the days leading up to their inevitable confrontation with the sylinth, they set out to complete their quest.

Makauric led them unhesitatingly through the jungle, and like with the first leg of their journey with him, he guided them around trouble and hazards alike. He was exceedingly tight-lipped, hardly speaking at all, and Kari assumed it was because he was still upset about what Erik said to him in the czarikk village. While brys were not well-known for holding grudges, Makauric had proven to be anything but ordinary for one of his kind, and Kari couldn't shake the feeling that they were very, very lucky to have met him.

Three days passed quietly before they emerged from the jungle onto a broad savannah that stretched from horizon to horizon east to west, and to a mountain range that was barely peeking over the northern edge of the world. Though the jungle was beautiful – particularly once they had the brys to guide them through its mysteries – and reminded Kari of the elven lands of Terrassia to an extent, she was glad to be free of its humid, oppressive heat. The rains that were prevalent while they traversed the southern end gradually tapered off over the course of their journey, and the lack of deep rivers near or north of the czarikk gave gave Kari a good idea of why the czarikk lived where they did.

The savannah was different from the rolling plains of Terrassia where Kari had spent a lot of time traveling, but it was open and more arid, which she preferred. The golden grasses bent low to the ground in a hot wind that blew west to east, and after allowing his companions a few minutes to take in the sight, Makauric set out to the east. He seemed less tense out on the savannah, though his eyes scanned the horizon in all directions constantly, and he led them away from the edge of the jungle, likely to avoid the possibility of ambushes from within its shadows. He explained that the great cats and hyenas were their biggest concerns on the open lands, but that humanoid enemies likewise hunted there and he would do his best to avoid them.

He shot down a young antelope from an incredible distance as the afternoon wore on, and when they made their evening camp under a low, nearly horizontal-growing tree, Makauric prepared the carcass and started a cooking fire with what wood he could find. He set some of the beast's meat to cook on a spit while he chewed on a raw flank, and his eyes began to glow in the twilight, watching over the grasslands for trouble. Even in the failing light, vultures circled high overhead and the braver ones landed and hopped into range of the firelight, looking for a chance to steal some of the carcass.

After cutting several more strips of meat from the animal for their morning meal, the brys hefted it over one shoulder, ignoring the blood that dripped down his arm. He walked a good distance from the camp and deposited the body there for the predators and vultures to do with as they pleased. When he returned, Makauric sat back down under the tree, took off his leather breastplate, and cleaned the blood off of it with his tongue. Kari put a hand over her mouth, not prepared for such a sight. Makauric looked up at her surprised features, and his brow knitted. "Am I bothering you?" he asked.

She reminded herself that he wasn't trying to be rude, but that brys simply spoke their mind plainly and to the point. "That was gross," she said quietly.

"Then I will not eat in front of you in the future," he returned. He put his breastplate back on and then climbed the tree to get a better vantage point from which to survey the land.

"I didn't mean to be rude," she called up to him, and Erik shook his head.

"I did not think you were," came the brys' voice from the treetop. "It did not occur to me that you have only seen me eat meat that has been cooked. If eating raw meat disturbs you, I will refrain from making you watch." He dropped down from his perch, landed softly in the grass, and glanced around once more. "We should each urinate a short distance from the camp before retiring for the night, so that the animals know not to approach. The scent of several lionesses is upon this tree, and they may return here in the night."

"Is anything troublesome close by?" Erik asked, but the brys shook his head.

"I imagine they're enjoying the feast he left them not long ago," Kari said.

"Indeed," Makauric said. He walked a short distance before he began tagging the area with a urinary mark, and when she realized what he was doing, Kari turned her attention to Erik.

"We should be able to reach Talvor tomorrow if what the czarikk said is accurate," she commented. "We can re-supply there and maybe enjoy hot baths and some fresh food at an inn before we make our way to the sylinth's lair."

"Depends what time of day we reach the city," Erik said. "If it's early, I don't think we should indulge ourselves. We need to get rid of this sylinth and meet with the others as soon as possible. Much as I'd like a drink and a bath, I'm not sure we have time for either."

"Of course," Kari said as Makauric came back into the camp, and she looked to the brys. "I didn't think your piss had any scent, how are you marking the camp?"

The demon regarded her for a moment and then moved to sit at the base of the tree. "It has a scent, just one that few creatures can detect," he said. "Animals are much more sensitive to such things. It will be faint but they will sense it, and know to avoid what left it." He looked at Erik and nodded his head toward the larger male. "His may convince them to live elsewhere."

Erik rose to his feet with an uncomfortable expression. "I'll see what I can manage," he said. "I haven't been drinking much, so I doubt I'll be much help."

"Have you been to Talvor before?" Kari asked Makauric when her partner walked away.

The brys shook his head. "I have seen its gates but found no reason to risk entry."

"You should wait out here on the grasslands when we go in," she said, and he silently agreed. "We may spend the night there if the day is mostly gone when we arrive, but if it's still early we'll only be stopping in to re-supply before we get underway again. As Erik said, we need to keep moving to try to stay on schedule."

The brys regarded her curiously. "What schedule?" he asked.

"We're supposed to meet with Erik's siblings as soon as possible after we're done, so the less time we spend tracking and killing this thing, the better."

"So your presence is also related to the rumors of war?" he stated as much as asked.

"Yes," Kari said, and she held his stare. "If you really care about this island, then perhaps you can help us." He said nothing, but as his gaze

245

drifted away she could tell he was thinking about it.

Kari took advantage of his distraction to go out and take her own part marking the area with their scents once Erik returned. She could hear the two men talking while she was away from them, but couldn't make out whatever it was they were saying. When she returned, it was hard to tell what they'd been speaking of based on Makauric's expression, but the way he held Erik's stare, she guessed it wasn't pleasantries.

The night passed calmly. Only the occasional calls of hyenas got their attention, but the savannah was otherwise mostly quiet. The next day's travel brought them to the outskirts of the city of Talvor. Before they approached, Makauric found a tree to hide in while his companions made their way toward the gates. Kari and Erik left him behind and approached the city, and they saw that it was walled but had open archways rather than closed gates, and didn't seem particularly unwelcoming. They both reconsidered that thought once they reached the gates and guards stepped forward to halt their progress.

The terra-rir guards called inside and a third soon appeared, wearing the stripes of an officer. His eyes widened at the sight of the two visitors, and he stepped up before them with an appraising, hard-eyed glare. He started to speak, but Kari reached inside her breastplate for her tags and he stepped back defensively. The other two guards moved in front of the officer with their hands to the hilts of their blades.

Kari pulled her dog tags out slowly and she fixed the three with a glare of her own. "You might want to consider your first words very carefully," she said.

The officer motioned for his guards to stand down. He came forward once more to fix Kari with a scowl, but it didn't even faze her. "What business have you in the city?" he asked.

"We're on official demonhunter business for Zalkar," she returned. "We're stopping in to re-supply and then we'll be on our way."

The officer looked to Erik, and Kari wondered how hard he would push the point. She had the distinct feeling that they had walked right up to a bastion of Gaswell supporters or, at the least, sympathizers. Kari wiggled her fingers subtly in preparation to defend her partner if need be, but then the officer waved them through. "See that you are," he said. "The last thing this city needs is the kind of trouble demonhunters bring."

Kari shook her head, which drew a growl from the officer, but she headed through the gates without further incident. Despite the initial impression she got, the city was picturesque: a port town that sat on the inner corner of a sparkling, deep blue bay. The land graded downhill toward the water, and Kari could see the jungle high above on cliffs to the southwest. Waterfalls fed the bay from the higher jungle, lending a calm and beauty to the city and its port. The houses were made of brick or wood, and while they weren't extravagant, they suggested that the city was fairly wealthy. Kari couldn't see any obvious churches or temples from where they entered, so she and Erik resolved to simply re-supply and then leave as promised.

Thankfully they found a general goods store just inside the gateway and were able to make their purchases. Kari tried to ask the proprietor about a church to Zalkar within the city, but he all but refused to speak to her and Erik about anything but their purchases. To make matters worse, he clearly charged them far more for their goods than they were worth, and it didn't take them long to confirm Kari's suspicions. Taking their goods, they left the shop and then the city as quickly as possible. They ignored the stares of the guards as they passed through the archway into the savannah, and soon they returned to the tree where their brys companion hid. He seemed surprised to see them again so soon, but the shock dissipated quickly and he dropped gracefully from the tree and reinitiated their trek to the northeast. He didn't bother asking what happened within the city; Kari assumed her facial expression said enough.

She and Erik followed the brys for another three days and the savannah climbed up into the lightly wooded foothills of a mountain range that jutted up along the east coast. They crested the first hill and Makauric stopped and moved toward a tree. He glanced up into its leafy crown before he hopped up and off of its trunk to land on one of its thick lower branches, where he squatted down and gazed at the surrounding landscape intently. Kari approached and could see that Makauric was perturbed, which was unusual for him. "What is it?" she asked. "Trouble?"

"This is as far as I go," he said simply. "It will not be difficult for you to find the trail of the demon from here. Head to the base of this mountain and then follow its edge to the north. If you do not find wanton slaughter, I will be surprised. Simply follow the trail to the door of the sylinth's lair."

Erik sighed and wagged his head. "Why aren't you going with us?"

Makauric shook his head. "The last time I drew close to this creature you hunt, it nearly overtook my mind. I dare not approach again."

"Fine," the larger male said, and he began heading farther into the hills.

Kari lagged behind momentarily and touched the brys' hand, though he drew away from her unexpected touch. "Thank you for your help," she said.

Makauric nodded shortly. "I will wait here for your success," he said. "I will see you if you cross out of the hills, so do not look for me; I will find you. From there, perhaps I can be of assistance with this warlord of yours to the west."

The terra-dracon woman nodded and bid him farewell, and she followed after her partner. When she caught up to Erik, he rolled his eyes with another shake of his head. Kari patted his shoulder but said nothing. He wasn't going to change his attitude toward the brys even if Makauric did decide to go with them. They picked up their pace as they sensed they were closing in on their quarry. The travel was familiar and easy: the hills were rolling and covered in soft dirt and grass, with a few trees breaking up the strong sunshine coming in from the west. The peaks to the east weren't as high as the Barrier Mountains of Askies Island, but they formed an imposing wall between the demonhunters and the ocean, standing in silent vigil over the lush hills at their feet. It was an odd formation, though Kari had seen stranger things in her travels across Askies and Terrassia.

Kari paused as they crested yet another rise, and she knelt in the dirt and looked north and south. Erik came over to see what she had found, and she pointed out the tracks he had missed. They were animal tracks, and Kari pointed out that by the spacing, the deer or similar creatures that left them had been heading south at considerable speed. They followed the tracks to the north. After several hours, with the sun sliding rapidly toward the western horizon, they ducked low to a hilltop beneath a tree as they saw a cave at the base of the peak they were circling. It took only a few minutes to confirm that it was the cave Makauric described: there was a refuse pile strewn about outside the door, and a narrow stream trickled near the cave entrance from farther up the mountain. Kari exchanged a brief glance with Erik and they dropped their packs under the tree, drew their weapons, and circled to the north to approach from the blind side.

"Follow my lead," Erik whispered sharply when they reached the base of the mountain on the cave's north side and crept slowly to its mouth. "Keep your mind clear of anything but what we're here for; don't let it try to trick you. We'll pin it between us and cut off its tail."

Kari nodded silently, and soon they were at the mouth of the cave. They did their best to ignore the wretched stench from the refuse pile and from within the cave itself. The entrance was quiet but they could hear the sylinth moving around inside. After gesturing to Kari briefly, Erik started forward slowly and kept tight to the wall to try to make as little noise as possible. His heavy plate and chain armor wasn't designed for stealth, though, and soon there was a hiss of surprise. Erik dashed into the cave and Kari followed close behind him.

"By the gods," Erik muttered, stuttering to a stop. Kari came in behind him and her reaction was nonverbal but just as surprised. It was no ordinary sylinth: the creature towered well over nine feet tall when it straightened itself out. Its tail extended just as far, and the demonhunters quickly realized the kill would not be as straightforward as they expected.

A pale blue glow lit the chamber as Zalkar's symbol drew itself on Kari's breastplate, and her swords began to drip with red blood though they'd been clean only a moment before. Kari circled to her right, putting the massive creature between her and her partner, but its reptilian eyes moved in opposite directions to keep both of the demonhunters within its sights. It let out a long hiss, apparently amused, and picked up a massive spear with blades at both ends. It twirled the weapon menacingly, lashed its tail, and regarded each of its enemies.

"Is this the best they sent?" it asked venomously with another hissing chuckle. "Two pathetic whelps to take on Ressallk, the greatest of Sekassus' sons? I will kill you and rape your corpses, and then deliver them to my father to do the same."

Kari had no time to attack before the creature closed its eyes and the hood of its cobra-like head fanned, and a wave of mental energy pulsed out from it. It struck her like a wall of wind and she staggered back under its crushing weight. Kari shook her head as images manifested themselves in her mind's eye, and the creature attempted to insert itself into her memories as an ally. Kari tried to sort through the images the creature placed in her mind to build a false web of trust stemming from a history that she knew was not true, but she couldn't easily dismiss it. The creature was her friend. They had spent so many years fighting together, clearing the lands of their enemies: the people who threatened war for no good reason.

You trust me, its sibilant voice echoed in her mind. *I am like your father, you love and respect me, and together we battle our enemies.*

Kari's eyes opened slowly and she scowled at the sylinth. Its mental assault had nearly fooled her, and were it not for the creature comparing itself to her father, Kari wasn't sure if she would've seen through it. The sylinth brought its weapon up before it defensively, narrowed its eyes, and hissed threateningly, but then it flashed its long, venomous fangs in a wicked grin and slithered to its side as Erik came forward. It took Kari only a moment to realize that he was under the demon's influence, and she brought her twin scimitars up before her defensively.

Ressallk moved to the side, where it placed one end of its spear into the ground and simply stood watching. The arrogance of demons never ceased to amaze Kari, but she brushed those thoughts aside at Erik's approach. Kari drove Erik's blades aside with her right blade as he rushed in, and she slapped him in his armored rump with her left. She hoped it might shake him free of the demon's influence, but it served only to enrage him, and he came in once more with a measured, careful combination. She knocked his half-hearted swings aside easily and gave up ground, but she circled to ensure she didn't get pinned against a wall or between Erik and the sylinth.

Erik seemed to be considering a new angle of attack, so Kari moved to beat him to the punch. She corkscrewed, hitting high-low-low-high with her blades as they came around, and she kicked the inside of his knee with a strong thrust as he blocked the final high blow. Erik stumbled back, tripped over an outcropping of stone, and clattered to the ground in his heavy metal armor. For a moment he appeared to be breaking free of the demon's hold on him, but then he rose to his feet with a snarl and approached again. Kari sighed; she was hesitant to demonstrate too much fighting her companion, since she didn't want the demon to learn her reactions and strike sequences before she actually engaged it. But Erik was no slouch and she could only afford to toy with him for so long before she would have to wound or even kill him.

His next move surprised her: he led with his longsword. Though Kari was familiar with changing her own sequence of attack, she had never seen Erik do it in all their days practicing together, and she wondered if the sylinth was partially controlling his actions. She brought her right scimitar across in an upward swing to deflect the unexpected thrust, but she was thrown off her rhythm and couldn't bring her weapon back quickly enough to stop his follow-up slash. She spun after her initial parry and brought her left blade around to stop his own scimitar, but he cut high over her block and slashed through her wing, tearing through the membrane and severing the outer bone support.

Kari screamed in pain and stumbled away from her partner, but she spun suddenly and cut across his throat with a blind slash. Her blade ripped through his throat guard, bringing forth a spray of black blood, and she pushed in to continue the attack, blind to how much damage she might've done to him. The blade fell from Erik's right hand and he reached up to his wounded neck. Kari cut under both of his arms and inside both of his knees in a dazzling pattern, severing the straps of his armor. Even as he started to stumble, she tucked her right arm close and drove her shoulder into him, leveling the much larger male.

Kari stared down the demon and approached Erik warily, and she worked to get her emotions back under control. Erik's eyes came up to meet hers, and Kari could see that he was finally free of the sylinth's grip. He grasped at his throat, breathing uneasily and with a slight gurgle, and Kari was glad to see what damage she'd done was not immediately life-threatening. It wasn't often she hit someone in blind fury – certainly not a friend – but she was left with little choice when she considered the prospect of being killed by a demon-controlled Erik. Her partner shook his head *no* ever so slightly at her approach, and he motioned for her to forget him and go after their enemy. Kari continued to watch Ressallk, but she knelt beside Erik and struck him cleanly in the chin with her sword gripped in her fist, knocking him out cold.

Kari grimaced. The wound to her wing was a sharp pain that she fought to push aside, and she folded her wings tightly behind her to try to avoid more damage. She stepped over her fallen companion and made her way to the center of the chamber. There she faced down the demon, which stood with its weapon still tip-down before it, regarding her with narrowed eyes. Kari came to a stop a dozen feet away and crossed her blades before her chest, and then she slid the left down the back of the right, banged them against the cave floor, and spat on the rocks before the creature. "You will pay for what you've done to the czarikk," she said. "When I'm done with you, you'll beg for death, and I'll send you to your father with my name on your lips."

The creature let out its hissing laugh once more. "Boldly you speak, but look about you, woman: you stand in my home, and I have taken your partner from you without even lifting my weapon against you. Surrender yourself to me, I will take your life quickly and you will feel nothing when I ravage you."

Kari shook her head slowly. "Snake, you just said that to the wrong person," she said.

She brought her blades up and stalked in toward the demon. It towered over her and its dual-bladed spear came at her in a deceptively simple one-two combination that it finished by spinning the haft around its hand and then uppercutting with the lower blade. Kari dodged the attacks easily by hopping out of range of the first two and then spinning back in around the third, and she ducked low and threw a pair of crossing slashes at the sylinth's lower belly. She knew her enemy well and struck where it was least mobile: since it was unable to hop out of the way, it brought a spear blade down to stop her first swing, but her second cut a shallow gash along its lower belly. It was a minor hit, but the creature hissed in anger, and Kari used a heavy flap of her wings to hop back out of attack range.

251

She yelped in pain and nearly swooned, her knees threatening to give out, but she kept the presence of mind to not reach for her wounded wing. Getting her legs solidly back beneath her, she circled and slapped mockingly at the spear blades that came at her as the sylinth closed and attacked. Kari was patient and acclimated herself to her enemy's fighting style, just as she had done to Erik, Typhonix, and countless other warriors before. They exchanged a few more routines, and though Kari was unfamiliar with the type of weapon Ressallk wielded, she wasn't particularly impressed with its skill. Ressallk was clearly a capable fighter, but she laughed in the back of her mind at the thought that it might be the greatest of its father's sons.

Kari shook away the thoughts and deflected yet another attack sequence. She reminded herself that she was under the influence of her deity's presence. Her skills were formidable, to be sure, but her reactions were just a little quicker, her swings had a little more bite, and her parries were stronger than normal, all on account of her lord's influence. She knew she wouldn't win the battle if she were to take her god's strength for granted and waste the opportunity. She had to keep her wits about her, to stay focused only on killing the creature and making sure she survived. She was not here for glory: she was here to enact justice and protect her charges, and she had sworn an oath to her deity and the czarikk that she would not fail.

Kari tensed as Ressallk approached once more, and she waited for the most opportune moment to counterstrike. Tumureldi's style was primarily one of counterattacks, capitalizing on opponents' mistakes, and trying to frustrate them to the point where they would lose composure and attack recklessly. Tumureldi won dozens of fighting tournaments and duels, and led a more-than-successful career among the elite rangers of the shakna-rir empire on Terrassia, thereby proving that his style was not just one of showmanship, but of undeniable skill. Karian Vanador had been his sole student: the only person whose character and teachability had ever impressed the king enough to share his secrets. She trained with him for a grueling nine months, listening to his lessons, practicing routines, and sparring with arguably the greatest sword-fighter to ever walk the face of Citaria. She'd entered his tutelage with only rudimentary knowledge of the scimitar, but had left a master, possessed of a fighting spirit and a style that left most slack-jawed. She was good enough, she realized, to beat Ressallk. She had all the tools: the experience, the style, the reflexes, and the strength to cut down even the son of a demon king. And everything she had, everything she brought with her along with what the Tesconis siblings taught her was being augmented by the power of her god.

Ressallk's right arm flashed forward suddenly, but Kari ignored the coming attack, recognizing it was a feint. She tucked and rolled like Aeligos had taught her, came up to her knees beside it, and took a double swipe at the demon's exposed side as she spun to her feet. Ressallk cringed slightly in pain as she cut a little deeper into its scaly armor and drew blood, and it turned to bring its weapon before her. Kari pressed the attack, quick stepping in and to the sides at angles to present a hard target to hit while battering the sylinth's defenses with wicked, sinuous strikes that gave the impression of a scorpion fighting a snake. The demon worked furiously to defend itself and offered little offense while Kari buried it under a flashy routine designed to infuriate it.

Ressallk coiled its tail and Kari broke off her attack, bracing her blades before her as she quick-stepped backward. The demon stopped when she recognized its intention, and it hissed in anger, lashing its tail violently side to side. Ressallk's hood flared out once more and Kari felt the push of the mental attack against her, but her determination and the presence of her deity's power turned it aside harmlessly. Kari turned to an angle and pointed low at the creature with her front blade while her right blade arced high over her head like a scorpion's tail. "Is that the best you've got?" she taunted it. "I've beaten an erestram before; I figured you'd be tougher."

Ressallk's eyes narrowed and it hissed and flared its hood once more, though no mental attack came this time. Instead it spat suddenly, and Kari was barely able to turn her head and bring her uninjured right wing up before her as a shield. Kari flapped her wing quickly to try to get the poison off of it, and was relieved to find the venom wasn't caustic. Sensing no ill effects from the venom, she returned to her earlier posture and smiled confidently. Ressallk came in once more, feinted to draw the woman in to attack, and brought the haft of its dual-bladed spear up to block the obvious attack from her scorpion-tail blade. Ressallk then moved to block her other sword before she even began to follow up on the combination, but Kari surprised him when it was her right sword again, not her left, that came in for the second attack. She struck the haft of the demon's weapon again and again, all the while moving her left blade in a distracting pattern as her head swung side to side, and she rang out a seven-hit sequence that bit deep into the wooden haft of Ressallk's weapon and threatened to sunder it.

The demon tried to back up and moved to parry her right blade when Kari quick-stepped in, but this time her left blade flashed forward. The sylinth cried out in frustration and fear as she landed a second seven-hit combination upon the haft of its weapon, all coming from her left blade.

The dual-bladed spear snapped in two in Ressallk's hands, and the demon nearly fell backward, but it righted itself at the last moment and coiled its tail. Kari did not miss the coiling and was already dodging to her left when the demon sprung at her. Its envenomed fangs snapped on a mouthful of her hair where her body had been only a blink of an eye before, but it was unable to grip her silky strands in its maw.

Kari slashed as she fell, an off-balance and off-target strike that drew blood from the side of the demon's neck, but again only from a minor wound: its scaly armor was quite thick. Her hand touched the ground and she gritted her teeth, crushing her knuckles beneath the pommel of her sword to cart-wheel and come up on her feet once more. She had a flash from her training under Tumureldi and, on instinct, she spun left as she stepped right, and her left blade came around and ripped through one of the demon's eye sockets when it attempted a second bite.

Ressallk screamed and dropped one of the halves of its destroyed weapon to reach up to its ruined eye. Its face was a bloody mess: Kari had nearly cloven its skull and killed it outright. Its remaining reptilian orb fixed on Kari hatefully, though the demon did not rush to attack again. Kari took in the scene before her, and moved between the demon and her fallen companion. She guessed it was most likely to attempt to kill Erik before being killed itself. Once she saw that it was not following, she knelt beside her partner and touched his breastplate, and confirmed that at the very least he was still breathing.

Ressallk straightened out and took account of its wounds, and it screamed an echoing cry of frustration that forced Kari to press her arms over her pointed ears. Staring her down through a single, narrowed eye, the demon let forth a hateful hiss, then threw back its head and screamed, "Father! I have failed you; spare me and give me the means to kill this insect!"

Kari stood and spoke, but it was not her voice that came forth, and the thoughts behind the words were not her own. She hissed, fixed the sylinth with a glare, and then let forth a raspy chuckle. "Your father has no power here, snake," she said sibilantly. "For harming my people, your punishment is death, and there shall be no escape for you. This instrument of the gods has been given over to me, and I will drink blessed wine in celebration as she destroys you."

"What is this?" Ressallk bellowed.

Kari shook her head lightly as whatever presence had taken hold of her to speak gently released her, and she felt a tingle in her mind that manifested as a pat on the shoulder. "I think Sakkrass wants you dead," she said quietly, and she began to stalk toward her enemy.

"Who is Sakkrass?" the demon demanded. It backed away and held up the single end of the ruined spear in its left hand.

"The god of the czarikk – the people whose eggs you smashed like a coward," she said. "You're pathetic. Is there a spine in that rancid body of yours, or can you only kill children to satisfy your father?" The demon hissed in anger, and Kari continued to stalk toward it, even when it coiled its tail beneath it. "I told you you'd pay for killing the czarikk children. Besides failing your father, you've made him a target for the anger of several gods."

Kari leaned backward, braced herself with one leg, and brought her blades up to catch the sylinth's head between them as it sprang to bite her once more. Its one remaining eye widened when she pushed back against it, and before that single eye could blink, Kari severed its head. She closed her eyes and turned away as she was sprayed with a blast of foul blood, and she quick-stepped away from the thrashing headless corpse. Kari wiped the blood from her eyes and then pushed her matted hair back to keep it from dripping onto her face, and she watched the demon's death throes until they slowed and came to a stop.

Once the adrenaline drained from her blood, a heat passed through Kari's belly and into her chest. She fell to her knees in sudden agony and wondered if she'd inadvertently swallowed even a drop of the creature's foul blood. She felt as though she'd been poisoned, and she forced herself to her feet and stumbled out of the foul-smelling cave. She staggered desperately toward the stream outside and crashed into the mud. She tried to dip her snout into the stream to take a few quick sips of the cold liquid, but before she could draw in even a mouthful, she curled up into a ball and vomited. She dry heaved twice immediately afterward, so she splashed water onto her face, trying to get the demon's blood off of her.

Kari vomited again and desperation overtook her as she felt the heat passing from her chest and belly into her arms and legs. It was as though she were burning from the inside out and she nearly cried out for help, but she knew that there would be no one to answer: Makauric was far from the cave and Erik was unconscious. She gritted her teeth in determination and dragged herself halfway into the stream, and at last she forced several mouthfuls of water down her throat. It did nothing to quell the heat that burned at her core, but it didn't come right back up, either. She took several more sips of the water and dragged herself back out of the stream, where she lay down on its uncomfortable rocky shore and closed her eyes. The heat finally dissipated when it reached her fingers and toes, and her eyes snapped back open and she lifted her head to look around. She was thankful to find that she was not lying in a golden field in her deity's realm or anything of the sort: she was quite alive and well, and found the strength already returned to her body. She stood up and took off her breastplate, and when she lifted her padded shirt she saw that her lord's symbol was no longer upon her chest.

Kari sighed lightly and leaned down to take up a double handful of water and drink, and then she splashed more water on her face and washed off as much of the demon's blood as she could in a few seconds. She ran back into the cave, picked up the blades she had dropped on her way out, and moved quickly to her fallen companion. Erik was still breathing, and when Kari removed his breastplate she found his heartbeat was still strong. She placed her hand over the wound on his throat and channeled some of her deity's power to seal it, and she turned him on his side so any blood that had trickled in could come forth easily if he coughed. She took up her canteen and splashed a bit of water on his face but he didn't wake, so she retrieved a few of the animal furs the sylinth had slept on, bundled them, and put them under Erik's head. The furs smelled horrible, but she figured if he woke up to complain it would be a blessing. She put another over him, and moved toward the demon's corpse.

Ressallk's head lay staring at her through its single, glazed-over eye in utter disbelief, and she nearly laughed but for the implications. Killing the son of a demon king would carry more consequences. Ressallk said it was the son of Sekassus the Calculating, who was far from being some minor lord: he was one of seventeen demon kings who sat upon the underworld council. Kari knew from experience that some of the demon kings were nearly on par with the gods in terms of raw power: while Chinchala rarely displayed his full fury, Kari had heard enough stories of his battle prowess to know that angering Sekassus had to be very dangerous. She let out a sigh and hoped that she would never come face to face with Ressallk's doubtless-volatile father.

A quick search of the lair turned up nothing of value, and Kari wondered why a demon would be content to sit in a cave and not even collect trinkets or slaves. Ressallk had apparently done little other than slaughter a lizardman tribe's defenseless children and who- or whatever's remains lay outside the mouth of its lair. Clearly there had to be more at work in the situation, and she wondered how or if the demon's presence had anything to do with Gaswell's plans. She found it unlikely: she didn't see how having one race fight against all the others made any sense unless the demons were simply trying to cause havoc. She realized she would need to report the odd developments to Zalkar's church as soon as possible to let his clergy confer with each other and their lord for an answer to the puzzle. When Kari looked at her disabled companion, though, she realized she couldn't carry him and couldn't realistically drag him very far, even if she made a litter. She glanced out of the cave mouth and laughed at herself, realizing she wished Makauric were there, if for nothing else than to keep her company.

Kari walked over and touched Erik's shoulder briefly, and the unconscious male let out a pained groan, though he didn't stir from his forced slumber. She wondered how hard she'd hit him, and hoped that she didn't hurt him too badly. She decided that only time would tell, and after pulling the smelly blanket up fully over his chest, she took up her blades and made her way out of the cave to retrieve their bags from the hillside. She slung the bags over her shoulder and screamed as a sudden sharp pain reminded her that she had a severed wing bone. She let her heartbeat slow down, and then she slung the bags over her other shoulder and walked wobbly-legged to the cave to set them beside her companion. She stripped the smelly skins off of Erik and laid out her bedroll. She prodded Erik to roll onto it, and then she put her pack under his head and her cloak over him. Satisfied that he was at least comfortable, she took up the hollow staff that housed her bow and moved back out of the cave and to the stream.

Kari looked around for several minutes while she pulled her bow and two arrows from the hollow staff and strung the weapon. She set it down just on the edge of the stream, and after taking off her armor and clothes, she knelt by the water's edge to wash them. She cleaned her blades after and noted that the blood they secreted when the Blood Oath manifested was gone. She smiled grimly, satisfied that she had at least kept her word to the czarikk. The stream was only knee-deep, but she stepped into its cold waters and crouched down to wash herself. It took several minutes to get the demon's blood out of her hair, and she shivered in the twilight air. Once finished, she took up her equipment and returned to the cave briefly before she collected dry wood from the nearby hills. She hoped that nothing came upon her while she was dressed only in the shouldered bow. Once she collected a sizeable pile of sticks, she returned to the cave and built a fire just outside.

Kari used the fire to dry her clothing and armor, and then dressed herself in the warm garments. She sat near Erik and lay back with her head on his warm belly, and she closed her eyes. She did her best to stay awake but she was exhausted physically, mentally, and spiritually, and within only a few minutes of lying down she was fast asleep. Kari woke a few hours

257

later and the cave mouth was lit only by the dim light of the fire's embers. The cave was quiet and her eyes began to glow softly with their inner luminescence, her stronger night vision taking over. There was nothing else in the cave, so she sat up to check on Erik and saw that he was still not awake but his breathing seemed steadier and deeper.

She put her armor back on and then dug through her pack, and Kari pulled out the trail rations and ate her fill of them. She didn't like being off her normal eating and sleeping schedule, but wielding her deity's power had burned her out – even more so than on previous occasions – and she realized just how taxing it must be for Grakin to do all the time. She tilted Erik's head to the side slightly and dripped water from her canteen onto his tongue, and he swallowed it uneasily without waking. She patted his cheek with a sigh, and then made her way to the cave mouth. The night outside was quiet but for the soft trickle of the stream and the calls of insects and toads. After looking around, Kari was satisfied that there would be no trouble from animals, doubly so because the demon had likely killed nearly every living thing within a mile or more of its cave. After a contemplative minute, she returned to Erik's side, gathered up the fetid furs and skins that belonged to the demon, and deposited them at the cave mouth to further deter curious critters.

The refuse pile drew her attention, though only for a couple of minutes before she couldn't bear the stench anymore. There didn't appear to be anything of value among the bones and bits of hides and other armor. The skulls appeared to be from gnolls, and she wondered where the hyena-like humanoid creatures made their homes and how they had ended up tangling with the sylinth. She thought of the finger-bone necklaces the czarikk wore, and wondered if those, too, were from gnolls. Whatever the case, Kari was glad for the skulls' presence, as they indicated that the gnolls surely knew that it was a demon's cave and they would likely stay far away from it.

"Kari," she heard Erik whisper, and she made her way back into the cave. She dashed to kneel beside him and stroked his brow. His blue eyes were glowing and he tried to keep his gaze steady with hers, but his eyes rolled back every so often before he would blink and refocus on her. "I...can't move..."

Kari's stomach dropped. She put one hand on his chest and brought the other up to the end of her snout. She jumped slightly in shock when his hand came up to lie atop hers. "What can't you move?" she asked after letting forth a sigh of relief.

He shook his head lightly, but his eyes rolled again and he cringed in

258

pain. "I can move everything," he said quietly, "but I'm going to be sick if I do. It'd help if you could make the cave stop spinning."

"Lie still, then," she said, and she put her hand over his eyes to make him close them. "I didn't think I hit you that hard but I guess your head hit the floor after I punched you."

"Kari, I'm...sorry....," he began, but she gently clasped his snout shut.

"Don't even think about it," she said. "It could have just as easily been me, or both of us...we could be on our way to kill the people we swore to protect right now. But we're not: we're safe, and the sylinth is dead."

He let out a short sigh. "Good...work," he said weakly, and she felt him go limp as he slipped into unconsciousness again.

Kari pulled a towel from her backpack and soaked it in the cool stream so she could put it on his head. She stopped short when she saw a brys watching her from the nearby hilltop, and it began to approach after a moment. She made her way into the cave without waiting to see if it was Makauric. She assumed that not being attacked meant it was him, and she wanted to be near her weapons if it turned out she was wrong. When she reached her blades, she turned to see that the brys had followed her inside, and at the closer range her night vision revealed it was indeed Makauric. She knelt down and wrapped the cool, wet towel about Erik's head, and the brys looked around the cave. When she was done, Makauric came and squatted by her partner. He looked the larger male over for a minute, checking his breathing and touching small, clawed fingers to the side of Erik's neck before he looked to Kari for explanation.

"I knocked him out when he was under the sylinth's control," she said. "I didn't think I hit him that hard, but he's dizzy and can't move without wanting to throw up."

Makauric checked Erik's ears, and then he reached behind the half-guardian's head. He ran his fingers through the larger male's hair and they came up clean. He gave a slight nod, sat back on his heels, and met Kari's questioning stare. "He seems to have a concussion," he said, but he saw that she didn't understand. "A type of brain injury. Let him rest a day or two, and see how he feels then."

Kari beheld the brys for a moment, surprised that their anatomical knowledge would also include things healers like Grakin would know. Makauric stood up and walked toward the back of the cave to inspect her handiwork. He inspected the corpse and its wounds, the severed head, and the destroyed weapon, and then he cast a gaze at Kari that she was quite familiar with. He said nothing, though, and Kari watched him pry open the sylinth's mouth to inspect its fangs. He pulled out a sharp knife and began slicing open its palate. She guessed he was looking for its venom glands, and Kari approached and looked over the rest of the corpse. She wanted to burn it, but she knew she needed help moving the body outside of the cave, and she doubted Makauric had the strength to be much use.

She grabbed one of Ressallk's arms, braced her feet against the stone floor of the cave, and tried to drag its body. The corpse was heavy but slid easily over the blood-slicked rock, and Makauric came over to help when he noticed what Kari was doing. As she suspected, he lacked the muscle mass to help as well as Erik would have, but the brys had a lean strength and together they managed to get the body outside. Makauric returned for the severed head while Kari gathered more wood from the nearby hills.

When Kari returned with two armfuls of wood, she found that Makauric had stacked the remains of the demon's victims along with its body in preparation for burning. They left the body in a place where the smoke from the fire was unlikely to enter the cave, and they stacked the wood around the remains and set it ablaze. They watched for several minutes to make sure the demon corpse actually burned, and once its flesh began to blister and char they moved back inside. Erik was still asleep. Kari yawned, which prompted the brys to point at her partner.

"Lie down and rest," he said. "I will watch over you until the dawn comes."

Kari shook her head. "Wake me when you get tired," she said. "I'm still on a military schedule anyway, so I pretty much expect to get woken up a few hours before dawn."

The words *military schedule* piqued his interest, but as usual he didn't ask. "As you wish," he said, and he took up his bow and moved to sit outside the cave mouth.

Kari stretched out on her bedroll beside Erik, pulled her cloak over herself, and cuddled close to him to share his warmth. She fell into a light and dreamless sleep, and she felt as though she'd only slept a few minutes before Makauric shook her shoulder to rouse her. She took up her own bow with a yawn and headed outside while the brys lay down next to her bedroll.

Kari sat on a rocky outcropping near the cave mouth and saw that the first of the three moons was already dipping toward the western horizon. She guessed that dawn was close. It made little difference what hours they slept if Erik was going to take a couple of days to recover, and she was glad that Makauric trusted her as much as she trusted him. Unlike Erik's guardian demon forebears, the brys could not go extended periods without food, water, or rest. Kari knew it would do none of them any good if

Makauric were to exhaust himself on her behalf.

The remainder of the night passed quietly, and after only a few hours Makauric came out of the cave, bow in hand, and motioned for Kari to go in and get more sleep if she wanted. Ressallk's body and the rest of the remains with it had burned down to ash and bits of bone by first light, and after surveying the area, Kari retired within and lay down beside Erik. She didn't sleep again, but once she felt refreshed she channeled more of her deity's power to help her partner's throat wound heal a little faster. It already looked better, the lower layers of flesh sealed and the upper layers beginning to come back together.

Kari took the towel from around Erik's head and wet it in the stream again. While she replaced it about Erik's head, Makauric returned with a young deer over his shoulder. Kari couldn't help but smile for his efficient nature that required nothing in the way of orders or direction. It was no wonder that the brys had arguably been Seril's favorite creation: Kari had wished for soldiers like Makauric so often during the war campaign. He noticed her stare and gestured outside with his head, and after patting Erik's chest, Kari followed the brys. They prepared the carcass, rationing out the meats for several days in case it took Erik longer than expected to recover, and then Makauric burned the remains so as not to attract scavengers.

Kari studied the brys at length while they worked, and though he didn't show it, she knew he wasn't comfortable under her scrutiny. She thought it a good thing, since it might force him to be more honest when she questioned him. "Why didn't you come help us kill the sylinth?" she asked quietly, trying to keep the inquiry from sounding like an accusation.

Makauric regarded her for a moment and sighed for the first time that she could remember. "I was afraid," he admitted. "Afraid it would enrapture me a second time and force me to turn on you. I was under its power once, and it was an experience I wish to never repeat."

Kari stared at him for a moment and he met her eyes with his typically confident gaze. "You didn't mention that before," she said. "You said it clouded your mind and you fled."

The brys nodded. "That is what happened, in a sense," he said. "I believe I was under its control, or at the least not in my right mind for a time after I ventured close to its lair. Once I was a good distance from its cave, I broke free of its influence."

"Did you kill the czarikk children?" she asked evenly.

Makauric held her gaze and didn't blink. "I did not," he said. "This I swear to you. I still had the same complement of arrows after my mind cleared as I did before, and my blades were still clean, so to my knowledge,

261

I did not harm anyone or anything. I was also far from the czarikk when I broke free; it was not I who destroyed their eggs."

Kari nodded; what Makauric said agreed with what little the czarikk were able to tell her, and based on his mannerisms she believed he was telling the truth. "Did its presence still linger after you broke free?" she asked.

The brys nodded shortly. "It did. That is why I came to you after the creature was killed. I sensed its demise when the cloudiness in my mind dissipated completely."

Kari didn't press the issue further. She patted the brys' shoulder and then filled their canteens from the mountain waters flowing nearby. The stream proved clean and refreshing, and Kari and Makauric enjoyed the clean water and venison as the rest of the day and the next passed uneventfully. The brys was his usual quiet, reserved self and provided Kari little in the way of conversation, but simply having him there made the boredom more bearable. Though Makauric was unable to tend to Kari's wounded wing at all, he was able to patch up the straps of Erik's armor. Kari was looking forward to seeing Grakin again, and though being apart from him hurt, she took comfort in the ache since it told her that her feelings for him were absolute.

On the third day, Erik was awake, coherent, and able to speak. Kari knelt beside her partner and hugged him when he sat up. "How do you feel?" she asked as she pulled away and gripped his face.

"Hungry and thirsty," he said, and he didn't hide his shock when Makauric brought a canteen and some of the roasted venison. Erik reached up, touched his neck, and winced. "Neck's still sore but my head's clear, and I think I can stand without throwing up."

"If you feel good enough to travel, it's best if we head back to the czarikk as soon as possible," Kari said while Erik began to eat. "With any luck, the others have reached the shakna-rir by now, and perhaps even farther west."

Erik looked around while she spoke, and met her gaze as he sipped the water. "Where's the sylinth?" he asked.

"We burned it the other night," she said, and she could see the question in his eyes. "You were out for two days. Gods, when you woke up the first time and told me you couldn't move, I almost pissed myself."

Erik chuckled. "I'm amazed I could even talk. I couldn't figure out if I dreamed that or it really happened. You'll have to tell me all about the fight when we're walking back to the czarikk village."

He got up and was stiff-legged at first, but he showed no immediate signs of trouble from the concussion. Kari and Makauric began gathering up their things, and Erik approached and touched Kari's wing gently. "This looks bad," he said, eyeing the smooth edges of the severed bone poking out of the wound. "I think Grakin can fix this, but it's beyond anything I can do."

Kari winced only slightly; the pain was sharp but she was getting used to it, so long as she avoided jolting it. "It's a clean cut," she said. "It hurts, but we don't have anything to try to keep it together until we get back to your brother. I just hope it doesn't tear any further."

"Well at least you made Ressallk pay for it," Erik said, but he paused when Kari fixed him with her stare. "Oh, no, don't tell me *I* did this to you…"

"Forget it," she said, waving her hand. "It wasn't your fault."

Erik sighed and went out to wash up in the stream. Once he donned his armor the three began the return trip to the czarikk village. Makauric took the point and led them unhesitatingly across the savannah, and as they walked, Kari filled her partner in on what had happened.

Chapter XIV - Protection

Kulthon was a beautiful city, but struck Aeligos as sleepy despite its busy nature. The rigidly ordered structure of shakna-rir society eliminated most of the intrigue and excitement he and his companions had hoped to find while waiting for their appointment with the queen. Ty and Serenjols were allowed to spar freely in the arena and even duel some of the braver citizens, but most were dubious about even stepping into the circle with either of the massive warriors. The two were able to entertain themselves and many a spectator, and took the opportunity to help Sherman and Katarina hone their skills.

As Aeligos suspected, the stone streets and buildings of the city retained heat that they slowly released overnight, keeping the city warm and its inhabitants comfortable. Despite Sonja's teasing, he refrained from finding a bedmate, since he was unsure how these shakna-rir regarded casual relations and didn't want to draw any sort of negative attention prior to their audience. Sonja didn't attract any inquiries from the local males at the taverns, though it didn't seem to bother her at all. She seemed just as happy to not look where she knew she wouldn't find anything permanent, but Aeligos was annoyed that she didn't attract any attention.

The dark male spent several hours each night looking for any leads that might point to a thieves' guild or similar organization but, like in Tingus, he found nothing. He assumed the militaristic shakna-rir simply had no tolerance for organized crime, and that their punishments deterred nearly all criminals from even trying to ply their trade. On the one hand he found it impressive and a testament to the dedication of the desert people, but on the other it was frustrating, as it cut him off from one of the more reliable sources of information when he was in a new place. While he could get information easily enough using charm and diplomacy with the common people and the royalty, money would get him less well-known and consequently much more valuable information from rogues and similar shady sorts. It certainly didn't hurt that he was strikingly handsome for one of his kind, as it made getting information from women even simpler and more enjoyable as well. And though that didn't sit well with Erik or Sonja, Aeligos looked at it as simply being willing to do more and go farther to accomplish their ends than his more uptight siblings were.

Sonja regarded Aeligos as they made their way up toward the palace and he grimaced inside. He knew that she picked up surface thoughts from undisciplined minds, much like their mother could. Usually he guarded his thoughts more carefully from mental eavesdropping, but he'd become quite lax in doing so during their ocean voyage and in the sleepy cities of Tsalbrin. Sonja smiled after a moment and patted his shoulder lightly, and he managed a smile of his own, glad that with the power she had, she was usually understanding and rarely openly judgmental.

High noon was approaching fast when they reached the palace district, and Aeligos greeted the guards at the gateway and introduced his sister. They were more amiable this time, since they knew that he had an audience with the queen, and they gave Sonja only a brief glance before waving the pair through the gate. The guards watched her as the two moved away, and Sonja had a broad smile on her face that Aeligos didn't miss. He touched her shoulder briefly with a chuckle, and they made their way to the palace door.

The two guards outside the palace doors opened the portal wide for them, and Aeligos led Sonja inside and stopped to wait for the inner guards to direct them where to go. The guards looked Sonja over for a minute and then directed the two to the rear door leading to the throne room's antechamber. The antechamber was a cozy square room with decorative curtains on the stone walls and padded benches on each side, with another set of double doors directly across from where the half-demons entered. It was kept well lit by several wall sconces, which also served to keep it quite warm despite not seeing sunshine. On the left bench sat Haicer, who looked up from his red leather book, and he took a minute to look over Aeligos' more casual attire as well as his sister.

"Chamberlain, this is my sister Sonja," Aeligos said, and Haicer stood up and shook the woman's hand lightly with a short bow of his head.

"Haicer Dorsereldi," he greeted her. "Her Majesty is just finishing up a civil trial. If you will but have a seat, she will see you in a few minutes."

The two nodded and took the opposite bench, and the chamberlain looked through his red leather book once more. "Busy day for the queen?" Aeligos asked casually.

Haicer sighed. "No more than usual," he said. "Though other than yourself, all of Her Majesty's appointments today are related to justice rather than diplomacy. Normally such duties put Her Majesty in a foul mood, but I could tell she is looking forward to seeing the two of you."

"How old is she?" the rogue asked, and Haicer regarded him curiously.

"She is in her thirty-first year," he answered. "Why do you ask?"

Aeligos shrugged. "I know Aurun Ch'Gurra has had some young queens in its history."

Haicer nodded pensively. "Yes, due to assassination as often as not. To be frank, there are just too many noble houses in Aurun Ch'Gurra, and tempers and jealousy run hotter than the desert sun. This kingdom has seen no such problems for as long as my family has lived here: the noble families are few and very supportive of their matriarch. Like her mother before her, Her Majesty is very protective and nurturing of her people, and our kingdom flourishes."

Aeligos considered the man's words and remembered that despite their simple look, even the peasants and laborers of the lower city seemed content and secure. It was heartwarming to see a monarchy devote its power entirely to the welfare of its people, and such certainly appeared to be the case in Kulthon. It gave Aeligos further hope that the queen would do whatever was necessary to protect her people from the threat of Gaswell, and that he could trust her judgment in deciding whether or not war could be avoided. He assumed that she might be more in favor of war given the nature of the shakna-rir people as a whole, but her protectiveness meant it would not be a blind decision.

His contemplations came to an end when the double doors to the throne room opened and a shakna-rir male was escorted out roughly in shackles. The prisoner looked to the chamberlain but Haicer simply shook his head, and the guards pulled the man along and passed through the outer doors, leaving the trio in silence. The chamberlain motioned for the guests to wait where they were, and he entered the audience chamber. He kept the doorway propped open, announced Aeligos and Sonja in a loud voice, and then gestured for them to enter.

The throne room was not as large as Aeligos expected but it was an impressive sight nonetheless. A long, red carpet led from the double doors up to the dais at the back, which rose three steps to the throne. The room was brightly lit by chandeliers, its walls were decorated with curtains like the antechamber, and to Aeligos' surprise there was only a single pair of armed guards inside the doorway. No guards flanked the queen like he expected; only a single armed and armored shakna-rir male stood leaning against the throne. Despite the lack of sunlight within, the audience chamber was still bright and warm.

The throne was a simple one of polished wood with no gold or gems adorning its sturdy frame; there were merely red cushions on its seat and back for the queen's comfort. Sitting upon it was a pretty and stately-looking shakna-rir woman dressed simply in a golden gown, with a thin silver circlet set high on her brow. Her hair was long and red like Sonja's, and she had it braided to lie over her right shoulder and down over her

267

breast. Her bright ruby eyes regarded the half-demons with interest, and she looked to the male standing beside her briefly before she crossed her legs and leaned slightly to the side in her throne.

Aeligos and Sonja approached and, without even exchanging a glance or receiving an instruction from the chamberlain, they stopped at the base of the dais and bowed down to one knee. After a moment the queen motioned for them to rise and smiled warmly. She was very pretty despite the worry-lines around her eyes, and in her confident gaze Aeligos could see that she was a woman unburdened by the weight of a crown. It was obvious just to look at her that she had sat the throne for a number of years, as she seemed quite comfortable – a fact further attested to by the few guards in the throne room itself. It made Aeligos wonder how long she'd sat the throne and what might have happened to her mother, but he spared only a moment on such thoughts.

Aeligos had left his weapons at the inn, something he usually hated doing. Normally in such situations he still had knives and even a stiletto or two hidden under his clothes or within the folds of his cloak. In the queen's court, however, he was confident that he would need no such precautions, and he was wary of doing anything that might provoke the queen or her guards. Haicer had warned him that even bringing a weapon into the queen's presence was punished – not punishable, he thought to himself, but punished – by death. He could only imagine what they did to someone that made the mistake of using magic, no matter how harmless, in her presence.

The two continued to stare at the queen, waiting for her to speak, but after a few silent moments the male beside her spoke. "It is customary for guests to introduce themselves first in the Queen's court," he said, his stern demeanor softening somewhat in an obvious attempt to make the two more comfortable.

Aeligos found that odd since Haicer had announced them, but he nodded and bowed. "Your Majesty, I am Aeligos Tesconis, and this is my sister Sonja," he said, and his sister gave a surprisingly graceful curtsey. "It is our honor to visit your kingdom and your court."

"And it is our honor to welcome you to it," the queen said with a short nod. Like her gaze, her voice was powerful, but it lacked the forcefulness that marked many a leader as lacking self-confidence. "I am Queen Omalias Tuvurasti, and this man beside me is my mate and warlord, Maktus Tuvurasti. Our time is now yours."

"Your Majesty, we come before you today in regard to Braxus Gaswell," Aeligos said.

The queen's brow furrowed for a moment before she turned to her mate. "The warlord in the south," Maktus said. "He is not a threat, so we have ignored his antics to date."

"I see," Queen Omalias said, turning her attention back to her guests. "And what have you to say on this matter?"

Aeligos paused a few moments, considering his words. The queen seemed to take the opportunity to look him over more closely. He was glad he had worn his casual attire: he was certain his armor and the various tools of the trade that adorned it would have brought a much different reaction from her. "We understand the strength of your kingdom and why you would not consider Gaswell a threat," he said at length. "However, you should consider that he may well be a threat to your allies or trade partners to the west and south."

The queen held her hand up, stopping his train of thought. "Why are you here?" she asked. "Have you come from Raugro or the other western cities to enlist our aid? Why have you come to my kingdom to ask me of someone who you have admitted is no threat to us?"

"We've come at the behest of Zalkar himself, Majesty," Aeligos said, and immediately both the queen and her warlord straightened up a little. "My elder brother is a demonhunter, and was sent here by Zalkar to try to prevent war. As he is currently busy tracking a demon to kill here on the island, he asked us to come ahead and speak to you on his behalf."

Queen Omalias nodded, and Aeligos paused to allow her to speak. She turned to her mate. "This warlord, is he related to Eric Gaswell?"

"Yes, my Queen," he answered.

"Yes, our people remember Eric Gaswell," she said, turning back to her guests. "The fool gathered an army many years ago to try to overrun the Isle of Kirelia. I assume you two are not from our island; do you know of Eric Gaswell and his ill-fated plans?"

"Not very well, Majesty," Sonja said.

"It was roughly a century ago that Eric Gaswell drew many other bloodthirsty fools to his side in an attempt to capture the Isle of Kirelia. It is believed his intention was to capture and subjugate our kirelas-rir brothers and sisters: to bend their war wizards to his will and use them to conquer Tsalbrin and perhaps beyond. At the time, the kirelas-rir were still a mystery to the rest of us, and our ancestors did not fully appreciate the scope of Gaswell's plan. Once it became clear that his plan of attack was not only quite real but likely to succeed given Kirelia's poor defenses, our ancestors moved swiftly to destroy him."

She shifted to lean the other way in her throne, reversing the crossing of her legs, and continued, "His army had already departed when our own forces reached his stronghold, and it took little effort to capture and execute him. His army quickly fell apart without his fanatical command, and were left to return to their normal lives without penalty as long as they caused no further trouble."

Aeligos nodded. "This is what we are trying to determine in the current situation, Your Majesty," he said. "We need to know what Your Majesty's intentions are, and those of the western cities, as Zalkar himself sent my brother to come here and try to avert war if at all possible."

Maktus looked to his mate, received a nod, and addressed their guests. "War is not so easily averted simply because the gods wish it so. If Gaswell has become enough of a problem that the Unyielding himself has taken notice, then clearly war has to be considered. Most often it is not enough to cut off the head in such a situation: in our peoples' last encounter with the Gaswell family, it was necessary to not only kill their leader but to answer them with such a force as to make any think twice about stepping up to take Gaswell's place."

"What option would Zalkar prefer?" Queen Omalias asked.

Aeligos looked to Sonja, who gave a slight shrug. "According to my brother, the slaying of Gaswell is to be done covertly, without upsetting the entire countryside in the process, Your Majesty," he said. "I believe the biggest concern is that the nations of Dannumore to the north will be tempted to go to war if they learn of unrest here on the island."

The queen regarded her mate, who nodded. "That is a possibility, my Queen."

Queen Omalias seemed to consider his words for a few moments. "Still, we destroyed Eric Gaswell, and if his descendant is tempted to make the same foolish mistakes that he did, then we will likely have no choice but to do so again. Though I will ask: what do you believe we should do? I am honestly curious that the gods would send *half-demons* to tell us their wishes. Not to insult you, but you must admit it is strange."

"No insult taken, Majesty," Sonja said, waving her hand dismissively, and Aeligos let her speak. "Our goal is to avert a *war*, but no one said anything about a battle or a short siege. If it turns out Gaswell's army is too large for a force such as ours to dismantle through subterfuge, then perhaps it would be best to have Your Majesty's army – and maybe those of some of the western cities – confront Gaswell to open up his lines to us. As long as the fighting is short-lived and word of it is slow to spread, then attention from the north may still be avoided, if it has been to date."

"Indeed," Maktus said. "My queen, I recommend that we begin

mobilizing our forces west through Saint John's pass. We will need to send emissaries to the town of Fahrem to inform them of our intentions beforehand, but if war is inevitable, then we should not hesitate to make ready. I also recommend we send scouts to the northern ports to keep eyes and ears open to trouble from Dannumore."

Queen Omalias shook her head. "I will not act rashly on this," she said. "Our kingdom has known peace for many years and I will not be the one to change that unless all other options are exhausted. Summon your generals so that they may give us their thoughts on these matters."

The queen turned her attention back to her guests. "Understand: it is not that I do not trust you or value your counsel, but this is a situation that my generals and my warlord have not seen fit to inform me of before now. I cannot, in good faith, mobilize my armies simply because you bring the tidings of Zalkar. I must make certain that my peoples' interests and lives are my highest priority. The Unyielding does not rule our people."

"Your Majesty is wise," Aeligos said, bowing his head. "I do not mean to press, but how long will you need to reach a decision?"

"We will render our decision by tomorrow at this time," Queen Omalias said, and she rose to her feet. She clapped her hands twice, and a young shakna-rir page made his way to the antechamber doors, opened them, and summoned the chamberlain into the queen's presence. Haicer approached the throne, bowed before his queen, and awaited her orders. "Clear our court schedule for the remainder of today and tomorrow," she said. "Tomorrow at noon, our half-demon guests will be returning."

"As you wish, Your Majesty," Haicer said.

"If I understand correctly, you said you are headed west to the other major cities of the island?" Queen Omalias asked her guests, and Aeligos responded affirmatively. "Tell me: if we are to mobilize our forces, would you be willing to act as our emissaries to the western cities, since you will already be ahead of our armies?"

"If Your Majesty trusts us with such a task, we will perform it gladly," Sonja said.

"Is there anything else the crown may do for you today, then?" the queen asked, and she sat back down upon her throne.

"No, Your Majesty," Aeligos said.

"Very well then," she said. "Please, enjoy the hospitality of our city and return here tomorrow at high noon. Then we will render our decision unto you."

Aeligos and Sonja bowed before the queen and followed the chamberlain from the throne room. In the antechamber, Haicer returned to the bench he'd been sitting on, took up his red leather book, and began crossing off names and appointments. He looked up after a minute when he realized the two half-demons were still waiting, and he gestured for them to depart. "Return tomorrow at noon," he said simply. "I will see you then."

Aeligos and Sonja returned to the inn and found the others finishing lunch. Sonja sat among them and Aeligos stood at the end of the table to address them. He glanced around at the sparsely populated common room before he spoke. "Pack your things and begin heading north along the mountains to Saint John's pass first thing in the morning," he instructed them quietly. "I have to meet with the queen again at noon tomorrow, but there's no reason for the rest of you to delay here while we wait to see what her decision will be. In fact, I should've sent you to the next city as soon as I found out we'd have to wait three days to see her in the first place."

"What about you?" Typhonix asked.

"I should be able to catch up to you easily enough," he said. "Assuming the queen and her council really do make up their minds by tomorrow. Either way, our priority now is to make sure that whatever the shakna-rir decide, the rest of the major cities and their ruling bodies are in agreement." He looked to Sonja. "I hadn't really considered it, but what you said makes perfect sense. We've been sent to stop a war, but no one said anything about a short siege or a battle."

Sonja nodded. "I hadn't thought about it myself until I considered what Erik said about someone else replacing Gaswell if he's simply killed. If we can align enough of the island's major armies against him and *then* kill him, his men will likely disband in the face of a superior force if they have no one to lead them."

Aeligos nodded. "And the armies will draw out his forces, making a covert strike more likely to succeed. All right, forget what I said. Pack your things and start making your way north this afternoon," he said. The others looked at him with raised brows, but he shook his head. "I'm not joking. Erik would do the same in my place. Get to it, we've got work to do and our timeline is getting shorter by the hour."

The rest of the group looked to Sonja and she nodded, which sent them all into action. Once the others headed up to their rooms to retrieve their things, Sonja approached Aeligos and touched his shoulder. "Be careful," she said. Her tone left little doubt as to what she meant, and he nodded and made his way up to his own room.

Aeligos saw his siblings and human companions off at the edge of the city an hour later, and passed the remainder of the day looking for trouble.

His efforts still yielded him no results in finding a thieves' guild or anything remotely like it, so he passed the night playing cards at a local tavern. He made back much of the money he'd spent during the trip before the other players grew tired of him and he returned to his room at the inn.

When the sun drew high overhead the next day, he returned to the castle and was quickly escorted into the queen's audience chamber. She seemed surprised that Aeligos had come alone, and he was likewise surprised to find the throne room much fuller than the first time. A half-dozen other shakna-rir flanked the area before the throne, three to a side, and Aeligos approached to stand between them and bowed to the queen. Each of the others was dressed in regal finery, five males and one female, and they appeared to be the generals the queen had spoken of at the previous meeting. They all regarded Aeligos for a moment before everyone turned their attention to the queen.

Queen Omalias shifted in her throne and spared a glance toward her mate before she stood up and held her hands out to the sides. "Welcome back to our court," she said to her half-demon guest. "My mate and his generals have conferred long with me on this matter, though we still have a few questions to make certain our chosen course is the correct one."

"I will be of any aid I may to Your Majesty," Aeligos said.

"To your knowledge, what is Zalkar's ultimate goal with respect to General Gaswell?" she asked. "Does he want him captured or killed, and what of his progeny, if any?"

Aeligos scratched absently at his snout. "We weren't given specific instructions outside of preventing a war. How Gaswell is removed from power was left up to us. Personally, I believe it would be best to capture him so we have the luxury of interrogation to determine if he was working for another. Killing him may simply make him a martyr, but he may leave us with little choice."

"Working for another? How do you mean?" the female general who stood at Aeligos' right asked.

"As I explained to Her Majesty yesterday, my elder brother Erik was the one tasked with coming here to stop Gaswell and war," he said. "He sent us ahead to speak to your Queen on his behalf because he was also tasked with finding and killing a demon. It's only speculation, but it's quite possible whatever demon he hunts is related to Gaswell and his plans. Until he and Kari – his partner – return, we won't know for sure."

The general nodded appreciatively and turned back to her queen. "I agree with Maktus on this, Your Majesty," she said, her voice clear and confident. "If these are to be trusted as you believe, then our best course of action in my opinion is to send our armies out in preparation, and then follow the lead of these servants of Zalkar."

The queen sat back down and rubbed a finger thoughtfully across her chin. "I would like further confirmation before we proceed," she said, and she clapped her hands once. A young page appeared from a side door and bowed before his queen. "Go to the church of Zalkar and bring their highest ranking priest to me right away. Go."

The page rushed from the throne room and the queen stood once more. "Our court shall recess until the priest has arrived," she said. "Evanja, please show our guest to the dining hall for refreshments and then show him around should time permit."

The female general nodded her head and gestured for Aeligos to follow her while the queen, Maktus, and the other generals made their egress through a side door. She led Aeligos through the opposite door and down a long hall decorated the same way as both the throne room and its antechamber. At its far end was the dining hall, a massive rectangular chamber with a table that had to easily seat fifty people. It was stately and warm despite its size, with several stone hearths standing at intervals around the room to keep it heated should the need arise.

Evanja made her way to the table and sat at its end, and she gestured for Aeligos to sit beside her. As he took his seat, he studied the woman more thoroughly, noting that she seemed to be at least a decade older than her queen. She was attractive, with wavy brown hair tied back in a neat tail and matching eyes that studied the half-demon warily and questioningly. It was a stare he was used to: he received it any time he tried to get information on an uncomfortable topic.

"Your queen doesn't seem to trust me entirely," he said as a servant brought them both goblets of wine.

The shakna-rir female beheld him curiously. "If Her Majesty didn't trust you, she would not have listened to your counsel," Evanja said before she took a sip. "She has sent for the priest merely for the sake of being thorough, not because she doesn't trust you."

"And what about you?" he asked, meeting her eyes.

Evanja seemed surprised by the question, and she took another sip of her wine before answering. "I was raised in Aurun Ch'Gurra, where I served in the military for many years," she said. "I only came here a few summers ago to escape the endless bickering of the nobility, to find a more peaceful and quiet kingdom to live in. I was made one of the warlord's generals because of my experience, but my contributions go well beyond the military. The Queen listens to my counsel where half-demons are concerned, as Aurun Ch'Gurra had many more of them than this kingdom sees."

"Oh? And what were your experiences with my kind like?" he asked.

She managed a slight smile. "Normally your kind weren't a problem, so long as the children were never subjected to their father's presence growing up. Of course, I've never been too familiar with *your* kind as such: I've never dealt much with anything other than half-corlypsi, half-brys, or rarely half-elites. You're half-guardian, unless I'm mistaken."

"You're not," he said with a smile. "So you trust half-demons normally?"

"No more or less than anyone else," she answered, and she took another sip of her wine while she thought to herself. "You see, the others don't seem to realize that we risk making the same mistake that Gaswell does: he relies solely on his own kind, and oftentimes we shakna-rir do as well. When the gods send a group of half-demons to our doorstep to ask something of us, clearly it requires a more open mind than we are accustomed to."

Aeligos nodded. "I can see you're very valuable to the crown. I wish every city, county, and kingdom had someone like you in it."

She smiled but said nothing, and the two finished their drinks in silence. Just after they finished, a page came to inform them that the priest of Zalkar had arrived and the court was about to reconvene. They made their way back to the throne room and found a robe-clad human among the others, and they took their places. The members and guests of the court stood at attention until Queen Omalias was seated on the throne and motioned for them to stand at ease.

"Good afternoon, Your Majesty," the human said. "I am Tomas Davidson, priest of Zalkar and representative of the Unyielding. What does the crown require of our church?"

"We welcome you to our court, Master Davidson," Queen Omalias returned. "We have called upon you this day to verify the words of this half-demon, Aeligos Tesconis. While we have no reason to distrust him, we have a decision before us that will affect the entire kingdom and all her people. We would like confirmation as to the Unyielding's role in this matter."

"I will be of what assistance I may, Your Majesty," the priest said formally.

"Does the Unyielding have demonhunters on the island named Erik Tesconis and..."

"Erijinkor Tesconis and Karian Vanador," Aeligos amended when the

275

queen paused and glanced at him.

"I was not aware they had arrived, Your Majesty, but our priesthood here on the isle was expecting them," the human said with a nod of his silver-haired head. "What has his brother said that you need verified?"

"He has told us that the Unyielding has sent them here to prevent a war," the queen said, and the eyes of the entire gathering fell onto the priest.

Tomas looked to Aeligos for a few moments before turning his gaze back to the Queen. "Your Majesty, I am aware of no such orders," he said. "I know only that two demonhunters were dispatched here to the island to deal with an *infestation* of a possibly underworld nature. However, it is also possible the Unyielding has issued other orders to his hunters that we are simply not privy to."

"It was supposed to be kept a secret as much as possible, Majesty," Aeligos said. "My brother's Order didn't want Gaswell to know who or what to expect, if anything."

Queen Omalias considered the two males' words for several long, silent minutes before she looked up to her mate. "I do not want to take our nation to war," she said.

"I understand, my queen," Maktus said. "The decision is yours, but we must consider that attacks upon our neighbors will soon become attacks upon us. It is better that we prevent war by destroying its source than to hide from it and hope it passes us by."

The queen looked to the sole female general before her. "And you trust the words of this half-demon?" she asked.

Evanja nodded and regarded Aeligos for a moment before turning her full attention back to her queen. "I do," she said. "We have verified his brother's existence and presence; now we need only decide whether we prepare for battle in defense of our island."

"And indeed we must," Queen Omalias said, though her quiet sigh told Aeligos it was not a decision she made lightly. She looked up to Maktus once more. "Mobilize the army. You are in command."

The warlord saluted his queen and motioned for his male generals to go carry out their monarch's orders, and then he gestured for Aeligos to come closer. "You will carry word to Fahrem and Raugro," Maktus said when Aeligos approached. "Inform them of our intentions, and tell their leaders that our armies will be stationed on the plains south of Brehl, where we will meet them should they wish to join us. I will prepare official documents for you to take with you, and have them ready by morning."

Aeligos cursed silently in the back of his mind, but he masked it

276

behind a smile and bowed before the warlord and queen. "Thank you," he said. "I will carry word to your neighbors and convince them to join you. When we meet again on the plains in the place you've specified, we will further develop a strategy."

"Go safely under the watchful eyes of the gods. We thank you for your warning, and your patience in delivering it," Queen Omalias said.

Aeligos bowed once more, and Evanja touched his elbow lightly. "Would you like to sleep the night here in the palace?" she asked quietly while Master Davidson bid the court farewell and made his way from the throne room.

"If that's not going to be an issue with Her Majesty...?" he asked. The last thing he wanted to do was sabotage his own work.

Evanja shook her head. "I know how it might seem, but she won't mind."

Aeligos considered the possibility the queen would want someone to stay close to him and gauge his behavior in the wake of their decision. On that note, he decided it might be even more suspicious if he refused than if he accepted. "Then I'd love to," he answered with a smile.

~~*~*

Kari decided to stop in the city of Talvor on their way back to the rainforest. She knew Erik didn't want to delay, but channeling Zalkar's power to heal her wing had managed only to stop the bleeding and protect it from infection. The membrane tore a little more every time Kari jolted it, and she wanted to find a healer that could at the very least repair the structural damage and prevent it from compounding. Erik and Makauric offered no argument, and after three days they arrived at the open archways of the bay city. Kari brought Makauric along with them to the gates, intending to bring him to Zalkar's church. He was initially unwilling to go, but she convinced him by assuring him he would be under her protection.

The guards wasted no time aiming their crossbows at Makauric when they approached, but Kari stayed in front of the brys with her hands up. The officer among them ordered his men to spread out and keep their weapons trained on the creature but await his command, and he fixed Kari with a scowl. Though it wasn't the same officer from their previous visit, his attitude didn't seem any better, and Kari wondered if they thought she was half-demon or if they just hated everyone. "What is the meaning of this?" the officer demanded. He stepped in front of Kari and brought his face uncomfortably close to hers.

The terra-dracon woman drew out her dog tags slowly, laid them across her chest and met the officer's stare. "My name is Karian Vanador, Shield of the Heavens, by Zalkar's grace," she said, drawing a look of unmasked surprise from the man before his face returned to a stern stare just shy of the previous scowl. "This brys is with us; we have to take him to Zalkar's temple."

The officer sighed, ran his fingers through his short white hair, and shook his head. "We are under strict orders to keep all trouble out of the city," he said, his defiance clearly overridden by Kari's profession and rank – or maybe it was Erik's stature. "Two half-demons and a full-blood..."

"I'm not half-demon," Kari said, and she showed her teeth. "And even if I was, I'm in service to Zalkar and don't have time for this. My wing's hurt and I'm in a lot of pain, please don't make an incident out of a simple request."

The officer inspected her wounded wing, and then he waved for his guards to lower their weapons and let the group through. "Very well. Head straight to the temple and stay out of trouble," he said, and then he turned to Makauric and pointed a finger in warning. "Keep that bow shouldered at all times! Zalkar's temple is straight down this avenue: go past two plazas and you'll see it ahead on your left."

Makauric nodded and Kari waved off the officer's comment. "He's with us, he won't cause any trouble," she said.

The terra-rir officer waved them along. The three passed into the city and ignored the questioning glances of its citizens, who appeared to be almost exclusively terra-rir. Kari considered it strange, as from what they had learned, Gaswell and his forces were situated almost entirely in the southwest. She wondered if the city's homogenous population had anything to do with the warlord at all, or if it was just a coincidence. She found it difficult to believe it was coincidence: with the rir peoples' aversion to sea and ocean-based travel, port cities without humans were nearly unheard of.

They passed through the city quietly but quickly, afraid to be exposed for too long with a brys with them. It was clean and tidy, and its citizenry was obviously wealthy. After two plazas they came upon Zalkar's temple on the left side of the avenue, and Kari dashed in quickly. She had only to point out her wounded wing to the acolytes within, and they called upon one of the priests to come minister his healing arts to her. Kari sat on a bench and glanced briefly at Erik and Makauric, who entered after a short delay outside. She wondered briefly what the issue was and whether they'd had an argument out of her earshot, but then she figured it was more likely

Makauric had hesitated to enter a temple to Zalkar.

Two of the human acolytes inspected her wound and then held the severed edges of the bone together. Kari gritted her teeth in pain, and then the priest and applied his blue-glowing hand to the broken bone. Kari screamed in shock as the edges of the bone immediately frayed and then knitted, and a mass of black scar tissue formed over the exposed area. A shiver coursed through her in the wake of the pain which, though it dissipated quickly, left her with a short burst of adrenaline running through her veins. She stood up and flapped her wing; the pain was now but a phantom memory. When she glanced over at Erik, though, she could see he still felt guilty that the wound was his doing.

Kari thanked the clergy, but when they noticed the brys among them, they fixed the demonhunters with incredulous stares. "What is this?" the priest asked. "You bring a demon into the very house of the demonhunter patron?"

Kari beheld the older human's impatience and could tell he wasn't as angry as his words made it seem. His cool blue eyes studied her evenly and he dismissed the acolytes so that he could speak with the guests alone. The younger humans moved to the rear of the temple, and the older robed human folded his arms across his chest as he waited for an explanation. Erik took a seat on one of the horseshoe-shaped benches near the temple's center and, after a moment, Makauric did likewise.

"This...*demon* is the reason we succeeded in our mission here," Kari explained quietly. "He guided us through the southern rainforest and put us in contact with a tribe of czarikk who'd been attacked by a sylinth. Then he led us to the sylinth's lair so we could destroy it. I know the Unyielding despises his kind, but this brys has earned both our trust and respect."

The human looked to Makauric for a minute, and he rubbed his chain thoughtfully. He nodded and met Kari's eyes. "I understand," he said. "So you destroyed a sylinth, fulfilling Zalkar's task for you here on the island?"

"Yes, Master," Kari said, and she and the priest moved to sit on the bench facing her partner and the brys. "We have some questions about it. Do you have any underworld records?"

"We do," the priest said. He turned toward the acolytes at the temple's rear and raised his voice, asking them to bring something called the Anthraxis Council Codex. Based on the name, Kari understood that it was obviously a record of the council of demon kings. The priest looked back to her and then Erik and gave a muted smile. "Forgive me. I am Master Tanner, ranking priest of our lord here in Talvor. I regret that I am not an

279

experienced healer or high-ranking priest of our lord, or I would have done a better job with your wound."

Kari waved off the comment. "I appreciate your work," she said. "I'm Karian Vanador, Shield of the Heavens, and this is my partner Erijinkor Tesconis, Demonhunter. The brys is called Makauric."

"Makauric?" the priest repeated, his brows arching. "Ah, I should have guessed. We've heard of this particular brys before: he ranges the forest and the savannah nearby, and we have had no reports of trouble from him at all. Unusual for one of his kind, if he will forgive my saying so."

Makauric made a dismissive gesture but said nothing, and Kari had to smile. "He certainly is unusual," she said. "I wish all of his brothers were like him."

That drew a short-lived smile from the brys, but it disappeared as quickly as it had come. Soon one of the young acolytes approached with the black book his superior had asked for. The younger human handed the book to the priest before returning to his duties, and Master Tanner began to flip through it. "So, you said it was a sylinth?" Tanner asked. "Killing a sylinth is quite an impressive feat, even for one of your rank. This codex will only list the demon if it was a prince or a very high-ranking noble. I don't suppose it happened to give you a name?"

"Actually, it did," Kari answered. "Its name was Ressallk. It said it was 'the greatest of its father's sons,' and claimed to be the son of Sekassus the Calculating."

The priest regarded her with wide eyes as she spoke, but then he shook his head when she finished. "No, whoever this Ressallk was, he was not Sekassus' firstborn," Tanner said, and he began flipping through the tome. He came to a page with a picture of a massive snake-like creature, though unlike the sylinth they had fought, the one pictured had a humanoid body. Kari read the caption below the picture: *King Sekassus the Calculating, the Cobra Lord, Sixth of the Council.* Her underworld historical and hierarchal knowledge was far from extensive, but she did know that Celigus Chinchala was only the seventh on the Council. She thought about how strong Chinchala was, and then tried to imagine the strength of the one above him in station on the Council.

"Had you fought Amnastru – Sekassus' firstborn – we would likely not be having this conversation," Tanner said with a solemn gaze. He continued to flip through the tome past the entry for Sekassus, and at last came to another that had no drawing beside it. "Here he is: Ressallk, eleventh-born son of the king, lieutenant in the king's army."

"I might have guessed," Kari said. "He didn't seem very strong or

280

experienced."

Tanner regarded her with interest. "Though he was still fairly young for one of his kind," he said, "killing a sylinth – let alone a sylinthian prince – is, as I said, an impressive feat. Did you learn anything of his intentions or reason for being here?"

"Not exactly," she answered. "He murdered the children of the czarikk, and they said he was trying to get them to bend knee to him. We think he might've been involved with Gaswell's sudden uprising, but we're not really sure how 'recruiting' the czarikk would've fit into that, given Gaswell's plans. How much do we need to worry about revenge from the Cobra Lord?"

The priest sighed. "That is hard to say," he said. "Sekassus has lost several sons in his time, but unlike his more hot-tempered counterparts on the Council, he is slow to react. His plans oftentimes take years to enact and come to fruition, but I will pass on word for those in the proper places to keep an eye on him and an ear bent to his plans. In the meantime, I would not worry too much about retaliation."

"That's a relief," Erik commented.

Tanner nodded. "I will pass along word of your success to your superiors in DarkWind, as was directed," he said. "Is there anything else I can do for you?"

"I'm just curious how you run a temple in the city if Gaswell has so many sympathizers here," Kari commented.

The priest waved off the comment, making an obvious effort to not laugh. "They talk tough, but like the man they consider following, they are cowards at heart," he said. "I see they failed to keep you from entering their city…even with a brys among you."

"Even still, I don't think it's a good idea to stay here," Erik said, rising to his feet, and his concerns were echoed by a nod from their brys companion.

"Yea, that's true," Kari said, and she saluted the priest. "Thank you, Master Tanner."

The priest rose to his feet and bowed before the demonhunters with a warm smile. "Be safe in your journeys," he said. "As I said, I will pass along word of your success."

"Farewell, Master," Erik said, and he led Kari and the brys from the temple. Afternoon was fading fast, so they made their way swiftly from the city. Fortunately, no trouble found them on their way out, and soon the grasses of the savannah were beneath their feet again. When twilight fell over them they set up camp under one of the sparse trees once more. They shared what little dried venison was left from their stay at the cave and enjoyed the meal together.

Makauric told them they could reach the czarikk in two days if they forced themselves to march into the night, and they agreed that it would be best even if it exhausted them. They headed toward the jungle the next morning and arrived in czarikk territory late on the second day, where they were met by a patrol that recognized them. The patrol allowed them to pass through hastily, and they arrived in the village just after sundown, when the evening meal was about to be served. Savarras greeted them when they entered the center of the village, and he invited them to sit with him and the chieftain on the logs near the central fire pit.

Kari took a seat and noted the joyous expressions on the faces of the lizard people, and she found that they were quite contagious. She thought perhaps they'd felt the sylinth's demise just as Makauric had, but after a minute she thought better of that and turned toward Savarras. "You spoke with Sakkrass," she said in elvish to the shaman, and his smile spread wider.

"Yes. Several days ago, when we fire danced, we felt his presence among us once again, and we knew you had succeeded," he said. "Sakkrass said that when you performed the fire dance, his spirit came upon you, and because he could not communicate through me, he did so through you instead. You have experienced something even I, his high shaman, have not."

Kari remembered Sakkrass speaking through her, but only now did she grasp the true importance of the event. Not only was this other peoples' god quite real and benevolent, but he'd trusted Kari to carry his spirit into battle and fight for him. She put her hand to her chest and smiled, and the happiness of the czarikk around her warmed her to the core. "It was my honor to carry your deity's spirit into battle," she said, doing her best to convey her joy to the holy man. "I know that slaying the sylinth has not eased the pain of your loss, but your people should be safe, and prosper in your next mating cycle."

Savarras nodded and his smile did not dissipate. "Indeed. We received further blessing from our lord as well," he said. He looked across the circle and beckoned for someone to approach. After a moment, a young female czarikk approached holding a hatchling cradled to her chest, and she knelt down before the shaman. "This is Aszera and her child. She hid her egg from the family, as she is not mated and was afraid of being shunned."

Kari studied Aszera, though her eyes were downturned and she wouldn't meet Kari's gaze. "Her egg survived because it was not with those of the rest of the tribe," Kari reasoned.

Savarras nodded and laid his hand on Aszera's shoulder. "Yes. What would normally bring shame has instead brought joy to the family. This is a blessing from Sakkrass," he said, and upon hearing their deity's name, the female looked up and managed a smile, though she didn't appear to understand what he was saying to Kari. "We have awaited your return, she who has made us safe from the sylinth. Tonight we will fire dance for our lord, and you will participate in the child's naming ceremony."

Kari bowed her head politely. "I would be honored," she said. Savarras translated their conversation quickly into his sibilant language for the female before them and his chief. Kari took the opportunity to likewise inform her companions of what was being said, and Erik smiled. Even Makauric's eyes betrayed one, though his face remained neutral.

They shared in the evening meal with their czarikk hosts, and soon after the meal was finished, a massive bonfire was started in the central fire pit. The dancers did not immediately begin their ritual praise to their lord, though, but waited as Savarras called the female with the hatchling to stand before him and Oshasis. He invited Kari to stand with them, and together the four stood by the fire while the entire tribe watched.

Aszera dropped to her knees and held the hatchling in both hands over her head and toward the shaman, and he made several gestures over the squirming babe as he spoke in their sibilant language. The female said something in return, and Savarras smiled briefly at Kari before motioning for her to take the child from its mother. The demonhunter did so after only a slight hesitation, and held the child up before the shaman and chieftain while the holy man repeated his gesturing and spoke once more in their tongue.

Savarras met Kari's questioning gaze when he finished the ritual, and he said, "Aszera has asked to name her hatchling in your honor. If you agree to this, then simply kneel before Oshasis as she has done, and hold the child up to him in offering."

Kari blushed, but after meeting the girl's gaze, she knelt beside her and held the child up in both hands, offering the hatchling to the tribe's chief. Savarras said something in the czarikk tongue, and Kari caught her name among his words. After a moment, Oshasis smiled and took the child from Kari's hands, and he held it high above his head in a careful grip. He bellowed in a loud voice, and again Kari heard her name mentioned in whatever was being said. When the chief had finished his declaration, the tribe cheered and its females let forth a hissing whistle that Kari found intriguing.

"The chief has welcomed the child among the people, and she will bear your name," Savarras said to Kari as she rose to her feet. Kari bowed her head with a smile. "Oshasis also wishes to make you and your companions family, that you will always be welcome among us should your travels bring you back into our homeland."

Kari found her eyes a bit misty. "Your people honor us, and we give thanks for your hospitality and friendship," she said.

Aszera bowed before the demonhunter and said what were obvious thanks in her language. Aszera bowed again to Kari, her chief, and the shaman, and then she made her way back among her people, who welcomed her with touches and hugs.

Savarras turned to speak with Oshasis, and Kari sat down beside Erik and Makauric and began to explain what had happened. Erik gave her shoulder a squeeze and pulled her in for a hug after a moment. It was clear he was very proud of her, both for slaying the demon and the simple act of diplomacy she had accomplished with a people whose language she did not speak. "Are you going to dance with them tonight?" Erik asked.

"Yes," Kari answered. "Savarras told me that when I danced with them, their god saw and put his vengeful spirit upon me to help with our mission. So I'm going to dance with them to say thank you for his strength. And you two will get to see me naked again."

Erik laughed, and both he and Kari were surprised when the brys did as well. Makauric seemed embarrassed when fixed with both of their amused gazes, and Kari was amazed to see so much expression from the normally unreadable creature. "I would be lying if I said I did not enjoy that," he said quietly.

Kari patted her partner's shoulder. "You know, if the two of you put your duties aside for a while, maybe you could find your own women," she said. "Then you can stare at your own naked mate instead of someone else's."

Erik snorted with a dismissive wave, and Makauric shrugged. "I have nothing to offer one," the brys said.

"You might be surprised," Kari countered. "Maybe there's a reason your brothers are all on the west side of the island. Maybe there's a lot of rir rangers who patrol those woods, and it's possible they've let your brothers into their circles."

The brys didn't seem at all convinced. "Perhaps," he offered, but let the matter drop.

"Maybe I'll try to find whoever Annabelle Sol'ridachi is and ask to court her," Erik said dryly, trying to suppress a chuckle. Kari fixed him with wide eyes. "I've been meaning to ask you who that is since you mentioned the name."

Kari shook her head, took a deep breath, and sighed uneasily. "Honestly, you don't even want to know," she said, glancing off into the depths of the village as she beat back the memories of her past. "She was a friend of mine once, but…"

Kari went silent and Erik regarded her curiously. "Now you've got my curiosity piqued," he said. "You'll have to explain some time when you feel up to it."

Kari gave a noncommittal shrug and rose to her feet. She removed her armor and clothes as the czarikk began painting their dancers in preparation for the ceremony. To her surprise, no females came to paint her. Instead, Oshasis and his high shaman took up the task. The designs they painted were different, and it took Kari only a few moments to recognize the symbols and glyphs she'd seen carved and painted within the shaman's teepee. At first Kari was nervous about having the two touching her body so intimately, but she relaxed and reminded herself that they would not violate the sanctity of their ceremony.

She waited by her friends, her body painted in a beautiful array of orange, yellow, red, and blue symbols and markings whose meaning was lost on her. She was confused when the other czarikk finished their painting but did not dance, and after a few moments she realized the eyes of every member of the tribe were upon her. She bit her lip anxiously, but then she stepped close to the fire, turned to her right, and stomped her foot twice as she initiated the dance. She repeated the dance that she had performed for so many hours on her first visit, trying to stay as true to the czarikk ritual as possible, and if she made any mistakes, no one made any sound or move to correct her. Once she completed the first circuit, a male joined her, and then a second, then a female followed by another female, and so it went with each pass that four more dancers joined them. The voices of the tribe rose in exultation and Kari felt the heat of the fire pass through her skin and to her very soul. Soon, all of the dancers had joined her in the ceremony.

Kari felt the presence of Sakkrass in her mind, just as she had the moment he spoke through her in battle with the sylinth. In her primal core she felt his scaled body press against her as their minds danced together. She continued her dance around the fire to the ebb and flow of the sibilant voices of the czarikk, and she moved in perfect harmony with the dancers who had performed the sacred rite for years. In her mind it was only she and Sakkrass that danced around the fire, and her body reacted to his mental touch. Theirs was not a dance of lovers, but a dance of protector and protected: Sakkrass' body pressed tight against her in her mind, and it was as if he was wrapping her in his scaly flesh to protect her from harm. His reptilian snout touched lightly at the base of her neck where Grakin had kissed her innumerable times, but Sakkrass did not kiss her. He sniffed lightly at her skin, and she could feel him smile. Gently he released her and she spun away from him, and then she came to a stop and stared across at him.

Kari blinked several times in surprise when she realized the czarikk were no longer singing and no dancers remained around the fire. All of the lizard people had prostrated themselves before a single czarikk who stood completely naked before her. It didn't take Kari long to figure out what had happened, and while her companions gaped in disbelief, she dropped to one knee before the reptilian male.

"Arise, please, my friend," Sakkrass said in his sibilant voice, and he stepped forward and held his hand out to help her to her feet. Kari nearly choked as he in turn knelt before her, and his glowing red eyes came up to meet hers. "If any should bow, it should be I to you, in thanks for what you have done for my people, for what I could not."

Kari looked him over more thoroughly and beheld what she assumed was a perfect specimen of a *mulrassa* czarikk. He wore no clothing, showing off every perfectly sculpted muscle beneath his dark green scales, though his scales did bear several scars that marked him as a warrior. She wondered if he had once been mortal, as was the case with many of her own pantheon's deities, or if he was in fact a lizardman deity who had a hand in the creation of the czarikk people. She touched the end of her snout lightly with one hand as he rose to his feet and drew closer. He towered over her, though not so much as Erik did.

"It is an honor to meet you," she managed after a few silent moments, and the czarikk male smiled. Kari suddenly realized that they were conversing in the common tongue, but the other czarikk around the camp seemed to understand them as well.

"You and your gods do not know me, and yet you afford me the respect you would one of their peers," Sakkrass said. "Your honor convinces me that I should make myself known among their number, if only to grant them another ally in their struggles against the demon kings."

"I'm sure they would welcome you as a brother," she said, and she reached toward him tentatively. He bowed his head toward her hand, and Kari touched his face and felt the smooth scales of his cheek, and the gentle flitting of his eye when her hand passed over it. "Just as I welcome your shaman and his chief as mine."

Sakkrass turned and stepped away from her when she finished speaking, and he held his hands out to the sides. "Arise, my people; your lord is moved by your love, and I wish to watch you dance. Dance not for me, but for yourselves, and for the children I will bless you with. The work of the demon shall not diminish my devotion to you."

Again he had spoken in what sounded to Kari like the common tongue, but the czarikk rose to their feet and let forth the same cheers and hissing whistles they had for Aszera's child, and soon the dancers were underway again. Kari hesitated for a moment and stood by Sakkrass' side, and Oshasis and Savarras approached to kneel before their god. Kari had never met an avatar before – other than those who served as such in title only – but she knew instinctively that what stood before her was a true physical representation of the czarikk god. She was amazed at the blessing their people had received, and was proud to be a part of it.

Sakkrass touched the chief and shaman each on the top of their heads, and motioned for them to rise. "I know each of you feels responsible for what has happened to my people. I hold you free of blame. You have served me well, and it was no fault of yours what befell them," he said. He turned his attention to Savarras, and Kari could see that his features hardened. "Know that I would never abandon you, and certainly never hurt my own people to spite them."

"Forgive my foolishness," Savarras said, and Kari found that she could understand him perfectly despite the fact that he had clearly spoken in the czarikk tongue. Savarras knelt in supplication before his lord, and Sakkrass touched his shaman's head in absolution.

Sakkrass turned back to Kari, and his reptilian eyes blinked slowly as the warm smile returned to his handsome features. "I cannot remain long upon your world without attracting the attention of enemies," he said. "I owe you a great debt, one I am not certain I can repay. Ask of me anything, and if it is within my power to grant, I shall."

Kari shook her head. "You don't owe me anything," she said, but Sakkrass waved away her words and waited for her to ask something of him. She looked at Savarras and Oshasis for a moment, and then to Erik and Makauric, and it seemed they, too, were able to understand all that was being said. Kari turned back to Sakkrass and said, "Teach me the language of your people."

The lizardman god considered her for a few moments and then smiled. He reached up, laid his hand on the top of Kari's snout, and whispered into her mind. It felt as though a soft breeze blew across her brain, cooling and

287

tickling, and glyphs and characters began to draw themselves within her imagination. She started to recognize what they said, and she watched as the deity wrote an entire book of his peoples' histories into her mind. Most curious of all were the images of the czarikk people interacting with both the elves and the luranar, as Kari had suspected. There wasn't much immediate explanation, but Kari found the lizard peoples' connection to the elves heartwarming. When Sakkrass finally removed his hand from her, Kari's mouth fell open in wonder. "Speak to me," he said softly.

"I am called Karian Vanador," she said, trying to emulate the sibilant accent of the czarikk as she spoke their tongue. "And I will always remember you, Sakkrass of the people."

"And I shall always remember you, Karian Vanador. I will watch over you, just as your own god does, as if you are my daughter," he said. Just the word daughter was enough to bring tears to Kari's eyes, but Sakkrass' clawed fingers wiped them away gently, and he cradled her face gently in his scaly palm. "Be safe, my child."

And then he was gone, leaving his people stunned. Kari turned immediately and spun to reinitiate the flow of the dance. She listened to the czarikk take up their beautiful song once again, and she understood each word as it was intoned in melodic harmony. Kari began to sing with them while she danced, and her participation in both dance and song seemed to spur them to greater joy. Soon she found her partner dancing just behind her, painted like she had been the first night, though he wore his loincloth. She smiled and the joy of her expression was mirrored upon his face as he did his best to mimic her dance, though he was clearly not a dancer.

"What are they singing?" Erik asked, his voice raised so she could hear him.

"*Up from the roots, we are Sakkrass' seed! His love and blessing are all we need. We dance for him by stars and fire. To be his children to what we aspire!*" she sang to him in the common tongue. It wasn't an exact translation, but it was what came to mind when Kari tried to interpret the song. The czarikk did not just worship Sakkrass as their god: they served him as their father, and being good children to him was the most important thing in their lives. Kari thought briefly of her prayer to Gori Sensullu before she'd departed for Tsalbrin, and she thought that perhaps her people and the lizard-folk were not all that different.

Erik smiled but didn't interrupt her further as she continued in the ceremony. Kari knew she had only a modest singing voice, but the sound of the czarikk language flowing from her tongue without effort was simply beautiful. Kari danced until the night was deep and the fire had burned down to a warm glow, but unlike their previous visit, the czarikk did not retire to their homes until she had finished. They cheered and let out the hissing whistles when she brought the ceremony to a close, and she smiled broadly and bowed before them. She felt at home among them, which surprised her; only a few weeks before, she had never really felt at home anywhere.

Savarras allowed the guests the use of his teepee once again. Makauric bid Kari and Erik goodnight and climbed the nearest tree to recline in its higher branches. Kari and Erik headed toward their loaned tent but stopped when several female czarikk came and stood by its doorway. They glanced at Kari briefly but then gazed at Erik expectantly, and Kari laughed, lifted the flap over the entryway, and started to slip within. Erik stopped her. "What do they want?" he asked.

Kari wondered if he was really that naive or just pretending to be for modesty's sake. "You shouldn't have to speak czarikk to know," she said. She was surprised when he blushed: though it was impossible to see a half-demon blush, she could tell by his expression that he was doing so. "Erik, if you have any doubts about how good-looking you are, this should put them to rest. You're handsome, you just saved their tribe from a demon, and they want to thank you. Be polite: if you're not interested, say so and head inside. Otherwise, go enjoy yourself."

"Kari…," he muttered, almost a whine.

She rose up straight before him and touched a finger to his snout. "Erik, they know what they're asking for, and you're an adult – you can make your own decisions. I'm not going to think differently of you no matter what you decide. If you want to go play with them, then by all means, go enjoy yourself for a night. Zalkar's not going to strike you with lightning."

"Are you sure?" he asked.

Kari could tell that his discomfort was genuine. "I'll be honest with you, Erik: Grakin's not the first man I've ever been with. I don't think he thinks any less of me because of it. If you want to go, then go," she said. She laid her hand on his chest and met his eyes evenly. "Maybe you should think about what *you* want rather than what your siblings might think for a change. You might find that they're holding your love life back more than your job."

Erik still didn't seem entirely convinced, but he gave the barest of smiles and nodded to Kari's words. He gave her a chaste kiss on the side of her snout in farewell, and then let himself be led away by the czarikk girls.

He looked over his shoulder once, and Kari could see that his discomfort was genuine, but he was trusting in Kari's words. She ducked inside the tent, lay in the soft, warm furs of the shaman's home, and closed her eyes. She felt Sakkrass' ethereal touch in her mind and whispering across her skin, but it was not his spectral hand that caressed her body: it was the feeling of a blanket being drawn up over her, and as its warmth settled into her naked form, Kari fell fast asleep.

Chapter XV – Small Blessings

It took Aeligos a week to reach Fahrem. While leaving the desert, he carried a simple tent to sleep under during the day and traveled by night in the hopes that he could overtake the rest of the group. He never did, and it surprised him that the time Maktus had cost him by delaying the preparation of the sealed documents allowed his siblings to outpace him. On the other hand, the Warlord's delays had allowed him to spend time with Evanja. He enjoyed his time with her and found that they had quite a few things in common, but she wasn't able to tell him anything useful that he didn't already know with regards to the situation with Gaswell or any other facets of politics on the island. Aeligos suspected the delays that kept him from overtaking his siblings would get blamed on their tryst, despite the truth. He was pretty sure he would hear it from Sonja when he met the others in Fahrem.

He attributed the rest of the group's faster movement to their decided lack of caution compared with him, as he rarely traveled on the road itself. He headed north out of Kulthon near the dirt road that followed the base of the mountains, but Aeligos picked his way through the rocky hills that footed the higher peaks, uncomfortable traveling where the fact that he was alone compounded his exposure. Traveling up in the rocky foothills allowed him to camouflage himself while he slept thanks to the coloration of his tent. Staying off the road added time to his journey, but without having to lead his siblings and their human friends, he was able to travel longer through the night and into the early morning before he stopped to rest, so he was able to make up some of the time.

He found Saint John's pass horrifying: within minutes of reaching the eastern end of the pass, he prayed that his siblings had thought better of traveling directly through it. Not so much a pass as a roofless tunnel, it was a natural funnel that canny bandits or any military commander could use to decimate an enemy force. The cliffs formed a remarkably straight line, which left Aeligos to wonder if the pass had been cut through the stone in ancient times or if it was natural. While the cliffs were high enough to pose a serious problem should the need to climb arise, they were not so high that a squad of archers would have any issue slaughtering travelers to a man.

Naturally, Aeligos scaled the cliffs and found that the top was a smooth, wide area that did indeed house a military force. To his relief, it was a unit of shakna-rir soldiers stationed there to make certain that no one used the pass for what Aeligos had feared. The soldiers immediately approached and demanded Aeligos identify himself. He explained the situation with his siblings and friends and his concern for them, and he presented the sealed documents from Maktus. Satisfied that he could be trusted, the guards let him go without incident, though they told him that they hadn't seen the group he described. Aeligos wondered at that, but thanked the soldiers for their help and continued his journey. Free of the desert's heat, he began traveling during the day and into the night, and returned to a normal schedule.

Saint John's pass opened into a beautiful expanse of grassy plains, and the landscape was dotted in places with massive, solitary trees. To the north of the pass was the patterned vista of farmland, and nestled at the base of the hills on the eastern end of the farmland was an unwalled town. It took Aeligos a couple of hours to walk to the town of Fahrem and he arrived just before sundown, which came much later without the imposing wall of peaks that had choked out the light while in Kulthon. Fahrem was a small town with only a single inn, so he found his siblings easily enough, and his sister greeted him when he arrived at last.

Sonja's red eyes showed relief and she asked, "I was expecting you'd overtake us, what happened?"

Aeligos shrugged off his travel pack and hung his cloak on the back of a chair, and he sat down across from his sister. "It took Maktus longer than I expected to have official documents prepared," he said. "I'd expected to leave the city the same day but ended up leaving closer to noon the next day. I also got held up coming through the pass; I didn't like the look of it. I climbed up top and traveled the higher ground after I spoke with the soldiers up there."

"That's my Aeligos," Sonja said with a smile.

"Did you walk through the pass?" he asked. "The guards said they didn't recall seeing you all move through the area."

Sonja nodded. "I used a chameleon spell to mask our presence for the most part," she said, and then she chuckled. "All I could think of was you hopping up and down saying, *'No! It looks like an ambush point!'*"

Aeligos laughed and wondered if he looked as silly as his sister's pantomime. "I nearly did just that when I reached the eastern end of the pass," he said. "I'm not sure why it surprised me that the shakna-rir had a military force stationed at the top of the cliffs. That spot would be a murder hole for bandits otherwise. Those green-skins really have their affairs in order."

Sonja sat back and fixed her brother with an amused gaze. "So, a missive came to us not long after we got here," she said, her tone dripping with mischief. "The courier mistook Grakin for you, and delivered a letter from Eryn. Oddly, though, it's about wanting to have sex with you, and the…interesting things she wants to do to you."

Aeligos chuckled and held his hand out. His sister produced the letter, and she simply shook her head as she handed it to him. He ignored her, opened the letter, and read through it quickly. It said exactly what Sonja hinted at, but the amount of articulation confirmed what the rogue suspected: to anyone else reading it, it appeared to simply be a letter detailing dozens of naughty things Eryn wanted to do to him. To those like Aeligos, however, it said something completely different.

He laid the letter out on the table and asked Sonja for a writing implement and some paper, and Aeligos reread the letter while she went upstairs to get them. When she returned to find him smoking the cigar he'd received in Tingus, she gave him a rather dubious look but handed him the items he'd asked for. "Aeligos, how did Eryn know where to find you?"

The rogue looked up at his sister and smiled around the cigar between his teeth. He glanced around the common room of the inn, which was nearly deserted, and none of his other siblings or their human companions was present. "Can you keep a secret?" he asked. Sonja continued to regard him curiously, but after a few moments she nodded. "Every time you saw Eryn and me fight on the ship, it was an act."

Sonja considered his words. "So Eryn going her own way was your plan all along?" she concluded.

Aeligos took the cigar from his teeth and put it in the ashtray. "Sonja, what do you think Erik's reaction would've been if he knew Eryn wanted to infiltrate Gaswell's army?" he asked.

His sister titled her head and pursed her lips. "He'd have told you it was too great a risk," she said. "And he would've forbid her from trying."

"And we'd be walking into this situation with an army at our backs, but completely blind otherwise," Aeligos added. "We needed to know what we're dealing with *before* we show up at Gaswell's doorstep. And if you think this letter has anything to do with sex…"

He trailed off and Sonja sat down and studied him while he worked. He began decoding the letter, and while he worked, the rest of their siblings and companions made appearances for dinner. Sonja motioned for everyone to remain quiet while Aeligos worked, and they shared a meal together in relative silence while the younger of the dark brothers diligently translated Eryn's missive.

At last he laid down his quill, and he sat back and took a long sip of his ale. He looked over the faces of each of his companions and nearly choked imagining what their expressions must have looked like after reading Eryn's letter. He didn't expect any of them to understand, despite the fact that it was no mystery that if Eryn wanted to do such things to him, she wouldn't have bothered writing about it. He flashed a lopsided smile as he considered that there was a lot he had to teach his siblings and friends about speaking in code.

Aeligos glanced around the common room casually but diligently and the group finished their meals. He took account of the many human and shakna-rir faces around them and was satisfied that the town was unlikely to be full of Gaswell supporters. "I'm sure you all got a good laugh out of this letter from Eryn," he said, and chuckles resounded around the table. "I can assure you there's nothing sexual about it, despite what it appears to say."

He spun the page he had been writing on and pushed it toward his companions, and their eyes widened at the sight of a carefully drawn map of a fortress. Marked with arrows and tick marks referring to a legend along the right side were more than a dozen apparent ways to enter it. The amount of detail was astounding, and even in the first brief minute many of the Silver Blades could see that there were further markings revealing troop positions, patrol routes, and notations of how high the walls and towers were. They continued to look it over with great interest for several minutes before Aeligos picked it up and sat back in his chair studying it.

"How do you know that's what the fortress looks like?" Sherman asked.

"Everything I drew and wrote is in this letter," Aeligos said, touching the fingers of his right hand to Eryn's missive. He looked over his shoulder briefly to see if anyone was listening in, but there was almost no one near them, and those who were paid them no obvious or even subtle attention. "Trust me when I tell you: Eryn doesn't talk about the things she wants to do, she just does them. Each of the things she described in this letter was a reference to *sensitive* areas of the fortress. Every time she described what sounded like a part of my body, she was drawing a verbal image of how the fortress is laid out. All the explicit stuff told me the best spots to invade." He glanced at Sonja briefly. "I was wrong about her, as usual; the old girl really came through for us."

"Old girl?" Katarina echoed as Aeligos shook his head at himself for show. "Isn't she still in her teens, like us?"

The rogue laughed, as did his siblings. "No, she's a half-brys," he said. "She doesn't show her age – doubly so because her kind are so small to begin with – but she's sixty-two."

The humans' eyes went wide, and their half-demon friends smiled knowingly: the twins had much to learn about half-demons. Sherman and Katarina exchanged a glance and then began laughing, and soon the rest of their companions joined them. "That letter was...rather explicit," Sherman said after a minute.

"I almost fell from grace just *reading* some of those things," Katarina quipped.

"Of course it was explicit," Aeligos said, and he gestured toward the group. "It's written so that anyone who reads it will think it's a proposition rather than a verbal schematic of how the enemy lair is laid out. Even if the letter was opened by a spy or other nosey third party, they likely didn't get any more out of it than you lot did. Gaswell or one of his men probably read it before it was even sent, obviously to no effect, but that's part of why it was sent here and not into shakna-rir territory or one of the bigger cities on the island. From what I gather, she's actually serving in his castle, and so far he and his people have no idea she's not what she appears to be."

"So she hasn't tried to kill him yet?" Sonja asked.

Aeligos shook his head. "No. One of the descriptive parts says he has two lieutenants who are very close to him and would likely take up his position if he were killed. She doesn't think she could kill all three of them before raising too much suspicion and having to flee, and I can sense there's something else going on there that she couldn't make mention of at all in the letter. I suspect it may be the demon Kari and Erik are hunting, and that that's what's truly behind all this." Aeligos held the letter up and gestured to a particular spot. "This seems to say that she's expecting us to bring an army close to his home to draw his garrisons out, and then we can invade the fortress with a small force."

"So that's our plan?" Sonja asked. "Cause a small battle to prevent a massive war?"

"I don't see any other choice," Aeligos answered. "We don't have the manpower to do anything while his army is sitting comfortably in and around his fortress. All we can do is our best. If war breaks out, there's not going to be anything we can do about it, and the gods will have to seek other options. Our best course of action is to go forward with Queen Omalias' plan, since Eryn is thinking along the same line with much more information."

"I'm sure Erik would agree," Sonja said.

"Anyone have any questions?" Aeligos asked. "I'm not going to go over everything I have here until our companions have had time to join us."

"Yea, I've got a question," Typhonix said, and he leaned forward on the table with his brows knitted. "Does Eryn really do those things to you?"

There were chuckles around the table, but Aeligos was not amused. He rose to his feet with a sigh and took up the letter and translation. He folded them carefully before putting them into a pocket inside his cloak. He threw the garment over his shoulders and walked out the door, and left his siblings and the two human teenagers staring after him in shock.

*****

Sonja saw that the others were all shocked, and their stares settled on Typhonix after a silent minute had passed. The blonde warrior shrugged and held his hands out to the sides.

"He has seemed on edge for some time now," Grakin said with a yawn.

"Eryn can bring out the worst in him, but I think her absence specifically brings out the worst in him," Sonja returned with a sigh.

The priest shook his head. "She is not what brings out the worst in him," he said. "He worries about what we think of her, and of the two of them together, and that is what brings out the worst in him. Clearly your having read that letter when it was addressed to him specifically was a mistake. Now he is not only unhappy, he is embarrassed."

"He's too sensitive," Typhonix said. "You'd think he didn't grow up with four brothers."

"A couple of months ago I might have agreed with you," Grakin said. He rose to his feet, pushed his chair in, and gripped its back as he faced his siblings. He bit his lower lip for a moment, and then gave a slight shrug. "Now I think I understand the way he feels."

Sonja regarded Grakin curiously, but he bid the group goodnight and headed upstairs. Sherman and Katarina followed his lead as they had done on many things since he had taken up teaching them several weeks before. Typhonix regarded Sonja for a moment before making his way to the bar, and the expression on his face said that he felt Grakin's words were primarily aimed at him. Serenjols patted Sonja's shoulder and made his way upstairs as well. Alone at the table, Sonja regarded the book before her only briefly. She wasn't in the right frame of mind to read; she was more caught up in Aeligos' words regarding Eryn, and Grakin's words.

She turned toward the door and sighed, wondering where Aeligos had gone to. She thought about what Grakin said, and her brother's words gave her pause as she considered it was entirely possible that Aeligos' promiscuity was a result of the way his siblings treated him and his lover. She thought perhaps he spent so much time in strangers' beds because he knew that no one would ever question who they were or what his intentions toward them were. As she thought about it, it made her think about herself and the reason she attracted so little attention from men. She wondered if it was possible – or more accurately, probable – that many men had been taken with her but were afraid to approach her because of her siblings. Kari had said more than once that Sonja was beautiful, and though Sonja never thought of herself in such a light, Aeligos' exit and Grakin's words made her wonder. It made her consider her own happiness: she thought of how good Kari and Grakin were together, and whether she herself should look for a similar relationship away from her siblings.

As she thought about Aeligos' words that he'd asked her to keep secret, Sonja ultimately had to wonder if everything she thought she knew about Aeligos and Eryn's relationship was just a façade. If their fights during the voyage had all been staged, and all of the bumps and rough spots in their relationship were as well, then Sonja had no idea what to think of the two. She knew Aeligos and Eryn were both crafty manipulators – their skill at cards barely scratched the surface – but had they completely fooled Sonja for this long? Or was making her think they had just a part of the greater deception?

She shook the thoughts off; trying to figure Aeligos and Eryn out was sure to give her a headache. She took a sip of her ale and opened the book before her. She'd been reading *The Ascension of Saint Bakhor*, as she wanted to see how often and how much the book mentioned her terra-dracon friend, though she had yet to come across any references. She was curious to see how her friend and the legendary saint first met, and whether the Karian described in the book's pages would be like the one she knew. Her thoughts turned to Erik and her sister-in-law then, and she wondered if their mission was successful or if they were in trouble, hurt, or worse.

She swallowed hard, took a calming sip of her drink, and offered a prayer to Kaelariel in her mind. She closed her eyes as she thought of losing them. It would be especially devastating, for not only would they lose their brother and group leader, as well as their sister-in-law, but Grakin, who was already quite withdrawn, would be completely crushed. Sonja took a deep breath and let it out in a long but quiet sigh, and she looked up when Aeligos sat across from her once again.

Sonja looked him over as he sat before her silently, and he would not meet her eyes. She wondered if it had something to do with his late arrival from Kulthon, but even as she considered it, Grakin's words came to her again. The priest wasn't wrong: no matter who Aeligos spent his nights with, he received a hard time about it. When he was with Eryn, he had to deal with Erik's disapproval and the attitude that came with it. When he slept with other women, he had to deal with the same, but also with Sonja's disapproval, Typhonix' harassment, and the anxiety of his sex life being the center of attention.

Sonja leaned forward, reached across the table, and gave her brother's hand a squeeze, and some of the tension seemed to drain from his face. "Aeligos, I think you're doing a great job," she said. "Erik will be very happy, and proud, just as I am."

He looked over his shoulder briefly and grimaced. "The others don't respect me," he said. "They're more interested in what I'm doing on my time than what I'm saying on theirs."

"I know," Sonja said, partially cutting him off. "I'm sorry if I've come across as judging you too often. Just know that when I've been upset with you for being with other women, it's because I felt bad for Eryn. I like you and Eryn as a couple, and I mean that."

Aeligos fixed her with a hard stare that clearly said he didn't believe her. "Just keep in mind that you don't really know anything about our relationship," he said. "What you think you know is just what we've let you see."

Sonja pursed her lips and bit back a response; she understood that now and didn't want to argue or press him when she was trying to ease his tension. "In the end, you're only responsible for your own happiness," she told him with a shrug. "What the rest of us think really doesn't matter when it comes to choosing a mate."

Aeligos smiled, and he rose and moved around the table to give her a kiss on the side of her snout. "I dropped off sealed documents from the shakna-rir at the mayor's office while I was out, so our work here is done. We can get moving again first thing in the morning. Goodnight, Sonja," he said. He made his way upstairs, and Sonja watched as Aeligos and Typhonix looked at each other briefly and exchanged nods.

Alone at the table again, Sonja's thoughts turned back to Erik and Kari, though she wasn't thinking so much about their safety as their ability to get along. It seemed that no matter what passed between her brothers, the boys always shrugged it off in the end and remained friends. With Erik, though, she knew he was distrustful of Kari, and that it was very likely that once they were away from the others he confronted her on her apparent "deception." Sonja thought perhaps she could have done more to convince Erik that Kari really was who she said she was. She sighed, worried that

298

the two demonhunters' mission may have been sidetracked before it ever began because of personal issues.

Sonja left her book on the table and made her way outside. She looked down one of the town's long roads toward the eastern horizon, which was dominated by the high mountains. The first of the three moons had crested the high peaks, full and bright, and as Sonja beheld its polished white surface, an incantation came forward in her mind. Her finger came up and traced the glyph she saw in her mind's eye in the air before her, and a soft incandescent glow followed after it. Soon the surface of the moon appeared larger, and as Sonja made a soft turn of her wrist, the heavenly body likewise shifted. She closed her eyes and guided the lunar orb with thoughts rather than sight, picturing Kari and Erik in her mind, and after a few moments she looked up once again to behold their reflected images on the moon's surface. Sonja smiled: they both appeared to be healthy and in good spirits, and she opened her fist slowly to widen the angle of her celestial eye. She could see that they were headed north, nearly clear of the rainforest, but when she saw that they were traveling with a brys, she wondered if they had even accomplished their demon-hunting mission yet. She sighed: her magical spying had created more questions, but she was thankful that the most important question had been answered.

She ceased her concentration on the spell and the moon's exaggerated proportions dissipated from her sight. Sonja glanced around briefly and then made her way back inside the inn. She bounded up the stairs with unusual grace for a woman her size and soon came to Grakin's door, and she knocked gently on it. Thankfully, he didn't appear to have gone to sleep: he was still mostly dressed, and he let her into his room.

"I got impatient," she told him. "And a little practice with divination is never a bad thing. I saw Kari and Erik! They're both fine and appear to be on their way north, hopefully to us. I don't know if they finished their other mission yet, but they were close to leaving the rainforest."

Grakin smiled and closed the door gently behind his sister before he returned to sit on his bed cross-legged. "That is good to know," he said. "Could you tell how far away they are?"

Sonja shook her head. "Not just from looking, but based on our own travel time...," she said, and she thought to herself. "If I had to guess, I'd say they're probably two weeks from us, maybe a little more."

"Did Aeligos return?"

"Yes, he'll be all right," she said. "He's upset. He doesn't think the rest of us respect him. He doesn't appreciate the fact that everyone followed Erik's orders without question but seems to be fine with second-guessing his. Honestly, he's just not used to being in charge."

Grakin shook his head. "No, he is used to working alone, or with people like Eryn. I do not imagine he expected to be put in charge of the rest of us. He feels trapped for many reasons, and when treated with disrespect – even jokingly – he takes it very much to heart, as he is afraid of bringing us to harm should he make the slightest misstep," he explained, and Sonja nodded in full agreement. "I do not suppose you could summon my mate to me tonight, could you?"

Sonja chuckled. "If only," she said, and she took the cue and opened the door to leave. "I'll let you get back to your meditations. Sleep well, Grakin."

The priest bid her goodnight, and Sonja returned to the common room to continue reading her book. Early in the morning they would continue west toward Raugro, the largest city on the island, whose jurisdiction on military matters covered nearly the entire northwest. She imagined they would find the remaining help they needed to enact their plan against Gaswell there, and then Aeligos would divulge Eryn's information to the rest of them. If Sonja's calculations were anywhere near accurate, Erik and Kari would reunite with them shortly after they reached the metropolis.

A smile dominated her features as she skimmed through her book, and when she found the spot she'd left off at and continued reading, she finally came across what she was looking for:

We weren't really sure what to expect, even with the assurances I'd received from CB. Before that point, I had only ever met demonhunters on a few occasions, none ever higher than perhaps the fourth or fifth rank. To be instructed to seek out someone of Kari's renown was humbling, in a sense, as we needed to ask her for her help and had no idea what type of reaction we would receive. Given who my deity is, it was quite possible the woman might've looked at me as a "demon servant" and attacked; given that she allegedly slew an erestram in single combat (gods, I'd have hated to face one with my entire group at that point), we knew that we might be heading into a volatile situation.

What we encountered could not have been further from expectations. When one is told to go introduce themself to a 'devil-slayer,' it puts many images into the mind. The mere mention of Turik Jalar's name strikes fear into the hearts of demons everywhere: they know he is Avatar of Vengeance, and one wonders what they imagine when they hear that title. When one thinks of a devilslayer, I imagine they think of a giant, imposing, muscle-bound warrior with fire in his eyes and scars that tell tales of his glory. Not so with Kari. I have met bigger, stronger, prettier, and smarter women in my life, but still none has ever left an impression upon me the way Kari did. I can still remember that first meeting as though it were yesterday.

We were directed by numerous townspeople in Solaris that Kari could be found nightly at an inn called The Pyre Peaks. Arriving there after the dinner hour, we had half-expected this famous demonhunter to be surrounded by people basking in her glory and listening to her many tales of fantastic battles. Instead, we found a lone terra-dracon girl sitting at the bar, nursing a double godhammer (I still can't stomach those) and largely being left alone by the other patrons. Hrothgar started to move forward, but I insisted that I should be the first to speak to her, as her reaction to my station as a priestess to CB would tell us whether or not we would receive her help within moments.

As I approached and spoke her name, those intense ebon eyes locked with mine for the first time, and I could see an immediate change in her expression. Again it went against all expectations, as before I could even introduce myself, she rose to her feet, took one of my hands in hers, and said, "You are Carly Bakhor, the priestess?" She then informed me that she had heard much about me, and invited us all to sit with her and share the details of what we required of her. No comments about how my deity was technically a "demon," no accusations of being a traitor to our people or any of the other nonsense I had heard countless times since I began my field ministry. To anyone that didn't know me, it may have seemed as though I were a priestess of Zalkar based on Kari's reaction.

Even as we described the details of what CB had asked of me, it was clear that Kari was as interested in our work as I was. Once the others retired to their rooms, I sat with Kari for several hours, impressed with the way the woman held her liquor, but even more impressed with the way she held herself. This was someone whose name was spreading across the land like a wildfire, whose accomplishments as a demonhunter, whose having won the heart of the shakna-rir king, and whose reputation as a law enforcement official were known or at least whispered nearly everywhere. And yet, as I sat there speaking with her about our lives and the passion of our divine missions, I found something else.

I found my sister.

Sonja closed the book and cradled it tight to her chest, and she fought back tears as she thought of her sister-in-law and the impact Kari had on her friends' lives. It was already late, and even Typhonix had gone upstairs while she read, so Sonja decided to retire to her own room. She passed the

301

doors of her siblings' rooms and opened her mental awareness. She found naught but the softly dreaming psyches of sleeping males. She smiled, climbed into bed, and whispered a silent prayer to Kaelariel. She prayed for her friends' safety and success in both their missions, and drifted off into a peaceful slumber.

~~*~*

Kari yawned and stretched, and she felt a soft weight dissipate from her, as if something had slept beside her and backed off when she awakened. A smile came to her face thinking of Sakkrass and his vow to watch over and protect her. Her thoughts threatened to turn dark as she considered his words: that he would watch over her as if she was his daughter. Despite knowing that he meant that in the most loving and protective way possible, the only father she had ever known had been an abusive, molesting bastard, and that remained painfully in the front of her mind. Kari tried to keep perspective: she tried to imagine that she might have something akin to a real father for the first time in her life, and she let that thought permeate her being as she breathed slowly to calm herself.

She thought of Grakin, and of Sonja's words that night when the scarlet-haired woman mentioned that she was the only woman in the family. Kari wondered if their father had been abusive as well and driven their mother away in similar fashion to the way Kari was driven from her home. She bit her lip and considered she and her mate possibly had yet another sore, painful thing in common, but as she continued to try to keep perspective, she smiled. It was entirely possible they had both been abused as children, but she forced her mind to consider a more prominent fact: both of them had turned out good people regardless, and everything that had happened had brought them together.

Tears welled up in her eyes as she thought about it, but she felt her body relax when a soft breeze blew through her mind, tingling in her brain and sending a shock of tickles below her skin. Sakkrass' presence was not as strong as it had been the two previous times she'd felt him in her mind, but it still registered as a loving, comforting touch, and she couldn't help but laugh. She wiped the moisture from her eyes, her heart lightened, and she looked down at her naked form, covered with the slightly smudged but still unmistakable glyphs of the czarikk. Kari had to wonder if they had facilitated the lizardman god's appearance. They were some kind of ritual glyphs, so she wondered if Oshasis and Savarras knew that painting her in such a way before she danced would bring forth an avatar of their lord. In

302

the end it mattered little: Sakkrass had come on account of her, and she found it both humbling and uplifting, a blessing she doubted many of the czarikk themselves could ever attest to having seen, let alone experienced. Hers was a life of protecting and serving, and though Kari didn't seek after the rewards such work brought, she had to admit to herself that receiving such an unprecedented and unexpected boon was as pleasing as it was surprising.

The terra-dracon woman rose to her feet, stretched out once more, and then exited the teepee to step into the muted sunshine of the jungle morning. Many of the czarikk were out and about, tending to the ashes of the fire pit, preparing morning meals, or making ready for their patrols. They beheld Kari's painted, naked form with smiles before they returned to their work. Kari had no doubts they felt the same way about her relationship with Sakkrass as she did, and it made her feel as though she truly was a member of their tribe instead of just an honorary one. Only weeks before she had known little of the czarikk and nothing of their god, but after the previous night she felt as though she knew both as intimately as if she were one of them.

She moved over to Savarras when she saw him sitting near the central fire pit with a female czarikk beside him. Both looked up at Kari's approach, and they smiled and bowed their heads to her in unison. The female was a dark green like her mate, but with a deepening pink coloration across her collarbone and breast, and she had reddish-brown fins that began behind her eyes and ran over the ridgelines of her skull to the base of her neck, where they became frilly. Kari hadn't studied the females in much detail before, but she found their forms no less handsome than those of their males.

"Good morning," Kari said in the czarikk tongue, and the two were still surprised to hear her speak their tongue, and so well.

"Blessed morning it is," the shaman returned. He took his mate's hand in his before he met Kari's eyes again. "If you remember our lord's words last evening, he has blessed us more than we expected: our females have gone into season a second time."

Kari smiled and touched the shaman's cheek, and she leaned down and kissed him on the side of his scaly snout, which surprised the female beside him. "My heart warms to hear this," Kari said with a pat to the side of his face. "Have you seen my companion this morning?"

"He is down by the river, bathing," the female czarikk said.

"This is my mate, Ansha," Savarras said, gesturing toward the female with his eyes. Kari bowed her head and Ansha did so in return. "You and your companions are welcome to stay among us as long as you wish. Our people are beginning to associate your presence with the blessing of our lord."

Kari smiled again. "I am flattered," she said. "However, my companion and I must meet with his siblings; we still have work to do here on your island. Though we enjoy your company and hospitality, time is short and we must leave this morning, preferably."

"Would you like me to show you to the river to bathe?" Ansha asked. Kari nodded and followed the slender female through the woods to a fairly wide but slow-moving river. Erik was sitting on a rock near the river's edge and covered himself when the two women approached. Ansha waved her hand toward him and the river, and said, "I will leave you to yourselves."

Kari waded out into the river once Ansha left, and the terra-dracon woman submerged herself quickly. She rubbed the paint off of her skin in the gently moving waist-high waters, and she turned to look at Erik while she bathed. Kari flashed him a smile, trying to gauge what he thought of his own actions during the night. He smiled in return, but there was uncertainty in it that she could see even from the distance between them. She guessed he wasn't entirely comfortable with what he had done, but he had enjoyed himself, and was trying to reconcile what he felt with what Kari had told him the night before.

"I wonder what your siblings would think if you brought a czarikk girl back with you," she said after a couple of silent minutes.

Erik started laughing and shook his head. "I wouldn't even want to find out," he said.

Kari emerged from the river, and she moved to sit beside him on the sunny rock. "Don't find them attractive or pleasant to be with?"

The blue-eyed male waved off the question. "It's not that," he said. "I find them likable enough, but my siblings – and my parents, for that matter – have certain expectations. Even though Serenjols is the eldest, the expectations that come with being the eldest male have sort of fallen to me, since he's so shy and quiet. I'm pretty much expected to find a good woman – someone like you – and have a number of children."

Kari sighed. "I guess one of the positives that came from being a runaway is I've never had to satisfy anyone's expectations but my own," she said. She took his arm and turned to look at him. "You know you're never going to be happy if you spend your life trying to make other people happy. Sometimes you have to be a little selfish."

He looked out over the river and asked, "Why do you assume I'm not happy?"

Kari shook her head. "Erik, I'm not the smartest girl you'll ever meet, but I'm not stupid," she said. "You live for Zalkar and to make your siblings and parents happy, and you don't seem to ever take a minute to tend to yourself. You're thirty-six and you don't have a mate, and I know it's because you're not even looking. Don't tell me it's because you think you have more time as a half-guardian: it's because you don't think you can live up to what your family expects."

Erik looked at her and squinted for a moment, then shrugged. "Do I seem unhappy?"

Kari nodded. "You do," she said, and she touched his face gently. "You seem to lash out at people around you without even realizing it. Just think about the way you treated me when we first came into this rainforest – you thought I was an impostor? Have you given that any thought since you decided to believe me?"

He shrugged. "I guess it was pretty stupid," he admitted. "Willful stupidity, since I think it was as much not *wanting* to believe it was true as not being able to believe you could've been returned from the dead."

"And the way you treat Eryn…"

"She's a murdering bitch!" Erik snapped. Kari recoiled slightly, and Erik's mouth tightened, flustered. "She and the people she works for are no better than the demons we hunt. Sorry, Kari, but I'm not wrong about her."

Kari shook her head impatiently. "There's more to her than that," she said, and she put a finger to the end of Erik's snout to stop him from interrupting. "Not the least of which is: she's your brother's mate. You don't have to like her, Erik, but at the very least, for your brother's sake, you should try to treat her with some respect. You're not just Aeligos' brother, you're his leader, and it makes it hard for him to trust you when you don't trust him because of his mate. Consider how you'd feel if you did what I said and brought one of these scaly girls back with you, only to have your siblings hate her and make you both feel unwelcome around them."

He considered her words - and the slight moisture about her eyes - for a couple of minutes before he nodded. "You're not wrong," he conceded.

Kari leaned against him. "Love's a weird thing, Erik," she said. "You don't exactly plan to fall in love with someone. I've been in love a few times, and every time it's been different. When I first met Grakin, I wasn't sure he liked me, since he never talked to me and never even met my eyes, but I couldn't have been more wrong. I don't know what made Eryn and Aeligos fall for each other, but there's obviously something there, and just because we don't understand it doesn't make it any less real. You don't know who you're going to fall in love with until it happens, and when it does, what your siblings think should be the *last* thing on your mind."

Erik wrapped an arm around her and hugged her. "You're right," he said. "That's a good way to look at it. You're a good woman, and a good friend, Kari. And my brother is a very lucky man...makes me wish you had sisters."

Kari's thoughts almost turned dark, but she fought the memories back and chuckled along with him. "Don't want to save yourself for Annabelle Sol'ridachi?" she teased, though she could still barely say the name without tensing up. She stood up and, when she met his stare, she could see he was still curious to know who Annabelle was. "I'll tell you about her on our way north, but we'd best get ready to go."

Erik nodded and pulled on his loincloth as he stood, and he and Kari headed back into the village. They gathered their belongings, dressed, and then met with Oshasis and Savarras near the fire pit. The two czarikk males seemed genuinely sorry to see them leave, and Kari took the expressions of the lizard people as a whole as a compliment. Makauric joined them as they sat with their czarikk hosts for the morning meal, and the three prepared to take back to the road immediately after.

"I have one last thing to give you before you go," Savarras told Kari while she belted on her swords and shouldered her pack. "Sakkrass granted a vision to me of his travels with the wolf spirits of the celestial forests, and he has asked that I bless you with their speed and stamina, to bring you to your friends and destination more quickly."

Kari bowed her head in thanks, and the entire village gathered to watch the shaman work. He began to chant and waved a hand over his guests. Makauric seemed as though he were ready to attack if the spellweaving proved to be a deception of some sort, and Kari had to suppress the urge to chuckle at him. As Savarras chanted, three blue spectral wolves appeared from the ether, howling in a ghostly shrill that sent shivers down Kari's spine – and apparently everyone else's as well. The wolves circled the three companions several times before brushing against them, and when one touched her, Kari felt a surge of power flow through her. It was a strange feeling, almost like a rush of adrenaline, but it didn't cause her body to shake with the explosive release of energy. She felt as though she could run forever, and the pathways between the trees around the village seemed to grow larger and much more accommodating. Suddenly the jungle was not such an unusual place, and Kari felt more at home within it and its muted sunshine. The scents of the village and its scaled people came more strongly, and without thought Kari's feet scraped gently at the earth, her clawed toes digging slightly in anticipation.

"Go," Savarras said. "Go with the thanks of the people, the blessing of our chief, and the favor of our lord. Sakkrass be with you."

"Until we meet again," Oshasis added. "Be well, and know that you are welcome to return to us whenever you wish."

Kari bowed before her gracious hosts, and then she beckoned for her companions to take to the road. Erik and Makauric hesitated for a moment, but Kari broke into a run, bounding along through the village and out into the forest. Her two companions were soon following in her wake, and as her surefooted steps took her speedily through the drifts of fallen leaves and along the cool soil of the pathways, she found that her breathing remained steady and her heart beat comfortably strong. She felt as though she could run all day, and was amazed at how the forest seemed to split before her.

They ran for hours and stopped only for lunch before rushing off through the forest again. They travelled into the early evening, and found themselves out on the savannah before they finally became weary. Kari marveled at the blessing of the shaman, and she and her companions set up a camp as night fell and Makauric headed out to hunt for them. Erik regarded Kari with a smile and they chatted happily about how the shaman's blessing would likely cut their travel time in half. It had seemed such a minor boon when he had given it, but as Kari considered the results that went beyond just their quickened pace, its actual value became so much clearer.

Makauric returned with a slain antelope, and he prepared several days' worth of meat for their journey before he offered the remains to the scavengers a fair distance from the camp. The three enjoyed a quiet dinner, and Erik ordered Makauric to sleep first. Kari assumed he wanted to prod her about Annabelle before she took her rest. The brys offered no argument. He curled up and fell asleep in moments, and Kari placed her cloak over him to keep him warm.

"You want to know about Annabelle Sol'ridachi, don't you?" Kari asked when she turned back to her partner.

Erik nodded. "You've kept me in suspense long enough," he said. "So what's the story behind the name?"

Kari fixed him with a steady gaze. "Ever fought a vampire?" she asked. His eyes went wide, and Kari blew out a short sigh to keep her thoughts calm. "Annabelle was a friend of mine, a fellow demonhunter I worked with on occasion. She was there when my friends and I killed the red dragons…"

"Wait a second, you killed a red dragon?" Erik asked incredulously.

Kari nodded shortly. "I guess I'm going to have to see what the history books actually say about my career sometime," she said. She motioned for Erik not to interrupt. "Yes, with the help of a fairly large group, I once killed a few red dragons. But that's a story for another time. Anyway, Annabelle helped with a couple of my tougher demon kills when I was younger. I got a message from her on one of my stops through Solaris asking me to help her kill a demon that was proving too difficult for her to kill on her own. So I headed up north to a place called Fort Sabbath, which at the time was a known base for a bunch of thieves-turned-outriders. They were unpredictable, but I figured if Annabelle trusted them enough to stay there, then they must be helping her, or at least not interfering with her mission."

"When I got to Fort Sabbath, the place was deserted. At first I guessed they were all out fighting something that had threatened the fort. But it didn't take long to figure out that wasn't right: there were no guards whatsoever, so I started looking around. No bodies, no blood, and no signs of struggle: the place was simply deserted. The whole situation was just wrong. At first I suspected maybe a brys or two had attacked, but there would've been blood and signs of a fight even if that had been true."

Makauric popped an eye open when she said *brys*, and the two demonhunters chuckled as he smiled and closed his eye again. Kari continued, "I wasn't sure what I'd find inside, so I went up to the keep, picked the lock, and went in."

"You picked the lock?" Erik repeated with a raised brow.

"You pick up quite a few skills when you live on the streets of a city like Solaris for five years," she said, and his other brow joined the first. "It's not like I was adopted when I got to Solaris, Erik. I lived on the streets for five years before I managed to scrape up enough money to buy passage to Askies to get to DarkWind."

Erik shook his head and Kari waved off her own comments before he could prod her further. "But that's a story for another time, too. Once I got inside the keep, I started to find the bodies. They all had their throats torn out, so I suspected the demon that Annabelle needed my help with had attacked the fort, to beat her to the punch. I went upstairs with my blades drawn, but when I got there, all I found was Annabelle: no demon, no sign that anyone or anything else was or had been there. And when I saw her face, I knew something was terribly wrong."

Kari paused for a minute to get her emotions back in check. Erik propped himself up on his side with his head in his palm. "Take your time," he said softly.

Kari bit back a sob. "Annabelle was my friend," she said, and she bit her lip. "To see her that way, a friend and fellow demonhunter...all I wanted to do was find and kill whatever had done that to her. When she saw me, she tried to...I don't know, she tried to put me under a charm or something – like the sylinth did – trying to convince me that she could give me the same gift she had received. It didn't work Just the sight of her pale face and those cold, dead eyes...I tried to kill her, but she slipped away down the stairs. So I chased her into the keep's lower level, and found myself face to face with..."

She paused and swallowed, looking away into the night, and Erik sat up a little straighter. "Another vampire?" he prompted. "Or the demon she was hunting?"

"The biggest black dragon I've ever seen," she said when she met his gaze again. "But it wasn't just a black, Erik: it was a *vampire* dragon. I had no idea such things even existed."

His eyes were wide and he shook his head. "Neither did I. What did you do?"

Kari sighed and said, "I just turned and ran. There was nothing I could do against a demonhunter-trained vampire and a dragon. I felt like such a coward, and expected to be called one when I went to the temple of Zalkar in Dira Ch'Tori. But they told me I did the right thing, and that they would gather a force to take care of the problem. But when I returned with a strike force, the fort was guarded again by a bunch of undead that we assumed might all be vampires. So we returned to Dira Ch'Tori, and I think the task was appointed to another."

Erik crawled forward a bit and touched Kari's hand as she frowned. "Give yourself some credit," he said. "You're no coward, I can tell you that for sure, and at least you didn't rush headlong into a fight you had no reasonable chance of winning to try to prove otherwise."

Kari nodded but her frown remained. "It hurts just to think about her, and the fact that she might still be out there with that dragon," she said, looking off into the darkness again. "Or that they might be terrorizing the northlands of Terrassia to this day."

"You did what you could," Erik said. "No sense worrying about it now. If Zalkar needs it taken care of, he'll ask. Vampires and dragons aren't exactly our specialty."

Kari nodded, but was hardly satisfied with his approval. She felt and had always felt that she'd let her friend down. Erik told her to get some sleep, so she laid out her bedroll and blanket and forced herself to sleep.

She was surprised when she wasn't awakened in the early hours of the morning, but at first light: Erik and Makauric had stood watch in turns and let her sleep the night through. Kari was thankful and made sure to let them know. After they shared a breakfast of reheated meat and trail rations, they set their feet on the road once more, running across the savannah under the effects of the shaman's blessing.

Makauric suggested they travel to the metropolis of Raugro, the largest city on the island and the most likely place Erik's siblings would have gone after the shakna-rir kingdom if they were trying to raise an army. He didn't know exactly where to find it, but based on things he'd heard from other travelers and fellow serilian demons, his best guess put it less than four days west of Saint John's pass. When they paused for lunch, the brys cleared some grass away and drew them a rough map of the island in the dirt, and he showed them their northward route to the pass, and then west to Raugro. In the end they agreed to avoid other cities and head straight to the largest, where they would either find their companions or else be able to send out couriers to the nearby cities to find them.

The savannah gradually turned to longer grassy plains as they continued their steady trek north, and after two and a half days of travel across the grasslands they came into the foothills of a long chain of jagged mountains that stabbed into the belly of the heavens. Makauric led them across the base of the foothills, and flew above them for most of the day so that he had a better vantage point from which to spot trouble. The threat of war kept most of the intelligent, hostile humanoids of the hills and plains out of sight, so their progress remained unimpeded.

Two and a half more days brought them to the pass through the mountains, and from there they turned their journey west. The plains turned to farms and grazelands, and Makauric began walking between his demonhunter companions to avoid drawing attention. He didn't hunt in the grazelands, wary of upsetting the locals if he happened to kill someone's livestock, and his companions surrendered the remainder of their meats to him and went back to their trail rations. There were established roads, but the group decided against following them, and instead cut across the grazelands and avoided the farms as they approached the metropolis.

After another two days of their shaman-enhanced travel they crested one of the hills close to the city, and Kari's mouth fell agape as she beheld something unlike anything she'd ever seen. *Metropolis* hardly began to describe the size of the city of Raugro. Even Kari's childhood in the cities of Flora, Solaris, and DarkWind didn't compare to the staggering sight. From the hilltop she could see whitewashed stone buildings built atop twin hills on opposite sides of a river, with the largest man-made bridge she'd ever seen connecting the two sides. Kari guessed it had to easily be three times the size of Solaris, which to her was almost unfathomable. It had a high white wall, with farmhouses in the fields outside and gates at regular intervals. Kari considered for a moment that it could take them more than a day just to find their friends in such a place.

Makauric expressed doubt about entering the city, but Kari reminded him of Talvor and how she had managed to get him not only within its walls but also into the temple of Zalkar without incident. The brys relented and they took to the main road, and headed to the largest of the gates to the city. Kari was glad to find that traffic into the city wasn't too slow despite its volume, and she led her companions to the gate. There were almost a dozen guards posted at the gate at ground level, and Kari pulled her dog tags up to fall over her breastplate. She was shocked when two of them brought up their crossbows, and before she could even speak, the *click* and *snap* of the weapons being fired preceded the startled scream of a brys in pain.

Chapter XVI – Charisma

Aeligos led his siblings and their human companions west just after breakfast the next morning, and they traveled along the major road toward Raugro. They passed by the farms and grazelands quietly, enjoying the landscape as they moved along, though Aeligos had his thoughts focused solely on the mission ahead. He knew that in Raugro, he would once again have to convince a government to send its armies into a preemptive war, but this time he wouldn't have the advantage of speaking to a militaristic, warlike people. It was possible that they wouldn't need the help of the people of Raugro, but Aeligos knew the larger the opposing force they could marshal outside of Gaswell's gates, the more likely they would either draw out his entire garrison or else quickly overpower it.

It took them nearly four days to reach the metropolis, and Aeligos and his companions stood in awe of its majesty. It was even more impressive than the sight of Kulthon, which was the most breathtaking city the rogue could remember visiting. Like the seat of the shakna-rir empire, the city was built so that it ascended a hill, though unlike Kulthon, Raugro was built on two hills: one on each side of a wide, sun-streaked river. Its buildings were made of white stone, and a similarly colored wall surrounded the city, with only farmhouses and a few guard towers outside. Spanning the river was a massive stone bridge of masterful construction that was obvious even at the distance from which Aeligos first saw it. It had six large towers and arced over the river in such a way that smaller ships could easily travel under it. As Aeligos and the others made their final approach to the city gates, he wondered whether it was two cities linked by the bridge, or if Raugro included both sides. Either way, it seemed most likely that the city was the largest on the island, and that it was the seat of non-shakna-rir civilization.

The guards at the main gate regarded the group only briefly and waved them through even before Typhonix remembered to show his dog tags. Aeligos led his companions up the main thoroughfare into the heart of the eastern city. The main road ran straight southwest to the bridge, with other roads that ran at angles to form a diamond that was bisected by the main road. The city was clean but noisy: a bustle of activity surrounded the friends on all sides, and Aeligos had to make sure they didn't lose themselves in the rush and flow of the busy citizens. Like Erik had done so many times, Aeligos led them to a plaza down one of the side streets, where he found a cozy little inn called *Guzman's Hearth.*

Aeligos arranged for rooms for his siblings and their human companions, and then he bid the others stay near the inn and out of trouble while he explored. Sonja offered to go with him, so once the innkeeper told them where to find city hall, he returned to the streets with his sister. Their travels took them over the bridge, which looked wide enough for more than six carts to cross abreast. Its towers had catapults mounted atop them to defend the city in case of a water-borne attack, and the bridge itself was a meticulously cleaned, cobblestoned expanse.

The west side of the city was set up almost exactly the same way as the eastern side, except that the main avenue had a circular plaza at the top of the hill, and in the center sat the white, domed building the innkeeper had identified as city hall. Made of marble and gorgeously crafted with columns and arching windows, it was a stately home for a governing body. The traffic outside of it seemed light, and after passing by a fountain with a statue of a robed judge standing within, Aeligos and Sonja entered through the oaken front doors.

The interior was no less impressive. The open marble foyer floor was imprinted with a metal seal depicting Zalkar's symbol in its center, with the words *Love of Justice, Application of Mercy, Annihilation of Lawlessness* inscribed around the outer edge. A desk flanked by two sets of double doors stood directly across the foyer, and other doors led off of the entry chamber on two levels. A mocha-skinned human woman with dark eyes and her hair set high in a bun sat behind the desk, but she didn't look up until Aeligos and Sonja approached.

"Good afternoon, and welcome to city hall," she said, her angular face flowing into a smile as the pair drew up to her desk. "What can I do for you today?"

Aeligos regarded her for a moment and wondered if her accent was common for all the people of the city; the innkeeper had a similar one. "We need to make an appointment to see your governor or city council," he said.

The young woman nodded. "The council session for today ends in a half-hour," she said. "Tomorrow's session is a general assembly, and all citizens and visitors to the city are allowed a turn to speak if time so allows. Do you need a specific, private appointment?"

"Yes ma'am," Aeligos replied. "If you could inform the council that I bring official sealed documents from the shakna-rir of Kulthon, I'd appreciate it."

The young woman took the documents from Aeligos, and she broke the wax seal and unfurled the scroll. Her brows arched as she read it, and once finished, she looked back up. "These appear to be in order," she said. "I will pass them along to the council, and let them know you've requested a private meeting at the earliest possible time. Where are you staying?"

"Across the river, at a place called Guzman's Hearth."

The young woman nodded. "I'm familiar with it," she said. "Go on back and relax. I'll have a courier come inform you of your appointment time once I've spoken with the council."

"Thank you," Aeligos said. Sonja nodded to the young girl and the two turned to leave. They returned to the inn and found the rest of their companions already gathered for dinner, and the group shared the evening meal. The innkeeper served them a thick, hearty beef stew with freshly baked bread and butter, and large steins of ale. Aeligos dug into the dinner hungrily, glad to finally have something other than roast pork or trail rations. The others regarded him for a few moments before returning to their meals, and remained quiet until everyone had finished.

"So did you get an appointment with whoever's in charge?" Typhonix asked before he sat back and took a long sip of his drink.

Sonja nodded. "We're not sure when, but the documents Aeligos brought from Kulthon should allow us to see them without too much waiting."

"I'm just glad Maktus gave me those scrolls," Aeligos said. "As nice as these people seem so far, I'm not sure I'd have wanted to walk into the city and ask for a meeting without them, considering we're half-demon."

"You could always ask Katarina and me to go in such a situation," Sherman said.

Aeligos nodded but waved off the comment. "I appreciate your offer, but with all due respect, you're just not experienced enough in dealing with people to handle this sort of thing."

Katarina took up her brother's line of thought. "True, but perhaps you could take us along with you, both to ease tensions and teach us how you go about such diplomacy."

"Can't argue that point," Sonja said.

"Indeed, it would be beneficial to their training as paladins," Grakin added. "We should be taking every opportunity to teach them whatever we can. If we want them to remain a part of our group after this mission is over, it would benefit us to *make* them a part of our group *now*."

"Yes, but I'm not sure what Erik will want to do when we're done here," Aeligos said.

"I am not interested in what Erik thinks," Grakin countered. "I am

315

interested in what *you* think. And if you think this young man and woman are worth our time to train and initiate into how we do things, then now is the time to do so more seriously."

The rogue looked to his other brothers, who both nodded, and when his gaze fell over Sonja, she did as well. "You're right," he said, and he looked to his teenaged companions. "All right, I want you to come with us when we go to meet with the city council. For now, what you two can do for me is a little information gathering." He held a finger up to stifle Sonja before she could even say something, and he gestured for her to let him finish. "I don't want you in taverns or near any of the docks; stick to inns and shops, and do your best to fit in. Shops and inns run by humans – like this one – are your best bet."

"What would you like us to try to find out?" Katarina asked.

"Everything you can," Aeligos said, resting his elbows on the table. "Impress me. See what you can find out and give me a full report on the city and its movers and shakers tomorrow at dinner. But you have to be smart about it: don't give people the impression you're paladins or possibly agents of the city watch trying to find out secrets. Act like you're tourists thinking about moving to the city, and see what the people are willing to share. Let them tell you all about what's great about their city, because what they *don't* talk about is what we want to know. But don't ask about those things: their silence will tell us enough for now."

"Are you sure that's the best way to go about it?" Sonja asked.

Aeligos could see that she was mindful of second-guessing him even as she asked, but the question didn't bother him. "Grakin's right, we need to get them acclimated to functioning on a team, and practicing swordplay with Jol and Ty every day won't change Erik's mind when the subject of them staying on with us comes up."

"So you want us to stay on with you?" Sherman asked, trying to mask his surprise without much luck.

Aeligos waved a hand dismissively. "Look, I won't make any promises," he said. "But if this is the kind of work we're going to be doing in the future, a large, well-balanced team is only going to make things easier. Certainly a pair of paladins will make a welcome addition regardless of what else you bring to the table, since as you've already suggested, sending you ahead to *break the ice*, so to speak, will really make our lives easier."

The two humans smiled, and there was a silent accord around the table. "Just out of curiosity, what do I bring to the table other than muscle?" Typhonix asked.

"Nothing," Aeligos said, but then he bobbed his head to the side. "Well, that's not true. You bring irrelevant but amazing socio-political and economic information to the table. Frankly, muscle is all you need to contribute, since I don't think any of us scare people as easily as you do – not even Jol." The largest of the brothers smiled at that statement, and Typhonix laughed.

"With any luck, we'll receive word of an appointment by the morning," Sonja said. "I believe Kari and Erik may be here within a few days, but if we can get the meeting with the council taken care of before they arrive, it will expedite things."

"Is there anything the rest of us should be doing while we wait?" Grakin asked.

Aeligos shook his head. "Just stay out of trouble," he said. "We don't want or need any negative attention while we're here. If you need any supplies or such for our impending trip south, go ahead and pick them up tomorrow on the off chance we're out of the city sooner than expected. Other than that, enjoy yourselves...as inconspicuously as possible."

The group played cards for a few hours, and then most of them retired to their rooms, leaving only Aeligos and Sonja at the table in the common room. "If you can manage it, I'd like you to use your magic to see where Kari and Erik are," Aeligos said, and Sonja tilted her head curiously. "It's not that I don't want to be in charge – although I still don't – but we have a lot to fill them in on, and we may be leaving the city earlier than expected. It would help to know how much longer it will take them to get here, or if they're even headed here in the first place."

"I'll do so right now," Sonja said. Aeligos followed her out into the street, where both of them looked around before she began to work her magic. He watched her while she stared at the moon and some unseen image in the sky, and she turned her hands gently and tilted her head every so often. After a few minutes, a smile came to her face. She blinked away whatever it was she was seeing and turned to look at him. "They're just south of Saint John's pass! They should be here in less than a week, even if they stop at Fahrem first."

"Hmm, unless they make the mistake of going to Kulthon," Aeligos said quietly, but then he shook his head. "I think it's safe to assume they'll come here first, given how long we've been at our task. Go get some rest; we may have a busy day before us tomorrow." She nodded, and the two retired to their rooms to get some sleep.

The courier arrived the next morning while the group took their breakfast, and the young human informed them that the council would meet with them the following day at midmorning. While not surprised, Aeligos was disappointed: he'd hoped the council might suspend even an hour of its open session for such an urgent matter. Sherman and Katarina bid the group goodbye and made their way into the city. Aeligos was a little nervous about sending the teenagers out alone, but felt he had prepared them as well as he possibly could, and in the end he reasoned that they needed to learn to interact with the rest of the world without being *babysat*, as Erik had put it. He doubted they would find out anything of any real worth, but he was willing to hope he might be pleasantly surprised. In any case, he would find out if they were useful for doing the sort of work he and Eryn did. Except possibly for Grakin's healing skills, Aeligos had always felt that his was the most important and difficult of the group's roles: the rest of them were effectively useless if he couldn't do his job.

Aeligos shook off the anxiety eventually and separated from the rest of the group to go do something he hadn't done since before the War. Down by the docks, he was able to purchase a simple fishing pole and line along with some bait, and he spent several hours fishing on the edge of the river near the bridge. There were many people doing the same, and he was able to make small talk with several humans and rir while he passed the day lazily. The people of Raugro seemed to pay little to no attention to the fact that Aeligos was half-demon, and he found that to be a welcome change. They didn't offer much in the way of information other than the fact that the city was prospering and life was generally peaceful. Curiously, there wasn't anything said about Gaswell, and while alarming, the rogue also found it somewhat comforting.

When Aeligos returned to the inn at dusk, Sherman and Katarina spent the dinner hour telling him all about the city and its people, though as he expected, they didn't tell him anything of particular use. They were quite thorough, however, in explaining that the east side of the city was primarily populated by humans and shakna-rir, while the west side was mostly terra-rir with a smaller human population. They also mentioned that the humans had a second dialect, and that was the reason for the accent the group noticed right away. Aeligos sat forward with interest as they began to describe the ruling body: there was a council of five, with a governor who oversaw the execution of the council's wishes as well as the day-to-day running of the city. The twins were also able to tell Aeligos that there were three humans, a terra-rir, and a shakna-rir on the council, and that the governor was also human, though they seemed embarrassed that they couldn't remember any of their names.

The rogue waved off their concern, and told them that he hadn't really

318

expected the people to tell them anything of use, so he was quite pleasantly surprised at what the twins had discovered. He asked about how difficult it was for them to question the people without seeming too inquisitive, and Katarina told him that the people of the city were very open and happy to share on virtually any topic. While glad the twins hadn't marked themselves as conspicuous people, in the back of his mind Aeligos sighed, cursing the fact that in the one city where he didn't need to do any digging, information had proven to be soft and fertile ground.

The Silver Blades passed the night playing cards again, and retired to their rooms well before midnight. After sharing a meal the next morning, Aeligos decided that the entire group should go to the capitol as a show of solidarity if nothing else, and that all of them could use a refresher in diplomacy. He led his siblings and his human charges into the domed building, and when he stepped up to the desk, the young human girl looked up to him with a smile.

"Welcome back. The council is ready to see you. You may head into the assembly chamber when you're ready," she said with a gesture toward the double door to her right. After looking briefly to the rest of the group, Aeligos thanked her and proceeded through.

The assembly chamber was massive, comprised of a semi-circular seating gallery that surrounded an open floor affronted by a long podium behind which five people sat. As Sherman and Katarina had informed the group, there was a single human seated at his own desk on the right side of the open floor, at the same elevation as the raised podium. A shakna-rir woman sat at the center of the longer council podium, and to her right sat two humans, with a terra-rir and another human to her left. The council watched with interest as the half-demons passed through the gallery, and the governor waved them forward casually.

Aeligos was surprised to find the gallery full of people: he didn't expect anyone else to be in attendance since the council hadn't agreed to see them during their open session. He moved to the railing that separated the gallery from the floor and stepped through its swinging gate, and he took only a few moments to regard the chamber's décor before he stood in the center. Normally he would've liked to take in his surroundings more carefully, but he decided to focus on the task at hand and not waste a single moment the council gave him. His companions followed him, and they took seats on benches just inside and to either side of the gate itself.

"Please state your name and city of origin for the record," the governor said.

Aeligos saw there was a trio of scribes to the left, across from the governor, and they went into action as soon as the governor had spoken. "Aeligos Tesconis of Latalex," the rogue answered, which drew surprised glances from all six of the people before him and hushed whispers from the gallery behind.

"Latalex, on Askies?" the governor responded, and Aeligos nodded. "You have come a long way, indeed. Very well, the council recognizes Aeligos Tesconis of Latalex. You have the floor; please state your business before the council this day."

Aeligos gave each of the six people before him quick but appraising glances and noted the names that were clearly etched onto wooden plaques in front of them. "Am I correct in assuming you received and reviewed the documents I brought from Kulthon?" he asked.

The governor, an older man with graying hair whose plaque read Gov. David Potter, nodded and held up the scroll from Maktus Tuvurasti. It was obvious just from a glance that he had held his post for quite some time, and Aeligos had no doubt the man had worked in either law or politics – or both – for most of his life. "Yes, we have," Potter said. "The documents state that you bring word from the warlord of the Tuvurasti kingdom, and that your news is of great import. So tell us then, what would you and our shakna-rir neighbors have of us?"

Aeligos stood at attention with his wings folded tightly behind him, and accentuated his words with soft gestures of his hands. "I'm sure the council is well aware of the rise of General Gaswell in the south and the army he has been amassing. My brother Erijinkor was assigned by Zalkar's Demonhunter Order to come here to your island and do everything in his power to prevent any sort of prolonged war from breaking out. While he is busy taking care of a demon-hunting mission on the other side of the island, he asked us to come ahead and speak to you about Gaswell. I'm curious to know where you stand on this matter."

The shakna-rir woman – Petra Sil'Duranti – leaned forward to speak, and Aeligos was surprised that her accent was closer to that of the innkeeper at *Guzman's Hearth* than that of the desert people of Kulthon. There was an obvious strength about the woman as she began to speak, and Aeligos could tell she was the de facto head of the council. It didn't take him long to recognize that she was both well-named and married to a terra-rir. "Yes, we're aware of Gaswell and his forces; however, to date we have not considered him to be a threat. Our sources have informed us that the general's plans involve pushing all but the terra-rir from the island. As alarming as such a proposition sounded initially, we quickly decided that such a plan is doomed to fail without any action on our part."

320

"How so?" Sonja asked before Aeligos could, and she rose and approached to stand beside him. "Forgive me; I am Sonja Tesconis, Aeligos' sister."

"The council recognizes you, Sonja Tesconis," Potter said. "Mr. Duvall?"

The terra-rir to the right of Petra leaned forward on his elbows to speak. He appeared to be the youngest of the councilors, but while Aeligos could see the impatience of youth in his eyes before the man even spoke, the rogue could also sense that being called on first to speak by the governor held some subtle meaning. "As Mrs. Sil'Duranti said, the general's plan was recognized as doomed to fail without outside interference. Every city on the island has a mixed population, and anyone who has not already flocked to his call is unlikely to do so. It stands to reason that he will encounter resistance from those he finds in each city – and then from his own soldiers if he orders them to kill their own kind while trying to secure the island for them."

"And you think that will stop him?" Aeligos asked incredulously; that had to be one of the stupidest things he'd ever heard. Based on the way Sonja reached up and scratched the end of her snout as if suppressing a laugh, he guessed she either thought the same thing or had managed to overhear his thoughts.

Avery Nash, the human male on the far left end, leaned forward and spoke next. Avery was a middle-aged human who seemed rather unconcerned with the topic at hand, and with only a brief study, Aeligos could tell the human would be the toughest councilor to convince. There was a calm about him that went beyond age or experience; the rogue interpreted it to mean that Avery was a born politician, and that he was already looking at how best to use the situation to his political advantage. "We don't believe his army will ever begin its ill-fated march," Avery said. "In order to sustain its advance, Gaswell would need to find new soldiers and supporters in each town as he conquers it. As it stands, none of the cities nearest to his stronghold have a population that would benefit him to attack. Markho and Vagan are both primarily human towns, but with enough of a rir presence to give him doubts about attacking them. He stands to lose too much, and if the terra-rir are all he will press into his forces, he has little to gain."

Avery sat back and the human woman beside him, whose plaque read Sadessa Alvarez, took up his line of thought. Sadessa appeared to be in her late twenties, and Aeligos got the impression that she was a citizen servant and not a born politician. She had the look of a laborer about her despite her important position, and the rogue assumed that she came from a working-class family and would be more inclined to protect the people than Mr. Nash. "Lanz, too, has a primarily human population like Markho and Vagan, so Gaswell stands to gain little by moving south to secure his rear flank," she said with the wondrous accent of the secondary dialect. "As the others have said, there are no cities for him to conquer that will not offer stiff resistance, and even if victorious, he will not be able to replenish his ranks enough to sustain an advance."

That made a little more sense, but Aeligos was still left to wonder if the council had or had access to even a single tactician. "With all due respect, you're forgetting a couple of important facts," Aeligos said, but he made soft gestures to make his words seem less hostile. "First and foremost, Gaswell is far from sane. Your assumptions are based on the belief that he is thinking rationally and that he's not going to do anything self-destructive. To have even come this far, he is clearly not in his right mind, and the results of any pending attack beyond victory are likely unimportant to him. At this time, you have to consider that if he attacks, it's not a sustained advance you need to worry about so much as the immediate results: the razing of one of your neighboring cities. If he razes one of your cities and it looks like this crusade of his might actually succeed, he'll start attracting more followers and insurgents in these other towns."

Max Soroza, the only councilor who hadn't spoken, leaned forward, and Aeligos paused to let the human speak. Max, like Sadessa, had a working-class look to him, but he was easily twice his counterpart's age and his eyes were full of skepticism as he listened to Aeligos speak. "Yes, you are correct in that regard," the middle-aged human male said with the same accent as Sadessa. "We have scouts in each of our southern neighboring cities, as well as ranging the plains north of Gaswell's stronghold to monitor his armies for movement. Rest assured that when they mobilize, we will send a sufficient force to deter them."

"Again, with all due respect, deterrence won't be enough," Aeligos countered. "When faced with a madman, you cannot simply put an opposing force in front of him and hope that he backs down. If he goes so far as to mobilize and attack, he's not going to give up unless there's a significant enough force to crush him; scare tactics will be ineffective."

"Where exactly do our shakna-rir neighbors stand on this matter?" Potter asked.

"I expected the sealed documents I brought along to explain that," Aeligos answered. "Were they unclear?"

"They were affixed with the personal seal of Maktus Tuvurasti, the warlord of the kingdom and mate to the queen, but he did not include actual details on what they intended. His letter stated that the bearer would make their intentions clear due to the possibility the message would be intercepted by Gaswell's forces. The shakna-rir are nothing if not thorough," the governor said, and his quip drew a short chuckle from Petra.

Aeligos regarded his sister for a moment before he sighed and began to explain. "The Tuvurasti are already moving their forces south to stonewall any advance by Gaswell. They would like to attack, dismantle his forces, and depose him as soon as possible, but since they are crossing lands in your jurisdiction, they want your consent and help in this matter. They clearly wanted your council to send whatever military aid it could to assist them, and make sure that the battle, once joined, is short and successful."

"And they felt they needed our help in such a matter?" Max asked. "The shakna-rir are far stronger than we are in matters of war. I find it strange they would need our help."

"It's because this needs to be done as quickly as possible," Aeligos said. "The other fact you're forgetting is the threat of invasion from the north. When I spoke to the Tuvurasti queen and her warlord, they agreed that should the kingdoms of Dannumore to the north become aware of fighting here on the island, they may take the opportunity to invade."

"Dannumore?" Petra echoed. The gallery erupted into mumbling, and Petra folded her arms before her as Potter banged his gavel to restore the silence. "We've heard nothing from the mainland in the way of trouble for decades; they have been locked in the throes of civil war for over a century. Why do the Tuvurasti assume that would change?"

"I can't say for sure," Aeligos returned. "It was something the queen, her warlord, and his generals were all in agreement on, and one of the primary reasons my elder brother was sent to the island. The Tuvurasti even went so far as to send scouts to their northern and neighboring cities to watch for any sign of trouble from Dannumore. What kind of trouble would they be expecting from the north?"

"You come from Askies, was that land not invaded by a people called the bakatur many years ago?" the terra-rir, Carson Duvall, asked.

Aeligos glanced at Sonja and then looked back at his siblings. Serenjols and Typhonix were students of history, but Aeligos wondered if Jol would be comfortable speaking in front of a room full of people. Under the rogue's gaze, Serenjols spoke. "I am Serenjols Tesconis of Latalex," he introduced himself, though he did not stand. "The bah'qitur invaded shortly before the Fifth Demon War."

323

Carson continued, "Dannumore is primarily inhabited by the bakatur, and though their society nearly collapsed after their failed attempt to attack Askies, they have regained much of their military strength. However, for the last century and more, they have aimed their hostilities inward, culling their own people in some purification war. We have continued to trade with their coastal cities, which have sizeable rir and human representation among their populations, but we have heard no rumblings of war aimed outward."

Aeligos gave a respectful nod to Carson's historical knowledge, and noted in his mind that the young man may have recently finished university schooling. The rogue beckoned for Jol to come forward and, after hesitating for a moment, the massive male did so. His size drew wide-eyed gazes from the councilors before Aeligos prodded him further. "What happened in the war with the bakatur?" the rogue asked.

"They landed and established a hold in the northeast, near Ceritopolonis," Serenjols said. "They found victory easily initially, but they drew the ire of Seril, and soon found themselves fighting against two opposing forces. With the rir and humans as well as the serilian demons attacking them, they were forced to withdraw, and many of their ships were destroyed from the air by fire-wielding brys and corlypsi. More than half of their vessels were destroyed and their people drowned. It is believed that less than a quarter of their attack force returned home."

Aeligos patted his brother on the shoulder in thanks, amazed at how much Jol had spoken – almost more than he had in the previous few months combined. "I can't admit to knowing much of these people other than what my brother just shared," the rogue said. "But if the Tuvurasti and the gods themselves are concerned, it stands to reason you should be as well. My brother's orders are very specific: war is to be avoided at all costs. My sister and I came to the conclusion that while *war* is to be avoided, a single, quick battle that deposes Gaswell and scatters his forces should accomplish our goal without provoking the northern kingdoms. They're far less likely to attack a unified Tsalbrin than they are several scattered armies."

"I'm curious," Petra said. "Why did Zalkar not inform us through the clergy here? Why was your brother sent here to do what any man could have done?"

Aeligos accepted an offered glass of water from an officer of the court, and Sonja took up his line of thought. "As we understand it, our brother was assigned to look into a demonic threat to the east. While he didn't give us many details, we've been suspicious that whatever he and his partner are looking into might also have something to do with Gaswell and his rise to power. A civil war is a serious enough matter, but a civil war sparked by a demon represents a threat to everyone. To be fair, it's only speculation at this point, but until my brother and his partner arrive in a few days, we won't know for sure."

Potter looked to each of the councilors before speaking again. "This situation is getting more complicated by the minute," the governor said. "Let us assume for a moment that our most prudent course of action is to send the provincial armies south to confront Gaswell: what is the shakna-rir plan once we join them?"

Aeligos touched his sister's shoulder to silence her, and he looked over the gallery before speaking. "With all due respect, sir, I don't think it's a good idea to divulge any specifics with the gallery full," he said.

"Yes, you are correct," the governor said. "We will adjourn for a short recess, and the court officers will clear the gallery before we come back into session in one hour."

Potter banged his gavel on his podium, and the councilors stood and exited through a back door. Aeligos watched their egress and turned around to supervise the clearing of the gallery by the court officers. His siblings approached, and he folded his arms lightly across his chest and glanced at his human companions. "That went about as well as I could've hoped," he said. "At the very least we haven't been shoved off on account of our race."

"That was very keen of you to hold your tongue on our plans with the gallery full," Sonja said. "It hadn't occurred to me until you touched my arm to stop me from speaking."

"Probably unnecessary, but better to be cautious than reckless," he returned with a nod. "On the off chance Gaswell had a spy in the gallery, they haven't learned anything they didn't already know. They must know what's going on with the shakna-rir, and that the Tuvarasti would ask for help from this city. Let's go get something to eat while they're adjourned."

Aeligos led the group to a local tavern for a snack, and they chatted lightly while they waited for the council to come back into session. The rogue spent the time explaining the basics of how to get more information than you give in a seemingly two-sided conversation, and the young humans took his lesson in eagerly. He also explained what he saw in each of the councilors simply based on their appearance, and how their words had altered those perceptions. He was happy to have gotten as much out of the council as he had, but he knew there was still a lot he had to learn if he wanted to convince them to follow his plans. He explained that the more he knew of them and the way they thought, the easier it would be to convince them, and they would end up making the decision he wanted without any real effort on his part.

They finished their meal and made their way back to the city hall's assembly room. The gallery was empty, and only the three scribes and two court officers were present when the group took the places they had occupied during the first part of the meeting. Aeligos paced the floor, and it didn't escape his notice that Sonja was once again working to stifle a laugh as she watched him. For all his dislike of being in charge, Aeligos understood that it was a role he filled well when the situation demanded it; Sonja's behavior made that clear. Aeligos didn't have the imposing physique of Erik, but what he did have was the charisma to draw people to him and make them listen to what he had to say.

The council arrived in the chamber and took their seats, and the governor banged his gavel three times to bring the meeting back into session. He regarded his fellow councilors for only a moment before he sat back and fixed Aeligos with a curious gaze. "Now that we've cleared the gallery, we'd like to hear what you and our shakna-rir neighbors have planned."

"Well, foremost I can tell you that our intention is not to try to defeat Gaswell by means of attrition," Aeligos said. "Assuming you send your provincial army south to meet up with Maktus and his forces…"

"Warlord Maktus leads this force personally?" Petra interrupted as her ears perked up. She made a slight gesture of apology when Aeligos paused and nodded. The shakna-rir woman turned and looked to the governor. "If Warlord Maktus has taken the field personally, then what our guest has said is no exaggeration. The warlord himself would not have left the city if they were expecting invasion from the north. If Maktus leads this force personally, then he goes to win this conflict quickly and decisively. Queen Omalias is clearly taking Gaswell and this young man's plan quite seriously."

"Indeed," Potter said, and he gestured toward their half-demon guest. "Please, continue."

"As I was saying, assuming you send your army south to join with the shakna-rir, the general idea is not to wage a war of attrition, but to draw Gaswell's army out onto the field. Once the bulk of his garrisons have been drawn out of the castle, your army and the Tuvurasti forces would engage them while a strike force infiltrates Gaswell's stronghold to kill him and secure the castle. With their leader dead and no base of operations to return to, we believe his army will simply scatter before the combined might arrayed against it."

326

"What if he isn't in the castle when this strike force invades his halls?" Avery Nash asked dryly, and he cupped his chin in his hand as he leaned on the podium.

"We're almost certain he will be," Aeligos said, holding up his hand to stifle any reply. "Even assuming he's insane – which I believe he is – this will be the first real test of his army. He's not going to take the field and risk losing everything before he's had a chance to see what cards his enemies are holding. Everything in my experience tells me he'll be holed up inside that fort, watching and waiting, ready to disappear should things look hopeless, to try another day."

"But again, if he isn't?" Nash prodded.

"If he isn't, then an attrition battle will be unavoidable, at least to start. If he takes the field, the strike force will still be able to secure the castle and cut off their retreat. Once his army starts being slaughtered by the superior force awaiting them, they'll lose morale. Gaswell is not a leader, he's just a man promising things and drawing fools to his side. He's also not a demon king: he doesn't rule this army by force or fear, only by the promise of victory and glory. Even if there's a demon behind all this, there's no reason to believe these men will die blindly for it. So the only way Gaswell can keep his army from abandoning him in the face of a superior force will be to rush in headlong to spur them on, and he'll be done in by his own impatience."

"And what of the demon, if indeed there is one?" Potter asked.

"We have three demonhunters among our number, sir," Aeligos said confidently. "If the demon doesn't flee, it's going to die."

"You seem very sure of how Gaswell will react," Carson Duvall said. "Exactly what experiences are you drawing on?"

"The Apocalypse," Aeligos answered. "I know your island probably saw almost no fighting, but my siblings and I were in the thick of the war from beginning to end. We did this sort of thing once before to a minor demon lord, and we accomplished similar tasks against other targets of opportunity. I'm not saying our plan is perfect or guaranteed to work, but given the dangers of inactivity and allowing Gaswell to gain more of a foothold than he has, I believe it is our best chance at succeeding in the task we've been given from above."

The shakna-rir woman in the center smiled. "Well spoken," Petra said, and Aeligos received the nods he was expecting from Max and Sadessa as well. Avery was still skeptical, and Carson looked as though he wanted to think on it further, but Petra continued, "So let us assume that Gaswell stays in his fortress as you believe he will: what kind of strike force are you planning to send, and what makes you believe they will succeed?"

"My siblings and this fine young man and woman before you," Aeligos said, waving a hand toward his companions. "Also, my elder brother Erijinkor and his partner when they've rejoined with us; that will make up the strike force. We also have another companion on the inside, serving within Gaswell's fortress to gather information for our strike."

"You managed to get someone inside his fortress?" Petra asked with wide eyes. "I see now why you were hesitant to speak before the full gallery."

Aeligos nodded. "Our insider is well disguised," he said, and in the back of his mind he hoped none of his companions would give away his ruse. "He's already provided us a detailed map of the fortress and the best ways to get in and out. He's given us a lot of information that should make getting in rather easy, coupled with my sister's ability to mask our movements. From there it will be a matter of finding and killing Gaswell, which I admit is far from a simple matter, but well within our capabilities, I believe."

"This is quite a daring plan, I have to say," the shakna-rir woman said, rubbing a finger under her chin thoughtfully. "What do you call yourselves?"

Aeligos regarded his companions before he turned back and said, "The Silver Blades."

There were clear nods of respect from nearly all of the councilors, and silence fell for only a moment before Governor Potter addressed them. "Well, let us put this to vote," he said, but he held up his hand when Aeligos looked at him. "Not on sending the army just yet, young man, but a vote to determine if this matter has satisfied our requirements to deliberate further on its merits. All those in favor of giving this matter our full consideration?"

Aeligos couldn't suppress a smile as all five of the council members said *Aye*, and he nodded to Sonja over his shoulder. "The council is unanimous," Potter said. "We will take the records of the scribes and the sealed documents of Warlord Maktus Tuvurasti into consideration, and should have our resolution for you in a matter of days."

"Days?" Aeligos repeated incredulously, but he mentally berated himself as soon as he'd spoken. Nearly all of the councilors and the governor himself seemed surprised by the outburst, and Aeligos made a gesture of apology. "Forgive me; I'm just a little impatient due to the nature of the matter. Please, take your time coming to whatever you consider the proper decision."

"You have the thanks of the city and her people for delivering this message to us," the governor said with a nod. "We will send a courier to you when we have reached a decision. In the meantime, do try to relax and enjoy the hospitality of our city."

"Thank you, and farewell," Aeligos said. He turned and motioned for his companions to make their egress. He was glad to have convinced the council to make a decision, but at the same time he could hardly believe they were going to waste days coming to that decision. It had already been a couple of months since Gaswell rose as a threat, so Aeligos couldn't imagine they needed to deliberate all that much on whether or not to stop that threat. He shook his head in disbelief but said, "I don't know if they'll do what we asked them, but I don't think that could've gone any better."

"Neither do I," Sonja said. "You should be very proud of yourself. I would certainly do as you asked were I in their position."

"Based on what you told us to watch for, I think two of the humans and the shakna-rir woman were clearly in favor of following your plan," Katarina said, and Aeligos nodded, glad to see his lessons had sunk into someone. "The other two seemed skeptical, but I cannot imagine they will ask the city to sit idly while Gaswell threatens them."

The Silver Blades returned to the inn, and Aeligos dismissed them to do as they pleased for the remainder of the day. He passed the afternoon fishing peacefully, and when he and his companions gathered for dinner, they spoke of the coming confrontation as quietly as possible. All of them were anxious – even the siblings who had fought in the Apocalypse for eight years – but as Aeligos looked to each of the faces around the table, he realized there was no one there he didn't trust in. There was no reason for them to fail unless every possible facet of luck turned in Gaswell's favor or some unforeseeable, catastrophic event took place. Aeligos was not the type to ever think that success was assured, but he couldn't imagine being any closer to it.

Raugro was surprisingly quiet and sleepy at night for a city its size, and the companions found little nightlife among the streets. It was just as well since Aeligos asked them to stay out of trouble: to be content to pass the time in calm boredom and simply look forward to Erik and Kari's return. He himself was looking forward to seeing Eryn again, but his mind was focused on his mission, his brother's imminent return, and finally getting to the bottom of the situation with Gaswell. What time he couldn't pass sleeping he passed playing cards with the others, or by himself, until finally he retired to bed after the midnight hour.

Aeligos was disappointed that no courier came to summon them to the council chamber on the following morning, so he passed the day fishing. Grakin joined him and the two spent the morning and afternoon chatting about everything from their lovers to their plans for the future. They kept the topic of the coming battle close in their minds but didn't speak of it in front of the locals. They tried to keep as upbeat as possible, as they didn't want the simple fact that they were half-demons to compound any negative attitude about them or tip the common folk off to the fact that danger was looming.

No word came the following morning either, and Aeligos decided to check in at city hall. The length of the decision was already making him nervous, and he couldn't help but think there was something bad coming as he crossed the bridge toward city hall.

Chapter XVII – Failures

"No!" Kari yelled. She fought back the urge to draw her blades, and instead turned and dropped to her knees beside the brys, who had crumpled to the ground. The guards fanned out around her and trained their weapons on the fallen demon, but Kari paid them little heed. She looked Makauric over and could see that his left leg was shattered by a direct hit, and the other bolt was lodged deep in his belly. Already his black blood was pooling around the wounds, and his eyes remained closed, his face set in a grimace of pure pain.

"Stand aside!" the captain of the guard yelled as his men moved to surround the creature.

Erik moved between Kari and the guards and held his hands up. "Stand down, we're demonhunters," he said.

"Makauric?" Kari asked, fighting to keep her voice steady. He didn't respond, still didn't open his eyes; he only let out a pained groan, and Kari whirled on the guards with a scowl. "You idiots! Did it occur to you he was walking with us for a reason?"

"Kari," Erik said warningly.

"What business do you have bringing a demon to the gates of our city?" asked the guard captain, a middle-aged terra-rir male. "If you're demonhunters, why is the creature still alive?"

Kari ignored the idiotic question, turned back to the brys, and put a hand to the wound in his belly. Makauric screamed in pain but Kari kept the pressure on it regardless. "Is there a temple to Kaelariel in the city?" she asked.

"You're not bringing him into the city," the captain said.

Kari rose to her feet and her hands dropped to her scimitar hilts, but Erik put his hand to her chest. "Kari, stop!" he said, his stare incredulous.

Kari glared at him, but after a moment she returned to her position at the brys' side, and put pressure on the worse of the two wounds once more. "This brys has been helping us, and is under my protection," she said. She looked at the captain over her shoulder. "You've already made one mistake, don't make things worse by standing in my way."

"How dare you!" the rir male replied, but he backed up when she sprang to her feet.

"Because we're demonhunters, you stupid ass!" she yelled. "You're supposed to help us, not kill our friends and then ask questions! Now show me to Kaelariel's temple or get the hell out of my way."

Erik tried to step between them and laid his hand on Kari's shoulder. "Kari, this isn't exactly how we should introduce ourselves to the city," he said.

"Erik, by the gods, he's going to die!" she barked at him. "Do something! Help me!"

He just stood staring at her, and Kari wondered what was wrong with him. The captain looked at her suspiciously, but once he took a closer look at her dog tags his eyes went wide. He motioned for his guards to stand down and ordered one of them to lead the demonhunters to the temple of Kaelariel. He started to offer an apology but Kari cut him off with an impatient wave of her hand. She picked up the wounded brys and cradled him to her breast, trying to keep pressure on his wounds even when her hands were full. The human guard led her through the gates and along a main thoroughfare to the eastern hill, but Erik lagged behind. At the top of the hill was a temple district, and they easily found the winged focus of Kaelariel. Kari wasted no time and hurried through the doorway. Several acolytes saw her enter with someone cradled in her arms, but even they seemed surprised when they saw it was a brys. Once they noticed his wounds, they had her lay him down on a stone altar, and they began to cut away his armor to inspect the damage.

Kari stood by, her hands, belly, and legs coated in the brys' black blood, and she knew the situation was dire. Makauric had lost a lot of blood, and even if the priests could stabilize him and seal his wounds, it would be a long time before he would recover, if he ever did. She sank to her rear end a few feet away from the altar and stared at her blood-covered hands, and she closed her eyes and held her breath to try to calm her racing heart. In a span of moments, she could recall nearly every time she had been covered in the blood of a serilian demon she had killed in defense of her people. Now she sat covered in the blood of a creature she had led to his death – which she had in effect killed after he had done nothing but help her – and she wanted to vomit. Kari's skin crawled as Makauric's blood cooled against it, leaving her cold and empty, and her hackles rose as she felt the chill of death run down her spine. She prayed silently to Kaelariel, asking him to spare the brys, and she unthinkingly offered herself to the god of death in the demon's place.

She opened her eyes when one of the acolytes called across the temple. With hurried footsteps he rushed to fetch a robed human who emerged from a back room. Together the two ran back to the altar where Makauric lay, and Kari saw the brys' blood run down the side of the white stone and begin to pool on the floor. Her attention was drawn to Erik when he arrived, and he spared the bleeding demon only a glance as he approached Kari.

"Let the priests do their work," he said, squatting to bring his face in line with hers. "We should start looking for my siblings, or for someone who might know if they've been here."

Kari met his gaze evenly and wondered how he could be so callous. "Makauric might not survive," she said quietly. Her gaze returned to the altar where the priest and his assistants worked at healing Makauric. "Don't ask me to walk away from him now."

"Kari, he's a *demon*," Erik returned with an unmasked sigh. "We've been trained to *kill* these things, not feel bad for them when they meet their end. Yes, he helped us and made our work here easier, but in the end, he's still a brys and they're still ruthless, murdering bastards. The world's not going to miss him and neither should we. Let him go."

"This is my fault, Erik!" she said, staring at him incredulously. "I told him he'd be safe under my protection. He never would have come here if he doubted me, and I failed him. You want me to just walk away from him because some of his kin are rotten?"

"Some?" Erik repeated. "Kari, *all* of them are rotten. You promised him he'd be safe, and you did everything that anyone could expect to keep that promise. He's reaping the rewards of being what he is, and that's not your fault. We're pretty lucky to even be alive, and a dead brys is a small price to pay for that. Right now we've got more important things to do than cry over a dead demon."

The priest looked at the demonhunters over his shoulder but said nothing. Kari drew her legs up to her chest and rested her head atop her knees. "He's not a demon," she said quietly.

"What?" Erik returned. "Kari, be sensible..."

"Go find your siblings, Erik," she said dismissively. "I want to be alone."

He stood up and shook his head. "Don't come apart on me, Kari," Erik said. "We still have a lot of work to be done. We don't have time for this."

Kari raised her eyes to meet his. "Erik, go find your siblings. Go spend a little time with them and ask yourself if you're going to be like this if one of them dies," she spat. Erik's brow came low, but ultimately he simply sighed and headed out of the temple.

Kari bit back a sob, determined to not feel sorry for herself or Makauric. Instead, she rose and approached the altar. "I can channel some healing; is there any way I can help?"

The human priest, whose robes were already stained with the brys' blood, shook his head. "I've stabilized him as much as I can and he feels no pain, but the wounds are too extensive," he said. He looked up to meet Kari's eyes and sighed quietly. "He will not last to evening. If you have anything to say to him, do so quickly if he regains consciousness."

Kari shook her head slowly, fighting back tears, but she let forth a single, biting sob. "This is all my fault," she said.

"No, it is not," Makauric rasped, and his dragon-like eyes opened and fixed on Kari. His eyes rolled but he fought to stay conscious, reaching his hand up toward her face. He managed a pained smile when she took his hand in her own. "This is my fault. I started to see myself as mortal because you treat me with so much respect for one of my kind. In the back of my mind I knew entering this city would be the death of me, but after our visit to Talvor, when I saw how far you would go to defend me, I thought perhaps I was wrong. I was not."

"I'm so sorry," Kari said. She moved beside the altar and laid a hand on his chest. "The priests say…"

"I will die, yes," he said. "I had no doubt about that when the guards shot me. Erik is not wrong, Karian. You should not feel sorry for me."

"But you're my friend," she said, and the brys' brows rose in surprise. She was amazed at how expressive he was, but she guessed that in the face of death those carefully constructed defenses and gruff exterior were no longer necessary. She didn't have time to think about it, but a part of her wondered if there was far more to a brys than she had ever imagined.

"Your friend?" he returned in amazement. Even the priest regarded Kari with interest, but she did her best to ignore the anxiety she felt under the scrutiny. Makauric watched her intently, but his pupils began to dilate as his eyesight failed, and he gasped lightly, his breathing becoming shallow and quick.

Kari gave his hand a squeeze and ran her other hand along his snout and down his cheek, and she bit off another sob. "Yes, my friend," she said.

"I am scared, Karian," he said, and she didn't bother to correct him. "I never gave my life much thought, but I never expected it would end like this."

She hushed him and shook her head; her suspicions that he was young for one of his kind were confirmed. "There's nothing to be afraid of. Death isn't the end, it's just a new beginning," she said. He met her gaze as evenly as he could, his dying eyes full of questions. "I've been dead before, Makauric. It's scary to pass, but when you do…it's beautiful. Like all the cares in the world fall away and you're left in its naked beauty."

The priest watched her intently but did not interrupt, and the brys squeezed her hand as tightly as he could. "Do I go to Kaelariel, though he was not my maker?" he asked.

Kari smiled. "I believe so. You've been a good friend, and gave your life for someone else's cause. There's reward in that, I promise you," she said. Kari leaned down and kissed him lightly on the side of his snout as his eyes closed and his breathing became even shallower. "And I will remember you, Makauric: you will not go quietly into the night."

"Go in peace," the priest intoned, and Makauric's last breath came forth in a quiet sigh.

Kari turned and walked away, and she sat on a stone bench a few feet away and hung her head in her hands. Away from Erik's judgmental gaze, she let herself cry for a few minutes to let the emotions play themselves out. She was vaguely aware of the priest issuing orders to his acolytes to clean the body and the altar as much as possible, and she came to attention when the priest sat beside her and put his hand comfortingly on her shoulder.

"Are you all right?" he asked when she looked at him.

Kari blew out a long sigh to further calm herself, and when she looked down to her black hands, still covered with the now-dried blood of the brys, she imagined her face was, too. "I never thought...I'd get attached to one of them," she said, staring at Makauric's body rather than the priest. "I've been hunting his kind for most of my life, I fought against them for eight years in the Apocalypse; Makauric was the first one that's given me pause."

She finally turned to meet the man's chestnut eyes. "I'm Karian Vanador, Shield of the Heavens, by Zalkar's grace," she introduced herself.

The priest shook her hand; his was also covered in the drying blood of the demon. "I am Samuel Tirar, ranking priest of Kaelariel here on Tsalbrin, though I am not very high up in the hierarchy across the world," he said. He gestured toward the dead brys. "Would you care to explain what happened?"

Kari braced her elbows on her knees, leaned forward, and let out a sigh. Samuel touched her shoulder lightly and told her to take her time, and the acolytes brought bowls of water for the two to wash their hands and faces. Kari cleaned off Makauric's blood and Samuel did the same, and once she finished Kari rose to her feet and approached the body of her friend. She touched his face gently and felt the chill already spreading through his normally warm flesh. She looked around the temple to clear her thoughts.

The décor was not at all what she expected: the white walls were accentuated with black drapes and tapestries depicting various scenes from Kaelariel's past. Most prominent was one of Kaelariel swearing brotherhood to Erijinkor, which marked the turning of the guardian demons to the service of the pantheon. Its make was intricate and intriguing, but Kari realized she had little time to indulge herself in the deity's past: there was no avoiding talking about Makauric. She glanced toward the three altars, one set at each major cardinal direction save the one on the side of the main entryway, and the stone benches that fronted each of them. The room was lighted by braziers, with torches on some of the simple columns, and the air was warm and quiet.

"Sorry to have made such a mess in your lord's house," Kari said, glancing down at the pooled blood at the base of the altar. She knew she was stalling, but even being mated to Grakin, she felt uncomfortable in the temple of the lord of serilian demons, given her profession.

"This is not our lord's house. It is a gathering place for giving thanks, and Kaelariel would be touched to see such a display by a demonhunter, regardless of the mess," Samuel said as he approached. He stood across the altar from Kari and regarded the dead brys for only a moment before his eyes met hers. "What happened?"

Kari blew out another calming sigh. "My partner and I were assigned to find and kill a demon - an underworld demon - somewhere on the island," she said. "We landed in Riverport when we arrived and headed into the rainforest, but we got lost pretty quickly. This brys, Makauric, found us and offered to guide us to a nearby village of czarikk, and eventually to the lair of the demon itself. Once we killed it, we headed here to meet with my partner's siblings and a couple of other companions, and Makauric agreed to accompany us to help with our other task. But when we got to the gate, the guards shot him without question...they didn't even seem to care that he was walking between two demonhunters and showed no signs of aggression. I thought I could protect him; he trusted me, and I failed him."

Samuel touched her hand as it lay on Makauric's chest. "You did what you could," he said. "Even the brys expected no more. We will take care of the body; go see to your partner;."

Kari growled. "To hell with him," she snarled, and she returned to the bench. "You serve Kaelariel; can you tell me why this brys would have helped us in the first place? My partner believed he would have betrayed or harmed us at some point, but I've been dealing with his kind for many years, and they've never been known for subtlety or fancy schemes."

The priest came over to sit beside her again. "Many things have changed even since the end of the War. Kaelariel is – in appearance, at least – a serilis-rir," Samuel said, and though the term serilis-rir piqued Kari's interest, she didn't interrupt. "He has taken those that remain under his wing as his people. With Seril's death, the malignant will that sustained the lesser of the serilis-rir – the solas and the kryons – was severed, and they lived no more. The stronger types, however – the corlypsi, brys, elites, and guardians – survived her passing, as they relied less on her power to sustain their life force than their lesser cousins. As a demonhunter, I assume you already knew that the elite and guardian demons broke free of the Devil Queen's will long before the Apocalypse?"

Kari nodded. "If I'm not mistaken, it was shortly after Kaelariel's rise to power as lord of demons," she said. She remembered as much from the years shortly before her own death, though such had not been the case when she attended the Academy. Kaelariel was born seven years after Kari, and his rise to power had only shortly preceded her death. When he ascended, he wrested control of much of the Devil Queen's army from her, and subsequently used it to fight against her in the Fifth Demon War and the Apocalypse.

Samuel nodded. "More or less. Once Seril was destroyed at the War's end, the others were also freed of her will. Though the corlypsi remain savage, cowardly, and stupid, the brys are much more intelligent and cunning. While many of the serilis-rir have been fighting against the mortals or their own kind for too long to ever change their ways, some have and continue to do so. It would seem that Makauric was one such brys."

"I think he was still just a child, if such a thing is possible. He seemed young and was a little, eh, underdeveloped when I saw him nude," she said slowly.

The priest regarded her curiously, and Kari wondered what he was thinking. "It seems you may have been closer to him than you thought," Samuel said. "If Makauric showed himself to you, then he found you attractive and was trying to see if you felt the same. As for being underdeveloped, brys are all like that. Their kind has not been on this island for long or in large numbers. It is entirely possible that he was only a 'child' by our reckoning, but the serilis-rir are not created as children. They are created whole at adulthood, with much of Seril's knowledge already imprinted upon them so that they are prepared to serve her immediately. It is tragic that he would be killed so young, but it is not as though he died a child."

"I understand," she said absently, still at a loss over Makauric being

337

attracted to her. "On our way here I heard others call the serilian demons serilis-rir. Why do you call them that?"

His stare drifted away from her for a moment. "This may be difficult for you to hear, especially being a demonhunter, Karian," he said.

"Kari," she interrupted, and his brows arched. "My friends call me Kari."

Samuel smiled. "Very well then, Kari," he said. "As I was going to say, it will likely be hard for you to believe, but the serilis-rir are not so different from your kind as you may think. Though they were created by Seril, the Devil Queen created them in a similar image to your lord – all, of course, but the solas, who were intended to be more beastial."

Kari considered his words for a few moments. "It's not that hard to believe, really. They can breed with us, and other than the wings and the immunity to fire…," she said. "And the others that called them serilis-rir referred to the half-demons as serilian-rir."

Samuel nodded. "The only other major difference would be the simple fact that Seril never created females for their kind," he said. "We have long believed this was so that the two races would become one over time, after she won. It was not because she was unable to do so, however, as Kaelariel was once able to create a female serilis-rir."

She regarded him with surprise. "He did? I had no idea."

The priest nodded. "He created only one, and it is a long and sad tale," he said. "Our lord has never created another, and seems to have no intention of doing so again. Nevertheless, they are no more or less *people* than you – or your partner, regardless of what he may think."

"I don't understand him," she said, and she shook her head and looked down at her hands. "I thought he'd be more tolerant, given he's half-demon himself."

"His attitude is very common among serilian-rir. For many generations they have been persecuted outcasts, and they place the blame on Seril and their fathers as much as on the rest of society. I cannot say I know him, but I think there is much in your partner's heart that he has yet to come to terms with, and killing *demons* acts as an outlet for him," Samuel explained.

"Makes sense," Kari said.

"Kaelariel is working to integrate his *people*, as it were, into mortal society, but this is something that will take many, many years. As I said, many of them have fought against mortals for so long that they will never acquiesce to their lord's wishes no matter how much he assures them. Others will come out slowly, moving into towns like Awlinscar's village, learning to live among mortals," he explained, but he paused when Kari glanced at him quizzically. "I assume you know of Awlinscar, the lord of the elite demons; he established a village many years ago where mortals and serilis-rir are both welcome to live together. And indeed, they have – and peacefully – for as long as he has been in charge of it. It is his hope – and that of my lord – that over time the serilis-rir may learn to coexist with our peoples in peace. But some will not, and will instead go to another place that was prepared for them."

"You don't mean he'll kill them...?" Kari asked, shocked.

Samuel waved off the comment. "No, he will not kill them," he said. "There was a place prepared for them where they could live apart from rir and humans alike. It is a secret place, and we are bound to not speak of its location. Our lord ushers the more...feral, I guess you could say, of his people to this place."

"May I ask you something?" she asked, touching his arm lightly. "If your deity is the lord of demons and mine is the hunter of demons...why don't they speak to each other?"

"I am sure they do," he said. "Kaelariel is now the head of the pantheon, and Zalkar was his ally during the War. I am not certain they speak of Kaelariel's plans, however; your lord has been long at his task, and your kind has hunted Kaelariel's charges for over a thousand years. It is entirely likely that Kaelariel is unsure how to approach your deity with his current plans, and if the behavior of your partner is any indication, I can understand why."

Kari shook her head. "Our gods need to talk to each other," she said, wringing her hands. "You can talk to Kaelariel, right?"

"To an extent; my contact with him is limited, but what did you have in mind?"

"Tell him my Order is still killing his people at will," she said. "Tell him he needs to talk with Zalkar, and he needs to tell the Unyielding everything you've told me. Our love is justice, but only when it's tempered with mercy. If we don't have to just kill the serilis-rir indu..."

"Indiscriminately?" Samuel offered as Kari stuttered.

"I think that's the word," she said. "If we don't have to do that, Zalkar will change his orders. But Kaelariel will never convince his people to trust our people unless we stop killing each other on sight."

Samuel nodded, and Kari walked over and kissed Makauric on the forehead. "I am sorry, my friend. But thank you for all you've taught me," she intoned quietly. She turned around and fixed the priest with a curious gaze. "Where has his spirit gone?"

"I am not certain," the priest replied. "My lord has dominion over death and the dead; he could have sent the brys' spirit anywhere he wished. He may have sent Makauric's spirit to his realm in the heavens or anywhere the young brys wished to go. But I cannot say for certain."

Kari smiled after a moment, and she laid her hand on the brys' chest. "I have a feeling I might know where he's gone to, if the choice was his," she said, and she sniffled.

"Kari!" came a call from across the temple.

She recognized Grakin's voice immediately. She looked up as he hurried toward her, and took him in a tight embrace. "Grakin!" she cried happily, and he held her tight and kissed her.

"I thought I may have lost you when Erik arrived alone," he said. He pulled back from her and cupped her face in his hands. Grakin's eyes were filled with tears, but after a moment he saw the corpse of the brys. "Oh no, is this the brys who was helping you?"

"Erik mentioned him?" Kari asked, surprised.

Grakin shook his head. "Nay. Sonja used her spells several days ago to monitor your whereabouts and mentioned that you were traveling with a brys. Erik told me I could find you here, but made no mention of him or that he had been killed," he said. Grakin pulled Kari back in for a tight hug as fresh tears rolled from her eyes. "You grew close to him?"

"He was a good friend," she said quietly.

Grakin drew away from her lightly and kissed the side of her snout, and he turned to the other priest. "Greetings, brother," he said. "I am Grakin Tesconis. Thank you for comforting my mate."

Samuel rose and shook the half-demon's hand with an unmasked smile. "Grakin, the healer?" he asked, and Grakin nodded. "I have heard much about your work. I am Samuel Tirar, ranking priest of our lord's church here in Raugro. Welcome to our temple, brother."

"What happened to the brys?" Grakin asked Kari, but she shook off the question.

"Can you cremate Makauric's remains so I can take them with me?" Kari asked Samuel. "I'd like to take him home to the rainforest when we leave."

"Yes, of course," Samuel said. "I will have his body prepared tonight; you may come for him in the morning. Is there anything else I can do for you, my lady?"

"Just what we discussed earlier," she said. "I'd like you to do it. Grakin is my mate, so I think the message will carry more weight coming from you."

"I understand," Samuel said with a polite bow. "Farewell to you."

Kari and Grakin bid Samuel farewell, and she walked with her mate as he led her to the inn. The others rose to greet her, and Typhonix nearly crushed the life out of Kari with a bear hug. It was an amazing feeling, like being welcomed home by family, something she could rarely remember feeling across her two lives. Once all of them said their hellos, she took a seat at the table with them and saw that they were going over some sort of map and a set of notes that sat before Aeligos. Erik's expression held the same impatience she recalled from so many times during their journey: the arrogance that came with his belief that he was correct and had little time for others' thoughts or feelings.

She didn't pay much attention to what Aeligos said initially. Instead, she stared at Erik and Typhonix and tried to understand how they could be demonhunters when they were serilian-rir. While demonhunters also hunted the demons of the underworld, most of their time and effort was spent combating the serilian demons. If the priest was accurate, if Kaelariel really did want to integrate his *people* into mortal society, then having serilian-rir hunting their full-blooded forebears, regardless of type, was as counterproductive as possible.

Erik's complete disregard for Makauric's death would have been understandable had the brys not been as good as a friend to them. Kari thought perhaps she'd been mistaken in not telling Erik of everything that transpired while he was unconscious: that the brys had guarded them, hunted for them, and that she believed he would have fought for them had the situation arisen. As she thought about it, though, she realized Erik had to have come to those conclusions himself, and that his disdain for the brys was a conscious choice in spite of the facts before him.

Kari had precious few good, true friends in her life, but despite all their differences, she couldn't deny that Makauric did everything possible to be a friend to her. She regretted that she never had the opportunity to fight by his side: she always wanted to witness the prowess of a brys in the heat of battle when its ire was not directed at her. While she served with a number of brys in Jir'tana's unit during the war, they were mostly scouts and ranged support, so it wasn't the same. Her mind flashed across the days she had traveled beside Makauric, and she recalled how accommodating he was toward her when everything in her training and experience pointed to such being unheard of for brys. And, of course, there was what Samuel had mentioned regarding Makauric being attracted to her; how had she missed it?

Kari looked around the table and realized she already missed him.

Though he wasn't overly personable or talkative, she had gotten used to his presence and the fact that she could talk to him without reservation and without fear that he would judge her. When it came to Erik, she was very cautious about things that were personal to her; she could talk to him about her many accomplishments, but she refrained from telling him about her personal life. She knew Makauric probably hadn't cared about most of what she told him, but whatever the case, he'd never given her dirty or surprised looks. He'd simply listened when she needed an ear.

Sitting at the table, she felt the weight of Erik's disapproval as he sat at the other end and spared her glances only now and then. After he confronted her in the rainforest when they first departed from the rest of the group, Kari thought perhaps he'd learned his lesson. She further thought his night with the czarikk girls might have changed his attitude, but she realized that if Erik ever changed, it would take a very long time to happen. She sighed lightly and closed her eyes, and Grakin's hand fell on her leg. Aeligos stopped speaking, and after a few moments, Kari rose from her seat and pushed it in.

"I'm sorry, I need some time alone," she said. The others watched her walk over to the innkeeper, and she asked him about a bath. The innkeeper gestured toward the back room and told her he'd bring hot water for her, and Kari escaped her friends' scrutiny quickly.

Mr. Guzman brought hot water for her and Kari settled into the tub. She always loved a hot bath to sit and think in, and the steamy water helped massage her body and feelings alike. Within minutes of settling in, there was a brief knock on the door and Aeligos approached. She was shocked that it was him and not Grakin. Aeligos knelt beside the tub and wrapped Kari in a hug, and she returned it after a tentative moment. When he released her, he sat back on his heels and studied her eyes closely, and he gave a soft shake of his head. Kari could see the light and the concern in his dark eyes, and she remembered how highly Grakin had spoken of his brother during their journey. In those brief moments, Kari could see her feelings about Aeligos were off-base, but she still wasn't sure what to make of him.

Aeligos picked up the scrub brush beside the tub and gestured for Kari to lean forward so he could wash her wings. "Are you all right?" he asked as he began to scrub the leathery folds.

"No," she said quietly with a sniffle. "I was expecting Grakin to come in."

"I know, but Grakin's just going to comfort you. I need to talk to you first," he said, and Kari turned to face him. "Did Erik do anything to you while you were tracking the demon?"

"Other than to accuse me of being a fake and tell me to leave his brother alone, no."

Aeligos shook his head again with a sigh. "I might have guessed," he said. "But he didn't hurt you, or put his hands on you at all?"

Kari grimaced. "He did this to my wing, but it wasn't his fault," she said. "He fell under a charm from the sylinth we fought, and it forced him to attack me."

"Did what to your wing?" Aeligos asked.

Kari took hold of her left wing to show Aeligos the scar tissue where the severed bone had been healed, but there was no trace of the wound whatsoever. Kari was confused; she didn't know how the wound had healed completely without the ministrations of an experienced healer. "Well, that's weird," she said. "He cut through one of my wings when he was charmed."

"That was all?" he asked and Kari nodded, though she was concerned at what he was implying. Aeligos touched her face and gave her a chaste kiss on the forehead. "I knew it was a bad idea to let you leave without trying to tell Erik the truth first. I'm sure you've seen the way he treats Eryn; I was afraid he might treat you the same way or worse when no one was around to mitigate his temper. He's more like our father than he cares to admit."

Kari beheld him curiously but said, "I can take care of myself."

"I know you can, but the point of being part of a family is not having to," he said. Kari looked at him in wonder and he flashed his boyish smile. "Sonja and I will talk to Erik and try to get this all sorted out. Do you want me to send Grakin in?"

Kari nodded. "Thank you, Aeligos," she said, reaching for a hug, and he obliged. They turned when the door opened and Grakin approached, and the priest smiled as he drew close and knelt beside his brother.

"I'll leave you two alone," Aeligos said, and he patted his brother's shoulder before he rose and left the bath chamber.

Kari met her mate's eyes as the door closed behind Aeligos. "We were just…"

Grakin waved off the comment. "Kari, I know. Aeligos is not just my brother, he is my best friend," he said. "If anything ever happens to me, I trust him to take care of you."

She wondered why she'd even bothered trying to explain it; he trusted her completely. She stroked his face and they kissed briefly. "It seems even after a few months, there's a lot about your family I still don't know," she said. "Aeligos seemed to be trying to tell me he thought Erik was going to hit me when we were alone."

"Did he?" Grakin asked, clearly perturbed by the thought.

Kari shook her head. "Grakin, if your brother had hit me, one of us wouldn't be here right now," she said. "Anyway, how was the journey for the rest of you?"

"Long, and lonely," he said, and Kari giggled with him. "I was unsure how well Aeligos would lead in Erik's absence, but he did well, and I am already beginning to wish he was still in charge. He is less demanding, and much more humble. Erik is just…"

"Erik's not a bad leader, he's just a hardhead when he thinks he's right," Kari said, but she waved her hand dismissively before Grakin could press the issue further. "I'd really rather not talk about it. Honestly, the hunt with him went very well, just not the beginning or the end. Tell Aeligos to get the others back together and we'll go over his maps and strategy when I get out of the tub."

"You are all right to be alone?" he asked, touching her jaw lightly.

"I lost a friend today," Kari said with a sniffle, but then she met Grakin's eyes evenly. "But I got six others back…and more importantly, you."

Grakin gave her a parting kiss and then made his way out to the common room, leaving her alone to wash and relax. Kari sank down into the water a little more, put her feet up on the far end of the tub, and let out a calming sigh. She tried to massage her feelings with reality, and she reminded herself that as long as she lived the life of a demonhunter, she would always be in danger of losing friends. It was simply the way of things. She could quit the life of the hunter and become a commoner, but the risk of death would always be present. It was not something one could shut themself away from.

Her thoughts turned to Trigonh, and she began to look at the erestram and what he had done in another light. He made no secret of the fact that he loved Kari in a romantic sense, and although she didn't share his feelings, she considered him a friend. They'd traveled together on only one occasion, but he'd shattered everything she knew about his kind in the span of a few weeks. He was an oddity among his kind, but that didn't diminish the kindness and gentle side he demonstrated during the short time they spent together. Even when she refused him, he stayed with her, and he was by her side when her end came.

As her heart fluttered once more with the thought of Makauric's death, Kari considered how Trigonh – and indeed even her friend Carly – must have felt when she died, and whether they went through the same turbulent emotions. It had to have been so, and she bit her lip as she considered how rude she was to Trigonh when she was resurrected and stood before him. He had given her a gift, and though she hadn't fully appreciated its scope and significance when she initially received it, she felt ashamed now at her reaction. She had a mate now, and many beautiful chapters of her life to write with him, all thanks to the selflessness of a *demon*.

She chuckled, considering the strange way life worked, and the sudden shocks of surprise it sent one's way when one became too deadset in their thinking. Kari thought about Erik, and although his attitude and closed-mindedness upset her, she realized that at times she had been like him. She remembered her first encounter with Trigonh and his master, Celigus Chinchala; she recalled her doubts when Kaelariel rose to power and the people began to trust some of the serilis-rir; and she was sharply reminded of the fact that the Light forces of the Apocalypse were led by the lord of the serilis-rir and a demon king.

Kari recalled an old human proverb and chuckled again as she considered that life was teaching her new tricks. A smile came to her face, punctuated by tears, though they were closer to tears of joy as she thought of her brys companion running free somewhere in the heavens, no longer hated or hunted on account of his skin color or who had created him. She was fairly certain she knew where he had chosen to go if Kaelariel indeed gave him a choice, and she smiled more broadly imagining it. *Run free, my friend*, she whispered in her mind.

Kari lost track of time, so she began washing herself more quickly, not wanting to keep the others waiting too long. After a couple of minutes there was a knock at the door, and Sonja entered. She seemed to be on the verge of crying, but when she knelt by the bathtub she met Kari's stare. Kari could see the amazement in her friend's eyes as they held each other's gaze, and she smiled to let Sonja know she was all right. After a moment, the larger woman reached for a hug, and Kari obliged. "I'm sorry to hear about your friend," Sonja said with a sniffle. "Are you feeling all right?"

"I'm all right," Kari said, and her smile didn't dissipate. "I just had an epi...epip..."

"Epiphany?" Sonja finished when her sister-in-law paused.

"Yea, one of those," the terra-dracon woman said. "It hurts, but I think I understand. He's teaching me as much in death as he did when he was alive."

Sonja nodded, but it was clear she didn't entirely understand. "Are you mad at Erik?" she asked. "I don't mean to butt in, but time is growing short and we can't afford any delays. If you two can't work together, that's something we need to address before we move forward."

Kari shook her head. She gathered her hair, wrung some of the water from it, and then threw it in a bunch over her shoulder. "I'm not mad at Erik," she answered. "I think your brother just is the way he is, and nothing's ever going to change that unless he wants it to. I know he wants to be Avatar of Vengeance, but it's honestly scary to think of him in that position, the way he brushes aside what other people think or feel. I'm a demonhunter, too, but as much as my duty to Zalkar means to me, it's not what makes me who I am, Sonja. With Erik, I don't think there's much more to him than his duty to the Unyielding...and to you, his siblings."

Sonja regarded her curiously but didn't disagree with her. "He raised the rest of us as much as our father did," she said. "I think he still sees himself as our father-figure, and worries more about us than himself. As you said, he rarely speaks of anything but his duty to Zalkar and advancement among the Order, and even when women show him interest he seems oblivious to it. He seems to push away or lash out at the things he can't control – like you."

Kari nodded solemnly. "Yea, the beginning of our trip through the rainforest was interesting," she said. She rose to her feet and took the towel Sonja offered her. Once she patted down her hair, she began drying off the rest of her body and continued, "He basically told me he thought I was a phony, and he wanted to know what I wanted from his brother other than sex."

Sonja sighed. "I had a feeling he would confront you as soon as you were away from the rest of us," she said. "I hope he wasn't too nasty with you?"

"No worse than the drill sergeants when I attended the Academy," Kari said with a shrug, and Sonja laughed aloud. "I thought sleeping with those czarikk girls might loosen him up, but he's very tense."

Sonja's eyes grew enormous. "What?! Erik, with czarikk girls?! Oh, do tell."

"Not my tale to tell," Kari said with a shake of her head, and she began to get dressed. "If he wants to share, he will. They were very happy when we destroyed the sylinth, though, and a few of them let him know it."

The larger woman started laughing, but she cocked her head and fixed Kari with a curious glance. "Not you, though?"

Kari shook her head. "I have a mate," she said simply, and Sonja smiled.

The two made their way back out to the common room. The others all watched when she came out of the bath chamber, and she walked around the table to give Grakin a kiss and a hug. "Feeling better?" Typhonix asked, his expression one of genuine concern.

"Much, thanks," Kari answered, and she gestured toward Aeligos. "Can you start again from the beginning? I was a little busy in my mind when you were speaking earlier."

"Sure, that's not a problem," the rogue answered, and he looked over his shoulder to the innkeeper. "Emil, could you give us the common room to ourselves for a half hour or so?"

The innkeeper nodded and made his way into the kitchen, and Aeligos drew forth the map and notes from his cloak pocket and slid them to the center of the table so everyone could see. "This is Gaswell's castle?" Kari prompted.

Aeligos nodded with a lopsided smile, and the others began chuckling before he spoke. "Yes, based on what Eryn wrote in her letter to me, which you don't want to read. This may not be entirely accurate, but what it does show is that there are multiple ways into the castle, most of which are on a second level, inaccessible from the ground – unless you have wings. There's also a back entrance through a sewer tunnel that runs out from the dungeons," he added and pointed to an exit marked on the south wall of the castle. "It runs off a cliff and out into the lake and has a grate over it, so it's unguarded, from what Eryn says. She thinks if we send two of our stronger members down that way, they should be able to pry the iron grate off of the sewer tunnel and make their way into the castle's belly. While it won't be the best-smelling entrance, it'll be the path of least resistance, and possibly lead to this kirelas-rir Gaswell has reportedly kidnapped."

"I'd almost forgotten about her," Erik commented with a nod. "Did Eryn mention what she does around the castle?"

"I think she's a porter," Aeligos said. "She's disguised herself as a terra-rir woman, but she's too small to be really useful as a guard or soldier, so Gaswell has her doing menial tasks around the castle. Basically, he's treating her like a housewife without the sex."

"Much to her relief, I'm sure," Kari said, which drew laughs from her companions. "How did she disguise her wings?"

"Eryn knows a little shapeshifting magic. It's not much but she's very good with it, and it's very hard to detect," the rogue answered, and he pointed to six other entrances located on the upper balconies and a second-floor patio of the inner keep. "These doors will be our most likely points of entry. She's in charge of making sure the doors are all secured, and she assured me that they can be opened from the outside. We'll obviously

347

attack under cover of night: terra-rir can see well in the dark, but with these patrol routes she's outlined for us, we can pick a lock in the least-heavily patrolled part of the keep. Using our wings, we slip in through the dark, unlock a door, and get inside. Once we're in, the rest of you will stay put while I explore the castle a little and find Eryn. Her letter did include a brief description of the inside of the keep, but since we'll be going in at night, we don't know exactly where Gaswell will be. He could be on his throne, in the dining hall, in his bedchambers…if we have to crash from place to place looking for him, we'll end up fighting everyone in the castle."

"So we're going to try to rescue the kirelas-rir girl that he captured?" Kari asked.

Aeligos nodded without looking at Erik. "Yes," he said. "I don't know if Gaswell has anyone else locked in his dungeon, but we can pretty safely assume that if he has prisoners down there, then they're probably our friends. This whole business about capturing a kirelas-rir girl doesn't make any sense unless he has other plans besides simply conquering the island. It was pretty obvious by Eryn's letter that there's more to this situation than what we see, and this kirelas-rir girl may be able to tell us what. In any case, she deserves our help."

Erik merely nodded, and Aeligos continued. "From what Eryn tells me, Gaswell has two lieutenants who are his right hand. Chances are when we find him, we'll find them, too. I don't think it'll be an issue given how many fighters we have, but we have to be prepared for an even fight; she wasn't able to tell me how many other guards to expect. It depends on how committed Gaswell is to meeting the shakna-rir forces and what sort of crew he leaves behind to man the walls and gate of the castle."

"She did good work," Kari commented.

"She always does," Aeligos returned with a grim smile. "So we have a basic plan of attack, but our first order of business is to get the city council here to send their forces south to meet with the shakna-rir under Warlord Maktus Tuvurasti. Once the two armies are together, we should be able to circle around to one of the castle's flanks so we're not crossing directly through enemy lines and we don't have to worry about getting caught in the middle when the two armies clash. As long as Maktus gives us enough time to get into position, the actual battle should be a short one: once Gaswell and his two lieutenants are dead, we can secure the castle and leave his army nowhere to retreat to. Their surrender is almost assured."

"If they don't surrender?" Sherman prompted.

"They'll be crushed between the castle and the combined armies,"

Aeligos said, but he sighed. "If they drag the battle out or are able to retreat to a nearby town, it may attract the attention from Dannumore that we're trying to avoid, but I doubt it. It's a risk, but a calculated one. This entire mission is, really."

Kari shook her head with a sigh. "This would be a lot easier if those idiots at the gate hadn't killed Makauric," she said, and the others glanced at her curiously. "Getting into the castle at night would be simple with a brys guiding us: they can see in the dark like it's day."

"True enough," Erik said.

Kari met Aeligos' gaze and realized he was waiting to see if she had anything else to add. "This is a good plan, Aeligos," she said.

The rogue smiled and nodded at last. He folded the papers and put them back in his cloak. He made his way over to the kitchen door and asked Emil to bring dinner for the group, and shortly after he returned to the table, the barmaid brought them all drinks and meals. They shared their dinner quietly and confidence settled in among them. After dinner they played cards for a while, and then everyone retired to their rooms for some rest, waiting for the courier to come summon them before the council the next morning.

Kari and Grakin retired to their room, and the priest had barely closed the door before Kari started undressing him. She didn't even wait to get to the bed before she began their lovemaking. He was shocked, and after a minute he drew away from her, so she followed him to the bed. They made love passionately: Kari's sorrow over having lost a friend mixed potently with the joy of being with her mate once more, and Grakin left her in control. There was no bed beneath them, no world around them: there was only the two of them melded together in the throes of passion.

They didn't speak after their passions had run their course: everything that needed to be said came out in their lovemaking. Kari fell asleep in Grakin's arms with her face pressed to his warm chest, and he folded his wings over them as well. She felt safe and warm, and her dreams were the same, though Makauric manifested within them at one point in the night. Contrary to what she expected, his appearance did not cause heartache or pain, but she had smiled in her sleep and enjoyed a last moment with him, ethereal as it was.

Kari and Grakin returned to Kaelariel's temple the next morning, and Samuel presented her with an urn containing the brys' ashes. She stowed it in Grakin's travel pack, since he was less likely to drop his in the face of trouble. They thanked the priest, and made their way back to the inn. Kari was surprised to find several guards at the inn when they returned, and the rest of her companions were seated around the table waiting for them. Aeligos made a gesture to the guards, who nodded, and he approached.

"You're not under arrest," he started, holding up a hand to stifle any reply, "but the city council has ordered you to appear before them for an inquiry. On the positive side, we've been summoned back to see them at the same time, so we should get all of our business taken care of this morning. The guards will escort you to city hall, but again, you're not under arrest."

"I understand," Kari said. She gestured for the guards to lead her along, and the rest of her companions rose and followed as well.

Chapter XVIII – Consequences

The guards escorted Kari and her companions to city hall, and after a short wait in the foyer they were escorted into the council chamber. The gallery was full. The guards gestured for Kari to follow them to the open floor, but ordered the others to stay behind. Aeligos started to protest, but Kari told him it was all right, and she moved to stand at attention several paces before the podium. She looked at the six people before her and waited for them to speak.

"Please state your name for the record," Governor Potter said from his place on the right.

"Karian Vanador, Shield of the Heavens, by Zalkar's grace," she replied formally.

The governor nodded. "Welcome to our city, demonhunter," he said. "While no formal charge was filed, we understand there was an incident yesterday involving yourself and one of our captains of the guard. The report states that you attempted to bring a demon into the city, and nearly attacked several guards when they refused to allow him entry. While we respect the authority of the Demonhunter Order, such an incident required a formal inquiry at the least. The report of the captain stands in evidence; what say you on this matter?"

Kari put her hands to her hips and looked at the floor, fighting to keep her emotions in check, and she blew out a short sigh. She looked back to the governor after a moment and said, "Your guards killed my friend yesterday."

The council was clearly surprised by the declaration, and the governor banged his gavel to restore order as the gallery erupted in mumbling. Once the chamber was quiet again, Potter leaned forward and fixed Kari with a curious gaze. "Please explain," he said.

"My partner and I were sent to this island to track down a demon," she said, trying to think of the best way to keep the story short and to the point. "Our search started in the Kavin Rainforest of the southeast, but we got lost out there, having expected to find the czarikk and ask them for help. We were approached by a brys who offered to show us the way to the czarikk and then to the demon we hunted, called a sylinth. Since our other task here needed to be done as quickly as possible, we had little choice but to accept the brys' offer."

She turned and looked at Erik over her shoulder. After a moment, the governor waved him forward and he approached to stand beside Kari. "The brys was a great guide, which wasn't surprising since he ranged the rainforest and the savannah north of it for years," she said, but then she paused for a moment. "I enjoyed his company, at least as much as you can enjoy the company of a creature with no sense of humor and little personality. During the fight with the sylinth, I was wounded and my partner got a...concussion. Makauric – the brys – didn't help us during the fight: he was afraid that he would be put under a charm by the sylinth, but after, when I was trying to care for my partner, he came for us. He hunted for us, guarded us while I slept, and helped me tend to my partner, and when we were ready to travel again, he led us here."

"The reward he received for his help was to be shot down without question by your guards, and that was *my* failure," Kari said, her eyes beginning to tear up, and she cut off the governor when he tried to speak. "That *demon* was under *my* protection, and I had to watch him die because your guards didn't use a shred of common sense when they saw red skin."

The chamber was silenced for a minute by her words. The councilors exchanged glances, and the gallery remained quiet, waiting to see what the council's reaction would be. Kari looked at Erik and he met her eyes, and he gave her a tight-lipped nod and patted her shoulder. Kari bit her lower lip. All at once she wanted to scream at Erik, the council, and every guard in the city; did none of them understand the value of Makauric's life? She curbed her emotions as best she could. The fact that she'd been called before the council for a hearing spoke of the damage the situation had already done, and the threat of it compounding was obvious. As much as she wanted to vent her anger, Kari knew that she also needed to patch things up if there was any hope of asking the council for their aid.

"Clearly the actions of the captain and his guards were rash, but understandable under the circumstances," Potter said at last. "But you say this brys was your friend?"

"I don't know what else to call someone that protects and provides for you," she said, and Kari bit her lip again as she caught her breath and tears rolled down her cheek. Erik put his hand on her shoulder once more. She was tempted to shake it off: to reject what she assumed was a false attempt to comfort her, but she decided not to make any more of a scene than her vehement declarations already had.

"What would you have us do, officer?" Petra asked, folding her arms before her.

The chamber was silent for several minutes, councilors, spectators, and friends alike awaiting Kari's next words. She remained silent; her eyes were on the council but her thoughts were on her slain friend. Soon she realized what it was the council was asking her. After a minute had passed, she calmly wiped the tears from her face and shook her head. "Nothing. What's done is done, and your people shouldn't suffer for what was…a mistake," she said quietly. "All I would ask is that they don't make this same mistake again."

"You're certain you do not wish the captain punished?" Potter asked. "As a high-ranking official of the patron of Law, you have the authority to demand it."

Kari shook her head again. "No. I'm no judge, and punishing him for protecting the city would be as much a crime as his men killing my friend," she said. "Just let it be. Explain things to him, since I can't. Knowing he was wrong should be his only punishment, since it'll calm his hand in the future." She glanced over her shoulder briefly and then fixed her gaze on Potter. "Have him look at the seal in the foyer, and remind him that it's not just words."

The council held her under their intense gazes, and Kari wasn't sure what they were thinking as she held their stares, until at last the shakna-rir woman in the center gave the barest of smiles. "Well spoken," Petra said with a nod.

The governor seemed to take Petra's words as a cue. "As you wish," Potter said. "What would you ask of the city as compensation for your friend's death?"

Kari was dumbstruck, and wondered what exactly they thought they could offer her in exchange for a life taken. She waved her hand dismissively. "I don't mean this to sound like a threat, but I'm not the one you should worry about compensating," she said, which drew more curious stares from the councilors. "If what Makauric told me is true, there are quite a number of brys in the forests to the north and west of you. They're the ones you should be worried about."

"How so?" Max Soroza asked.

"The brys are vengeful, and quite often consider each other brothers," Erik said, and Kari was thankful for the brief respite to collect her thoughts. "But they're also fairly predictable as serilian demons go. If they find out that their brother was killed at the gates of your city, they may come to collect a blood price: ten of yours for one of theirs is the standard. But an apology may go a long way with them. If they believe it was a mistake, they may leave you in peace."

"Would a handful of brys really pose a threat to our city?" Avery Nash asked.

"A handful of brys could sack this city if they put their minds to it and worked together," Kari answered. She blew out a short sigh as the councilors mumbled among themselves. It was apparent the city had little contact with serilian demons, and it left Kari to wonder whether the other brys on the island were anything like Makauric. "And they will if they're angry enough about Makauric being killed. He said he rarely saw his brothers, but that doesn't mean they won't care about his death. Also, what my partner said is only partially true: while their blood price is ten to one, *each* of them would collect it."

"This is alarming news, indeed," Potter said. "How would you recommend we go about offering an apology?"

Kari and Erik exchanged a glance, and Kari shrugged. "Your best option will be to send a ranger to the woodlands to get in contact with one of them," she answered. "They're not easy to find, but if there are a number of them in the forests, then the ranger networks must know of them at least, if they don't know them personally. Have a ranger take them an official, written apology; I'll write them something, too, so they understand. The word of a demonhunter should convince them your regret is real."

The governor sat back and nodded. "The council and I thank you for your insight on this matter," he said. "Thank you for your wisdom, and for your mercy; you are as fine an example of your Order as we have ever encountered. Is there anything else the council can do for you?"

Kari shook her head. "No, only the decision that my friends are waiting for," she said. "If you'll excuse me, I'd like to go out and get some fresh air."

"By all means," Potter said, and he gestured for Kari to take her leave.

Kari bade Grakin remain with his siblings and left the city hall alone. Out under a bright blue sunny sky, she took a long, deep breath to calm herself. The smells of the local bakeries and the fires of the smithies carried to her, punctuating the warmth of the early summer day, and the sound of drums and festivities echoed from one of the nearby plazas. Her tensions relaxed slightly. Tsalbrin was a lovely island, but her senses were still upside-down, her expectations thrown off completely by having gone from autumn to tropical weather and then into summer. She thought briefly of her slain friend, and the desire to drown her sorrows in a strong drink clawed at her mind. Kari set her feet toward the nearest tavern.

She found a cozy inn not far from the city hall, and the barkeep offered her the drink she asked for without reservation or question, which was a welcome change. Normally, requesting the highly potent beverage drew

354

surprise or even some form of judgment, and Kari could never figure out exactly why. She never understood whether it was because of her size, or the fact that she was a woman, or if it had something to do with the fact that she drank them at breakfast sometimes. The last thought gave her a laugh, so she asked the barkeep for something to eat.

Kari offered a silent toast to her departed friend and indulged herself in the intoxicating drink. She savored the bittersweet taste and thought of all that Samuel Tirar told her. It made her think of her conversation with Sonja aboard *Karmi's Sword*, when she had asked what it truly was they won in the Apocalypse. With the Devil Queen dead, the mortals still fought the serilis-rir, still fought with each other, and nothing was explained. Kari decided that hunting demons was no longer good enough: she now wanted the *why* to go along with the *what*.

The barkeep brought her biscuits and honey, and she ate quickly to avoid ending up tipsy. She thought of Makauric trying to live among mortals, and came to the conclusion that the only people he would likely have been comfortable among were the czarikk. They seemed tolerant of him once they were assured he meant them no harm, and from what she could tell from his normally emotionless demeanor, he found the people and their village intriguing. It was no secret that he'd enjoyed their food and their fire dances. *Then again*, she thought, *maybe he just enjoyed my fire dances*.

She chuckled and sighed wistfully, considering once more that Makauric had liked her enough to consider her in a romantic sense – or at least as romantic as a brys could possibly be. She turned in surprise when someone touched her back, and Erik stepped beside her. "Mind if I join you?" he asked quietly.

"Not at all," Kari said. In honesty, he was the last person she wanted to be around at that moment, but in the interest of fulfilling Master Surallis' wishes, she kept her feelings to herself for the time being. If Erik had left his siblings to come follow Kari, there must be something he wanted to say or ask her, so Kari tolerated his presence.

Erik asked the barkeep for whatever Kari was having, and she wondered if her partner had ever tried one of the potent drinks. Once the barkeep presented Erik with his drink, the two clinked their glasses. "To Makauric," Erik said quietly, and Kari repeated his toast after only the slightest of pauses. They each took a good sip of their drinks, and by his sudden change of expression, Kari guessed Erik hadn't ever tried one before. He coughed a couple of times and laughed at himself afterwards, but then he looked away from her and out the front door. "I can't even imagine what you must think of me right now."

"Don't worry, Erik, the way you treat me won't change my report," Kari said.

His blue eyes swung back to her and he shook his head. "That's not what bothers me," he said. "I don't know if I can explain it. Aeligos, Sonja and I had a long talk last night after you and Grakin went to bed, and a lot of what they had to say really came as a shock. Foremost being that what I thought of Makauric shouldn't have taken priority over how you felt, or how I should have treated you."

Kari held his gaze, trying to hold back tears, and Erik's mouth tightened. "I'm sure you're getting tired of hearing this, but I'm sorry, Kari," he said, his hands coming up before him helplessly. "Sonja said...she said I've always been like this to my siblings, and that it's only becoming apparent how wrong it is because you're not my sister and neither are the Morevilles. I'm sure you can imagine this was a lot to hear from my brother and sister in a single night."

"Keep going," Kari said, leaning on the bar. She tried not to seem too judgmental, but she wanted to grind Erik under her heel a bit: to make him sweat and remember the moment as something he never wanted to repeat. She wanted it to be a catalyst for change, no matter how small, because in her heart she knew he was a good man who'd apparently – as Aeligos said – simply taken too much after his father when it came to dealing with people.

"I'm a half-guardian," he said. "It's in my nature to protect my friends and my siblings, even from themselves if I think they're wrong. And, well, I tend to always think people are wrong when they don't agree with me. I'm not sure if that's because of my heritage or because I'm just hard-headed. I thought you understood after we talked in the rainforest, but you missed as much as you caught onto. It's hard for me to trust people, Kari: every time we meet someone new, it's an opportunity for one or more of us to get hurt. That's why I have such a hard time letting people get close to any of us – like you to Grakin."

"That's the real reason you didn't want to bring Sherman and Katarina?" Kari asked.

Erik nodded. "It's part of the reason I kept Makauric at arm's length, too," he said, shaking his head. "It honestly didn't even occur to me until you said what you did about him hunting for us, guarding us, and helping you tend to me. To think I not only owed my life to something I might've killed without a second thought on another day, but that he was a friend to us...I was...afraid that if I let myself like him, I wouldn't be able to do my job anymore. That I'd always have doubt and it would be my undoing at some point."

Erik went silent, and Kari could see that something was definitely changing in him, even if just a little. His contrition was genuine, and a part of her felt bad for him, even though he'd brought the situation on himself. "I admire you," Erik said suddenly, surprising her before she could speak. "I can't think of a better example of our lord's chosen than you, and it didn't take the governor long to see it, either. You're a great fighter, but your violence is tempered by the mercy the Unyielding demands, and a compassion I could hardly believe was real. Makauric's death was as much my failure as yours: anyone under your protection was also under mine, and I failed both of you. And now I don't just feel like I've failed, but like I've committed a crime. I still can't say I feel bad for *him*, Kari: I never let myself get close to him, so I don't really have any feelings for him. But I let him die, and that hurt you…and *I* hurt you, and that's going to haunt me for a long time. Can you ever forgive me, and do you think he ever could?"

"I already have," Kari replied without hesitation, but then she shook her head. "I don't hold grudges, Erik: life's too short for them. At the same time, life's too short to go around worrying about what the dead think. Where they are…where Makauric is…they no longer care. So it's left to you to learn your lesson but keep moving forward."

Erik stared into her eyes for a couple of minutes. "You're a good woman, Kari," he said. "I'm proud to call you my partner, and my sister."

Kari squared her jaw. "Make me proud to call you my brother," she said, and he nodded. "I lived my life pushing people away because I knew I was going to die, Erik, and it was a lonely life that didn't need to be that way. People are going to hurt you, and hurt your siblings, but that's part of what makes you stronger, and what makes you believe in what we fight for. If you don't let people in, your siblings will always be the only friends you have."

Erik shrugged but didn't disagree with her. "For a while I thought that was enough," he said. "I don't know how it was for you during the War, but we faced death on a daily basis, and we just grew closer and closer as the years and the trials passed us by. We've always relied on each other more than anyone else, given what our life was like growing up, and after the War it seemed there was nothing we couldn't accomplish together. It seemed like we never needed anyone else, but I guess I should've seen the folly in that when Grakin fell in love with you. Honestly, this is why our superiors should have just put you in charge in the first place."

Kari shook her head. "You don't learn as much following as you do leading. Even if you're making mistakes, you're learning, and if someone else is telling you what to do and how to do it, you're not necessarily learning the best way to do something. If you want to be Avatar of Vengeance, you have to have the conviction to make decisions and stand by them, and the wisdom to change course when you're wrong. You've definitely got the conviction…now you just need the wisdom to go with it. I think you've learned a lot; just make sure you remember all of it. Especially what you learned from those czarikk girls," she said, and she watched him over the rim of her glass as she took a sip.

Erik laughed and Kari did soon after, and the two clinked their glasses again. "I'll drink to that," he said.

Minutes later the others joined them, and it was apparent by Aeligos' triumphant smile that the council agreed to send the provincial armies to meet with the shakna-rir. The Silver Blades pushed together a few tables, and once they all had drinks they sat down to discuss what happened after Kari and Erik left. Sonja looked at Kari expectantly, and Kari smiled in a way that clearly said all was right again.

"We're on the road again first thing in the morning," Aeligos said. "The council and the governor have agreed to send the provincial army to join with the shakna-rir. Five hundred are already making ready to march south in the morning, and fifteen hundred more will follow them in three days. Messengers have been dispatched to the major neighboring towns and cities with standing garrisons, and each of their garrisons will also join with Maktus' forces. All told, the contribution from the provincial army should number between five and six thousand, though they won't all reach the war camp at the same time. They could send more, but not in the time frame we're looking at."

Erik stared at Aeligos and his astonishment was apparent to all. "Something tells me I should let you do all the talking in the future," he said.

Sonja laughed and patted Aeligos' hand. "He did excellent work, for certain," she added.

"In the morning we have to make our way toward Maktus' camp to explain our general plan to him," the rogue continued, turning to Kari and Erik. "I know you two could probably use some rest but we don't have that luxury right now. As it stands, it should take us about a week to reach the shakna-rir war camp. While we'll easily keep ahead of the garrisons heading south to join them, we're going to need more time to get into position for our strike."

"How much more time?" Erik asked.

Aeligos thought about it. "Depending on how fast the army moves after it's gathered, at least three to four days," he said.

"But it'll likely take more than a week for the garrisons to reach the war camp?" Erik pressed, to which Aeligos nodded. Erik gave the matter some thought, and he looked at Kari and Grakin before he shook his head. "We'll remain in town two more nights; we can make up the time on the road."

The others looked surprised. "Are you sure?" Sonja asked.

Erik patted Kari's forearm. "I'm sure," he said. "Relax and enjoy yourselves for a couple of days. Gaswell will still be there when we're ready."

~~*~*

Kari and her companions stayed in the city for two more days, during which Kari assisted the council in writing a letter to the brys of the north and west forests. Initially the council was tentative in its efforts, but with Kari's help, they crafted a letter that all felt would convey their sincerest regret. Kari ended up writing more than the council did, and she wrote passionately about her friend. She told Makauric's brothers of his bravery and sacrifice, about his selflessness that was a credit to all of their kind, and that without his help, a war with the underworld may have come to pass. She told them that it was an honor to know him, and that both she and the citizens of Raugro deeply regretted the accident that would deny others the same honor. In the end, she beseeched the brys to seek her out if they questioned her words and to leave the people of Raugro in peace.

The Silver Blades finally headed south on the third morning. Kari felt relaxed after getting to spend three nights with Grakin, and the fatigue of being on the road and the hunt for so long melted away. Makauric's death stayed close in her mind, but she tried to keep perspective and remind herself that the mission was the most important thing: if she failed, then Makauric's death would have been in vain. She and her companions traveled through farmlands for several days before the crops gave way to grazelands, and surveying the farmlands further reinforced Kari's thoughts. Eventually the Silver Blades encountered and passed through the southbound garrisons from Raugro. During their travels the rich plains turned into the more arid savannah that Erik and Kari had described from their own mission. They passed the city of Brehl, which sat on the shore of a great lake that seemed more like an inland sea. It sparkled under the sunrise and marked the eastern horizon for much of their journey.

After nearly a week they began to encounter scouts and patrols from the shakna-rir army, who let them pass and sent runners ahead to announce the approach of the Silver Blades and the provincial army. Late in the afternoon of the sixth day the companions reached the war camp, which was as fortified on the north side that faced Raugro as Kari imagined it would be on the south side. Aeligos explained that the shakna-rir were more than likely setting a false front for Gaswell's scouts to give the impression that the provincial army of Raugro might come and try to forcibly evict the Tuvurasti army. Kari found it odd, and wondered what relations between the shakna-rir and their neighbors were like during peaceful times.

Once they passed the fortifications, the Silver Blades found several large tents set up in the center of the camp, and they were ushered into the presence of Maktus Tuvurasti. He seemed glad to see Aeligos, and welcomed him and his friends into the command pavilion. Aeligos introduced the shakna-rir warlord to his other siblings, and then to Kari and the Moreville twins.

The shakna-rir warlord beheld Kari and Erik and gave them a respectful military salute. "It is an honor to meet you; all of you," Maktus said. "I would like to brief you on what we have seen since arriving here, but first I must ask: my scouts say there are several garrisons within a few days' journey of our camp here, but that they are not Gaswell's men or sympathizers; I take it this means your efforts in Raugro were successful?"

"Yes, quite," Aeligos said, but he shook his head. "I'm surprised you managed to get a force this large out here so quickly."

Maktus waved off the comment and gestured for his guests to sit on the rugs around the pavilion. He waited until his guests took seats and his servants served cups of red wine. "Saint John's pass is the most well-known route out of the great desert, and we did send several of our units by that route," Maktus explained. "But we have other ways out of our kingdom, ways that are fairly secret and well-guarded. We use these to move our military south when necessary, in order to avoid provoking Raugro and its allies."

The rogue nodded. "Makes sense," he said. "I assume there's no one here in the command tent that you don't trust?"

"Indeed," the shakna-rir warlord said. "Let us speak of the matter before us. Gaswell's army returned from their maneuvers once their scouts became aware of our presence. He is marshalling his forces, but strangely, they have made no move to attack or even provoke us. I believe it is safe to say they will not engage us until we draw within short range of their fortress, to avoid being flanked. Experience tells me that should we head south, he will meet us roughly halfway between our present camp and his base. Although they would have a tactical advantage fighting from within the fort, they do not know enough of our siege capabilities to risk their stronghold in the initial skirmishes. They are also unable to post scouts or spies north of our position, so they know nothing of the assistance coming from our neighbors in the northwest. They may assume Raugro is sending its forces, but I have been careful to keep a sizeable part of my forces facing north, as though we expect trouble."

Erik glanced at Aeligos briefly before asking Maktus, "When do you plan to attack?"

Maktus let forth a sigh. "That will largely depend upon your plans," he said. "I am not used to taking orders from any but my queen, but in this case, I understand the hands of the gods are involved. I will wait for several of the approaching provincial garrisons to arrive, but after that, I would like to move as quickly as possible. My armies grow impatient easily, and the longer we remain idle, the more likely our enemies are to discover that our forces will be larger than they expect. And to be honest, I do not like being away from my mate so long."

Kari looked at Grakin briefly and he smiled, though he didn't look directly at her. "Aeligos has an excellent plan," Kari said, turning back toward Maktus.

The rogue pulled the map and notes from his cloak pocket. "I have a written explanation of everything I'm about to tell you, and I'll give that to you after we're done," he said, to which the warlord nodded. "There was one major thing I didn't mention to you and your queen when we first met, because I wasn't sure it was true yet: we have someone inside Gaswell's fortress. She was able to pass us a wealth of information on when and where to strike, but I'll be honest with you: this entire plan of ours hinges on Gaswell sending out the bulk of his garrisons but staying in his fortress once battle is joined. If he leaves, it's going to be entirely up to you and your allies to crush him."

The warlord seemed impressed to hear that his guests had someone on the inside. "So you plan to remove him by means of subterfuge?" he asked, and he held up the map to study it. "Would you mind explaining your plan of attack? Perhaps I can help refine it should there be tactical flaws."

"Of course," Aeligos said. "The first thing we'll need to do is agree on a day when your army will engage his – not just move, but absolutely engage. If his army is still milling about outside his fortress when we attack, we're going to get pinned down and killed rather quickly."

Maktus nodded and produced a rough map of the island around Gaswell's fortress. He indicated an area and said, "If you are planning a covert strike, my scouts tell me this is an optimal spot for surveillance. It should take your group about four days to reach this point, and I trust you know how to get in once you're within striking distance. Once you leave the camp, I will give you three days before I mobilize my army. This will give you at least one more day to reach your destination before my forces encounter his, though it will more likely be a day and a half or two days. I assume you will attack under cover of night?"

"Yes," Aeligos said. "So you may want to march your forces so that you'll engage his just before nightfall."

Maktus grimaced; no commander liked fighting after nightfall, their soldiers' night vision be damned. "Not my favorite time to engage in battle, but the situation will demand it," he answered. "So once night falls and you are in position, what is your intent?"

"We'll be splitting into two groups: two of our number will go in through a sewer access here," the rogue said, pointing to the appropriate markings on the map. "The rest of us will be going to this second-story balcony. Our ally on the inside has indicated this is the weakest stretch of guard patrols, since there are no gates or ground-level entryways on that side of the castle. The second-story doors are easily worked from the outside, though, and our information indicates they're dormitories, so they should be empty just after nightfall, especially if there's a battle not far from the castle."

"Excellent," Maktus said, but his brow furrowed and he glanced at the sewer marking on the map. "Why do you have two going in through the sewers?"

"To free the prisoners," Kari piped up. She hoped she wasn't out of place speaking, but she felt like a fifth wheel and figured Aeligos would at least know she had paid attention when he explained the plan. "They have a kirelas-rir war wizard locked down there as far as we know, and there may be others. If we can release the war wizard, she may be able to help convince his army to surrender, or destroy them."

Maktus gave an appreciative nod. "Very good point," he said. "We had heard that he captured a kirelas-rir, but given how long ago that was and that we've heard nothing of her since, I assumed she had been killed. If not, however, she could indeed make a powerful ally as you've suggested. The might of the war wizards is well known even to our people. So then, I assume these young humans will be the ones going in through the sewers, since they cannot fly to your second-floor target entryway?"

362

"No," Aeligos said, and Kari saw that she wasn't the only one surprised. "Serenjols and Typhonix can carry the twins; the distance shouldn't be an issue. I don't think this is a good time to send them on their own to test them. There's too much at stake. With apologies for sending them into a sewer, I was thinking of sending the girls. Kari will be able to take care of anyone down there, and Sonja's magic should help with whatever they've done to subdue the kirelas-rir girl. There's no way this kirelas-rir war wizard is just sitting down there in shackles; she's got to be magically contained somehow or she would've freed herself by now."

"Good point," Sonja said. "Does that sound agreeable to you, Kari?"

Kari nodded. "As long as you're comfortable without my help," she said to Aeligos.

"I wouldn't say comfortable," he said with a wink, and Kari chuckled. "But I like our odds if we send you and Sonja to take care of the prisoners while the rest of us hunt down Gaswell. Even if we don't have the manpower to overpower Gaswell, once you and Sonja free the war wizard, the scales should tip in our favor anyway. Grakin, I think it's best if you stay behind, either here with Maktus and his people or else wherever we make our attack from. Any other time, I'd want a healer close at hand, but this is a do-or-die proposition. If it comes down to needing a healer once we're inside, we're pretty much finished."

"I understand," the priest said. "Is everyone in agreement on that, then?"

Kari nodded. She would never say so in front of his siblings, but she was much more comfortable with her mate staying behind where it was safe. Everyone else agreed as well, and Erik said, "Stay here with Maktus. I'm sure they'll have plenty for you to do once the battle has been joined."

"We certainly will," the shakna-rir commander said with a grim smile. "So that leaves you...six for the invasion of the keep itself? How do you plan to go about that?"

"Even with our companion's inside information, we're going on a few assumptions," Aeligos said, taking up his notes. "We'll be attacking just after nightfall, so there shouldn't be anyone in these bedrooms we're targeting for entry. My plan is to get us inside, and then have the others stay put while I explore the castle a bit. I should be able to find our insider, and once we know exactly where Gaswell is, we'll try to pin him down and capture him. But I have to find our insider first and speak to her before we go in."

"Why's that?" Erik asked.

Aeligos' mouth tightened and he sighed through his nose. He pulled

363

forth the original letter that Eryn wrote to him and gestured toward the end. "As much as Eryn said in this letter, it's what she *didn't* say that worries me," he said. He looked around at each of his siblings and friends, and Kari got the impression he was actually embarrassed to say what he was about to say. "Eryn always kisses me over the heart after we make love, and the fact that she didn't put that in her letter is a clear message that there's something else at the heart of all of this. It could be the demon you and Kari killed, or it could be something else entirely, but either way, this map and my plan are not complete yet. I need to talk to her, or we could end up walking into a trap."

"This is alarming," Maktus said. "Does it change my role in this matter?"

Aeligos shook his head. "No. Regardless of what's at the heart of this, our best chance of success still hinges on your people drawing out Gaswell's garrisons. It could be something very powerful in that castle or, like I said, it could've been the demon that Erik and Kari already killed. Based on timing, I think Eryn sent this letter before Kari and Erik finished their hunt, so if that demon was involved, that could be what Eryn was hinting at. In the end, as much as Eryn was putting me on alert for its presence, we can rest easier knowing that whatever it is, it's still been tentative to move even with an army at its command."

The warlord considered Aeligos' words for several minutes while the others remained silent. "This is a risky plan, but I see few other options outside of simply trying to overrun his forces and begin a lengthy siege of his castle," Maktus said. "Multiple battles or a lengthy siege may bring in further support for him from unknown quarters; this battle must be quick and decisive. With my queen's wishes to avoid the notice of the northern kingdoms, I think this is an acceptable risk. In the end, if you fail, we will be in no worse a position than we are now."

"We can handle this," Serenjols declared. "There will be little difference between this and what we did to Curlamanx, except that this castle is not full of demons."

"Curlamanx?" Maktus repeated.

Kari remembered the tale as she'd heard it during the Apocalypse and during the voyage on Karmi's Sword. She looked to Erik when he spoke. "A minor demon lord whose keep we infiltrated during the Apocalypse," he explained. "Jol is right, it's a fairly similar situation."

"I see. What are your plans once you capture Gaswell?" Maktus asked.

"We haven't given that much thought," Aeligos said. "We can turn him over to your people, or to the city council in Raugro, or even to the kirelas-rir to do with as they please. Ultimately, it's not important what happens to him as long as we remove him from power and keep him from starting another Apocalypse."

Erik regarded his brother curiously, and Kari wondered if he was thinking the same thing she was. Kari had been under the impression that Eryn was hired to assassinate Gaswell, but no one had ever said so outright. She wondered if it was possible that her slipping away to infiltrate Gaswell's army had been her and Aeligos' plan all along. It would certainly befit their devious natures.

"We'll make an effort to capture him. We should find out if he was working for another or even the sylinth, because if he was working for the demon, we need to know why and toward what end," Erik said. "After we capture him, we'll try to use a catapult or such to send a fiery signal to your forces that he's in custody and you can break off your attack. Then you can get in contact with his field commanders, tell them their leader and their home have been captured, and demand they surrender to you."

"I should be able to create a magical signal," Sonja offered.

The shakna-rir warlord stared at his guests, and by his expression he seemed satisfied with what he'd seen and heard. "See my quartermaster in the morning for any provisions you will need for your journey," Maktus said, rising to his feet. "Get a good night's sleep; you are perfectly safe while you are within our camp. In the morning I will receive updated positions on the coming garrisons from the provincial army, and then we will decide on a target day for you to leave and begin the final phase of your mission."

"Good evening, warlord," Aeligos said. Kari rose to her feet and saluted the shakna-rir warlord, and Erik and Typhonix did likewise. He returned their salute crisply and dismissed the companions out into the camp.

The Silver Blades were able to get hot meals from the cooks, and they chose a spot near the center of the camp to bed down for the night. The shakna-rir soldiers paid them little heed, and in the absence of their own campfire to provide light, the friends decided not to play cards. Instead, they passed the time chatting lightly, and made sure that all of them understood their roles in the coming attack.

~~*~*

It took only two days for three of the approaching garrisons to arrive in

365

the war camp, and they submitted themselves to Maktus' command. The warlord summoned the Silver Blades to his command pavilion and set them forth on their task, explaining that he was satisfied that he had enough men to confront the army his scouts had described. After gathering their things, Kari and her companions prepared to leave. Aeligos instructed the warlord that he should engage Gaswell's forces no more than four days later, and Maktus agreed and began issuing the orders through his subcommanders.

Grakin followed his companions to the edge of the camp, and he and Kari embraced. "I will never get used to this," he said.

"You're not supposed to," she replied, and she kissed the side of his snout. "Pray for us; we'll be back before you know it."

"You are always in my thoughts and prayers, my love, especially when you are far away," he said, touching her face gently.

Erik stepped beside Kari. "Don't overwork yourself trying to help everyone after the battle," he said to his brother. "Do what you can, but don't hurt yourself in the process."

"Worry not," Grakin said. He turned to the twins. "Be careful, and do as you are told. My siblings are experienced and will keep you safe as long as you let them lead you. Know that you go to protect others, and that what you do, you do for a righteous cause."

"We will. Be safe, and we will see you soon," Sherman said, and then the Silver Blades departed.

The group pushed themselves to travel quickly, and Sonja used a masking spell to keep them hidden from the few scouts that Gaswell had patrolling the lands around his keep. Erik deferred to Kari's tracking instincts, and with Aeligos' help she led them to the spot indicated on Maktus' map. Kari was cautious to avoid Gaswell's scouts completely, since she knew killing even one of the spies would alert Gaswell to the presence of a covert force. The Silver Blades traveled into the nights to keep ahead of schedule and pressed onward with urgency; they did not want to miss the chance that Maktus' attack would grant them. On the fourth day, they came to the edge of a cliff looking down over a massive lake, from which a river ran south.

On the cliff face to the east of them stood the fortress of Braxus Gaswell – apparently the same one that had been occupied by his ancestor during his ill-fated campaign to invade the Isle of Kirelia. From their vantage point, Aeligos could see that the castle was close in appearance to the one he had drawn based on Eryn's letter. Sonja continued to use a wide-area masking spell to keep their voices and firelights from being noticed. Despite Sonja's lack of confidence in her magical abilities, the strength of the spell and the concentration it required to keep it active for hours on end impressed her companions.

As night descended at their temporary camp, Aeligos slipped closer to the fort to examine the sewer outlet and the light from the second floor windows. He drew closer to the wall, and he could see there were few patrols along the battlements, just as Eryn had described. He bit his lip for a moment in thought, and then made a choice. He watched the patrols for some time to get a rough idea of how much time elapsed between the passing of each, and after the next patrol passed, he mentally counted out the minutes and then took wing. Aeligos flew up and landed lightly on the smooth-cut stone.

None of the moons had crested the castle itself, so the side he perched on was blanketed in deep shadows between the torches placed here and there. Aeligos glanced from side to side but, as he expected, there were no further patrols along the western wall. He looked from window to window on the second floor and then down into the courtyard. There was no one about, so he glided across to one of the balconies. He tucked his wings tight to his back and folded his cloak over them, and he readjusted them until they fit snugly underneath so he would appear to be a terra-rir to the casual observer. He pressed himself against the wall and then looked through the large glass double doors into what appeared to be a bedroom. With his enhanced night vision he saw that there was no one inside, the bed was empty, and the only light within was coming from the crack under the door exiting into the keep proper.

Aeligos examined the latch on the balcony door and reached a finger under his right bracer to draw out a set of fine lock picks and tools. He scanned the battlements for signs of the next patrol, still some time away, and he crouched down beside the door and tested the latch. He was hardly surprised to find it locked, and since he knew he didn't have the luxury of time, he set to opening it as quickly and quietly as possible. It wasn't a complicated lock, but picking it from the outside was more difficult. As he counted out the seconds, he knew he would be inside well before the next sentry walked past across the way. Soon enough he heard the satisfying *click* that told him the door was open. He depressed the latch slowly and carefully to make as little noise as possible, and once the door was open wide enough for him to slip through sideways, he did so. He closed and locked the door, and then he put his lock picks safely back under his right bracer.

The room was deathly quiet, so he crept silently on his toes to the doorway, crouched behind it, and listened for a while. There were no voices; no sound at all came from the hallway except for the gentle lapping of torch flames. He prepared to venture into the keep itself and his features began to shift. Though he wasn't as proficient with shapeshifting magic as Eryn, he was able to meld his wings into his back, lengthen his hair to a uniform warrior's style, and change his coloration to appear like an average terra-rir. Satisfied with the scout guise that would hopefully attract little attention, he moved to listen at the door again. Once certain there was no one close by, he gently swung the door open.

The hallway outside was indeed empty, and ran north to south by Aeligos' reckoning. The image of his map came up in his mind, and he guessed that Gaswell's throne room was to the south and closer to the center of the keep. Aeligos took a deep breath; if he were discovered it would make their mission impossible, whether he escaped or not. He couldn't afford to be detected at all and, thinking on that, he backed up and regarded a bookshelf in the bedroom. After a cursory glance, he found a promising title to take with him.

The corridor was quiet and warm as he made his way south, and soon he came to a four-way intersection. He thought of his map again, and realized that the keep was not nearly as large as it had appeared on paper: by his best estimate, if he turned left at the intersection, the throne room would be the first door on the right. Glad to have found a quick path to it, he thought about where the porter's quarters might be, and concluded they would be near the keep's main doors. He paused in his search, opened the book, and pretended to peruse its pages while he tried to remember if Eryn had mapped any of the stairways for him. He couldn't recall making any markings that looked like stairs, but assumed they were likely in the corners of the keep. A guard passed by him, but the rir paid him little heed. The hallway to his right appeared to have doors to more dormitories, so Aeligos continued straight ahead.

Farther down the first hallway he found another intersection, and on the right was a staircase leading down to the keep's first floor. He descended the stairs unhurriedly and passed another terra-rir dressed in finery, and Aeligos nodded to him absently while he continued to look at the book. When he reached the first floor, it appeared to be set up almost the same way as the upper level, and he retraced his direction to the north. He found the double doors leading out into the keep's bailey, and before them was a wide entry chamber that appeared large enough for the guards to build defensible fortifications and hold in the case of a breach. To each side of the open area were doorways, and Aeligos examined both briefly before he approached the one on the west side. There was a chip missing from the lower left corner of the door. With a grim smile, the rogue knocked lightly in a short, patterned sequence.

The door opened slightly after a moment, and Aeligos slipped in quietly, closed his book, and set it on a short table just inside. Soon Eryn's arms were around his neck, and she gave him a tight squeeze before she met his gaze evenly. "Where are the others?" she whispered, hardly paying any notice to Aeligos' shifted features.

"Safely outside, camped a distance away from the keep, waiting for the diversion that the shakna-rir will provide," he answered in hushed tones.

Eryn beheld him curiously. "What are you doing here?"

"I came to make sure I understood your instructions before I possibly lead my siblings to their deaths," he said. He watched as she locked the door and undressed. "What are you doing?"

"I've been cooped up in this castle avoiding any kind of personal contact for fear of being discovered," she said. "If your siblings aren't here and we have the luxury of time, I'm going to take full advantage of it."

Aeligos shook his head, but when Eryn climbed up on her bed, lay down, and beckoned to him, he did as she asked. He took his clothes off and joined her under the covers, and the two made love quickly and efficiently. There was no discussion about their differences or the issues that threatened to divide them; there was only the passion of two people who had been apart too long and who knew each other as intimately as was possible. Minutes later they were sitting on the edge of her bed, examining Aeligos' map and notes under the soft light of her lantern, and he gave her a couple of minutes to peruse everything he'd written.

"That's more or less everything I tried to tell you," Eryn said. "Gaswell is a good fighter, make no mistake, but he's been acting very strange lately. He seems to be having doubts about what he's been doing, but that's not enough to warrant stopping what we're here for. If the shakna-rir move this way, he'll send out his forces to meet them: the army has been idle for too long, and they're itching for a fight. But Gaswell won't go out with them. He's not that kind of leader."

"What about his lieutenants?"

"They never leave his side normally," she said. "They're not battlefield commanders, either. When you infiltrate the keep, they'll almost certainly all be together, unless Gaswell is sleeping. When do you plan to attack?"

"Tomorrow night, two hours after sundown," Aeligos answered.

"Sooner than I expected, good," she said with a decisive nod. "I'll try to get him into his throne room just after the dinner hour. If you can have

Typhonix and Serenjols start a melee in the barracks, it should keep them from being able to lock down the halls, and also keep the guards and soldiers off of you long enough for the rest of you to pin Gaswell in his throne room. The fool's ancestor didn't bother putting any back exits in the room, so once he's in there and you hold the doorway, he's not getting out."

"Perfect," Aeligos said. "What about the prisoners? We have Kari and Sonja going down there to release them."

"Prisoner," Eryn corrected. "It's just a kirelas-rir war wizard. I don't know why Gaswell is holding her, since he's made no mention of her people in the plans he shares freely. My best guess is he's holding her to make people think he's after Kirelia like his great-grandfather – which I assume you've heard all about from the other cities you've visited. Anyway, if Kari and Sonja can free this war wizard, she might kill Gaswell for you...from what I gather, she's extremely powerful. Let them know that they'll likely only find a single jailor if they come in through the sewer exit, and he's usually asleep at his post, so they shouldn't have much trouble. But they should be cautious anyway, since I'm not sure how the guards will react to the armies meeting, and there should be others in the lower level."

"All right, so that covers Gaswell," the rogue said. "What are we missing?"

"Tactically, nothing," she said with a shake of her head. She went silent for a moment, and Aeligos waited for her to complete the thought. "There was more to this at one time. I got here late in the formative stages, but there was a demon here when I joined Gaswell's forces."

The rogue nodded. "Kari and Erik killed a sylinth – one of those snake-demons – on the east side of the island...," he started, but he trailed off when she shook her head once again.

"I know, I've heard mention of that one as well, but there was another demon here...what are they called? Mallasti? The hyena-types...it was a female called Emma," Eryn explained. Aeligos tilted his head curiously in recognition and Eryn paused, but she stuck to her own line of thought instead. "It's been difficult to figure out just what she's been up to: obviously, I've never been welcome to be around when Gaswell and this *Emma* were speaking of whatever their plans were. I've been able to pick up clues here and there, though, and one of the conclusions I came to was that Emma doesn't really care about the results of this situation with Gaswell. He thinks she's going to provide him with soldiers from the underworld, but I know enough about thaumaturgy to know that demons can't just come here at will. Unless she can open a sizeable portal and maintain it, her promise to him is empty."

"Is she still here?" Aeligos asked.

"I don't think so," Eryn answered. "I've seen less and less of her ever since Kari and Erik killed the sylinth, and I could tell when they did because Emma's behavior changed slightly. The odd thing is: she seemed pleased. I think she's just been using Gaswell and that sylinth as a diversion while she looks for something. I've heard mention of something called 'Salvation's Dawn,' but referred to as an object, not a time. Does that mean anything to you?"

Aeligos shook his head. "Maybe we can ask Sonja, she's more versed in the arcane...."

"No," Eryn said with a shake of her head. "Not Sonja; Grakin. Whatever Salvation's Dawn is, it has something to do with the Temple of Archons. What I can't figure out is why Emma is here when the Temple is on Morikk, off the west coast of Askies. We need to know what Salvation's Dawn is, and why she's looking for it *here*."

"All questions for later," Aeligos said. "As long as you're reasonably sure that Emma isn't here anymore, we'll proceed with the plan tomorrow night."

Eryn shook her head negatively. "I'm almost positive she's not here. I suppose that's one thing we can thank the gods for. She's a sorceress, and a very powerful one. I don't know what the sylinth's place in all this was, but it was subservient to her. She started becoming more and more scarce after it died, and I haven't seen her for over a week – not since the first reports of shakna-rir battalions mobilizing from the north started to come in."

Aeligos was intrigued. "What has Gaswell been doing since then?"

"Biding his time," she answered, and then she chuckled briefly. "When the shakna-rir army gets close enough, he's going to let his army loose against them, because he thinks there's going to be a demon army flanking them. His scouts have confirmed that there's another force approaching them from the north, but if I know your sweet-talking ways..."

"It's the provincial army of the northwest, coming to reinforce the Tuvurasti," the rogue said with a grim smile. "I guess they have some people like us among their number passing along half-truths to throw Gaswell off-guard. It's funny, too, since I had considered suggesting that they make it seem like they're going out to confront the shakna-rir for that very reason."

Eryn smiled and kissed him, and the two giggled, pointedly reminded of how well they went together. "There's one other thing: I've never really

371

been privy to what's going on, since I've just been serving as the porter," the half-brys woman continued, "but being the porter means I can go all over the castle without ever really drawing too much attention. While I've always made sure to not be around when sensitive matters might have been being discussed, I've been close to Gaswell, his officers, and those demons enough to tell when something was going on just based on their behavior. And based on that and the fact that Gaswell's army has never mobilized except for maneuvers, I came to a conclusion after Emma disappeared."

She paused again, and Aeligos considered what it all meant. His eyes went wide. "This was all a dry run?" he asked.

Eryn nodded. "Someone in the underworld is testing us, Aeligos: testing our world's defenses and the reactions of the gods to a scenario like this. Emma really is after whatever Salvation's Dawn is, but she's just a pawn controlling other pawns. She was taking orders from someone else just as she was giving them to Gaswell and the sylinth. But this whole thing is just one giant diversion. Nothing else makes sense; it's like committing a petty crime to see what kind of reaction you get, so you know what to expect when you really hit a place hard. They touched this place in such a small way, and look at the reaction they got from the Demonhunter Order and the gods. Now they know what to expect if the Temple is their real target."

Aeligos nodded but gestured lightly with his hand. "The Temple's been sealed for as long as our people have been on this world; Salvation's Dawn must have something to do with unlocking it. I wouldn't worry too much about that at this point. As far as the demons testing our defenses, what else could anyone have done? At the very least, the demons needed to be driven out, and the threat of near-global war was no exaggeration. If things had been handled in typical fashion, and a massive war broke out…who knows? That may have been something the demons wanted. Or, more likely, it would've just helped mask what they were really up to, like when my siblings and I stopped Curlamanx."

"When you met Emma?" she prompted, surprising him only slightly.

"Yea," he said with a light sigh. "I don't know who she serves, but I think it's safe to say she doesn't serve Arku, seeing as she helped betray one of his vassals. She was a servant in Curlamanx' keep, and she knew exactly what I was up to when I started weaving my webs amongst his staff, working to turn them against him and against each other. But she never got in my way. In fact, she almost seemed happy to see what I was doing. Maybe she's just an agent of chaos, but if this was a dry run like you think, then her intentions likely run darker and deeper than merely chaotic. She's a lot more dangerous than I had assumed when I met her."

Eryn shook her head, her mouth tightened into a thin line. "I suppose as long as Emma is really gone, it's not important right now either way," she said. "But it's something we'll want to go over with Kari and Erik so they can tell the Order, and we'll want to get Grakin's insight on Salvation's Dawn and the Temple. Whatever's in there, it seems important enough to be of higher priority to the demons than a world war, and that can't be good. For the time being, I don't think we need to concern ourselves with the demons, though. We need to prioritize killing Gaswell and preventing this war the gods are leery about. Gaswell may have been part of a larger threat, but now he's just a man waiting to get killed, and I fully intend to oblige him."

"That makes two of us," Aeligos said. "Much as I like this island, I can think of a lot of other places I'd rather be. And--"

"And with your siblings should be one of those places," she interrupted, and she nudged him. "You'd best get going. I'll tell Gaswell to be in his throne room after dinner tomorrow for a tactical report from his officers, and then you can do your work. The castle should have little more than a skeleton crew defending it. The men know that beating the shakna-rir army will mean they've already effectively captured the island, so they're fully committed to winning this battle. On the same token, they know that if they get pinned inside the castle they'll be starved out or else crushed under a siege, so they won't fall back here unless all other options are exhausted. If Ty and Jol pin the guards in the barracks like I suggested, then all you need to do is bar the front door and the castle's own defenses will do most of your work for you. Don't expect to find me about when all this happens, I have to keep up appearances or they'll know they're being set up. And make sure you keep those kids out of harm's way!"

Aeligos kissed her. "I will. Thank you, Eryn; you've done a phenomenal job with this."

"Thank me when we're standing over Gaswell's corpse," she said, and he nodded. "Go."

Aeligos dressed himself and checked his appearance in the room's small mirror to ensure his disguise was still in effect. He took the book back with him and retraced his steps to the bedroom from which he'd entered, and he found it was still unoccupied. He put the book back into place on the shelf and then crouched by the balcony door to watch for the patrol to go by on the battlements. Since he'd need his wings to escape, he dispelled the shapechanging effect upon him. Once the disinterested-looking sentry made his way past, Aeligos counted out the minutes again, and slipped outside. He was careful to lock the door as he closed it behind him, and once the way was clear, he glided back over the outer wall and down into a thicket. He stayed hidden in the shadows until he was certain no one had seen or heard him, and then he picked his way back to the campsite cautiously. None of his companions noticed him until he stood among them, which nearly sent the group into a panic.

"Where have you been?" Erik hissed, trying to keep his voice down despite the masking spell and their distance from the keep.

"I was able to slip into the castle," the rogue answered.

"You did what?" his blue-eyed brother asked.

"I was able to get inside and locate Eryn, and she verified a lot of the information we went over in our strategy," Aeligos said. "She's going to get Gaswell into his throne room just after sundown tomorrow, and she went over some other things with me, too."

"Aeligos, what if you'd been captured?" Erik asked, fixing him with a stern gaze.

"I thought about that. Ultimately I decided that if I couldn't infiltrate that keep on my own, we wouldn't be able to as a group. Given the possibility that we all walk into a death-trap tomorrow night, I figured it was a worthwhile risk. Despite what Maktus said, the lot of us dying certainly changes things for *me*."

That drew laughs from his companions, and Erik conceded the point. "I suppose you're right," he said. "Did you find out anything new?"

"I was right about her letter," Aeligos said. "There was another demon involved here, but she seems to be gone now. There's a lot more to this situation that we have to review with your Order and with Grakin and his church, but right now none of it is really relevant. The demon has effectively abandoned Gaswell, so we're clear to proceed as planned. I found a spot to break in close to the throne room and the doors are easy enough to open, so I should be able to get us inside in less than a minute. One thing I'm not sure about is if they'll step up patrols after their forces engage the shakna-rir tomorrow. If they do, it may be a little trickier to slip in, but if not, it should be very easy. Eryn seems to think there won't be many soldiers about."

"So the demons *were* involved with Gaswell," Kari mused, and she glanced at Erik. When she turned back to Aeligos she added, "Did she mention anything about the dungeon?"

"Nothing specific about the dungeon itself, but she said there's usually only a single jailor sleeping down there, and that the kirelas-rir girl is the only prisoner," Aeligos answered. "I think it's still best if we send both of you down there, just in case there are more men than usual. Eryn suggested we have Ty and Jol go start a melee in the barracks to keep what soldiers and guards remain away from our backs while we engage Gaswell."

Typhonix backhanded his eldest brother in the chest lightly. "Something we're good for, finally," he joked, and Serenjols chuckled.

"Gaswell's throne room has no exits other than the main door," Aeligos said. "Eryn says once we pin him in there, there'll be no escape for him. We're only going to get one shot at this, so if he has more than just his two lieutenants with him, things could get hectic. What I'm going to recommend is that we have one of the twins watch the door, since with those greatswords they'll be able to keep anyone from rushing in. In the meantime, Erik, myself, and whichever of the twins isn't guarding the door will have to try to dispatch Gaswell and his men."

Erik considered his brother's words for a moment, a hand to his chin thoughtfully. "This is getting a little riskier than I like," he said. "If it's more than just Gaswell and his lieutenants in the throne room we could be outnumbered and overwhelmed fairly easily. Is it absolutely necessary for both Ty and Jol to go start trouble in the barracks?"

"Eryn seemed to think so, and I trust her judgment," Aeligos answered. "She said she won't be about when we attack, but once the fighting gets underway I don't imagine she'll be far from it. We can probably count on her help as well."

Erik looked to each of the others around him, gauging their reactions. "Anyone have any questions or concerns?"

"Maybe I should be in the throne room with you," Kari said. "If the dungeon only has one jailor, I'm sure Sonja can handle anything down there on her own, or with Katarina..."

Aeligos chewed his lip for a moment. "Again, we need to assume that the fortress is going to be a lot less sleepy once Maktus engages Gaswell's army," he said. "Eryn said that the war wizard down in the dungeon is very powerful. If we release her, she may end up killing Gaswell for us. If that's the case, it's more likely she'll be well guarded once the general alarm is raised through Gaswell's forces."

Erik blew out a sigh. "I don't think we can afford to second-guess ourselves or Aeligos' plan at this point," he said. He regarded Aeligos skeptically. "You're sure this other demon is gone?"

Aeligos shrugged. "Eryn seems to believe so. In any case, does it make a difference? We either go through with this or we abandon the plan and let things play out between Maktus and Gaswell. If she's still there, well, we have three demonhunters here."

Erik nodded and fixed his younger brother with a confident stare. "We're just going to have to be in top form."

The rogue grabbed his pack and began to dig through it, and he withdrew a pair of leather and metal gauntlets with katars affixed to them. Kari stared at the weapons in wonder: she'd never seen the young man fight with anything but his bare hands. Once he put them on, Kari watched him spar a bit with his elder brother. His style was mostly one of slapping parries, and he worked at getting inside Erik's range and throwing sweeping kicks. Erik proved a hard target to knock down, but any doubts Kari had as to Aeligos' ability in a melee were quickly dispelled. She knew that once he had his opponent on the ground, he was fully in control.

The night deepened and the group prepared to sleep in shifts. They gathered into a tight circle. In the absence of Grakin, Sherman took up the role of prayer leader, and together they prayed to the gods for the safety of their companions and the success of their mission. From the looks on everyone's faces when the prayers were complete, it was apparent that everyone was confident in their plan. Sleep came easily to them and, with the half-demon males keeping watch, the others took the first sleep shift.

Kari closed her eyes and let out a deep but quiet sigh. Aeligos had no doubt that her thoughts were fully upon Grakin, and he glanced at the fortress in the moonlight. Kari had made a promise that she would return to Grakin's side, and Aeligos silently made a similar promise to Eryn in his mind. No matter what befell them the following night, Aeligos was determined that he would either live or die with Eryn by his side.

Chapter XIX – Invasion

Dawn came, arid but breezy, and Gaswell's fortress stood silhouetted against the rising sun as it came over the eastern horizon. The Silver Blades waited patiently. Aeligos could smell war in the air, and he trusted in Maktus, so he and the others passed the day chatting quietly or practicing their fighting routines. Aeligos knew that nightfall would bring either stunning victory or crushing defeat, and he steeled himself, knowing the end of their mission was upon them. Come the following morning, they would either be making their way home, or Maktus and his armies would be doing everything they could to salvage the will of the gods.

They ate a light dinner. No one wanted to be weighed down by food or have too much in their stomachs to contest with their anxiety. Every eye in their camp watched the sun retreat over the western horizon. The hour was nearly upon them, and Aeligos almost willed the sun to disappear: for the waiting to at last be over and the time for decisive action to come. As the sky faded to pink and purple and finally to a deep bruise-blue, he prepared to head to the castle, and his companions offered each other last words of encouragement and hugs of support. And then night fell, and Kari and Sonja broke off from the rest of the group and picked their way along the edge of the cliff to where Aeligos told them the sewer entrance stood.

The land was dark, as the moons had not yet ascended, and the others followed Aeligos toward the castle wall. He had them hunker down in some brush while he crept closer and watched the sentries. Like his previous visit, he watched the patrols along the western rampart, but to his surprise, there was no change in the frequency of passing guards. He watched for a short while to be certain, and once satisfied that he and his companions would have ample time to pass without drawing attention, Aeligos returned to the others and beckoned for them to follow him as quietly as possible. They moved slowly given the weight of the larger brothers' armor, and crouched below a tree fairly close to the wall while they waited for the next patrol to pass. Once the terra-rir guard passed by, Aeligos motioned for patience and mentally counted out the minutes, and then he beckoned for Typhonix to pick up Sherman and follow him.

They flew up and over the wall, and the burly blonde showed little strain in carrying the armored human male in flight. Aeligos scanned the courtyard quickly before they glided over to the balcony he'd visited previously. He drew out his lock picks and tools and had the door open in moments, and he ushered his brother and human friend through. He had them crouch down in the dark of the bedroom, which was empty just as it had been the night before, and the rogue softly closed the balcony door and watched for the next patrol to pass. A minute and a half after the guard walked past, Aeligos flew back to the top of the wall and beckoned for Serenjols to carry Katarina and follow, and he led his eldest brother across the way to the room. He repeated the process for Erik, and soon all of them were safely inside.

Aeligos was concerned with the noise they had made: Erik, Ty, and Serenjols' armor was heavy and far from quiet, but the sound of armored men moving about the castle seemed to have attracted no attention. He watched one last sentry pass before he was satisfied that their entry had gone unnoticed, and he regarded his companions in the dark for a moment. The humans were having obvious trouble seeing in the near-lightless room. He motioned for all of them to remain still and silent and he opened the door into the hallway slowly.

The corridor was empty, so Aeligos altered his appearance and stepped out into the hall as if nothing was amiss. He headed south and then turned east at the first intersection and passed close by what he believed was the door to the throne room. There were no voices coming from within, which he found curious; he expected Gaswell and his lieutenants to be there. He put a hand to his chin thoughtfully but continued walking so as not to mark himself as a conspicuous target for any patrolling guards. He concentrated on his memory of the castle map in comparison to where he stood, and began to wonder if any of his notations were wrong and Eryn had merely missed it. She had said the map was accurate, so he was hesitant to second-guess their plan. Instead he made his way to the eastern hallway that ran north to south. It was entirely possible that Gaswell and his men were simply still having dinner and their plans had been delayed. He pushed down his anxiety and made a full circuit of the keep interior's upper level before he came back around to the dormitory where his companions were hiding.

He passed only a single guard who paid him little heed. Once he was satisfied that the hallway was empty again, he ducked back into the room with his friends. They regarded him for a moment, but he simply shrugged and motioned for them to remain patient. Espionage was a business that required a lot of nerves and patience, and a surgical strike such as the one they were performing was no different. Aeligos had done such missions many times in his fairly short life, but he knew his siblings and certainly his two human companions had not. He hoped they had the will and the calm to sit tight as long as needed, and he let out a silent sigh.

His ears perked up when he heard footsteps approaching down the hall, and he motioned for the rest of his group to remain absolutely still and quiet. As he feared, the footsteps stopped outside the room, and he rose to his feet silently and pressed himself to the wall beside the door. Someone depressed the latch and the door swung open, and a terra-rir stepped in and reached for the lantern beside the portal. In the blink of an eye, Aeligos sprang into action. He drove his knee into the man's groin, blasting the air from him in a rush, and then drove him face-first into the floor. Aeligos kicked the door closed and back-mounted the man, wrapping himself around the man's prone form and bringing his arm across the man's throat. Instinctively the terra-rir reached for the Aeligos' arm, so the rogue slipped his right arm under the man's armpit and behind his head. Aeligos rolled his victim over and squeezed with both his arms and his legs, choking the life out of the rir male. Aeligos held tight until his victim stopped thrashing and for several seconds after, and then rolled him back over.

Aeligos worked to steady his breathing as he stared at the still form before him, and after a moment he checked the side of the rir's neck and found a pulse. He bit his lip, unsure if he should kill what could be a guard, one of Gaswell's lieutenants, or even Gaswell himself, for all he knew. He decided against it, and instead pulled a small pair of manacles from his belt and locked the man's hands behind his back. He tied a short string around the end of the rir's snout so he would be unable to do more than groan, and then carefully dragged the unconscious form around to the other side of the bed and left him there.

The others regarded Aeligos when he returned near the door, crouched in the darkness, waiting, and Aeligos hardly registered that it had to have been the first time the twins saw him nearly kill someone. He trusted they would remember what they were told: that they were there to kill, but to do so in defense of others, and that they should not feel bad for those whose lives they took. Aeligos kept his thoughts focused, and no other footsteps approached in the hallway as the long minutes passed so silently that he could hear his pulse in his ears. He sat mentally counting out the minutes, but returned to their unconscious guest's side when he heard the captive stir. The rir's eyes came up and widened in surprise when they met Aeligos', and the rogue put a finger to his pursed lips and displayed one of his katars. The man nodded in understanding, and Aeligos patted him on the shoulder.

The rogue returned to the door and slipped quietly through it and out into the hallway once more. He repeated his earlier circuit in reverse, and paid particular heed to the voices he heard as he passed each door along the hallway. When he came around to the door he expected to find Gaswell and his men behind, he was alarmed to find there were still no voices. He briefly considered going down to find Eryn and ask if the general was hiding elsewhere or if his map had been wrong, but he was nervous about exposing himself to any more scrutiny than he had to. He ultimately decided it was a worthwhile risk: he needed to see if there was significant traffic between where his group was hidden and the barracks anyway. If Typhonix and Serenjols were spotted before they made it to the guard quarters, it would spell disaster: the general alarm would be raised, and they would be attacked from all directions, pinned down hopelessly in the hallways. Aeligos made his way quickly but unhurriedly to the southwest stairs, descended them, and listened for the sound of anyone approaching.

He found the lower level quiet – almost spooky – and he looked around briefly before he made his way northward toward the front door of the keep. He cursed his luck when he reached the entry chamber and found Eryn's door ajar with no light coming from within. He took a deep, steadying breath and opened the outer door to the bailey, and the two guards stationed outside turned to regard him as he looked around. "Any trouble to report?" Aeligos asked, keeping his voice steady and with an edge of authority to it.

"No, sir," said one of the guards. "The sentries up on the battlements have seen no one approach. The fighting is still a safe distance from our walls."

Aeligos nodded but said nothing, and he closed the door and blew out a quiet sigh as he rolled his eyes. He nearly laughed at how difficult Gaswell was proving to find in such a small keep, but he kept his wits about him and made his way back to the upper level. He walked a last circuit around the upper level, but lay down and pressed close to the southeast stairs when he heard voices approaching around a corner. He knew that if they came to the stairs or if anyone else came up, he would have to fight his way through, but he held his breath and remained perfectly still, his nerves hardened to icy steel.

The voices turned down the westbound passage, and they were speaking about the battle and the likelihood that fighting would reach the keep itself. Aeligos let his breath out in a quiet sigh, rose silently to his feet, and crept to the corner. Looking down the hallway he saw three terra-rir males enter the suspected throne room, and he ducked back around the corner, pressed his back to the wall, and gave a silent prayer of thanks to the gods. He wasn't sure it was Gaswell and his lieutenants, but the fact that *someone* had entered the room dispelled his growing suspicion that it was naught but a storage area. At the very least, he and his group would find *someone* to fight in there, and if all else failed, they might get some answers out of the wounded after.

Aeligos made his way back to the bedroom his siblings and human friends were hiding in and slipped quietly through the door. They looked up to him expectantly and he motioned for them to be as quiet as possible and follow him. They followed him from the room, and Aeligos led them to the southwest stairs, where he crouched down. He tilted his head down and tried to concentrate on any approaching sounds, but the castle was still and quiet. The others gathered close and Aeligos kept his voice down to a whisper.

"Ty, Jol, head down these stairs and then north," he said, gesturing the direction they had just come from. "Turn right at the first intersection, and the barracks will be on the left. I've no idea how many soldiers and guards will be in there, so be careful."

The two larger males nodded and began to make their way down the stairs, trying their best to be quiet in their heavy metal armor. Once they disappeared down the stairwell, Aeligos led the rest of the group back to the intersection and turned right. They crept up to the door on the south wall that Aeligos indicated, and the rogue spent a few moments listening at the door before he dispelled his alteration magic and nodded to Erik. The blue-eyed male moved to the door, took a deep breath, and then threw it wide and stepped in.

~~*~*

Kari and Sonja pried the grating off the end of the sewer slowly. The metal bent and gave under the combined strength of the two women, and they were mindful of how much noise it could make if they worked too quickly. Once free, they carried the grate to the side and laid it quietly against the pipe, and then they made their way into the dark interior of the square-cut stone passage. The stench was nearly overwhelming, and they had to give themselves a few moments to acclimate themselves to breathing as sparingly as possible. It wasn't quite as bad for Kari: she had grown up on the streets of Solaris and her nose had smelled far worse on her own forays through that city's sewer systems.

The sewer exit extended slightly over the cliff and was several hundred feet from the castle wall by her best guess. It would take them some time to get inside, assuming the dungeons didn't extend beyond the foundation

381

of the castle walls. Sonja explained it was likely the sewer was slightly graded and ran out through the foundation at exactly one point; she expressed hope that the sewer wasn't graded too steeply and that their climb through the muck wouldn't be any more difficult – or disgusting – than it already seemed. Kari found it odd that the sewer was large enough for people to walk through, but she assumed it was meant as an emergency exit should the castle be captured.

They picked their way along carefully, thankful that no disgusting flow engulfed their lower legs, but the slick remains of passing water and waste made the footing treacherous. Their eyes began to glow softly as they passed into the deeper darkness of the tunnel, and Kari put her hands high on the smooth-cut walls to brace herself in case her feet slipped even slightly. One misstep could easily send her tumbling into Sonja, and with the floor being slippery, it was possible they wouldn't be able to stop themselves and slide right out of the pipe and down onto the rocks far below. She kept her mind on the task at hand, and after a lot of slow progress, Sonja said they had likely made it to the outer wall of the castle. They stopped in their travels when Kari spotted a corpse ahead.

It was the body of a male shakna-rir – a scout judging by his armor – and Kari wondered how he'd gotten there. Sonja started to move past her to examine the body, but Kari stopped her, looking to the walls and the ceiling suspiciously. "What's wrong?" the larger woman whispered.

"Might've been a trap that got him," Kari returned quietly. "If I was going to put a sewer running out of *my* castle, I'd put some nasty surprises for anyone that tried to come in that way."

Sonja nodded and closed her eyes, and Kari watched her curiously. Sonja began to wave her finger in the air in front of her, tracing a symbol in a softly glowing amber line, and when she opened her eyes, they had changed from their normal glowing red to the same hue as the glyph. Kari waited patiently while Sonja examined their surroundings. Sonja shook her head after a minute and the amber color faded from her eyes, leaving the scarlet once more. "My incantation didn't reveal any sections of the walls, floor, or ceiling that move," she whispered.

"That's a handy trick," Kari said. "Maelstrom teach you that?"

Sonja shook her head. "Aeligos did."

That came as a surprise. Only Sonja had spent any time practicing the arcane arts during the voyage, so Kari expected she was the only one who could. Then again, she thought, if Eryn had used the arcane arts to disguise herself, it wasn't at all surprising that Aeligos knew a bit of the arts himself. "I had no idea he practices magic," she commented.

"Only a little," Sonja returned. "Just practical things that help with his espionage."

Kari nodded and gestured for her friend to wait while she crawled forward slowly. She ignored the feeling of the muck on her hands and approached the corpse cautiously. She looked for any sign on the walls or ceiling that might indicate what killed him. The walls near the body were smooth-cut stone, and she saw no holes that might suggest mechanical traps, so she examined the ceiling, keeping Sonja's words in mind, and saw nothing on the smooth stone above that would suggest any sort of mechanical trap, either. Finally, she moved up next to the body, and the first thing she noticed was the buildup of waste against his back, which faced farther up the tunnel. She looked to his faded eyes and surmised that he'd been dead for several days, and she gave him only a cursory examination as she suspected what had killed him. Kari beckoned for Sonja to approach, and she looked farther up the tunnel before turning her attention fully to her friend.

"I think he might've tried to escape this way, and poisoned himself to avoid capture when he realized he was trapped," Kari whispered. "I don't see any wounds, and the muck piled up against him says he's been down here a while. They probably didn't bother following him, figuring he'd have to come back out or they'd kill him when he came out of the pipe."

Sonja nodded. After offering a silent prayer for the fallen scout, the two continued along. Soon they came to a point where there was a hole in the ceiling, though it wasn't wide enough to climb up. They didn't remain underneath it for long, as Kari quickly realized what it was for, and they made their way farther up the tunnel, which began to shrink in size. They passed several more holes in the ceiling, until they finally came to a wall marking the end of the tunnel. The wall was wet and smelled of urine and worse, and even as they stared at it, a small amount of sewage trickled down its face. The ceiling was cut away, leaving barely enough room to climb up, and Kari looked at her friend. Kari held her hands cupped before her, and Sonja stepped within them, reached up, and grabbed the top lip of the wall, which – as they expected – turned out to be a dam of sorts. Once Sonja had a firm grip, she nodded down at Kari, and the terra-dracon woman climbed deftly up her friend's side until she could grasp the lip of the wall.

They pulled themselves up at the same time and glanced into the dungeon. Before them was a small rivulet of water mixed with the waste from the dungeon cells: the water apparently ran over the wall when the level reached a certain point. The dungeon didn't appear extensive, as though it were only a small part of the lower level, and from their vantage point Kari could see a door which led out, and six cells, three to a side. A lone guard sat in a chair with his feet up on a table, and over the sound of dripping water, Kari could hear the soft drone of a sleeping rir.

Kari motioned with her eyes for Sonja to stay put, and the larger woman nodded and braced her back and wings against the wall behind her to take some of the strain off of her arms. Kari pulled herself up silently and slipped into the cold and disgusting water before them without a sound. Kari regarded the cells around the room for a moment: only one of them was occupied, and the person laying within was still and silent. Kari moved farther out and stepped lightly and silently from the water onto the drier cut stones of the dungeon floor. She crept on her toes toward the guard, and after what seemed an entire painstaking minute, Kari gripped the sleeping man's chin and the back of his head and snapped his neck effortlessly. She grabbed the corpse and turned his chair so the body would lie up against the wall without sliding to the floor.

Kari beckoned Sonja to join her, and her friend hoisted herself up and approached as quietly as she could. "Watch the door a moment," Kari whispered. Sonja muttered a quiet incantation, and a massive two-handed sword appeared in her outstretched hands. Kari nodded, impressed, and made her way over to the occupied prison cell.

Kari examined the lock for only a moment before she returned to the guard's corpse and rifled through his pockets for the key. Once she unlocked the cell door, she approached the girl slowly and noted that her eyes were slightly open but glazed over. The girl was gaunt, as if she had scarcely eaten in weeks, she was lying in her own filth, and were it not for the pool of saliva gathering under her face, Kari would have suspected she was dead. Kari grimaced and wondered what had prompted the general to do such a thing to a pretty young woman. She continued to examine the prisoner. A touch to the girl's smooth neck proved that she was quite alive: her skin was cool but not deathly cold, and Kari could feel a weak but steady pulse. She brushed the young girl's fluorescent green hair back from her face and gave her a gentle shake, but there was no response. Kari peeled back one of the girl's eyelids and her blue eyes were dilated and didn't appear to be focused on anything. For a moment Kari wished Grakin was there.

She examined the shackles about the girl's wrists, ankles, and neck, and recalled what Erik said about the girl being magically subdued. She tried the cell key on the shackles to no effect. "Sonja!" Kari rasped, trying to get the woman's attention without yelling for fear there were other

384

guards outside the door.

"What is it? Oh, gods," Sonja said as she approached and saw the state the girl was in. "What did they do to you, sweetie?"

"These shackles are probably magical, do you think you can get them off?" the terra-dracon woman asked.

Sonja shook her head. "I don't have any spells of that sort yet," she said. "If she were trapped behind a dampening field or something, I could bring it down, but I don't have anything that would break locks. Usually we rely on Aeligos to take care of this sort of thing."

Kari patted her friend on the shoulder; she didn't want to give Sonja the impression that she wished someone else was with her. Kari moved over to the guard's table and found there were utensils left behind from his evening meal. She grabbed them up quickly and rushed back to the cell. Sonja regarded her curiously, and Kari smiled grimly. "You pick up a few things when you live on the streets," she said. "Keep watching the door, it'll take me a few minutes to impro...eh, make lock picks out of these. I should be able to get her out of these."

Sonja nodded and returned to the doorway. Kari had only been working for a few moments when Sonja returned. "It doesn't sound like they're coming this way, but I hear voices out there," she said. "Work as quickly as you can."

Kari nodded but said nothing. She worked deftly, bending the outer tines of the fork to specific angles, and she used a seam in the stone wall to bend the knife's blade slowly without breaking it. She moved to the other side of the cell so she could see Sonja, and every so often she would look up to see if the scarlet-haired woman heard anyone approaching. Once she had her improvised tools, Kari began trying to pick the locking mechanisms of the shackles. She moved slowly to make sure she didn't break them: she knew she would get no second chance. Her eyes widened in shocked joy as the first of the five locks popped open, and when she held up a single finger to Sonja, the scarlet-haired woman smiled. Kari moved on to the second and checked the girl's eyes for any sign of life, but she guessed whatever magic the shackles held would not be broken until she'd gotten several or all of them open. Biting her lower lip in concentration, Kari set to her task once more.

"Kari," Sonja called softly.

Without hesitation the terra-dracon woman put down her improvised picks, drew her swords, and moved toward the wall beside the door. She could hear footsteps coming down the stairs, and Kari motioned for Sonja to wait for her lead. A single terra-rir male came through the door and chuckled. He nudged the "sleeping" jailor, but he backed up a step in shock when his companion's head flopped limply to the side. He spun around and came face to face with Kari, and she drove her scimitars up and under his ribs, puncturing both lungs and leaving the man without an ounce of air to even groan with. She drove him backwards and into one of the empty cells, and she worked to lay the body down as quietly as possible. When she turned around, Sonja was staring at her, clearly surprised by the brutality of the kill.

"Do you have any spells that make noise, maybe sound like people talking?" Kari asked her quietly. "If there's others out there but they hear voices, they might think the guards are chatting. Otherwise, they might wonder why the relieved guard isn't coming out."

Sonja snapped free of whatever she was thinking. "I'll see what I can manage," she said, and she closed her eyes to concentrate.

Kari returned to the kirelas-rir girl and took up her improvised tools. The second wrist-shackle popped off after only a minute, but when Kari looked at the neck and ankle locks, she realized they were different and would probably prove more difficult. Suddenly she heard the soft murmur of voices from outside the cell, and she took up her blades and prepared for battle. She saw only Sonja, and she realized her friend must have thought of an appropriate spell.

She began working on the locks again, and to her elation, the ankle locks popped open even more easily than the wrist locks, but the girl still showed no sign of coherence. With grim determination, Kari swept the girl's hair to the side and began working on the neckpiece. Sonja backed over near the cell after a minute and Kari looked up, but Sonja motioned that she heard no other sounds from outside. With a nod, Kari set back to her task, and after several more minutes the final lock popped open.

She started to give the kirelas-rir girl a shake, but as soon as her hand touched the girl's shoulder, Kari's brain caught fire. She stumbled back out of the cell clutching her temples, and she was only just coherent enough to notice that Sonja was likewise affected. Kari fell to her knees in excruciating pain, and the shattering of her mind was worse than when she fought Ressallk. The depths of unconsciousness threatened to overtake her, but she fought the urge to scream, knowing that whatever happened, they could not alert the guards or all would be lost.

~~*~*

"What is this?" barked one of the men when Erik stepped in through

386

the doorway holding his blades. There were five terra-rir males in the room: two who appeared to be guards, two others dressed in intricately etched plate mail, and the fifth apparently the general himself. The general was dressed in a light-looking suit of armor with a crimson cloak draped over it, and he drew a pair of longswords as Aeligos and the others stepped in behind Erik. Soon four faced five, all had their weapons drawn, and they glared at each other for a moment before anyone moved.

"Intruders! Intruders in the castle!" one of the guards yelled.

"I am Erijinkor Tesconis, Demonhunter of Zalkar, and by his authority I have come to remove you from power, Braxus Gaswell," Erik said. "Stand down, and you and your men will be spared. Offer resistance and I have the authority to kill every last one of you."

"Boldly spoken, demonhunter, but do you have any idea what you face? Your army is in the process of being crushed by my underworld *friends*, and you fools have walked right into Emma's trap!" Gaswell said.

"He's bluffing," Aeligos whispered to Erik.

"If I were you, I'd be more worried about the trap *you* just walked into, Gaswell," Erik snarled, and he approached their enemies.

"Their god holds no power on this island! Take them alive, my brothers; we don't know if Emma's trinket is among them!" Gaswell yelled. His guards rushed to the attack, and his two lieutenants moved forward after the briefest of delays. The guards carried longswords but didn't have their shields with them. Each of the lieutenants wielded a longsword. Gaswell backed up behind his men and watched for an opportunity to join the fray.

Erik twirled his swords and beckoned for the lieutenants to come for him, and then he nodded his head toward the general. "Watch the corners, don't let them pin you! Katarina, the door; Aeligos with me!" he barked, and the rogue stalked around his brother's left side.

The room wasn't very large, and Aeligos and his companions worked to keep their enemies before them to prevent being flanked or allowing anyone to escape to find more guards. One of Gaswell's lieutenants engaged Erik, but the other moved along with one of the guards to engage the obviously young and inexperienced human to his right. Erik distracted the officer before him with a quick one-two combination and the strength of his blows clearly surprised the rir, but even as his longsword was parried, Erik turned it over in his hand and stabbed it backward at the lieutenant who had engaged Sherman.

Sherman backed up initially, but once Erik's attack drew the lieutenant's attention away, he swung his two-handed blade with a mighty chop. He surprised the guard, who expected him to take advantage of the lieutenant's distraction: the human kept his eyes on the lieutenant but swung for the guard, a trick Serenjols taught him and made him practice extensively during their long boat trip. The guard tried to thrust under Sherman's swing, but was shocked to find the greatsword descending for him and not his officer, and he collapsed in a heap, slammed with a crushing blow.

Erik executed a cross-pattern attack routine, something he had seen Kari do several times in practice, and he finished with a reckless spinning double-chop. It had looked impressive when Kari did it as part of her routine, and he expected the two lieutenants wouldn't know what to make of it. He was correct in his assumption: both were forced back a couple of steps and he came back to his ready position before them. He marked each with a baleful glare and stalked forward slowly to re-engage.

Aeligos blocked a swing from the guard on Erik's left, and he pushed the blade high and attempted to trip the man, going down to one hand and foot to sweep across with his other leg. The guard stumbled but didn't fall, but Aeligos followed him, not giving him even a moment to ready himself before burying him under a multitude of thrusts. The katars didn't have an optimal reach for engaging in combat with longswords, but Aeligos wasn't looking to kill his enemy, merely push him back and distract him. He spread his wings out suddenly to further distract the man, and then he turned and drove one of his katars deep in the side of the lieutenant beside him.

Working in tandem, Erik stabbed the same lieutenant Aeligos did, and ran the man through with his longsword. He continued his momentum, driving his longsword to push the man back, and Erik spun to bring his scimitar around and knock the thrust of the other lieutenant harmlessly wide. He drew his longsword from the gut of the dying one, but saw Sherman moving toward Gaswell. Erik shouted for the young human to wait.

Sherman didn't even hesitate once the guard fell before him. He drove the tip of his massive blade through the belly of the man's armor and then stepped over the corpse and brought the weapon up before him once more. He paid Erik's warning shout little heed, but made his way for Gaswell, his features hardened into a scowl. "Fool!" he shouted. "May the Armored Shepherd take you by my hand!"

Aeligos crouched and spun to face the guard once more. He feigned a high lunge but instead rolled forward and kicked out the man's leg. He brought his knee up to deflect the weight of the guard as he fell atop the

388

rogue, and Aeligos wrapped his legs around the man. The guard's sword clattered harmlessly to the floor, and Aeligos stabbed his katars in an alternating pattern up each of the man's sides until silver blood flowed warm and thick over his hands and out of the guard's mouth. The man was dead even before Aeligos rolled the corpse off of himself and got to his feet. He turned to see Katarina bringing her sword up to fend off a roving guard attacking her from the hallway, and Aeligos moved to help the young woman.

Sherman chopped at the general with a cleaving, overhead swing, but Gaswell deftly sidestepped and countered. He came in quickly with a combination of short swings and thrusts, and stabbed Sherman hard through the right shoulder. Sherman had never sparred with either Kari or Erik, and the quickness and deceptiveness of the general's movements overwhelmed him. Sherman yelped in pain, backed up, and tried to lift his sword to attack, but the blade was too heavy with a wounded shoulder. He cast the blade aside and drew the longsword that he wore at his hip, thankful that Erik had impressed on him the need for a backup weapon, and Sherman tried to fend off the general with his good left arm. He was far from proficient with his left hand, however, and found himself under a flurry from the more experienced terra-rir male.

Erik tried to help Sherman, but the remaining lieutenant circled to keep himself between the demonhunter and the injured human. The lieutenant pressed his attack. He wasn't much of a threat with his one blade against Erik's two, but he executed a brilliant feint to draw Erik's guard up on his left side, and with the half-demon's weapon out of position, the lieutenant slid next to his companion's corpse. He picked up the second longsword that belonged to his dead partner, and then he grinned and beckoned for Erik to attack once more.

"Coming through!" Aeligos yelled, and Katarina's instincts took over: she hopped back a half step and threw an arcing chop at the guard in the doorway. She caught her swing before it dipped below her waist. The cut was wicked enough to push the guard back, and Aeligos slid through the doorway at their feet and came up on the guard's side. Together the two pinned the guard in the doorway, but he was no green recruit: he accepted a stinging jab from one of Aeligos' katars while he ducked into the room to avoid Katarina's next attack.

Sherman slapped at the general's taunting thrusts, but as Gaswell pushed in harder, the young man panicked. He attempted to strike off the general's head, but Gaswell easily parried and twisted his blade around and under the human's, and pulled it from his feeble grip. Sherman attempted to back up, but the general rewarded his bravery with a stab to his other shoulder, and then he hacked brutally at Sherman's belly. The longsword tore through the chainmail, and Sherman screamed as he was nearly disemboweled. He grasped at the wound, fell to his back, and curled into a fetal position.

Erik squared off with the lieutenant and tried a few simple combinations to gauge how skilled the man was with two weapons. He found that his enemy had not picked up the second sword just for show, and Erik grimaced: Sherman wouldn't last long against the general. When he heard his companion yell in pain, Erik steeled himself, knowing the lieutenant would come in when he was distracted. Instead, Erik crouched as black flames burst forth from his skin, and he drove his shoulder forward into the rir's midsection. The lieutenant's swords glanced harmlessly off of Erik's plate armor, and the demonhunter grabbed hold of the lieutenant and held him in an incinerating grasp. Within moments their armor began to glow with absorbed heat, and the scent of searing flesh filled the air. The lieutenant screamed out in agony, and Erik dropped him to the floor and rushed to Sherman's aid.

Katarina saw her brother fall, but she kept her wits about her just as she'd been drilled to do so many times by Serenjols and Typhonix. She turned as if to approach her brother, but then she bounded three steps to her right and swung sideways at her opponent. The reach of her great sword's swing drove the guard back toward Aeligos, and the guard didn't realize his error until it was too late. Aeligos punched one of his katars through the guard's liver, and then he finished the man off with three more well-placed punches across the chest, with one last strike to the throat. Katarina turned to help her brother, but she saw that she couldn't stop Gaswell in time.

"Alarm! Alarm! Intruders in the castle!" came a shout from the hallway. Aeligos found that curious, but he moved to chase after whoever had yelled. He was stood up straight at the doorway by an arrow that whistled past his face and took down the man who'd shouted. Aeligos looked east down the corridor and saw Eryn standing at the intersection with her bow, no longer in the guise of a terra-rir woman. She nodded to him and notched another arrow, and she began scanning in all directions down the hallways.

Aeligos rushed to the intersection where the dead man lay, and then south toward the stairwell. Far below he could hear the sounds of a melee, and he smiled grimly: Typhonix and Jol were doing as they were asked. He rushed back to the intersection, whistled to gain Eryn's attention, and made a sharp gesture to ask her if more guards would be coming from the bailey.

She shook her head and made a gesture in return that clearly said she had barred the door, just as he had expected. Aeligos smiled, wanting to rush down and kiss the woman. Instead, he made another gesture to ask her if there was any sign of Emma. He let forth a sigh of relief when Eryn shook her head negatively.

Erik rushed sideways and threw a reckless double-chop at Gaswell to chase the general away from Sherman before he could perform a coup de grace. Erik's eyes were full of fury as he stood up before Gaswell, but the general simply backed away a few steps. "What do you hope to accomplish here, fool?" Gaswell asked, and he began to circle his enemy. "My death will change nothing, another will simply take my place."

"On the contrary," Erik said, crossing his swords before his chest, "your army is in the process of being completely demoralized by a much larger and stronger shakna-rir and human force. That army you think your demon allies have sent from the north...those are *our* allies. Your army is doomed. Don't you get it? The demons betrayed you. That's what they do. They got you to try to start a war for them, and then they left you. You're on your own, and your bloodline and your foolish quest both end here."

Gaswell glanced away however briefly, and Erik could see reality had sunk into the man. But then the general looked up and said, "My bloodline, perhaps, but the quest I was appointed to will not end with me. If Emma's found what she was looking for...you're all doomed." He tested Erik with a complex routine of diversionary, half-hearted swings and thrusts, and his more pointed attacks came in at odd angles. He was no slouch: his fighting style was similar to Kari's, and for a moment Erik wished that Kari was with him, if for nothing more than to see her pit her style and skill against the general.

Katarina dragged Sherman to a safe corner behind the door, and she knelt down and pulled up the shirt of his chainmail to survey the damage. "Oh, gods!" she cried, and she tore off a portion of her brother's tabard and pressed it to the bleeding wound on his belly. It was deep: the flesh and even the muscle were cut partway through, but she was by no means a healer like Grakin and couldn't tell how substantial the damage truly was. At the very least Sherman hadn't lost consciousness and no blood was coming forth from his lips. She took that as a good sign.

Aeligos returned to the doorway and surveyed the scene before him quickly. He rushed over to dispatch the lieutenant his brother had burned. The man was struggling to his knees in pain and offered little resistance as Aeligos gripped his head and gave a sharp twist, breaking his neck with a satisfying crack. Aeligos gave Erik only a cursory glance as his brother squared off with the general, and the rogue made his way over to Katarina and Sherman. Aeligos was no healer, either, but he patted the girl on the shoulder and told her to keep pressure on the wound. He then tore off two more pieces of the tabard and stuffed them under the chainmail at each of the young man's other two wounds.

Erik parried and dodged, threatening whenever the general overbalanced, but as he had learned from the weeks of sparring with Kari, the demonhunter didn't press his own attacks too hard. He knew that eventually the general would either tire or make a mistake, and like his partner had done so many times to him, Erik would be waiting to capitalize. Gaswell was a skilled swordsman and it seemed he may have earned the military title instead of simply taking it upon himself like so many would-be tyrants did, and Erik was hard pressed to keep the slashing blades away from himself. The advantage he had – and he wondered if Gaswell understood – was that he had the constitution of a half-guardian demon: there was no way a terra-rir would outlast him in a contest of endurance. At the very least, Erik knew he could outlast Gaswell.

"Aeligos!" Eryn called, and the rogue returned to the hallway once more. "I'm going out on the balcony to cause some havoc with the soldiers outside. I think you should go see how your brothers are doing downstairs!"

The rogue shook his head. "Sherman is wounded! I have to watch the door!"

He couldn't hear her, but he could clearly see her swear. "How bad?" she yelled.

"I think he'll live but he has to be tended to!" Aeligos called back. "Go ahead, I can keep the hallways locked down well enough from here!"

The woman nodded and was gone from sight in moments. Aeligos looked back once at his brother and the general fighting, and a grim smile came to his features; the deed was almost done. While Gaswell displayed obvious prowess, he could not outlast a half-demon, and the rogue thought he must know it. There would be no escape and no real chance of victory; the fight was done unless something truly and extraordinarily bad happened. In the back of his mind, Aeligos simply prayed that Eryn was right, and they would not come face-to-face with Emma before the fighting was done.

~~*~*

392

Kari kept her hands to her temples until the fire in her mind subsided. Once she got her wits about her again, she looked up to find the kirelas-rir girl floating within her prison cell. The girl was looking around as though trying to identify her surroundings, and when her glowing white eyes met Kari's they were full of wrath. Kari got to her feet but suddenly found that she could not move. She was pinned in place as if by an invisible hand, and the war wizard floated toward her in ghostly fashion.

"Where is the demon?" the kirelas-rir girl demanded. Her voice was light and playful like a young woman's despite the tone she tried to take.

"Which demon?" Kari managed. She was having a hard time breathing in the crushing grip of the woman's spell. Sonja lay beside her motionless, and Kari wondered if the war wizard had done something worse to her friend while she'd been fighting the mental fire.

"The serpent who captured me," the kirelas-rir girl clarified.

"The sylinth? It's dead; my partner and I killed it," Kari said and she gasped for a second, trying to suck enough wind in to speak. "My friend and I came here to rescue you."

A confused expression crossed the girl's face but she held Kari's gaze. She waved her hand dismissively and the force that had bound Kari in place dissipated. Kari fell to her knees and crawled over to Sonja, who began to rise even before Kari reached her. The two regarded the kirelas-rir girl curiously for a few moments, until at last the war wizard's feet touched the ground and her eyes became more solidly blue once again. She moved to sit on a dry patch of the dungeon floor, and her face scrunched up in disgust as she saw how filthy she was.

"Are you all right?" Kari asked, daring to approach and kneel before the girl.

"I…believe so," the kirelas-rir girl replied, and she blinked a few times before meeting Kari's eyes. "I am not certain what has happened. I know not where I am, or why. I know only that I am filthy, hungry, tired, and quite confused."

"But you mentioned the demon," Kari said. "You were captured by the sylinth?"

"It overwhelmed my senses," the girl said. "I could not tell up from down, or even who I was, before it was upon me. Your grabbing my shoulder was the next thing to happen to me that I was able to register properly. Where am I?"

"You're in the dungeon of a madman named Braxus Gaswell," Sonja said, and she rose to her feet. She took up her sword and moved toward the exit to listen for approaching guards.

"I recognize that name," the war wizard said. "It was an invitation from him to any and all terra-rir males of a proper age for military service to join him that drew me to this island. I was curious to see if he was truly a descendant of the fool that attempted to attack my people a generation ago, and if so, what his intentions were."

"Was he with the demon when you were captured?" Kari asked.

"I do not remember clearly, but I think so," the girl answered. She thought to herself but ultimately shook her head. "It is not important at this time. You have come to rescue me; does the castle rest in the hands of your allies, then?"

"No," Kari said with a shake of her head. "We have friends upstairs trying to capture Gaswell, and volunteers from across the island are fighting on the fields before the castle to make our mission possible. Now that we've freed you, our job is to get you out of here safely."

"Nonsense," the girl said, and she rose to her feet once more. "I will not hide in the shadows while your friends risk their lives for those of my people. Come, we will join with them and I will take you to safety when the general is in your hands."

"Other than the sewer exit, I'm not sure if there's an easy way out of here," Kari said.

The war wizard smiled grimly. "I was not interested in taking the easy way out," she said. Her feet rose off the floor as her eyes went white once more. The blue vertical stripes on the sides of her snout began to glow with mystic power and she hovered above the cool, wet stones, gliding like a banshee toward the doorway. With a gesture, she tore the door from its hinges and cast it aside into a nearby cell with a crash. Several alarmed voices came from farther up the stairway, and two rir males appeared at the far end of the tunnel and yelled for her to halt. Without a word, she held her hand forward and forked lightning shot forth up the staircase. Kari and Sonja turned away from the blinding light and covered their ears as a deafening thunderclap followed the display. Screams sounded from up the stairs only briefly, and when Kari rose to her feet, she could smell the curious scent of ozone mixed with that of charred corpses.

She and Sonja followed silently as the kirelas-rir girl floated without hesitation up the stairs, and the three ascended to a long hallway that ran east to west by Kari's best guess. Armed soldiers came around a corner from the west, but with a gesture the war wizard engulfed the entire hallway with flames, consuming the men in moments. Kari looked to Sonja in complete shock, and the scarlet-haired woman could only give a shrug that clearly said such magic was far beyond her skills. The

394

demonhunter shrugged in return, and they followed their kirelas-rir *guide* as she floated down the hallway to the east. Three more times they met armed resistance while the young woman floated undeterred down some specific route, and three more times she annihilated their foes utterly without a hint of effort. If she felt at all hesitant or bad for what she did, she didn't show it: there was no expression in her blank, white eyes or upon her face. Whatever she was doing, she apparently knew the way, and led them to a staircase before her feet finally touched the floor again.

She regarded her rescuers for only a moment when her eyes returned to normal, and she blew out a fatigued sigh. "I must conserve my energy for what is to come," she said. "Please defend me as we make our way to your friends."

"Sure thing, um...," Kari began.

"Triela," the girl said with the barest of smiles.

"Pretty name for a pretty girl," Kari said, and she bounded up the stairs before them. When they reached the top, they could hear the sounds of a melee from somewhere near, and Kari motioned for her two companions to remain on the stairwell while she went ahead to scout. From the nearby intersection she could see blood trails on the floor, and a corpse laying in a doorway down the eastbound passage.

"I think we found Ty and Jol," Kari called back over her shoulder, and she gestured for her friends to come forward. "We should probably look in on them."

Without a word, Triela once again floated above the floor, and she glided down the hallway without a sound and turned to face in the doorway. Kari watched the girl encase herself in a shell of crackling, arcing lightning, and Triela bellowed into the room where the fighting was taking place. "Lay down your arms or be incinerated!" she yelled, and after only a moment the sounds of fighting ended abruptly. Soon enough, Typhonix and Serenjols ducked past the girl and came up the hallway toward Kari and Sonja, and Triela yelled into the room once again. "Leave this castle and be far from it when it is destroyed. Remember what you have learned this day, and do not tempt fate by repeating this iniquity!"

Apparently that was all that needed to be said. Soon the soldiers that Ty and Serenjols had been fighting all ran past Triela and down the hallway without weapons in their hands. Kari couldn't help but chuckle as she tried to take a headcount. Ty and Jol had been fighting at least a dozen enemies, not including those they'd already wounded or killed. Ty and Jol weren't in prime condition: based on the black blood on their armor that was clearly theirs, they were each bleeding from dozens of wounds. Most of those appeared superficial, though, and neither man was staggered or too wounded to breathe or speak normally.

"I see you found the war wizard," Serenjols commented dryly, which drew laughs from Kari and Sonja.

"I almost pissed myself when she yelled at us all," Ty said, trying not to laugh. He sniffed the air a couple of times and glanced at Kari and Sonja. "You two smell wonderful."

"We came in through the sewer; what's your excuse?" Sonja shot back.

Ty scowled at his sister playfully and Kari chuckled, but she stood straight when the last of the soldiers fled past them and headed northward, to where she suspected the front door was located. "Triela, our friends are on the next level!" Kari yelled, and she was surprised when the woman simply nodded and then disappeared with a buzzing pop.

"This way!" Ty shouted. He led the others up the stairs to the next level, and within moments they were at the door Aeligos was guarding. The rogue was clearly happy to see them and let out a shout of triumph at their approach, but he jumped in shock when the kirelas-rir girl appeared beside him. He nearly took a swing at her but caught himself when he realized what she was. After giving her an obviously appraising glance, he made his way into the room.

Kari and the others entered soon after, and Sonja knelt down beside Katarina to check on Sherman. He was unconscious but appeared to at least be stable. Erik was still fighting Gaswell. Each had managed to inflict only minor wounds on the other, and both were apparently growing tired. When Triela floated into the room, the general balked, and Erik seized the opportunity to knock one of the blades from his hand. It mattered little: a moment later the other sword flew from his hand. It floated before Triela for only a moment before it melted into a glowing puddle of metal at her feet.

"Your time is at an end, Braxus Gaswell," she said calmly. She made a gesture and the terra-rir general suddenly stood in an odd pose, as though being crushed by the same spell the woman had gripped Kari with.

"Wait, don't kill him," Erik said, but he did a double take when he turned around and realized it wasn't his sister's magic that had disarmed and immobilized the general. "Um, please don't kill him, mistress. We should take him into custody."

"I will not kill him. His fate will ultimately be in your hands, not those of the people he truly sought to destroy," Triela said. She fixed her glowing white eyes upon Sherman and gave a casual wave, and what appeared to be a disembodied glowing blue hand passed over the young man's wounds. The bleeding was stanched in its wake, and Kari wasn't sure what to make of it; she'd never heard of wizards utilizing divine or any other type of healing power.

Erik nodded and turned his gaze to Ty and Jol. "Report, gentlemen?"

"The young lady scared away all the soldiers we hadn't killed yet," Typhonix said, but once he finished speaking, he put a hand to his belly and grunted.

"Are you hurt?" Erik asked.

"Couple of stab wounds, nothing Grakin can't fix," the blonde warrior said. He put his axe into the strap across his back and sat down, and despite his best efforts, Kari could see he was in pain.

"I am fine," Serenjols said.

"All clear in the prison?" Erik asked Kari, and she nodded. "Aeligos, go see if you can find Eryn, and let's get out of here with the general as soon as we can."

"Triela sent the soldiers out the front door, so if there was anyone outside waiting to get in, they may find themselves not wanting to do so anymore," Sonja added.

"It's over," Erik said with a satisfied sigh.

"No, it is not," Triela said, her head tilting curiously.

The blue-eyed demonhunter regarded her curiously. "What do you mean?"

Triela turned toward the door, and everyone followed her gaze. Eryn entered the room, and Triela did nothing to stop the half-brys woman as she approached, drew back her bowstring, and put an arrow through the head of the general at point-blank range. Gaswell could let out only a brief startled cry of protest before his head snapped to the side with the force of the impact. Triela released her holding spell to let the body crumple to the floor.

"Damnit, Eryn!" Erik barked.

"Look, I'm being paid to bring this idiot's head to my employer," the half-brys woman said calmly. "I waited until you could finish your mission, now I need to finish mine. Don't get in my way."

The blue-eyed demonhunter growled, but Kari approached and held her hand up. "It's over, Erik. We were never asked to take him into a court of law, just to stop him at any cost. We've done that, and we have Eryn to thank for it – don't give her a hard time."

Erik regarded Kari for a moment. "I wanted answers from him!"

"He wouldn't have told us anything," Kari countered. "Erik, if he was working with demons, he either would've kept his mouth shut, lied, or the demons would've killed him before he could tell us anything. The answers we can get, we'll get from Eryn."

Erik didn't seem convinced, but he sighed and nodded. "You're probably right," he said. He bowed his head toward Eryn. "Thank you for your help, Eryn."

"My pleasure," the assassin said, and she went to collect the grisly proof of her success.

"Where are your allies located?" Triela asked, and once Erik told her where the shakna-rir base camp was, the woman closed her eyes, concentrating, and then opened them after a moment. "Prepare yourselves."

She threw her arms to the sides and a shock of lightning rattled Kari's senses, and she soon found herself and everyone else within Maktus Tuvurasti's command post behind the front lines. The Silver Blades were immediately surrounded by the warlord's personal guard, but once they identified Aeligos and his friends, they stood down and sent for the warlord. Everyone turned as a thunderclap tore past the camp on the wind, and high over the battlefield they could see the lightning-encased form of Triela hovering above Gaswell's castle. For several minutes, not a person in the command post moved while the small form rained lightning upon the castle far in the distance, and interspersed between the thunderclaps were the sounds of the castle being blown apart. Even Maktus stopped to watch the display when he came forth from his pavilion.

Kari noted that the command post was closer to Gaswell's castle than she expected, and she guessed that Maktus' superior force was routing the general's men easily. She returned her gaze to Triela's display and smiled grimly: Gaswell's army was being dismantled and would soon have nowhere to run. Maktus said as much while he watched the display with his honor guard. Aeligos approached the warlord as Maktus ordered one of his subcommanders to take their battalion and strike out to the southwest, to cut off any retreat to the sea. The warlord saluted Aeligos at his approach, and the rogue returned the gesture.

A moment later, the ball of lightning over Gaswell's castle disappeared, and Triela suddenly stood in the middle of the command post near the Silver Blades. She collapsed almost immediately, and Kari's proximity and reflexes allowed her to catch the girl when she fell. Triela was exhausted, and Kari recalled Sonja's tales of how using her sorcery and Grakin's channeling of divine power burned them out rather quickly. At Maktus' direction, Kari carried the girl into the warlord's mobile pavilion, which was smaller than the one at the main camp but still quite spacious.

Serenjols carried Sherman into the pavilion as well, and he and Kari placed their unconscious friends on the cushioned floor. Kari put a blanket over Triela to keep her warm, and Typhonix stood beside Sherman while they waited for a runner to fetch Grakin.

Within minutes, Grakin entered the command pavilion and approached Kari, but she held her hand up to keep him at bay. "Don't touch me, I've been crawling around in a sewer for hours," she said, but he paid her warning no heed. He embraced her and held her tight until she finally pushed him away lightly. "Sherman's hurt pretty badly."

That was all she needed to say. Grakin turned and knelt beside his human companion, and helped to remove the young man's armor so he could properly tend to the wounds. Kari watched with interest while Grakin inspected the worst of the wounds, and after a moment the healer began his work. He closed his eyes as he began to tap into and channel his deity's divine power, and slowly he sealed the wound, causing Sherman to grit his teeth in pain. After a moment the priest's eyes opened and he fixed them on Katarina. "Place your hands over his shoulder wounds and concentrate on sealing them," he said quietly.

"I don't know how to," Katarina responded.

"You do; use your faith, like I taught you," Grakin said. "Put your trust in the Ghost that he will heal your brother through you. It is part of your service as a paladin. Simply believe in your deity, and in yourself. You can do this."

The young woman did as she was instructed and Kari watched her begin to channel the Ghost's divine power. Katarina's eyes widened in joyful surprise when Sherman's wounds began to close. Within minutes she and her mentor completed their tasks, and though the flesh was still raw around the wounds, the lacerations were sealed and the bleeding had stopped completely. With a satisfied but fatigued sigh, Grakin sat back on his haunches.

"He is stable, and I do not believe any damage was done to his organs. The wounds are sealed but he will need rest," the priest said. He turned to Typhonix and inspected the wounds he'd suffered, and Grakin asked, "How are you even still walking?"

"Too stubborn to die," Aeligos quipped. Kari chuckled, which caused Typhonix to do so as well before cringing in pain.

"You should've seen what *they* looked like," the blonde warrior joked as he lay down.

The shakna-rir warlord smiled quietly and Erik approached him. "I am glad to see you are all safe," Maktus said. "Was your mission a success?"

Eryn tossed the satchel containing the general's head to the warlord, and Maktus looked at it for only a moment before he returned it to the half-brys woman. Erik introduced the warlord to the assassin, and also told him who the unconscious kirelas-rir girl was. Maktus gave orders to his attendants in the pavilion to clothe the war wizard and tend to his guests, and even went so far as to order a makeshift bath prepared for the women.

"If you will excuse me, I will take the field myself now," Maktus said to his guests, and he put on his breastplate and helm. "I sent a good deal of Raugro's forces southeast to cut off any attempt by Gaswell's men to flee eastward toward Ursis or Talvor, and now I have another battalion cutting off their retreat to the west. Thanks to your young kirelas-rir friend, they now have nowhere to run. They may continue to fight, but I will go and offer them the chance to surrender before desperation takes hold. You have all done well. Rest now, and I will see you again in the morning."

Kari and Sonja washed off, and by the time they finished, Triela was conscious again. She washed off with help from Kari and Sonja, and soon the war wizard was seated on the cushioned floor of the warlord's pavilion eating. Kari wondered just how long Triela had been starved at Gaswell's hands. Kari found it amazing that after all Triela had been through, she didn't have any desire to personally kill the terra-rir general. Sitting safely in the command pavilion, the girl seemed concerned only with sating her long-standing hunger.

Kari sat beside the kirelas-rir girl and put her hand on the war wizard's shoulder, and after a moment Triela's blue eyes came up. "How do you feel?" the demonhunter asked.

"Very tired," Triela answered. "I would like to rest here for the night, and in the morning I will take you and your companions to my home. There are things you need to see and hear."

Kari patted the smaller girl's shoulder. "If that's what you think is best," Kari said. "Get your strength back; we're not going anywhere anytime soon."

Erik gave a noncommittal shrug. "We'll want to make our way back to Riverport at the earliest time. We don't know when *Karmi's Sword* will return, or any ship heading back home."

"I will take you to Riverport when our business on Kirelia is concluded; that will not be an issue," Triela said between bites of her food.

"If it's not too much to ask, I'd like to visit the czarikk one last time," Kari said to Erik. She half-expected him to say no.

"Do you think you can get us back to their village without Makauric to guide us?" he asked, and she nodded confidently. "We can go when we're done on Kirelia, then."

Once their hunger was satisfied, they retired to the general camp to bed down for the night. Though the camp was alive with the sounds of orders being issued and men going to and coming from the front lines, there was a peacefulness about the group, and Kari and Eryn slept in their lovers' arms, surrounded by their friends.

Chapter XX – Salvation's Dawn

The next morning was hazy and hot. Kari watched the sun rise, and the shakna-rir were already well under way in dismantling their camp. In the early hours of morning, the terra-rir forces formerly under the command of Braxus Gaswell had signaled their unconditional surrender, and their field commanders submitted themselves to Maktus' judgment. Kari had spoken briefly with the the shakna-rir warlord in the pre-dawn hours, and he informed her that he'd merely bid them disperse with a warning to undertake no such folly in the future, and he promised them that no further punishment would be forthcoming as long as they kept true to his wishes. Of course, he had his soldiers make certain that the enemy truly dispersed, and that they didn't all simply begin marching to the nearest city. Kari was nervous about the warlord's approach, but she trusted in his judgment.

Sherman was up and about with the sunrise, though he was still weak and his movements were obviously painful. Grakin had instructed him to eat and drink heavily until he regained his strength, and both Sherman and Triela were given priority on food. Triela already looked better by morning, though she was still gaunt, and under closer inspection by daylight Kari was able to see many of her ribs. Even still, there was strength of will in her eyes that clearly said no matter how bad her body looked, her spirit was still quite powerful. After the prior night's display, Kari had little doubt about that.

Kari shared the morning meal with her companions and listened while Aeligos debriefed Maktus on everything from the previous night. Kari made certain to mention the dead scout she and Sonja had found so that his family would have some closure. After breakfast, Maktus began issuing orders to get his soldiers busy preparing to return home, and then the warlord rejoined Kari and the others in his command pavilion. "Allow me to extend the thanks of Her Majesty for your help in this matter," he said, shaking Aeligos' hand. "I will be honest: I had my doubts about you when you first spoke to us in Kulthon. I am glad to see I was wrong."

The rogue nodded. "I'm sure you didn't expect so grave a warning and help to arrive in the form of half-demons," he said. "Your queen is wise, and you serve her well."

"I hope at some point you have occasion to visit our fair city when times are not so dire," Maktus said with a nod. "This is a beautiful island, and it is a shame that you only came to visit to see war upon it."

"It's possible," Erik said. "One never knows where the Unyielding will send them next."

The warlord smiled. "We do not see your Order here often," he said. "Given the small number of serilian demons here on the island, there normally isn't much call for your people to work here, but we are glad to have had your help."

Serilis-rir, Kari thought, but she kept it to herself. "And we're honored to be of service," she said. She touched her fist to her breastplate in salute, and Erik and Typhonix repeated the gesture, which drew a respectful military salute from the warlord.

"Go with the gods," Maktus said. "I understand our young kirelas-rir guest has things she must show you on her peoples' island, so I will keep you no longer. As it stands, I need get my forces moving northward as soon as possible."

"Farewell," Erik said on behalf of the group, and Maktus left the pavilion.

"If you are all ready, then?" Triela asked as she stood up.

"Are you sure this is a good idea?" Kari asked. "Could we simply take a boat to your island to let you conserve your strength?"

The war wizard waved off the comment. "Once I return home, my strength will return much faster," she said, and Kari had to smile for the jovial and juvenile sound of the girl's voice. "If there is nothing else we need do here, I will take you there now."

The group agreed. Triela threw her arms wide with a crackle of electricity and tore a hole through the bounds of reality, moving the friends across to a small island off the southwest coast of Tsalbrin. Despite having experienced it before, Kari was still astounded by the power of the woman and the flawless execution of her magical will. While Kari had been impressed by Sonja's displays – both aboard *Karmi's Sword* and during the course of their mission – it simply paled in comparison to Triela's wizardly prowess. It left the demonhunter to wonder where so young a girl had learned such things and gathered so much power.

As the war wizard's teleportation magic faded around them, Kari and her companions found themselves in a village that sat within a sheltered glade. All around them stood a lush forest of wondrous beauty, and nestled under the branches of the trees sat huts and tents made of wood or animal skins. It was not unlike the czarikk village in its simplicity, but there was a stark contrast between the people here and those of the reptilian tribe. There was stateliness and unmasked power that flowed through Triela's people, and it awed Kari and her companions as they looked around.

404

The kirelas-rir were reclusive, and it was well known that attempting to visit their island without being invited was a surefire way to get oneself in trouble. There was something about the way they thought and the way they carried themselves that made them much different than the other rir people, and drove them to keep themselves apart from the rest of the world as a whole. While it was not uncommon to meet a kirelas-rir here and there, they were rarely found outside their homeland in numbers. Consequently, little was known of the people or their home, or what secrets they hid so diligently.

The people of the village watched the arrival of the group, and they soon gathered around joyfully when they saw Triela amongst them once again. The girl greeted her people warmly and exchanged hugs with many of them, and she introduced the people informally to those who had rescued her. The people took an interest in their guests but, like the czarikk, they didn't impose themselves too much upon the strangers: they kept their distance, though their demeanor was a welcoming one. Like Triela, the people were all fairly small in size, though taller than Eryn, and Kari nearly laughed at herself when she realized being around Grakin's brothers was skewing her perceptions. The kirelas-rir all had light blue stripes on the sides of their snouts, which Kari found interesting. She'd assumed Triela's were arcane tattoos that had something to do with her wizardly might. Their hair colors were all fluorescent, bright and beautiful, and their eye colors were likewise all bright and exotic like the denizens of Salkorum.

Triela kept the friends gathered near the center of the village, and after a few minutes a kirelas-rir male in a deep blue robe approached. His shoulder-length hair was shockingly orange and set into small, beaded braids, and he had matching orange eyes that were startling to behold. He smiled as he approached, and he hugged Triela without hesitation. She clung tightly to him for several long moments before they split apart and she bowed before him. "My lord," she said quietly.

The male bowed before her in turn. "Your Eminence," he said.

Kari was intrigued. When she looked at her friends she saw they were similarly curious. Kari's mind flashed back to the previous night, when Triela had healed Sherman seemingly without effort, and she wondered if Triela was also a priestess. After a moment, Triela waved a hand toward Kari and her friends and introduced them to the male. "These are the ones who rescued me from my captivity," she said. "I do not know all of their names, but I call them my friends regardless. My friends, this is Icavior, the ruler of our people."

Kari and her companions bowed respectfully to Icavior and he bowed his head in return. "I bid you welcome to the Isle of Kirelia," he said. "We do not have visitors here under normal circumstances, but for you to have saved the life of our high priestess marks this as anything but a normal circumstance."

"High priestess?" Erik repeated with a raised brow.

"I thought she was a war wizard," Kari added.

Triela excused herself to go wash and change clothes, and Icavior looked over the gathered friends and smiled. "Yes...a war wizard," he said. "Or so our divine souls are called by your people when they leave our island to explore your lands. She is a master of the arcane, but her primary devotion is to the power of the gods."

"She practices both the arcane and the divine?" Grakin asked.

"She practices the arcane by way of the divine," Icavior clarified. He gestured for the group to follow him. "Come; let me show you what I mean."

He led them farther into the village, and Kari saw that the place where they had arrived was not truly the center, but rather *a* center. The village extended much farther into the reaches of the forest than had initially been apparent, and each clearing in the area served as yet another *center*, rather like plazas in a city. Like the czarikk village, many of the clearings had fire pits and stone ovens for cooking, and each section of the town was arranged around these circles. Kari looked around at the structures and the people, and she could see that though the village itself was simple, the kirelas-rir people clearly were not. For whatever reason, they seemed to prefer the simple living they enjoyed in harmony with their surroundings.

Soon Icavior brought them to another clearing, and it seemed to Kari that this one fronted his own home. The larger tent was decorated with glyphs and arcane symbols. In the center of the clearing was a massive stone fountain, though whether mortal hands had built it, Kari couldn't tell. It was flawless in its construction, not a single imperfection showing in its mortar or symmetry, and Kari and her companions stood agape at its beauty. Despite the limited direct sunlight, the fountain glowed with a radiance that was not reflected. Flowing within it was what appeared to be water, but it glowed with an inner light whose source was not immediately apparent, and it sparkled like liquid gold.

Icavior stood before the fountain. He held his hand over the water and closed his eyes, and a smile came to his face. He turned back to the group and gestured toward the fountain, but he watched silently as Grakin approached and held his hand out over the liquid. The priest's eyes widened in shock, and when he looked at Icavior, the kirelas-rir male nodded. Grakin turned to his friends, shook his head lightly, and tried to speak, but no words would come forth at first. His siblings and friends chuckled, but Kari approached and took his hand in hers.

"This…this is amazing," Grakin finally managed.

"What is it?" Erik asked, approaching, but he hesitated to put his hand near the water.

"This is a conduit of holy power," Icavior explained. "It is the reason men like Gaswell have sought to capture our island since the dawn of our creation. Such men believe that having a portal such as this would give them the power of the heavens and allow them to bend the will of the gods to their own schemes. They simply do not understand that the will of the gods cannot be subjugated - certainly not for evil purposes - and that without the proper mental discipline, the power of this well is useless."

"But Gaswell had no priests in his retinue," Erik said. "What use would this well have been to him?"

"It is not merely a well," Triela said as she came back among the group dressed in a beautiful black robe trimmed in light blue. With the garment blocking the view of the ribs that showed prominently through her skin, she looked much better than she had when they first rescued her. Her eyes were full of power, and when she moved closer to the fountain her eyes and the stripes on the sides of her snout began to glow with a radiant light that made Kari's jaw drop.

"This is a portal into the celestial realm, is it not?" Grakin asked Triela, and she touched his face tenderly with a smile.

"Your faith and your training serve you well," she told him. "Yes, this fountain is not only a conduit of power but a gateway into the heavens themselves, for those who know how to tap into its power. Gaswell, like his foolish ancestor before him, likely sought to capture it, in the hopes that they could enter the splendor of the celestial realm uninvited."

Triela turned and looked at Kari, and the terra-dracon woman almost faltered under the strength of the woman's blue-eyed stare. "The demon that captured me also sought to use this fount for its own evil purposes," the war wizard said. "That much I remember."

"Is this fountain called Salvation's Dawn?" Eryn asked. The half-brys woman's mention of Salvation's Dawn immediately drew Grakin's attention.

"No; it is called Arakiel's Chalice," Icavior said. "Why do you ask?"

Aeligos and Eryn exchanged a glance, and it was not lost on the rest of the group. "What is it?" Kari asked. "Does this have something to do with the other demon that was working with Gaswell?"

"There were *two*?" Triela interjected.

"There was a mallasti there when I arrived to join Gaswell's army," Eryn explained. "A female named Emma that Aeligos met when he and his siblings invaded Curlamanx's keep."

"Is that true?" Erik asked, and Aeligos nodded. "You never mentioned her before."

Aeligos made a gesture to let the matter drop, and surprisingly, Erik didn't push the issue. The rogue then gestured for Eryn to fill the others in.

"From what I was able to gather, Emma was looking for something called Salvation's Dawn," the assassin said, and Grakin folded his arms across his chest. "I'm pretty sure it has something to do with the Temple of Archons, but I'm not exactly well-versed on that. What confused me is that if it has something to do with the Temple, then why was Emma *here*? So I thought maybe it was this fountain...this portal that she was after. I guess not. Grakin, what does Salvation's Dawn mean to you?"

The priest sighed lightly. "It is not something that is discussed frequently within the churches of our deities, but you are correct with regard to its connection to the Temple of Archons. I will try to be brief: the Temple requires seven 'seals' to unlock. Six of the seals are guarded by powerful entities that have been entrusted with never surrendering them unless the gods themselves request them. The locations of these seals are a well-guarded secret; Kaelariel will not even speak of their locations. Even were some powerful entity to find and wrest the six seals from their guardians, they would be useless without the seventh seal, called Salvation's Dawn. For a demon to have knowledge of this is most distressing. It may mean that one – or several – of the pantheon's clergy have been compromised."

"But what *is* Salvation's Dawn?" Eryn prodded. "Is it here? Is that why Emma was here looking for it?"

"It is not that simple," Grakin said with a shake of his head. He thought to himself for a few moments before he began to explain in more detail. "I was taught that one cannot find a seal until the previous one in the sequence has been found. In order to protect them from discovery, they also cannot be found through arcane or even divine means. When the first is found, it will point the finder to the second, and the second to the third, and so on. Even then, when the sixth one is found, it does not lead to the seventh seal, because…"

He broke off for a moment, obviously uncomfortable sharing the secrets of the clergy, but when Kari put her hand on his shoulder, he looked at her and nodded. "Salvation's Dawn is not a seal…it is a person," Grakin

408

said with a quiet sigh. "And this person is or has the means of opening the gates of a Temple that has been sealed since the creation of our world."

Erik glanced around at his siblings, companions, and the two kirelas-rir. "Do you know who it is?" he asked the priest.

"No," Grakin said. "To my knowledge, even Kaelariel does not know who Salvation's Dawn is. It is the one secret his father never shared with him. Obviously, something of great power rests inside that Temple. Many of the clergy speculate that something within the Temple has the means of granting divinity: that it is the place Gori Sensullu took the great heroes of our history to make them into the pantheon we serve. Gori Sensullu must have planned for it to be opened and used one day to have bothered leaving the keys where mortal hands could find them, but just who, when, or why is anyone's guess. It is believed that a new Salvation's Dawn is born in each generation, else this person would have to be immortal, and their existence would be too conspicuous. That being said, if Emma was looking for it and holding Triela in the dungeon..."

All eyes fell over Triela, and the young woman seemed just as shocked as the rest of the gathering. "If I am Salvation's Dawn, that was unknown to me," she said. "I was under the impression that I was captured because I was a direct threat to Gaswell and his demon allies."

"No, that doesn't make sense," Eryn interjected. "Emma abandoned Gaswell a few weeks ago under the pretense of going to the underworld to bring back an army for him. If Triela was Salvation's Dawn, there's no way Emma would've left her shackled in the dungeon, at risk of being killed when war came to Gaswell's gates."

"Eryn's right," Aeligos said, and Kari nodded in agreement with them both. "If Emma had Salvation's Dawn, she would've brought them to the underworld with her before there was any serious threat to their well-being. It's entirely possible that she didn't find whoever it is at all, and that she figured out that she was looking in the wrong place. What really concerns me is the thought that Emma might already have the other six seals, and capturing Salvation's Dawn may have been the final stroke in a plan we've known nothing about to date."

"Had the other six seals been uncovered, the pantheon would surely have known, and others like ourselves would have been sent to intervene," Grakin assured his brother.

"Even with the Apocalypse going on?" Aeligos returned.

"It is more likely that Emma sought Salvation's Dawn first so that she would have a distinct advantage when wresting the seals from their guardians," Grakin argued calmly. "If she began collecting the other seals,

409

she would have attracted far too much attention to ever complete her quest, even with the Apocalypse reaching its climax. Consider it: if she had Salvation's Dawn in her possession when she began seeking the other seals, then only she would know her next destination as each one was captured. I believe she sought Salvation's Dawn first; one person going missing in the midst of or shortly after a war would hardly draw much attention, especially when one considers that no one even knows who Salvation's Dawn is. Clearly these developments will require research and consultation with the Demonhunter Order and the temples, but again, it is more likely that Emma did not find Salvation's Dawn here at all."

"But then why did she leave? Did she take anyone with her when she left?" Erik asked.

"Not that I'm aware of," Eryn responded. Normally such an answer would've left a lot of doubt, but given her work over the previous several weeks, Kari was satisfied that had Emma taken a hostage to the underworld with her, Eryn would've known. "As for why she left...I think this whole situation was a dry run."

"A dry run? What does that mean?" Erik prodded.

"It was a test," Eryn continued. "The demons are after Salvation's Dawn and the Temple of Archons, but Emma was testing how the gods, the temples, and the Demonhunter Order would react to her meddling. And what she discovered is that the gods and the Order were willing to send one of the greatest heroes in our history to come see to this personally. The gods threw down their hand before the bets were even in."

"What if...what if Salvation's Dawn is a priest, or a demonhunter...someone that would get sent to deal with this sort of uprising?" Aeligos ventured. "Is it possible Emma expected a specific person – maybe Kari – to be sent in response to her presence, and that this specific person also happens to be Salvation's Dawn? A world war could have been part of her intent - it would have covered up her hunt for the other six seals quite nicely - but think about it: she sat on her haunches long enough for opposition to arrive. It seems like Emma knew someone would come, and that perhaps she believed that Salvation's Dawn would be among their number."

"Maybe Salvation's Dawn is standing right in front of us," Typhonix said, and then he chuckled. "Hell, maybe it's me."

"Gods help us," Sonja muttered, and Kari had to put her hand over her mouth to stop from cackling.

Kari looked around at her companions, and when she glanced toward Triela and Icavior, they were both considering the strangers before them.

She turned back to Grakin and gave his hand a squeeze to get his attention. "How would we even know for sure?" she asked. "Is there some way to find out, other than collecting all of the other seals and then seeing if they can open the door?"

"I am not certain," Grakin answered. "Then again, perhaps we are best off if we do not know for sure. If Emma knew, would she not have intervened in the battle, to carry off her prize while the rest of us fought with Gaswell's people?"

Eryn grimaced. "I don't know. If Emma was intent on winning that battle, even after you killed the sylinth, I'm pretty sure she could have, with or without an army. If Emma had been in the fort when you invaded, I think we all would've been killed," she said. She eyed Triela briefly. "Triela may have been able to stand against her; I'm honestly not sure. But just walking past that mallasti girl made my hair stand on end, and she didn't keep her sorcery a secret at all. If she hadn't abandoned Gaswell – intentionally or not – this would've been a total disaster. Despite your orders, none of us would've been prepared for that kind of fight."

Erik held Eryn's gaze for a silent minute. Kari and the others watched closely, but then Erik gave an appreciative nod. "I guess we owe you our lives," he said.

The assassin made a dismissive gesture. "Comes with being part of a team," she said.

That seemed to shock Erik, and Kari laughed along with his siblings and friends. Erik took their chuckles in stride, but his eyes settled on Kari and he nodded his head toward her. "Maybe it's Kari," he said quietly. "How often do you hear of someone being resurrected?"

That drew Triela and Icavior's full attention. "You were resurrected?" Icavior asked.

The revelation didn't seem to surprise any of her companions, and Kari guessed they had all figured it out or been told the truth by now. She folded her arms across her chest lightly and shrugged. "I don't think it's me," she said. "Firstly, I wasn't born in this generation, so what Grakin said about a new one being born in each generation doesn't fit. And it would've all hinged on Trigonh even asking for me to be returned in the first place. Seems like something Gori Sensullu would've planned for well in advance, and not left to chance."

"She makes a valid point," Aeligos agreed. "But Grakin's right: maybe it's best if we don't know. If we simply alert the temples and the gods to the fact that they need to find and protect whoever this person is, it'll mean Emma will have the full weight of the pantheon to contend with

411

if she's still intent on abducting this person."

Erik turned to their hosts. "Is there anything you two would like to add or suggest?" he asked politely. "Since this entire plot dragged your people into it, you're as involved in it now as the rest of us."

Icavior deferred to Triela, and the young woman shook her head negatively. "Not at this time," she said. "Given our seclusion here, this conduit is the only divine structure of which the Night Runner informs me. However, in the future I shall pray to be kept abreast of the goings-on surrounding this Temple of Archons, that should Emma become a problem once more, I may lend my aid in subduing or killing her."

"The Night Runner?" Ty echoed.

"Garra Ktarra," Grakin clarified, and he bowed his head respectfully toward Triela. She returned the gesture, and Grakin added, "Clearly, Triela's involvement in this matter, no matter how awful, has been to our benefit. The involvement of a high priestess of the god of the night means that now, with the pantheon's attention focused on Emma and her underworld schemes, little that goes on even in the shadows of night will escape notice."

"Indeed," Triela agreed.

"Clearly, there's a lot we're going to need to discuss on the voyage home, and then pass that along to the Order and to Kaelariel when we get to DarkWind," Erik said, and there were nods of agreement all around. He turned to Triela and asked, "In the meantime, will your island and this conduit be safe?"

"I believe so," she said. "Now that I have felt the sting of a sylinth's mental attack, I will be better able to defend myself against them. If they try to capture me in the same manner, they will find a much different result, and our people as a whole are strong in the ways of the arcane. Even if it turns out the demons are also interested in this conduit, they would be fools to invade here, where we are at our peak strength."

"There are two other questions that linger," Serenjols said, surprising his siblings and friends. "First, we still must find how Emma and this sylinth were even summoned to this world. But more importantly, if it turns out that the demons were interested in this conduit, we must consider that Sekassus does not possess the power to invade the heavens on his own. If he is trying to break through into the heavens, then he either has more allies in the underworld willing to aid him, or…he has someone in the heavens helping him."

Kari wasn't sure what surprised her more: that Jol had said so much or what he'd said. "Is that even possible?" she asked, and an involuntary shiver coursed through her.

The eldest Tesconis male nodded. "You know there has been bad blood between some of the gods since the Koryonite pantheon joined with our own. Do not forget that with the Koryonite pantheon came gods who sit among our deities above, but also on the Council below."

Kari was at a loss; the merging of the pantheons had happened between her two lives, but Jol seemed to realize that after a few moments. "The merging of the pantheons happened before your resurrection...suffice to say there are two deities that came with the Koryonite pantheon that are also considered demon kings, and they sit upon the council below, just as Lord Chinchala does," Jol explained. "It is possible that Emma serves one of them, and they have agreed to help Sekassus in exchange for help unlocking the Temple. If this is the case, then whatever is in the Temple must be of great value, particularly in the wrong hands."

Grakin answered with a shrug. "These things, we will learn them in due time. For now we need only know if Triela and this conduit are safe again."

"Yes," Triela answered, and she looked to Icavior. "We will be more cautious in the future, and when my lord begs me to not leave the island alone, I will heed his advice."

The two chuckled, and Kari and her friends did likewise. There was clearly chemistry between the two, and Kari wondered if they might be lovers, or if they were just very familiar as leaders and defenders of their people. "Please stay the night here on our island and enjoy the hospitality of our people," Icavior said.

The friends all looked to Erik, who nodded his assent as if it shouldn't have even been necessary. Icavior began to lead them back to where they initially arrived, but Triela grasped Kari lightly by the arm and asked her to stay behind. Once the others left and the two were alone by the fountain, the young woman looked to the demonhunter with an expression that was a mixture of resolve and trepidation. Kari had seen it many times: it was the same expression the priests had on their faces when they told her of her terminal illness - the same one she imagined she'd had when she told Trigonh she was going to die.

"What is it?" she asked softly.

Triela sighed. "Forgive me, it is not my business, but when you touched me in Gaswell's dungeon, my defenses were not in place due to the shackles," she said, and Kari cocked her head. "When you touched me, I saw into your very soul, and all of your secrets poured into my mind."

Kari was perturbed by the girl's statement, and she folded her arms across her chest. "All of them?" she asked.

Triela nodded solemnly. "You guard your heart well, but not from a mind such as mine," she said. "Something has jumbled your memories, I can tell. It is my assumption that having been dead is a part of this. The return from death to life is jarring, and if those who brought you back were careless in doing so, they have left you fractured and confused. Am I incorrect?"

Kari shook her head. She tried to keep her emotions in check and reminded herself it hadn't been the girl's intention to read her like a book. "So why are you telling me this?" she asked, trying not to sound too aggravated.

"Forgive me, it may be forward of me to suggest this, but if you wish it, I can attempt to rearrange your memories and your thoughts to clear away the confusion," the war wizard said. "It will take only a few minutes, and if all goes as I hope, then you will be better prepared to keep the hurtful shadows of your past at bay, and the confusion that plagues you should cease."

Kari closed her eyes and bit her bottom lip. "Can you just erase those memories?"

Triela shook her head. "Attempting to do so is dangerous for more than one reason," she said. "Not only is there the danger that I erase more than just the hurtful memories you wish gone, but there is also the possibility that you undergo an irreversible change. It is quite possible that your love for Grakin would be gone when I was finished, or that you might not even remember who he and his siblings are. Your entire personality might be changed forever. As much as it pains you – it pains me just having had a glimpse of it – your past is what has made you what you are, Karian Vanador. And what you are is one of the best people I have ever met, let alone had a glimpse of from the inside."

Kari took a deep breath to steady herself, and the war wizard touched the side of her face lightly. Kari could feel the mental intrusion of the smaller female, but it was not one of brute force, but rather like a cat brushing up against her leg playfully. The hurt that had welled up at the young woman's words fled at the onset of the warmth of her touch, and Kari calmed down. She was hesitant to let anyone into her past – even her mate – but there was a calmness to Triela's presence and touch that filled the demonhunter's heart with warmth and her mind with an unbreakable strength.

"You can help me?" Kari asked.

"I believe I can," Triela answered, and she didn't take her hand from

414

its comforting place on the terra-dracon woman's cheek. "If you wish for me to do so, I believe I can help you keep those memories at bay, so you may draw strength from them without letting them hurt you on a consistent basis or interfere with the way you feel about your mate, or your friends."

"What do I need to do?"

"Sit down here," the war wizard said. She led Kari to the stone fountain, where both women took seats on its edge. "Now, in your mind you will confront your past. Gird yourself in the armor of Grakin's love for you, and arm yourself with the conviction that makes you a demonhunter. I will stand beside you and help you to contain what wounds you. It will not be easy, but together you and I will persevere – you know this. Close your eyes and open your mind to me."

Kari closed her eyes and soon felt a tingle in her mind as Triela established contact. She didn't physically touch the terra-dracon woman, but in Kari's mind the war wizard's presence manifested again as a cat brushing playfully against her leg. Then it was a more intimate touch, like Grakin's lips tracing up her back. Kari started to shift uncomfortably, but Triela's voice whispered into her mind. "Be at peace," she said. "I am wading through the most pleasant of your memories before we face what burns at your core."

Kari relaxed and the sensation of Grakin's kisses faded, and then she felt hands upon her shoulders shortly before the demonhunter found herself in Triela's embrace. She was shocked for a moment, and her eyes popped open, but when they did so she realized she stood not in the kirelas-rir village, but on a broad plain of sand that stretched from horizon to horizon. It appeared to be the Khalarin Desert of Terrassia, but there were no landmarks, no vegetation, nothing whatsoever to suggest that she was seeing a real place. Within moments the unforgiving heat began to seep through her skin, the glaring sun burned her with its intense stare, and her hair whipped violently to the side in a driving, sand-filled wind.

And then Triela was beside her. The kirelas-rir woman looked around for a few moments before speaking. "This is the place of discomfort without escape that your memories bring you to when you are not prepared to deal with them," the young woman said, her voice raised to counter the scorching wind that blew past them mercilessly. Though she had to speak over the screaming wind, Triela showed no other effects from the environment, as though she was immune to its grip. "Here we will trap them: that they may sit in this place of torment alone and the sound of their desperation will lend you strength in times of crisis."

From the sands before them a pair of gravestones arose: the same ones

415

Kari had seen in the graveyard in Flora. Kari bit her lip and steeled herself in the face of the trial. Despite the fact that they did not touch, she could feel Triela's comforting hand on her shoulder. Carved into the marble faces of the tombstones were the names of Kari's parents, and a rage welled in her breast: hatred for her father, but an even deeper hatred for her mother. She closed her eyes and tried to get her emotions under control, but she felt her eyes pried open by the will of the kirelas-rir woman.

"Do not push down your hatred," Triela whispered into Kari's mind. "It is not your emotion you must suppress, but the memory itself. Laugh, Karian! You live, and they are unable to touch you, unable to hurt you unless you let them. And you will not let them hurt you ever again, for they are trapped in this endless desert of torment, while you walk in the love of a god and your mate!"

Kari suddenly found herself in a dark corner of an attic: a helpless little girl curled up in a ball while the sounds of two angry voices fought below. Triela was not with her physically, but still she felt the strength of the kirelas-rir war wizard's presence. Soon the voice of her mother carried up the ladder to where she hid, the same way it always had when the woman had come, seeking to lend some false comfort well after the fact. Never had she stopped her husband from abusing their daughter, and in the deep recesses of Kari's heart, that hurt even more than all the abuse her father had piled on her. Kari started to close her eyes, but even as she did, her features hardened into a scowl, and she became acutely aware of the fact that she wore an adult body and – more pointedly – her swords. For the briefest instant, she thought perhaps it would quell her rage if she killed the ghostly memories of her parents.

Then a voice echoed in her thoughts: not her mother's, or her father's, or even Triela's. What she heard was the voice of Suler Tumureldi, her one time master and lover:

I will never let anyone harm you, Kari, his ethereal voice said softly. Your greatest enemy lies within: you allow others to harm you because you fool yourself into believing you somehow deserve it. You are a beautiful and loving woman, and you deserve nothing but the best. But you must be willing to accept it, and accept yourself – as you have accepted me.

Tears rolled from Kari's eyes as she closed them. "He always knew," she whispered to herself, but the voice of her kirelas-rir friend answered.

"Yes, just as Grakin knows and has chosen to stay by your side," Triela said softly, her words caressing Kari's shoulder as surely as her hand would have. "What was done to you was not your fault, and you have no reason to accept it or force down the hatred it has bred in your soul. You hate the demons because they hurt people without cause, Kari; on the same token, you should hate those who have hurt you this way without cause. This is no minor offense that is forgivable, and you should not let it tear you apart. You owe forgiveness to no one."

"I hate them," Kari said, crying softly. "But they made me who I am."

"No!" came Triela's voice more forcefully. "*You* made *yourself* what you are despite them taking away all that you had, all that you were! You have built yourself up from nothing, and become a woman loved and admired, even by the gods themselves! Even by a demon..."

Kari's eyes snapped back open and she found herself once again on the broad plain of sand. The tears that streaked her face evaporated in moments and she stared down at the tombstones. They served as a reminder that her parents were dead, but also of what they had done to her. An image of Trigonh appeared in her thoughts, and soon he stood beside her and Triela with a soft smile on his lupine features, though he said nothing. Kari met his icy-blue gaze and recalled all the things he had said to her over their all-too-brief time together, and she was poignantly reminded of how much he had changed on account of her. And then Grakin stood beside them, and then Suler Tumureldi, and then even the legendary Saint Bakhor. Kari nearly chuckled through her pain at the reaction of the kirelas-rir girl, who recognized the shakna-rir priestess.

A warmth spread through Kari's entire body. "I am a good woman," she said quietly, and all of those standing with her nodded their agreement. She looked down at the tombstones once more, but the anger had drained from her completely. While she could not summon the strength – or the desire – to forgive, she found herself filled with the conviction to bury them and never let them resurface. "And you...you can go to hell."

Kari felt an incredible release in her mind, and the gravestones before her sank back into the sands. The images of her friends softly faded. The screaming wind died down and left a serenity that pervaded the scene before her, and the temperature cooled and the sands began to be replaced by rolling, grassy plains. Kari took a couple of steps forward, treading over the place where the gravestones had been, but she felt nothing to suggest they were still there, and no pain welled up in her heart when she thought of them. Kari took a deep breath and let it out in a calming sigh, and then she looked to the kirelas-rir woman.

"Is that all?" she asked.

Triela shook her head in disbelief. "Is that all?" she repeated. "You are much stronger than you realize, Karian. Not many could have done such a thing; most would have crumbled at the very sight of what you faced. I have helped you trap the hurt of this memory here, but it was your strength of will that allowed me to do so."

"Are you done, then?" the terra-dracon woman asked.

"No, though the worst of it is over," Triela answered. "Now I will sort through your memories to alleviate your confusion."

Kari found herself in the kirelas-rir village once more, but she closed her eyes as she felt Triela begin to comb through her mind. It was an odd experience that left a tingling in her brain that was like an itch she could not scratch. It lasted only a few minutes, though, and then Triela withdrew from her mind and Kari felt herself more solidly within her body. When she opened her eyes, she could see that Triela was smiling.

"Now what?" Kari asked.

Triela waved off the question. "It is done," she said. "You should no longer be plagued by the side effects of your unexpected return from death."

Kari let out a sound somewhere between a laugh and a sob, and she took one of Triela's hands in her own. "How can I ever repay you?" Kari asked.

The war wizard's face scrunched up in confusion. "You saved my life," she said. "I will be forever indebted to you. This was the least I could do for you in thanks."

Kari hugged her, and after a few minutes the two went to join the rest of the Silver Blades for a meal. The day was quiet and peaceful, and Triela gave the group a short tour of the village and the nearby forest. They slept beneath the stars that night, and at dawn the next day, Triela used her magic to transport them across the island to a point near the city of Talvor. From there, Kari led them into the rainforest, and headed to the czarikk village for one final visit.

~~*~*

For much of the day and into the night Kari marched the friends unerringly southwest. After camping for a night in the humid depths of the jungle, they continued onward the next day. Kari amazed her friends as she guided them through the heavy forest almost without regard to any sort of landmarks; only a few small streams gave her any indication of where they were. It mattered little, though: after only a couple of hours on the second day, the group encountered a czarikk patrol. The lizardmen were shocked to find so large a group moving through their lands at first, but thanks to the gift she received from Sakkrass, Kari was able to speak clearly with them.

418

They remembered her and Erik, and Kari explained that the others were their friends. Sonja expressed surprise that Kari knew how to speak the sibilant language of the lizard people, and the others echoed her sentiments. Erik tried to explain what had happened on their previous visit, but ultimately he just said they'd see for themselves soon enough.

They were waved onward, and just as it began to grow dark they crossed the breastwork that marked the outer boundary of the village. The guards let them through, and Kari led her friends into the heart of the czarikk settlement, where she bid them sit near the central fire pit and wait for the shaman or chieftain to come greet them. The appearance of such a large group drew a lot of attention, but the czarikk were shy and didn't approach despite Kari's presence. Her friends marveled at the czarikk village, simple but large, and it was clear Triela had a healthy respect for the lizard people already.

"Do you know the czarikk?" Kari asked the war wizard.

Triela nodded. "There is a village of them that share our island," she said. "They are fishers and gatherers, and they trade with my people from time to time. We find them to be quiet and agreeable neighbors."

Kari smiled, and after only a few minutes Savarras came out to see what had caused such a commotion. He smiled and approached the group, and he bowed before Kari. She greeted him in his tongue as she returned the gesture. While the others watched, Kari introduced them by name to the shaman, and he nodded as she motioned toward each of her friends. Soon he was speaking rapidly to her in his flowing dialect, and Kari chuckled.

"This is Savarras," she said, gesturing toward the shaman, and he bowed his head toward the group. "He says that Erik and I are friends of the tribe, and that all of you are welcome as our friends. Oshasis, the chief, will be out to join us at dinnertime."

The friends began to relax, and Kari asked Grakin for the urn with Makauric's ashes. Savarras watched with interest as she took the container and approached, and his expression was questioning. "Our brys friend fell after we left your village," she explained in the czarikk tongue. "He seemed to enjoy our time here, so I have come to ask if you would let me lay his ashes around your sacred fire pit."

The shaman regarded her for a moment before he brought his hands together before his chest and tapped his clawed fingers together. "You will need to ask Oshasis for his permission, but I believe he will agree to it," he said. "The demon aided you in aiding us, and was named a friend to our family; I see no cause for our chief to deny your request."

"Thank you," she said, touching his face tenderly. He seemed surprised by it at first, but then he smiled and returned to the chieftain's tent.

"What did you ask him?" Erik inquired once Savarras had left.

"I asked if I could lay Makauric's ashes around the fire pit," Kari answered. She took a deep breath through her nose. "He liked it here; I think he'd want to be laid to rest here."

Erik regarded her for a few moments, and at last opened his arms to hug her. Kari embraced him and he held tight to her for a minute. When Erik drew away he met Kari's gaze evenly. "You are a good woman, Kari," he said, and then he turned to his brother. "You're a lucky man, Grakin."

"That I am," the priest agreed.

"What is this?" Triela asked, gesturing toward the urn.

Kari sighed, trying to keep her heart light. "Before we came to rescue you and remove Gaswell, we hunted down the sylinth, like I told you," she said. "A brys helped us not only find our way through this rainforest, but also to survive while we recovered from the fight with the sylinth. He was killed by the guards at the gates to Raugro, who saw red skin and just shot him."

The war wizard's eyes were intense as she considered Kari's words and tone. "And he became a friend to you?" she stated as much as asked.

Kari shrugged, unsure if Triela expected an explanation. "I wasn't expecting it to happen."

"Neither was he, I am certain," Triela said, and a smile came to her pretty face. "I think it says much about the kind of person you are to have been able to befriend one of the very creatures you were trained to hunt."

Erik laid his hand on Kari's shoulder and she turned to face him. "It does," he said. "I could learn a lot from a woman like you."

"That's why they partnered you with her, genius," Typhonix said, drawing laughter from the gathered friends. "They may as well have put her in charge of all of us."

"I think we all learned a lot from each other," Kari said, and that drew sage nods from each of the group members. The demonhunter stared in particular at her half-brys friend, and the two exchanged broad smiles. Their conversation came to a halt as more czarikk began to filter into the center of the village and take seats around the large circular clearing. The females preparing the evening meal began moving about at a hectic pace when Oshasis emerged from his tent along with his shaman, and the two came to take their places near where the Silver Blades were gathered. Kari had all of her friends bow in respect to the chieftain at his approach, and Oshasis bowed his head in turn to them.

"Welcome back, my friend. I see you have brought all of your companions with you. Savarras has explained that friend Makauric was slain, and that you wish to lay his ashes to rest around our sacred fire pit?" Oshasis asked, and he bobbed his head as Kari nodded solemnly. "I believe this would please Sakkrass. The small demon helped defend this village and avenge the slaying of our children; we owe him this honor at least."

"Will the people fire dance this night?" Kari asked.

Oshasis tapped a finger on his chin, and for some reason Kari found it funny to see one of the lizard-folk do so, though she kept her mirth on the inside. "We had not planned to, but we will send our friend to the hereafter with song and dance," he said. "If it so pleases you, we will fire dance in his honor."

"I would appreciate it," she said, and Oshasis bowed his head in agreement.

They shared in the evening meal, and Kari's friends were surprised at the variety of the foods the czarikk prepared, from gathered fruits and the leaves of plants to roasted spiders and insects, along with more traditional meats that they recognized. They tried to be gracious and ate whatever was offered to them without too much fuss, and Kari could see they were pleasantly surprised at how delectable many of the odd foods turned out to be. The Silver Blades watched while the czarikk began gathering wood in the center of the circle, and within minutes it was piled high enough to last well into the evening. The czarikk began to paint each other's bodies in preparation for the fire dance, and Kari's friends watched with interest as she stood up and began removing her armor and clothing. The czarikk chieftain and shaman began to paint her with the same symbols and glyphs as on her previous visit, and Kari suspected her friends – and her mate – must be wondering what she was doing.

"Prepare to be amazed," Erik said from behind her.

"Wait a second! Is Sherman old enough to watch this?" Typhonix joked.

"Are *you?*" Sonja quipped in return, and the others laughed as the blonde fixed his sister with a squinty-eyed scowl.

The joking quieted down, and Kari felt the eyes of all of her friends upon her as she walked over to assist in the lighting of the bonfire. Kari spread Makauric's ashes in a circle around the bonfire as the crackling flames danced up through the center of the wood pile. After a moment she tilted her head back and let out a shrill cry that skirted the line between

421

anguish and exultation. In her mind, Kari imagined the brys running through the celestial forests with the czarikk deity. Based on her impressions of him and Savarras' words when he blessed Kari and her friends, she assumed Sakkrass was a wilderness runner in the forested lands of the celestial realm. Kari believed in her heart that Makauric's love of ranging the forest would have drawn the brys' spirit to the czarikk deity's side, if Kaelariel had allowed it.

"As I commit Makauric's ashes to the land, I salute thee, Sakkrass, Lord of the People, and friend of mine," Kari called out in the sibilant tongue of the lizard-folk. "Tonight, we dance for you, and for our fallen friend; may his memory live in you forevermore."

The people took up a cheer and the females let forth the hissing whistle Kari remembered from her previous visits. After stomping her right foot twice, Kari initiated the fire dance. Her friends watched her dance with the czarikk for hours, though none of their number worked up the courage to join her. Despite Typhonix's joke, it was clear to Kari each time she passed her friends that Sherman, like his sister, saw Kari's performance as an expression of how much she cared, and that he was taking careful note of her passion. Grakin couldn't tear his gaze away from Kari, mesmerized by the sway of her hips and the dance of the flames behind her, and each time she passed him, he smiled broadly.

The dance was a celebration of life, and the weight of Makauric's death slowly dissipated from Kari's heart. She recalled the blessing the czarikk people had received after Sakkrass' visit, and considered the cycle of life and death that the elves had taught her to respect rather than despise. She felt at peace by the dance's conclusion, and in her mind she bid her friend a final, silent goodbye. With the fire burning low behind her, she stood before her friends in the deep gloom of night, and without having to speak a word, Kari could see they understood that the ceremony was something she felt she needed to do. Her eyes met Erik's after a moment and he nodded silently to her steady gaze; it seemed he finally understood. It brought a smile to her face, and she turned to Savarras as the shaman approached her.

"You dance so effortlessly with our people," he said. "It is as if you truly are a child of Sakkrass. You doubtless make him very proud, just as you do make all of us proud."

"It is my honor to dance with your people," she replied with a bow of her head.

"Your friends are welcome to bed down here near the remains of the fire," he said. "If you wish, you and your mate may share my tent, if such will not cause you discomfort."

"We appreciate your hospitality," Kari said, sparing Grakin a glance. "I will let the others know. Thank you."

Savarras nodded and his mate came up beside him, and they made their way to their tent. Kari filled the others in on what Savarras said, and with an anxious smile, Grakin took Kari's hand and followed her to the shaman's teepee. The two czarikk were already wrapped up in their blankets when the two entered, so Kari and Grakin bedded down on the opposite side of the tent. Grakin regarded Kari with no small amount of alarm when she began to undress him completely.

"What are you doing?" he asked with a slight edge to of his voice.

Kari paid the sharpness of his voice little heed, as rare as it was. "What do you think they're doing?" she asked, nodding her head toward the bundle of movement on the other side of the tent. Grakin hesitated, but Kari leaned in close and kissed him passionately, and he eased up slightly. "I have to tell you, though: I've long since run out of the herb. We've been gone longer than I expected, and I haven't bothered getting more since we got here."

"And you still…?" Grakin began but he did not finish the thought, and Kari nodded. "If this is what you want."

She cupped his face in her hand and kissed him again. "It's what I want, Grakin," she said, her eyes welling up with tears. "More than you can imagine."

He smiled and undressed the rest of the way, and with only a single, short glance toward where their czarikk hosts lay, he lay down with Kari to make love to her.

~~*~*

The czarikk bid Kari and her friends farewell the next morning, and Triela transported them to the city of Riverport with her magic. News was already spreading of the dismantling of Gaswell's army, and unlike their first trip to the city, the Silver Blades found that an aura of calm pervaded the port. The people still went about their jobs but there were far fewer curious stares or distrustful glares, and when the friends returned to *The Port* they found the innkeeper in a much better mood. They were able to purchase the rooms without incident, and Marshall's service was much more hospitable than it was during their first visit.

Triela gave the group a lengthy thank-you and farewell, and promised that they would meet again in the future. And then she was gone, leaving the Silver Blades to the quiet beauty of Riverport while they considered how to get home. There were no large ocean-going vessels in port when they arrived, so they paid for their rooms for several days in advance and began to enjoy what little entertainment the city offered. They found that many of the taverns doubled as gambling establishments on the upper tiers, and most of the group wasted time losing their money on games of chance.

Aeligos investigated the city more thoroughly than he had the first time around but found nothing exciting or out of the ordinary. He was able to find out the schedule of ships coming through the port. There was no word on *Karmi's Sword* or its next scheduled stop in Riverport, but her sister ship *Karmi's Flail* was expected a week later. According to what the port authority knew of the ship's manifest, she would be sailing eastward to Flora and then around the northern end of Askies to DarkWind. The ship was of the same make as *Karmi's Sword*, and the harbormaster said it was quite likely they would be willing to take the group on as passengers.

Kari told her friends that Master Surallis had mentioned her return trip taking her to DarkWind, and they wondered if he had known the ships' schedules. Seeing little other choice, the group spent another week in the port and made the best of the time with their feet on dry land, as they knew soon enough they would be cooped up on a ship for several months. *Karmi's Flail* arrived in port after seven days. Her crew wasn't as colorful as that of *Karmi's Sword*: they were more businesslike, less personable, and certainly less accommodating. But they were also a compassionate crew, and they stopped at Salkorum to drop off supplies and visit with the seterrarir just as the crew of *Karmi's Sword* had done. With no pressing schedule before them, the Silver Blades were happy to spend time on the island, and enjoyed the sun, the sea, and the rum, and Kari was overjoyed to have a chance to see Dowain and Saisha's newborn child. Sherman and Katarina got to visit with Elleraus and their old friends and told them of the excitement and sense of pride the mission had provided. The crew of *Karmi's Flail* decided to remain there for a week of shore leave, and even Erik was agreeable to the relaxing vacation.

After nearly a month out of Salkorum's harbor, the ship came within sight of the city of DarkWind on Askies' east coast. The city was familiar to most of the group, since many of them had lived or trained there at some point, and it was always an exciting and somewhat dangerous place to be. Kari and her friends stood at the bow of the ship, and they watched as her crew brought her slowly and steadily into port at the direction of the harbor master. Most of her friends seemed glad just to be back on Askies – even the Moreville twins who had never even set foot on the continent before.

For Kari, it was simply nice to be home, and she looked at her distracted friends before she touched her clawed hand briefly to her lower belly. Only Grakin saw, and there was a light in his eyes as his fingers interlaced with hers in a firm grasp and the word echoed in Kari's mind once again: *Home.*

###

Appendix A: The Many Unique Races of Citaria

Terra-rir (TEH-ra reer): the first of the rir, black-skinned, silver-blooded, mammalian draconic species created by Gori Sensullu. Very similar to humans in anatomy with the exception of more draconic heads, tails, and small claws on their hands and feet. They are born of a magical process which involves a pregnancy, but they have no navels.

Terra-dracon (TEH-ra drah-CONE): a mutation of terra-rir that possess leathery dragon-like wings; highly susceptible to a genetic defect called Dracon's Bane that slowly kills them.

Terra-bengal: subspecies of rir that possesses white tiger-like stripes, and soft pads on their feet; much more lithe and graceful than a typical terra-rir.

Shakna-rir (SHOCK-nuh reer): green-skinned, desert-dwelling variants of rir; matriarchal, highly populous, and very militant; resistant to heat and flame.

Fures-rir (FYOR-iss reer): matriarchal, cold-dwelling variants of rir; all possess hair and eyes in shades of blue and are virtually immune to their cold climate.

Kirelas-rir (kur-ELL-ahs reer): mystical variant of rir differentiated by stripes on the sides of their snouts and mental powers; reclusive and few in numbers.

Seterra-rir (seh-TEH-ra reer): red-blooded variant created to be more human-like; their pregnancy is like that of humans, and accordingly, they possess navels.

Serilis-rir (SEH-rill-iss reer): also known as serilian demons; red-skinned, vicious creatures that come in six varieties, each with their own characteristics, personalities, strengths and weaknesses. The types are called *solas, kryon, corlyps, brys, elite,* and *guardian.* All serilis-rir are male except for the solas, who are genderless.

i

Serilian-rir (sur-RILL-ian reer): the result of a serilis-rir crossbreeding with any other type of rir. Also commonly called half-demons, they are as varied as their fathers' types, and are accordingly named (*half-kryon, half-corlyps, half-brys, half-elite,* and *half-guardian*). Persecuted and despised by most people throughout history.

Bah'Qitur (BAH kih-TOOR): commonly miscalled *bakatur*; the bah'qitur is a very large, human-like race that has some reptilian features. They are very aggressive but are also a highly devout people. Virtually exclusive to the continent of Dannumore.

Czarikk (Sah-REEK): the lizardmen of Citaria come in two varieties: the more humanoid mulrassa, and the more reptilian sulrassa. Very reclusive people.

Luranar (LOO-ruh-nar): bipedal wolfmen common to the southeast of the continent of Terrassia; considered savage and uncivilized by outsiders, though those who travel through civilized lands are typically well-behaved and therefore accepted.

Kwarrasti (Kwah-RAHS-tee): bipedal catfolk common to the southeast of Terrassia; nomadic and aloof, they are somewhat reclusive and rarely travel into more 'civilized' lands.

Appendix B: The Merged Citarian-Koryonite Pantheons

The Citarians: These are the deities exalted by Gori Sensullu to keep watch over Citaria.

Gori Sensullu, "The Creator": more common name for Arakiel, the creator of Citaria and its indigenous peoples; killed at the end of the Apocalypse.

Kaelariel Arakiel Jir'tana, "The Ascending Dawn": son of Gori Sensullu who appears to be a guardian demon; god of freedom and death, lord of serilis-rir, and leader of the pantheon after the Apocalypse.

Sechre Tori, "First in Battle": terra-rir god of righteous battle and patron of the military; the oldest Citarian deity exalted by Gori Sensullu.

Kris Fletcher, "The Ghost": a human also called The Armored Shepherd; he is the god of honor and loyalty, and the patron of paladins.

Kerry Kijana, "Garra Ktarra": terra-rir deity of the night, explorers, and skill; considered the greatest fighter among the pantheon; patriarch of the bloodline that bore Kaelariel.

Zalkar the Unyielding, "Avatar of Vengeance": human god of law and the patron deity of demonhunters; called primarily "the Unyielding" by his followers.

Tisa Ch'Brakkh, "The Dawn of Hope": terra-bengal descendant of Garra Ktarra and mother of Kaelariel; goddess of beauty; ascended directly to deity status.

Karmi G'Dorrinn, "The Lady of the Depths": human goddess created by Gori Sensullu to be caretaker of the oceans and those who travel upon them.

Mitreus & Zitenius Satachi, "The Sandur Striders": twin human rangers who were appointed as caretakers of nature and its defenders.

Carlos Bouron, "The Beast": human ranger reincarnated as a sylvan beast; deity of shapeshifters, lycanthropes, and the more savage humanoid species.

Seril, "The Devil Queen": terra-bengal goddess and mate to Gori Sensullu who turned on him; creator of the serilis-rir and enemy of the Light forces in the Apocalypse; killed at the end of the Apocalypse.

The Koryonites: These are the principal deities of the Koryonite pantheon who agreed to merge with those of Citaria to aid in the Apocalypse.

Ambergaust Coramin, "The Wellspring": human leader of the Koryonite pantheon who agreed to merge his own pantheon with that of Citaria; god of life and marriage.

Carsius Coramin, "The Mother of Truth": Ambergaust's human wife and goddess of birth and motherhood; matron to female paladins.

Bek Coramin, "The Resultant Truth": daughter of Ambergaust and Carsius; human goddess of wisdom and piety; nearly a paladin in her own right.

Cabal Coramin, "The Iron Fist of Heaven": son of Ambergaust and Carsius; human god of courage and battle.

Tigron Coramin, "The Celestial Mender": younger brother of Ambergaust; human god of healing and life.

The Outsiders: These are Koryonite deities who merged with the Citarian pantheon but have limited influence or even contact with the people of Citaria.

Krollmar Stonetender, "The Celestial Smith": dwarven god of craftsmen who merged with the Koryonite pantheon and subsequently the Citarian pantheon; impromptu god to all of the "little peoples."

Belgrin the Wanderer, "Tender of the Roots": half-elven god of nature, the arts, and peace who joined the Koryonite pantheon at Tigron's insistence, and subsequently also joined the Citarian pantheon.

Korbaz the Constant, "Lord of the Second Law": human god of decay; has limited influence over the Koryonite pantheon, and less over the Citarian pantheon.

Braum the Clairvoyant, "The Magnificent Intellect": human god of knowledge; eons-old friend of Ambergaust who serves as advisor to the head of the pantheon.

Ellen Dragonborn, "Fruit of the Great Tree": half-elven deity of love; mistrusted by many of her fellow deities.

Appendix C: Geography and History

The Continents: The five major continents and their *associated islands*.

Askies, The Motherland: This island, located on the western and southern hemispheres, respectively, was the birthplace of the rir people and their civilization. Control of Askies was the main focus of the Apocalypse.

The Isle of Morikk: This island runs parallel to Askies' west coast; it was the birthplace of the seterra-rir and is where the Temple of Archons is located. Since the war that nearly wiped out the seterra-rir, the island has been deserted.

The Crystal Isles: These small, uninhabited rocky islands off the southeast of Askies were so named due to their polished, reflective surfaces.

Terrassia: Located on the northern and western hemisphere, Terrassia is the birthplace of numerous races: the fures-rir, the shakna-rir, the luranar, the kwarrasti, and the elves. It was the site of the Third Demon War, and saw a fair amount of fighting during the Apocalypse.

Senkiro's Solace: Also called Druidia, this tiny island off of Terrassia's southern coast was home to a secret priesthood for hundreds of years. The island is now considered haunted and is avoided by even the staunchest adventurers.

Isle of the Maelstrom: This tiny island located north of Terrassia is sealed off by a magical vortex and is home to the High Council of Wizardry. It is so named because of the Council's founder.

Masceria: Made up of many large islands, this continent lies north of Askies. Its inhabitants – mostly terra-rir and humans – prefer to remain isolated from the rest of the world, and are rumored to be far more technologically advanced than the rest of Citaria.

Dannumore: This massive continent spans most of the eastern hemisphere. Populated primarily by the bah'qitur, much of it remains unknown and uncharted to non-bah'qitur society. It is rumored to have a population greater than the rest of the world combined.

Tsalbrin: This semi-tropical island sits in a sea that juts into the east side of Dannumore's northern half. It is home to humans and several species of rir, some of whom have spread onto the coasts of Dannumore. Tsalbrin is also home to several tribes of czarikk, a few of the more savage humanoid species, and also several dragons.

Arkalman: This sparsely populated, smaller continent is south of Dannumore. It has a mixture of races, but tensions between them keep any from claiming dominance over the island.

The Wars: These are the major wars recorded throughout the history of Citaria; ME denotes "Modern Era."

The First Demon War (ME 92): The first major clash between Seril's serilis-rir and Gori Sensullu's terra-rir; involved a nine-month siege of the holy city of Sarchelete. The war was ultimately won by the terra-rir thanks to the help of the recently-arrived humans and their adaptability. The serilis-rir were unable to tolerate the cold winter and those that could not flee north were slaughtered.

The Second Demon War (ME 822-824): Seril's second attempt at eradicating the terra-rir came shortly after the founding of the city of Gnarr. The war was fought primarily in the heartlands between Barcon and Gnarr, and was mainly an attrition-based war that left the rir and human populations of the heartlands badly decimated. Victory came after a being, rumored to have been an archangel, engaged Seril and forced her to retreat from Citaria.

The Succession Wars (ME 1422-1484): As the rir and human populations continued to thrive and expand to the four corners of Askies, several wars broke out between the dominant cities of each province as they sought to crown a king. Gradually the elders of the noble families of Barcon, Gnarr, Oge, DarkWind, Latalex, and Ceritan lost power or died off, and the wars came to an end as the younger nobles agreed to form ducal councils. Askies was divided into counties and duchies, and while a king eventually came to power in the Strekan Province, his authority was limited to keeping the peace between the various duchies.

The Third Demon War (ME 1484-1487): While the Succession Wars were coming to a close, Seril attempted to capture the continent of Terrassia. During the initial years of the conflict, two new species of rir surfaced: the shakna-rir and the fures-rir. With the shakna-rir attacking from the balmy south and the fures-rir attacking from the frozen north, the armies of the serilis-rir were flanked and crushed. It was during the Third Demon War that the first recorded underworld invasion took place as well: a race of serpent people led by a sorcerer simply called Tempis'ra tried to establish a foothold in the southern jungles of Terrassia. In the ensuing clash between Tempis'ra and the wizards of the rir armies, the southern jungles were completely destroyed, leaving a desert in their place, but the serpent people were exterminated.

The Fourth Demon War (ME 1832-1835): With her armies replenished, Seril once again attempted to conquer Askies. In a move reminiscent of the First Demon War, the Devil Queen attempted to capture the holy city of Sarchelete and destroy the grand temples of her enemies. Better prepared to deal with the harsh winters of the south, the serilis-rir army laid siege to the city for well over a year, but was unable to break the city's defenses. Reinforcements arrived from the east, and Seril was forced north to avoid being flanked, as she was during the Third Demon War. Her army was able to hold its own and inflict devastating casualties on their enemies, but the Devil Queen accepted a stalemate and retreated to the underworld by all reports.

The False Apocalypse (ME 2452-2453): When the guardian demon called Erijinkor turned on his creator, many of the various priesthoods of the rir believed it marked the beginning of the Apocalypse. Soldiers from every major city were sent to Sarchelete to protect it from possible attack, but the attack never came. With the major cities and their leaders distracted, Seril launched one simple, brutal assault and captured the city of Oge. She made the city her base of operations, and rebuffed several attempts by the mortals to recapture it. To the surprise of many, the residents of Oge largely supported the Devil Queen once she took power. It was during this time that the major assassins' guilds in Oge were merged into one guild called the Five Clans. The Five Clans was run by the brys known as Olgaryn, and under his leadership they answered to the Devil Queen herself.

The War of Purity (ME 2878): With the appearance of the seterra-rir, the collective rir species of Askies launched an invasion of Morikk, seeking to wipe out what they believed was an attempt by Seril to infiltrate their very bloodlines. Curiously, the humans did not take part in this war. The seterra-rir population is believed to have been annihilated in this short, six-month conflict.

The Bah'Qitur Invasion (ME 2879-2880): No one is quite sure what prompted the bah'qitur to invade Askies, but they sent a fleet to Askies' northeast coast, near the city of Ceritopolonis. They captured the city and its surrounding territory easily, granting their army a port into which to bring reinforcements. Unfortunately for the bah'qitur, their plans to conquer Askies angered Seril, and she sent her serilis-rir army to bolster the mortal forces and drive the bah'qitur from "her" island. Few of the invaders returned home.

The Fifth Demon War (ME 2880-2882): Once the bah'qitur were dealt with, Seril turned on the mortals once again. This time, however, a massive portion of her army turned on her, swearing fealty to the new lord of the serilis-rir, Kaelariel. The guardian demon Serenjols delivered the most significant victory of the War when he killed Seril's firstborn son, Urukh. Seril's forces were decisively defeated in a massive battle at DarkWind, and the combined army of mortals and those serilis-rir loyal to Kaelariel drove the Devil Queen back to Oge. Kaelariel decided against a lengthy siege of Oge, as he believed the cost of life would be far too great with the Devil Queen herself living in the city. Satisfied that she was beaten, the newly sanctified god of freedom and death instead began working on relations between the mortals and his people.

The Fall of Terrassia (ME 2880-2884): Aided by an unknown source, the demon king Celigus Chinchala invaded the continent of Terrassia in the year ME 2880. With Kaelariel and the mortal forces largely focused on defeating Seril in the Fifth Demon War, Chinchala was opposed only by the residents of Terrassia itself. Chinchala formed a foothold in the northwest of the badlands, and launched his first invasion directly into the shakna-rir empire. Despite numerous attempts by the northern cities to draw him off from his attack on Aurun Ch'Gurra, Chinchala's tactical brilliance left his enemies completely dumbfounded. Chinchala captured the shakna-rir capital of Aurun Ch'Gurra with little trouble, and invaded the palace himself to force the queen, Gwendolyn Tumureldi, to surrender. Curiously, Chinchala allowed the queen to continue ruling her people so long as she ultimately answered to him. Chinchala then moved on to capture Solaris, Dira Ch'Tori, and even the frozen capital of the fures-rir kingdom, Castle Tenari. Chinchala never bothered with the elves of Laeranore, and relinquished his command of the major kingdoms after a short – and prosperous – five years, saying only that a time would come when he would reclaim the thrones he was vacating. To date, no one is quite sure why Chinchala conquered the island in the first place or why he promised to retake it in the future.

The Culling (ME 2880-Present): After the defeat of their imperial army on Askies, war broke out on Dannumore between those bah'qitur loyal to the church and those loyal to the imperial line. Little is known of the reasoning behind this war, or its results, but by all accounts it rages even still.

The Apocalypse (ME 3050-3058): The final war between Gori Sensullu and Seril, the Apocalypse saw perhaps Seril's greatest effort in conquering Askies. Using the trust garnered by Kaelariel's loyalists against them, Seril was able to weaken most of the major cities of Askies from within before her actual attacks began. In one long, calculated move, she was able to capture most of the major cities and nearly all of the important smaller ones within weeks. Under the command of Kaelariel and the demon king Celigus Chinchala, the mortal forces sought first to bolster those cities not already captured and to seal off the west side of the island from attack – thus protecting the holy city of Sarchelete. The two sides traded victories for years as the mortals worked to liberate each of the captured cities. The brilliance of Kaelariel's son, Kris Jir'tana, along the Barrier Mountains and the stonewall tactics of Chinchala along the Ceritan Mountains kept Seril's forces contained to the heartlands of the continent. The breaking of the siege of DarkWind was one of the most significant victories for the mortals, as it broke the spine of Seril's most powerful battalion. Soon after, the archmage Percival Cintalas was able to kill Seril's mate, the warlock Shawn Gobrae, leaving the Devil Queen with few allies. Once the Devil Queen was driven back to Oge, Kaelariel besieged the city and fought her to the death. At the same time Kaelariel killed Seril, Gori Sensullu also died, bringing the conflict between the two to a close.

Thank Yous & Acknowledgements

Thank you for reading Salvation's Dawn! If you enjoyed this book, please leave a review on Amazon and let other people know what you liked (and even what you didn't like). As an indie author, reviews are especially important for getting the word about the strengths of my work, and it only takes a minute or two; you don't have to write a term paper about my book! http://amzn.to/1SWoipF

No book would be complete without thank-yous and acknowledgements. While I am the author of this book, to say it is the work of one person would be only a half-truth, at best. A number of people have helped with this work in some way, whether in the building of the world itself, an encouraging word after reading, or in having helped edit it so it sounds a little less like something written in one's spare time watching baseball or in the café of Barnes & Noble (both of which are true).

No one could take the top spot of thanks over my Lord and Savior, Jesus Christ, whose guiding hand brought me to a place in my life where I had the time, the maturity, and the mental wherewithal to see to this book's completion. All the glory belongs to Him.

Thank you to Richard Samanic, who introduced my friends and I to the world of AD&D, wherein this book's entire pantheon, world, and races were created. And many thanks go to the players who helped me build the world up from a barely-conceived Sci-Fi mess to a fully realized alien world: Robert Rothman, Pascal, Lenny, Dave, Mike Orlandi, Dave Christopher, Vincent DeBoer, Thanas Tsioplakis, Louis DeBoer, Erin Groppe, and Rachel DeBoer.

Special thanks go to Erin Groppe, who tirelessly read and re-read the rough drafts of this, offered suggestions, corrected errors, and, again, helped turn it from an amateurish mess into a polished amateur work. On the same token, many thanks to my other test readers and feedback crew: AJ Merrick, Thanas Tsioplakis, and Carl Souza. Asking people to read a 475+ page manuscript and give honest feedback is a tall order, so to those who took the time to go through the book's rougher versions and critique it honestly, thank you.

Thank you to Andreas Zafiratos for the gorgeous cover and to Adam Wayne for the original incarnation. Being someone who can write but can't draw to save my life, it is amazing to see someone bring the characters of the book to life in detail, and come so close to what I envision.

And last but certainly not least, thank you to my darling wife Crystal, whose patience and encouragement are the only reason this book has made it to this point. While most of my test readers went through this book once in one of its various incarnations, and Erin probably went through it three or four times, I don't think it's an exaggeration to say my wife has probably read it no less than ten or fifteen times. She saw this work in its very rough, very incomplete first draft, and she's seen it in its final state as published here. And she is the main reason I say that this book is not solely my work; she has been with me every step of the way, offering guidance, character observations, plot suggestions, grammar and spelling checks, and the encouragement to put this work out for the whole world to see. Thank you, Crystal, with every fiber of my being.

I will also add a thank you here at the end for some of my favorite fantasy authors, whose works helped to inspire me by way of their masterful storytelling, their technique, and/or their brilliant characterization: RA Salvatore, Tad Williams, Raymond E. Feist, Elaine Cunningham, and Alison Sinclair. And this list is only of those in the Fantasy genre; there have been plenty of other influences as well. Other names will join this list as my reading expands and my writing progresses.

Printed in Great Britain
by Amazon